Thomas Pynchon

The Chemical Forces

Anatiposi

Thomas Pynchon

The Chemical Forces

Reprint of the original, first published in 1871.

1st Edition 2023 | ISBN: 978-3-38216-919-0

Anatiposi Verlag is an imprint of Outlook Verlagsgesellschaft mbH.

Verlag (Publisher): Outlook Verlag GmbH, Zeilweg 44, 60439 Frankfurt, Deutschland
Vertretungsberechtigt (Authorized to represent): E. Roepke, Zeilweg 44, 60439 Frankfurt, Deutschland
Druck (Print): Books on Demand GmbH, In de Tarpen 42, 22848 Norderstedt, Deutschland

THE CHEMICAL FORCES

HEAT—LIGHT—ELECTRICITY,

WITH THEIR APPLICATIONS TO THE EXPANSION,
LIQUEFACTION AND VAPORIZATION OF SOLIDS: THE STEAM ENGINE:
PHOTOGRAPHY: SPECTRUM ANALYSIS: THE GALVANIC BATTERY: ELECTRO-PLATING: THE
ELECTRICAL ILLUMINATION OF LIGHT HOUSES: THE FIRE ALARM
OF CITIES: THE ATLANTIC TELEGRAPH:

AN INTRODUCTION TO

CHEMICAL PHYSICS,

DESIGNED FOR THE USE OF

ACADEMIES, COLLEGES, AND MEDICAL SCHOOLS.

ILLUSTRATED WITH NUMEROUS ENGRAVINGS,
AND CONTAINING COPIOUS LISTS OF EXPERIMENTS WITH DIRECTIONS FOR PREPARING THEM

BY

THOMAS RUGGLES PYNCHON, M. A.,

SCOVILL PROFESSOR OF CHEMISTRY AND THE NATURAL SCIENCES,
TRINITY COLLEGE, HARTFORD.

———• • •———

NEW YORK:
TAINTOR BROTHERS.
678 BROADWAY.
1871.

Entered according to Act of Congress, in the year 1869, by

THOMAS RUGGLES PYNCHON,

In the Clerk's Office of the District Court for the District of Connecticut.

TO THE MEMORY

OF

DR. JOSEPH BLACK,

DURING A LONG LIFE, PROFESSOR OF CHEMISTRY

IN THE UNIVERSITIES OF GLASGOW AND OF EDINBURGH,

THE FRIEND AND ADVISER OF

JAMES WATT,

AND THE DISCOVERER OF THOSE LAWS OF LATENT HEAT

WHICH LED TO THE WONDERFUL IMPROVEMENTS IN THE STEAM ENGINE

THIS VOLUME, DEVOTED CHIEFLY TO THE ELUCIDATION

OF THE SAME AND KINDRED SUBJECTS,

IS RESPECTFULLY INSCRIBED

BY

AN ARDENT ADMIRER OF

HIS GENIUS

PREFACE.

This Treatise has been prepared for the use of the general reader, as well as for that of Students in Academies, Colleges, and Medical Schools, and is designed to embody the most important facts and principles of the Physical Forces,—Heat, Light, and Electricity, that have any connection with the production of Chemical phenomena, and to form an introduction to the study of the science of Chemistry. With that science these subjects are so closely associated that they may be said to constitute a part of it, and a thorough knowledge of them *is* absolutely indispensable to its satisfactory study. They are also possessed of great intrinsic interest, and are intimately connected with all the most important scientific inventions of the Age,—the Steam Engine, Photography, the Electric Telegraph, and others, as well as with many of the great processes of Nature, in constant operation around us, and these cannot be understood without a thorough knowledge of their elementary Principles.

At the same time they are among the most difficult portions of Physical Science, and for their thorough understanding a considerable amount of minute explanation and illustration is required. The author has, therefore, treated them with some copiousness of detail, and has endeavored to avoid that meagreness of statement which aims to present only the bare facts of science; while at the same time he has sought not to exceed the limit beyond which his readers would be unable to follow him without the aid of Mathematics. All matters of which a knowledge could equally well be obtained from any good treatise on Natural Philosophy have been omitted; and those points have been elucidated with special care, which a somewhat extended experience as an Instructor has shown to be peculiarly difficult of comprehension by the student.

The subjects which have been most carefully elaborated, are *Heat; Radiant Heat; the transmission of Heat through media; Latent Heat; the Steam Engine; the Chemical Influence of Light; Photography; Spectrum Analysis; the Galvanic Battery, and its heating, illuminating, chemical and magnetic effects; the Electric Telegraph; the Atlantic Telegraph; Electro-Magnetic Engines; the Fire-Alarm of Cities; the Induction Coils of Page and Ruhmkorff; the Magneto-Electric Machines of Saxton, Page, Holmes, Wilde, and Ladd, and their various applications to Electro-Plating and Gilding, to the illumination of Light-Houses, and to Medicine.* Much attention has been paid to the modern *Theory of the Correlation, Convertibility and Equivalency of the Physical Forces.* Great pains has also been taken to trace the history of the various scientific discoveries described, and to give to their Authors the merit which is justly their due. And at the end of every Section *copious Lists of Experiments* have been introduced, with minute directions for their preparation and performance, arranged with reference to the convenience of teachers as well as of students. It is believed that these Lists are much more complete than any heretofore published.

An attempt has been made, both in the arrangement of paragraphs, and in their printing, to place the subject before the student in a distinct light, and in a clear and systematic manner. Besides a full catalogue of subjects at the beginning, for general use, a running title has been put at the top of each page, and every paragraph provided with a heading printed in heavy type, for the purpose of furnishing a continuous Table of Contents, subject by subject, and also of enabling the teacher to select those portions which he may deem the best adapted to the wants of the student, whenever, for any reason, it is thought expedient not to attempt the study of the whole.

As the merit of an elementary treatise like the present, must consist rather in the judgment shown in the selection and arrangement of materials than in the originality of its contents, the Author has not scrupled to avail himself of aid from every quarter. The works most frequently consulted have been Ganot's *Traitè de Physique*, Pouillet's *Elements de Physique, and* Miller's *Chemical Physics*. The illustrations, where not original, have been drawn from sources equally varied.

Should this volume meet with public favor, it will be followed by a second on the same plan, upon Inorganic and Organic Chemistry. The Author takes this opportunity of expressing his acknowledgements, for many important suggestions, to several valued friends, and particularly to Mr. S. H. Clark, of Hartford, for the great pains which he has bestowed upon the engravings, and for the fidelity and skill with which he has executed them.

T. R. P.

HARTFORD, September 1st, 1869.

TABLE OF CONTENTS.

CHAPTER I.

INTRODUCTION.

SUBJECT MATTER OF CHEMISTRY; USES; HISTORY. THE CHEMICAL AGENTS.

PARAGRAPH.	PAGE.
1. ORIGIN of name,	1
2. Chemistry investigates the composition of Matter,	1
3. What is Matter?	2
4. Matter inert, but affected by external forces,	2
5. The three states of Matter, Solid, Liquid and Gaseous,	3
6. The properties of Solids,	4
7. The properties of Liquids,	4
8. The properties of Gases,	5
9. The Atmosphere a type of Gases. Its properties,	5
10. The properties of Matter treated of by Natural Philosophy,	7
11. The properties of Matter treated of by Chemistry,	7
12. The study of Matter also forms the subject of Mineralogy, Botany and Zoölogy,	8
13. The difference between Natural Philosophy and Chemistry illustrated,	8
14. Chemistry is a science of Experiment,	9
15. What is a Chemical Experiment?	9
16. Chemistry is connected with many processes in the Arts,	10
17. Chemistry explains the nature of Medicines,	10
18. Chemistry explains Respiration,	11
19. Chemistry connected with Agriculture,	11
20. Chemistry explains the extraction of Metals,	12
21. Chemistry connected with the manufacture of Gas,	12
22. Chemistry explains Combustion,	12
23. Importance of Chemistry,	13
24. Chemistry exhibits striking proofs of Design,	13

TABLE OF CONTENTS.

PAR.		PAGE.
25.	The history of Chemistry,	13
26.	Chemistry depends upon the Balance,	14
27.	Apparatus required in Chemistry,	15
28.	The Fundamental Principles of this Science,	15
29.	Simple and Compound substances distinguished,	16
30.	The term Element defined,	16
31.	The number of the Elements,	17
32.	The constitution of some of the most important Chemical compounds stated,	17
33.	Chemical Affinity defined,	18
34.	The active Agents of Chemistry,	19
35.	The Chemical Agents,—Heat, Light, Electricity, why called Imponderables,	20
36.	The study of Chemistry begins with the Chemical Agents,	21

CHAPTER II.

THE FIRST CHEMICAL AGENT, HEAT.

DIFFUSION OF HEAT,—EXPANSION; LIQUEFACTION; EBULLITION; EVAPORATION; SPECIFIC HEAT; SOURCES OF HEAT; NATURE OF HEAT.

§ I. Diffusion of Heat.

37.	The Nature of Heat,	22
38.	Heat exists in two states,	22
39.	Heat present in all bodies,	23
40.	Heat and Cold relative terms,	23
41.	Heat, the repulsive principle of Matter,	24
42.	Heat tends to an Equilibrium,	24
43.	Three modes in which Heat seeks an Equilibrium,	25
44.	First mode.—Conduction,	26
45. 46.	Bodies differ in conducting power,	26
47.	Density favorable to Conduction,	27
48. 49.	Relative conducting power of the Metals,	27
50.	Porous bodies bad conductors,	28
51.	Illustrations of Conduction,	30
52. 53.	Applications in the Arts,	31
54.	Animals and Plants protected by non-conducting coverings,	32
55.	Liquids poor conductors,	33
56.	The Gases poor conductors,	34
57.	The conducting power of different Gases different,	36

PAR.		PAGE.
58.	The second mode of diffusion,—Convection,	37
59.	Convection in Liquids,	37
60.	Convection in Gases,	38
61.	Illustrations of Convection,	38
62.	What makes heated Water and Air ascend,	40
63.	The ascension of heated Liquids and Gases illustrated,	41
64.	The third mode of diffusion,—Radiation,	42
65.	Radiant Heat follows the same laws as Radiant Light,	43
66.	Nature of surface affects the rate of Radiation,	43
67.	Other circumstances affecting the rate of Radiation,	45
68.	Radiation takes place from points beneath the surface,	46
69.	Practical applications,	46
70.	The radiation of the Earth,	47
71.	The theory of Radiation,	48
72.	The reflection of Radiant Heat,	48
73.	The Law of the reflection of Heat,	48
74.	Concave Mirrors,	49
75.	Experiments with two Concave Mirrors,	50
76.	The different reflecting powers of different substances,	52
77.	The apparent radiation and reflection of Cold,	53
78.	The material of Mirrors affects their reflection,	53
79.	Practical applications,	54
80.	The reflection of Heat by Fire-places,	55
81.	The absorption of Radiant Heat,	56
82.	The absorption of Heat affected by Color,	57
83.	Transmission of Radiant Heat,	57
84.	Transmission of Heat depends upon the source from which it proceeds,	58
85.	Transmission of Heat from different sources of equal intensity, different for the same substance,	59
86.	Transmission of Radiant Heat from the same source, different for different substances—Diathermancy,	61
87.	Diathermancy not proportioned to Transparency,	62
88.	Melloni's experiments on diathermancy of Solids,	62
89.	The diathermancy of Liquids,	64
90.	The diathermancy of Gases,	65
91.	Diathermancy explained on the supposition that there are different kinds of Heat,	66
92.	The existence of different kinds of Heat proved,	66
93.	The different kinds of Heat separated from each other,	69
94.	Different kinds of Heat emitted by different sources of Heat,	70

PAR.		PAGE
95.	Unequal diathermancy of Heat from different sources, due to the different kinds of Heat emitted,	72
96.	Unequal diathermancy of Heat from the same source, owing to a property in bodies called Thermo-chrosis,	72
97.	The refrangibility of rays of heat may be altered by re radiation,—Calorescence,	74
98.	The double refraction and polarization of Heat,	75
99.	The different processes through which Heat may pass in seeking an Equilibrium,	76

EXPERIMENTS ON DIFFUSION OF HEAT,—76, 77, 78, 79.

§ II. Effects of Heat,—Expansion.

100.	Expansion produced by Heat,	79
101.	Expansion of Solids proved,	80
102.	The expansion of Solids unequal,	80
103.	The expansion of Metals,	81
104.	The force of Expansion,	81
105.	Illustrations of Expansion,	83
106.	The force of Contraction equal to that of Expansion,	83
107.	Applications in the Arts,	85
108.	Injurious effects of Expansion,	86
109.	Glass fractured by Expansion,	86
110.	Fracture produced by sudden cooling,	87
111.	Metallic instruments injured by Expansion,	88
112.	Harrison's Compensation Pendulum,	88
113.	Other Compensation Pendulums,	89
114.	The Compensation Balance,	90
115.	The expansion of Liquids,	91
116.	The expansion of different Liquids unequal,	91
117.	The expansion of the Liquids produced by the condensation of the Gases,	92
118.	The expansion of Gases,	92
119.	The expansion of Air,	92
120.	The expansion of Air the cause of the draught of chimneys,	93
121.	Exception to the general law of expansion by heat;—Water at certain temperatures contracts from Heat and expands from Cold,	95
122.	Important effects of this exception,	96
123.	This peculiar constitution of water proved by experiment,	97

TABLE OF CONTENTS. xiii

PAR.	PAGE
124. Water expands in freezing,	98
125. Illustrations of this Force in Nature,	99
126. Other substances also expand in Solidifying,	100
127. The Thermometer,	100
128. The Air Thermometer,	101
129. The Differential Thermometer,	102
130. The Mercurial Thermometer,	103
131. Construction of the Thermometer,	104
132. Fahrenheit's Scale,	105
133. Other Thermometric Scales,	106
134. Different forms of the Thermometer,	108
135. Register Thermometers,	108
136. Metallic Thermometers,	109
137. Pyrometers,	110

EXPERIMENTS; EFFECTS OF HEAT,—EXPANSION,—110, 111, 112.

§ III. Effects of Heat,—Liquefaction.

138. Heat of Composition,	112
139. Liquefaction produced by Heat,—melting point,	113
140. Disappearance of a large amount of Heat during Liquefaction,	113
141. The amount of Heat absorbed during the melting of Ice,	114
142. The amount of Heat thus absorbed, shown by experiment,	115
143. The Heat of Fluidity,	115
144. Solids cannot be heated above their point of fusion, until the whole of the solid is melted,	116
145. The Heat absorbed in Liquefaction is given out in solidification,	117
146. Liquefaction always produces a reduction of Temperature,	118
147. Freezing Mixtures,	119
148. Salts and Acids dissolved in Water lower the freezing point,	120
149. Two substances mixed, often melt at a lower temperature than either separately,—Fluxes,	121
150. Refractory Substances,	121
151. Facility of Liquefaction proportioned to the quantity of Latent Heat required,	122
152. Important results in Nature of the absorption of Heat in Liquefaction, and its evolution in Solidification,	123
153. The beneficial effects of this Constitution,	124
154. Dr. Black, the discoverer of the Laws of Latent Heat,	124

§ IV. Effects of Heat,—Ebullition.

PAR.		PAGE
	EXPERIMENTS; EFFECTS OF HEAT,—LIQUEFACTION,—	125, 126
155.	Vaporization,	126
156.	The physical properties of Vapors,	127
157.	Difference between Evaporation and Ebullition,	127
158.	Ebullition,	127
159.	Absorption of Heat in Ebullition,	128
160.	The heat absorbed in Vaporization given out again in Condensation,	129
161.	The amount of Heat absorbed not the same for all Vapors,	130
162.	The Boiling point variable,—influenced by atmospheric pressure,	131
163.	Wollaston's Hypsometer,	133
164.	Influence of adhesion on the boiling point,	133
165.	Air dissolved in Water favors Ebullition,	134
166.	Solids dissolved in a Liquid elevate its boiling point,	134
167.	Increase of pressure elevates the boiling point,—Diminished pressure lowers it,	135
168.	Elevation of the boiling point indicates increase of pressure,	135
169.	The culinary paradox,—Water made to boil by the application of Cold,	137
170.	The amount of expansion of Liquids in Vaporization, especially Water, in producing Steam,	138
171.	The Condensation of Steam by decrease of Temperature,	139
172.	Wollaston's Steam Bulb,	140
173.	The Steam Engine,	140
174.	The two forms of the Steam Engine,	142
175.	The Condensing and Non-condensing Engine,	142
176.	The Steam Engine in its most complete form,	143
177.	Latent Heat of the Condensing Engine,	145
178.	The Boiler,	146
179.	The Boiler is an apparatus for forming and compressing Steam,	147
180.	Law of the propagation of pressure through Fluids,	149
181.	Mode in which pressure is transmitted from the Boiler to the Cylinder,	150
182.	Explosion of Boilers,	150
183.	The Boilers of Locomotives,	152
184.	The alternating movement of the Piston, how produced. The Valves,	153
185.	Steam may be used expansively,	155
186.	The expansive power of Steam increases with its Temperature,	155

PAR.		PAGE.
187.	No economy of fuel in boiling Water at a low Temperature,	156
188.	No economy in using Liquids which boil at a lower Temperature than Water,	158
189.	Super-heated Steam,	158
190.	Papin's Digester,	159
191.	The Spheroidal state,	160
192.	The Spheroidal state explains the explosions of Boilers,	162
193.	Distillation,	164
194.	Uses of Distillation,	166
195.	The separation of two Liquids by Distillation,	166

EXPERIMENTS; EFFECTS OF HEAT,—EBULLITION,—167, 168, 169.

§ V. Effects of Heat,—Evaporation.

196.	Evaporation,	169
197.	Evaporation takes place at ordinary Temperatures. Heat, its cause,	169
198.	The amount of Vapor formed, and its elasticity proportioned to Temperature,	170
199.	These truths illustrated by Experiment,	171
200.	The rapidity of Evaporation varies with the pressure. In a vacuum it is instantaneous,	172
201.	The amount of Evaporation of different Liquids in a vacuum at the same Temperature, is unequal,	173
202.	The elastic force of Vapor in a confined space does not vary with pressure, but with Temperature,	174
203.	The elastic force of Vapor in two connecting vessels cannot rise above the elastic force proper to the colder vessel,	177
204.	The rate of Evaporation of different Liquids in Air is unequal,	179
205.	The presence of Vapor in Air affects its bulk and density,	180
206.	The circumstances which influence Evaporation,	181
207.	Absorption of Heat,—diminution of Temperature produced by Evaporation,	181
208.	Removal of Atmospheric Pressure hastens Evaporation, and increases Cold,	183
209.	Cause of the Cold produced by Evaporation,	184
210.	The Cryophorus,	184
211.	The Pulse Glass,	186
212.	The cold of Fountains and Earthern water jars,	186
213.	Effect of Evaporation on Animal life,	186
214.	Effect of Evaporation on Climate,	187

PAR.		PAGE.
215.	Effect of the condensation of the watery Vapor of the Air,	187
216.	The amount of watery Vapor contained in the Air,	188
217.	Hygrometers,	188
218.	Daniell's Hygrometer,	189
219.	Effect of reducing the Temperature of the Air upon the amount of watery Vapor contained in it,	191
220.	Dew is produced by reducing the Temperature of the Air,	191
221.	Constitution of Gases,—difference between Vapors and Gases,	194
222.	Pressure required for condensing Gases,	194
223.	The amount of pressure varies with the Gas,	195
224.	Thilorier's process for solidifying Carbonic acid,	196
225.	Solid Carbonic acid,	198
226.	The solidification of other Gases,	199
227.	The pressure exerted by condensed Gases,	200
228.	The present constitution of the Globe dependent upon its Temperature,	201

EXPERIMENTS; EFFECTS OF HEAT,—EVAPORATION,—202, 203.

§ VI. Specific Heat,—Capacity for Heat.

229.	The amount of Heat in different bodies of the same Temperature unequal. Specific Heat,	203
230.	Proof that different bodies of equal weight contain unequal amounts of Heat. Method of mixture,	204
231.	Specific Heat determined by the time required to heat equal weights of different bodies equally,	205
232.	Specific Heat determined by rate of cooling,	206
233.	Specific Heat determined by the amount of Ice melted,	207
234.	The Calorimeter of Lavoisier and Laplace,	207
235.	Specific Heat determined by the rise of Temperature produced in equal weights of Water,	208
236.	The Specific Heat of Water,	209
237.	The Specific Heat of Solids,	209
238.	The Specific Heat of Liquids,	209
239.	The Specific Heat of Gases,	210
240.	Regnault's determination of the Specific Heat of Gases,	212
241.	The Specific Heat of a body may be changed by altering its density,	213
242.	The Specific Heat of a body changed by altering its physical state,	214

TABLE OF CONTENTS. xvii

PAR.		PAGE.
243.	A change in the Specific Heat of a body affects its Temperature; an increase of Specific Heat diminishes Temperature; a diminution of Specific Heat increases it. Change of density affects Temperature,	214
244.	The Fire Syringe,	218
245.	The distribution of Temperature in the Atmosphere, the formation and disappearance of clouds, the production of Rain and Snow, explained by change of density in the Air,	219
246.	The condensation of Vapors by pressure explained on this principle,	220
246.*	Summary of Principles; Applications; Illustrations,	221

EXPERIMENTS ON SPECIFIC HEAT,—222, 223.

§ VII. The Sources of Heat.

247.	The Sources of Heat,	223
248.	The Sun,	223
249.	The internal heat of the Earth,	223
250.	Chemical Action,—Combustion,	224
251.	Electricity,	225
252.	The absorption of Liquids and Gases,	225
253.	Vital Action,	226
254.	Mechanical Action, Friction and Percussion,—the Mechanical equivalent of Heat,	227

EXPERIMENTS ON SOURCES OF HEAT,—228.

§ VIII. The Nature of Heat.

255.	The material theory of Heat,	228
256.	The mechanical theory of Heat,	229
257.	Proof that Heat is produced by Motion,	229
258.	Proof that Motion is produced by Heat,	230
259.	Heat not the sole cause of Motion, while Motion is the sole cause of Heat,	230
260.	The amount of Heat produced by a definite amount of Motion, and the Motion produced by the same amount of Heat, exactly equal,	231
261.	Some of the common phenomena of Heat explained on the Mechanical theory,	232
262.	The Mechanical theory confirmed by several simple facts,	233
263.	Heat may be converted into Light,	234

xviii   TABLE OF CONTENTS.

PAR.   PAGE
264. The convertibility into one another of the Forces which act upon
     Matter, and their indestructibility, - - - - - 235

CHAPTER III.

THE SECOND CHEMICAL AGENT,—LIGHT.

THE NATURE OF LIGHT; SOURCES; REFLECTION; REFRACTION; SOLAR SPECTRUM; SPECTRUM ANALYSIS; EFFECT OF LIGHT ON PLANTS; CHEMICAL EFFECT OF LIGHT; PHOTOGRAPHY; RELATIONS OF LIGHT AND HEAT.

265. The nature of Light, - - - - - - - 236
266. The sources of Light,—Solar Light, - - - 237
267. The ignition of Solids a source of Light, - - - 238
268. Electricity a source of Light, - - - - 238
269. Exposure to the Sun's rays and to Electricity a source of Light, 239
270. Decaying Animal and Vegetable matter a source of Light, 239
271. Luminous animals a source of Light, - - - - 239
272. Crystallization a source of Light, - - - - 239
273. The reflection of Light, - - - - - - 240
274. The refraction of Light, - - - - - 241
275. The double refraction and polarization of Light, - 242
276. The compound nature of Solar Light. The illuminating rays, 243
277. The number of vibrations required to produce the different colors of the Solar Spectrum, - - - - 246
278. The Heat rays of the Solar beam, - - - - 246
279. The Chemical rays of the Solar beam, - - - 248
280. The range of the Chemical rays in the Solar Spectrum,—Fluorescence, - - - - - - - 249
281. The triple character of Solar Light, - - - - 250
282. The spectra produced by Artificial light and colored flames, 252
283. The Solar Spectrum not continuous, but crossed by fixed dark lines,—Fraunhofer's Lines, - - - - 253
284. Spectra produced by the light of the Nebulæ, and by Artificial light, crossed by bright, instead of dark, lines, - - 255
285. Spectrum Analysis, - - - - - - 256
286. The Spectroscope, - - - - - - - 258
287. The new metals discovered by Spectrum Analysis, - - 259
288. The dark lines of the Solar Spectrum exactly coincident with the bright lines of spectra produced by the metals, - - 261

TABLE OF CONTENTS. xix

PAR.		PAGE
289.	The bright lines afforded by Metallic spectra converted into dark lines. The dark lines of the Solar Spectrum explained,	261
290.	The effect of Solar Light on the Vegetable kingdom,	263
291.	Summary of the effects of Light on Vegetation,	264
292.	The effect of Solar light on Chemical compounds,	265
293.	The Daguerreotype process,	266
294.	Photographs,	267
295.	The Photographic Camera,	269
296.	Photographs produced solely by the Chemical rays of the Solar Beam,	270
297.	Practical importance of distinguishing between the Illuminating and Chemical rays of Light,	271
298.	All surfaces are affected by the Sun's light,	272
299.	The relations of the rays of Heat, Light and Chemical effect, in the Solar Spectrum,	273

EXPERIMENTS ON LIGHT,—273, 274, 275.

CHAPTER IV.

THE THIRD CHEMICAL AGENT,—ELECTRICITY.

STATICAL ELECTRICITY; GALVANIC ELECTRICITY; ELECTRO-MAGNETISM; MAGNETO-ELECTRICITY; THERMO-ELECTRICITY; ANIMAL ELECTRICITY; THE RELATIONS OF THE CHEMICAL AGENTS.

§ I. Statical Electricity.

300.	Electricity,	275
301.	The nature of Electricity,	276
302.	The fundamental facts of Statical Electricity,	276
303.	The sources of Electricity,	277
304.	Electrical attraction and repulsion,	278
305.	Two bodies similarly electrified repel each other,	279
306.	Two bodies differently electrified attract each other. Two kinds of Electricity,—Vitreous and Resinous,	279
307.	The Electroscope,	279
308.	Conductors and Non-conductors,—Insulation,	280
309.	Vitreous electricity cannot be produced without a corresponding amount of Resinous electricity, and *vice versa*,	281
310.	Induction of Electricity,	282
311.	The intervention of solid matter no obstacle to Induction,	283

TABLE OF CONTENTS.

	PAGE
312. The theory of Induction,	284
313. Electricity confined to the external surface of bodies,	285
314. Theories of Electricity,	286
315. Development of large quantities,—The Electrical Machine,	287
316. The Leyden Jar,	288
317. Mode of charging the Leyden Jar,	290
318. The theory of the Leyden Jar,	290
319. The Electrophorus,	291
320. The Hydro-Electric Machine,	292
321. The effects of Electricity,	293

EXPERIMENTS ON STATICAL ELECTRICITY,—296, 297.

II. Galvanic Electricity.

322. Galvanic Electricity,	297
323. Discovery of Galvanic Electricity,	298
324. Galvani's theory,	298
325. Correction of Galvani's theory, by Volta,	299
326. The Voltaic Pile,	300
327. True theory of the Pile,	301
328. Chemical constitution of the substances used to produce Voltaic Electricity,	302
329. Proof that Chemical decomposition is the source of Galvanic Electricity,	303
330. The decomposing plate is the point of departure of the Electrical current,	304
331. Mode of transfer of the Hydrogen,	305
332. The part played by the Copper plate,	306
333. The polarization and transfer of the elements of the Liquid, and the polarization of the Solid particles of the circuit, necessary for the electric force to circulate,	307
334. Proof that a state of electrical Tension exists in the plates before the actual passage of the current,	309
335. The energy of the current proportionate to the Chemical activity,	310
336. The direction of the current dependent upon the direction of the Chemical action,	311
337. Direct metallic connection between the generating and conducting plate, not necessary,	312
338. Effect of the discharge of Hydrogen on the conducting plate,	312
339. The Gas Battery,	313
340. The Galvanic Battery,	315

PAR.		PAGE.
341.	Batteries of Intensity, and Batteries of Quantity,	316
342.	Improved Batteries,	317
343.	The Sulphate of Copper Battery,	319
344.	Daniell's Battery,	319
345.	Grove's Battery,	321
346.	Bunsen's Battery,	322
347.	Smee's Battery,	323
348.	Management of Batteries,	323
349.	De Luc's Pile,—the dry Pile,	325
350.	Proof of the similarity of the electricity of the Battery and that of the Electrical Machine,	326
351.	The difference between Galvanic and Statical Electricity,	327
352.	Galvanic Batteries of Historic note,	327
353.	Heating effects of the Galvanic current,	328
354.	Ignition produced,	329
355.	Luminous effects,	330
356.	Duboscq's Electric Lamp,	331
357.	Discovery of the Electric Light,	332
358.	The Electric Light not the result of Combustion,	332
359.	The properties and intensity of the Electric Light,	333
360.	Connection between the heat of the battery and the Mechanical equivalent of Heat,	333
361.	Heating effects are best produced by batteries of Quantity,	334
362.	The Chemical effects of the Galvanic current,—decomposing power,	334
363.	The constitution of Water,	334
364.	The decomposition of Water by the Battery,	335
365.	The decomposition of Water is effected by the polarization and transfer of its component elements,	336
366.	The decomposition of other compound Liquids,	338
367.	The decomposition of Metallic Oxides in solution,	338
368.	The decomposition of Metallic Salts in solution,	339
369.	The decomposing Tube,	339
370.	The Glass Cup with porous diaphragm,	340
371.	Secondary decomposition,	341
372.	The experiment of three cups connected by Syphons,	343
373.	Sir H. Davy's experiment in which the Acids and Alkalies, under the influence of the current, seem to lose their ordinary affinity,	344
374.	Exception in the case of the production of insoluble compounds,	344
375.	The successive action of the same current on different vessels of Water,	345

PAR.		PAGE
376.	The successive action of the same current on vessels containing different compound Liquids,	346
377.	Electro-Negative bodies,	347
378.	Electro-Positive bodies,	347
379.	The Law of Chemical decomposition by the electrical current,	347
380.	The amount of Zinc dissolved from the generating plate, is proportioned to the amount of Chemical decomposition produced, and *vice versa*,	348
381.	The Voltameter,	348
382.	Electro-plating and gilding,	349
383.	Electrotyping,	350
384.	The protection of the Copper sheathing of ships,	352

§ III. Electro-Magnetism.

385.	Magnetic effects of the current,	353
386.	What is a Magnet?	355
387.	The poles of the Magnet,	355
388.	The mutual actions of the Poles,	355
389.	The directive action of the Earth upon the Magnet,	356
390.	The Astatic Needle,	357
391.	The induction of Magnetism,	358
392.	All substances are either attracted or repelled by the Magnet,—Magnetic and Dia-magnetic bodies,	358
393.	The dia-magnetism of Gases,	359
394.	Oxygen, a magnetic substance,	360
395.	Magnetic and Dia-magnetic bodies,	361
396.	Reason why a magnetic needle assumes a position at right angles to the conducting wire,	361
397.	The Galvanic current produces magnetism,—Electro-magnets,	362
398.	Molecular movements during the magnetization of bars,	364
399.	The Galvanometer,	364
400.	The Astatic Galvanometer,	365
401.	The Liquid part of the Voltaic circuit acts upon the magnetic needle,	366
402.	The Laws of Electro-magnetism,	367
403.	Ampere's Theory of magnetism,	367
404.	The magnetic effect of the wire carrying the current accounted for by Ampere's theory,	369
405.	The most powerful form of Electro-magnets,—the Horse Shoe Magnet,	372
406.	The Magnetic Telegraph,	373
407.	Morse's Electro-magnetic Indicator,	376

PAR.		PAGE
408.	The Telegraphic manipulator, and Morse's alphabet,	377
409.	The Relay,	379
410.	The transmission of messages,	381
411.	Telegraphic Batteries,	382
412.	Caillaud's Battery,	383
413.	The Sand Battery,	384
414.	The Earth as a part of the Telegraphic circuit,	384
415.	The velocity of the telegraphic current,	387
416.	The Submarine Telegraph,	387
417.	The Atlantic Telegraph Cable,	389
418.	Thomson's Reflecting Galvanometer,	391
419.	The actual arrangement of the Cable,	392
420.	The Rate of transmission,	393
421.	History of the Atlantic Telegraph,	394
422.	Application of Electro-magnetism to the production of Motion,	395
423.	The Electro-motor of M. Froment,	396
424.	The Electro-motor of M. Jacoby,	398
425.	Electro-magnetic Locomotives,	398
426.	Page's Electro-magnetic Locomotive,	398
427.	Stewart's Electro-motor,	400
428.	The expense of Electro-magnetism compared with Steam,	400
429.	Electro-magnetic Clocks,	401
430.	The Electric Fire-alarm,	403
431.	Electric Gas-lighting,	406
432.	Progress of discovery in Electro-magnetism,	407

§ IV. Galvanic Induced Electricity.

433.	Volta-electric Induction,	409
434.	Faraday's Experiments,	411
435.	The inductive effect of the Primary current often takes place through a considerable distance,	413
436.	Induction of a momentary Secondary current by the approach and removal of the primary current,	415
437.	The conditions of Induction, and properties of induced currents,	417
438.	Induction of a current on itself. The extra current,	417
439.	Induction of a Secondary current in the primary wire itself,	419
440.	Induced Tertiary currents. Henry's Coils,	422
441.	History of the discovery of Volta-electric Induction,	424

§ V. Magneto-Electricity.

442.	Magneto-electric Induction,	425
443.	Electricity induced by induced magnetism,	426

TABLE OF CONTENTS.

PAR.		PAGE
444.	History of the discovery of Magneto-electricity,	428
445.	Volta-Magneto-electric Induction,	429
446.	History of the discovery of the Induction of Electricity by Electro-magnetism,	430
447.	Arago's Rotations,	432
448.	The magnetism of the Earth induces secondary currents of Electricity in metallic bodies in motion,	434
449.	Magneto-electric Induction confirms Ampere's Theory,	435
450.	Volta-Magneto-electric Coils for inducing secondary currents,	435
451.	Page's Separable helices,	436
452.	The Circuit-breaker,	438
453.	Ruhmkorff's Coil for inducing secondary electrical currents,	440
454.	Ruhmkorff's Coil complete,	444
455.	Ritchie's improved Ruhmkorff's Coil,	445
456.	The management of Ruhmkorff's Coil,	448
457.	The mechanical effects of Ruhmkorff's Coil,	450
458.	The Physiological effects,	450
459.	The Heating effects,	450
460.	The Luminous effects,	452
461.	The Light intermittent, and affected by the Magnet,	456
462.	Application of Geissler's Tubes to medical purposes, and to the illumination of Mines,	458
463.	Application of Ruhmkorff's Coil to Spectrum Analysis,	459
464.	Chemical effects,	460
465.	Conversion of Carbon into the Diamond by the long continued action of the Coil,	463
466.	Magneto-electric Machines. The principles on which they depend,	466
467.	Saxton's Magneto-electric Machine,	466
468.	Page's Magneto-electric Machine,	469
469.	Magneto-electricity used in the Arts in place of Voltaic electricity, especially for the illumination of Light-houses,	471
470.	Holmes' Magneto-electric Machine, for illuminating Light-houses,	472
471.	Wilde's Magneto-electric Machine,	475
472.	Improvements upon Wilde's Machine. Ladd's improvement,	481
473.	Points of difference between the electricity of the Machine and that of the Battery,	482
474.	Points of resemblance between the electricity of the Machine and the secondary electrical currents induced by the primary current, and by Magnets,	485

TABLE OF CONTENTS. XXV

PAR.		PAGE
475.	The quantity of electricity produced by the Battery immense, and its magnetic effect far superior to that of the Machine,	485
476.	The action of electricity and magnetism on Light, - -	487
477.	Progress of discovery in the induction of electricity, and the construction of Induction Coils and Magneto-electric Machines,	491

§ VI. Thermo-Electricity.

478.	Heat produces Electricity, - - - - -	493
479.	Thermo-electric Battery, - - - - -	495
480.	Thermo-electric Battery of Nobili, - - - -	496
481.	Thermo-multiplier of Melloni, - - - -	497
482.	Farmer's Thermo-electric Battery, - - - -	498

§ VII. Animal Electricity.

483.	Animal life produces Electricity, - - - -	500
484.	Physiological effects of the Galvanic current, - - -	502
485.	Various sources of Electricity, and its relations to the other two Chemical Agents, Heat and Light, - - - -	505

§ VIII. Conclusion of the Chemical Forces.

486.	The relations subsisting between the three Chemical Forces, Heat, Light and Electricity. They are convertible, and probably due to the motion of the molecules of bodies, - -	506
487.	In every case of the convertibility of the Chemical Forces, there is an expenditure of the original Force, and a reduction of its strength exactly equivalent to that of the new Force produced,	508
488.	The convertibility and equivalency of Forces true of all the Forces which act on Matter, - - - -	511
489.	The Indestructibility and Conservation of Force. The Correlation of The Forces, - - - - -	511
490.	Heat and Electricity the chief agents used by the Chemist in his investigations. The Lamp and the Galvanic Battery his chief instruments, - - - - - -	512
491.	The Conclusion of the Chemical Forces, - - -	513

EXPERIMENTS ON GALVANIC ELECTRICITY; ELECTRO-MAGNETISM; MAGNETO-ELECTRICITY; RUHMKORFF'S COIL; THERMO ELECTRICITY, AND ANIMAL ELECTRICITY,—514, 515, 516, 517, 518, 519, 520, 521, 522, 523, 524, 525.

THE
CHEMICAL FORCES.

HEAT—LIGHT—ELECTRICITY.

CHAPTER I.

SUBJECT-MATTER OF CHEMISTRY: USES: HISTORY: THE CHEMICAL AGENTS.

1. Origin of the name Chemistry. The name Chemistry, is said to be derived from the Arabic word *Kimia*, something *hidden* or *concealed*, and from this, to have been converted into Χημεία, a word first used by the Greeks about the eleventh century, and meaning the art of making gold and silver. Between the fifth century and the taking of Constantinople in the fifteenth century, says Dr. Thomson, in his History of Chemistry, the Greeks believed in the possibility of making gold and silver artificially; and the art which professed to teach these processes was called by them, Chemistry. This idea, however, has long since been thoroughly discarded, and is now no longer heard of.

2. The nature of Chemistry. It explains the composition of Matter. Chemistry is now a science of well-established laws and principles, the object of which is the study of the composition of Matter. It informs us of what the various sub-

---

1. What is the derivation of the name Chemistry? What was the meaning of the word among the Greeks? Is it any longer regarded as the art of making gold and silver?—2. How is it now regarded? Enumerate its objects.

stances in nature, the rocks, the soil, the water, the air, the trees, the plants, the animals, and all the various solids and liquids of the earth are made. It teaches us, also, the number and properties of these elementary substances, and the action which they exert upon each other when mingled. It studies the laws which regulate their union, ascertains the proportions in which they combine, devises means for separating them when combined, and seeks to apply such knowledge to the explanation of the phenomena of Nature, and the improvement of the various Arts.

3. Matter, what it is. Chemistry, it will be seen, treats of the subject of Matter. The question therefore arises, What is Matter? The name Matter may be given to any substance which is cognizable by any one or all of the senses. Every thing not cognizable by the senses, passes under the name Immaterial. All matter possesses the four properties of Extension, Impenetrability, Inertia, and Weight. We know that a body possesses Extension, from its occupying a portion of space; we know that it possesses Impenetrability, from its not allowing another body to occupy this space at the same time with itself; we know that it possesses Inertia, from its want of power to change its state, to move if at rest, to cease to move if in motion; we know that it possesses Weight, from its effect upon the balance, and from the fact that it falls to the ground if its support be withdrawn.

4. Matter, though Inert, capable of being affected by External Forces. Matter is in itself inert, but it is subject to the control of certain forces,—1st. *Cohesion.* This force binds together particles of matter of the same kind, with more or less strength, producing solid bodies of different sizes, and various degrees of hardness and toughness. It acts only at insensible distances, the closest proximity of the particles being required in order to admit of its exercise. When this proximity has once been destroyed, its restoration is a matter of great difficulty.— 2d. *Adhesion.* This is the force which unites unlike particles of matter, when brought near to each other. Thus, if a rod of glass be dipped in water or oil, particles of the liquid will adhere to its surface. In common language, the rod is said to have become wetted; in the language of science, adhesion has taken place between the particles of glass and those of the liquid with

---

3. Give the meaning of the word Matter? What four properties does it possess? What is meant by Extension? by Impenetrability? by Inertia? by Weight?—4. What four Forces is Matter subject to? Define Cohesion. Define Adhesion.

which it has been brought in contact. By the same force, liquids are raised in fine tubes, provided there be adhesion between them and the matter of which the tubes are made; in such cases, it constitutes a force which is called Capillary Attraction. In other cases it is the force which operates in the use of cements and glue. It is unlike cohesion, in tending to unite particles of different kinds, and in not requiring such close proximity for its action.—3d. *Repulsion.* This is the force which prevents particles of the same body from coming into actual contact, and from being so tightly bound together by the force of cohesion as to be incapable of separation. It is supposed to be due to the presence of heat in bodies, and is always the antagonist of cohesion. The state of a body as to softness and hardness, depends upon the relative proportion existing between these two forces. When repulsion predominates, the substance will be very soft; but when cohesion is superior, it will become proportionally hard and tough. We possess the means of increasing and diminishing the force of repulsion in any substance, and, consequently, of affecting many of its physical properties, by elevating or depressing its temperature.—4th. *Gravity.* This force operates upon particles of matter, whether like or unlike, and tends to draw them toward each other. It does not require close proximity for its action, though its power is increased as the square of the distance diminishes. This is the force which tends to draw masses of matter towards the centre of the earth, and to attract the earth itself, with all the planets, to the sun. It is not confined, however, to such large masses of matter as these. A pendulum, in vibration, will be sensibly affected by the presence of a mountain in its neighborhood; and even smaller masses of matter, if susceptible of motion, tend to approach each other under its influence.

5. The Three Principal States of Matter: Solid, Liquid, and Gaseous. Matter exists in three principal states, the Solid, the Liquid, and the Gaseous. When the particles of a body are in close proximity, and so firmly united as to be incapable of any considerable change of place in reference to each other, the body is said to be a Solid. When the particles are far enough apart to admit of a very appreciable degree of motion, they form a Liquid; and when they are separated so far as to cease to be drawn towards each other at all, they constitute a Gas, like the atmosphere, or a Vapor, like steam.

---

4. Define Repulsion. Define Gravity.—5. State the three principal forms of Matter. State the difference between Solids, Liquids, and Gases.

The difference between gases and vapors, is that the former are permanently aeriform at all ordinary temperatures, the latter are the aeriform fluids, that are formed, by the addition of heat, from various liquids, such as alcohol, ether, water, and mercury, and they remain in the aeriform state only so long as their temperature is maintained above a certain point; when their temperature is reduced below this point, they immediately return to the liquid state from which they sprung.

The existence of matter in one of these states in preference to the others, is chiefly due to the relative strength of the forces of cohesion and repulsion. When Cohesion predominates, the body is in the solid state: when the two forces are in equilibrium, the body is in the liquid state; and when Repulsion preponderates, the body assumes the gaseous state. As we have the means of varying the force of repulsion by the addition or abstraction of heat, oftentimes the same portion of matter may be made to pass from the first of these states, through the second, into the third, and then to return to its original condition. Thus, ice, by the application of heat, may be converted into water; this water, by the further addition of heat, into steam; and when this heat is withdrawn, the steam will return first into the state of water, and then into that of ice. In the same way, many of the permanent gases, by the combined influence of the abstraction of heat, and mechanical pressure, may be reduced to the liquid, and finally to the solid state.

6. The Peculiar Properties of Solids. Solids possess, to a marked degree, the distinctive properties of matter, such as Opacity, Transparency, Softness, Hardness, Elasticity or the reverse, Color, and Density. Their particles are also nearly immovable, and pressure operating upon them is propagated through them in right lines, or in a right line which passes through their centres of gravity.

7. The Peculiar Properties of Liquids. Liquids exhibit the characteristic properties of matter with less positiveness than solids. They are all, with the exception of mercury, more or less transparent. They are compressible only to a very limited extent, and, therefore, very slightly elastic. They differ from solids, in propagating pressure, made at any one point, equally in all directions; consequently, a pressure of one pound to the square inch, upon the side or bottom or any part of a liquid,

---

5. To what is this difference owing? Show the effect of increasing and diminishing the force of repulsion in the case of Ice.—6. State the peculiar properties of Solids. How is pressure propagated through them?—7. State the peculiar properties of Liquids. Show how pressure is propagated through them.

will be propagated in such a way that the same pressure of one pound will be experienced by every other square inch throughout the liquid, and by every square inch of the vessel containing it. The weight of a solid immersed in a liquid is diminished by the weight of the mass of liquid which it displaces. All liquids therefore have a certain buoyant power. Water is taken as the type of liquids, because it possesses their marked characteristics in an eminent degree.

8. The Peculiar Properties of Gases. Gases possess the distinguishing properties of matter to a much less extent than either Solids or Liquids. They are all transparent, and many of them colorless; their particles are capable of an unlimited degree of motion; they are very compressible, and highly elastic, and tend, when compressed, to return with great force to their original dimensions. As they are in a state of constant compression, in consequence of the atmospheric pressure to which they are always subjected, they are never in a state of permanent equilibrium, but are continually striving to increase in volume, and tending powerfully to expand. This is their principal characteristic. They are greatly dilated by heat; pressure is propagated through them, as through liquids, equally in all directions; some of them, by pressure and the abstraction of heat, can be reduced to the liquid, and even to the solid state; but the greater part of them, like the atmosphere, resist every attempt at solidification, and remain permanently gaseous at all temperatures. They also, like liquids, diminish the weight of all solid bodies immersed in them, by the weight of a bulk of the gas equal to that of the body immersed. They consequently possess also a certain buoyant power, and all bodies therefore weigh less in air or other gases than they do in a vacuum.

9. The Atmosphere a Type of all Gases. Its Properties. The Atmosphere possesses the properties of the Gases in the most marked manner. It is perfectly clear and transparent. It is very compressible, and by pressure may be made to occupy much less space than it ordinarily does. It is highly elastic, and tends, when compressed, to return to its original volume. The space which it occupies, depends upon the pressure to which it is subjected: if the pressure be doubled, its volume is diminished one-half; if the pressure be diminished one-half, the space

---

7. What is the type of all Liquids?—8. State the peculiar properties of Gases. Show how pressure is propagated through them.—9 State the principal properties of the Air. What is the effect of pressure upon the space which it occupies?

occupied is doubled. The atmosphere possesses weight, and presses with an average force of about fifteen pounds upon every square inch of the earth's surface. This pressure is the weight of a column of air resting upon a base whose area is one square inch, and extending from the lowest to the highest limit of the Atmosphere. By the pressure of one atmosphere is always meant, a pressure of fifteen pounds to the square inch.

The weight of the atmosphere varies continually, and this variation is measured by the rise and fall of the mercury in the tube of the barometer. When the air is heavier, a longer column of mercury will be supported; when lighter, a shorter column only can be sustained. When the pressure is exactly equal to fifteen pounds, it will sustain a column of mercury thirty inches high, the weight of a column of mercury of that height, and with a base one square inch in area, being exactly fifteen pounds. One hundred cubic inches of air, at 30 inches of the barometer, and 60° Fahrenheit's thermometer, weigh 30.829 grains. The body of a man of medium size, exposes a surface of about fifteen square feet, and he must consequently sustain a pressure of more than 30,000 pounds, or about fifteen tons. This vast weight is carried without effort, because, in consequence of the propagation of pressure by the air, equally in all directions, the external pressure is counterbalanced by an equal pressure exerted from within, through the medium of the air which penetrates into the interior of the body. As there is the same amount of pressure upward, as there is downward, the air, in fact, exerts a certain buoyant power, which tends to support his body and render his movements even more free and easy than they would be in a vacuum. As we ascend in the atmosphere, its weight and pressure diminish; and at 2.7 miles its pressure is but seven and a half pounds to the square inch, and the barometer stands at only fifteen inches. The height of the mercury in the tube of the barometer, is therefore an excellent measure of altitude. On the contrary, as we descend below the level of the sea, the atmospheric pressure increases, and the mercury in the tube of the barometer has been known to rise to forty-five inches. The extreme range of the barometer between the highest altitudes reached in balloons, and the greatest depth beneath the level of the sea, is from thirty-three to thirty-

---

9. What is the pressure of the Atmosphere to the square inch? By what instrument is the atmospheric pressure measured? What is the amount of this pressure upon the body of a man? What change takes place in the atmospheric pressure as we ascend into the air? What is the range of the barometer? What is the variation of pressure upon the body of a man within these limits?

four inches; and as the variation of one inch produces a change of pressure upon the body of a man, of 1,000 pounds, the variation of pressure experienced in these cases amounts to thirty-three or thirty-four thousand pounds. The distance to which the atmosphere extends above the earth cannot be very accurately determined, but is estimated at about forty-five miles.

10. The General Properties of Matter, as Solid, Liquid and Gaseous, are treated of by Natural Philosophy. These general properties are essential to Matter, and must be taken into view in forming a correct idea of it. They constitute the subject of Natural Philosophy, and it is to that science that we must resort for a detailed and systematic description of the general properties of the matter of the universe, as it exists in the three different states, solid, liquid, and gaseous. But *particular kinds of matter*, forming the various special substances that surround us, possess additional properties which it is the peculiar province of chemistry to investigate. The general properties of matter must, however, first be understood; and therefore an acquaintance with the first principles of natural philosophy is a necessary preliminary to the study of chemistry; while, on the other hand, a knowledge of chemistry is a necessary supplement to natural philosophy, if it be wished to have a complete understanding of the true nature of the various forms of matter which surround us.

11. Chemistry treats of the same Properties of Matter as Natural Philosophy, and of others beside. The properties of Matter treated of by natural philosophy are very different from those investigated by chemistry. Natural philosophy makes no other distinction in bodies than that of solids, liquids, and gases. In her view all solids are alike, all liquids, and all gases, because they all possess the same general properties. Chemistry, on the other hand, treats of every particular solid, liquid, and gas, and shows in what respects each differs from every other. Natural philosophy takes notice only of the external and obvious properties of bodies, such as Color, Weight, Density, Elasticity, and those which belong to all matter in the mass, whether solid, liquid, or gaseous. Chemistry, on the other hand, deals with the internal constitution of Matter, seeks to take it to pieces, to resolve it into its elements, to ascertain of

---

9. What is the height of the Atmosphere?—10 What science takes note of the general properties of solids, liquids, and gases? What science treats of special kinds of Matter?—11. What is the difference between natural philosophy and chemistry? Why is chemistry a science of analysis?

8   PROVINCE OF CHEMISTRY.

what simple substances every variety of it consists, and to study the properties and relations of each. It is essentially a science of *analysis*, and its great object is to find out what all substances are made of, and what action they exert on each other when brought into contact; to study the nature of the compounds which they form, and to ascertain the character of the force which produces their union.

12. **The Study of Matter forms the Subject of other Sciences besides Natural Philosophy and Chemistry, viz., Mineralogy, Botany, and Zoology.** If we regard material objects in reference to their external form, the different arrangement of their parts, their power of growth, of motion, and of reproducing other objects like themselves, in short, if we regard Matter as entering into the structure of minerals, plants, and animals, and classify these according to the degree of resemblance found in their internal and external organization, we are led to the three descriptive sciences which constitute Natural History, viz., Mineralogy, or the description and history of minerals, Botany, or the description and history of plants, and Zoölogy, or the description and history of animals. If, on the other hand, we regard material objects entirely apart from their form and organization, and only as composed of matter in general, we are confined to the sciences of natural philosophy and chemistry.

13. **Difference between Natural Philosophy and Chemistry illustrated by an Example.** Take a piece of marble, for instance: it possesses weight, and is influenced by the force of gravity; it has color, density, opacity; it is composed of small particles bound together by the force of cohesion, and these particles, however minute, are yet, each of them, as truly marble as any portion of the mass, however large. These are the only properties of the marble which are noticed by natural philosophy; but there are others, besides. Each little particle of the marble, however small, is a compound substance, made up of three elements, very different from marble, and very different from each other in all their properties, viz.: a metal named Calcium, common charcoal or Carbon, and a gas named Oxygen. These three substances, when brought into close proximity, exert a certain *action* upon each other: they are drawn toward

---

12. What other sciences does the study of matter include? What is Mineralogy? What is Botany? What is Zoology?—13. Illustrate the difference between natural philosophy and chemistry by a piece of marble. What force unites the particles of marble of which a mass of marble consists? To what science does the consideration of the force of cohesion belong? What are the three substances of which each particle of marble is composed?

each other, and tend to unite to form a fourth substance entirely distinct in all its properties from those of the elements that enter into it. There are more than sixty such elementary substances, all of which tend to act upon each other, and to unite so as to form new substances, whenever they are brought into contact. It is the properties possessed by these elements, and by the compounds which they form, the force which unites them together, and the character of the action which they exert upon each other, that constitute the subjects of which chemistry takes cognizance.

14. Chemistry is a Science of Experiment. With many varieties of Chemical Action we are familiar. Sugar dissolves in water; bright iron rusts in the air, and when heated in the fire, becomes covered with black scales; wood and coal burn, and are converted into invisible gases; illuminating gas gives forth light and heat, and then disappears; soda powders, when mingled in water, produce a large quantity of gas, which escapes in foam; charcoal, when inflamed, gives forth an invisible gas which puts out lighted candles, and destroys life. With these, and many other instances of the action of different kinds of matter on each other, we are already familiar, for they fall under our notice every day; but it is chemistry which investigates and explains them. Where this explanation is not easy, experiments are invented for the purpose of ascertaining the truth. Chemistry, consequently, is a science of experiment.

15. A Chemical Experiment: what it is. A Chemical Experiment is a process devised for the purpose of eliciting or illustrating some important chemical truth. Suppose we wish to ascertain of what common Salt is made: we pour some common sulphuric acid or oil of vitriol, which may be procured at any druggist's, upon a little table salt in a glass flask provided with a cork and a piece of bent tube like that in *Fig.* 1. Sulphuric acid is a compound of sulphur and oxygen gas, and is a thick and oily liquid. As soon as it touches the salt, an effervescence is produced, and a white, pungent vapor formed, which es-

Fig. 1.

A Chemical Experiment.

---

13. How many elementary substances are there? Mention the subjects of which chemistry takes cognizance.—14. Mention some instances of chemical action.—15. If we wish to know of what common salt is composed, what do we do? What is sulphuric acid?

capes into the air. If now the end of the tube discharging the vapor be dipped into a wine-glass partly filled with a solution of purple cabbage, the purple color is immediately turned to red; if dipped into water, the water becomes acid. We conclude, therefore, that common salt contains a substance, which, when driven out by sulphuric acid, has a most pungent and irritating odor, an acid taste, and the property of turning vegetable blue colors red. We say, therefore, that salt, when treated in this way, gives forth an acid. This is what is called a Chemical Experiment; and the science which devises processes like this, and traces their results, is called the science of chemistry.

16. Chemistry is connected with many Curious Processes in the Arts. If into the flask used in the experiment just described, still containing oil of vitriol and salt, we put a little oxide of manganese, and apply heat, the white vapor disappears, and is replaced by a gas of a green color; and what is very singular, if this green gas be made to pass into a wine-glass containing a solution of purple cabbage, or some of the liquid turned red in our last experiment, these liquids almost at once become colorless, and we observe, as the bubbles of gas escape, that they diffuse a very disagreeable odor. Here we have another experiment illustrative of a Chemical process of a very curious and important character, one which is daily performed upon an immense scale, in the arts, for the purpose of bleaching the cotton and linen fabrics which we wear, and of making the rags from which writing and printing papers are manufactured, fair and white. The green gas in this experiment is called Chlorine, and it is contained in common salt, united with a bright and shining metal named Sodium. Common salt is composed exclusively of these two elements, and takes from them its chemical name, Chloride of Sodium.

17. Chemistry explains the nature of Medicines. If, again, into this green Chlorine gas, we dip a little hot Mercury, the metal immediately begins to burn, and to emit a white cloud, producing a substance known in medicine as Corrosive Sublimate, a virulent poison composed of chlorine and metallic mercury. The medicine Calomel is also composed of chlorine and

---

15. What takes place when sulphuric acid is poured on the salt? What effect has the substance driven out of the salt, on vegetable blues?—16. What process in the arts is explained by chemistry? What is the green gas named that is driven out of the salt? What other substance besides chlorine is contained in salt?—17. What is the effect of putting hot mercury into chlorine? What is the difference between corrosive sublimate and calomel?

mercury, but it has double the quantity of mercury in it that corrosive sublimate has. Calomel may therefore be made by adding an additional quantity of mercury to corrosive sublimate. Here we have another chemical process of great importance in the preparation and administration of medicines.

18. Chemistry explains the change which Respiration produces in the Air. If, through a piece of glass tube, we breathe air from the mouth into a tall wine-glass containing lime-water, the water will immediately acquire a white color and become turbid; and if, after breathing some minutes, we gently lower a lighted taper almost to the surface of the water, it will be at once extinguished. A small insect, introduced in the same manner, will soon die. From this experiment it is evident that there issues from our mouths in breathing, an invisible substance which has the power of turning lime-water white, extinguishing lights, and destroying animal life; and this explains why it is, that if a number of persons are confined in a small closed room, unprovided with means for ventilation, they are soon suffocated. This invisible gas is called Carbonic Acid, and is a compound of Charcoal and Oxygen. It is produced by the burning of charcoal, and gas, and oil, as well as by the breathing of animals, and this accounts for the fact that death is so often caused by the burning of these substances in closed apartments, and shows the necessity of free ventilation. Here we have a great danger, the real nature of which is made known to us, as well as the importance of guarding against it, by the science of which we propose to treat.

19. Chemistry is connected with Agriculture. The farmer, as is well known, if he wishes to increase the amount of his crops, plentifully manures his fields. Chemistry teaches us that one of the most important constituents of all animal manures is the gas Ammonia, and shows how its escape into the air, before the manure is worked into the soil, can be prevented. It teaches us that ammonia is itself composed of two other distinct gases, Nitrogen and Hydrogen, in the proportion of one atom of the former to three of the latter, and that it is the substance which gives to common hartshorn its pungent odor and other

---

17. Of what use is chemistry in the manufacture of medicines?—18. What takes place when breath is forced from the lungs through lime-water? What happens to a lighted taper introduced into the wine-glass? To an insect? What change is produced in the air by respiration? By the burning of gas and oil? Why is ventilation necessary?—19. What valuable substance does chemistry disclose in manure? What is ammonia? What has it to do with guano?

12   USES OF CHEMISTRY.

characteristic properties. Chemistry shows us how we can apply it to plants in other forms than that of barn-yard manure, especially in the state of guano, points out the special manures that different plants require, and teaches us how to manufacture them. It is to chemistry that we are indebted for our knowledge that Phosphorus is valuable as a fertilizer, particularly in the culture of wheat and other grains, that it is a simple substance contained in bones, and that bone-dust and the phosphates of Lime, which are made from bones, are of great value for enriching the soil. That plants require ample supplies of proper food in order to thrive, and that without it they must languish and die, is another truth of the greatest importance, for which we are chiefly indebted to this science.

20. Chemistry treats of the Extraction of Metals from their Ores. It is Chemistry that shows us how to extract iron and other metals from the stony ores in which they are found in the earth, and explains how, by heating these, after they have been ground and mixed with charcoal and lime, the pure metals are left behind, and the impurities with which they were mingled are separated from them. It is therefore to chemistry that we are indebted for the iron employed in the construction of railroads, steamboats, and every kind of machinery, as well as for the other metals which are used so abundantly in the various arts. It is chemistry also, by teaching how to extract phosphorus from bones, that enables us to manufacture the common friction match abundantly and cheaply.

21. Chemistry is connected with the Manufacture of Gas, and with most of the Useful Arts. The printing of calico, and all processes for dyeing cloth, the preparation of illuminating gas from coal and oil, the making of soap and candles, the distillation of perfumery, the raising of bread, the manufacture of soda water, and innumerable arts of a similar kind, all depend upon chemical principles.

22. Chemistry explains the Great Natural Processes of Respiration and Combustion. Finally, it is Chemistry that explains why atmospheric air is essential to the life of animals

---

19. What substance, valuable as a fertilizer, is found in bones? What great agricultural truth is taught by chemistry?—20. What science explains the extraction of metals from their ores? To what science are we indebted for the cheap and abundant supply of iron? Of phosphorus and friction matches?—21 What other arts are dependent upon chemistry for successful prosecution?—22 What light does chemistry throw upon respiration and combustion? Has it anything to do with the life of animals and plants, or with the lighting of fires, the generation of steam, or the movement of machinery?

and plants, and that it is by the rapid combination of the Carbon and Hydrogen of wood and coal with the Oxygen of the air, that combustion is produced. Thus Chemistry teaches us what it is that keeps vegetable and animal life in existence, and what it is that furnishes the heat required in most of the arts, in cooking, in warming houses, in generating steam, and setting in motion steam engines, steamships, and all the rest of our varied and complicated machinery.

23. The Importance of Chemistry. Thus we see very plainly how important a knowledge of its principles must be to every manufacturer of cotton and paper, to every physician, farmer, and worker in metals; to all makers of locomotives and steam engines; to all manufacturers of gas, and indeed to all persons, whatever their occupations, since it enables them to carry on their various pursuits successfully, and to preserve their health, while, at the same time, it gives them an intelligent appreciation of the great operations of Nature which are continually going on around them. The phenomena of combustion, of respiration, of artificial illumination, and of the action of the atmosphere on the soil, are all explained by it, and a knowledge of its principles should be possessed by every intelligent man.

24. Chemistry furnishes Striking Proofs of Design. No Science furnishes more striking instances of Design in Creation, more convincing proofs of the existence of God, or more satisfactory illustrations of His Power, Wisdom, and Goodness. It teaches more forcibly than any other Science, our entire dependence from moment to moment, for life and breath, upon a Being higher than ourselves, and that it is not in man, whose breath is in his nostrils, to direct his own steps; shows how impossible it is to violate any even of the Physical Laws of the Almighty with impunity, and conduces powerfully therefore to the promotion of principles of Humility, Devotion, and Obedience.

25. The History of Chemistry. The History of Chemistry commences with the first efforts of man to appropriate the natural world to his use, and to fabricate out of rude matter, articles of luxury and necessity. A practical knowledge of the chemical properties of common substances must have been possessed from the earliest ages, by all persons engaged in the extraction

---

23. To what trades and professions is a knowledge of its principles essential? Why should all persons desire to know something of this science?—24. What light does it throw upon the relations of Man to his Creator? What does it show in regard to the character of God?—25. Trace the History of Chemistry.

14   USE OF THE BALANCE.

of metals from their ores, and in the manufacture of soaps, dyes, and glass. The art of making leavened bread required a knowledge of practical chemistry. The lighting of a common fire is one of the most beautiful and striking of all chemical processes; and the earliest chemist, beyond all question, was the man who first struck a spark from the flint, in order to produce flame. Experience daily added to the stock of chemical knowledge. In the course of time this knowledge was greatly increased by the invention of ingenious experiments, and by the researches of the Alchemists. These singular men professed the art of converting the baser metals into gold: this they believed could be effected by means of the Philosopher's Stone, which they described as being a red powder having a very peculiar smell. They also entertained the opinion that there was a great similarity between the mode of purifying gold and curing disease, and that the Philosopher's Stone was also an Elixir of Life, by the use of which the existence of man could be indefinitely prolonged. But it was not until about the year 1774 that Chemistry became fairly entitled to rank among the Sciences, when, in the hands of the illustrious Lavoisier, the Balance was called in, for the purpose of applying its rigorous test to the results of all chemical experiments. Since that time its progress has been rapid and brilliant; and hardly any names shine more brightly on the rolls of fame, than those of the Philosophers who have devoted themselves to this Science. Priestley, Cavendish, Watt, Lavoisier, Davy, Faraday, and Liebig, possess a reputation limited to no age or country.

26. Weight and Proportion of Great Importance. Modern Chemistry depends upon the Use of the Balance. As Chemistry undertakes to teach the composition of matter, it not only requires that the different substances entering into a compound should be pointed out, but also the proportions in which they combine. This demands the constant use of the Balance, and renders the subject of weight one of the greatest importance to the chemist. Nearly all the great chemical truths have been rigorously examined and tested by this instrument, and it is therefore of as much importance to the chemist as the telescope is to the Astronomer. It is constructed with the greatest accuracy, and so much importance is attached to its indications, that the general division of substances into Ponderable and Impon-

---

25. Who were the Alchemists?—26. How is the subject of proportion connected with chemistry? Why is the Balance necessary? How should it be constructed?

derable is founded upon them, the former class embracing everything that has, the latter, everything that has not any appreciable weight.

27. Other Apparatus required in the Study of Chemistry. Besides the balance, the most important apparatus required in chemistry is an air pump, an electrical machine, a powerful gas lamp, alcohol lamps, a platinum crucible, a small galvanic battery, a pneumatic cistern, bell glasses for the collection of gases, graduated jars for their measurement, precipitate glasses, flasks, retorts, glass tubes of various sizes, India rubber bags and tubing, all of which may be obtained at no great expense; and there is no one who may not very easily attain such a knowledge of the science as to be able to add something to the stock of chemical knowledge.

28. The Fundamental Principle of Chemistry is the Indestructibility of Matter. The most striking of all Chemical phenomena is *the indestructibility of Matter*, a truth verified only by the constant use of the balance. Whatever changes may be made in the appearance and form of matter by any chemical process, none of it is destroyed. The sum of all the results of every chemical process weighs exactly the same as the sum total of the weight of all the matter that entered into the process. This is true of the combustion of wood and coal in air. If the coal be weighed on the one hand, and on the other, the air which surrounds it, and which serves to produce the combustion, it can be proved with perfect exactness that the sum of the ashes left, and of the water and gas that are formed, is equal in weight to the sum of the weights of the coal and of the air which has been consumed. When mercury is heated in a vessel of confined air, it is eventually converted into a mass of red scales, by uniting with one of the elements contained in the air, and the volume of the air within the vessel is at the same time considerably diminished. If the red scales be now weighed, they will be found exactly equal in weight to the sum of the weights of the mercury and of the air, which have disappeared; in other words, the weight of the compound produced is exactly equal to the weight of the elements which have combined in order to form it. All chemical processes may therefore be expressed in the form of an

---

26 What is the difference between Ponderable and Imponderable substances? 27. What other apparatus is required besides the balance? Is it within the power of all persons to acquire a knowledge of this science?—28. What is the fundamental principle of chemistry?

equation. On one side should be placed all the substances that enter into the process; on the other, all the results, solid, liquid, and gaseous; in every case, these are exactly equal to each other. The principle laid down by Lavoisier, and established by the use of the balance, is, THAT IN NATURE NOTHING IS LOST, AND NOTHING CREATED. Substances may be combined, or separated from each other; but whether combined or separated, they exactly preserve their weight. The end, therefore, which chemistry seeks to attain, is the thorough study of all the ponderable matter of which the earth consists, whether organic or inorganic, animal or vegetable, mineral or metallic, liquid or gaseous. Since Lavoisier conceived the happy idea of introducing the balance into the study of chemical phenomena, this science has advanced with steady progress, determining the composition and ascertaining the mutual relations of all the different kinds of matter, showing that they are composed of a comparatively small number of elementary or simple substances, united in regular proportions, and proving that the great chemical processes unceasingly going on in Nature, result from the action of these simple and compound substances upon each other.

29. Simple and Compound Substances, what they are. A compound substance is one which can be taken to pieces and separated into two or more distinct substances having different properties: thus, Water is a compound substance, and may be separated into two gases, Hydrogen and Oxygen, one of which, Hydrogen, is inflammable, and much lighter than the air; the other, Oxygen, not itself inflammable, makes combustible bodies burn with great fury and brilliancy, and is heavier than the air. Neither Oxygen nor Hydrogen, however, can be separated into other substances, nor can any other substance be extracted from them; consequently they are called Simple substances, or Elements.

30. The Meaning of the Word, Element. When it is said that a chemical substance is an Element, it is only meant that so far as we at present know, it is incapable of decomposition. Future researches may show that many of those now regarded as simple substances are really compound, and that

---

28. How may all chemical processes be expressed in the form of an Algebraic Equation? What great principle was laid down by Lavoisier? What has been discovered in regard to the simple and compound substances of which matter is composed?—29. What is a compound substance? What is a simple substance? Illustrate this difference in the case of water. Is oxygen simple or compound? Why is it called a simple substance?—30. What is an element? Are we absolutely sure that any substance is an element?

some of those now considered compound are really simple. Chlorine was for a long time considered a compound of Oxygen and Muriatic acid; but Davy showed that it is truly a simple substance. Potash, on the other hand, was universally regarded as a simple substance, until the same philosopher proved that it was composed of the metal Potassium, and Oxygen.

31. The Number of the Elements. The number of the Elements is not as great as might be supposed. Chemists have as yet discovered only sixty-five. Of these, fifteen are called metalloids, the remainder are metals. The metalloids are very extensively diffused, but the greater part of the metals are quite rare; not more than one-third are used in the arts, and some of them are found in such small quantities as to have been detected only by the most refined analysis. The list of the elements is steadily increasing; four new metals, Cæsium, Rubidium, Thallium, and Indium, have been discovered within the last four years.

32. The Constitution of some of the most Important Chemical Compounds. By the steady prosecution of chemical research, the composition of nearly all the different forms of matter upon the earth has been determined. The metals are all simple substances, and therefore incapable of decomposition; so also are sulphur, carbon, phosphorus, iodine, bromine, and the gases, oxygen, hydrogen, nitrogen, and chlorine. Water is composed of eight parts by weight of oxygen, and one part by weight of hydrogen; air, of four-fifths by volume, nitrogen, and one-fifth oxygen; sulphuric acid, of sulphur and oxygen; sulphurous acid, also, of sulphur and oxygen, but less oxygen than the preceding; nitric acid, of nitrogen and oxygen; nitrous acid, of nitrogen and oxygen, but less oxygen than the preceding; chloro-hydric acid, of chlorine and hydrogen, and is sometimes called muriatic acid; carbonic acid, of carbon and oxygen, and is an invisible gas, like the atmosphere; illuminating gas is a compound of carbon and hydrogen; ammonia, of nitrogen and hydrogen. Potash is an oxide of potassium, and is composed of oxygen and the metal potassium; soda is the oxide of sodium, and is composed of the metal sodium and oxygen; lime is the oxide of calcium, and is composed of the metal calcium, and

---

30. How was chlorine formerly regarded? How is it now regarded? How is potash regarded?—31 What is the number of the elements? How many of them are non-metallic? How many are used in the arts? What is said in regard to their abundance? Have any new elements been recently discovered? What are they? 32. What is the composition of water? of air? sulphuric acid? carbonic acid? sulphurous acid? nitric acid? nitrous acid? chloro-hydric acid? muriatic acid? carbonic acid? potash? soda? lime?

oxygen. The compounds of oxygen and the different metals are called oxides: thus, there is the oxide of mercury, of iron, of lead, of tin; the compounds of chlorine and the metals are called chlorides, as the chloride of sodium, or common salt, the chloride of mercury, or corrosive sublimate, the chloride of ammonia, or sal ammoniac; the compounds of iodine with the metals are called iodides, as the iodide of mercury, the iodide of potassium. The compounds of sulphuric acid with the different metallic oxides are called sulphates, as the sulphate of iron, composed of sulphuric acid and oxide of iron; sulphate of lime, of sulphuric acid and lime, or the oxide of calcium; sulphate of soda, of sulphuric acid and soda, or the oxide of sodium; sulphate of potash, of sulphuric acid and potash, or the oxide of potassium. The compounds of nitric acid and the metallic oxides are called nitrates, as the nitrate of lead, composed of nitric acid and oxide of lead; nitrate of iron, of nitric acid and oxide of iron. The compounds of chloro-hydric acid and the metallic oxides are called chloro-hydrates, as the chloro-hydrate of iron, composed of chloro-hydric acid and oxide of iron; chloro-hydrate of lime, of chloro-hydric acid and lime, or the oxide of calcium. The compounds of carbonic acid and the metallic oxides are called carbonates, as carbonate of potash, composed of carbonic acid and potash; carbonate of soda, of carbonic acid and soda; carbonate of lime, of carbonic acid and lime, &c.

33. Chemical Affinity, or the Force by which the Elements are united. The force by which the elements are united into the different compounds of which matter chiefly consists, is the force of Chemical Attraction or Affinity. There is no element which has not a powerful tendency to unite with others, and this is the reason why simple substances are so seldom found uncombined in Nature. This tendency is not possessed by them all in an equal degree, and hence some are found in a free state much more frequently than others. This force of Affinity differs both from Cohesion and from Gravity. It differs from gravity, in that it acts at insensible distances. It differs from cohesion, in that it tends to unite only particles of different kinds, while cohesion tends to unite particles of the same kind. Thus, a piece of marble is a collection of small particles attached to

---

32. What is the composition of oxide of mercury? oxide of iron? chloride of sodium? sal ammoniac? chloride of mercury? iodide of mercury? sulphate of iron? sulphate of lime? nitrate of lead? nitrate of ammonia? carbonate of potash? carbonate of lime?—33. What is the force by which the elements are united? Describe this force. How does it differ from cohesion? How does it differ from gravity? Illustrate the nature of affinity in the case of a piece of marble.

each other by cohesion: these are called *integrant* particles, and each of them, however minute, is as perfect marble as the mass itself. Each of these integrant particles, however, consists of three distinct substances, calcium, carbon and oxygen, which are different from one another, as well as from marble, and are united by Affinity: these are the *constituent* particles of marble, and it is of these that Affinity has the exclusive control. The study of this force is essential to the chemist, and, indeed, chemistry may be defined, the science whose object is, to examine the relations that Affinity establishes between bodies, ascertain with precision the nature and constitution of the compounds it produces, and determine the laws by which its action is regulated.

34. The Active Agents of Chemistry. But, while Affinity is the force by which the Elements are united, it is itself controlled and modified by the three great agents, Heat, Light, and Electricity. Thus, the electricity produced by a small galvanic battery can effect the decomposition of water, a firm and stable chemical compound; and this decomposing action of the battery is not limited to water, but extends to a very large number of compound substances. In like manner, heat will decompose limestone, or the carbonate of lime, and drive off the carbonic acid; it will also decompose chlorate of potash, oxide of mercury, oxide of manganese, nitrate of potash, and, in fact, the larger part of all chemical compounds. Light, though acting with less intensity than the two preceding agents, nevertheless produces analogous effects, and decomposes many compound substances. This is shown in a striking manner in its destruction of the colors of various bodies, and especially in the power which it gives to the leaves of plants of decomposing carbonic acid. On the other hand, these agents will often effect the union of substances which under ordinary circumstances refuse to combine. Thus, oxygen and hydrogen will remain uncombined for years, though mingled in the same vessel in proper combining proportions; but if the smallest particle of any substance in active inflammation be applied to the mixture, they will unite instantaneously with a violent detonation, at the same time forming a small quantity of pure water. The same is true of carbon and oxygen, which will remain uncombined for ages, though in the closest proximity; but if the smallest particle of

---

34 By what is Affinity controlled? What are the Active Agents of Chemistry? Give some instances of decomposition produced by them: of combination.

the carbon be heated red-hot, combination will immediately ensue and proceed with the greatest intensity. In like manner, electricity, if made to pass through a mixture of oxygen and hydrogen, will cause them to unite with a violent explosion; and if a succession of electric sparks be transmitted through a mixture of oxygen and nitrogen, we shall find that they have been made to combine and form nitric acid. In the same manner, a beam of bright sunlight, allowed to fall upon a mixture of equal volumes of chlorine and hydrogen, will cause them to combine with a violent explosion, and form chloro-hydric acid. It is evident, therefore, that the force of Affinity is to a great extent under the control of these agents, and it is in their application for the purpose of modifying this force, that the chemical arts chiefly consist. Their nature ought therefore to be thoroughly understood. They are also closely connected, in some mysterious manner, with the constitution of matter, so that this constitution can not be altered without their manifestation. They play a prominent part in the most brilliant phenomena of Nature; they meet us on every hand; they are everywhere present, and are possessed, therefore, of a paramount interest. No chemical process, whether performed on a great scale in Nature, or on a small scale in the arts or in the laboratory, can be carried on without the development or the action of these three agents. Thus, in the experiments already described, the rapidity of the process in every case is much increased by the application of Heat. In some of them great Heat is produced; in others, currents of Electricity are set in motion; and oftentimes the result of both is the production of vivid Light.

35. The Chemical Agents, Heat, Light, and Electricity, are commonly called Imponderables. From the active and energetic nature of Heat, Light, and Electricity, they are called the Chemical Agents; and from the fact that they possess no appreciable weight, so that a body is no heavier for their accumulation, or lighter for their abstraction, they are named the Imponderables. They can not be confined or exhibited in a mass, like ordinary bodies; and can only be collected through the intervention of other substances. Their title to be considered material is therefore questionable, and the effects produced by them have accordingly been attributed by some to certain

---

34. Why should these agents be thoroughly understood? Is it possible to change the constitution of any substance, without meeting with them?—35. Why are heat, light and electricity called Imponderables? Has their title to be called material ever been questioned?

motions or affections of common matter. By some they are considered as only *modes of motion*, and as convertible into each other; and this view is beginning, of late, to attract considerable attention. It must be admitted, however, that they appear to be controlled by the same powers which act on matter in general, and that some of the laws which have been determined concerning them are exactly such as might have been anticipated on the supposition of their materiality. Hence it follows that we need only regard them as subtile species of matter, in order that the phenomena to which they give rise may be explained in the language and according to the principles which are applied to material substances in general; and as such they will be considered in what immediately follows, the thorough discussion of their true nature being reserved until we have become familiar with the principal facts connected with them.

36. The Study of Chemistry should begin with the Chemical Agents. As Heat, Light, and Electricity exercise a controlling influence over Affinity, and are possessed of so much interest and importance in the explanation of chemical phenomena, it is necessary to commence the study of this science with an examination of their principal qualities. We can then proceed to the study of the composition and chemical properties of the different kinds of matter, and the various and extraordinary changes which result from their mutual action.

Chemistry is therefore usually divided into two portions. The first treats of the Chemical Agents, Heat, Light, and Electricity, and is commonly called Chemical Physics; the second, of the Chemical properties and relations of the various kinds of matter. The second of these two portions is, however, itself also divided into two parts, the first treating of the chemical properties of the Inorganic, the second of the chemical properties of Organic matter. The general arrangement of every complete treatise on Chemistry will therefore be as follows:—

Part I. Chemical Physics: Heat Light and Electricity.

Part II. Inorganic Chemistry. Part III. Organic Chemistry.

This treatise is devoted exclusively to the 1st Part, viz., Chemical Physics: Heat, Light and Electricity.

Inorganic and Organic Chemistry are reserved for another volume.

---

35. What other view is taken of them? Which view meets with the most favor? Why is it convenient to regard them as material? What view is taken of them in the present work? When will their true nature be considered?—36. With what should the study of chemistry commence? What subject immediately succeeds the Chemical Agents? Into how many parts is chemistry divided? What does the first part treat of? What is chemical physics? What does the second part treat of? What is the general arrangement? What is the subject of this volume?

CHAPTER II.

THE FIRST CHEMICAL AGENT:—HEAT.

DIFFUSION OF HEAT: EXPANSION: LIQUEFACTION: EBULLITION: EVAPORATION: SPECIFIC HEAT: SOURCES OF HEAT: NATURE OF HEAT.

§ 1.— Diffusion of Heat.

37. The Nature of Heat. Heat is known only from its effects. It has never been isolated, or completely separated from material substances, so as to be obtained in a perfectly pure and uncombined state, and consequently its true nature is altogether a subject of inference and hypothesis. There are two theories in regard to the nature of Heat, which serve with nearly equal completeness to explain all the phenomena to which it gives rise. According to the first, Heat is material, and subject to all the laws, which control ordinary matter. It is regarded as an extremely subtile fluid, pervading all space, entering into combination with bodies in different proportions, producing the various effects, of change of temperature, expansion, liquefaction and vaporization. The second theory regards it as the effect of undulation or vibration, produced either in the constituent molecules of bodies themselves, or in a subtile fluid which pervades them. Modern science seems to lean at the present moment decidedly towards the latter of these theories; but as the former is simpler and more easily understood, and greatly facilitates the demonstration of the principal properties of Heat, it is the one generally preferred for the explanation of the effects which are produced by this agent.

38. Heat exists in two states. Heat exists in two states: first, as free and sensible; second, as combined and latent. In the first state it gives rise to what is called the sensation of heat, affects the thermometer, and produces all the familiar results invariably ascribed to its agency: in the second, it enters into combination with bodies, and tends to alter their condition, producing the liquefaction of solids, and converting liquids into vapors; when such a change in the state of matter is accomplished, a large amount of heat disappears, ceases to exhibit its usual properties, and seems to be buried and lost, in the body

---

37. Why is the nature of Heat hypothetical? State the first theory in regard to it. State the second. To which theory does Modern Science incline?—38. In what two states does Heat exist?

in question; in this second state it is called heat of composition, or Latent Heat. The subject of the combination of heat with matter, will become more clear as we proceed. At present we shall consider only the properties, which Heat possesses in its free and uncombined state.

39. Heat Present in all Bodies. Heat seems to be present in all bodies, and there is no process by which it can be wholly abstracted from any substance: for however cold any substance may be, if it be carried to a place where the temperature is still lower, it will again give out heat, and continue to do so until its temperature has become the same with that of the surrounding medium. Thus if a piece of ice at zero of Fahrenheit's thermometer, were transported to any region where the temperature was 60° below zero, it would begin to emit heat, and continue to do so until its temperature had become reduced to that of the surrounding air. In such an atmosphere, the ice though at 0° would be a hot body, and would communicate heat to all objects in its vicinity. Place the same piece of ice, thus reduced to a temperature 60° below zero, in an atmosphere 80° below zero, and here again, compared with the surrounding medium, it would be a warm body, and would again give forth heat, until an equilibrium was established between its temperature and that of the objects around it. As this process might be carried on without limit, it is quite clear that heat is present in all bodies, however cold, and can not be entirely abstracted from any substance.

40. Heat and Cold are Relative Terms. No body is hot or cold, absolutely of itself, but only so, in comparison with other bodies near or in contact with it. So far as our sensations are concerned, heat and cold depend upon circumstances. The same medium will feel warm at one time, and cold at another, though possessing the same temperature, depending upon the varying temperature of our own bodies. Thus the air of a cellar, the temperature of which is very nearly the same both in winter and summer, will feel cool when we enter it on a warm summer's day, but warm on a cold day in winter. A traveler descending from the summit of Mount Etna, will find his garments uncomfortably warm, when half way down, while at the very same

---

State what is meant by sensible Heat, by heat of composition, or Latent Heat.—Which state of Heat do we consider at present?—39. Show that Heat is present in all bodies, however cold.—40. Show why heat and cold are relative terms. Explain why a medium of the same temperature will feel hot at one time and cold at another. Give the illustration of a traveler on Mount Etna.

place another traveler, ascending the mountain from the warm regions below, will find the air inconveniently cool, and will wrap his garments more closely about him.

The White Bear, from Greenland, and the Elephant, from Hindostan, are seen to suffer, the one from heat, and the other from cold, in the atmosphere of the same menagerie. Even to the same person, the same temperature may seem both hot and cold at the same moment. Thus if one hand be placed in water at 40° and the other in water at 150°, and then both hands be plunged together into a third vessel, in which the water is at 90°, one hand will experience a sensation of heat, and the other of cold, though the temperature to which both are exposed, is the same. *Fig. 2.*

Fig. 2.

Sensations of Heat Relative.

41. Heat, the Repulsive Principle of Matter, and opposed to Cohesion. Heat is the great repulsive principle of Nature, and tends to separate the molecules, and consequently increase the dimensions of every substance into which it is introduced.

It is opposed to cohesion or that force which tends to draw the particles of substances together, and to bind them closely to each other; and it is upon the relative strength of these two forces, that the condition of matter as solid, liquid and gaseous, depends. When cohesion predominates over heat, the body has the form of a solid; when they are of nearly equal strength, the solid is converted into a liquid; and when heat predominates over cohesion, the gaseous state results. As we have the means of increasing and diminishing the heat of a body within a very wide range, and therefore of changing at will the strength of the repulsive principle, the form of most kinds of matter may be varied at pleasure: solids can be converted into gases, and gases into solids: snow and ice changed into steam—an invisible vapor; and, on the other hand, carbonic acid, an invisible gas, condensed into a white, flaky solid, in appearance resembling snow.

42. Heat tends to an Equilibrium. One of the most obvious properties of heat is, its tendency to an *equilibrium*, that is,

---

Of the Polar Bear and the Elephant. Give the illustration of the two hands placed in a central bowl of water at 90°.—41. Why is heat called the repulsive principle? To what force is it opposed? Show how the state of bodies as solid, liquid, and gaseous depends upon the balance between heat and cohesion.—41. What is the obvious property of heat?

HEAT SEEKS AN EQUILIBRIUM. 25

its disposition to pass from a hot body to those colder than itself. Thus if several bodies of different temperatures be placed in the same room, the warmer body will continue to impart its heat to those which are colder, until they all indicate the same temperature by the thermometer. This tendency to an equilibrium is so strong that it is impossible to maintain the temperature of any body permanently above that of the medium in which it is placed. As soon as heat accumulates in any body, it immediately begins to diffuse itself through the matter which surrounds it.

43. Three Modes in which Heat seeks an Equilibrium. Heat attains this equilibrium in three different ways: 1st. By *Conduction*. This takes place only in solids. Thus when an iron bar is heated at one end, the heat passes from particle to particle through the whole bar, until every part has reached the same temperature. 2d. By *Convection*. This takes place only in the liquids and gases. In these, every particle is in turn brought into contact with the portion of the vessel where the heat is applied, until they have all attained the same temperature. 3d. By *Radiation*. In this case the heat darts through an appreciable space, and so passes from a hot body to one at a considerable distance. By this process a hot stove sends forth rays of heat in every direction, that pass through the air without heating it, but raise the temperature of all bodies upon which

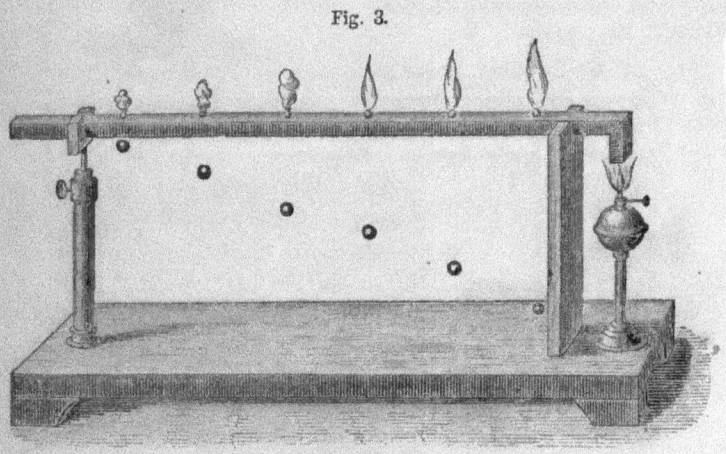

Fig. 3.

Conduction Gradual.

What is the effect of this tendency? —43. What are the modes in which Heat seeks an equilibrium? Describe them.

26 CONDUCTION OF HEAT.

they strike. In like manner the earth is warmed by rays which emanate from the sun, and have passed through the air without raising its temperature.

44. First Mode in which Heat is Diffused.—Conduction. When heat is conducted through bodies, it does not flash through them instantaneously, like electricity, but passes successively from particle to particle, requiring an appreciable time for the passage. In the accompanying figure there is a bar of iron, having a lamp at one extremity. Upon the upper surface are arranged small bits of Phosphorus, at equal intervals; on the lower a number of marbles have been attached by bits of wax. The marbles do not all drop at the same time, nor do the bits of Phosphorus take fire at the same instant, but successively; and this shows that the passage of the heat is gradual. *Fig.* 3.

45. Bodies Differ in Conducting Power. Heat passes through different bodies with different degrees of rapidity. Some permit it to pass through them quite rapidly; others only very slowly, and some almost entirely intercept its passage. Thus, one can hardly hold a brass pin for a moment, in the flame of a lamp, without burning his fingers, while a piece of glass of the same size, may have one of its ends melted, without warming the other. This can be proved by holding a bit of iron wire by one hand and a piece of glass rod by the other, in the flame of a spirit lamp. *Fig.* 4.

Fig. 4.

Difference in Conducting Power.

Fig. 5.

46. The same fact can be very plainly shown by the apparatus, represented in *Fig.* 5. Rods of different substances of the same size and length, are covered with wax, to the distance of an inch from their free extremities, tipped with little bits of phosphorus, and then inserted into sockets upon the side of a brass vessel, filled with hot water. The phosphorus is inflamed, and the wax

Difference in Conducting Power

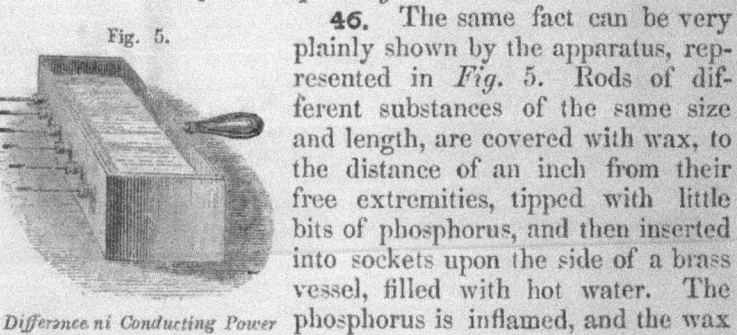

44. Show that in conduction, heat passes from particle to particle. Describe Fig. 3.
45. Prove that bodies differ in conducting power.—46. Describe Fig. 5.

commences melting upon the different rods at different intervals of time; upon the best conductor first, and successively upon the others, in the order of their conducting power.

47. Density Favorable to Conduction. Bodies which are most dense are generally the best conductors. Thus the metals conduct better than stones; stones better than earth; earth better than wood; and wood better than charcoal, cloth or paper. But sometimes there is no relation between the density of the body, and its power to conduct heat. Thus platinum is the most dense of the metals, but it is not by any means the best conductor among them, and glass is a worse conductor than many substances of much less density.

48. Relative Conducting Power of the Metals. The following table presents the results of a series of careful experiments by M. Despretz, in regard to the conducting power of the metals and some other substances. The substances employed were made into prisms of the same form and size. At one extremity heat was applied from the same source, and its passage along the prism in each case was estimated by small thermometers, placed in holes drilled at regular intervals, and filled with mercury.

Despretz' Table of Conductivity for Heat.

Gold,	1000	Tin,	304
Platinum,	981	Steel,	218
Silver,	973	Lead,	179
Copper,	898	Marble,	24
Brass,	441	Porcelain,	12
Iron,	374	Brick-clay,	11
Zinc,	343		

49. The succeeding table of the conduction of heat compared with conduction of electricity, was prepared by MM. Wiedemann and Franz. Their apparatus was arranged in the same manner as that of M. Despretz, except that instead of estimating the progress of the heat by thermometers, it was done by a small thermo-electric pile, the most delicate known instrument for measuring heat, to be described hereafter. The results that they reached were very different from those of M.

---

47 To what other property in bodies is conduction generally proportioned.—48. Describe the apparatus of Despretz for determining conduction. Give his table of conduction.

28 CONDUCTION FOR HEAT COMPARED WITH ELECTRICITY.

Despretz, and showed that the conducting power of the metals for heat, is very nearly the same as their conducting power for electricity, and that the conducting power of Platinum, notwithstanding its great density, is very low.

Table of Conductivity for Heat compared with that for Electricity.

	Heat.	Electricity.
Silver,	100	100
Copper,	74	73
Gold,	53	59
Brass,	24	22
Tin,	15	23
Iron,	12	13
Lead,	9	11
Platinum,	8	10
German Silver,	6	6
Bismuth,	2	2

50. Porous Bodies Bad Conductors. Solid substances conduct heat in all directions, whether upward, downward, or sideways, with nearly equal facility. A notable exception to this is seen in the case of certain crystals, such as quartz, which conduct heat with greater facility in the direction of their optic axis, or of their greatest length, than at right angles to it. Wood is also said to conduct heat with greater rapidity in some directions than in others, and more easily with the grain than across it. Of all solids, those which are most porous conduct heat with the least rapidity. On this account flannel is warmer in winter than silk or linen. It is owing to the air, which loose, spongy substances contain, that they resist the passage of heat better than those of a closer texture. Thus eider-down, and fur, make the warmest clothing, because they contain the most air in their interstices, and for the same reason cotton batting is much warmer than the same weight of cotton cloth.

Some curious experiments were made by Count Rumford in 1792, for the purpose of ascertaining the relative conducting power of materials used for clothing. He arranged a thermometer in the interior of a glass cylinder, having a bulb blown at one extremity, in such a manner that the bulb of the ther-

---

49. What did Wiedemann and Franz ascertain in regard to the conducting power of bodies for heat and electricity? Give their table. Do all bodies conduct heat with equal facility in all directions? Give the exceptions to this rule.—50. What kind of conductors are porous bodies? To what is their non-conducting power due? Describe Count Rumford's experiments upon the relative value of substances used for clothing.

CONDUCTION OF POROUS BODIES. 29

mometer occupied exactly the centre of the bulb of the cylinder, and filled the space between them with the substances to be examined. The apparatus was then dipped in boiling water, until the thermometer marked 212° in every case; it was then transferred to melting ice, and the exact time consumed during the sinking of the thermometer through 135° noted. When there was nothing but air between the thermometer and the cylinder, the cooling took place in 576 seconds: when the space was filled with twisted silk, in 917"; with fine lint, in 1032"; with cotton wool, in 1046"; with sheep's wool, in 1118"; with raw silk, in 1284"; with beaver's fur, in 1296"; with eider down, in 1305"; with hare's fur, in 1315". The general practice of mankind is, therefore, fully justified by experiment. In winter, the animal heat is retained as much as possible by covering the body with bad conductors, such as woolen stuffs, furs, and eider-down; while in summer, cotton or linen is used for the purpose of increasing as much as possible the escape of heat.

The imperfect conducting power of snow also arises from the above cause. When newly fallen, a great proportion of its bulk consists of the air which it contains, as may be readily proved by the comparatively small quantity of water it produces when melted. Such a provision was designed for the benefit of man, in preventing the destruction, during the cold of winter, of delicate shoots and roots imbedded in the earth. Farmers, in cold climates, always lament the absence of snow in winter, because as a consequence, the frost penetrates to a great depth, and does much injury to the grain sown the previous autumn. So great is the protecting effect of snow, that in Siberia, it is said, when the temperature of the air has been 70° below the feezing point, that of the earth, under the snow, has seldom been colder than 32°. It has also been often observed that the heaving of the ground by frost is much less when it is protected by snow, than when it is uncovered and exposed. For the same reason, many substances which, in the solid state, are quite good conductors of heat, when reduced to powder, become very poor conductors. Thus rock crystal is a better conductor than bismuth or lead; but if the crystal be reduced to powder, the passage of heat through it is exceedingly slow. Rock salt, when in the solid state, allows heat to pass through it with

---

Give his results. To what is the non-conducting power of snow owing? What is the effect of pulverization on conduction?

great facility, but common table salt in fine powder obstructs its passage almost entirely. Sawdust, powerfully compressed, allows heat to pass through it with the same facility as solid wood of the same kind, but when loose and unconfined, it is one of the poorest conductors known.

51. Illustrations of Conduction. Our ordinary sensations every day convince us of the different powers of various substances to conduct heat. In the winter the articles in a cold room impart very different sensations to the hand. A pair of tongs will conduct away so much heat as to give a painful sensation of cold; while a piece of fur or flannel, scarcely feels cold at all, and yet both are of the same temperature, when tested by the thermometer.

A piece of anthracite coal lighted at one end, can not be touched with impunity, even at the distance of six inches from the source of heat, while a piece of burning charcoal or of flaming wood may be held without any sensation of heat at the distance of only 1-20 of an inch from the flame. Hot water in an earthen pitcher will feel only moderately warm on account of the poor conducting power of the earthy material which contains it, while the same water poured into a tin cup held firmly in the hand, will be found too hot to be endured, on account of the excellent conducting power of the tin. A saucepan, having an iron handle, can with difficulty be removed from the fire with the naked hand, while if it be provided with a handle of wood it can be moved with ease. The large amount of iron required for castings of great size, is often more than can be melted in a furnace at one heating. As each successive furnace full is melted, it is emptied into a large iron vessel elevated several feet above the ground, and having a conduit, which may be opened at pleasure, leading from the lower part to the mould embedded in the earth. This vessel has a lining of clay or fire brick, and the melted iron is also covered with a layer of fine charcoal. In consequence of the extremely poor conducting power of this substance, and of the earthen lining just described, the melted iron may be preserved in a liquid state for several hours, until a sufficient quantity has been accumulated to make any casting, however large.

52. Applications in the Arts. These principles admit of many useful applications in the arts, and explain many natural phe-

---

51. Give illustrations of conduction—the tongs—the carpet—anthracite coal—tin cup of hot water—iron furnace lined with fire-brick.

ILLUSTRATIONS OF CONDUCTION. 31

nomena. Thus, stoves are lined with fire brick, of bad conducting power, for the purpose of preventing the iron covering from being heated too hot. Furnaces are lined with the same material to prevent the heat from escaping; houses are built of non-conducting materials; locomotive boilers and cylinders are provided with casings of wood; steam-pipes are bound with canvas; instruments used in the fire are provided with wooden handles; tea-pots are made of earthern-ware, or, if of metal, are handled with woolen holders; and, in the best of them, the metallic handles are separated from the body of the vessel by bits of ivory, (an excellent non-conductor,) for the purpose of preventing the transmission of the heat. On the same principle, metallic articles exposed to a very low temperature are never handled without woolen or leather gloves, lest the heat of the hand should be too rapidly abstracted; or, if so handled, they are provided with leather or woolen coverings of their own.

53. Sand, an excellent non-conductor, is placed beneath the hearths of fire-places, to guard against accidents by fire. At the siege of Gibraltar, the red-hot balls fired by the English, were carried from the furnaces to the guns in wooden wheelbarrows protected only by a thin covering of sand. Ice is prevented from melting in summer by wrappers of flannel. It is also exported to warm countries, and conveyed to the most distant portions of the earth, packed in saw-dust and shavings.

Refrigerators are provided with double walls, between which are enclosed shavings of cork or powdered charcoal. Fire proof safes have also double walls, the space between them being filled with ground plaster of Paris. Near the summit of Mount Etna, ice has been discovered beneath currents of lava, which have poured over it in an incandescent state. It was prevented from melting only by a thin layer of volcanic sand. The ice gatherers of the same mountain, export their ice to Malta, and distribute it through Sicily, protected by envelopes of coarse straw matting. Asbestos, a fibrous mineral substance, is woven into an incombustible cloth of such poor conducting power that red hot iron may be handled with gloves made of it.

Glass is another excellent non-conductor; and a glass tumbler filled with hot water may be handled with impunity, when

---

52 State some of the applications in the arts; stoves, furnaces, locomotive boilers, &c.—53. Cannon balls, how kept red-hot? Ice, how prevented from melting?

a metallic vessel filled with the same, would severely burn the hand. This property of glass exposes it to the danger of cracking when suddenly heated. The surface immediately in contact with the source of heat expands; but the non-conducting power of the glass preventing the heat from passing inward, the inner portions remain in their unexpanded state, and, as a consequence, a violent separation of one from the other is apt to take place. On this account, glass ought never to be suddenly exposed to a high degree of heat. Both surfaces should be heated, if possible, at the same moment, and when once thoroughly heated through, the glass should never be touched with any cold metallic substance by which the heat, at a particular point, might be suddenly abstracted. This is the reason why heated glass and earthen vessels, filled with hot substances, are often broken by being heedlessly placed upon the head of a nail which happens to project from the wooden floor.

So poor is the conducting power of glass, that a large, red-hot molten mass of it may be ladled into cold water, and the interior remain visibly red-hot for several hours; and if a large crucible full of melted glass has once solidified by the decline of the fire, it is almost impossible to melt it again. For the same reason, the vitreous matter of which lava is composed is a long time in cooling, and its heat is given out so slowly that many months after its irruption, eggs may be cooked, and water boiled, in the crevices with which it is filled.

54. Animals and Plants Protected from the Cold by non-conducting Coverings. Nature also makes use of the same principles in her operations. Animals are protected against the excessive cold of winter, which tends to reduce their temperature to such a degree as to destroy life, by thick furs, an excellent non-conductor, while in summer these are exchanged for thinner coverings.

Birds, which from their rapid and lofty flight, are especially exposed to a dangerous reduction of temperature, are covered with feathers, and often beneath the feathers, with fine down, which is one of the most perfect non-conductors known. The vegetable kingdom supplies illustrations of the same principle. It has been found that wood, always a poor conductor, opposes much greater resistance to the passage of heat in a direction

---

Illustrate the non-conducting power of glass. Explain how glass may remain red-hot in water.—54. How are animals protected from the cold of winter? What is the advantage of the non-conducting power of wood and bark?

BY NON-CONDUCTING MATERIALS. 33

across the grain, that is, from the centre toward the bark, than in the direction of its length; it is, therefore, difficult for the heat to escape from a tree, even in the coldest weather; and generally the temperature of the interior, near the pith, is much higher than that of the cold air on the outside. This may be shown by boring a hole into the centre of a tree, on a cold winter's day, and inserting a thermometer. Indeed, one of the most important offices of the bark is to confine the heat as much as possible, to the interior of the tree; and so, instead of being dense and firm like the woody fibre beneath, it is porous and spongy in its texture, so as to enclose a large amount of air. A tree stripped of its bark, is liable to perish from loss of heat, like an animal stripped of its fur, or a bird of its plumage. The general effect of this provision of nature is to maintain the tree at a uniform temperature, both in winter and summer. In the case of young and tender trees, it is usual to surround them with an external covering of straw, for the purpose of still further confining the heat, and guarding them against the effects of severe cold. For the same reason this substance is placed upon garden beds, in order to protect the flowering plants and roots.

55. Liquids are Poor Conductors of Heat. Liquids are exceedingly poor conductors of heat, and have even been thought to possess no conducting power whatever. Their slight conducting power may be shown in the following manner. Into a vessel of water, whose temperature has been carefully determined by a thermometer, pour a little sulphuric ether. In consequence of the superior lightness of this liquid, it will float upon the surface of the water, without mingling with it. Now apply a lighted match, and when the flame of the burning ether has entirely gone out, the water will be found to possess precisely the same temperature as before, which could not be the case if it possessed any power of conducting heat whatever. Again, if a delicate thermometer, as in *Fig.* 6, be placed in a jar of water, with its upper bulb just beneath

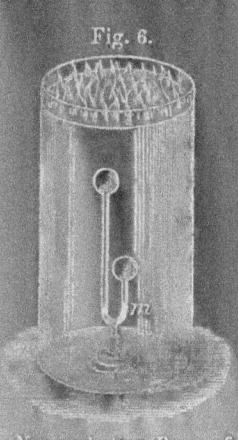

Fig. 6.

Non-conducting Power of Liquids.

How are trees maintained at a uniform temperature in winter and summer? What is the design of straw coverings for trees and plants?—55. What is the conducting power of liquids? How can their feeble conducting power be shown? Describe the experiment in Fig. 6. Describe the experiment in Fig. 7. Describe Dr. Murray's experiment.

2*

34   LIQUIDS ARE POOR CONDUCTORS.

the surface, and a small quantity of sulphuric ether be poured upon the water and inflamed, intense heat will be produced, but in consequence of the poor conducting power of the water, no effect will be experienced by the thermometer, though its bulb be no more than one twentieth of an inch distant from the flame. In like manner, if ice be formed at the bottom of a glass test tube, and secured in its place, water may be boiled in the upper part of the tube, by holding it in an inclined position in the flame of a spirit lamp, as represented in *Fig.* 7, without melting the ice in the smallest degree. Count Rumford found that the heat from a hot iron cylinder could not pass downwards, through a thin stratum of olive oil not more than two tenths of an inch in thickness.

Fig. 7.

Non-conducting Power of Liquids.

By other experiments, however, it has been ascertained that liquids do conduct heat to a very slight degree. Dr. Murray established this fact in the following manner. At the bottom of a vessel of ice, he placed a delicate thermometer, in a horizontal position, and then poured in olive oil, until the bulb of the thermometer was just covered; a second vessel, of iron, was then introduced, filled with boiling water, and secured in such a position that it almost touched the bulb. In seven and a half minutes the heat from the boiling water had been conducted by the oil to the bulb of the thermometer, in sufficient amount to raise the temperature from 32° to 37½°.

Under ordinary circumstances, however, liquids may be considered absolute non-conductors of heat. This is true of all liquids except mercury, which, from its metallic nature, conducts heat with great facility, and is an exception to the general rule.

56. The Gases are Poor Conductors of Heat. The air and other aeriform fluids are, in like manner, exceedingly poor conductors of heat. This may be shown by the operation of double windows. A thin stratum of air being confined between the opposite sashes in such a way that it can not escape, and all communication with the external air being cut off, has the effect

---

56. What is the conducting power of the gases? How is their feeble conduction shown by double windows?

of preventing the passage of heat from the inside to the outside of the window, or the reverse. The internal heat is prevented from escaping, and the external heat from entering, and consequently the house is rendered much more comfortable in both winter and summer. The same fact is also proved by the construction of ice pitchers, which are really made double, and consist of a pitcher within a pitcher. The stratum of air enclosed between them is found to be an excellent non-conductor of heat, and to obstruct the passage of the external heat into the pitcher almost altogether. The same fact is also illustrated by the double roofs of ice-houses, and double walls of fire-proof vessels and safes. Double walls to houses make them much warmer in winter by preventing the escape of heat, and much cooler in summer by obstructing its entrance. In all these cases it is essential that the air be *closely confined*, and that no opportunity be allowed for the establishment of currents, by openings above and below; otherwise the escape of heat is facilitated. The non-conducting power of air is also shown by the poor conduction of heat by substances which, like fur and down, contain a large quantity of it inclosed in their texture.

57. The Conducting Power of Different Gases supposed to be different. It has been asserted that the conducting power of the gases for heat is very unequal. This opinion is founded upon the different cooling effects exerted by the various gases upon the temperature of a platinum wire heated white hot by a galvanic battery. Such a wire is cooled more rapidly when surrounded by air than when in a vacuum, more rapidly by hydrogen than by air, and less rapidly by sulphurous acid gas and chloro-hydric acid gas, than by air. These experiments were performed with an apparatus represented in *Fig.* 8. Let o be a glass vessel, which can be exhausted of air through the lower stop-cock, s; let s be another stop-cock, by which air or any other gas may be introduced into the vessel at pleasure; b is a metallic rod, passing through a stuffing box airtight, yet capable of sliding so that it can be adjusted at any height; c is a similar metallic rod, connected with the brass cap at the lower part of the vessel; h n is a fine platinum wire by which b and c are now connected. The glass vessel being full of air, the connections with the poles of the galvanic battery are formed at b and c, and in a few moments the heat

---

By ice pitchers? By ice houses? By furs? Why is it necessary that the air should be closely confined in these cases?—57. Is the conducting power of gases for heat equal?

36   GASES DIFFER IN CONDUCTING POWER.

Fig. 8.

Different Conducting Power of Gases.

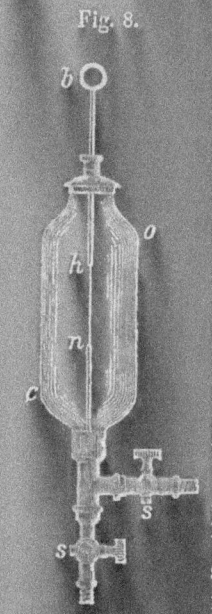

is great enough to make the platinum wire faintly luminous. Let the air now be withdrawn by an air pump, and the wire almost in an instant glows more brightly: introduce the air again, and it glows more feebly. This reduction of temperature from a white heat to bright redness seems to show that the air, when it is readmitted, has so much conducting power for heat as to lower the temperature of the wire very sensibly. Now let the vessel be exhausted a second time, and in place of air, let Hydrogen gas be introduced: the wire, which began to glow with a white heat on the exhaustion of the air, as soon as this gas is introduced ceases to glow altogether, and it will be necessary to more than double the power of the battery in order to raise the wire again to a white heat. This seems to show that the conducting power of Hydrogen for heat is much greater than that of air. If the Hydrogen were withdrawn, the energy of the current would now be great enough to fuse the wire. The cooling effect of the other gases may be ascertained in the same way. Illuminating gas, ammonia, and the vapors of alcohol and ether, also exert a greater cooling influence upon such a wire than air. It has also been found that if heat be applied at the closed top of a vessel, it is conveyed more quickly to a thermometer placed at some distance from the top when the vessel is filled with Hydrogen, than when it is filled with air. This is the case even when the vessel is loosely packed with cotton wool or eider down. From these experiments it has been argued that Hydrogen conducts heat like a metal. On the other hand it is contended that Hydrogen, being the lightest of the gases and more than fourteen times lighter than air, this effect may be due to the superior mobility of its particles over those of air. This would hardly seem adequate to account for all the effects observed, and on the whole it would appear that the gases do differ somewhat in their power of conducting heat.

Describe the experiments illustrated by Fig. 8. What is the general conclusion?

CONVECTION IN LIQUIDS. 37

58. The second mode in which heat is diffused through bodies—Convection. The question at once arises: If liquids and gases are such poor conductors, in what way is heat propagated through them at all? Heat is conveyed through all liquids and gases by a change of place among their particles; and this constitutes the process of convection, or the second mode by which heat seeks an equilibrium and is diffused through matter. When a vessel of water is placed over a fire, the particles nearest the flame are expanded, and becoming specifically lighter than those around and above them, whose temperature is as yet unaffected, they rise to the surface. At the same time the cold particles above descend, in order to supply their place; these becoming heated in turn, also rise to the surface, and are succeeded by a fresh supply of colder particles from above. In this manner all the water is gradually brought into contact with the source of heat, and the whole mass finally becomes uniformly warmed throughout.

59. Convection in Liquids. The manner in which liquids circulate on the application of heat can be easily shown. Into a glass flask containing water, see *Fig.* 9, throw a small quantity of any insoluble powder, such as amber, rosin, or even saw-dust, as nearly as possible of the same specific gravity with the water. When placed over a lamp the circulation will soon begin; the warm currents will rise in the centre where the heat is greatest, and the cold will descend upon the sides, and their exact direction will be indicated by the solid particles which they carry with them. The water ascends and descends in this manner just the same, whether the solid particles are in the flask or not; these only serve to make the motion more plain to the eye. Even after the liquid has begun to boil, this same circulation will continue. It may therefore be stated as a general truth, that in order to raise the temperature of liquids and make them

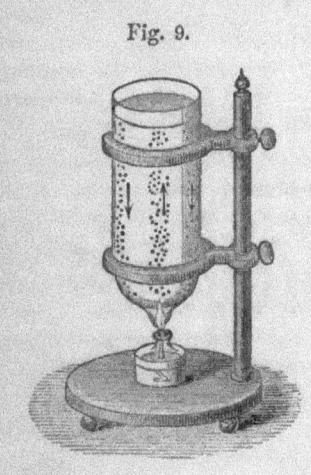

Fig. 9.

Convection of Heat in Liquids.

---

58. Describe the mode in which heat is propagated through liquids. What is convection?—59. How may the currents produced in liquids be shown to exist?

boil, heat must be applied at the bottom; they can not be heated from the upper surface. This is a matter of great practical importance in the construction of the boilers of steam engines, and in all cases where heat is to be diffused through large quantities of liquids.

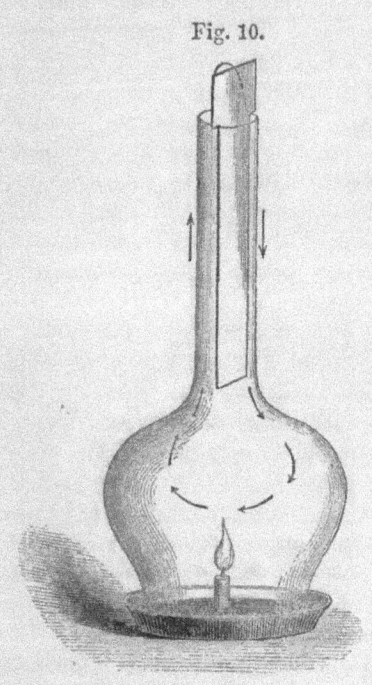

60. Convection in Gases. Similar currents are established in air and all the gases, upon the application of heat. The only difference is, that the heat is diffused through them with much greater rapidity than through liquids, in consequence of the greater mobility of their particles. The fact of the establishment of currents in air by the proximity of any source of heat, is clearly shown by *Fig.* 10, where a lamp chimney is represented over a lighted candle placed upon a plate filled with water, to prevent the entrance of air from below. The chimney is divided by a pasteboard partition, and on dropping a bit of smoking paper into it the movement of the smoke will show that the air is ascending on one side of the chimney, and descending on the other, exactly as in the case of the bits of floating amber in the vessel of heated water.

Fig. 10.

Convection of Heat in Gases.

61. Illustrations of Convection. The existence of currents produced by convection is seen on a great scale in Nature, in the cases of the Gulf Stream and the Trade Winds. The air and the water are heated in both these cases, not by the direct rays of the sun, but by heat which emanates from the earth. The rays of heat proceeding from the sun pass through the atmosphere without perceptibly heating it, and being absorbed as soon as they strike upon the earth's surface, gradually com-

---

60. How is heat propagated through gases? How may the existence of currents be proved?—61. Give illustrations of the existence of currents in the atmosphere and the ocean.

ILLUSTRATIONS OF CONVECTION. 39

municate their heat to the lower portions of the atmosphere, and to the water immediately in contact with it. These heated particles of water and air ascend, in consequence of their diminished density, and as their places are supplied by descending currents of cold water and air, they flow off to the north and to the south of the equator, carrying the heat with which they are charged, and imparting it to the cold water and air of the temperate regions; while on the other hand the cold water and air from the temperate and arctic regions are drawn steadily towards the tropics, charged with the cold which they have received from the poles. There is therefore a current of hot air in the upper regions of the atmosphere setting towards the north and south poles, and a current of cold air near the surface of the earth, moving from the poles to the tropics. The same is true of the waters of the ocean; a current of warm water upon the surface is setting towards the north and south, and of cold water beneath it moving from the north and south towards the equator; see *Fig.* 11. Thus the excessive heat and cold of the

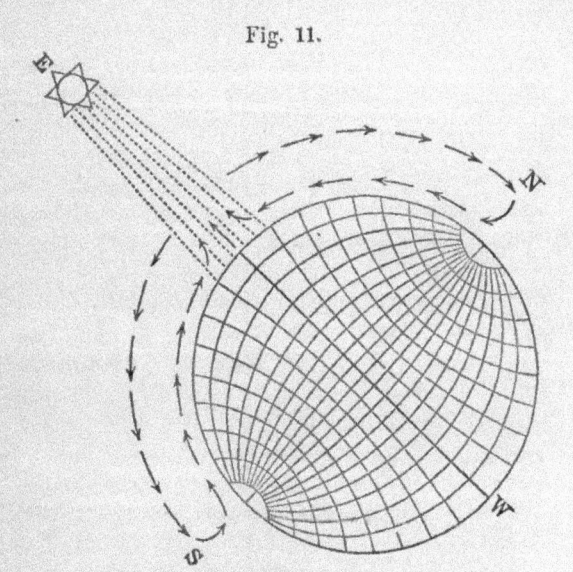

Fig. 11.

Convection Illustrated by Trade Winds and Gulf Stream.

opposite portions of the earth are moderated, and the general

---

How are the Trade winds produced? The Gulf stream? The land and sea breezes of the tropics?

temperature of the globe rendered more nearly equal. To the same cause the sea breezes, which temper the excessive heat of tropical islands, are due. The hot air rising from the heated surface of the earth floats off seaward, and the colder air of the sea flows in near the surface of the earth to supply its place: at night this process is reversed; the earth being colder than the sea, the warm air of the sea flows towards the land, while the cool air from the land is borne out to the ocean.

62. What makes the heated Water and Air ascend? As the absolute weight of the heated portions of liquids and gases is not diminished by the increase of their temperature, the question at once arises: What makes them ascend? The answer to this question requires an accurate knowledge of the principles of Hydrostatics, for which reference must be made to some good treatise on Natural Philosophy. It may however be stated in general, that the heated particles rise, because their density has become less than before, and less than that of the colder particles immediately around and above them. Take for instance the case of a cubic inch of liquid, near the bottom of a flask of water; as long as it is cold, it remains at rest and without any tendency to move, because the pressure of the water above it, and its own weight, which tend to make it sink, are exactly counterbalanced by the pressure from below tending to force it upwards. So long as these two pressures remain exactly equal, the cubic inch of water will continue fixed in its position; but let the equality of these two pressures be destroyed, and the cube of water will necessarily move in one direction or the other.

These two pressures may be represented by two columns of water placed side by side, one of which has the lower surface of the cube in question for its base, and extends vertically upwards to the surface of the water; the other is placed directly by its side, and possesses a base of the same dimensions, the same altitude, and the same density. Under these circumstances the cube of water will remain in equilibrium. Let this cube be now enlarged by the expansive effects of heat until it has attained the size of two cubic inches; its weight remains exactly the same as before, but its density has been diminished one half. The downward pressure is now represented by a column of water having a base of two cubic inches, and extending from the lower surface of the double cube of water in question

---

62. Explain the ascension of heated particles of liquids and gases.

ASCENSION OF HEATED LIQUIDS. 41

upwards to the surface of the liquid. The upward pressure is now represented by a column of water placed by the side of the first, also having a base of two cubic inches, and extending upwards to the surface of the liquid. These two pressures are, however, now no longer equal, because the density and weight of the two cubic inches at the base of the first column are only one half the density and weight of the two cubic inches at the base of the second column. The pressure upwards is therefore greater than the pressure downwards by the amount of this difference in weight between the two lowest cubic inches in the second column and the two lowest cubic inches in the first. The two cubic inches of expanded water will therefore be pressed upwards by a force equal to this difference in weight. The cold water which takes its place will undergo the same process, and rise in turn, and thus a steady current will be established which will continue to flow until the water has acquired the same temperature throughout, or the source of heat is removed.

This is also the cause of the ascension of heated air and of the currents that are established in the atmosphere when brought into contact with any source of heat.

63. The ascension of heated Liquids and Gases illustrated by a Figure. This process is illustrated in *Fig.* 12, where *a b* and *c d* represent the two columns of water which exactly balance each other, with the exception of the two cubic inches at the base of each. A cubic inch of cold water at 60° weighs about 252 grs. By the application of heat, such a cubic inch has been expanded to two cubic inches without any increase or diminution of its weight. The two cubic inches of hot water weigh precisely the same as one cubic inch of cold water; their density is

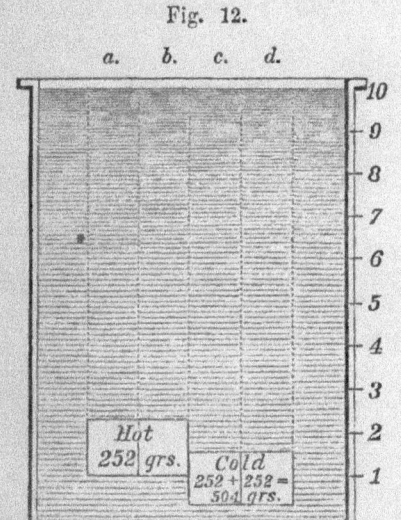

Fig. 12.

Cause of the Ascension of Heated Liquids and Gases.

63. Explain the process indicated in Fig. 12.

therefore diminished one half, and they are pressed upwards by the particles of cold water about them. The equal pressure, therefore, of the two columns $a\ b$ and $c\ d$, is destroyed, in consequence of the inequality in the weight of the two cubes at the base of each, the two cubes of cold water weighing $252+252=504$ grs., while the two cubes of hot water weigh only 252 grs.; the column $c\ d$ is thus made heavier than $a\ b$, and tends to press it upwards. The importance of this process of convection in the arts, as well as in Nature, can not be too highly estimated, and the principle on which it depends should be thoroughly understood.

64. The third mode in which Heat seeks an equilibrium—Radiation. Radiation is the name applied to the third mode in which heat seeks to distribute itself equally through bodies, viz., by darting from a hot to a cold body through an appreciable interval of space.

That heat is so transmitted is easily proved by standing before a fire, or holding one's hand at some distance from a hot body suspended in the air. In both these cases it is clear that the heat is not transmitted by *conduction* from particle to particle of the intervening air, because, as we have seen, the conducting power of air is extremely small; nor is it by *convection*, for this would only tend to propagate the heat vertically, by the establishment of an upward current: moreover it is found that the process goes on in a vacuum with three times the rapidity that it does in air; consequently we infer that no medium whatever is necessary for the passage of heat by this process.

It is called *radiation* because the rays of heat proceed from every point upon the surface of the body equally in all directions, like radii from the centre of a circle. The fact of radiation may also be proved more satisfactorily by placing several thermometers at equal distances from a hot body which is suspended in the air. They will begin to rise at the same moment, and at the expiration of a given time will all be found to indicate the same temperature, with the exception of the one placed immediately above the ball. This will be found to stand higher than the others, because it has been influenced by the ascending currents of hot air produced by convection, as well as by the rays of heat which have reached it by radiation. If the experiment were performed in a vacuum the thermometers would all be affected equally.

---

64. What is the third mode in which heat seeks an equilibrium? Is any medium necessary? Why called Radiation? How may the fact of radiation be proved? Why does the upper thermometer stand higher than the others?

65. Radiant Heat follows the same laws as radiant Light. Rays of heat proceed from the hot body in right lines like rays of light, and with a velocity equal to that of light; and their effect diminishes as they recede from the hot body, not in proportion to the distance, but to the *square* of the distance. A thermometer at two feet from the radiant body will not indicate one half as much heat as the thermometer placed at the distance of one foot, but only one fourth as much, i. e., four times less: in this respect also, radiant heat follows the same law as light. When radiant heat falls upon other bodies it is either *absorbed*,—in which case it raises their temperature,—or it is *reflected*, i. e., turned back towards its source; or it is *refracted*, i. e., bent out of its originally straight course, which occurs only when it falls at an angle less than a right angle, upon some medium which it is capable of traversing; or it is *transmitted*, i. e., passed through unchanged when it falls perpendicularly upon some medium capable of transmitting it, although this rarely takes place without more or less absorption. Radiant heat does not affect the temperature of the media through which it passes. A tube full of ether may be held in the focus of a convex lens without becoming sensibly warmer, but if any of the rays are absorbed by the introduction into the ether of some solid substance, such as a bit of charcoal, the heat thus absorbed is communicated from the charcoal to the liquid by convection; the ether soon begins to boil and is finally dissipated. The heating of the earth by the sun is the grandest instance of radiation found in Nature. The heat radiated from this great luminary passes through the air without perceptibly affecting its temperature, and finally striking upon the solid earth, is absorbed by it. The heat thus gained by the earth is communicated to the atmosphere and propagated through it by the process of convection, as has been already described. The amount of heat radiated by the sun in the course of a single day upon one acre of land in the latitude of London, is estimated to be equal to that produced by the combustion of one hundred and eighty bushels of coal.

66. The nature of the surface affects the rate of Radiation. The principal fact connected with radiation is, that the nature and condition of the surface of the hot body has a powerful

---

65. In what direction do the rays of heat from a hot body proceed? In what proportion does their effect diminish? In what four ways is radiant heat, when it falls upon bodies, disposed of? Does radiant heat affect the temperature of media through which it passes? What effect does it produce if absorbed? How can this be proved?—66. What influence has surface upon radiation?

EFFECT OF SURFACE.

effect in promoting or checking the escape of heat from it by this process.

Where other circumstances are equal, the rate at which heat escapes from bodies by radiation is *directly* proportional to the roughness and dullness of their surfaces, and in the *inverse* proportion to their polish and smoothness; in other words, those surfaces which are rough and dull radiate most rapidly, and those which are bright and polished most slowly. Sir J. Leslie, who was one of the earliest experimenters upon this subject, ascertained this fact by the following experiment. He covered one side of a brightly polished cubical tin vessel with lampblack, another with writing paper, a third with a thin plate of glass, while the highly polished surface of the fourth side was allowed to remain uncovered. The vessel was then filled with boiling water, tightly closed by a cork, through which a thermometer was inserted, and placed at some distance before a concave mirror having a delicate differential thermometer in its focus, somewhat as represented in *Fig.* 13. The radiating effect was esti-

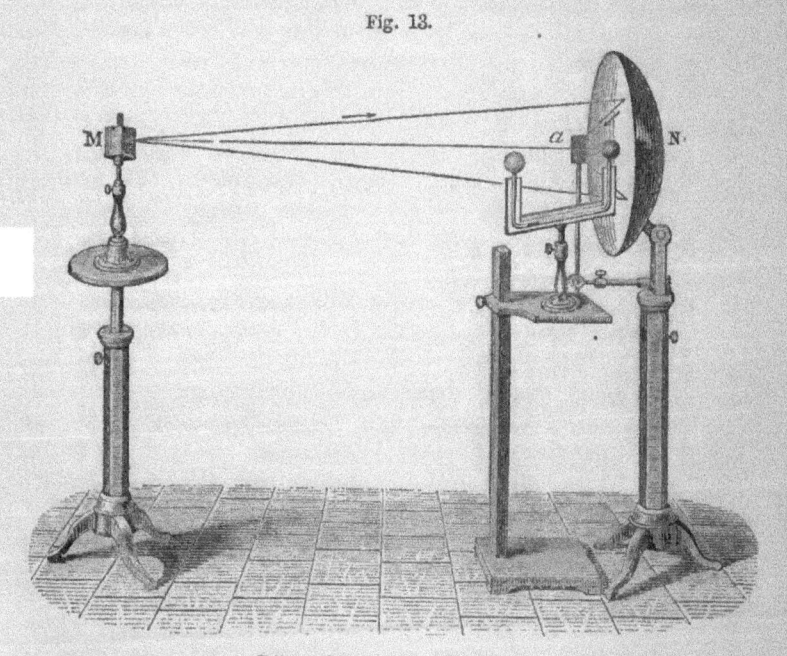

Fig. 13.

Effect of Surface on Radiation.

mated by the depression of the thermometer in the canister and

Describe the experiments of Leslie.

CIRCUMSTANCES AFFECTING RADIATION.

the elevation experienced by the differential thermometer in the focus of the mirror. On turning the side covered with lampblack towards the mirror the thermometer in the canister soon sank several degrees, while the one in the focus of the mirror rose at nearly the same rate: with the papered side the effect upon the thermometer was nearly the same; with the glass side the effect was decidedly less; and with the bright metallic side the influence upon the thermometer was very slight. Taking the quantity of heat radiated by the lampblack as 100, that radiated by the paper was found to be 98, that by the glass 90, and that by the bright metal only 12. From this experiment the extremely feeble radiating power of brightly polished metallic surfaces is very apparent. The same fact can be readily shown by using the tin cube alone without the mirror. Thermometers placed at equal distances from its four sides will be unequally affected, and the one opposite the side covered with lampblack will rise highest in a given time. The difference in the amount of heat radiated can be readily perceived by placing the hand successively near the four sides of the vessel; the impression produced by the lampblack side will be decidedly the most powerful. This experiment may be varied by using, instead of one vessel with differently constructed sides, three canisters of sheet brass, having exactly the same dimensions, but with different surfaces, the first having its surface highly polished, the second covered with whiting, the third with lampblack, filling them with boiling water from the same vessel, and then allowing them to cool. At the expiration of half an hour the blackened canister will be found by the thermometer to have lost the most heat, and to have the lowest temperature, the whitened canister to have lost somewhat less, and the polished one the least. Leslie also ascertained that by roughening brightly polished metallic surfaces they could be made to radiate nearly as well as lampblack; and that by scratching them with lines which crossed each other at right angles the effect could be greatly increased. This is probably owing to the increase of the amount of surface exposed, and in the number of radiating points thus produced.

67. Other circumstances affecting the rate of Radiation. It has also been ascertained that a *variation in density* makes a difference in the amount of heat radiated. A hammered silver plate will radiate much less than a cast plate of the same metal.

Describe the experiment with three canisters. Explain the effect of roughening a polished surface.—67. What other circumstances affect the rate of radiation?

At one time it was thought that color also had an effect upon radiation, and that black radiated more heat than any other; but it has now been ascertained that color has no effect whatever on radiating power.

68. Radiation also takes place from points below the Surface. It has also been found that radiation does not take place solely from the particles which compose the surface of a hot body, but that it also takes place from those which are situated a small distance beneath the surface. This was ascertained by Mr. Leslie, by covering one side of a vessel containing hot water with a thin coating of jelly, and putting upon another side four times the quantity. The nature of these two surfaces was precisely the same as to material and smoothness, but they were found to radiate very differently; the thinner film depressed the thermometer in the canister 38°, while the thicker depressed it 54°. The increase of radiation continued until the coating amounted to the thickness of 1-1000th of an inch, after which no further increase took place.

69. Practical Applications. Vessels intended to preserve liquids at a higher temperature than that of the surrounding air for as long a time as possible, should be provided with bad radiating surfaces. Water in a bright silver tea-pot will retain heat much longer than one made of earthen-ware or porcelain. A tea-kettle is in its most efficient state when its bottom is black and rough with soot, and its sides and top brightly burnished, because then the parts exposed to the fire are in the best condition for receiving heat, and those exposed to the air in the best condition for preventing its escape. For the same reason the exposed portions of locomotives, such as the cylinders and steam dome, which require to be maintained at a temperature considerably higher than 212°, and which are much cooled by rapid motion through the air, are covered with burnished brass in order to prevent the escape of heat, and are kept brightly polished, not so much for ornament as for utility. There is also generally a space of several inches between the outside covering and the true surface of the cylinder and of the dome; and this is either filled with confined air, which, as we have seen, is a poor conductor of heat, or stuffed with some non-conducting solid substance, such as felt, wool, or shavings of wood, in order to oppose an effectual barrier to the escape of heat. Pipes in-

---

68. Prove that radiation may even take place from points beneath the surface.—69. State the practical applications of the principles of radiation. How is the heat of the locomotive prevented from escaping?

tended for the conveyance of hot water, steam, or heated air to a distance, should be kept perfectly bright and highly polished; but when they are designed to impart heat rapidly to the surrounding air they should be roughened, or coated with some good radiating substance. Stoves and stove-pipes should be made of rough and unpolished iron in order to secure the greatest heating effect; but if it be wished to carry a stove-pipe through a room without heating it, or to use a portable furnace without its warming the room in which it is placed, they should both be provided with a brightly polished metallic covering. By attending to such apparently unimportant circumstances the consumption of fuel may be greatly economized.

70. The Radiation of the Earth. As the earth receives its heat from the sun by means of radiation, so it, in turn, gives out heat itself by the same process. When the sun sets and the influence of his rays is withdrawn, the earth then becomes a radiating body and sends forth the heat which it had acquired during the day into space; but it does so very unequally. All other things being equal, those portions of its surface which, from their peculiar conformation, are good radiators, send forth heat much more freely, and are more reduced in temperature, than those which, from any cause, are poor radiators. Thus a bright metallic vessel placed upon the ground at sunset will have its temperature reduced indeed, but not nearly as much as an earthen-ware dish or a piece of wood of the same size. A glass cup placed in a silver bason which has been left upon the ground in the evening will become much colder during the night than the bason itself; and at the same time the grass and leaves of plants will become much colder than the smooth roads and paved streets; rough and fuzzy leaves will radiate more heat, and become much colder, than those which have a bright and polished surface. So much heat is thus radiated that on a clear and starry night the earth will sometimes be found, by a thermometer placed upon its surface, to be as much as seventeen degrees colder than the air ten or twelve feet above it. There is a close connection between this reduction of temperature and the formation of dew and frost, for these are nothing but the condensed vapor which previously existed in the air in an invisible form, deposited upon different substances

---

What surface should pipes intended to convey hot steam and air possess?—70. By what process does the earth lose its heat after sunset? Explain the reason why a rough board or rough leaf becomes colder at night than glass and polished metal. State the connection between radiation and dew.

whose temperature has been reduced by radiation. The better the radiating surface the lower will be its temperature, and the greater the quantity of dew and frost collected upon it. This subject will be more fully explained when we come to speak particularly of the watery vapor contained in the atmosphere.

71. The Theory of Radiation. Two theories have been proposed to account for the phenomena of radiation, suggested respectively by Pictet and Prevost. According to the former, when bodies of unequal temperature are brought near each other, there is a radiation of heat from the hotter to the colder, but none from the colder to the hotter; this continues until they have both reached the same temperature, when all radiation ceases. Prevost, on the contrary, is of the opinion that *all bodies*, whatever their temperature, are constantly emitting rays of heat in every direction; that the temperature of a body falls whenever it radiates more heat than is radiated to it; its temperature is stationary when it receives exactly as much heat from other bodies by radiation as it radiates to them, and that its temperature rises when it receives more heat than it radiates. According to this theory, which is now generally adopted, all bodies, whatever their temperature, are continually exchanging rays of heat with each other; and this is supported by the analogy of Light. Luminous bodies mutually exchange rays of light; a feeble light sends rays to one of greater brightness, as well as receives rays from it; and the quantity of light emitted by each does not seem to be influenced by the vicinity of the other. It is probable, therefore, that the radiation of heat takes place in the same manner.

72. The Reflection of Radiant Heat. When radiant heat falls upon a solid or a liquid body it is either reflected, absorbed, or transmitted. All the rays which are not absorbed or transmitted are reflected. The fact of reflection may easily be proved by standing before a fire in such a position that the heat can not reach the face directly, and then placing a piece of tinned iron in such a position as to allow of seeing the fire by reflection; as soon as it is brought into this position a distinct impression of heat will be perceived.

73. Law of Reflection.—Angles of Incidence and Reflection equal. In every case of the reflection of heat the angle of incidence is equal to the angle of reflection. In this respect heat follows the same law as light. This law has long been known

---

71. State Pictet's theory of radiation. Prevost's. Give the analogy of light.—72. What is meant by the reflection of heat?—73. State the law of Reflection.

LAW OF REFLECTION. 49

in regard to heat associated with light, as in the case of the sun's rays and those which are emitted from a red-hot ball; but that non-luminous heat, like that which proceeds from vessels of hot water or from other bodies heated below redness,—that these invisible rays of heat are subject to the same law of reflection as those which are accompanied by light, is a modern discovery, first established by Saussure and Pictet, at Geneva. This very interesting fact may be proved thus: In *Fig.* 14, let *m n* be a mirror of tinned iron, polished, and let a ball, heated to any degree below redness, be placed somewhere upon the line A B; the ray of heat falling upon the mirror will be reflected so as to reach a thermometer placed upon the line C B; and on measuring the angle A B D which the incident ray makes with the perpendicular at the point of incidence, it will be found to be exactly equal to the angle C B D which the reflected ray makes with the same perpendicular. It follows from this law that with a concave parabolic mirror the rays of non-luminous heat, like those of light, may be collected to a focus; and with two such mirrors, some very interesting experiments may be performed illustrative of the laws of radiation, as well as those of reflection.

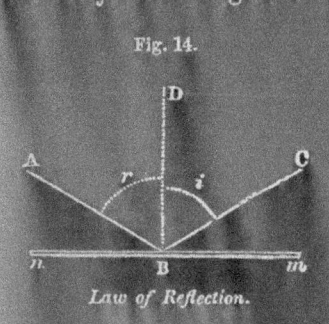

Fig. 14.

Law of Reflection.

74. Concave Mirrors. Concave mirrors, or reflectors, are parabolic or spherical surfaces of metal or glass, which serve to concentrate rays of light or heat upon one point called the focus. In *Fig.* 15, a section is given of a spherical mirror of this description. M N is the mirror, A. is its middle point or centre, C is the centre of the sphere of which the mirror forms a part, and A B is a line perpendicular to the middle point of the mirror. Now upon the line A B—the principal axis of the mirror—let any source of heat be placed at such a distance that the rays E K, P H, G I, L D can be considered as parallel to each other: the ray E K falling on the mirror will then be reflected in such a direction that the angle C K F, which is the angle of reflection, will be equal to the angle C K E, the angle of incidence; because any one point, as K, may be re-

---

How may it be proved in the case of a plane mirror?—74. Describe the concave mirror.

3

garded as a plane mirror, and the line C K is a perpendicular drawn to it. All the other rays, P H, A I, L D, will be reflected in the same manner, and concentrated upon the same point, F, situated upon the line A B. It follows in consequence of this concentration, that there will be a greater elevation of

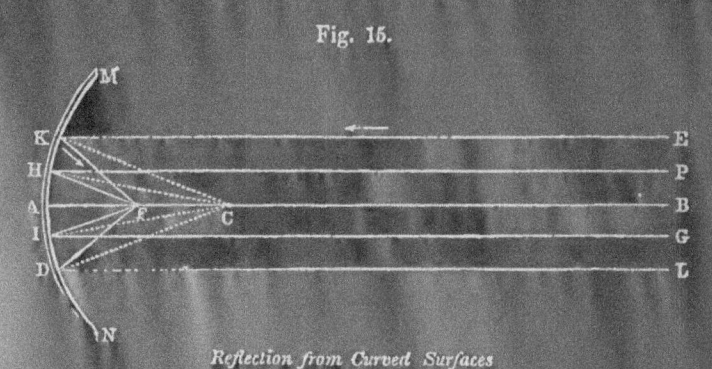

Fig. 16.

Reflection from Curved Surfaces

temperature at F than at any other point. This point is therefore called the Focus, and F A, the distance from the focus to the centre of the mirror, the focal distance. In the figure, the rays of heat are passing from E to K to F, in the direction of the arrows; but, reciprocally, if the hot body be placed at F, the rays of heat will pass from F to K, to H, to A, to I, to D, and from these points be reflected in lines parallel to each other; should these rays then fall upon a second spherical mirror exactly opposite to the first they will be reflected a second time, and concentrated at its focus.

75. Experiments on Radiation and Reflection with two Concave Mirrors. Let two concave mirrors, made of polished brass, and from twenty to thirty inches in diameter, be placed exactly opposite to each other and ten or fifteen feet apart; *Fig.* 16. In the focus of one mirror place a flask of hot water, and in that of the other a thermometer, with a screen of paper or glass between them; the focus of mirrors of this size is about $4\frac{1}{2}$ or 5 inches from their centres. Remove the screen, and the thermometer will at once begin to rise. If a cannon ball heated below redness be employed instead of the bottle of hot water, the effect upon the thermometer will be more decided. That this effect is due not to direct radiation from the ball to the thermometer, but to a double reflection from both mirrors, may

Show how heat is reflected by it.—75. Describe the experiments with concave mirrors.

EXPERIMENTS WITH MIRRORS. 51

be shown by moving the thermometer from the focus toward the hot ball, when it will be seen that the mercury falls instead of rising; and still more conclusively by placing a screen be-

Fig. 16.

Reflection of Heat.

tween the hot ball and its mirror, the thermometer being in the focus of the other mirror. In the latter case there is an opportunity for direct radiation of heat from the ball to the thermometer, but none for reflection, and yet the mercury falls; remove the screen so as to allow the reflected heat to fall again upon the thermometer, and the mercury will at once begin to rise, showing that the effect is due in both cases, not to radiation, but to reflection. When a red hot ball is placed in the focus of one mirror, water may actually be boiled, and tinder, phosphorus, and gunpowder ignited in the focus of the other. Similar experiments may be performed with a piece of gilt paper rolled into the form of a hollow truncated cone, open at both ends, the metallic surface being inside, and a hot ball placed opposite the larger opening of the cone. The rays of heat which enter

---

Show that the effect is due to reflection, and not to direct radiation.

the cone will be reflected in such a way as to be concentrated at a focus beyond the smaller end, in which phosphorus and gunpowder may be fired, *Fig.* 17. A silver spoon held in such

Fig. 17.

Reflection of Heat by Gilt Cone.

a position before the fire as to reflect the light to a focus will also concentrate the rays of heat to such a degree as to burn the hand and scorch a piece of paper.

76. The different Reflecting Powers of different Substances. This was determined by Mr. Leslie with an apparatus represented in *Fig.* 13: M is a cube of boiling water, at 212°; it is placed in front of the mirror N, on a line perpendicular to its middle point. The rays of heat proceeding from the cube are reflected by the mirror upon a plate a made of the substance whose reflecting power is to be determined, which is placed exactly in the focus of the mirror. By this plate the rays of heat are reflected a second time upon the bulb of a differential thermometer, and the number of rays reflected, or the reflecting power of the plate, is measured by the effect which is produced upon this instrument. Taking the reflecting power of brass as 100, it was found by this process that silver was 90, tin 80, steel 70, lead 60, India ink 13, glass 10, oiled glass 5, glass moistened 0, lampblack 0. Thus it was proved that the reflecting power of the metals is much greater than that of other bodies, and it has since been shown by Melloni that of all the metals mercury possesses the greatest reflecting power.

Describe the experiment with cone of gilt paper.—76. Describe Leslie's experiments for the purpose of determining the relative reflecting power of different substances. State his results.

77. The apparent Radiation and Reflection of Cold. There is an interesting experiment originally performed by the Florentine Academicians, which seems to prove the radiation and reflection of cold. If a piece of ice be placed in the focus of one of the mirrors, a thermometer in the focus of the other mirror will immediately descend, and then rise again as soon as the ice is removed. From this, it might be inferred that there are frigorific rays, possessed of the power of communicating coldness; but it is evident that in this case, according to the theory of M. Prevost, the thermometer falls because it radiates more heat than it receives, and not in consequence of the influence of frigorific rays. In relation to the ice the thermometer is really a hot body, and its temperature sinks when placed in the focus of the mirror, because it radiates more heat to the ice than is radiated to it by the ice: as soon as the ice is removed the thermometer receives as much heat as it radiates, and its previous temperature is restored. It is on the same principle that a sensation of cold is experienced on approaching a wall or a building whose temperature is much lower than our bodies, viz., because we radiate more heat than we receive.

78. The material of which Mirrors are made affects their power of reflecting Heat. There is a remarkable difference between the substances of which mirrors are made with respect to their power of reflecting heat, though their polish may be equal. Thus if the experiments already described be made with a concave *glass* mirror covered in the usual manner with amalgam, they will not succeed. A red hot cannon ball or a basket of burning charcoal placed in the focus of such a mirror can not be made to inflame phosphorus or tinder in the focus of the other. The mirrors themselves become warm and apparently absorb the heat without reflecting it, while they reflect light in the usual manner, as may be shown by substituting a blackened card for the phosphorus in the focus of one of the mirrors; a bright spot of light will immediately be formed, which is evidently the result of reflection. It is necessary that mirrors should be made of brightly polished metal in order to reflect both light and heat. If, however, solar light be used in these experiments, instead of artificial light, it is found that glass mirrors will reflect the sun's light and heat without becoming

---

77. What effect is produced if ice is introduced into the focus of one mirror? Does this prove the radiation and reflection of cold?—78. What effect has the material of which the mirrors are made? If solar light be employed, does the material of the mirrors exert any influence?

sensibly warmed themselves. This shows that the source from which the heat proceeds, as well as the material of which the mirrors are made, has a great effect upon the amount of heat reflected.

79. Practical Applications. The power that brightly polished metallic surfaces possess of throwing off the rays of heat which fall upon them, is often used for the purpose of protection against high temperatures, and for preventing bodies from becoming dangerously heated. Thus andirons, if brightly polished, will remain comparatively cool, notwithstanding their proximity to the fire, while, if rough and unpolished, they will become too hot to be touched. Water contained in a burnished silver pitcher can with difficulty be heated, even when placed directly before the fire: the same amount of water in a rough iron kettle at an equal distance from the fire would speedily be made to boil. Nor is it necessary that the protecting surface should be of any great thickness. The thinnest coating of bright metal reflects heat as perfectly as a solid metallic plate; a mere covering of gold leaf will enable a person to place his finger within a very small distance of red hot iron or other incandescent body, while the hand would be burned at ten times the distance if unprotected. If a piece of red hot iron be held over a sheet of paper upon which some letters have been gilded, the uncovered intervals will be scorched, while the letters will remain untarnished. Wood work in the vicinity of stoves and furnaces can be perfectly protected by a covering of bright tin. If the bulb of a thermometer be coated with tin foil it will remain comparatively unaffected by changes of temperature. The polished metallic helmet and cuirass worn by soldiers are cooler than might be imagined, because the polished metal throws off the rays of the sun and can not easily be raised to an inconvenient temperature.

In like manner heat can be *concentrated* by reflection. The Dutch oven reflects the heat of the fire upon the meat placed within it, provided its inside surface be kept brightly burnished. The most refractory substances can be melted, and even the diamond can be ignited and wholly consumed in the focus of a concave mirror, placed so as to concentrate the full strength of the solar rays. It was by a large number of plane mirrors, each one held by a single man, and so adjusted as to reflect the

---

79. Describe some of the practical applications of reflection of heat. Is it necessary that the reflecting surface should possess any great thickness? Describe the process by which Archimedes set fire to the Roman fleet.

heat of the sun upon a single point, that Archimedes is said to have set on fire the Roman fleet before Syracuse. The celebrated French Philosopher, Buffon, repeated this experiment in the last century, and constructed burning mirrors which were able to accomplish similar results. These mirrors were made of a great number of highly polished pieces of plane glass, eight inches long and six broad, which were placed in such a manner that the rays reflected from every piece could be concentrated on one point. By employing 128 such pieces of glass Buffon succeeded, at a distance of 220 feet, in firing a pitched wooden plank by the heat of a summer's sun.

80. **The Reflection of Heat by Fire Places.** The first great improvement in the construction of fire-places consisted in building the sides at an angle to the back, so that the heat proceeding from the fire might be thrown into the room instead of being reflected from one side to the other until it was finally absorbed. The upper part of the back of the fire-place was also inclined forward at an angle to the lower part, for the same reason and for the purpose of contracting the throat of the chimney. The angles of inclination should be 135°, as represented in the accompanying figures, and the brighter the sides and the back of the fire-place the greater the amount of heat reflected into the apartment. The ground plan of the old construction is represented in *Fig.* 18; of the new, in *Fig.* 19.

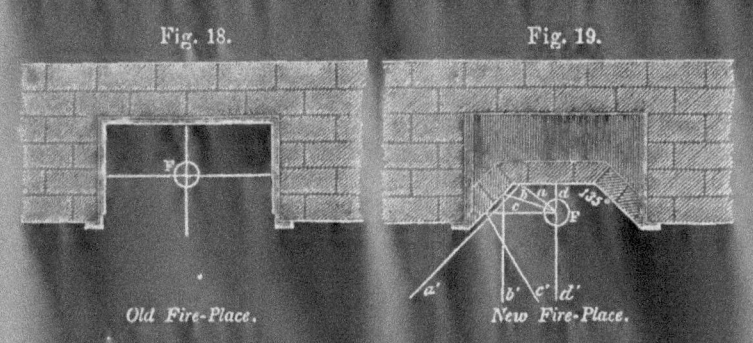

Fig. 18.　　　　　　　　　　Fig. 19.

Old Fire-Place.　　　　　　New Fire-Place.

The angle of incidence is the angle which the ray of heat that falls upon the side of the fire-place makes with the line drawn perpendicular to that side at the point of contact of the incident ray, and the angle of reflection being equal to the angle of incidence, it is evident that in *Fig.* 19 the incident rays, $a\ b\ c$ and

---

Describe Buffon's repetition of this experiment.—80. State the application of these principles to the construction of fire-places.

d will be reflected in the directions a' b' c' and d', and thus find their way into the room; while in *Fig.* 18, the rays must necessarily fall in such a manner upon the side of the fire-place that the greater part of them will be reflected from one side to the other, until they are ultimately dissipated and lost in the chimney, those only which fall perpendicularly upon the back being reflected directly into the room. In *Fig.* 20 is shown the same fire-place in elevation. This improvement was made by Dr. Franklin, and is found in the old-fashioned Franklin stove, which possesses also this additional advantage: that all the heat which is absorbed by the iron is diffused through the air of the apartment by convection, and thus prevented from being lost.

Fig. 20.

Franklin's Improvement.

Though the mode of warming houses by means of fire-places has nearly passed out of use, this improvement of Dr. Franklin's deserves to be remembered as being truly philosophical in its character. It would greatly conduce to the public health if our houses were more commonly warmed in this manner, because, by keeping up a continual draught it favors ventilation and produces a mild and gentle temperature.

81. The Absorption of Radiant Heat. Bodies differ very much in their power of absorbing radiant heat. The absorbing power of a body is always in the inverse proportion of its reflecting power; if it be a good reflector, it is a poor absorber, and *vice versa*. To determine the absorbing power of bodies, Leslie made use of the apparatus which he employed for determining their reflective power, see *Fig.* 13; omitting the plate a, and placing the bulb of the thermometer exactly in the focus of the mirror. This bulb was covered successively with lampblack, varnish, gold, silver and copper leaf, and the thermometer, under the influence of a constant source of heat, M, rose or fell, as the substance with which it was covered absorbed more or less heat. In this way it was found that the absorbing power increased as the reflecting power diminished. It was also discovered that those bodies which are good radiators also

---

81. How is the absorption of radiant heat determined? What is its relation to the power of reflection?

absorb heat readily, and that the power of absorption is directly proportional to the power of radiation. Thus lampblack, which is a good radiator, is also a good absorber; and in general, the more rough and uneven the surface, the more freely does it allow radiant heat to enter it.

82. The Absorption of Heat is much affected by Color. The color of a body has a great effect upon its absorbing power. Black absorbs the most, and white the least. This fact was first noticed by Dr. Franklin, who placed pieces of different colored cloths upon the snow in the sunlight, and observed that the melting extended to the greatest depth under those which had the darkest color. If pieces of copper be painted of different colors, placed upon a cake of wax and exposed to the sun, a similar result will follow. If the bulb of a thermometer be covered with paints of different colors and placed in the sun, the mercury will rise the highest when the darkest colors are employed. This is not only true of heat associated with light, but of *non-luminous* heat also. Thus when different colored wools were wound upon the bulb of a thermometer, and the instrument inclosed in a glass tube immersed in hot water at 212°, it was found that the effect upon the thermometer varied with the color of the wool. When black wool was used the mercury rose from 50° to 170° in 4' 30''; dark green, in 5'; scarlet, in 5' 30''; white, in 8'. Practical application is made of these facts in the selection of clothing; black colors should not be used in summer, because they absorb heat readily; but white, because they absorb slightly and reflect powerfully. Black and dark colored glass may be used with advantage in green-houses and hot-beds, because it absorbs heat, and elevates the temperature to a much greater extent than clear and transparent glass. In the Alps, the mountaineers accelerate the melting of the snow by scattering earth, ashes, and other dark colored substances upon its surface.

83. Transmission of Radiant Heat. When radiant heat is not reflected or absorbed by the surfaces on which it falls, it must of necessity be transmitted. If it be entirely transmitted, no elevation of temperature is produced in the body through which it passes. There are but few substances, however, which thus transmit heat; generally a portion of it is absorbed, and an elevation of temperature in the transmitting body produced.

---

82. Show that the power of absorption is affected by color. Is non-luminous heat affected in the same manner? How can this be proved? State some of the practical applications. —83. When radiant heat is not reflected or absorbed, what becomes of it? If heat be entirely transmitted, what effect is produced upon temperature?

84. The Transmission of Radiant Heat by any substance depends, to a great degree, upon the source from which the Heat proceeds. If a piece of glass be held between the bulb of a thermometer and the *sun*, scarcely any diminution of temperature will be observed in the thermometer, and scarcely any elevation of temperature in the glass itself. But if the same plate of glass be held between a brightly *burning fire* and the thermometer, it will be found to intercept nearly all the rays of heat, while at the same time its own temperature will be greatly elevated. The common glass lens, called the burning glass, collects the heat of the *sun's* rays to a focus so as to produce combustion without having its own temperature at all increased, but if exposed to any source of *artificial* heat and light, it will collect the rays of light to a focus as before, but will not concentrate those of heat, or any longer produce combustion. On the contrary, it absorbs the rays of heat as fast as they fall upon its surface, and in consequence of this, its temperature rapidly rises. In like manner, with a lens made of ice, Mr. Faraday succeeded in concentrating the sun's rays so as to inflame gunpowder; but the same lens held before a brightly burning fire, while it would concentrate the light as before, would no longer allow the passage of the heat; absorption of heat at once took place, and the lens was rapidly melted. In like manner the rays of the sun may be so concentrated by means of a parabolic mirror as to produce a bright spot of light and inflame a combustible substance, or even fuse metals and the precious stones, and if a screen of glass be interposed between the sun and the mirror, or between the mirror and the substance to be melted or burned, the effect will be but little, if at all, diminished. But let a powerful lamp, or a brightly burning fire, be substituted in place of the sun in this experiment, and it will be found, on interposing the screen of glass, that the heating effect of the mirror, instead of remaining undiminished as before, is reduced almost to nothing, while the brightness of the spot of light remains wholly unchanged. In the experiments above described upon the radiation and reflection of heat by two concave mirrors, in which the heat is derived from some artificial source, if a screen of glass be interposed between them, the rays of heat will be entirely intercepted, and the glass itself become sensi-

---

84. Is there any connection between the amount of heat transmitted and the source from which it proceeds? Give illustrations. State the difference between solar and terrestrial heat as to concentration by a lens. What experiment may be performed with a lens made of ice? State the effect of a concave mirror upon heat proceeding from different sources.

bly warmed. For this reason glass is preferred to every other material for the manufacture of fire screens, because it absorbs all the rays of heat that proceed from the fire, without obstructing the cheerful light. So too, it is used to fill the apertures for observation in porcelain and metal furnaces, because on account of its transparency it allows of close inspection of what is passing in the interior, while at the same time, in consequence of its complete absorption of the rays of heat, it shields the eyes and face from the excessive temperature to which they would otherwise be exposed. It is not to be understood, however, that perfectly transparent glass is absolutely impermeable to *terrestrial* heat, but only that its power of transmission is very small. The intense heat of charcoal ignited by galvanic electricity does produce a certain effect upon the air thermometer when concentrated by a glass lens, and thin plates of glass will also slightly transmit the heat of a powerful gas burner.

85. Transmission of Radiant Heat of equal intensity from different sources different for the same substance. These facts were confirmed by some experiments made by Melloni, an Italian philosopher, who paid much attention to this subject. In these experiments four different sources of heat were employed, viz.: 1st, the naked flame of an oil lamp; 2d, ignited platinum; 3d, copper heated to 750° F.; and 4th, copper heated to 212° F. Although these different sources differed in temperature, the experiments were arranged in such a way that the heat proceeding from each was in all cases of precisely equal intensity; this was accomplished by varying the distances from the different sources of heat at which the bodies in question were placed. The proper points were determined by noting the distances at which a differential thermometer, *Fig.* 21, whose bulbs were covered with lampblack, was required to be placed from each source of heat in order to rise an equal number of degrees in the same time. Then thin plates of rock salt, fluor spar, alum, and other substances whose power of transmission was to be determined, were placed in turn at these ascertained points opposite the various sources of heat employed.

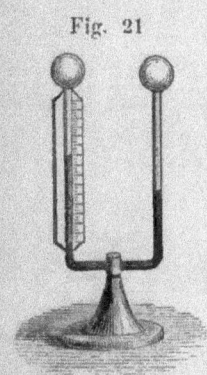

Fig. 21

Differential Thermometer.

Why is glass admirably adapted for fire screens? Is glass impermeable to terrestrial heat of every kind?—85. Give an account of the experiments of Melloni.

TRANSMISSION OF HEAT.

In this manner the heat which fell upon each plate from every one of the sources employed was made to be of exactly equal intensity. Finally, the amount of heat transmitted by each substance was ascertained by observing the effect produced upon a delicate thermo-multiplier placed in succession at an equal distance from each plate on the side opposite to that from which the heat proceeded. The results are contained in the following table. The figures not only indicate the comparative capacity of different substances for transmitting heat from the *same* source, or their *diathermancy*, as it is called, but also demonstrate the remarkable fact that this capacity varies in most cases with the source from which the heat proceeds, notwithstanding the intensity of the heat that is received from each is exactly equal. The explanation of this singular fact is, that there are different kinds of heat emitted by different sources, and that a body which is permeable to one kind is not necessarily so to all. The only exception to this rule is found in rock salt, which, it will be observed, transmits heat equally well from whatever source it may proceed. This substance is in all cases perfectly transparent to heat.

Melloni's Table, showing the amount of Heat from different sources, but of the same intensity, that is transmitted by different substances.

Each Plate was 0.102 inch thick.	Naked Flame.	Ignited Platinum	Copper 750° F.	Copper 212° F.
Rock Salt, limpid,	92.3	92.3	92.3	92.3
Sulphur, Sicily,	74	77	60	54
Fluor Spar,	72	69	42	33
Rock Salt, cloudy,	65	65	65	65
Beryl, greenish yellow,	46	38	24	20
Iceland Spar,	39	28	6	0
Plate Glass,	39	24	6	0
Quartz, limpid,	38	28	6	3
Quartz, smoky,	37	28	6	3
Topaz, white,	33	24	4	0
Tourmaline,	18	16	3	0
Citric Acid,	11	2	0	0
Alum,	9	2	0	0
Sugar Candy,	8	1	0	0

These experiments establish the general truth that the amount of heat transmitted by any substance is dependent, to a certain extent, upon the source from which the heat proceeds. Solar

---

State the results of his experiments. Why is salt called a perfect diathermic? What important truth is established by his experiments?

DIATHERMANCY 61

radiant heat finds a readier passage through transmitting media than that from any other source.

86. Transmission of Radiant Heat from the same source, different for different substances. Diathermancy. The amount of radiant heat transmitted depends not only upon the source from which the heat is derived, but also upon the nature of the transmitting substances. Thus the rays of heat from a brightly burning fire are hardly transmitted at all by a piece of clean, transparent, colorless glass, but very readily by a piece of black glass. Transparent alum is nearly as impermeable to heat as colorless glass, while rock salt, which is almost perfectly opaque, will transmit it with the greatest readiness. This power of transmitting radiant heat is called Diathermancy. Those bodies which give it a ready passage are called diathermanous, while those which allow it to pass with difficulty, or intercept it altogether, are called adiathermanous. Rock salt is the most perfect diathermanous body known, and its wonderful power in this respect can be shown by the apparatus represented in *Fig.* 22. Let s be

Fig. 22.

Diathermancy of Rock Salt.

a plate of rock salt, and G one of glass, both at equal distances from the ball of iron, which is heated nearly to redness. Let P P be bits of phosphorus, supported at equal distances from the plates S and G, behind which they are respectively placed. The plate of rock salt is four times thicker than the plate of glass, and is also nearly opaque; but notwithstanding this, the

---

86. Is the transmission of radiant heat from the same source the same for all media? How is the relative diathermancy of different solids determined? Describe the experiment illustrated by Fig. 22.

phosphorus behind it will be inflamed some time sooner than that which is behind the glass. In like manner, if the hands be placed, one behind each plate, the difference in transmissive power will be very perceptible, and if two large air thermometers be used, this difference will be made very manifest by the rising of one much higher than the other.

87. Diathermancy is not proportioned to Transparency. Diathermancy bears the same relation to radiant heat that transparency does to light. Transparency and diathermancy are, however, by no means proportional; on the contrary, often the most transparent substances are by no means as diathermanous as those which are opaque. Black glass will allow the rays of terrestrial heat to pass through it much more readily than that which is perfectly clear and transparent. Transparent alum and ice intercept the rays of heat almost entirely, while brown rock crystal and rock salt, which are quite *opaque*, furnish it a ready passage. Pure water arrests radiant heat almost entirely, while the reddish liquid, chloride of sulphur, allows it to pass with freedom. Sulphate of copper allows the passage of blue *light* abundantly, but arrests the rays of *heat* entirely. Mechanical arrangement has much influence upon diathermancy. Pulverization almost completely destroys the power of transmitting heat. Rock salt powdered is almost completely adiathermanous, and the same is true if it be dissolved in water; a solution of rock salt is nearly as adiathermanous as a solution of alum. This is in analogy with the effect of change in mechanical arrangement upon the transmission of light. Pure sugar candy is transparent, but ground to powder, it becomes opaque; and the clearest glass, if pulverized, loses its transparency and becomes entirely impervious to light.

88. Melloni's experiments on the Diathermancy of Solids. In these experiments, from which the greater part of our knowledge on this subject is derived, the heat transmitted was measured by the thermo-multiplier, an instrument much more sensitive to small degrees of heat than any thermometer. It is, in fact, the most delicate measure of heat known, and is now employed almost exclusively in researches of this description. The principle upon which it is constructed is, that heat has the power of exciting electricity, and the more intense the heat, the

---

87. What is diathermancy? Is there any relation between diathermancy and transparency? Give illustrations. What effect has mechanical division upon diathermancy? Give illustrations.—88. Describe the thermo-multiplier used by Melloni in his experiments.

DIATHERMANCY OF SOLIDS.

more powerful the current of electricity. This electricity may be measured with great accuracy by the galvanometer, an instrument which will be described hereafter, under the head of electro-magnetism. The general arrangement of Melloni's apparatus may be seen in *Fig.* 23; G is the galvanometer, by which the intensity of the electric current is measured; D C represents the thermo-electric pile by which the electricity is produced; T T, are cases which fit over it and protect it from the influence of surrounding objects; x and y are wires which convey the electricity to the galvanometer. At s the substance is placed, whose transmissive power is to be determined, and to the left of it, but unrepresented in the figure, stands the lamp or other source of heat employed. The results of these experiments may be seen from an examination of the different columns of the table previously given, § 85. Thus in the first column, where the results are those which were obtained by employing the naked flame of an oil lamp, the diathermancy is as follows:

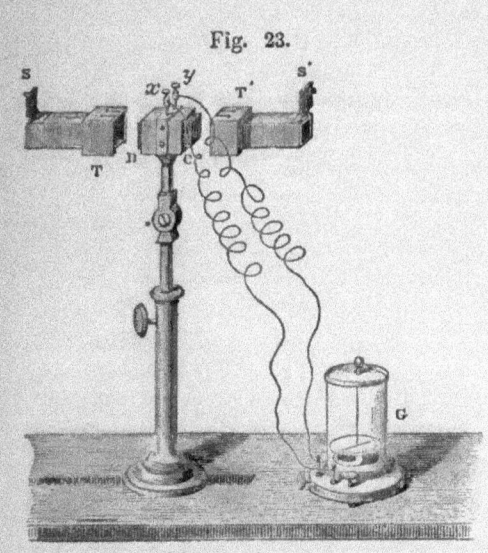

Fig. 23.

Melloni's Apparatus.

Melloni's table of Diathermancy, showing the amount of heat from the same source that is transmitted by different substances.

Each Plate was 0.102 inches thick. Source, naked flame.

Rock Salt,	92.33	Quartz, limpid,	38
Sulphur,	74	Quartz, smoky,	37
Fluor Spar,	72	Topaz, white,	33
Rock Salt, cloudy,	65	Tourmaline,	18
Beryl, yellow greenish,	46	Citric Acid,	11
Iceland Spar,	39	Alum,	9
Plate Glass,	39	Sugar Candy,	8

It is evident, therefore, that substances of equal transparency and equal thickness differ most remarkably in their power of transmitting heat from the same source. Melloni's apparatus was so delicate that the heat proceeding from the hand was at once made apparent by its effect on the galvanometer, and a temperature less than $\frac{1}{1000}$ of a degree, F., could readily be detected. It is the only instrument with which experiments of this kind can be satisfactorily performed.

89. The Diathermancy of Liquids. In like manner it was ascertained that liquids differ very much in their power of transmitting radiant heat. The source of heat was an argand lamp, and the liquids were confined in a trough of glass, the opposite faces of which were distant from each other 0.362 of an inch. Turpentine was found to transmit 31 out of every 100 rays, while rape seed oil transmitted but 30, olive oil 30, ether 21, alcohol 15, and distilled water only 11. Yet all these liquids are almost equally transparent. On the contrary Chloride of Sulphur, which is of a reddish color, and nearly opaque, allowed 63 out of every 100 of the incident rays to pass through it, showing in a striking manner the entire independence of transparency and diathermancy. Pure distilled water is one of the most adiathermanous liquids known, eighty-nine per cent. of the rays of heat which fall upon it being absorbed without perceptibly raising its temperature. A beam from a powerful electric light may be sent through a mass of ice, without melting it, provided the light be first made to pass through a stratum of water. The heat seems to be completely strained out of the beam and absorbed by the water, raising its temperature speedily nearly to the boiling point, while the light passes on without obstruction. A very thin stratum of water is quite sufficient to cut off all the heat that may be thrown upon it without perceptibly interfering with the light. It therefore makes excellent screens for the protection of workmen from the excessive temperatures of furnaces, while at the same time it allows them to keep a watchful eye upon all that is going on within. In consequence of the great capacity of water for heat, its temperature is but slightly affected by the heat proceeding from common sources.

What instrument is employed to measure the intensity of the heat? Prove the extreme delicacy of this instrument. What fraction of a degree can be measured by it? Give the general results of Melloni's experiments as contained in the table.—89. Is the diathermancy of all liquids equal? How was their diathermancy determined? State the diathermancy of several important liquids,—water, alcohol, ether. Is there any connection between the diathermancy and transparency of liquids? What is the effect of ice and water upon radiant heat? Why do they make excellent screens?

90. The Diathermancy of Gases. It is also found that the different gases, though they may be equally transparent, transmit very unequal quantities of terrestrial radiant heat. Perfectly dry and pure Air appears to transmit all the heat that falls upon it without the slightest absorption. The same is true of Hydrogen, Nitrogen and Oxygen. But Carbonic Acid, which is equally transparent with these gases, has a transmissive power, Air being taken as 1 of only $\frac{1}{50}$. The Illuminating gas of cities has a transmissive power of only $\frac{1}{970}$. Ammonia $\frac{1}{1195}$. It has also been found that moist air has much less transmissive power than dry air, and that if the air be perfectly saturated with watery vapor its transmissive power is diminished $\frac{1}{20}$. The effect of perfumes diffused through the air is the same, and the vapor of alcohol, ether and ammonia produces a similar result. It is the elementary gases, i. e., those which are incapable of decomposition, that in general have the greatest diathermancy and the least absorptive power. The compound gases and vapors, on the other hand, possess the least diathermancy, and the greatest absorptive power. In the case of solids it has been shown that good absorbers are good radiators. The same is true of the gases; those of them which have the least diathermancy, i. e., those which are the best absorbers of radiant heat, are also the best radiators, and allow heat to escape from them most readily. The amount of heat transmitted by the same gas, under the same circumstances, depends very much upon the source from which the heat proceeds.

The diathermancy of the gases mentioned above was determined with heat of low intensity, and derived from various *terrestrial* sources. The heat of the *sun* passes through them with much less absorption. If, however, this solar heat be allowed to fall upon the earth it is radiated again as terrestrial heat, and this re-radiated heat, strange to say, passes with great difficulty, and in some cases is entirely unable to pass at all through the air and other transparent media which, as solar heat, it had penetrated with the greatest ease. The moisture of the air, which then had little power to obstruct its passage, now stops it, and effectually prevents it from being transmitted into space and lost. The watery vapor in the atmosphere has

---

90. Are all gases equally diathermanous? What is the difference between the simple and compound gases in this respect? What influence does the source of heat have upon the diathermancy of gases? What effect is produced upon solar heat when re-radiated after absorption by the earth? What effect has the watery vapor of the air upon the escape of heat from the earth?

the same effect, therefore, as an envelope of glass would have in confining the heat, which tends to escape from the earth, while it allows a free passage to the solar radiant heat which is tending towards the earth. The practical utility of this, in maintaining the earth's temperature, is obvious. In the same way the perfume which rises from a flower-bed prevents the escape of a large proportion of the radiant heat which is constantly striving to pass from the earth, and thus assists materially in keeping the soil warm and productive. This must have a powerful effect upon the development of vegetation.

91. Diathermancy explained on the supposition that there are different kinds of Heat analogous to the different colors of Light. The reason why heat of a certain intensity and known effect, proceeding from one source will pass readily through certain transparent media, while heat of the same intensity and the same effect, as estimated by the thermometer, but proceeding from a different source, altogether fails to pass, is, that there are different kinds of heat, just as there are different kinds of light. A medium which will transmit one kind of heat will not necessarily transmit another; just as one piece of glass, if held up to the sun, will allow only the red rays of light to pass through it, absorbing all the other kinds, while another piece will only allow the green rays to pass, absorbing all the others; or just as a piece of red glass will allow all the light from flame of a red color to pass through it, but will not allow that from flame of a blue or green color to pass through it at all. The different kinds of light are sufficiently distinguished from each other by a difference in color, which is a visible property; the different kinds of heat not being thus distinguished, but being all equally invisible, it is necessary to resort to some other means of distinguishing them. This is found in the different degrees to which they are bent out of their original course, or the amount of *refraction* they undergo when passed through a perfectly transparent prism of rock salt. This substance is used both because it is the most perfect of all diathermanous substances, and also because it is equally diathermanous to all kinds of heat.

92. The existence of different kinds of Heat proved by the separation of a beam of Solar Heat by a Prism into rays possessed of different Refrangibility and different heating power. When the rays of heat fall at an oblique angle upon the surface

---

What effect have perfumes?—91. What reason is assigned for heat from different sources but of the same intensity, passing through the same medium with unequal facility?

of any substance capable of transmitting them, they are bent out of their course in passing through, or in other words, are *refracted*. The law of refraction for heat is very nearly the same as that for light. This is proved by the operation of the common burning glass, for it refracts both the heat and the light of the sun's rays to nearly the same degree, and concentrates them at nearly the same point, so that the brilliant spot of light which it produces is also the point of greatest intensity for heat. The fact of the refraction of rays of heat may also be proved by the use of a triangular glass prism. It is well known that if a beam of solar light be transmitted through such a prism, it is separated by refraction into several rays differing in color and refrangibility. Thus if a beam of sunlight be allowed to enter a darkened room through a fine slit, and fall upon a triangular prism, *Fig.* 24, it will not pass through the prism in a straight line and form a bright spot upon a screen of the same size as the opening, but it will be bent out of its course and throw upon the screen an elongated spot of light composed of different colors, arranged in a regular succession, and always in the same order. This elongated spot of light is called the solar spectrum, and is composed of the following colors: violet, indigo, blue, green, yellow, orange, red. The violet rays are the most refracted from the original course of the beam; while the red rays are the least refracted, and the highest illuminating effect is found to be in the yellow ray. Now on applying a delicate thermometer to the different colored rays it is found that the rays of heat are in like manner not collected at one point, but are diffused through the whole spectrum, and consequently a beam of solar heat is composed like a beam of solar light, of rays of heat of different kinds, and possessed of different degrees of refrangibility. It is also found that as

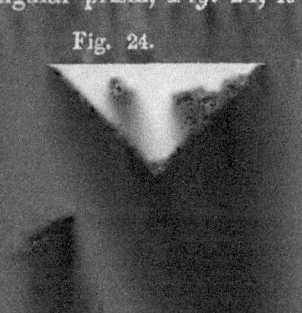

Fig. 24.

The Decomposition of Light.

---

92. Prove that there are different kinds of heat. How are the different kinds of heat distinguished? What is meant by refraction? What is the law of refraction for heat? Describe the refraction of solar light, and state the colors produced. Describe the refraction of heat.

the rays of light differ in color, as well as in refrangibility, so the rays of heat differ not only in refrangibility, but also in temperature. Thus, if a thermometer placed in the blue ray of the spectrum indicates a temperature of 56°, when brought down into the yellow ray it will indicate a temperature of 62°. If it be moved into the orange, the mercury will rise still higher, and continue to indicate a steadily increasing temperature as it approaches the lower part of the spectrum, until it finally attains its maximum of 79° in the extreme lower portion of the red ray, 23° higher than in the blue, and 17° higher than in the yellow ray, and indicating a progressively increasing temperature from the extreme violet to the extreme red end of the spectrum. What is still more remarkable, if the thermometer be moved to a point below the red ray, and entirely outside of the spectrum, it will be found to rise even higher than in the red ray itself, and a certain heating effect is found to be exerted at a point very considerably below the limit of the spectrum. This is shown in *Fig. 25*, where the different rays of heat marked H., may be traced from the red ray of the solar spectrum, R., as far down as b. The point of maximum heat depends upon the nature of the substance of which the prism is composed: when made of crown glass it is in the red ray; when made of flint glass it is just below the red; when of hollow glass, filled with water, it is in the yellow ray; when made of rock-salt it is some distance below the red ray. The whole range of the rays of heat extends from v. to $b.$, that is, through all the luminous portion of the spectrum, and also through a space which is non-luminous. These results of Sir W. Herschel were confirmed by the experiments of Sir H. Englefield, who proved that the thermometer rose in the different rays in the following order:

Fig. 25.

Unequal refrangibility of the Chemical, Illuminating and Heating Rays in the Solar Beam.

Do the rays of heat differ in temperature? What is the point of maximum intensity for heat? Is it ever found below the red? Are these invisible rays of heat associated with solar light?

RAYS OF HEAT MAY BE SEPARATED.   69

In the blue rays, in 3 min., from 55° to 56°, or 1°.
In the green "   in 3 "   "   54° to 58°, or 4°.
In the yellow "   in 3 "   "   56° to 62°, or 6°.
In the full red " in 2½ "   "   56° to 72°, or 16°.
In edge of red "   in 2½ "   "   58° to 73½°, or 15½°.
Below the red "   in 2½ "   "   61° to 79°, or 18°.

Sir W. Herschel ascertained that the invisible rays exerted a considerable heating power at a point 1½ inches distant from the extreme red ray, even though the thermometer was placed at a distance of 52 inches from the prism. From this it is evident that a solar beam contains rays of non-luminous as well as luminous heat, the former being much less refrangible than the latter; or rather the solar beam contains rays of heat mixed with the rays of light, some of which are of the same, and others of less refrangibility than the rays of light. The solar beam also contains a third class of rays more refrangible than those of heat and light, possessed neither of heat nor color, but exerting a peculiar chemical power. Of these we do not now speak particularly. They may be seen in *Fig.* 25, extending from v to c, and included in the bracket marked c.

93. This Difference is so marked that we may separate one kind of Heat from others with which it is mingled, and employ it exclusively at our pleasure. By employing a lens of Rock Salt, and placing it in the bundle of invisible rays of heat, extending from R to b, these rays may all be gathered up and concentrated at one focus, with the production of intense heat, but without a particle of light, and thus completely separated from those kinds of heat of greater refrangibility which fall between v and R, and are mingled with the rays of light in the luminous part of the spectrum. Again, there are some substances which possess the remarkable power of absorbing all the rays of light contained in the solar beam, but transmitting all the rays of heat. Glass colored black by carbon, and bi-sulphide of carbon containing iodine in solution, are particularly distinguished for this power. On transmitting the solar beam through the latter substance the rays of light are all absorbed, and those of heat alone allowed to pass. These invisible rays of heat thus transmitted may also be concentrated at an invisible focus by a lens of Rock Salt, and combustible substances actually inflamed. In like manner, if the electric light produced by the passage of a powerful galvanic current between pieces of charcoal be employed, instead of the light of the sun, and con-

---

93. How can the rays of heat in the sun's beam be separated from those of light? What effects can be produced by concentrating the invisible rays of heat by means of a lens?

centrated at a focus by a concave mirror, the intense light which is emitted will be entirely absorbed by the above-mentioned solution of iodine in bi-sulphide of carbon, placed between the focus of the mirror and the charcoal points, and the rays of heat alone allowed to pass. These invisible rays of heat will still be concentrated at the same focus, as before the solution was interposed, but with no visible mark to indicate the spot; the focus, in short, will be entirely invisible. The heat, however, is intense, and on placing in this dark focus pieces of wood and paper, they are immediately inflamed,—lead, tin and zinc are melted; if the invisible focus be thrown upon a piece of charcoal, suspended in a receiver of oxygen gas, the charcoal will be ignited and burn with splendid scintillations; if the charcoal be suspended in vacuo, it will be heated red hot. If blackened zinc foil be placed in the focus it will immediately be set on fire, and burn with a purple flame; the metal magnesium will burn in like manner with a splendid light.

94. Different kinds of Heat are emitted by different sources of Heat, just as different kinds of Light are emitted by different colored Flames. In the case of rays of light, if instead of employing the sun as a source of light to form the prismatic spectrum we make use of the red light which is produced by Nitrate of Strontia dissolved in alcohol, it will be found that the kind of light emitted is very different from that of the sun, that the greater part of the rays are those of small refrangibility, and that they are collected at the lower part of the spectrum, causing the point of maximum intensity for light to fall within the red ray. Just so with rays of heat: by changing the source of heat we obtain different kinds of heat, varying in refrangibility and altering the position of the point of maximum intensity for heat in the heat spectrum, in proportion as the rays of one degree of refrangibility preponderate over those of another. This takes place according to a certain fixed rule. The less intense the source, the lower the refrangibility of the heat radiated, and the nearer to the red end of the spectrum is the point of maximum temperature. The more intense the source of heat, the more abundant the emission of the kinds of heat possessed of high refrangibility. Thus the sun, the most intense of all the sources of heat, emits the more refrangible kinds of heat, containing rays which, when passed through a prism, undergo pow-

---

Describe the experiments with the invisible rays obtained from the electric light.—94. Show that different kinds of heat are emitted by different sources. How does the point of maximum intensity for heat vary with the source?

THE HEAT OF THE ELECTRIC LIGHT. 71

erful refraction, and are distributed over the whole spectrum, extending as high even as the extreme violet. The naked flame of a lamp, a less intense source, emits rays of less refrangibility, hardly extending above the blue portion of the spectrum. Ignited platinum, a still less intense source, emits those kinds of heat which have a still lower refrangibility, extending not much above the red. Copper, at 750°, emits those of even a still lower degree of refrangibility, while from hot water, at 212°, only those kinds of heat are emitted which are possessed of the lowest possible refrangibility. In the case of the electric light, which, after the sun, is one of the most intense sources of heat, the proportion of the more refrangible to the less refrangible kinds of heat is shown in *Fig.* 26. The rays extend from A to E, and perpendiculars erected at various points represent the calorific intensity, or the amount of heat of that particular refrangibility existing at those points: Then the ends of all these perpendiculars being united, we have a curve which shows at a glance the manner in which the heat is distributed through the electric spectrum. The luminous portion of the spectrum is unshaded, the non-luminous, or dark portion, is drawn in black. It will be observed that while this source emits kinds of heat of refrangibility equal to the blue, these are small in quantity; that the less refrangible kinds are larger in amount as we advance from E to D, where the luminous portion of the spectrum terminates: that these still further increase in quantity as advance is made below the red into the invisible portion of the spectrum, and finally attain their greatest

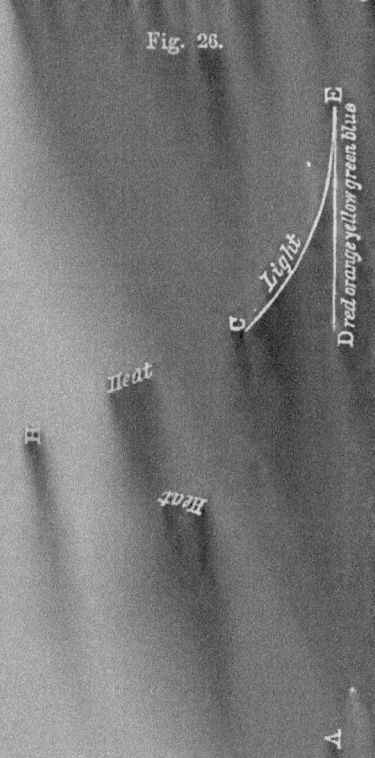

Fig. 26.

Curve showing the distribution of the heat in the spectrum of the Electric Light.

What is the relation between the intensity of the source of heat and the refrangibility of the rays? Explain Fig. 26.

intensity at II, a point considerably below the red end of the spectrum. If the heat spectrum of the sun were drawn on the same plan, the point II would be found opposite a point a little above D, and would fall within the light or illuminated portion of the spectrum, instead of wholly in the dark or invisible portion.

From all this, it seems clear that as there are different kinds of radiant Light, distinguished by a difference in refrangibility, and also by a difference in color, so there are different kinds of radiant Heat, distinguished from each other also, by a difference in refrangibility, but not distinguished from each other by color; and that different sources emit these different kinds of heat in various proportions.

95. Consequently the unequal Diathermancy of the same medium for Heat proceeding from different sources seems to be owing to the different kinds of Heat emitted by the different sources. This being so, it is easy to see that the reason the rays of heat proceeding from the sun can traverse glass and experience but little obstruction, when the same plate of glass can hardly be traversed at all by heat proceeding from a common fire, a lamp, or any other source of terrestrial heat is, that the rays which glass transmits are those of the more refrangible kinds of heat alone, and it is these which are the most abundant in the solar beam; while the rays of heat proceeding from the fire are those of the less refrangible kinds, and these glass is almost entirely incapable of transmitting at all; in the same manner precisely that a piece of blue glass will transmit perfectly all the rays of light proceeding from a Roman candle, while it will not allow any of the rays of light proceeding from a flame of a green or red color to pass through it at all.

96. The unequal Diathermancy of different substances for Heat proceeding from the same source seems to be owing to a property in bodies in relation to Heat, analogous to the property of color in relation to Light, and called Thermochrosis. The other peculiarity brought out by the experiments of Melloni, viz., that heat radiated from the same source, and therefore of the same kind, is transmitted completely by one substance, and imperfectly by another, seems to be owing to a property in bodies for heat exactly analogous to the property of color in relation to light. Thus, 92 out of every 100 of the rays of heat proceeding from an oil lamp are transmitted by a piece of

---

95. How does this explain the transmission of heat from one source, and non-transmission of heat from another source, by the same medium?—96. Prove that there is in bodies a property for heat analogous to the property of color for light.

Rock Salt, while only 9 out of 100 are transmitted by a piece of alum of equal transparency and thickness. The reason is, that Rock Salt is nearly perfectly transparent to heat, while alum acts like a piece of colored glass upon the sun; it will stop a considerable proportion of the rays and allow only a part of them to pass through. Thus, if clear glass be held up to the sun it will allow all the seven kinds of light of which white light is composed to pass through it, while a piece of blue glass will absorb a certain portion of the rays and only allow those of a blue color to pass through it. This unequal absorption of light of different kinds is the cause of the different colors of bodies, and this absorption is effected by some peculiar property which we call color; a body of a red color is one which absorbs all the rays of light except those which are red; of a blue, all the rays except the blue, &c. In like manner with the rays of heat proceeding from a lamp, Rock Salt will allow them all to pass without absorption, and they all go through unchanged, while alum, having the peculiar property of absorbing all the rays of heat except those of a particular kind, only allows the latter to pass through. This peculiar absorptive property for heat, corresponding with color for light, has been called *thermochrosis*, or tint for heat.

This is confirmed by another point of agreement between light and heat. In the case above mentioned, of a piece of blue glass which has absorbed all the rays of light except the blue, and allowed these alone to pass, it is found that if these blue rays be allowed to fall upon a second piece of blue glass they undergo no further absorption, but they all pass through it unchanged; the reason is, because all the rays of light which the second piece of blue glass could absorb have already been absorbed by the first piece, consequently it transmits all the light which has reached it from the first piece. In the same manner, if the rays of heat which have succeeded in passing through one piece of alum be allowed to fall upon a second piece, they will undergo no absorption, but all pass through unchanged, because all the rays of heat which the second piece of alum could absorb have already been absorbed by the first piece; consequently all the heat which reaches the second, after having passed through the first piece, is transmitted.

On the other hand if, instead of making use of a second piece

---

What is meant by the calorific tint of bodies? What light does this throw upon the transmission of solar heat by glass, and the non-transmission of artificial heat?

of blue glass, we make use of a piece of red glass, in the above mentioned experiment upon light, the rays of light which have passed through the blue glass will not pass through the piece of red glass, because the rays which red can absorb have not been all taken out of it by the blue; these will therefore be absorbed by the red, and the result will be that no rays of light whatever will be able to pass through. In like manner with the rays of heat which have passed through the first piece of alum, if they be allowed to fall upon a piece of ice, instead of a second piece of alum, as before, instead of passing through unchanged, they will all be absorbed, because the calorific tint of ice is not such as to allow them to pass.

It is evident, therefore, that bodies possess a *calorific* tint for heat precisely analogous to their *colorific* tint for light. The only substance which seems to have no calorific tint, but to be perfectly transparent to heat of all kinds, as clear glass is for light, is Rock Salt. In all experiments upon radiant heat this is the substance that should be used for the prisms and lenses which are required. Its diathermancy is so perfect that the rays of heat proceeding from the human hand will pass through it with scarcely any absorption, and produce a perceptible effect upon the thermo-multiplier.

97. The refrangibility of rays of Heat may be altered by re-radiation—Calorescence. When heat has once been absorbed, whatever may have been its original source, it acts in all cases in the same manner in producing expansion; and when radiated again it does not necessarily retain the peculiarities of the source from which it originally proceeded, but its refrangibility depends entirely upon the temperature of the surface which emits it the second time. Hence it is immaterial, so far as the common effects of heat are concerned, whether it were originally derived from the sun, from actual flame, from ignited platinum, or from a non-luminous body. It will in all cases be much affected by the nature of the substance from which it is re-radiated. If the temperature of the second radiating substance be lower than that of the original source, the refrangibility of the rays of heat will be lessened, and on transmission through a prism, will be found nearer the point b, in *Fig.* 25. On the other hand, if the temperature of the second radiating substance rise

---

97. Do the different kinds of heat, if of equal intensity, differ in their effect upon the dimensions of bodies? If heat be absorbed and radiated again does it still possess the peculiarities of its original source? Is any effect produced upon the refrangibility of heat by re-radiation? Explain calorescence.

DOUBLE REFRACTION OF HEAT. 75

higher than that of the original source, the refrangibility of the rays will be increased, and on transmission through a prism, will be found nearer the point R, in *Fig.* 25. Indeed, their refrangibility may be so much increased that non-luminous rays are sometimes, by re-radiation, rendered luminous. Thus the combustion of oxygen and hydrogen gases produces a flame which contains only rays of heat of low refrangibility, and consequently emitting very little light; but on introducing a cylinder of lime into the flame, the refrangibility of the rays is so greatly increased that they emit light too intense for the eye to bear, and on transmission through a prism the point of maximum intensity for heat is found to be nearly as high as y in the colored part of the spectrum, *Fig.* 25. In like manner the rays of *solar* heat are possessed of high refrangibility, but when reradiated from the earth their refrangibility is very much lessened, and they can no longer pass readily through the air and watery vapor which they previously traversed with the greatest ease. This alteration in the refrangibility of heat is sometimes called *calorescence*, and is analogous to a similar alteration in the refrangibility of light, treated of hereafter, called fluorescence.

98. **The double refraction and polarization of Heat.** It is well known that when a ray of light falls obliquely upon the surface of a crystal of Iceland spar it is divided into two distinct rays which proceed in two different directions through the crystal. One is in the same plane with the original ray, and is called the ordinary ray, represented at O, in *Fig.* 27; the other is not in the same plane with the original ray, and is called the extraordinary ray, represented at E. In like manner, if a ray of non-luminous heat from the lower or red end of the solar spectrum be thrown obliquely upon the surface of such a crystal, it will be found to be divided also into two rays, which will be refracted according to the same law, and exactly in the same manner, as the rays of light. The two rays of

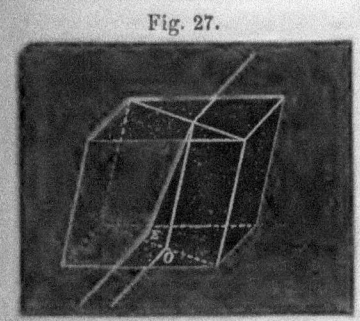

Fig. 27.

Double Refraction of Heat.

---

98. Explain the double refraction of light and heat. What is meant by the polarization of the doubly refracted rays of light and heat?

light produced by transmission through a doubly refracting crystal are found to have received a peculiar modification called polarization, the effect of which is briefly this:—A mirror placed in an inclined position at a certain angle above or below either of the two refracted rays, is capable of reflecting either ray in the ordinary manner; but if placed at the same angle of inclination on either side of this same ray, it becomes utterly incapable of reflecting it. The other ray is similarly affected, but the position of the reflecting side is reversed. In like manner, the two rays into which a single beam of heat is divided by a doubly refracting crystal, are found to possess the same properties of polarization. From these facts it appears that while there are many points of close analogy between Heat and Light, and each is capable of conversion into the other, yet as one may exist without the other, and when associated together one may be separated from the other without any diminution of the intensity of either, they are consequently in all probability entirely distinct agents, or, according to the undulatory theory, are the result of two different rates of vibration.

99. The different processes through which Heat may pass in seeking an Equilibrium. In seeking an equilibrium heat may go through the processes of conduction, convection, radiation, absorption, reflection, transmission, refraction, double refraction, and polarization. When, however, by any of these processes it is made to accumulate in any substance, it always produces certain effects, and it is to these effects thus produced by heat that we next turn our attention.

Experiments on Diffusion of Heat.

1. Conduction. To show that sensation is no test of temperature, arrange three bowls containing water at $32°$, $96°$, $150°$, respectively Dip the two hands into the first and third bowls, and then at the same instant into the centre bowl, containing water at $96°$. To one hand it will feel cold, to the other warm. See *Fig. 2*.

2. To show that heat is transferred from a hot body to one that is colder, introduce a small tin cup of mercury at $60°$, into water at $212°$ A thermometer placed in the cup will soon rise to $212°$, and the mercury will become uncomfortably warm to the hand.

3. The same fact is shown by holding a rod of iron in the flame of a spirit lamp.

4. That different substances conduct heat with different degrees of facility may be shown by holding with one hand a rod of metal, and with the other a rod of glass, in the flame of the same spirit lamp, or a rod of brass and a bit of charcoal. The charcoal may be inflamed and held in the fingers, not more than ¼ of an inch from the flame, without any uneasiness.

5. That different metals conduct heat with unequal rapidity may be shown by cones or rods of different metals tipped with Phosphorus, placed upon a metallic tray at equal distances from the flame of a lamp below.

6. The difference in the conducting power of bodies may be shown by surrounding three canisters of tin, of the same size, with cotton, charcoal powder, and iron turnings, contained in cylinders of pasteboard, filling the canisters with hot water from the same

---

99. State the different processes through which heat may pass in seeking an equilibrium.

EXPERIMENTS ON CONDUCTION, 77

vessel, and placing a thermometer in each; at the end of half an hour they will have cooled very unequally.

7. That heat progresses from particle to particle may be shown by a rod of iron, one end of which is heated in the flame of a lamp, having bits of phosphorus placed in order upon it. They inflame successively. See *Fig.* 3.

8. Wrap a piece of linen cloth, or of writing paper, tightly around a smooth brass or iron knob, and hold it in the flame of a spirit lamp. The paper will inflame with difficulty in consequence of the rapid conduction of the heat by the metal. Wrap the same substances around a piece of wood, and note how much more rapid the inflammation is in consequence of the poor conducting power of the wood. On this principle may be explained the melting of a bullet of lead smoothly wrapped in a bit of paper, and held over a lamp, without burning the paper.

9. The imperfect conducting power of glass may be shown by cracking it with hot iron; the heat of the iron can not penetrate into the glass; the outside, therefore, only expands, the inside retaining its original dimensions, and the two are torn apart.

10. Prince Rupert's Drops. Break the long end.

11. The imperfect conducting power of water compared with metal, may be shown by pouring water, of a temperature just supportable to the finger into a tin cup, grasped by the hand; it immediately becomes intolerably hot, owing to the excellent conducting power of the metal.

12. The poor conducting power of liquids may be shown by placing a differential thermometer at the bottom of a jar filled with water so as just to cover very slightly the uppermost bulb; pour a little ether on the water and inflame it. The heat is intense, but no effect whatever is produced upon the thermometer, though a very slight heat applied to the bulb, like that of the hand, will cause the thermometric fluid to move through several inches. See *Fig.* 6.

13. The poor conducting power of liquids may be shown by freezing a little water at the bottom of a test tube, filling the tube nearly full of water, and holding the upper portion in an inclined position over a spirit lamp; the water may be made to boil without melting the ice: see *Fig.* 7. The ice may be formed by introducing the tube into a freezing mixture composed of equal parts of snow and salt.

14. The same fact may be shown by pouring into a similar tube a small quantity of decoction of blue cabbage, then filling it with water and holding it in an inclined position in the flame of a spirit lamp, it can be made to boil on the surface without disturbing the blue decoction below at all.

15. **Convection.** To show that liquids must be heated from below, bring the lower part of the tube used in the preceding experiment over the spirit lamp; the blue liquid will immediately begin to diffuse itself and rise to the surface, in consequence of its particles becoming specifically lighter by expansion.

16. To prepare the decoction of blue cabbage, used for many purposes in chemical experiments, pour boiling water on purple cabbage cut into fine pieces, and let it steep for an hour. Strain carefully and bottle, with a little strong alcohol.

17. To show that liquids are heated by convection, fill a flask with strong solution of carbonate of potash; throw in some bits of amber, and dilute with water until the specific gravity of the solution becomes equal to that of the amber. Apply the heat of a spirit lamp below, when the bits of amber will be seen to rise in the centre of the vessel, and descend at the sides, following the motion of the water in which they are suspended.

18. Heat the solution of carbonate of potash, not over a lamp, but by dipping it in hot water; the particles of amber will rise at the sides and descend at the centre; as soon as it arrives at the same temperature with the surrounding water the motion ceases. Take the flask from the water and the current is reversed, descending upon the sides and rising in the centre.

19. That gases conduct heat slowly may be shown by filling a hollow cubical vessel of metal with boiling water, and noting the cooling at the end of an hour. Fill another vessel of the same size, made of metal only half as thick as the first, but placed within another metallic vessel an inch larger than itself, arranged so that the air between the two can not escape, making a cube within a cube, and note the cooling during the same time; it will be much less in the last than in the first, though the thickness of the two vessels in the last case is just equal to that of the one vessel in the first.

20. The currents produced in air by heat may be shown by placing a small wax taper under a tall bell glass; and also two small vessels containing ammonia and chlorohydric or muriatic acid respectively. A cloud is produced which circulates with the heated air.

21. **Radiation.** That heat leaps, as it were, from hot bodies through an appreciable interval, may be shown by holding a thermometer near a ball of metal moderately heated.

22. That the effect diminishes with the square of the distance, may be shown by actual measurement, one thermometer being placed at the distance of one foot from the hot body, another at two feet, and noting the effect.

23. That the escape of heat from a body by radiation varies with the nature of the

surface, may be shown by filling three canisters of thin brass, one having a polished surface, the second coated with lampblack, and the third with whiting, with hot water from the same vessel, and testing the temperature at the end of an hour. The first will be the hottest, the second the coolest, and the third intermediate.

24. The same fact may be shown by placing a thermometer at an equal distance from the four sides of a brass cube filled with boiling water, of which one side is brightly burnished, the second has the natural surface of the brass, the third is covered with a coating of whiting, and the fourth with a coating of lampblack; the polished side will affect the thermometer the least, the lampblack the most, &c.; the hand placed near the four sides successively will also detect the difference in the radiating power.

25. Absorption. To show that absorption is affected by the nature of the surface, and is proportional to the radiating power, place the three canisters of experiment 23, filled with water at 60°, at equal distances from the same stove; at the expiration of an hour they will be of very different temperatures, the blackened canister being the warmest.

26. The same fact may be shown by placing three thermometers, one having its bulb roughened with lampblack, the second covered with whiting, the third with tin foil, at equal distances from the same hot ball. The blackened thermometer will rise the highest in a given time, then the one covered with whiting; the one covered with tin foil the least.

27. To show the effect of color upon the absorption of solar heat, place pieces of sheet copper, two inches square, colored respectively black, brown, blue, green, red, yellow, and white, upon cakes of cerate composed of equal parts of beeswax and olive oil melted together, cut a little less than two inches square; expose them to the sun's rays and note the depth to which the cerate is melted under each piece.

28. The same fact may be shown by exposing different thermometers, having their bulbs differently colored, to the sun's rays, or by using thermometers filled with differently colored alcohols. In equal times the effect in both cases will be different.

29. To show that there is a difference in the effect of color upon solar and terrestrial heat, blacken one bulb of a differential thermometer, cover the other with whiting, and place it in the sun; the blackened bulb will be affected the most; place the same instrument near a heated ball, and no such result will take place.

30. Reflection. The reflection of heat may be shown by placing a hot ball and a thermometer on opposite sides of an opaque screen; the latter remains unaffected. Then hold a plate of tin, or a common looking-glass, in such a position that a line drawn from the ball to it will make with a perpendicular at the point of contact, an angle equal to that formed with the same perpendicular by a line drawn from the thermometer to the tin at the first point of contact; an immediate effect will be produced upon the thermometer, and the angle of incidence will be equal to that of reflection. Heat is therefore reflected like light. A vessel of hot water may be used instead of the ball.

31. That rays of heat may be concentrated by parabolic reflectors, to a focus, may be shown by placing a cube of hot water in front of a parabolic reflector, and a thermometer in its focus, and interposing a small screen between the bulb of the thermometer and the cube. The mercury will immediately begin to rise in consequence of the reflection of heat from the mirror.

32. If, instead of one parabolic reflector, two be used, a thermometer placed in the focus of one, and a cube of hot water in the focus of the other, a small screen being interposed so as to cut off all direct communication, the rays of heat striking the first mirror will be reflected in right lines to the second, and then be reflected to the thermometer in its focus, precisely in the same manner as light would be.

33. If the sides of the cube be variously coated the effect upon the thermometer will vary with the surface which is exposed to the mirror, showing the effect of surface on *radiation.*

34. If the thermometer be made with a cubical bulb of metal, and its four sides be differently coated, the mercury or colored fluid in the stem will rise to different heights, according to the side which is presented to the mirror, showing the effect of surface on *absorption.*

35. If a spermaceti candle be placed in the focus of the mirror the effect will be less than when an alcohol lamp is used, thus showing that the amount of heat emitted by a flame is not in proportion to the light.

36. If a ball of iron, heated so as not to be quite red hot, be placed in the focus of one mirror, and a candle tipped with phosphorus and chlorate of potash in the focus of the other, the candle will be inflamed. A common match may be lighted in the same manner, and water may be boiled.

37. To show that all bodies, even those not called hot bodies, are continually radiating heat to those colder than themselves, place a thermometer in one focus, and a lump of ice in the other. The thermometer will radiate more heat to the ice than is radiated to it by the ice, and its temperature will immediately sink.

38. To show the effect of bright surfaces in throwing off and reflecting rays of heat, coat the bulb of a thermometer with tin foil, and it will hardly be affected at all by the heat from a hot ball when held near it.

39. To show the effect of transparent screens in obstructing the passage of non-luminous heat, while they offer no impediment to that of solar heat, interpose a screen of glass between the mirrors, having a hot ball in one focus, and a thermometer in the other, and the heating effect will be at once cut off. Interpose the same screen between the sun and a thermometer placed in the focus of one of the mirrors, and no such obstruction will take place.

40. The same fact may be exemplified by holding a burning glass before a fire, and in the rays of the sun; the glass is powerfully heated in the first case, but not at all in the second.

41. **Diathermancy.** To show that diathermancy is not proportioned to transparency, employ the apparatus represented in *Fig.* 22. The screens of glass and rock salt need not be more than three or four inches square, and may be set into blocks of wood. The experiment may be varied by using an air thermometer instead of the bits of phosphorus, and observing also the effect upon the hands. Instead of a hot ball, a flask of boiling water may be used. Pieces of glass of various colors may be employed also, instead of the transparent glass.

42. For these experiments a delicate air thermometer is useful, which may easily be constructed from a common flat bottomed glass flask, by pouring in alcohol colored red by cochineal, or blue by litmus, to the depth of an inch, and then inserting a tightly fitting cork through which passes a long glass tube, a yard in length and of fine bore, fitting tightly and extending to the bottom of the flask beneath the surface of the liquid. On blowing through the tube air will be forced into the flask, and the fluid will rise in the stem. A scale of wood divided into equal parts may be attached to the stem by wire. The air in this case is the thermometric fluid, and such a thermometer will indicate very slight differences of temperature very plainly to the eye. The flask may be coated with lampblack or whiting rubbed in a mortar with spirits of turpentine, and when no longer wanted, these coats may be washed off by spirits of turpentine.

§ II.—Effects of Heat:—Expansion.

100. Expansion produced by Heat. When Heat is accumulated in bodies it produces very powerful effects. In general, it causes expansion, and alters the dimensions of bodies. Heat is antagonistic to Cohesion, or that attraction which tends to unite the particles of the same kind, of which matter is composed; and upon the balance between these two forces depend the dimensions of bodies, and their state as solids, liquids, and gases. At ordinary temperatures, heat and cohesion mutually balance each other, in all solids; but if temperature be increased, heat, or the force which tends to push the particles of the body apart, becomes stronger than cohesion, or the force which tends to bind them together; and the dimensions of the body are therefore necessarily enlarged. If the heat be increased, the relative strength of cohesion is still further diminished, the particles acquire mobility, and a liquid is produced. If it be

---

100. What is the first effect produced by heat? To what force is heat opposed? How does the balance between these forces determine the state of matter? What is the cause of liquidity?

still farther increased the liquid becomes a gas. The first effect of heat, therefore, is to expand all bodies into which it enters, and to make them larger. The ratio of this expansion, however, differs greatly in different substances. Thus with the same increment of heat, liquids expand more than solids, and aeriform bodies more than liquids. There is also a considerable difference in the expansibility of different solids and different liquids; but the aeriform fluids, as air and the gases, all expand equally with the same increase of temperature.

101. Expansion of Solids. The expansion of a solid is readily proved by fitting a piece of metal, when cold, to an orifice or notch, and then putting it into the fire; as temperature rises it will steadily increase in size, and soon become too large to enter its former measure.

Fig. 28.

Fig. 29.

Expansion of Solids.

Ring of St. Gravesande.

The piece of brass attached to the handle in *Fig.* 28, is exactly fitted to the notch in the plate, so as readily to enter it when cold, but when heated, its dimensions are so enlarged as to render this impossible. The same fact may also be shown by the ring of St. Gravesande, in *Fig.* 29, where the ball, a, after being heated, becomes too large to pass readily through the ring, m, which formerly admitted of its easy entrance.

102. The Expansion of Solids unequal. Different solids expand unequally for equal increments of Heat. The ratio of expansion may readily be shown by an instrument called

---

Of the aeriform state? How does the expansion of liquids and gases compare with that of solids?—101. How can the expansion of solids be proved? Describe the ring of St. Gravesande.—102. Is the expansion of different solids equal, or unequal? How can it be proved?

the Pyrometer, one form of which is represented in *Fig.* 30. A metallic rod, A, is placed upon the supports, and one end fastened firmly by the screw, B, while the other end is left unfastened, and arranged so as to touch the short arm of the lever, K. The rod is then heated by the spirit lamp, and its gradual expansion is shown by the motion of the long arm of the lever

Fig. 30.

The Pyrometer.

along the graduated circle, a very small expansion at the short arm of the lever causing the long arm to traverse an arc of considerable size, and very evident to the eye. In comparing different substances by means of this instrument, it is necessary that all the rods should be of the same size and length, and that the heat of the lamp should be applied the same space of time.

From experiments made with the pyrometer, it appears that, in most instances, there is a relation between the expansion of the metals and their fusibility, and in general, that those which are most easily fusible, expand most with equal increments of heat. Thus lead, tin and zinc, expand much more from the same increase of heat than copper, silver and iron, and the former are much more readily fusible than the latter.

103. Expansion of Metals. Among solids, the metals expand the most; thus lead, in being heated from the freezing to the boiling point of water, i. e., from 32° F. to 212°, expands much more than glass, earthen ware, and porcelain. The metals, however, differ very much among themselves in expansi-

---

Describe the pyrometer.—103. Give the order of expansion among metals. Is the same expansion produced by equal increments of heat at all temperatures? How is the total expansion of a body calculated? Do bodies, after being heated, contract, on cooling, to their original dimensions?

4*

bility from the same addition of heat, as will be seen from the following table:

Relative Expansion of different Solids.

1000 parts at 32° F.	become at 212°,	or are lengthened.
English Flint Glass,	1000.811	1 in 1248 parts.
French Glass Tube,	1000.861	" 1148 "
Platinum,	1000.884	" 1131 "
Steel,	1001.079	" 926 "
Antimony,	1001.083	" 923 "
Iron,	1001.182	" 846 "
Bismuth,	1001.392	" 718 "
Gold,	1001.466	" 682 "
Copper,	1001.718	" 582 "
Brass,	1001.801	" 536 "
Silver,	1001.909	" 524 "
Tin,	1001.937	" 516 "
Lead,	1002.848	" 351 "
Zinc,	1002.942	" 340 "

The expansion of the more permanent solids is very uniform within certain limits. Thus their expansion from 32° to 122° is equal to that between 122° and 212°, but above 212° the expansion proceeds more rapidly as the temperature rises, and becomes greater for equal increments of heat. Ten degrees of heat, therefore, added to any solid above 212°, produce a greater expansive effect than the same number of degrees added below 212°. The total increase in bulk of any body which has undergone expansion from heat may be ascertained by trebling the number which expresses its increase in length. Nearly all solids, after having been expanded by heat, return exactly to their original dimensions when they are allowed to resume their original temperature. Lead, however, constitutes an apparent exception; it is so soft that the particles slide over each other in the act of expansion, and do not return to their former position. A lead pipe used for conveying steam permanently lengthens several inches in a short time, and the leaden lining of sinks and gutters is soon thrown into ridges from the effect of the hot water.

104. The Force of Expansion. The expansion of metals by heat, and their subsequent contraction, are often employed with great advantage in the Arts, and frequently act as most efficient mechanical powers. The amount of force which pro-

---

104. What is the force of expansion equal to? Give illustrations.

THE FORCE OF EXPANSION. 83

duces these expansions and contractions is enormous, being equal to the mechanical power required to stretch or compress the solids in which they take place to the same amount. On heating an iron sphere of $12\frac{1}{2}$ inches diameter, from $32°$ to $212°$, its expansion exerts a force of 60,000 lbs. upon every square inch of its surface, or 30,000,000 lbs. upon the whole sphere. A bar of iron one square inch in section is stretched $\frac{1}{10000}$ of its length by a ton weight; the same elongation and an equal amount of force is exerted by increasing its temperature $16°$ F. In a range of temperature from winter to summer of $80°$ a wrought iron bar 10 inches long will vary in length $\frac{5}{1000}$ of an inch, and will exert a pressure, if its two ends be fastened, of 50 tons upon the square inch.

105. Illustrations. The immense force of expansion is clearly proved in many notable instances. Thus, Southwark Bridge, over the Thames, is constructed of iron, and surmounted by stone, and the arches rise and fall one inch within the usual range of atmospheric temperature. The Hungerford chain suspension bridge crosses the Thames with a span of 1352 feet in length; the height of this chain road way varies in the hottest day in summer, and the coldest in winter, to the extent of eight inches. The Menai suspension bridge weighs 20,000 tons, and this is raised and lowered fourteen inches by the change of temperature between winter and summer. The Britannia Tubular bridge, over the Menai Straits, expands and contracts in length from one to six inches daily. The Victoria bridge at Montreal, is exposed to great vicissitudes of heat and cold, and it is found that beams of iron, 200 feet in length, are subject to a movement of three inches in the climate of Canada. The Steeple of Bow Church, in London, has been nearly thrown down by the expansion of rods of iron built into the mason work. Bunker Hill Monument is sensibly deflected from the perpendicular by the influence of the sun's rays, so that its summit describes an irregular ellipse.

106. The Force of Contraction Equal to that of Expansion. The force of contraction is equal to that of expansion, and quite as irresistible. Its immense power was strikingly illustrated some years since in Paris. The two sides of a large building, the "*Conservatoire des Arts et Métiers*," having been pressed out by the spreading of the arched ceilings and the immense weights supported by the floors, M. Molard undertook to

---

105. Describe noted cases of expansion produced by heat. Southwark bridge. Menai bridge. Victoria bridge, &c.—106. To what is the force of contraction equal?

84   THE FORCE OF CONTRACTION.

remedy the evil by boring holes in the walls at the base of the vaulted ceilings, and opposite to each other, through which strong iron rods were introduced, so as to cross the interior of the building from one side to the other. On the projecting ends of the bars on the outside of the building were placed strong iron plates, which were screwed, by means of nuts, tightly against the walls, *Fig.* 31. The rods were then heated by means of

Fig. 31.

Restoration of a Building by the Force of Contraction.

rows of lamps placed under every alternate bar, and being lengthened by the expansion, the nuts and plates were pushed out to the distance of an inch or more beyond the walls. While in this condition, the nuts were screwed a second time tightly against the wall. The lamps were then extinguished, and the rods, contracting as they cooled, drew the walls together with a

---

Describe the restoration of the building at Paris.

force almost irresistible, and to a distance as great as that to which they had been lengthened by expansion. These bars being then left in their new position, the *alternate* bars, which had remained unheated, and by the contraction of the others had been also made to project beyond the walls, were again tightly screwed against the building. These were in turn expanded and lengthened by the application of the lighted lamps, and once more screwed up tightly against the walls. The lamps were then extinguished, and by the contraction of the second set of bars the walls were drawn still further towards each other. These were then left, in turn, to hold the building in its new position, and the first set of bars a second time brought into requisition. And thus the process was continued until the walls were drawn into their proper vertical position; and, the bars being left in their places, they have remained firm and upright ever since. In this manner a force was exerted which the power of man could scarcely have applied by any other means. The same process has since been applied to the restoration of other buildings which were threatening to fall.

107. Applications in the Arts. Advantage is taken of this force of contraction in many of the Arts. The iron tire of wheels is always made somewhat smaller than the wheel. It is then enlarged by being heated red hot and placed upon the wheel while still in that condition; cold water is then thrown on, contraction ensues, the parts of the wheel are bound together with great firmness, and the tire so tightly fastened in its place that nothing can pull it off. The tire of the wheels of locomotives is put on in the same way. The iron hoops of casks are applied when hot. The great vats of the London Breweries, some of which are large enough to float a seventy-four gun ship, and which contain liquid enough to produce a freshet if they should burst, are confined by enormous iron hoops, weighing from one to three tons, which are put on while hot. The plates of iron or copper of which steam boilers are made, are joined together by rivets which are inserted and hammered down while red hot, and the joints are thus made perfectly steam and water tight. This is il-

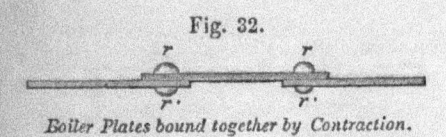

Fig. 32.

Boiler Plates bound together by Contraction.

---

107. State some of the applications of this force in the arts. Explain the manner in which boiler plates are made steam-tight.

lustrated in *Fig.* 32. The strong iron bands used in the manufacture of the Parrott and Armstrong guns are put on and welded down at a white heat. Moulds for casting objects in metal must be made larger than the intended size of the object, in order to allow for contraction in casting. The moulds for casting cannon balls must always be made larger than the calibre of the guns, on account of the contraction and shrinking of the ball in cooling; if of the same size as the bore, the balls will be too small for the gun.

108. Injurious Effects of Expansion. The expansion occasioned by heat often produces injurious effects, which need to be guarded against. A closely fitting iron gate, which can readily be opened on a cold day, is held tightly in its place on a warm day, in consequence of the expansion both of the gate and the fence. The pitch of a piano rises with the diminution of the temperature, in consequence of the contraction of the strings. Clocks go faster in winter than in summer. Nails driven into mortar get loose from expanding and contracting more than the mortar. Not unfrequently carriage wheels are set fast in consequence of the expansion of the axles, produced by the heat of friction; and the pistons of steam engines become bound too tightly to move, when exposed to excessive heat. Metallic roofs, whatever be the metal, from their exposure to the sun, expand and contract enormously, and must be constructed in such a manner as to admit of a certain amount of motion between the various parts. The shoes of horses, if nailed on when too hot, distort the foot by contracting too much as they cool. The iron rails of railroads will be thrown from position by the heat of the sun if the ends are permitted to touch. 3,000 feet of rails will expand nearly 3 feet between 0° and 110° Fahrenheit. From Liverpool to Manchester, the rails are 500 feet longer in summer than in winter.

109. Glass often Fractured by Expansion. The injurious effects produced by expansion are particularly apparent in the fracture of glass, especially if thick, upon the sudden application of heat. The outside surface is expanded by the action of the heat, and it not being permitted to penetrate the interior in consequence of the poor conducting power of the material, the external and internal portions are violently torn asunder.

Why must moulds for casting metallic objects be made larger than the desired size? 108. Mention some of the injurious effects of expansion. What is the effect upon clocks? Upon railroads, &c.?—109. Describe the effect of sudden expansion on glass.

When glass is to be exposed to great extremes of temperature, it should be made as thin as possible, and in all cases very gradually heated. When hollow, the heat should be applied upon the inside at the same moment as upon the outside, in order that the one surface may be expanded to the same degree with the other. This is the reason why a thick glass tumbler, if immersed in hot water, will escape cracking, if the hot water reaches the inside at the same moment with the outside. Thick glass mirrors are liable to be fractured by bright gas lights placed too near them, and plate electrical machines by careless heating with a lamp in order to dry them.

110. Fracture produced by Sudden Cooling. On the same principle, glass that has been expanded by the action of a powerful heat, is very liable to crack by the application of sudden cold. Hence, the glass roofs of green-houses, and skylights, expanded by the sun, and suddenly contracted externally by cold showers, while the internal portions are still considerably expanded, are very likely to be cracked. And for the same reason, any glass vessel, filled with hot liquid, is very sure to break if placed upon an iron nail in the floor, or upon any metallic support. Consequently, neither glass, nor any other brittle material of poor conducting power for heat, can bear to be either heated or cooled suddenly. For this reason glass ware, when first made, being nearly or quite red hot, if permitted to remain in cold air, is infallibly shivered, and is therefore always cooled gradually, or annealed, by being carried at once to a long hot oven, the temperature of which gradually diminishes from the front to the rear, through which it is slowly pushed, until quite cold. All these precautions would be unnecessary if glass were a good conductor of heat. Advantage is taken of this property in the manufacture of glass. The glass-blowers cut out patterns in glass by drawing a cold iron over it when in a heated state; and the Chemist shapes and alters his flasks and bottles by drawing over the cold glass a rod of heated iron. Watch crystals are obtained from globes of glass, very large and very thin, by applying to the surface heated metallic rings. On the same principle, rocks, which are generally poor conductors of heat, may be split by building a fire along the line of intended fracture, and then pouring on cold water. At Seringapatam, in India, rocks eight feet in thickness and eighty feet in length have been detached by this simple means.

---

110. Describe the effect produced on glass and rocks by sudden contraction.

88 RATE OF CLOCKS ALTERED.

111. Metallic Instruments injured by Expansion. The metals being expanded much more for a given increase of heat than other solids, and very considerably altered in their dimensions by slight variations in temperature, delicate metallic instruments are often seriously deranged by this means. All measures of length are considerably lengthened and shortened by the heat of the atmosphere.

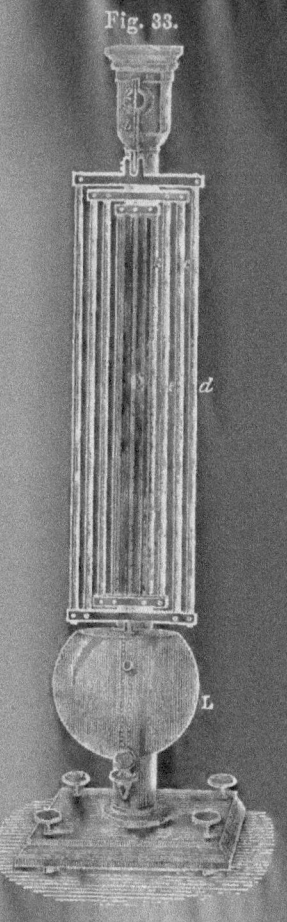

The rate of going of clocks is much affected by changes of temperature. If the pendulum be lengthened, the clock goes slower; if it be shortened, the clock goes faster. If the bob of the pendulum be lowered $\frac{1}{100}$ part of an inch, the clock will lose ten seconds in twenty-four hours. Now it has been found that an increase of temperature to the amount of 30° F., will lengthen a seconds pendulum $\frac{1}{128}$ part of an inch, and cause it to lose eight seconds in twenty-four hours. Of course the clock would gain eight seconds daily, if the temperature should sink 30° F. This continual variation in the movement of the clock destroys its value as an accurate measurer of time. The difficulty has been remedied by several contrivances.

Fig. 33.

Gridiron Pendulum.

112. Compensation Pendulums. In the gridiron pendulum of Harrison, represented in *Fig.* 33, the bob is suspended by a rod i, from the lowest of the three upper horizontal cross-bars. This rod passes freely through holes in the two lower cross-bars. The cross-bar of suspension is supported by a pair of vertical rods of brass, a, which rest upon the upper of the lower cross-bars.

---

111. What effect is produced upon the rate of time pieces, and upon measures of length?—112. Describe the gridiron pendulum of Harrison.

This cross-bar depends by means of iron rods, e, from the second of the upper cross-bars, which in turn is supported by vertical brass rods, c, and these again by iron rods, d, from the upper cross-bar, which is directly attached to the point of suspension, b. When the temperature increases, the iron rods d and e expand downwards, while at the same time the brass rods, c and a, expand upwards. These expansions in contrary directions, are so adjusted as to counteract each other, and the bob of the pendulum is thus maintained at the same distance from the point of suspension. The process is reversed when the temperature sinks. This pendulum gained the reward of £20,000 offered by the British Government for a pendulum that did not lose more than a fraction of a second in a year, and would enable the longitude to be determined within thirty miles.

113. The second mode of obviating the same difficulty is by using a hollow cylinder of glass for the bob of the pendulum, and filling it with quicksilver. As the rod of the pendulum expands downwards, the quicksilver expands upwards, so that the centre of gravity of the bob is maintained at the same distance from the point of suspension. A third mode consists in using compound bars of metal to adjust the point of suspension. If two metals, as brass and iron, one of which expands much more than the other, be firmly united throughout their whole length, and then heated, the brass expanding more than the iron, will bend the bar into a curve. If it be cooled instead of heated, the brass contracting more than the iron, will bend the compound bar in the opposite direction. This is represented in *Fig.* 34; the lower bar represents the compound bar (the brass being uppermost) in the state in which it is at the mean average temperature; the second line represents the same bar, when heated above this point; the upper line represents it when cooled below it.

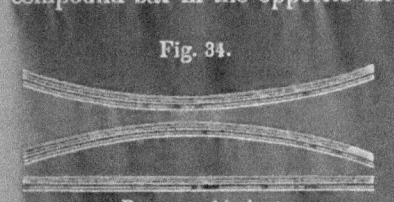

Fig. 34.
Bars curved by heat.

The application to the pendulum is represented in *Fig.* 35. The point of oscillation is formed by two such compound bars, fastened firmly at one end, and at the other extremity left free, and nearly touching each other, only leaving room for the passage of the delicate spring, by which the pendulum is sus-

---

113. Describe the compound bar. The compensation pendulum.

90 COMPENSATION BALANCE.

pended. At the mean temperature, the compound bars are perfectly straight, as represented in the second figure. When the temperature rises, the pendulum rod is lengthened, and the ball lowered; but at the same time the compound bar is bent

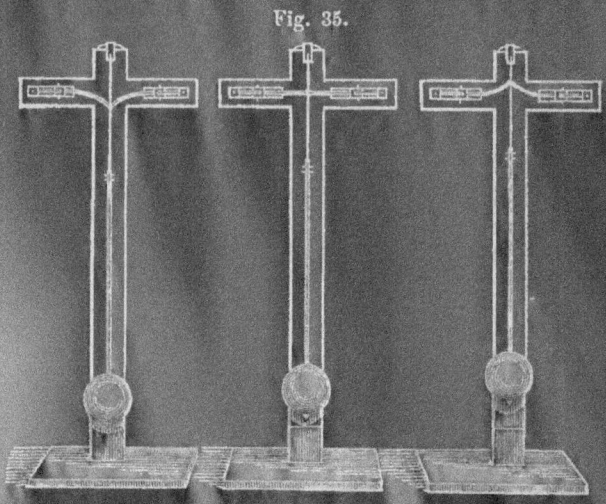

Fig. 35.

Compensation Pendulum.

downwards, and the point of suspension lowered to the same amount, so that the distance between the centre of the ball and the point of oscillation, is the same as before, and the rate of going is not altered. This is represented in the figure to the left. When the temperature falls, the rod is shortened, the ball rises, but the compound bars being then bent upwards, as is seen in the figure to the right, in consequence of the greater contraction of the brass, the distance between the point of oscillation and the ball is still the same, and the rate of movement remains unaltered.

114. Compensation Balance. The compensation balance wheels of watches are constructed on the same principle. In warm weather the diameter of the ordinary balance is lengthened, and its circumference increased; in cold weather it is shortened, and its circumference diminished. In the compensation balance, *Fig.* 36, the rim of the wheel is divided into four parts. These parts are made of compound bars of different metals, the most expansible being outermost, and hav-

---

114. Describe the compensation balance.

EXPANSION OF LIQUIDS. 91

Fig. 36.

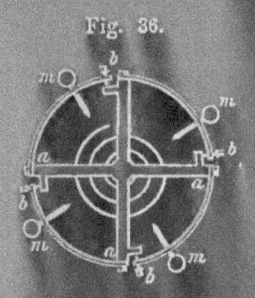

Compensation Balance.

ing one end fastened to an arm of the wheel. The other end is loose, and has a small screw attached near its free extremity. When the temperature rises the outer metal expanding more than the inner, curves the end of each quadrant more towards the centre and so counteracts the general expansion of the wheel. The reverse takes place when the temperature sinks, and in this manner an equal motion is secured at all times. This is an application of immense advantage in the construction of chronometers, for determining the longitude at sea. There are many other applications of the same principle, of nearly equal value to Science and the Arts.

115. The Expansion of Liquids. Liquids expand more for a given increase of heat than Solids. The fact of expansion may be shown by dipping a common thermometer into warm water, or by heating a larger tube and ball, partially filled with water, over a lamp: *Fig.* 37. If the liquid be colored alcohol,

Fig. 37.

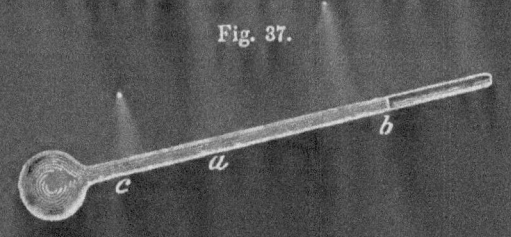

Expansion of Liquids.

its rise in the tube is more rapid and more apparent to the eye than if filled with water. It will speedily rise from c to a, from a to b. This expansion takes place with so much force that all closed vessels filled with liquids burst on the application of heat.

116. Expansion of different Liquids unequal. The unequal expansion of different liquids for an equal increase of temperature, may be shown by filling two bulbs of the same size, to the same height, with different liquids, and dipping them into the same vessel of hot water. If the fluids be alcohol and water, it will be found that the alcohol will rise in the tube twice as high

---

115. How does the expansion of liquids compare with that of solids? How can the expansion of liquids be proved?—116. How can the unequal expansion of liquids be shown?

EXPANSION OF GASES.

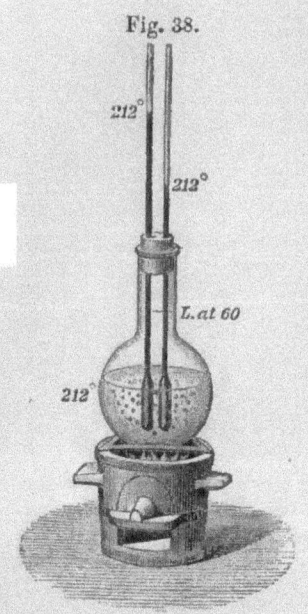

Fig. 38.

Unequal Expansion of Liquids.

as the water. If they be olive oil and water, standing at the same level at 60°, we shall find that when the water in which they are immersed boils, and they have been raised to 212°, the one has expanded much more than the other; *Fig.* 38. Alcohol, on being heated from 32° to 212°, increases in bulk $\frac{1}{4}$; olive oil $\frac{1}{10}$; water $\frac{1}{23}$. Twenty gallons of alcohol measured in January, will become twenty-one in July.

117. The Expansion of the Liquids produced by the Condensation of Gases. By compression, combined with great reduction of temperature, several of the aeriform, or gaseous forms of matter, may be condensed into liquids. These liquids differ from all common liquids in their enormous expansion on the application of heat. In general, the air, and other gases, expand more from equal increments of heat than any other substances; but these peculiar liquids exceed them in this respect, and are the most expansible substances known. Thus liquid carbonic acid, in being heated from 32° to 86° F., expands from 20 volumes to 29, which is more than five times as much as air. Liquid sulphurous acid, and cyanogen, expand to nearly the same degree.

118. The Expansion of Gases. Aeriform fluids are greatly expanded by heat, and much more than either solids or liquids for the same increase of temperature. With equal increments of heat, they all expand equally. If, therefore, the ratio of expansion for one gas, as oxygen, be known, then the ratio for common air and for all the other gases will be known also. The rate of expansion for all gases has been found to be about $\frac{1}{480}$ of the volume which the gas possessed at 32°, for every degree of Fahrenheit's thermometer. This calculation is based upon the experiments of Gay Lussac, who found that 1000 cubic inches of atmospheric air, raised from the freezing point,

---

117. What peculiarity is possessed by the liquids formed by the condensed gases?—118. How can the expansion of gases be shown? What is the rate of expansion of all gases for one degree F.?

EXPANSION OF AIR. 93

32° F., to the boiling point, 212°, were expanded so as to make 1375 cubic inches. It follows, therefore, that one cubic inch of atmospheric air at 32°, will, if raised to 212°, or heated by 180°, be expanded to 1.375 cubic inches, and for every additional 180° of temperature it will receive a like increase of volume. The ratio of expansion being $\frac{1}{480}$ for 1°, if any volume of air at 32° be raised to the temperature of $32°+490°=522°$, it will expand to twice its volume; and if it be raised to a temperature of $32°+(2°\times 490°,)=1012°$, it will be expanded to three times its volume, and so on. Later experiments have slightly altered this ratio, and shows that the different gases do not all expand to exactly the same degree for equal increments of heat; the inequality may, however, be disregarded for all practical purposes. In general, the gases and vapors all dilate equally and to the same degree as atmospheric air.

119. Expansion of Air. The fact of the expansion of air may readily be shown by filling an India Rubber bag with air, closing it tightly, and holding it near the fire. As the air expands the bag will become more and more tense, and finally burst with a loud report. A more elegant experiment is, to take a glass tube, terminated by a bulb, and put in so much water as to about half fill the tube, and then, having immersed it in a vessel of water, as represented in *Fig.* 39, apply the heat of a lamp to the bulb. As the heat rarefies the air in the bulb, the water will be forced down the tube, but will slowly rise again to its former level by the pressure of the atmosphere on the fluid, when the lamp is removed, and the air in the ball allowed to contract.

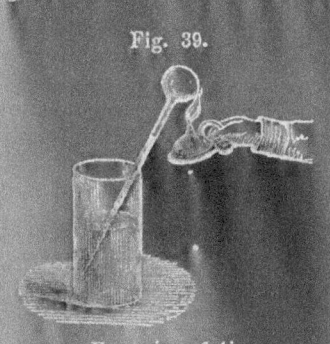

Fig. 39.

Expansion of Air.

120. The expansion of Air of great practical utility.—The Draught of Chimneys. The great increase in the bulk of air, produced by heat, diminishes its density and renders it specifically lighter, i. e., lighter than an equal bulk of air at a lower temperature. The consequence is that the heated air being thus made less dense tends to rise, just as a cork does in water, or a

---

119 How may the expansion of air be shown?—120. Why is the expansion of air of great practical importance?

balloon in the air; this creates a rush of air from every side to supply its place, and in this manner powerful currents are produced, and a general circulation kept up in the atmosphere, which is of the greatest practical utility, and one of the most beneficent arrangements in Nature. It is by the inequality in the weight of the column of air C D, within the chimney, compared with the weight of a column of cold air A B, on the outside, of equal base and height, that the rush of cold air into the chimney from below, in order to restore the equilibrium, is produced, which creates the draught; *Fig. 40*. This inequality is produced by the diminution in the density of heated air consequent upon its increase in bulk; see *Fig. 12*. It is upon this expansion produced by heat, therefore, that the draught of chimneys depends; a continued stream of fresh air is supplied to the fire, and the injurious products of combustion are removed, and without it, all processes of illumination and combustion, such as fires, lamps, and candles, would cease, or be maintained only by a costly and complicated machinery. Every six tons of coal consumed, requires at least seventy-two tons of air to produce perfect combustion, i. e., twelve times as much air by weight is required, as coal. Now the whole of this quantity, if it were nor for this extremely curious provision of Nature, would have to be supplied artificially; and it can readily be seen what a check this would place upon many of the arts essential to the comfort of man. Upon the same diminution in density depend all processes of ventilation, and all the atmospheric currents, such as the Trade winds, by which the commerce of the earth is wafted on its way, and the land and sea breezes, by which the heat of tropical climates is mitigated. At the equator, the hot air, rising in a steady stream, flows off, after it has reached a certain height in

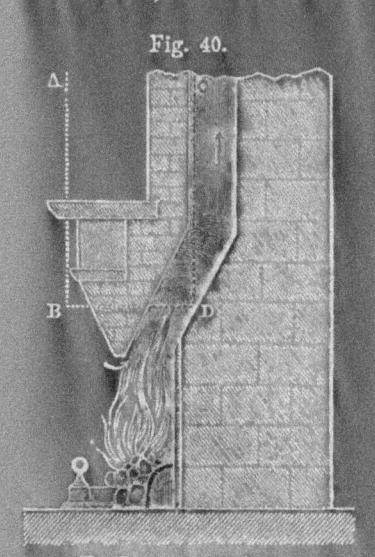

Fig. 40.

The Draught of Chimneys.

Explain the currents which it produces in the atmosphere. What has this to do with ventilation? The burning of lamps, and fires? Show how the draught of chimneys is produced. What saving does this effect in fuel?

WATER EXPANDS FROM COLD. 95

the atmosphere, both to the north and to the south, and this necessitates a steady current near the surface of the earth, from the north and the south, towards the equator. In our own climate, in summer, the hot air over the earth rising in the day time, produces a flow of cold air from the sea, and at night the process being reversed, and the warm air over the sea rising, produces a current of cold air from the land. In this way the extremes of climate are moderated, and the heat of the globe more equally distributed, the purity of the atmosphere is preserved, and many processes absolutely essential to the welfare and civilization of man proceed with undeviating regularity.

Fig. 41.

121. Exception to the general law of Expansion by Heat.—Water at certain temperatures contracts from Heat, and expands from Cold. It is a striking fact, and a most conclusive proof of design in the constitution of Nature, that water, at certain temperatures, does not obey the usual law of expansion from heat, and contraction from cold. Between 32° and 40°, if water be heated, it contracts; if it be cooled, it expands. If, therefore, water, at the temperature of 60°, be cooled, it will contract until it reaches 40°; and then, if it be cooled to a lower degree than this, it will begin to expand. At 40°, therefore, water is said to possess its maximum density, because if it be heated or cooled above or below this point, it becomes less dense. To show this, fill a flask with water at a temperature of 60°, and adapt to it a cork, through which passes a glass tube of small bore, *Fig.* 41, and a thermometer. Insert the cork and tube, and fill the tube with water to the height

Expansion of Water in cooling from 32° to 40°.

What is the connection between the expansion of the air and land and sea breezes? What effect has this on climate and the purity of the air?—121. Describe the exception presented by water to the general law of expansion by heat. At what temperature does water begin to expand by cold? How can this be proved? Describe Fig 41.

of two or three inches above the flask. Then immerse the flask in a freezing mixture of salt and ice at 0°. The water will immediately begin to contract and sink in the tube. But presently this will cease, and it will begin to rise again, showing expansion. The volume of the water has, therefore, first been diminished by the reduction of temperature, and then, secondly, increased. The thermometer shows that this increase begins to take place at 40°, and by the time its temperature has sunk to 32°, the water will have risen in the tube a considerable distance above its original position, and acquired the same bulk as it would have done if heated to 48°, so that it expands just as much in cooling 8° below 40°, as it does in being heated 8° above that point. It has been ascertained by experiment that the expansion of water continues even below 32°, for if kept perfectly quiet and undisturbed, water may be cooled as low as 12° without freezing, and it was expanded as much in some of the experiments by cooling, as it would have been, if heated to 75°.

122. Important results of this exception to a general Law of Nature. The most important effects result from this remarkable peculiarity of water. If water became steadily heavier as it cooled, and its density continued to increase until it froze, as is the case with mercury, ice would be heavier than water, and as soon as formed, would subside to the bottom in successive portions, until the whole of the water, however deep, had become solid. It is quite evident, that under these circumstances, in the autumn, and early winter, the water of lakes and rivers gradually imparting its heat to the atmosphere, would soon reach a uniform temperature of 32° throughout the whole mass, be converted into one solid body of ice, and occupy a very long time in resuming the liquid form in the spring. According to the present arrangement the instant that any portion becomes colder than 40°, in consequence of the diminution of its specific gravity by expansion, it rises to the top and collects upon the surface; and as water parts with its heat very slowly, for reasons hereafter to be explained, the upper portions may sink as low as 32°, while the great mass below is at the temperature of 40°. Consequently, during the whole of a long winter, while the upper portions of water are at 32°, or actually frozen, the lower rarely sink below 40°, and the greater part escapes solidification altogether. At the instant of freezing, a great additional expansion takes place, in consequence of which the specific gravity

---

122. What important consequences result from this peculiar constitution of water?

PROVED BY EXPERIMENT. 97

of ice becomes considerably less than that of the cold water at 32°, from which it is formed, and it floats upon the surface; thus the ice is kept where it can be most readily reached by the sun's rays, and the process of melting in the spring be easily accomplished. In general, therefore, however cold the weather, and however thick the ice which is formed, the great body of water never sinks below the temperature of 40°, too high to freeze, and thus the greater part of the water of seas and rivers even in the Arctic zone escapes solidification.

123. This peculiar constitution of Water proved by experiment. This peculiar constitution of water can be readily shown by a very simple experiment, *Fig.* 42. Let the tall glass

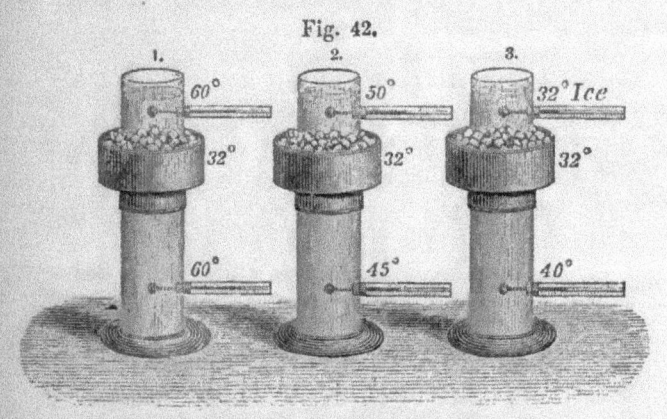

Fig. 42.

Warm Water Collecting at Bottom of Lakes in Winter.

vessel, 1, be pierced so as to admit of the insertion of two thermometers, one near the top, the other near the bottom. Just beneath the upper thermometer a brass cup is fitted around the glass vessel, and filled with broken ice at the temperature of 32°. Water at 60° is then poured into the glass jar, and both thermometers of course stand at the same point, viz., 60°. The effect of the melting ice is, to cool the water in the upper part of the vessel, and its density being thereby increased, it sinks to the bottom, while the warm water collects at the top. At the expiration of a few moments the apparatus will be in the condition indicated in vessel 2; the lower thermometer will have sunk to 45°, the upper one will be at 50° or 55°. This process will go on until the lower thermometer has sunk to 40° F. The

---

123 How can the collection of warm water at the bottom of lakes be proved? Describe the experiment with the three jars.

98   WATER EXPANDS IN FREEZING.

upper thermometer will then begin to sink, and soon stand also at 40°. Instead of remaining stationary, however, at this point, it will descend until it reaches 32°, and at the end of half an hour the apparatus will be in the condition indicated in vessel 3, i. e., the warmer water of 40° will be at the bottom, the colder water of 32° will be at the top. This represents the condition of a lake in winter, cooled by the contact of the cold atmosphere on its upper surface, and it is explained on the principle mentioned above.

124. Water expands in freezing. At the moment of congelation water also undergoes a still farther expansion; and this takes place with irresistible power, so that the vessels in which it is confined, if they be full, are infallibly broken. This is the cause of the bursting of water pipes at the approach of winter. This expansion is supposed to be due to the crystallization of the water as it freezes, and to the fact that the crystals which are formed do not lie side by side, closely packed together, but cross each other at angles of 60° and 120°, thus leaving large interstices. The water, therefore, necessarily occupies more space than it did before. The expansion of water in cooling and freezing is well shown in *Fig. 43*. A glass flask is filled with water, and a cork inserted, through which passes a tube, open at both ends. The water rises into this tube some distance, and this point is marked upon the scale. A thermometer is also passed through the cork for the purpose of indicating the temperature of the water. The whole apparatus is then immersed in a jar containing a mixture of ice and salt, at temperature of 0°. The first effect is the rising of the water in the tube, produced by the contraction of the glass flask in consequence of the cold of the mixture. This, however, is only momentary. The next effect is the rapid falling of the water in the tube, which goes on until the thermometer sinks to 40°. It then begins to rise steadily, and continues to do so until congelation takes place, when there is a sudden and very great expansion, and the flask is generally

Fig. 43.

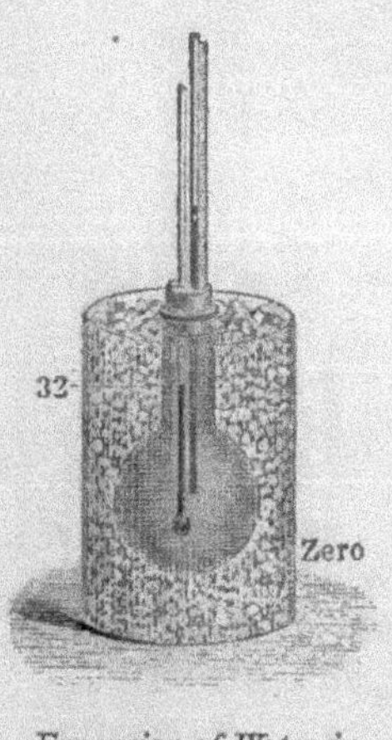

Expansion of Water in Freezing.

---

124. What effect has freezing upon the bulk of water? Describe Fig. 43. Show the great force with which this expansion takes place.

broken. The force with which this expansion takes place is very great, and cannon filled with water and plugged at the muzzle, may readily be burst. In 1784-5 Major Williams, at Quebec, made some experiments upon this subject, in one of which an iron plug three pounds in weight, was projected from a bomb-shell to the distance of 415 feet, and shells one and a half, and two inches in thickness were burst, by the freezing of the water. The Florentine Academicians burst a hollow brass globe, having a cavity of only an inch, by freezing the water with which it was filled; and it has been estimated that the expansive power in this case was equal to 27,720 pounds.

125. Illustrations.—Mountains broken down. It is this expansion of water in congealing that makes the freezing of vegetables and fruits, in the early winter, destructive to their organization. The farmer makes use of this force to break up the land, by heaping it in ridges in the autumn, and exposing, therefore, a large surface to the action of the frost. The water, in freezing, separates the particles of the soil, and when melting takes place in the spring, the whole settles down into a fine and comparatively dry powder, very favorable to early vegetation. Nature makes use of this force upon a large scale, to break down and grind up into fragments the cliffs and mountains, and thus to modify very materially the face of the earth. The water running into cracks and fissures in the rocks, freezes in the winter, and by its expansion breaks off large masses, which for the time are held in their places by the strong cohesive power of the ice; but on the approach of spring this melts, and the mass is precipitated into the valley below. In the same manner, vast masses of earth are loosened from the smooth surfaces of mountains, and slide down, in the spring, into the valleys. Hardly any other agency in nature has so much effect as this in altering the face of the earth. This force also operates powerfully in overthrowing and deranging the works of man. Railroads are thrown out of level by the expansion of the frozen ground beneath them; fences are raised out of line; buildings are elevated in the air; the walls of cellars are driven inwards. These effects are especially exhibited in stiff clay soils, on account of the adhesiveness of the clay, and the great amount of water which it contains. The posts of fences raised from their beds by the expansion of the frost, do not return to it when this frost melts in the spring, and the fence is perma-

---

125. Give illustrations of the operation of this force in Nature.

nently deranged. A single stone projecting into the clay on the outside of the cellar of a building, if within reach of the frost, will give to the heaving earth a lever by which the heaviest building may be raised from its foundation. For the same reason banks of clay thrown up against the underpinning of houses are very apt to push them in and undermine the building.

126. Other substances beside water expand as they solidify. Water is not the only liquid which expands as it solidifies. The same effect has been observed in a few others, which assume a highly crystalline structure on becoming solid. Melted antimony, bismuth, iron and zinc, are examples of it. Mercury is a remarkable instance of the reverse, for when it freezes it suffers a very great contraction. It is on account of this property that fine castings can be made from iron. The metal, as it cools and solidifies, expands so as to be forced into the most delicate lines of the mould. Antimony possesses this property in a high degree, and for this reason is mixed with tin and lead to form type metal and give the mixture the property of expanding into the moulds in which the types are cast. It is because gold and silver do not possess this property, but on the contrary shrink greatly as they cool in moulds, that coins can not be made by casting, but require to be stamped.

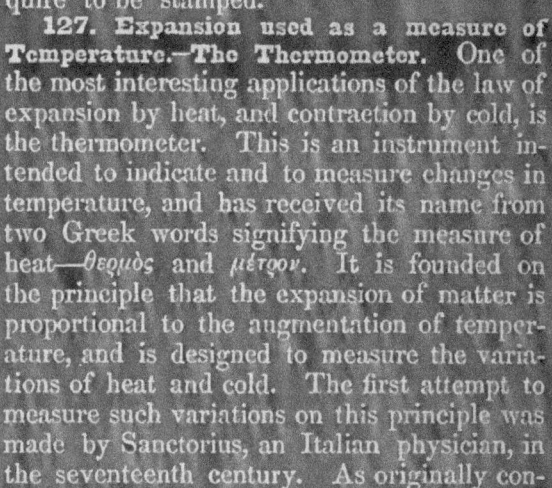

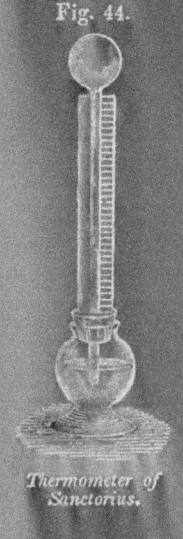

Fig. 44.

Thermometer of Sanctorius.

127. Expansion used as a measure of Temperature.—The Thermometer. One of the most interesting applications of the law of expansion by heat, and contraction by cold, is the thermometer. This is an instrument intended to indicate and to measure changes in temperature, and has received its name from two Greek words signifying the measure of heat—θερμὸς and μέτρον. It is founded on the principle that the expansion of matter is proportional to the augmentation of temperature, and is designed to measure the variations of heat and cold. The first attempt to measure such variations on this principle was made by Sanctorius, an Italian physician, in the seventeenth century. As originally con-

---

126. What other substances besides water expand as they solidify? What practical applications are made of this in the casting of metals?—127. What is the thermometer? What is the principle on which it depends? Who invented the instrument? Describe the first form of it.

THE AIR THERMOMETER. 101

structed it was a rude instrument, and it has reached its present state of perfection only by degrees, and after successive improvements by some of the most distinguished philosophers. These labors have been directed towards the improvement of its form, the selection of a good thermometric fluid, and the arrangement of the scales, by which the rise and fall of this fluid are indicated. The thermometer of Sanctorius is represented in *Fig.* 44. He employed a glass tube blown into a ball at one extremity, and open at the other. After expelling a small part of the air by heating the ball, the open end was plunged into a vessel of colored liquid, and as the air in the ball cooled, this colored liquid ascended the tube. Any variation of temperature, by expanding or contracting the air in the ball, would then cause the liquid in the tube to rise or fall, thus forming an imperfect air thermometer.

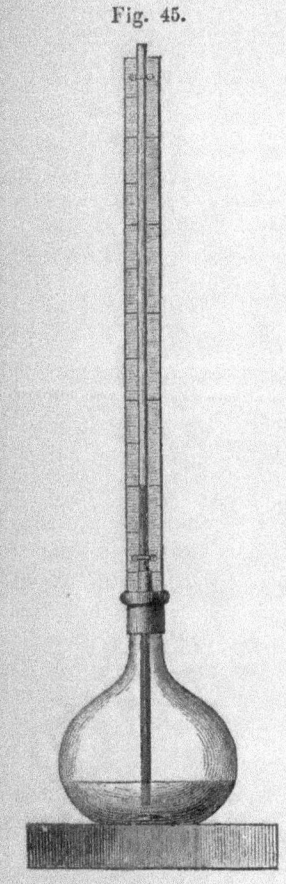

Fig. 45.

Air Thermometer.

128. Air Thermometer. A better construction for an air thermometer is represented in *Fig.* 45. It consists of a glass flask, with a bottom flattened so as to stand firmly upright, containing a small quantity of alcohol, tinged red by cochineal, and stopped closely by a cork, or by a stopper of brass, screwed tightly to a ring of the same metal cemented to the neck of the flask. Through this stopper is passed a tube of one-eighth inch bore, and a yard in length, open at both ends. This tube is cemented tightly into the stopper, and dips into the liquid. A scale of wood or metal, divided into equal parts, is attached to the tube by fine wire. There is, therefore, a quantity of air confined within the flask which can not escape, and when this expands by the ap-

---

128. Describe a second form of the air thermometer. What are the defects of such thermometers?

102   THE DIFFERENTIAL THERMOMETER.

plication of heat, the colored alcohol is forced up the tube. Thus the height of the fluid will indicate the expansion of the air, and consequently, the degree of heat to which the instrument is exposed. There are, however, two objections to the employment of air for this purpose. Its expansions and contractions are so great, even from small changes of temperature, that a tube several feet in length would be required to measure them; and as the tube is necessarily open to the air, the continual variation in the pressure of the atmosphere elevates, and depresses the colored liquid without any reference to the variations in temperature; and thus the instrument is converted into a rude barometer, and made a measure of the pressure of the atmosphere, as well as of temperature. It is, however, an exceedingly useful instrument in the laboratory for experiments on heat, to detect on the spot and make plainly manifest to the eye, sudden variations in temperature and small degrees of heat.

129. The Differential Thermometer. For the above reasons the air thermometer, for common purposes, is both inconvenient and inaccurate, and therefore has long since been laid aside. There is, however, a modification of this instrument, invented by Mr. Leslie, and called the *differential* thermometer, which, for certain purposes, is a very elegant and useful instrument. A drawing of this instrument is represented in *Fig.* 46, and it is designed, as its name imports, to show the difference of temperature between two places at short distances from each other. It consists of a glass tube terminated at each end by a bulb, and bent as shown in the figure. The tube is partly filled with some colored fluid, as sulphuric acid tinged with carmine, or alcohol colored by cochineal, the bulbs and other parts of the tube being filled with air. It is obvious, from the construction of this instrument, that it can not indicate the temperature of the atmosphere, since an equal expansion of the air in both bulbs would press equally on the fluid in both arms of the tube, and consequently it would rise in neither. But if one bulb be exposed to a higher temperature than the other, then, the expansion of air in this will be greater than in the other, and

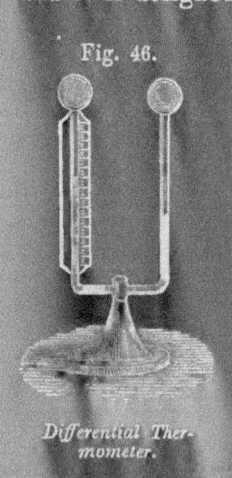

Fig. 46.

Differential Thermometer.

---

129. Describe Leslie's differential thermometer. What is its most important use?

consequently the fluid will move toward the bulb in which the air is least expanded. The use of this thermometer consists in showing the difference of temperature to which the bulbs are exposed, as in the experiments on the radiation of heat, already described. The scale affixed to one of the arms is divided into 100 degrees, and indicates the amount of expansion. The arms are six inches long, and the bulbs an inch, or a little more, in diameter. It is of special advantage in detecting the amount of heat which proceeds from any given source, such as that which is transmitted through rock salt, in experiments on diathermancy, without danger of part of the effect being due to some extraneous source, as for instance the heat of a neighboring fire or lamp. This extraneous heat, though it would affect a common thermometer, exerts no influence upon the differential thermometer, so that whatever effect is produced upon it, is due exclusively to the particular source of heat which is employed.

130. The Mercurial Thermometer. Aeriform fluids being inapplicable to the construction of thermometers for the purpose of measuring the varying temperature of places and things, on account of their great expansibility, it is necessary to make use of solids or liquids. Solid bodies, however, are equally unfitted for this purpose, from an opposite property, their slight expansibility, it being so small as not to be appreciable without the adaptation of complicated machinery. A perfect substance for this purpose would be a fluid, which would expand uniformly with equal increments of heat, and neither freeze nor boil at any temperature to which it might be exposed. Mercury approaches nearer to these conditions than any other substance, and therefore, this is the fluid now almost universally employed. Its boiling point is 662°, and its freezing point −40°, which enables it to measure a very wide range of temperature; and it possesses also this singular advantage, that though it expands more for an equal increment of heat at a high than a low temperature, this additional expansion is corrected by the increased capacity of the glass bulb and tube which contain it, so that the indications of the instrument are very nearly correct for all temperatures between freezing and boiling water; for higher temperatures the compensation is not so exact. The total expansion of mercury for three progressive intervals of 180° F. is, between 32° and 212°, 1 part in 55.08; between

---

130. Describe the mercurial thermometer. Why is mercury a good thermometric fluid?

212° and 392°, 1 in 54.61; between 392° and 572°, 1 in 54.01. The temperature of 572° F., as measured by an air-thermometer, if measured by the expansion of mercury, in an ordinary thermometer, would be indicated as 586°, showing that the expansion of the mercury increases as the temperature rises.

131. Construction of the Thermometer. The blowing of an accurate thermometer-tube and bulb requires much experience, is performed only by skillful artists, and is the most difficult part of the construction of the instrument. The delicacy of a thermometer depends upon the fineness of the bore of the tube, and the large size of the bulb. The bore must also be of equal calibre throughout; this is determined by introducing a small portion of mercury, and then ascertaining by means of a pair of dividers if it occupies the same space in all portions of the tube. The bore being extremely fine, the mercury can only be introduced by heating the bulb, expelling a portion of the air within it, and then inverting the open end of the tube into a vessel of the liquid metal. As the air within contracts by cooling, the pressure of the external atmosphere forces the mercury to enter the tube in order to supply its place. The bulb, and about one-third of the tube having thus been filled, a spirit lamp is applied to the bulb, until the mercury has been made to boil, and driven to the extreme upper end of the tube. By this process the air and moisture mixed with the mercury are completely expelled. At this instant, before the lamp is withdrawn, and while the mercury still completely fills the stem, the flame of the blow-pipe is darted across the end of the tube, and it is immediately melted up, or hermetically sealed. When the lamp is removed the mercury contracts to its former dimensions, leaving a vacuum between itself and the extremity of the tube. Consequently there is no aeriform fluid to be compressed by the mercury as it expands, and by its reaction keep the level of the liquid below the point it should properly reach. For this reason, in a properly constructed thermometer, if the tube be inverted, the mercury will freely run to the extremity of the instrument, there being no air within the tube to impede its motion.

Having sealed the end of the tube, the next step in the construction of the thermometer is its graduation. This is done by marking two fixed and invariable points on the stem,

---

131. Describe the construction of the thermometer. How is the air expelled? What are the fixed points of the scale?

FAHRENHEIT'S SCALE. 105

which indicate the same temperatures in every thermometer, and then making a scale of equal divisions between these two points. These are the freezing and boiling points of water which, under the same circumstances, always indicate constant temperatures. The freezing point is found by immersing the bulb of the thermometer in melting snow or ice, for it has been ascertained that the temperature of water flowing from melting snow or ice is everywhere the same, whatever may be the heat of the atmosphere where the experiment is made. The boiling point is slightly affected by a variation in the pressure of the atmosphere; but the thermometer will be sufficiently accurate for all ordinary purposes, when this point is ascertained by immersing the bulb in pure boiling water, open to the air, and at the level of the sea, during pleasant weather. The freezing and boiling points are marked, with a diamond or file, on the tube, and a scale is attached, upon which the degrees are clearly marked. The interval between these points is differently divided in different countries. In England and the United States, the division generally adopted is that of Fahrenheit.

132. Fahrenheit's Scale. Fahrenheit was a philosophical instrument maker of Amsterdam, who constructed thermometers in so admirable a manner that they soon spread all over Europe. On his scale the freezing point of water was marked at 32°, and the boiling point at 212°. The interval between these two points was then accurately divided into 180 equal parts, called degrees, which are continued below 32° to 0°, and above 212° as high as 662°, or the boiling point of mercury, if need require. The scale is often carried much lower than 0°, and in this case the degrees always have the prefix — *minus*, to indicate this fact. Thus — 40° indicates a temperature 40° below 0°. The scale, therefore, really commences at 32° below the freezing point of water, this being the point at which the 0° is placed; the freezing point of water is placed at 32°, and the boiling point of water at 212°, and when a higher or lower temperature is to be measured, the scale of equal parts, as has been stated, is continued beyond these points. It has been thought that Fahrenheit took the zero, or commencement of his scale from the degree of cold produced by mixing snow and common salt, that being the greatest degree of cold known in his time. The zero was, however, in reality, taken from the greatest cold observed in Iceland, and the principle which dictated

132. Describe Fahrenheit's scale.

106   OTHER SCALES.

the peculiar division of the scale was the following. When the instrument stood at the greatest cold of Iceland, or at 0°, it was computed to contain 11,124 equal parts of mercury, which, when plunged in melting snow, or freezing water, expanded to 11,156 parts; hence the intermediate space was divided into 32 equal portions, and 32° was taken as the freezing point of water. When the thermometer was plunged into boiling water the mercury was expanded to 11,336 parts, and therefore 212° was marked as boiling point. Though the principle on which this scale is founded is not reliable, yet it possesses in practice decided advantages over every other on account of its extensive range and the lowness of its 0°, which ordinarily dispenses with the necessity for using negative degrees, and also on account of the smallness of its degrees which makes the use of fractions unnecessary.

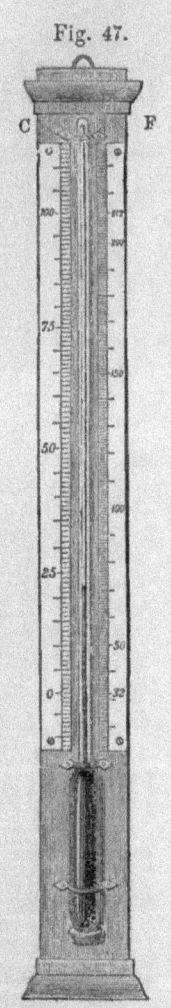

Fig. 47.

Mercurial Thermometer.

133. Other Thermometric Scales. Besides the scale of Fahrenheit, in which the distance between the freezing and boiling points is divided into 180 equal parts, there are in use in France and on the Continent in general, two other scales, the Centigrade and Reaumur's. In the former, the distance between the freezing and boiling points is divided into 100 equal parts, the 0° being placed at the former, and 100° at the latter. In Reaumur's scale, 0° is placed opposite to the freezing point, and 80° opposite to the boiling point. Consequently, 212° F. correspond to 100° C. and to 80° R., and 32° F. correspond to 0° C. and 0° R. In order to compare these scales together it is necessary to resort to calculation. The first thing to be done is to establish the ratio of the scales; and as the number of degrees between the freezing and boiling points of water in the three scales are 180, 100, and 80, the scales consequently bear these proportions to each other, which by reduction to their lowest terms become 9, 5, and 4. Consequently the Centigrade and Reaumur degrees are larger

---

133. Describe the Centigrade scale. That of Reaumur Reduce 140° Fahrenheit to Centigrade. Reduce 140° F. to Reaumur.

than those of Fahrenheit, 5° of C. and 4° of R. being equal to 9° of F. If, then, it be required to reduce 140° F. to the Centigrade scale, we first subtract 32° from 140°, because the two scales do not start at the same point, but the Centigrade begins at a temperature 32° higher than Fahrenheit; this gives us 108°. Then, as the scale F. is to the scale C. as 180 is to 100, we establish this proportion: 180 : 100 :: 108 : x, or 9 : 5 :: 108 : x; reducing, we have $\frac{108 \times 5}{9} = x$, or $\frac{540}{9} = x$; $x = 60°$ of the Centigrade scale. Consequently, 140° Fahrenheit are equal to 60° of the Centigrade scale. To reduce 140° F. to Reaumur, we first subtract 32° as before, and then establish the proportion 180 : 80 :: 108 : x, or 9 : 4 :: 108 : x; reducing, we have $\frac{108 \times 4}{9} = x$, or $\frac{432}{9} = x$; $x = 48°$ Reaumur. Consequently, 140° Fahrenheit are equal to 48° of the scale of Reaumur. In reducing Centigrade and Reaumur to Fahrenheit, we reverse the process and add 32° to the answer, instead of subtracting it, for the reason already explained. Thus, to reduce 60° Centigrade to Fahrenheit, we have 100 : 180 :: 60 : x, or 5 : 9 :: 60 : x; reducing, we have $\frac{60 \times 9}{5} = x$, or $\frac{540}{5} = x$; $x = 108°$ F.; adding 32° we obtain 60° C. = 140° F. To reduce 48° Reaumur to Fahrenheit, we have 80 : 180 :: 48 : x, or 4 : 9 :: 48 : x; reducing, we have $\frac{48 \times 9}{4} = x$, or $\frac{432}{4} = x$; $x = 108°$ F.; adding 32° we obtain 48° R. = 140° F. The following formulae, express the steps of these calculations very clearly:

Fahrenheit to Centigrade, $\dfrac{(F-32) \times 5}{9} = C.$

Centigrade to Fahrenheit, $\dfrac{C \times 9}{5} + 32 = F.$

Fahrenheit to Reaumur, $\dfrac{(F-32) \times 4}{9} = R.$

Reaumur to Fahrenheit, $\dfrac{R \times 9}{4} + 32 = F.$

Sometimes thermometers have two scales attached to the same stem, as in *Fig.* 47, where Fahrenheit's scale is placed on the right hand, and the Centigrade on the left. With such an arrangement there is no necessity for any calculation. This arrangement is still further improved by graduating the glass tube itself with one of the scales, and placing the other two upon the sides.

How are Centigrade and Reaumur reduced to Fahrenheit? Explain the principle of these reductions. Show how reduction may be obviated by thermometer with two scales, or with three.

108   REGISTER THERMOMETERS.

134. Different Forms of the Thermometer. The thermometer is arranged in many different forms, but in all, the principle is the same. For use in the laboratory it is specially advantageous to avoid the employment of wooden, ivory, or metallic scales, on account of their liability to corrosion from gases and liquids. The best chemical thermometers are therefore constructed with scales cut upon the glass, as in *Fig.* 48, which represents two thermometers graduated on the tube, and with bulbs elongated in order to render the mercury more susceptible to variations of temperature.

Fig. 48.

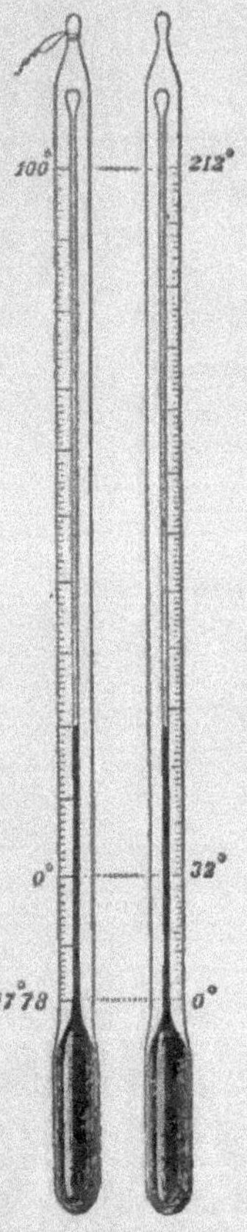

Chemical Thermometers.

135. Register Thermometers. Several methods have been devised to make thermometers mark temperature in such a manner as to leave permanent indications of the highest and lowest points which the mercury has attained since the last observation. Thus, in attempting to find the temperature of the deep ocean by the common thermometer, it is easy to see that the object would be defeated by the increase in the temperature of the water as the instrument is drawn toward the surface. If, however, a mark could be left at the point where the mercury stood when it was at the greatest depth, then the object in question would be attained, and this is what the self-registering thermometer performs. It also indicates the highest and lowest temperatures which may be reached during the day or night, in the absence of the observer. One of the simplest and most efficient forms of this instrument was invented by Rutherford, and bears his name. It is represented in *Fig.* 49, and consists of two thermometers, with their bulbs bent at right angles to the stem, and placed in an inverted position in reference to each other. The upper one is filled with mercury, the lower with alcohol. In the former a small piece of steel is introduced, which is pushed forward by the expansion of the

---

134. Describe different forms of the thermometer.—135. Describe Rutherford's Register thermometer.

mercury, and left when it again contracts. The lower side of the steel indicates, therefore, the highest point which the mer-

Fig. 49.

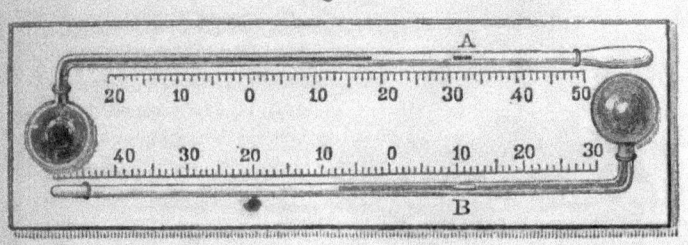

Rutherford's Register Thermometer.

cury has reached during the absence of the observer. In the latter, there is inserted a small bit of glass, which floats in the alcohol, and is carried down by it, when it contracts. When it expands again, the bit of glass is not pushed forward, but is left at the point at which the alcohol remained stationary. Thus the upper end of the bit of glass indicates the lowest point to which the thermometer has sunk during the absence of the observer. It is evident that the instrument needs to be adjusted before it can give these indications a second time. This is accomplished by inclining it upon the end towards the left and gently tapping the instrument. The steel descends to the level of the mercury, and the piece of glass flows down to the end of the alcoholic column. The thermometer is then adjusted and fitted to make a second registration.

136. Metallic Thermometers. When it is desired to measure temperatures lower than the degree at which mercury freezes, i. e.—40°, it is necessary to use thermometers filled with alcohol, a liquid which has never yet been solidified. On the other hand, when it is desired to measure temperatures higher than the degree at which mercury is converted into a vapor, we must employ thermometers made of metal. Metallic thermometers depend upon the expansion and contraction of solids, multiplied by means of machinery and accurately measured by a graduated scale. In *Fig.* 50, there is a representation of Bréguet's metallic thermometer. It consists of a strip of metal, composed of slips of platinum, gold and silver, which, after being soldered together, are rolled into a thin ribbon, which is then

---

136. Why are metallic thermometers useful? Describe Breguet's metallic thermometer

110   PYROMETERS.

Fig. 50.

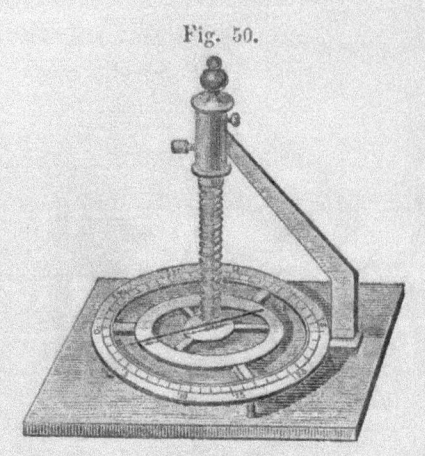

Breguet's Metallic Thermometer.

formed into a spiral or helix. The silver, which is the most expansible of these three metals, is placed upon the outside of the helix; the platinum on the inside, and the gold between the two. One end of the spiral is fixed, the other is connected with an index, and graduated circle. As the temperature rises, the silver expanding the most, twists the spiral and causes the index to move from left to right. When the temperature falls, the spiral turns in the opposite direction. It is an exceedingly delicate and beautiful instrument. There are others constructed upon the same plan, but arranged in a more compact and convenient form.

137. Pyrometers. This name is given to instruments intended to measure high degrees of temperature, such as the heat of furnaces and kilns. The most celebrated is the one invented by Prof. Daniell, depending for its action upon the expansion of a rod of platinum. The amount of the expansion is measured by nicely adjusted scales. Platinum is infusible at most artificial temperatures, and is therefore well fitted to test the heat of the hottest furnaces. Wedgewood's pyrometer depends upon the contraction of bits of clay, by heat, in consequence of the loss of water, which they suffer when placed in a very hot furnace. The amount of this contraction is measured by a scale, and thus it affords a tolerably accurate measure of temperature. By means of Daniell's pyrometer it has been ascertained that red heat takes place at about 980° F.; silver melts at 1 873°; cast iron, 2 786°; gold, 2 016°; and that the highest heat of a wind furnace is about 3 280°.

Experiments:—Effects of Heat: Expansion.

1. **Expansion of Solids.** That solids expand from heat may be shown by fitting a brass rod, provided with a wooden handle, into an iron plate, cut so as just to receive it. Heat the rod and it will no longer enter this cavity. Cool it by immersion in a freezing mixture, and it will enter it much more easily than it did at first.
2. Heat any metallic ball, and it will no longer pass through a hole in a plate of cop-

---

137. What are pyrometers? Describe Daniell's pyrometer. Describe Wedgewood's. Mention some of the temperatures determined by the pyrometer.

per or a ring, through which, when cold, it easily passed. Allow it to cool and it recovers its original dimensions.

3. To show that different metals expand unequally for the same additions of heat, expose rods of different metals to the same source of heat, i. e., the same lamp for an equal length of time, and measure the expansion by the moving of an index over a graduated arc of a circle, as in the ordinary pyrometer: the expansion will be different in each case.

4. Rivet together along their whole length, two strips of brass and zinc, and throw the compound strip into a vessel of boiling water. It will be curved by the greater expansion of the more expansible metal, the zinc.

5. Throw the same compound strip into a freezing mixture of ice and snow, or ice water, and it will be bent in the opposite direction, by the greater contraction of the same metal.

6. That solids expanded by heat return to their original dimensions when permitted to resume their former temperature is shown by experiment 2, with ball and ring; also by suspending a 56 lb. weight by an iron wire from the ceiling in such a way as to just clear a block placed under the weight; then tie upon the wire, at intervals of a foot, bits of tow; saturate them with alcohol and apply a match. The wire will be lengthened by the expansion, and the weight no longer clear the block. Allow the wire to cool and the weight will be drawn up to its former position.

7. That poor conductors of heat are readily broken by sudden heating is shown by applying a hot iron to a glass flask; it will be broken along the path of the iron.

8. Invert a bottle having a glass stopper, and cautiously heat the neck of the bottle on the outside with a spirit lamp; the stopper will soon drop out, showing the real expansion of the glass when slowly heated.

9. Grind a glass rod accurately into a hole in a metallic plate, and then heat slowly in a spirit lamp, or by immersion in hot water; it will no longer fit the hole.

10. Heat the glass stopper of a bottle, and it will no longer enter the mouth of the bottle.

11. **Expansion of Liquids.** To show that liquids expand, dip the bulb of a thermometer into hot water.

12. Fit a cork, with a long tube passing through it, into a flask filled with water. The water will rise into the tube three or four inches; tie a string around the tube at the level of the liquid, and dip the flask into hot water; first the water will sink and then rise very rapidly in the tube.

13. Fill a large test tube entirely full of alcohol, and then place it carefully in a jar of hot water; it will very soon overflow the rim. Or, fill a flask, like that described in the preceding experiment, 12, with alcohol colored red by cochineal, and note the additional amount of expansion.

14. Fill a dropping tube entirely full of sulphuric ether or alcohol, and apply heat to the bulb, the thumb being applied to the larger end. The liquid will be forced out through the small orifice, in a steady stream.

15. That different liquids expand unequally from the same increments of heat is shown by filling two bulbs, of the same size, one with alcohol, and the other with water, to the same height, and dipping them into the same vessel of hot water; or by filling a large bulb to a certain point first with water, and placing it for ten minutes in a vessel of boiling water; then emptying it, cooling in cold water, filling it with alcohol to the same point, and exposing it for ten minutes in the same vessel of boiling water. Note the difference in the expansion in the two cases by means of scale.

16. Apparent Paradox. Dip a flask of water, with tube, as in experiment 12, into a vessel of boiling water. The water for a few seconds will sink considerably in the tube, instead of rising. This is owing to the expansion of the glass flask, by which its capacity is increased.

17. Immerse the same flask in a vessel of ice and water; the liquid will rise instead of sinking, owing to the diminished capacity of the flask.

18. **Expansion of Gases.** That gases expand from heat is shown by applying heat to the bulb of the large air thermometer, described in Art. 128. *Fig.* 45.

19. Invert a glass tube, having a long bulb at the end like a large thermometer tube, in water colored blue by sulphate of copper: support it so that its beak just dips beneath the level of the liquid; apply the flame of a lamp and the air will be driven out, showing expansion: remove the lamp and the liquid will rise into the stem, showing contraction; apply heat again and the air will again expand, driving the colored water down before it. This forms a simple air thermometer.

20. Heat a well corked empty bottle by immersing it in hot water, or exposing it to the fire: the cork will be driven out.

21. Heat a tightly closed India rubber bag, partially filled with air; it will distend, and finally be ruptured.

22. **Exception by Water to the Law of Expansion.** Provide a flask, similar to the one used in experiment 12, but having a thermometer also passed tightly

through the cork; mark the height of the water by a string, and note the temperature. Then immerse in a freezing mixture of pounded ice or snow, and salt; the water will steadily sink in the tube until the thermometer indicates about 40°; as the temperature decreases, the water, instead of obeying the same law, begins to expand, and continues to do so until the thermometer indicates the temperature of 32°, when it will suddenly shoot up and overflow the end of the tube, on account of the freezing of the water in the flask. In consequence of this exception, cold water at 32° floats on the top of warmer water at 40°.

23. Repeat the experiment described in Art. 123, taking care to fill the brass cup with a mixture of ice and salt, instead of ice alone.

24. Thermometers. Test the freezing and boiling points by immersing them in melting ice and boiling water; the mercury should stand in the one case at 32°; in the other at 212°.

25. Note the temperature at which water boils in a glass flask, and observe the effect of throwing in some iron filings.

26. Invert a thermometer and observe if the mercury runs to the end of the stem.

27. Squeeze the bulb between the fingers and note the rising of the mercury. This shows the elasticity of the glass. The thermometer in this experiment should stand at 100°.

§ III. Effects of Heat:—Liquefaction.

138. Heat of Composition. It has been stated that heat exists in two states: first, as heat of temperature; second, as heat of composition. Having considered the effects of heat in the first of these states, we now proceed to consider those which it produces in the second. When heat merely flows into a body, without combining with it, the only effect produced is an elevation of temperature, together with a proportionate enlargement of its dimensions; but when it enters into a body so as to combine with it, the body is changed from the state of a solid to that of a liquid, or from the state of a liquid to that of a vapor. In this case a portion of the heat disappears; the whole of the heat which enters the body does not appear as heat of temperature, but a portion is expended in changing its state. The heat no longer appears as heat; the solid into which it has entered no longer appears as a solid. The heat and the solid have combined so as to form a new liquid or gaseous substance, differing essentially in its appearance and properties from both the substances which have entered into it. The process is analogous to that which takes place when the two invisible gases, oxygen and hydrogen, unite to form the visible substance, water, differing in all respects from the two elements which have combined to form it. It is a

---

138. What are the two states in which heat exists? What are the effects produced upon bodies by heat of temperature? What are the effects produced upon bodies when heat enters into composition with them? What change of state is produced by heat of composition? When two substances combine, what is the universal law?

LIQUEFACTION PRODUCED BY HEAT. 113

universal law that when two substances combine, the compound formed possesses properties different from those of the component elements. In this view, water is a compound of ice and heat; melted iron is a compound of solid iron and heat, because in both these combinations a large amount of heat has combined with the ice and iron, and no longer appears possessed of its most striking property, viz., the power to elevate temperature; while at the same time both the ice and iron have lost all their solid properties and been converted into liquids. The first of the effects of combined heat is Liquefaction; the second, Vaporization.

139. Liquefaction produced by Heat.—Melting Point. When heat enters a solid its first effect is to produce expansion; as it accumulates, the particles gradually become so far separated as to move easily upon each other and readily change their position, and finally, if the heat be increased still further, a state of complete liquidity is the result. This process is called Liquefaction. The degree at which it takes place is different for different substances, and is called the melting point. Ice melts at 32°F.; spermaceti at 132°; sulphur 226°; tin 442°; lead 612°; iron 2786°; silver 1873°; gold 2016°.

Fig. 51.

140. Disappearance of a large amount of Heat during Liquefaction. The most important fact connected with liquefaction, is the disappearance and absorption of a large amount of heat. The fact of this absorption may be easily proved. If a flask full of ice at 0°, with a thermometer inserted in it, be placed over a fire, the mercury will immediately commence rising, and continue to do so until it has attained the temperature of 32°; but when it has reached this point it will suddenly stop and refuse to rise any higher. *Fig.* 51. This elevation of temperature in the ice takes place without the melting of any portion, however small.

Absorption of Heat in Liquefaction.

In this light what may melted iron be regarded as composed of?—139. What is the cause of liquefaction? Is the temperature at which it takes place the same in all substances? Give the melting points of different substances.—140. What is the most important fact connected with liquefaction? How may the absorption of heat in liquefaction be shown?

114   ABSORPTION OF HEAT IN LIQUEFACTION.

As soon, however, as the thermometer has risen to 32°, the ice ceases to indicate any increase of temperature, and begins to melt very slowly. Now it is evident that in the five minutes immediately after the thermometer has ceased to rise, the ice must be receiving heat at the same rate as it did in the five minutes immediately before. What has become of this heat, since it produces no effect on the thermometer? It has evidently disappeared and been absorbed in the process of liquefaction, and its force has been expended in effecting this change of state. It has combined with the ice and produced a substance in which neither its own properties as heat, nor those of the ice, as a solid, any longer appear. The heat thus absorbed is said to have become *latent*, and the amount of it varies with the particular solid substance which is liquefied.

141. Amount of Heat absorbed in the melting of Ice. In the liquefaction of ice, the heat absorbed is sufficient to raise the temperature of an equal weight of water 140°. Thus, if a pound of ice be melted, the heat absorbed is sufficient to raise the temperature of a pound of water from 32° to 172°, or 140°. This may be proved by the following experiment: *Fig. 52.* Let a pound of broken ice at 32°, and a pound of water also at 32°, be introduced into two separate glass jars, of the same size and thickness, and in every respect exactly alike, and let both be placed in a shallow metallic pan, filled to the depth of an inch with water. Let a thermometer be placed in each jar, not arranged as in the figure, with its bulb touching the bottom, but suspended so that each bulb just dips beneath the surface of the broken ice and of the water. Each thermometer will stand, of course, at 32°. Now let a lamp be placed beneath the metal-

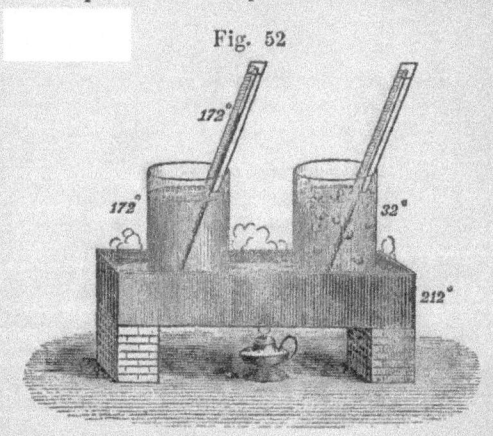

Fig. 52

Amount of Heat absorbed in Liquefaction.

What has become of the heat absorbed, and how has it been expended?—141. How much heat is absorbed in the melting of ice? Describe the experiment by which this amount is determined.

lic pan, and the water contained in it be slowly heated. Both jars receive heat at the same rate, and we should suppose that the thermometers would indicate a temperature increasing at the same rate in both; but instead of this, they are found to be very unequally affected. The thermometer in the jar containing water at 32° immediately begins to rise, while that in the jar containing ice at 32° remains stationary, and does not begin to rise until the ice is entirely melted. If at the instant when the last particle of ice disappears and while its temperature is still at 32°, we observe the thermometer in the jar containing water, it will be found to have risen from 32° to 172°, showing that the water has received 140° of heat. The ice in the other jar has necessarily received precisely the same amount, yet its temperature remains unaffected. What has become of this 140° of heat? It has obviously been absorbed in causing the ice to liquefy, and in so doing has become insensible to the thermometer. As soon as the ice has entirely melted, the thermometer will begin to rise, just as it did in the jar containing water, because the heat received from the lamp is no longer expended in producing the change from the solid to the liquid state, and exerts the ordinary effects of heat of temperature.

142. **The amount of Heat absorbed in the Liquefaction of Ice shown by a second experiment.** If a pound of water at 32° be mixed with a pound of water at 172°, the temperature of the mixture will be intermediate between them, or 102°,—the mean temperature. But if a pound of water at 172° be added to a pound of ice at 32°, the ice will quickly dissolve, and on placing a thermometer in the mixture it will be found to stand not at 102°, but at 32°. In this experiment the pound of hot water which was originally at 172°, actually loses 140° of heat, all of which enters the ice and causes its liquefaction, but without affecting its temperature; whence it follows that a quantity of heat becomes insensible during the melting of ice sufficient to raise the temperature of an equal weight of water by 140° F. This explains the well known fact on which the graduation of the thermometer depends, that the temperature of melting ice or snow never exceeds 32° F. All the heat which is added becomes insensible until the liquefaction is complete.

143. **Heat of Fluidity.** The heat thus absorbed in the liquefaction of solids is called the heat of fluidity, and is essen-

---

142. Describe a second experiment by which the same fact may be proved. Why can not melting ice rise above 32° until the whole is melted?—143. What is meant by heat of fluidity?

tial to the existence of the substance in the liquid state. It varies very much in different bodies. In ice, as we have seen, the amount of heat absorbed is 140°; in beeswax it is 175°; in lead 162°; zinc 493°; tin 500°; bismuth 550°; all of which is in each case given out when the body returns to the solid state. The heat in all these instances is not lost, but is simply rendered insensible to the thermometer. It enters into the constitution of the substance in question without raising its temperature. When the process is reversed, and the substance is reconverted into a solid, the heat which has been rendered insensible is again given out, and the temperature of the body rises. Consequently, whenever a solid is converted into a liquid, there is an immense absorption of heat, accompanied by a diminution of temperature; whenever a liquid is changed into a solid, there is an immense evolution of heat, accompanied by an increase of temperature. Similar variations in temperature are effected by simple change of density, without any such change in state as to produce either liquefaction or solidification. Condense any substance, and its temperature rises; expand it, and its temperature sinks.

144. Solid substances undergoing liquefaction can never be heated above their point of fusion, until the whole of the Solid is melted. When a solid is undergoing liquefaction, all the heat that enters it, is expended in producing the change of state, and none of it goes to raise the temperature until every particle of the solid has melted. Thus we have seen in the case of melting ice, that the temperature of the ice can not be raised above 32° until the last particle of the solid has disappeared. In the same way, if a mass of tin have its temperature raised to 442° it will then begin to melt, and its temperature can be raised no higher until the last particle of tin be melted, after which the temperature will rise as usual. In like manner lead will begin to liquefy at 594°, and notwithstanding the constant addition of heat, its temperature will not rise above 594° until its fusion is complete. The same is true of beeswax; it can not be raised above its melting point, however great the heat applied, so long as any wax remains unmelted; and even in the case of iron, which melts at 2786°, notwithstanding the intense heat of the furnace, it can not be raised above this point so long as any solid iron remains, because

---

Is it the same in amount for all bodies? What is the effect of liquefaction upon surrounding temperature? What is the effect of solidification upon temperature? What is the effect of change of density upon temperature?—144. Why can not solids undergoing liquefaction be heated above the melting point?

SOLIDIFICATION ELEVATES TEMPERATURE.

all the heat that enters it, however great, is entirely expended in producing liquefaction, and none at all goes towards the elevation of temperature.

145. The Heat absorbed in Liquefaction given out in Solidification. The heat thus absorbed in liquefaction is given out and rendered sensible again when the liquid returns to a solid state. This may be shown by immersing a vessel of water at 60°, containing a thermometer, in a freezing mixture of ice and salt, at 0°. The thermometer will immediately sink, and continue to do so, until it reaches 32°, when it will suddenly stop; and though the freezing mixture is at 0°, the water in the vessel persists in remaining at 32°, and at the same time slowly freezes. It loses heat at the same rate after it reached 32° as it did before; why does not its temperature sink? manifestly because the water in freezing is giving out the 140° of heat which it had absorbed in liquefying, and this it is which keeps up its temperature: *Fig.* 53. The same fact may be proved by another experiment. If water be kept undisturbed it may be cooled to 12° or 20° below its freezing point, 32°, without congealing, but upon the least agitation a small portion is made to solidify, and the heat given forth by this small portion in passing from the liquid to the solid state, is sufficient to raise the temperature of the whole mass of the water from 12° to 32°. Melted phosphorus, acetic acid, and sulphuric acid, also admit of being cooled down several degrees below their points of solidification, but if touched or agitated they immediately solidify with the evolution of heat. The solidification of metallic bodies is attended with like results; a liquid alloy of potassium and sodium may be formed by pressing together the two metals, which at common temperatures are quite soft; if a drop of mercury be added to them they instantly solidify, and in doing so emit heat enough to set fire to the naphtha which is used to protect them from the air. The freezing of water, and solidification in general, under all circumstances, strange as it may appear, is attended with the evo-

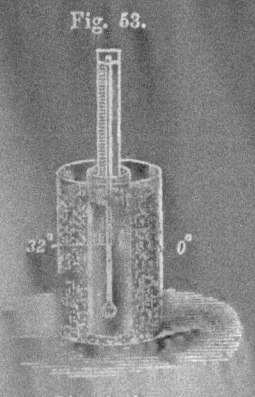

Fig. 53.

Heat of Liquefaction given out in Solidification.

---

145. Show that the heat absorbed in liquefaction is given out again in solidification. Explain the rise of temperature in water at 12°, when it is frozen. Explain the combustion produced when an alloy of sodium and potassium is mixed with mercury.

118   LIQUEFACTION LOWERS TEMPERATURE.

Fig. 54.

Heat produced by Solidification.

lution of heat, and is a warming process. When a pound of water is frozen, sufficient heat is given out to raise another pound of water from 32° to 172°, and to impart to it 140° of heat. If a ton of water be frozen, the same fact is true; the heat given out is sufficient to raise another ton of water from 32° to 172°, or to heat 140 tons of water 1°. A similar extrication of heat occurs in all cases of solidification. The precipitation of matter in a solid form from a state of solution always produces heat. Make a saturated solution of sulphate of soda, or Glaubers salt, in warm water at 90°, and set it aside until it cools, having first tightly corked it; on shaking the bottle, the solution will suddenly crystallize, and its temperature rise several degrees, as shown by the thermometer. If we prepare a saturated solution of acetate of soda in boiling water and allow it to cool without agitation, on pouring it over a bulb, the beak of which is dipped beneath the surface of water in a bowl, it will immediately solidify, and in so doing give out heat enough to drive out a part of the air, in bubbles through the water. See *Fig.* 54, where the water occupies a portion of the stem, and descends rapidly on the application of the solution.

146. Liquefaction, by whatever cause produced, always attended by a Reduction of Temperature. Liquefaction produces cold. This is not only true when solids are melted by the application of heat, but in every case in which solid matter is liquefied, by whatever means. Liquefaction can not take place without the absorption of a large amount of heat; consequently, if we can effect or compel liquefaction without the direct application of heat, a strong demand for heat is at once created, which must be satisfied at the expense of the heat of surround-

---

146. Why is liquefaction, by whatever cause produced, always attended by a reduction of temperature?

ing bodies, and their temperature consequently sinks. Now we have the means of causing bodies to liquefy suddenly by chemical means, without the application of heat; and consequently of producing a diminution of temperature in surrounding objects, by the demand for heat which is thus created.

147. Freezing Mixtures. On this principle depends the operation of what are called freezing mixtures. One of the simplest of these is composed of ice and salt. When mixed, these two solids combine in such a way that both are liquefied, heat is absorbed, surrounding temperature sinks, and the thermometer speedily falls to $-4°$, or $36°$ below the freezing point of water. Care should be taken that no heat be furnished either by the vessel in which the liquefaction takes place, or from any other external source. It follows, therefore, that the heat which is absorbed must be supplied by the substances themselves which compose the mixture, and which must suffer a diminution of temperature proportioned to the quantity of heat thus rendered latent. The cold produced will be increased by reducing the temperature of the substances in question, before mixing them. The vessel in which the mixture is made should be placed in a larger vessel, also containing some of the freezing mixture, for the purpose of cutting off every supply of heat to the inner vessel from the outside. The solids employed must be pulverized so as to dissolve quickly, and if salts, must not have lost their water of crystallization, or have become anhydrous. There are freezing mixtures more effective than ice and salt. Thus, chlorohydric acid 5 parts by weight, and snow or ice, 8 parts, will sink the temperature from $32°$ to $-21°$. Again, if equal weights of snow and common salt, at $32°$, be mixed, they will liquefy, and the temperature will fall to $-9°$. If 2 lbs. of chloride of calcium, and 1 lb. of snow, be separately reduced to $-9°$ in this liquid, and then mixed, they will liquefy, and the temperature will fall to $-74°$. If 4 lbs. of snow, and 5 lbs. of sulphuric acid, be reduced to $-74°$ in this last mixture, and then mixed, they will liquefy, and the temperature will fall to $-90°$. Again, if 1 lb. of snow be dissolved in about 2 quarts of alcohol, the mixture will fall nearly to $-13°$. If the same quantities of snow and alcohol, after being reduced in this mixture to $-13°$, be then mingled, the temperature of the mixture will be reduced to $-58°$, and the same process being

---

147. What are freezing mixtures? Explain the principle on which they depend. Give some of the most important freezing mixtures.

repeated, with like quantities in this second mixture, a further reduction of temperature to — 98° may be effected, and so on. The lowest known temperatures, however, have been produced by liquefying, and then evaporating some of the gases. Temperatures have been thus produced, varying from — 120° F. to — 220°. At such temperatures, mercury, which freezes at — 40° F., is easily solidified, and it is said that even alcohol, a liquid which has hitherto resisted all attempts at solidification, has been reduced to the consistency of oil and melted wax. These processes will be described hereafter. The extreme cold thus produced will perhaps be better understood by comparison with some of the lowest natural temperatures. The severest natural cold ever noted was in Siberia, lat. 55 N., where the thermometer was observed to indicate — 91.75° F. At Jakertsh, the mean temperature of the month of December is — $44\frac{1}{2}$° F., and it has been known as low as — 58°. In the expedition in Khiva, in December, 1839, the Russian army experienced for several successive days a temperature of — 41.8° F.

148. The solution of Salts and Acids in Water lowers its Freezing Point. The freezing points of liquids are generally lowered when salts are dissolved in them. The freezing point of pure water is stationary at 32°; but sea water, which contains several different salts dissolved in it, chiefly common salt, freezes at 27.4° F., the salt separating, and the pure water floating in the form of ice; whilst water which is saturated with sea salt sinks as low as — 4° F. before freezing. In like manner the strong acids, like the sulphuric acid, and the nitric, will very considerably reduce the freezing point of the water with which they are mixed. The icebergs, therefore, which float in the sea, and all the ice formed in the ocean in winter, consist of perfectly pure water. In like manner, if water hold in solution a small quantity of alcohol, and be frozen, the ice will be found to contain no admixture of alcohol, but to be the ice of perfectly pure water. This method is sometimes practiced to give increased strength to weak wines, for, as the water freezes, the remaining liquid becomes proportionably stronger. In the process of freezing, as it goes on in Nature, solidification does not proceed continuously, but the ice is formed in successive layers, and in the intervals between these layers is a stratum of ice, slightly more fusible than the mass either above or below.

---

148. What is the effect upon the freezing point of water of dissolving salts in it? What effect has the mixing of acids with water upon its freezing point? What is the effect of freezing upon salt water? What is the effect of freezing upon water containing alcohol in solution?

FLUXES.

149. Sometimes two different substances mixed, fuse at a temperature much lower than either separately.—Fluxes. Salt may be said to be a flux for ice, because it tends to liquefy the ice without the application of heat, at a lower temperature than it would melt without; in the same manner other substances, when mixed, often tend to fuse at a temperature much lower than the fusing point of either separately. In this way many very infusible substances are melted by mingling with them other bodies with which they tend to unite. Silica, the most important constituent in glass, is not fusible by any heat of the most powerful wind furnace, but if soda, potash, lime, and lead, be mixed with it, fusion takes place very readily at a comparatively low temperature. These substances are hence called *fluxes*. In the manufacture of porcelain, fluxes are employed; and also in the reduction of the metals from their ores. For this reason iron ore is always mixed with lime before it is subjected to the action of the blast furnace. In the case of some of the salts, the lowering of the point of fusion is very extraordinary; thus nitrate of potash melts at 642° F., the nitrate of soda at 591° F.; but a mixture of the two, in equivalent proportions, liquefies as low as 429°, or 162° below the melting point of the most fusible of the two salts. In like manner some of the alloys of different metals will often melt at much lower temperatures than any of the metals employed separately. An alloy of 8 parts of bismuth, 5 of lead, and 3 of tin, melts at a temperature below that of boiling water, and an alloy of 496 parts of bismuth, 310 lead, 177 tin, and 26 mercury, fuses at 162.5° F. If a thin strip of this alloy be dipped into water that is nearly boiling hot, it will melt like wax. Some bodies, like water, pass at once from the complete solid to the complete liquid state without passing through any intermediate condition; while others, like wax, tallow, and phosphorus, become soft at temperatures much lower than those at which they are liquefied; and there are others, like glass and platinum, which never, under any circumstances, attain absolute fluidity.

150. Refractory substances. Bodies, whose fusion is exceedingly difficult, or which resist it altogether, are called refractory. No substance can be said to be absolutely infusible, except carbon, which, under all its forms, of pure carbon,

---

149. What are fluxes? How may salt be said to be a flux for ice? Describe the use of fluxes in the making of glass and porcelain. What is the use of the lime employed in the smelting of iron? How does the melting point of alloys compare with that of the metals which enter into them?—150. What are refractory substances?

charcoal, anthracite, graphite, and diamond, has resisted fusion at the highest temperature which has yet been produced. There is reason to believe that even carbon may yet be fused by long subjection to the intense heat of Ruhmkorff's coil; § 465. Of the metals, platinum is the most infusible, and it can not be melted except by the oxyhydrogen blow-pipe, an instrument to be described hereafter, and by the galvanic current. Wrought iron is also extremely difficult of fusion. Among the most refractory bodies are the earths,—lime, alumina, baryta, strontia. Some compound substances can not be melted, because decomposition takes place before the degree of heat necessary for fusion has been attained. Thus marble, ordinarily, can not be melted, because, at a red heat, it is decomposed, and one of its constituents, the carbonic acid gas, escapes; but if it be tightly confined in a strong gun-barrel, so that nothing can escape, and intense heat be applied, its fusion can be accomplished.

151. Facility of liquefaction proportioned to the quantity of latent heat required. The different degrees of facility with which bodies are liquefied depends in part upon the relative amounts of heat which are rendered latent in the process. Thus ice liquefies very slowly, because the latent heat required is very great, water containing more latent heat, or heat of composition, than any other known substance. Phosphorus and lead, on the other hand, whose latent heat is small, melt very easily; ice can not be liquefied until it has received sufficient heat to raise an equal weight of water $140°$, while lead and phosphorus are melted by as much heat as would raise their own weight of water by $9°$. If but little heat is absorbed, and becomes latent, all the heat that enters the body in question goes at once towards its liquefaction; whereas, if a large quantity becomes latent, it is obvious that but a small amount can go towards the liquefaction, and the rapidity of that process is proportionably retarded.

152. The important results of the absorption of Heat in Liquefaction, and its evolution in Solidification. The absorption of this large amount of heat in liquefaction, and the proportional evolution of heat in solidification, lead to two most important results. 1st. The solidification of large bodies of water sets free an amount of heat previously latent in the water which is of the greatest value in mitigating the rigors of a cold

---

Which is the most infusible of all known substances? Which is the most infusible of the metals?—151. To what is the facility of liquefaction proportioned? Give illustrations of this in the case of water and phosphorus.—152. What important results flow from the absorption and evolution of heat in liquefaction and solidification?

climate. The act of freezing liberates heat, and very perceptibly moderates the temperature of the atmosphere. As soon as ice begins to form upon the surface of a lake in winter, the temperature of the atmosphere is immediately elevated. In the severest weather of winter, if a snow storm occur, the air at once becomes warmer from the heat, previously latent in the watery vapor, now given forth by its condensation and solidification. For the same reason water is often placed in cellars for the purpose of preventing frost by the heat given forth by its own congelation. 2d. The large amount of heat required for liquefaction tends to make the melting of solids slow and gradual, and the large amount of heat given forth in solidification tends to make the congelation of liquids equally slow and gradual. A check is thus placed upon the rapidity of both these processes, and matter is prevented from suddenly passing from one state to the other in either direction. We see the importance of this provision in the impediment which is thus placed in the way of the sudden liquefaction of large masses of snow and ice in the spring; if it were not for the immense amount of heat required, and which can not readily be obtained, the ice and snow that had accumulated during a long winter would, at the first approach of mild weather, be at once converted into water, and sweep away not only the works of man, but also those of Nature herself,—the trees, rocks, and hills. The difficulty of suddenly supplying so vast an amount of heat necessarily makes the process of melting very gradual. What would be the consequences if there were no such provision can be imagined from the destructive effects that are produced in spite of it, by the melting of ice and snow in the spring; if the vast body of water which is produced were formed in the course of a single day, it is evident that every thing would be swept before it. Occasionally catastrophes of this kind do occur, when a volcano, such as Etna, pours forth a stream of lava over fields of ice and snow; the destruction which is produced by the torrents of water is even greater than that of the lava itself. As we advance towards the north the transition from winter to summer is very rapid, taking place almost in a day, and it is evident that the beneficial results of this constitution of matter in countries where the masses of snow and ice accumulated in winter are immense, must be altogether incalculable. Again,

---

What effect is produced upon the temperature of the air by the freezing of water in the autumn? What effect is produced upon the rapidity of the melting of snow in the spring by the absorption of so large an amount of heat?

when in the autumn large masses of water are frozen, the heat latent in the liquid, and essential to its liquidity, is given forth, and this has the effect of elevating the temperature of the remaining water, and also of warming the atmosphere in contact with it. The evolution of this large amount of heat has the effect of retarding the freezing process, and limiting its effects. An impediment is thus placed in the way of the sudden freezing of large bodies of water. So happily adjusted are all the arrangements of Nature to subserve the comfort of man, and the preservation of animal and vegetable life.

153. The beneficial effects of all the laws of Nature, and of their exceptions in special cases. All animal and vegetable life depends upon the preservation in a permanently liquid state of vast quantities of water. To secure this end, the freezing of water is made a slow process, by the latent heat which is given forth as soon as it begins to take place. A similar provision, as we shall see, prevents it from too rapidly evaporating. Both those arrangements show the wisdom, power and beneficence of the Most High most emphatically and plainly, as indeed do all the laws to which he has subjected the world of matter. But especially are these attributes shown in the exceptions which he has made to his own laws, when their regular operation would be injurious to the welfare of man. These display a very peculiar and refined design which demands our highest admiration; and perhaps the most striking of these exceptions is shown in the exemption of water from the ordinary law of expansion and contraction, when its execution would be injurious to man. When water has cooled to a certain point, the ordinary law is reversed, the warm water sinks, and the cold water floats upon the surface. In what powerful language does this single fact in Nature speak to every religious mind!

154. The discoverer of the laws of Latent Heat. It is to the celebrated Dr. Joseph Black, Prof. of Chemistry in the University of Edinburgh, that we are indebted for the greater part of our knowledge on this subject. It is stated that an observation of Fahrenheit, recorded by the celebrated Boerhaave, " that water would become considerably colder than melting snow without freezing, and would freeze in a moment, if disturbed, and in the act of freezing emit many degrees of heat,"

---

153. How is the permanently liquid state of large amounts of water secured? What special design is shown by the peculiar constitution of water and its exception at certain temperatures, to the law of expansion from heat.—154. Who was the discoverer of the laws of latent heat? What directed his attention to the subject?

first suggested to Dr. Black the idea that the heat received by ice during its conversion into water is not lost, but is contained in the water. He instituted a careful train of experiments which fully established the immense absorption of heat in liquefaction and vaporization, and its corresponding evolution in condensation and solidification. These experiments may be found fully detailed in his own words, in his Lectures, one of the most instructive and interesting works on chemistry to be found in our language. This discovery of Dr. Black unfolded the true theory of the steam engine, and suggested to Mr. Watt many of his most important improvements.

Experiments: Effects of Heat.—Liquefaction.

1. **Liquefaction.** That heat produces liquefaction may be shown by heating ice, lead, or any other solid easily fusible.
2. That liquefaction is accompanied by the disappearance of a large amount of heat may be shown by heating a cup filled with ice at 0°, and containing a thermometer, over a lamp. The thermometer will rise to 32° and then remain stationary until all the ice has melted, notwithstanding it has been receiving heat at the same rate all the time. What has become of it? Evidently it has been absorbed. The ice may be reduced to 0° by immersion in a freezing mixture of ice and salt.
3. The same fact is shown by dissolving common salt, nitrate of potash, nitrate of ammonia, chloride of calcium, and in general all the salts, in water, and noting the great diminution of temperature which results, as tested by the thermometer.
4. Take 207 parts of lead, 118 of tin, 284 of bismuth, melt them together in a crucible, and reduce them to a finely divided state by throwing into cold water. On dissolving this alloy in 1017 parts of mercury, the thermometer will sink from 64° F. to 14°, and water may be frozen by the process.
5. The amount of heat absorbed in the melting of ice may be shown to be what would heat an equal weight of water 140°, by pouring a pound of water at 172° upon a pound of ice at 32°. The ice will be melted by the heat of the hot water, but the temperature of the whole mixture at the conclusion of the experiment will be only 32°, i. e., 140° of heat will have disappeared and been absorbed.
6. The same fact is shown by the experiment described on page 114. Two glass beakers, one containing a pound of ice at 32°, the other a pound of water at 32°, each having a thermometer suspended in it, with the bulb a little distance below the surface, are placed in a shallow tin pan kept boiling by a lamp. They receive heat at the same rate, and the temperature of the water rises, while that of the ice remains stationary at 32°. By the time the water has reached 172°, or received 140° of heat, the ice, which has received just as much, will only have melted, and the temperature of the vessel containing it will still be only 32°. See *Fig.* 52.
7. **Solidification produces Heat.** Potassium and Sodium pressed together in a mortar produce a liquid alloy; add mercury, and this liquid becomes a solid, and heat enough is set free to inflame the naphtha adhering to the potassium.
8. To a strong solution of chloride of calcium or muriate of lime, add a drop or two of sulphuric acid; a solid results, and much heat is produced.
9. Water and quick lime mixed, solidify with the production of much heat. If phosphorus in a watch glass be placed upon the mixture it will be inflamed, and water in a test tube may be boiled.
10. Place a small jar of water at 60° or 70°, and containing a thermometer, within a larger jar, and let the space between them be filled with a freezing mixture of snow and salt at a temperature of 0°, as shown by a second thermometer. The water in the inner vessel will steadily sink in temperature, until its thermometer indicates 32°, but at this degree it will remain stationary, though the mixture around it is at 0°, or 32° lower; the water at the same time will slowly freeze. Why is this? It is manifestly owing to the heat given out in the solidification of the water. See *Fig.* 53.
11. Dissolve sulphate of soda in water at 91° F. until the water refuses to take up any more of the salt; cork the bottle containing the saturated solution tightly and set it

aside to cool. The bottle should be entirely full and be permitted to stand very quietly. If it be agitated, the bottle will become perceptibly warm to the hand from the rapid crystallization and solidification of its liquid contents. If shaking the bottle be not sufficient to produce crystallization, extract the cork and drop in a bit of stick or a small crystal.

12. Prepare a saturated solution of acetate of soda, and when cold pour it over the bulb of an air thermometer. The air will immediately expand, showing the evolution of heat.

13. Freezing Mixtures. 1. To sulphate of soda, 8 ounces, add 5 ounces, by weight, of chlorohydric or muriatic acid. Temperature will sink from 50° to 0°.

2. To 20 ounces by weight of a mixture of equal parts of sulphuric acid and water, previously mingled and cooled, add 30 ounces of snow or pounded ice; temperature will sink from 32° to —23°.

3. To sulphate of soda, 10 oz., add 8 fluid oz. of a mixture of equal parts of sulphuric acid and water, cooled; temperature will sink from 50° to 3°.

4. Dissolve powdered sal ammoniac in water and note the diminution of temperature.

5. Dissolve nitrate of ammonia in water; temperature will sink from 50° to 49°.

6. Dissolve a mixture of equal parts of sal ammoniac and nitre in water.

7. Common salt, 1 part by weight; snow or pounded ice, 2 parts; temperature will sink to —5°.

8. Common salt, 5 parts by weight; nitrate of ammonia, 5 parts; snow or ice, 12 parts; temperature will sink to —25°.

9. Chlorohydric acid, 5 parts by weight; snow or ice, 8 parts; temperature will sink from 32° to —27°.

10. Chlorohydric acid, 5 parts, poured upon 8 parts of sulphate of soda, will reduce temperature from 50° to 0°.

11. Crystallized chloride of calcium, and 2 parts of snow, will reduce temperature to —40°, and freeze mercury.

12. If the chloride, in the last experiment, be cooled to 32°, the mixture will cause a thermometer to fall to —60°.

§ IV.—Effects of Heat:—Vaporization.—Ebullition.

155. Vaporization. It has been seen that the first effect of heat is, to separate the particles of bodies from each other, and at the same time to elevate their temperature; that then, as the heat accumulates, the force of cohesion is weakened to such a degree as to admit of the easy movement of the particles upon each other, and the solid becomes a liquid; and that this takes place *without* any elevation of temperature. If the heat be still further increased a *third* and final effect is produced. In the case of some substances the particles are pushed so far from each other as to acquire unlimited freedom of motion, and the substance passes into the state of an invisible gas, or vapor, resembling the atmosphere. This process is called *vaporization*. There are some substances, such as ice, arsenic, sulphur, camphor, which can yield vapor without passing through the intermediate state of liquidity; but in general all solid bodies are first liquefied, and then by a further application of heat, are converted into vapors.

---

155. What is the first effect of heat on solids? What is the second? If the heat be pushed beyond the degree required for liquefaction, what results? What is vaporization? Do all solids, in vaporizing, pass through the state of liquefaction?

156. The physical properties of Vapors. Vapors are transparent and colorless, like the gases; though there is a small number of colored liquids which produce colored vapors. In general, they possess the same physical properties as gases; the chief difference between them is, that a vapor is readily condensed into a liquid by a diminution of temperature, while a gas remains in the aeriform state at all common temperatures. The effect of pressure upon vapor is the same as upon gases, provided they are not condensed by it, i. e., the volume which they occupy is inversely as the pressure. Double the pressure and the volume is reduced one half. The expansion of vapors by heat is also the same as that of gases, i. e., for every degree of heat added to them they expand $\frac{1}{480}$ of the bulk which they occupy at 32°. This law does not hold good unless the quantity of the vapor heated remains the same, and does not apply to cases where fresh portions of vapor are continually rising from the liquid by which they are produced; but when there is no addition made to the quantity of the vapor, then they expand just as an equal volume of air would do, and thereby exert a certain amount of mechanical force. It is always to be borne in mind that a vapor, unless it be colored, is as invisible as the atmosphere, and that its particles are so far removed from each other as to oppose no obstacle to the passage of light.

157. Difference between Evaporation and Ebullition. Vapor is rising at all times, and at all temperatures, from the surface of liquids, but the higher the temperature, in general, the more rapid the process. When it goes on quietly and slowly, at natural temperatures, from the surface of liquids, it is called *evaporation;* but when, by the application of a large amount of heat, vapor is formed so rapidly at the bottom of a vessel as to produce violent agitation in the liquid, it is called *boiling,* or *ebullition.* The subject therefore naturally resolves itself into two parts, evaporation and ebullition; we will consider the latter first.

158. Ebullition. Ebullition, or the rapid and violent formation of vapor, takes place in different liquids at different temperatures; but in the same liquid, under the same circumstances, always at the same temperature; and this is called its boiling point. Thus, pure water boils at 212° F., alcohol at

---

156. State the physical properties of vapors. What is the difference between a vapor and a gas? What are the effects of pressure on vapors and gases? Of heat? Are vapors always invisible?—157. State the difference between evaporation and ebullition.—158. Define ebullition. Is the boiling point of the same liquid always constant? State the boiling points of water. Sulphuric ether. Mercury, &c.

175°, sulphuric ether at 96°, sulphuric acid at 620°, turpentine at 316°, mercury at 662°.

159. Absorption and disappearance of a large amount of heat during Ebullition. The most important fact connected with this process is, that it is attended by the absorption of an enormous amount of heat, which becomes insensible to the thermometer, just as in the case of liquefaction. The fact of this absorption may be proved by the following experiment: If we half fill a flask, *Fig.* 54, with pure water at 62°, suspend a thermometer in it, and place it over a lamp or fire, the thermometer will steadily rise until the water reaches the temperature of 212°. It will then cease rising and continue permanently at this point until the water is all boiled away. Suppose at the commencement of the experiment that the water was at 62°, and that it rose to 212°, the boiling point, in six minutes. It gained then, in these six minutes, 150° of heat, or 25° each minute. This is the rate per minute at which heat entered the water. The time occupied by the water in boiling entirely away was forty minutes. As it was receiving heat at the rate of 25° per minute, and was forty minutes in boiling away, it is quite evident that in the process it must have received 1000° of heat; yet the thermometer during the whole time did not rise above 212°. What then has become of this 1000° of heat? It has evidently entered into the steam and become latent, or insensible to the thermometer. It has been ascertained by the pyrometer, (§ 137,) that red heat takes place at 980°. Consequently, an amount of heat has been imparted to the water which, if it had been a solid substance, like iron, would have heated it red-hot; and yet the water has indicated only the temperature of 212°! This simple experiment furnishes satisfactory proof that in the process of vaporization a vast amount of heat is absorbed and becomes

Fig. 54.

212°

Heat absorbed in Boiling.

---

159. What is the most important fact connected with ebullition? How may this be proved? How much heat is absorbed or made latent in the boiling of water? How much more time is required to convert a given weight of water into steam, than to heat it from 32° to 212°?

latent and insensible to the thermometer, that it requires from $5\frac{1}{2}$ to 6 times as much time to convert any given quantity of water into steam, as it does to raise the same water from 32° to 212°, or heat it 180°, and consequently that $5\frac{1}{2}$ or 6 times as much *heat* is absorbed in the conversion of water into steam as is necessary to raise it from 32° to 212° or heat it by 180°, i. e., about 1000°.

160 The heat absorbed in Vaporization given out in Condensation. The heat thus made latent in the conversion of a liquid into a vapor, is again given out and made sensible when the vapor is condensed and re-converted into a liquid. This may be proved by the following experiment, *Fig.* 55. Let *a* be a strong copper vessel, having a brass tube bent twice at

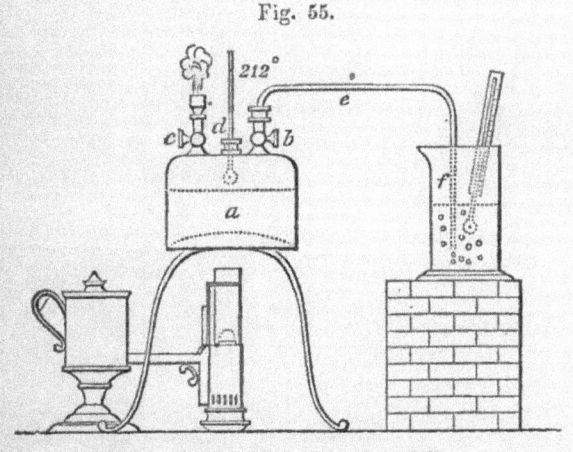

Fig. 55.

Heat given out in Condensation of Steam.

right angles connected with it, and dipping beneath the surface of water, of the temperature of 32° in the glass cup, *f*. At *d* there is a thermometer for measuring the temperature of the water; *c* is a stop-cock opening into the air; *b* another stop-cock commanding the entrance to the tube. A powerful lamp is placed beneath, and the water in *a* made to boil; *c* is then closed, and *b* opened. The steam rushes into the cold water in *f*, and is condensed by it, until this also has reached the temperature of 212°. The water in *f* will then begin to boil, and the steam commence rising into the air. The amount of cold

---

160. Is this heat annihilated? Can it be obtained again by condensation? How is this proved? How much latent heat is given out in the condensation of steam?

6*

water, at 32°, contained in f at the beginning of the experiment was 11 cubic inches; at the conclusion of the experiment the amount of water has been increased to 13 cubic inches, at temperature of 212°. It has increased in volume by two cubic inches, and has done so by the condensation of steam, at temperature of 212°, from the copper boiler. The latent heat, therefore, contained in two cubic inches of water in the form of steam, of the temperature of 212°, has raised the 11 cubic inches in the glass cup from 32° to 212°. The amount of heat, therefore, latent in two cubic inches of water at 212°, in the form of steam, is sufficient to raise the temperature of a volume of water in the liquid state, $5\frac{1}{2}$ times greater than itself, from 32° to 212°, i. e., by 180°. Consequently, the sum of the heat given out by the condensation of this amount of steam is equal to $180 \times 5\frac{1}{2} = 990°$. The raising the temperature by 180°, of an amount of water $5\frac{1}{2}$ times greater than the amount which has been condensed, is the same thing as raising the temperature of an amount of water equal to that which has been condensed by $5\frac{1}{2}$ times $180° = 990°$; from which we see very plainly that the amount of latent heat given forth in the condensation of steam, and its reconversion into a liquid, is equal to the amount of latent heat absorbed when water is converted into vapor, i. e., about 1000° in each case. These important facts were first demonstrated by Dr. Black, shortly after his discovery of the heat made latent in the process of liquefaction, and a full account of it may be found in the 1st volume of Dr. Black's Lectures, already referred to.

161. The amount of heat absorbed is not the same for all Vapors. Equal weights of different liquids require very different amounts of latent heat to convert them into vapor. Thus, while water absorbs and renders latent 1000° of heat, ammonia absorbs 830°, alcohol 386°, ether 162°, turpentine 133°. The amount of heat which is rendered latent in each case may be determined by distilling over a given weight of the liquid, and condensing it in a large volume of water, the temperature of which is noted at the beginning of the experiment, and also at its close; *Fig.* 56. The liquid to be tried is placed in the flask A, the neck of which is connected with a glass receiver, B, furnished with a spiral condensing tube terminating at D; this receiver is placed in a vessel C, with a considerable quantity of water, the weight of which has been accurately determined. The liquid

---

161. Is the amount of heat made latent the same for all vapors? How may this amount be determined for each?

BOILING POINT VARIABLE. 131

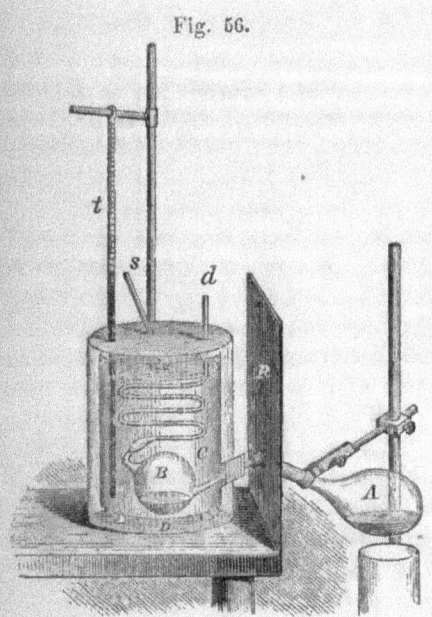

Fig. 56.

Determination of the Latent Heat of Vapors.

in A is distilled over into B; the quantity that condenses is carefully weighed, and the rise of temperature experienced by the water used for condensation is estimated by a thermometer, t. The whole is enclosed in an outer tin plate vessel, and is still further protected from the radiation of the lamp by the tin plate screen R. S is a glass rod for agitating the water. A pint of water converted into steam will, on condensation, raise the temperature of 10 pints 99° and a fraction. A gallon of water converted into steam, at 212°, and then condensed, will raise 5½ gallons of water from 32° to 212°, or 180°. It requires, therefore, 5½ times as much water at 32° to condense steam, as the water from which the steam was originally formed. If the condensing water be not so cold as 32°, a larger quantity of it will be needed. By careful experiments of this kind the latent heat of all vapors may be determined.

162. Boiling Point variable—Influenced by the pressure of the Atmosphere. The boiling point of the same liquid is not to be considered perfectly constant; it depends upon circumstances, the most important of which is the pressure of the atmosphere upon its surface. This pressure is equal to 15 lbs. (see § 9,) upon every square inch; it operates upon liquids, as well as solids, and its effect is to keep the particles of liquid down, and prevent them from passing into the vaporous state; this it does by the compression which it exercises, and it amounts to the same thing as adding just so much to the cohesion existing in the liquid, tending to keep its particles together. This additional cohesion can only be counteracted by heat, and no liquid can boil until it has acquired heat enough

---

162. Is the boiling point ever affected by circumstances? What is the effect of a variation in the atmospheric pressure? Explain this.

132   MEASUREMENT OF HEIGHTS.

to overcome this pressure of the atmosphere. The elasticity of the vapor, or its tendency to expand, must be equal to the force which tends to prevent it from expanding; in all cases where a liquid boils in the open air, the elasticity of the vapor, and the pressure of the atmosphere, exactly balance each other. Now if the pressure of the atmosphere be diminished, the elastic force required to balance it will be diminished also; and as this depends upon the temperature, the heat required will be less. Consequently, if the atmospheric pressure be diminished, boiling will take place at a lower temperature; if, on the other hand, the atmospheric pressure be increased, more elastic force must be possessed by the vapor before it can rise, and this it can not have without additional heat; boiling, therefore, must take place at a higher temperature. This can readily be shown by experiment. Remove the pressure from warm water by means of the air pump, and it will boil at the temperature of 70°, *Fig.* 57. Sulphuric ether, in a vacuum, will boil at —46°, or 140° lower than in the open air, at a temperature such that water will easily freeze in contact with it, as may be proved by experiment. As we ascend in the atmosphere the pressure of the air diminishes, consequently the boiling point is lowered. So regularly does this decline take place that it affords a measure of height. A fall of 1° F. indicates an elevation of 596 feet. On the contrary, at the bottom of mines the boiling point is raised in consequence of the increase of the atmospheric pressure. At the Hospital of St. Bernard, on the Alps, about 8,400 feet above the sea, water boils at 196°; on the top of Mount Blanc, at 184°. In consequence of this low temperature, it has been found difficult to cook food by boiling at these high points, as the solvent power of water, and its efficacy in cooking meats and vegetables, depends upon its temperature. This difficulty has been obviated by the use of Papin's Digester, an instrument to be described hereafter. It is evident, from this, that it is necessary to take the height of the barometer into the account in all experiments upon the boiling points

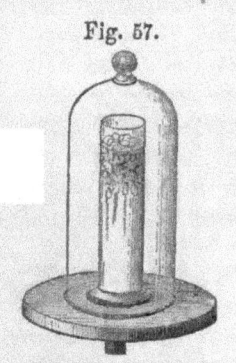

Fig. 57.

Water Boiling at 70°.

What is the effect of removing the atmospheric pressure altogether? What is the effect of elevation in the air upon the boiling point? What practical difficulty results from this? What is the variation of the boiling point within the ordinary range of the barometer?

of liquids. A variation of one-tenth of an inch makes a difference of more than $\frac{1}{20}°$ F., so that, within the ordinary range of the barometer, the boiling point of water may vary 5°.

163. Wollaston's Hypsometer. It has been stated that the lowering of the boiling point, in proportion to the elevation above the level of the sea, is made use of as a means of measuring the height of mountains. It is only necessary to note the temperature of water boiling at the base of the mountain, and then at the point of elevation. (1° F. is equivalent to 596 feet in height.) An instrument for taking these observations successfully, was invented by Archdeacon Wollaston, arranged in such a way that a 1000th part of a degree of the thermometer might be read upon the scale, and so delicate was it that the effect produced upon the boiling point by the height of an ordinary table could readily be ascertained.

164. Influence of adhesion on the boiling point. Adhesion of the liquid to the surface of the vessel has a decided effect upon the boiling point; and as the degree of adhesion depends upon the substance employed, the material of which the vessel is made has some effect upon the boiling point. Thus water sometimes boils at 214° in a glass vessel, but falls to 212° if a few iron filings be dropped in; this was first noticed by Gay Lussac. If the inside of a vessel be varnished, the boiling will sometimes not take place short of 221°, and then will proceed irregularly, the temperature falling to 212°, at every occurrence of boiling. The presence of a little oil upon the surface of a liquid also elevates the boiling point. After sulphuric acid has been boiled in a glass flask, the boiling point is said to be elevated five or six degrees. In all these cases the effect is due to the attraction of adhesion exerted by the surface in question upon the water, which tends to retain it in the liquid state, and this can only be overcome by an addition to the temperature. It takes place with other liquids, as well as water, and with some of them to a much greater extent. Though the temperature of the boiling water may be thus elevated, the temperature of the vapor formed is always at 212°, or at whatever point the atmospheric pressure at the time may require. As a general rule, however, the temperature of the liquid boiling, and the vapor formed, are exactly the same.

165. The Air dissolved in Water favors its Ebullition.

163. Describe Wollaston's Hypsometer.—164. What is the effect of adhesion on the boiling point? Give some illustrations.—165. What effect has the air dissolved in water upon its boiling? If air be entirely expelled from water, what results?

Water possesses the power of dissolving air. This may be proved by heating water in a flask, over a spirit lamp, when the air may be seen to separate from the water in the form of bubbles, and rise to the surface. These bubbles of air furnish, as it were, an avenue of escape to the steam; and at the same time, the presence of so large an amount of aeriform matter tends to diminish the cohesion of the particles of water, and to facilitate the separation that is necessary to enable them to assume the state of vapor. If the air be expelled from water by long continued boiling, it may be heated in an open glass vessel to the temperature of 360°, without boiling. The heat thus collected in the water causes it to flash into steam almost instantaneously, with a loud report, when it does boil, and the vessel is generally broken; the temperature of the vapor formed is only 212°, and that of the water immediately sinks to the same point. It is extremely difficult to expel all the air from water: boiling *in vacuo* for some time will not effect it. If water, however, be slowly frozen, the air is entirely expelled, and if a lump of this ice be immersed in heated oil, or turpentine, so as to melt without coming into contact with the air, it may be heated to many degrees above 212° without boiling, and will then suddenly be converted into vapor with great violence. Liquids which contain but little air, and which require but little latent heat to pass into vapor, such as alcohol, ether, and sulphuric acid, boil with great irregularity, and with sudden bursts, instead of with the regularity and steadiness of water.

166. Solids dissolved in a Liquid elevate its Boiling Point. The boiling point of a liquid is not changed by the presence of foreign bodies, which are mechanically diffused through it like sand or mud in water; but it is changed by all substances which are capable of forming a true solution with it. Thus rosins dissolved in alcohol, retard its boiling; salts dissolved in water, elevate the boiling point; acids the same; alcohol seems to lower it. This is owing to the attraction of adhesion, exerted by the substances in question, which tends to bind the particles of water closely to itself, and to prevent them from escaping. A saturated solution of common salt boils at 227°; of nitre, at 240°; sal ammoniac, at 238°; chloride of calcium, 355°.

167. Increase of Pressure elevates the Boiling Point;— Diminished Pressure lowers it. If water be boiled in a close

---

What is the effect of introducing ice into heated oil of turpentine?—166. What effect has the solution of solids in a liquid upon the boiling point?—167. What is the effect of increased pressure on the boiling point?

vessel, the steam collecting in the upper part soon presses on the surface of the water with so much force as to put an entire stop to the whole process of ebullition, and it will not recommence until the water has been heated considerably above 212°. This may be shown by boiling water in a strong glass flask, provided with a stop-cock, and having a thermometer immersed in the fluid. The stop-cock being open, the water will boil at 212°; but if the stop-cock be closed, in a few minutes the boiling will be seen to cease, so that there will be no agitation of the surface, and it will not recommence until the thermometer has risen several degrees. If, then, at this moment, the stop-cock be opened, the steam will rush out, pressure will be removed, boiling will recommence with great violence, and the thermometer immediately sink to 212°; *Fig.* 58. It is quite evident from this experiment that increase of pressure elevates the boiling point. If the spring safety valve screwed upon the stop-cock be removed, and air be forced into the flask, the stop-cock then closed, and the flask placed over a spirit lamp, a longer time will be required than before for the water to boil, and it will not do so until the thermometer has risen considerably above 212°, depending upon the amount of air forced in; this also proves the effect of increased pressure in elevating the boiling point. On the contrary, if a flexible tube be attached to this flask, and the air be exhausted by the air pump, the water will boil at a temperature lower than 212°, because the natural pressure of the atmosphere is removed from it.

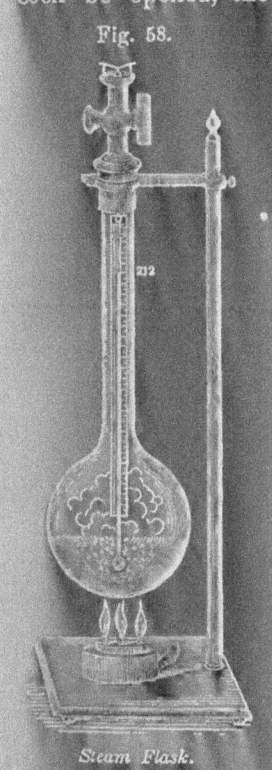

Fig. 58.

Steam Flask.

168. Elevation of the boiling point indicates Increase of Pressure. This principle is very satisfactorily illustrated in the apparatus of Dr. Marcet, represented in *Fig.* 59. B is a strong iron globe, about half filled with water, and having mercury at the bottom to the depth of

---

Describe the steam flask.—168. How may increase of pressure be inferred from the elevation of the boiling point?

about an inch; *t* is a thermometer screwed steam tight into the globe and graduated as high as 500°. It indicates the temperature of the steam in the upper part of the globe; *c* is a stopcock, which can be opened or shut at pleasure; *a* is a long and strong tube, graduated into inches and parts of an inch, open at both ends, and the lower extremity dipping beneath the level of the mercury. The water is made to boil vigorously by the flame of the lamp, and the stop-cock being open and steam escaping, the thermometer will indicate the temperature of 212°, and the mercury remain stationary at the foot of the tube. The pressure of the steam at this moment, in the interior of the apparatus is sufficient to drive out all the air, and amounts to 15 lbs. upon every square inch. If the stopcock be now closed, the steam, having no avenue of escape, begins to collect in the top of the globe, and to react upon the water. The pressure thus created puts a stop to the boiling of the water. The heat proceeding from the lamp is no longer wanted in order to become latent in the vapor, there being no vapor formed; the temperature of the whole apparatus rises, and the thermometer every moment indicates a temperature steadily increasing above 212°. At the same time the increased pressure causes the mercury to rise in the tube, *a*, and it at length makes its appearance above the globe, so as to be plainly seen. As the temperature rises higher and higher, the mercury in *a* advances steadily upwards, indicating the gradual increase of the pressure in the interior of the boiler. When the mercury has reached the height of 30 inches, it is an indication that the pressure in the interior of the boiler is now two atmospheres, or twice 15 lbs. to the square inch, i. e., 30 lbs.; and if the thermometer be noted at this moment it will be found to stand at 250°. When the thermometer

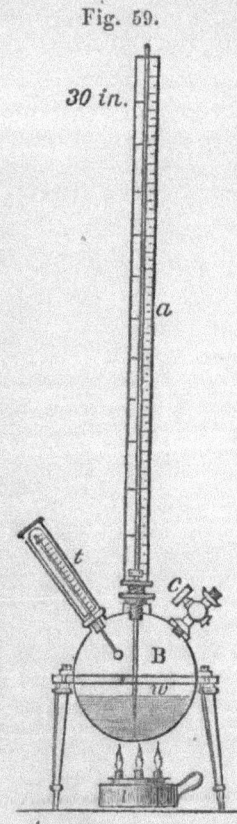

Fig. 59.

Marcet's Apparatus.

Describe Marcet's apparatus. What reduction must be made upon the actual pressure in order to calculate the explosive force?

THE CULINARY PARADOX. 157

has reached 275° the mercury will have risen 60 inches in the tube, and the pressure will be 45 lbs. to the square inch; when it has attained 294°, the mercury in the tube will have ascended 90 inches, and the pressure will have increased to four atmospheres, or 60 lbs. to the square inch. As temperature rises, pressure steadily increases, because with every addition of heat the greater the tendency of the water to flash into steam, and eventually the globe will be burst by the process. If now, under these circumstances, the stop-cock be suddenly opened, the pressure will be removed from the surface of the water, a large quantity will flash into steam, absorbing an immense amount of heat, and the mercury in the thermometer will immediately sink to 212°. It is evident, therefore, that the temperature of the steam in a boiler is a sure exponent of the amount of the pressure in the interior.

The pressures just given are the actual pressures produced by the elastic force of the vapor, but as the atmosphere presses upon the outside of the globe with a force of 15 lbs. to the square inch, the pressure tending to burst the globe is found by deducting this amount from the actual pressure, and consequently 250° of the thermometer is said to indicate a pressure of 15 lbs., 275° a pressure of 30 lbs., 294°. a pressure of 45 lbs. to the square inch. The sudden falling of the thermometer to 212° on opening the stop-cock is explained by the immense absorption of heat consequent upon the rapid passage of so much water from the liquid to the aeriform state. That it is not owing to the escape of the steam, but to its formation, might be shown by discharging the steam into a closed vessel, heated to 212°, from which none of it could escape. At the close of the experiment the steam in the closed vessel would be found to be only at the temperature of 212°. The water in the boiler has then lost heat, but nothing else has been apparently heated by it. The diminution of temperature is due, therefore, to the sudden passage of a quantity of water into the state of vapor, by which a large amount of heat has been made latent and become insensible to the thermometer.

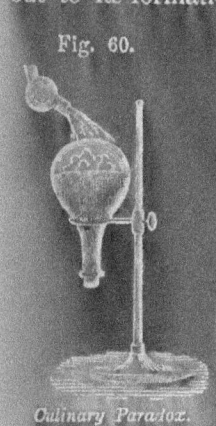

Fig. 60.

Culinary Paradox.

169. The Culinary Paradox. Water made to boil by the application of Cold. We

---

169. Describe the culinary paradox, and explain it.

138   EXPANSION OF WATER IN FORMING STEAM.

have seen that boiling has been made to cease in the steam flask, *Fig.* 58, by closing the stop-cock. It can be made to recommence by the application of cold water. The effect of the cold water is to condense the steam in the upper part of the flask; consequently there is a vacuum formed; pressure is removed from the surface of the water, and it will recommence boiling with great violence. If, at the moment when the water first begins to boil again, the stop-cock be opened, the air will rush in with a hissing noise, showing conclusively the existence of the vacuum. This experiment may be performed with an ordinary glass flask. Boil a little water, and when the steam is escaping, cork it tightly; take it from the lamp and pour cold water over the upper part; the boiling will recommence and proceed with vigor; apply hot water, and it will again cease. Remove the cork beneath the water and the inverted flask will be at once filled, showing the formation of a vacuum by the condensation of the steam. *Fig.* 60.

170. Expansion of Liquids in passing into Vapor,—especially water, in forming Steam. Vapors occupy more space than the liquids from which they are produced. Water, at its point of greatest density, viz., 39.5°, expands in passing into vapor, 1696 times, or in round numbers, 1700 times; i. e., a cubic inch of water makes about a cubic foot of steam. Alcohol expands 659 times; ether, 443 times. The amount of this expansion in the case of water may be readily shown by the apparatus represented in *Fig.* 61. The cylinder, *b*, is fitted with a steam-tight piston, *a p*. The weight of the piston is accurately balanced by means of the weight, *w*, so that it will remain stationary in any position in the cylinder in which it may be placed, without tending to move up or down, and exerting no pressure upon anything placed below it. Now let a very small quantity of water be introduced into the cylinder below the piston, and the heat of a lamp applied. The temperature of the water will steadily rise to 212°, after which

Fig. 61.

Expansion of Water.

170. What is the expansion which different liquids undergo in vaporizing? How may this be proved in the case of water? If water be boiled below 212° what effect has this on expansion?

it will remain stationary, and an invisible vapor or gas will be formed, and the piston gradually rise. This process will go on until the whole of the water has been converted into steam. On measuring the space occupied by the steam and comparing it with the space occupied by the water at the commencement of the experiment, it will be found to be 1696 times greater; in other words, the water, in passing into vapor, has expanded 1696, or nearly 1700 times; and as a cubic foot contains 1728 cubic inches, we may say in round numbers, that a cubic inch of water will make a cubic foot of steam. This expansion takes place against the pressure of the atmosphere, (the piston lifting the atmospheric column as it rises) which amounts to 15 lbs. on every square inch. If this pressure were diminished the water would expand more than 1700 times in passing into steam; if it were increased, it would expand less. In general, however, as the average pressure of the atmosphere is about 15 lbs. to the square inch, we conclude that water, passing into the state of steam, in the *open air*, expands 1700 times. If water be boiled at a temperature lower than 212° the expansion which it undergoes in passing into vapor will be proportionably increased; thus, if it be made to boil at 77°, one cubic inch will expand into 23,090 cubic inches of vapor; if it boil at 68°, it will expand into 58,224 cubic inches. This expansion of water, in passing into steam, is one of the moving forces in the steam engine, and the efficient working of this extraordinary machine depends upon this simple fact.

171. Condensation of Steam or its reconversion into Water, by decrease of temperature. One of the most remarkable properties of steam is its ready condensation into water, occupying 1700 times less space than itself as soon as its temperature is reduced below 212°. Thus, if into the cylinder, represented in *Fig.* 61, in which the piston has been driven up by the conversion of the water into steam, a little cold water at 32° be introduced beneath the piston, the steam will be instantly condensed into water, occupying 1700 times less space than the vapor; a vacuum will consequently be formed beneath the piston, and as the cylinder is open to the air at the top, the pressure of the atmosphere will drive the piston down with a force of 15 lbs. to every square inch. If the piston possess an area of one square foot the atmospheric pressure will be ob-

---

171. How may steam readily be reconverted into water? What effect is produced upon the steam in a steam cylinder by injecting cold water? What force is brought into play by this condensation?

140   THE STEAM ENGINE.

tained by multiplying 144, the number of square inches in this area, by 15=2160 lbs.; in other words, the atmospheric pressure, in this case, will be almost one ton. The completeness of the vacuum, and the degree of atmospheric pressure, will depend upon the temperature of the condensing water; if it be not so cold as 32° the vapor will not be entirely condensed, the vacuum not so perfect, and the atmospheric pressure proportionably diminished. Hence we have a second force, brought into play by the vacuum created by condensed steam. Both these forces, the expansion of water in vaporization, and the atmospheric pressure, are employed in the condensing steam engine.

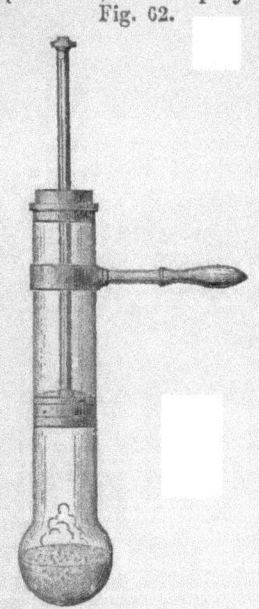

Fig. 62.

172. Wollaston's Steam Bulb. Both these forces are admirably illustrated by a little instrument represented in *Fig. 62*. It consists of a metallic bulb, surmounted by a cylinder of the same, into which a steam-tight piston is fitted. The bulb should be half filled with water and held over a lamp. When the water boils it expands, in passing into steam, 1700 times, and drives the piston up. Now remove the lamp and dip the bulb into cold water; immediately the steam is condensed, a vacuum is formed, the pressure of the atmosphere is brought into action, and the piston is driven down with very considerable force. In the steam engine this double process is repeated alternately on each side of the piston for every stroke. The great improvement of Mr. Watt, in the steam engine, consisted in condensing the steam in a condenser, separated from the cylinder, so as to avoid the necessity of cooling the cylinder below 212°, or the boiling point of water, for every stroke of the piston.

Wollaston's Steam Bulb.

173. The Steam Engine. This wonderful machine was perfected by Mr. James Watt, of Glasgow, in Scotland, about the year 1765. His great improvement consisted in the condensation of the steam in a vessel appropriated exclusively to this purpose, called the condenser. He was thus led to notice the

172. Describe Wollaston's steam bulb. What two forces does it illustrate?—173. Who invented the steam engine?

MR. WATT'S IMPROVEMENTS. 141

immense absorption of heat which takes place when water is converted into steam, and its evolution again when the steam is condensed into water,—a subject which had been previously investigated by Dr. Black, who was at that time Prof. of Medicine and Lecturer on Chemistry in the University of Glasgow, and an intimate friend of Mr. Watt. The following is the account given by Dr. Black of the successive steps in the improvement of the steam engine: "About that time Mr. Watt came to settle in Glasgow, as a maker of mathematical instruments; but being molested by some of the corporations, who considered him as an intruder on their privileges, the University protected him by giving him a shop within their precincts, and by conferring on him the title of 'Mathematical Instrument Maker to the University.' I soon had occasion to employ him to make some things which I needed for my experiments, and found him to be a young man possessing most uncommon talents for mechanical knowledge and practice, with an originality, readiness, and copiousness of invention, which often surprised and delighted me in our frequent conversations together. A few years after he was settled at Glasgow, he was employed by the Professors of Natural Philosophy to examine and rectify a small model of a steam engine which was out of order. This turned a part of his thoughts and fertile invention to the nature and improvement of steam engines, to the perfection of their machinery, and to the different means by which their great consumption of fuel might be diminished. He soon acquired such a knowledge on this subject that he was employed to plan and erect several engines, in different places, while at the same time he was frequently making new experiments to lessen the waste of heat from the external surface of the boiler, and from that of the cylinder. But after he had been thus employed a considerable time he perceived that by far the greatest waste of heat proceeded from the waste of steam in filling the cylinder. In filling the cylinder with steam, for every stroke of the common engine a great part of the steam is chilled and condensed by the coldness of the cylinder before this last is heated enough to qualify it for being filled with elastic vapor, or perfect steam; he perceived, therefore, that by preventing this waste of steam, an incomparably greater saving of heat and fuel would be attained than by any other contrivance. It was thus that, in the beginning of the year 1765, the fortunate thought occurred to

---

Give the history of its improvement.

him of condensing the steam by cold, in a separate vessel, or apparatus, between which and the cylinder a communication was to be opened for that purpose every time the steam was to be condensed, while the cylinder itself might be preserved perpetually hot, no cold water or air being ever admitted into its cavity." Such is Dr. Black's account of the invention of the steam engine. It was soon brought, by Mr. Watt, to the highest degree of perfection, so as to leave hardly anything to be desired, either in regard to its principles, or mechanical details. The model alluded to by Dr. Black is still preserved in the Cabinet of the University of Glasgow.

174. Two forms of the Steam Engine. There are two forms of it, differing essentially from each other, viz., the condensing and non-condensing engine. In the former, both the two forces described above, viz., the expansive force of steam, and the pressure of the atmosphere brought into play by its condensation, are employed; hence this is called the condensing engine, or, the low-pressure engine. In the latter, only one of the two forces described, viz., the expansive force of steam, is employed; and as only this one force is used, it is necessary, in order to obtain an equal effect, to make use of steam possessing an expansive power of at least 15 lbs. to the square inch greater than in the condensing engine; consequently this is called the non-condensing, or high-pressure engine.

175. Condensing and Non-condensing Engines. The difference between the two forms of the steam engine is indicated in *Fig.* 63. In 1, the piston having been driven down by the steam, is rising again by the pressure of a fresh supply from the boiler through the pipe, B. The steam that drove it down is issuing through the stop-cock at the top, which is open for its escape, into the air, and it is very evident that the piston in rising is acting against the pressure of the atmosphere, and has to lift a column of air of the same area with itself, extending to the upper limit of the atmosphere, and pressing with a weight of 15 lbs. upon every square inch; all of which the steam below the piston is obliged to raise. In order to raise this immense weight, amounting to nearly 2200 lbs. to the square foot, the steam must be of high pressure; and as it is also let off into the air and escapes after having done its work in driving the piston,

---

174. What are the two forms of the steam engine? State the difference between them. —175. Describe Fig. 63, showing the difference between the condensing and non-condensing engine.

THE MOST COMPLETE FORM 143

without being condensed, this form of the steam engine has received the name of the High-pressure and Non-condensing engine. In 2, the piston having been driven down by the force of the steam, is ascending by the pressure of a fresh supply from

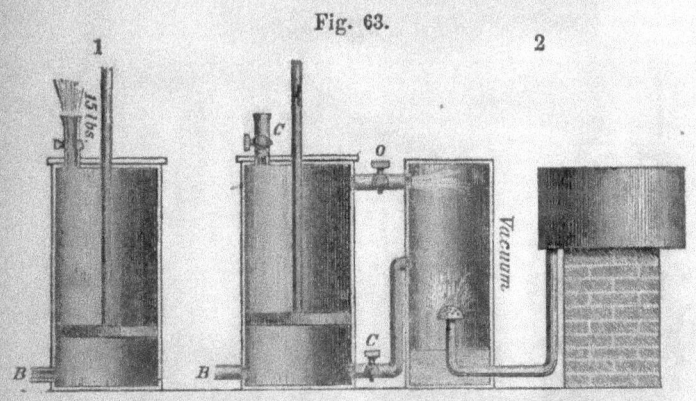

Fig. 63.

Principle of Non-condensing and Condensing Steam Engines.

the boiler through the tube B. The steam that drove it down, however, instead of escaping through the stop-cock C, which is closed, passes through the stop-cock O, into an adjoining vessel, C, called the condenser, where it comes into contact with a stream of cold water, by which it is immediately condensed into a quantity of water 1700 times less than itself, and a vacuum at once created. As soon as this takes place, the steam still remaining in the cylinder, rushes through O, into the condenser, where it is also at once condensed; thus the process goes on, until a vacuum, more or less perfect, depending upon the coldness of the condenser, is produced, not only in the condenser, but also extending into the cylinder. There being, therefore, a vacuum in the upper part of the cylinder, it is evident that the piston has no atmospheric column to lift, pressing with 15 lbs. to the square inch, and it need not, therefore, possess as much expansive force by exactly this amount: hence its name of Condensing and Low-pressure.

176. The Steam Engine in its most complete form. In the steam engine, in its complete form, there is an arrangement by which the steam from the boiler can be supplied to both sides of the piston alternately, and then, having done its work,

---

176. Describe the condensing steam engine in its most complete form. Show how the piston is made to work in a vacuum.

144   IS THE CONDENSING ENGINE.

Fig. 64.

The Condensing Steam Engine.

be discharged from both sides alternately into the condenser. In *Fig.* 63, the discharge pipes into the condenser are seen at o and c. Consequently there is always a vacuum in the cylinder, extending into it from the condenser, on that side of the piston opposite to that on which the steam from the boiler is pressing; so that, in moving in both directions, the piston is working in a vacuum, and the pressure of the atmosphere is altogether taken off. This constitutes the most perfect form of the steam engine, and is represented in *Fig.* 64. A represents the cylinder, having a portion of one side removed to show the interior. s is the pipe, through which steam enters from the boiler. U is the pipe conveying the steam from the cylinder to o, which is the condenser. Here it is condensed into water by cold water thrown in through the pipe T, by the pump R. The water thrown into the condenser for this purpose, and that which is formed by the condensation of the steam, is drawn off by the pump M, in order that the condenser may be prevented from filling, and is discharged continually into the well N. It is very hot from the latent heat given forth by the condensed steam, and advantage is taken of this by using it to replenish the boiler, which is done by means of the pump Q. The piston, therefore, it will be seen, works continually in a vacuum, and the motion communicated to it is transmitted by means of the working beam L, and the connecting rod I, to the crank K, by which an impetus is imparted to the fly wheel V. From the direction of the arrows it will be seen that the piston is going down, the connecting rod I is going up, and the fly wheel is turning towards the left. The non-condensing or high pressure engine resembles the above, exactly, except in the omission of the apparatus beneath the upper plate, viz., the condenser O, the pumps M and R. The pump Q is retained to feed the boiler. The pipe U, instead of continuing to O, is broken, turned upwards, and discharges steam by puffs into the air.

177. Latent Heat of the Condensing Engine. It is evident from the principles laid down above, that the condensation of this large amount of steam is attended by the giving out of the enormous quantity of latent heat which it contains, viz., 1000°, which has a tendency to heat the condenser very hot, and to impair its efficiency. It is evident, also, that if the condenser becomes heated to 212°, no more steam can be condensed. To prevent it from becoming thus heated, a great quantity of cold water must be used. The condensing engine can not, therefore, be employed except where a large amount of cold water can readily be obtained. It is unfitted, therefore, for use in locomotives. In consequence of the additional size of the engine and the larger amount of machinery required, it is unfitted for use in confined situations of limited extent, and in steamboats on shallow waters. The magnificent marine engines of ocean steamers are, however, always condensing engines, and so also are the ponderous engines used for draining mines and pumping water for aqueducts. The Cornish steam engine is a peculiar form of the steam engine used in the mines of Cornwall, for the purpose of raising water.

---

177. Explain the large amount of heat set free by the condensation of the steam in the condensing engine.

146 THE BOILER.

178. The Boiler. The steam engine consists of two parts, quite distinct from each other: 1st, the machinery, by which the power is made to produce motion; (this has been already described,) and 2d, the apparatus in which the power itself is generated. The Boiler is the instrument for the production of power. It consists of a strong copper or iron vessel, *Fig.* 65, made of

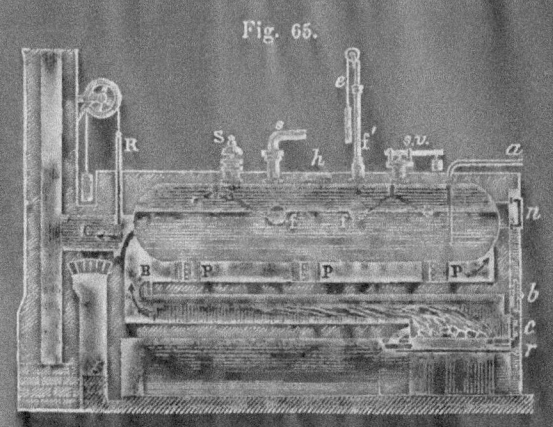

Fig. 65.

Boiler of Steam Engine.

well rolled plates of metal strongly riveted together. Usually it is cylindrical in shape, and if possible, the fire box containing the coals, and the flues by which the smoke is carried off, are contained within the boiler, in order that every particle of heat generated may go to the production of steam. The steam, as it is formed, collects in the upper part of the boiler, and fresh portions being continually added to it, all of which tend to occupy a space 1700 times greater than the water from which they are formed, it is obvious that its tension is steadily increasing, and a very powerful pressure exerted upon the water and the sides of the boiler. The temperature, at the same time, steadily rises, and if there be no opportunity for the steam to escape, the boiler will finally explode. To prevent such a catastrophe, a safety valve is provided; see $s\,v$ in *Fig.* 65. This consists of a small piece of iron or brass fitting tightly over an aperture in the top of the boiler, and confined in its place by a heavy weight. So long as the steam exerts a less pressure upon the under side of the movable plug, than the weight, it will remain

---

178. Into what two distinct parts may the steam engine be divided? Describe the construction and arrangement of the boiler.

in its place, and the steam can not escape; but whenever it has accumulated to such a degree as to press upon the plug with a power greater than the weight, it will raise it, and escape into the air, until the pressure in the inside is made equal to the pressure on the outside. Usually, this movable plug is kept in its place by a lever, from one end of which the weight is suspended. This may be seen at sv, in *Fig.* 65; also, at A, in *Fig.* 71. The pressure in the interior may be measured by means of the mercurial gauge that has been described in the account of Marcet's apparatus, (§ 168,) or by others depending on different principles. By the operation of the safety valve, and a careful observation of the gauges, the danger of explosion is guarded against. When the temperature of the water has risen to 250° there is a pressure of 30 lbs. to the square inch in the interior of the boiler; when it has mounted to 275°, there is a pressure of 45 lbs.; at 294°, a pressure of 60 lbs., &c.; but as the atmospheric pressure on the outside of the boiler, tending to bind its plates more firmly together, amounts to 15 lbs. on every square inch, the actual internal pressure tending to burst the boiler, or the working power of the steam, is the excess of the total pressure over 15 lbs., and is found by subtracting 15 from the number indicating the total pressure. The explosive force for 250° is, therefore, 15 lbs.; for 275°, 30 lbs.; 294°, 45 lbs. This fact must be constantly borne in mind in all calculations upon the pressure upon the inside of boilers. The steam, when formed, collects in the upper part of the boiler, and is conveyed to the cylinder by the pipe s, which is commanded by a stop-cock, under the control of the engineer; a is a pipe for supplying the boiler with water; n is an opening by which it may be entered and cleansed; b is a lower portion of the boiler, communicating with the upper by means of the tubes P P P, and intended to facilitate the production of steam; c is the fire box; r the grate; the course of the smoke and flame is indicated by the arrows; after passing beneath the lower boiler, they circulate around the upper, and finally escape by the chimney E, commanded by the damper R. The locomotive boiler, as will be seen presently, is arranged upon a somewhat different plan.

179. The Boiler is not only an instrument for converting water into vapor, but also for compressing this vapor. In order to obtain any mechanical power from steam, it is not sufficient simply to convert the water into vapor; if this be all that

---

179. How is the requisite compression of the vapor formed in the boiler effected?

is done the steam would have no more mechanical power than an equal volume of air of the same temperature: all that would have been accomplished would have been to convert water into an aeriform fluid, no more. In order to obtain any mechanical power from steam, it must be compressed, just as in the case of air. If we wish to make use of the elasticity of air as a moving power, we must compress it by powerful forcing pumps; a large quantity of air is thus packed into a small space, and as it tends to return to its original volume in consequence of its elasticity, it is evident that we have here a very considerable source of power. In the same way, if we wish to obtain power from steam, we must compress it, and at the same time elevate its temperature. Both these conditions are requisite. If steam be compressed without any addition to its temperature, a portion is reconverted into water, and its elastic force remains unchanged; if, however, it be powerfully compressed, and at the same time elevated in temperature, its elastic force is enormously increased. This will be made more clear hereafter. These conditions being preserved, the more powerfully it is compressed, the more violently does it tend to return to its original volume. The only difference is, that instead of compressing the steam by pumps, we do it by forming more and more steam from the water within the boiler, and every fresh formation more forcibly compresses that which existed before, and proportionably increases its elasticity. This soon generates an enormous power, which not only endangers the boiler, but also reacts upon the water, and tends to stop the formation of additional steam; to overcome this tendency the temperature must be steadily elevated. It is therefore by increasing the heat that the expansive power of steam is augmented; but the two do not increase at an equal rate; the power increases much faster than the temperature, and when we reach very high temperatures, such as 400°; an addition of 4° or 5° to the temperature of the boiler adds as much to the elastic power of the steam as 40° added to it at the temperature of 212°. It will be observed that for this process to go on, there must be a continued supply of water in the boiler; if the water has all boiled away then the steam is only increased in volume by the increase of temperature, at the same rate as so much air would be, i. e., for 1°, $\frac{1}{480}$ of the space it occupied at 32°. The steam being thus formed and thus compressed, tends to rush forth with great fury. It presses upon all areas of the boiler of equal size, with equal

MODE IN WHICH PRESSURE IS 149

power, and if a section of the boiler were movable, it would press it steadily outward.

180. Law of the Propagation of Pressure through Fluids. This equal distribution of pressure is owing to the law of the propagation of pressure through fluids, both in the state of liquids and in that of vapors or gases, viz., that a force applied to a fluid at one point, is propagated through it equally in all directions. This is illustrated in *Fig.* 66, where a closed vessel being entirely filled with water, and having a number of pistons pressed down upon the liquid on all sides, and there being two weights of five pounds each or a force of 10 lbs. applied upon the piston A, this pressure of 10 lbs. is propagated equally in all directions, and every one of the other pistons, B, C, D, E, having an equal area, tends to move outwardly with the same force, viz., 10 lbs. The same would be true if the vessel were filled with air, or any other aeriform fluid, like steam. Nor does it make any difference whether the internal pressure be produced from without as in *Fig.* 66, or from within by internal expansion, as it would be if this water were converted into steam, occupying 1700 times more space than before. In any case the pressure which is exerted upon any area of the inside surface of the boiler, as a foot square, for example, will be exerted to an equal degree upon every other area of equal size. Nor does the shape of the vessel make any difference, however irregular this shape may be. If a tube be carried from one vessel to another, at some distance, so long as this tube is open and the passage free from obstruction, the pressure upon any definite area in the first vessel will be propagated through the fluid in the tube, whether it be liquid or vapor, and be exerted to the same degree upon every equal area in the second vessel. Consequently if there be a pressure of 60 lbs. to the square inch at one point of the internal surface of a boiler, there is the same pressure to the square inch at every other point in the boiler, or in any closed vessel connected with the boiler by an open tube or pipe.

Fig. 66.

Pressure Propagated in Fluids.

---

180. State the law of the propagation of pressure through fluids.

181. Mode in which the Pressure is transmitted from the Boiler to the Cylinder. On attaching to the upper part of the boiler, B, a tube leading to the bottom of a cylindrical chamber, in which there is a movable piston, as is represented in *Fig.* 67, it is evident that the steam will at once fill the tube; the cylinder c will become a part of the boiler, and the steam will press upon the lower side of the piston P with the same force precisely as upon an equal area of the boiler. If the steam exert a pressure in the boiler of 60 lbs. to the square inch, it will exert the same pressure in the cylinder. If the piston in the cylinder have a weight upon it, which presses it down with the force of 60 lbs. to the square inch, it will not be moved from its position; but if it be pressed by a weight less than 60 lbs. to the square inch, it will be driven to the top of the cylinder. If, when it has reached this point, the steam through another pipe be brought to bear upon its upper side, while at the same time it is shut off from the lower side, and the steam confined there, be let off into the air, it is evident that the piston will be driven down again with the same force as it was driven up. The piston, then, may be looked upon as a movable section of the boiler, which is alternately driven up and down by the steam admitted upon its under and upper side; and if machinery be attached to this movable piston, it will participate in its motion.

Fig. 67.

Pressure transmitted from Boiler to Cylinder.

182. Explosion of Steam Boilers. A boiler like that represented in *Fig.* 65, if made of good materials, may be gradually heated to a degree much higher than 212°, without any danger of bursting, so long as the engine is working and the water covers all the parts which are exposed to the direct action of the flame, because, under these circumstances, no portion of the boiler can be heated hotter than the temperature of the water itself. But if the water should, from any cause, fall so low that some of the parts exposed to the flame should have no

---

181. How is the pressure transmitted from the boiler to the cylinder? Why may the piston be regarded as a movable section of the boiler?—182. What is the cause of the explosion of steam boilers, and how may they be prevented?

THE EXPLOSION OF BOILERS. 151

water upon the inside to keep them cool, these might become red-hot, and when the boiler was replenished with water, this coming into contact with the red hot iron, would instantly produce a vast volume of steam of immense expansive power, and before it could raise the safety valve and escape, the boiler would explode. Such accidents are very likely to happen immediately upon setting an engine in motion, after stopping it for a short time. During this interval of quiet, the water steadily boiling away, and its level falling, may at length sink below the top of the flues, and a portion of the boiler become heated very hot, no water being forced in to supply the place of that which is evaporated, in consequence of the stoppage of the pumps. If, at the same time, the safety valve be shut, the steam formed will react upon the surface of the water with so much force as finally to stop the ebullition, and keep its surface perfectly quiet, but still with a constantly increasing tendency to boil with vehemence, as we have seen illustrated in the steam flask, (§ 167.) Now, under these circumstances, let this pressure be removed by the starting of the engine. The water will recommence boiling with so much fury that it will be dashed against the top of the boiler, and coming into contact with the too highly heated portions, it will flash into steam of such expansive power that nothing can control it, and an explosion will result. Or, suppose that, the water boiling away, and the boiler becoming too hot, the safety valves at first are opened, so that the steam, as fast as formed, escapes, and the boiling is not checked as before, and afterwards, at the instant of starting, that these valves are closed; then the pumps beginning to work at the same time with the engine, speedily bring up the level of the water to the too highly heated iron, and an explosion results as before. It is a point, therefore, of the first importance, for the engineer to keep a vigilant eye upon the level of the water in the interior of the boiler. This may be observed by having stop-cocks at different levels, which from time to time must be opened to ascertain if they discharge water or steam; or by a curved tube of glass, connected with the boiler, in such a way as to show the height of the water. See o, in boiler, *Fig.* 126.

There are other means by which the same end may be attained. Let s, in *Fig.* 65, represent a steam whistle, which can be made to sound by pulling a wire from below, attached to the float, *f*, and let it be arranged in such a way that when the float

---

Why is it necessary to keep a vigilant eye upon the height of the water in the boiler? How may this be ascertained?

has sunk to a certain fixed point it will sound the whistle, then, whenever the water in the boiler has declined so far as to endanger its safety, the float descending with it will open the whistle, and sound the alarm. Again, let e be a weight, attached to a cord passing over a pulley, and descending through the upright pillar, f, until it enters the boiler and is attached to the float, f; as the float falls from the gradual sinking of the water, it draws the weight up, and being placed in full view of the engineer, indicates the danger within.

183. Boilers of Locomotives. The boilers of locomotives are constructed somewhat differently from others. One peculiarity of the locomotive consists in its rapid motion, and proportionably great consumption of steam. Four cylinders full of steam are required for every revolution of the wheels. The boiler must therefore be constructed in such a way as to produce steam very fast. To this end the fire box, D, *Fig.* 68, is entirely surrounded by water, so that all the heat produced is obliged to go to the formation of steam; the flame and smoke are then carried through a large number of small pipes, indicated by the arrow in the figure, which pass through the boiler, and terminate in a chamber immediately beneath the chimney. These tubes expose a very large heating surface, and are also surrounded by water; all the heat produced is therefore compelled to enter the water, and the formation of steam is made wonderfully rapid. In the figure, E represents the steam dome, from the upper part of which the steam is conveyed to the cylinders through the pipe F. In this manner the spray and water are prevented from surging into the cylinders. As the smallness of the tubes tends to diminish the draught, the steam, after having done its work in the cylinder, is discharged

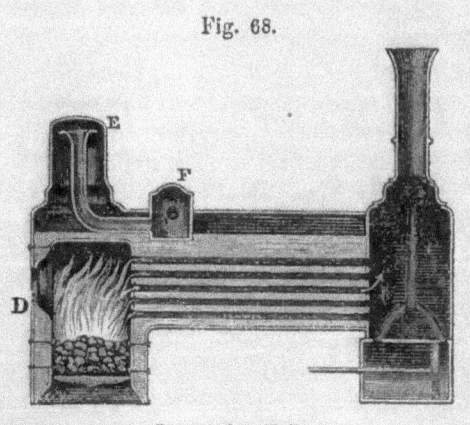

Fig. 68.

Locomotive Boiler.

---

183. Describe the boiler of the locomotive. Why is it necessary to make steam so fast? How is the draught maintained?

through a pipe directly into the air chamber beneath the chimney, and rushing violently upwards, drives all the air before it, precisely as the plunger of a pump would, if similarly situated. A vacuum is consequently created behind it, in the lower part of the chimney and air chamber; and this must be supplied by a rush of air through the fire grate, the fire box, and the tubes. The combustion is at once increased and made more and more vigorous with every puff of steam. In this way a draught is created equal to that of a chimney 80 or 90 feet in height; the more rapid the movement of the engine, the more powerful the draught, and the more abundant the production of steam. This mode of increasing the draught by discharging steam into the chimney is the great improvement made in the steam engine by Mr. Geo. Stephenson, by which it was adapted for use upon railroads.

When steam is discharged in jets through a pipe into the lower part of another tube, it always tends to produce a vacuum below it, and an arrangement of this kind is often employed for the purpose of ventilation. Steam thus escaping expands enormously as it enters the atmosphere, and so much heat becomes latent by this expansion that the hand placed in the jet actually experiences a sensation of cold, even though the temperature of the steam may be considerably higher than 212°. The cooling effect is increased by the rapid intermixture with the air.

184. The alternating movement of the Piston, how produced.—The Valves. It now remains to consider the means by which the steam is admitted alternately above and below the piston. This is accomplished by means of the valves. There are many different forms of valves; but the simplest, and on the whole the best form, is the sliding valve represented at G, *Fig.* 69. Upon the side of the cylinder is fitted a chest through which all the steam which is admitted to the piston must pass. This is called the steam chest. The object of the valve is to direct the steam from the steam chest first to one side of the piston and then to the other, at the same time allowing that upon the opposite side to escape either into the open air or into the condenser. In order to accomplish this end the two tubes conveying the steam to the two ends of the cylinder are made to terminate quite near each other, as is represented in *Figs.* 69 and 70, and over them there is made to slide, steam tight, the piece of metal, G, which is moved by means of the rod, E,

---

Show how steam can be used for ventilation.—184. Explain the mode in which the alternating motion of the piston is produced.

154 OF THE PISTON.—THE VALVES.

through the steam-tight packing box, B. When it has slid over one passage, it has opened the other, and *vice versa*. In *Fig.* 69, the passage, I, is open, and the passage, H, is closed. The steam is consequently pressing upon the under side of the pis-

Fig. 69. Fig. 70.

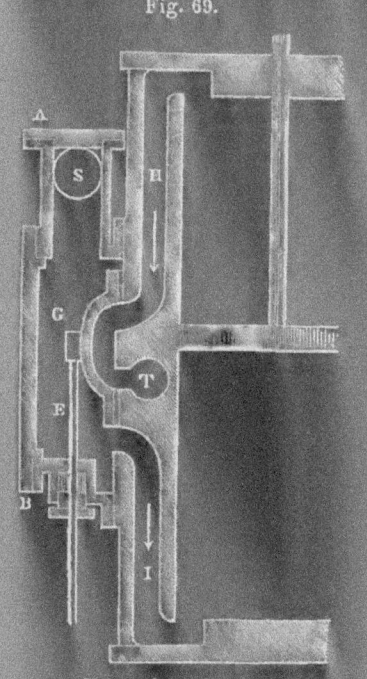

Valve driving Piston up. *Valve driving Piston down.*

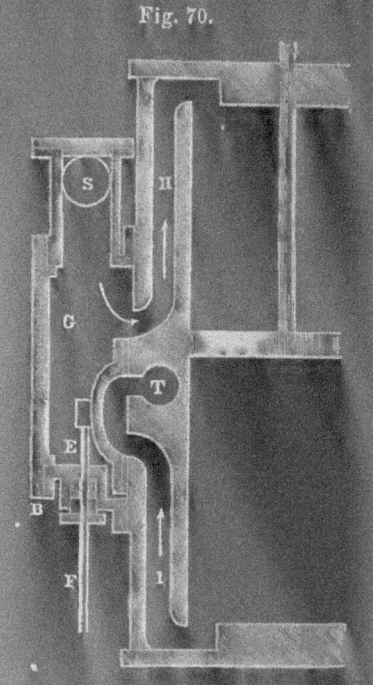

ton, and it is rising to the upper end of the cylinder. When it reaches the top, the valve is moved by the action of the engine so as to open the passage, H, as in *Fig.* 70, when the passage, I, becomes closed, and the piston begins to descend. In this manner, by moving this slide, the steam is admitted first to one side and then to the other of the piston.

The next point is to provide for the escape of the steam from the end of the cylinder towards which the piston is moving, into the open air, or into the condenser. This is accomplished by making the under side of the sliding valve hollow, so that, at the same time that it cuts off the tube over which it is moved from communication with the steam of the steam chest, it furn-

Describe the valves.

ishes a way of escape for the steam in the cylinder into the escape pipe, T. In *Fig.* 69, the steam from II is passing into the escape pipe, T, through the under side of the valve. In *Fig.* 70, the steam from I is passing into the same escape pipe through the groove on the underside of the valve. By this simple contrivance the alternate motion of the piston is produced.

185. Steam may be used expansively. When it is desired to make use of the direct pressure of the steam from the boiler for a portion only of the stroke of the piston, the steam is shut off, at the proper point, by a cut-off valve. The steam that has been admitted into the cylinder having been strongly compressed in the manner described in § 179, has still great elastic force, and tends powerfully to enlarge its volume, and it will continue to urge the piston to the end of the cylinder by the action of this expansive tendency, notwithstanding the connection with the boiler has been entirely broken. This is called using steam expansively, and is one of the inventions of Mr. Watt. The cut-off valve may be arranged so as to cut-off the steam at any portion of the stroke of the piston, when it has moved $\frac{1}{8}$, $\frac{1}{4}$, $\frac{1}{2}$ or $\frac{3}{4}$ of the length of the cylinder. It is obvious that the sooner the connection with the boiler is cut off the greater the saving of the steam, and the more economical the working of the engine. The cut-off is sometimes a separate valve, sometimes merely a modification of the slide valve. It is capable of adjustment by the engineer, according to the work to be performed by the engine.

186. The expansive power of Steam increases with its temperature. The expansive power of steam increases amazingly with the temperature at which it is formed, so that, if a portion of the material of the boiler, in consequence of the want of water, should have become heated to 415° F., the expansive force of the steam produced would be 300 pounds to the square inch; or upon one square foot 43,200 pounds, more than 20 tons. This pressure, however, must be diminished by 15 pounds to the square inch, because the pressure of the atmosphere on all sides of the boiler tends to counteract the expansive force of the steam to this extent. It is quite evident that a force of this degree of power would burst almost any boiler, however great its strength. The following table, founded

---

185. What is meant by using steam expansively? What is the advantage of cutting off steam?—186. What is the effect upon the expansive power of steam of increasing its temperature?

upon the experiments of Regnault, shows the increase in the pressure of steam corresponding with the increase in its temperature.

Regnault's Table showing the Pressure of Steam at different temperatures.

Pressure in atmospheres 15 lbs. to square inch.	Actual expansive pressure.	Temperature ° F.	Rise in temperature for each additional atmosphere.	Pressure in atmospheres 15 lbs. to square inch.	Actual expansive pressure.	Temperature ° F.	Rise in temperature for each ad. ditional atmosphere.
1		212°		11	150 lbs.	364°.2	7°.6
2	15 lbs.	249°.5	37°.5	12	165 "	371°.1	6°.9
3	30 "	273°.3	23°.8	13	180 "	377°.8	6°.7
4	45 "	291°.2	17°.9	14	195 "	384°.0	6°.2
5	60 "	306°	14°.8	15	210 "	390°.0	6°.0
6	75 "	318°.2	12°.2	16	225 "	395°.4	5°.4
7	90 "	329°.6	11°.4	17	240 "	400°.8	5°.4
8	105 "	339°.5	9°.9	18	255 "	405°.9	5°.1
9	120 "	348°.4	8°.9	19	270 "	410°.8	4°.9
10	135 "	356°.6	8°.2	20	285 "	415°.4	4°.6

This table corresponds very nearly with one constructed many years since by Dulong and Arago. They made the temperature of steam at 30 atmospheres, 418°.46; at 50 atmospheres, 510°.60. It will be observed that the number of degrees required to add an additional atmosphere is much smaller at high than at low temperatures, i. e., the greater the pressure, and the higher the temperature, the smaller the number of degrees necessary to be added in order to increase the elasticity and expansive power of the steam. Thus, if the steam be at 212°, it is necessary to add 37°.5 of heat in order to increase its pressure by 15 lbs.; while if it be at 410° only 4°.6 are required. This is one of the principal reasons for the increased economy of power in using steam at a high, rather than at a low pressure.

187. No economy of Fuel in boiling Water at a low temperature. As water may be made to boil at a temperature of 70° in a vacuum, it has been a question whether, by the removal of the atmospheric pressure from the boiler, a great economical advantage might not be gained in the saving of fuel. Mr. Watt ascertained, by careful experiment, that nothing is gained in this manner, because the lower the temperature at which the steam is formed, the greater amount of latent heat which it con-

---

Give the general results of Regnault's table.—187. Why is there no economy of fuel in boiling water at a low temperature? Who ascertained this fact?

tains. By condensing steam formed at this temperature, and observing the quantity of heat which it communicated to a given weight of water, he ascertained that its latent heat, instead of being about 1000°, was between 1200° and 1300°. It is now a well recognized principle that whatever be the temperature at which steam or vapor may be formed, the sum total of the heat contained in it, both sensible and insensible, is nearly the same. Thus, according to the experiments of Clement and Desormes, a certain weight of steam at 212°, condensed into water at 32°, gave out,

   Sensible heat, ... 180°.
   Latent heat, ... 950°. Total, 1130°.
The same weight at 250°, gave out,
   Sensible heat, ... 218°.
   Latent heat, ... 912°. Total, 1130°.
The same weight at 100°, gave out,
   Sensible heat, ... 68°.
   Latent heat, ... 1062°. Total, 1130°.

Consequently, whatever the temperature at which steam is formed, the total amount of heat required is nearly the same. Mr. Watt was of the opinion that this was strictly true; but Regnault has shown that the sum of the sensible and latent heat increases as the temperature rises; the amount, however, is so small that it may be neglected in practice. It will be remembered that the lower the temperature at which water boils, the greater the amount of its expansion in passing into vapor; consequently, the greater the amount of latent heat necessary.

Regnault's Table showing the sum of sensible and latent heat in steam at different temperatures:

Temperature.	Latent Heat.	Sum of Latent Heat and Sensible Heat.	Temperature.	Latent Heat.	Sum of Latent Heat and Sensible Heat.
32°	1092°.6	1124°.6	248°	939°.6	1187°.6
50°	1080°.0	1130°.0	266°	927°.0	1193°.0
68°	1067°.4	1135°.4	284°	914°.4	1198°.4
86°	1054°.8	1140°.8	302°	901°.8	1203°.8
104°	1042°.2	1146°.2	320°	889°.2	1209°.2
122°	1029°.6	1151°.6	338°	874°.8	1212°.8
140°	1017°.0	1157°.0	356°	862°.2	1218°.2
158°	1004°.4	1162°.4	374°	849°.6	1223°.6
176°	991°.8	1167°.8	392°	835°.2	1227°.2
194°	979°.2	1173°.2	410°	822°.6	1232°.6
212°	966°.6	1178°.6	428°	808°.2	1236°.2
230°	952°.2	1182°.2	446°	795°.6	1241°.6

How may it be proved? Give the general results of Regnault's table.

188. No economy in using Liquids which boil at a lower temperature than Water. As alcohol and ether boil at lower temperatures than water, it might be thought that it would be economy to use them, instead of water, as sources of power. This, however, would not be the case, even though they could be procured for nothing, for two reasons: first, on account of the comparatively small expansion of these liquids in passing into vapor. Thus, a cubic of water yields 1700 cubic feet of steam; a cubic foot of alcohol yields only 493 cubic feet of vapor. It is necessary, therefore, to boil away more than 3 cubic feet of alcohol in order to make 1700 cubic feet of alcoholic vapor and create a moving power equal to that of steam. A cubic foot of ether yields only 212 cubic feet of vapor; it is necessary, therefore, to boil away 8 cubic feet of ether to make 1700 cubic feet of ethereal vapor. This would require a corresponding enlargement of the boiler, and many of the other parts of the engine. Secondly, to form 1700 feet of alcoholic and ethereal vapor would require more heat than to form 1700 cubic feet of steam. Thus, the latent heat of steam is 1000°; the latent heat of an equal volume of alcoholic vapor is 1575°; the latent heat of an equal volume of vapor of ether is 2500°. Their cost in fuel would be proportionate to the sum of the sensible and latent heat of equal volumes; it is evident, therefore, that the advantage would be decidedly on the side of water. This may be clearly seen from the following table:

The Latent Heat contained in equal volumes of Water, Alcohol, Ether, and Spirits of Turpentine:

A cu. ft. of Water yields 1700 cu. ft. of Steam, latent heat, ... 1000°.
A cu. ft. of Alcohol yields 493 cu. ft. of Vapor, latent heat, 457°.
   493 cubic feet : 457° :: 1700 cubic feet : $x°$ = ... 1575°.
A cu. ft. of Ether yields 212 cu. ft. of Vapor, latent heat, 312°.
   212 cubic feet : 312° :: 1700 cubic feet : $x°$ = ... 2500°.
A cu. ft. of Spts. Turp. yields 192 cu. ft. of Vapor, latent heat, 183°.
   192 cubic feet : 183° :: 1700 cubic feet : $x°$ = ... 1620°.

The heat, therefore, required to produce an equal amount of mechanical power from water, alcohol, ether, and spirits of turpentine, is as 1000° to 1575° to 2500° to 1620°.

189. Super-heated Steam. Steam which receives an accession of heat after it has been separated from the water that

---

188. Why is there no economy in using liquids which boil at a lower temperature than water? Show this from the table in the case of alcohol, ether, and spirits of turpentine. —189. What is meant by super-heated steam?

formed it, by passing through a series of hot pipes, acquires some important properties which distinguish it from ordinary steam. In the first place, it has more expansive power, and this may be imparted to it without any additional expenditure of fuel. Secondly, it is not so readily condensed as common steam; ordinary steam returns at once to the liquid state as soon as its temperature is at all reduced; but in the case of super-heated steam no part of it can return to the liquid state until it lose all the heat which has been imparted to it by the super-heating process. For this reason super-heated steam is often employed in high-pressure steam engines, in which it is considered important to prevent the condensation of the steam as much as possible during its progress through the cylinder; in this manner all condensation is avoided until the steam has been allowed to escape into the air. It is formed by causing the steam, after it has been made in the boiler, to pass through a series of very hot tubes before it is allowed to enter the cylinder.

190. Papin's Digester. The solvent powers of water are greatly increased by the high temperature which may be given to it by pressure. Thus, as we have seen, at the pressure of two atmospheres, or 30 pounds to the square inch, the temperature of water is 250°; at three atmospheres, 275°. This increased solvent power is turned to good account in Papin's Digester, which consists of a very strong metallic vessel, upon which the lid, c, fits steam tight and is confined by a powerful screw; a safety valve is provided to prevent explosion. The water and the substances to be dissolved must be introduced before the top is screwed down. By this instrument gelatine and albumen have been extracted from bones and applied to the formation of various valuable products. These bones might be boiled at the temperature of 212° for an indefinite period, without change. This apparatus is of the greatest utility for boiling vegetables and meats at points of great elevation, where the pressure of the atmosphere is so low that the heat of water at the boiling point is not sufficient for cooking. By enclosing these articles in a vessel of this description the heat may be increased to the required degree without the slightest difficulty. On the same principle, the cooking of vegetables at ordinary levels may be quickened by covering the pot containing them with a lid firmly held in its place by a few bricks. Steam, heated to a high temperature by passing through red-hot pipes, may also be used for the same purpose; and for converting

---
190. Describe the construction and use of Papin's digester.

160   THE SPHEROIDAL STATE.

Fig. 71

Papin's Digester.

wood into charcoal by driving off all the volatile portions, leaving the pure carbon behind; also for the distillation of oils, and the extraction of lard and fat from the bodies of animals. Steam may be heated hot enough to melt lead and to set wood on fire.

191. The Spheroidal State. Though heat is the cause of ebullition, and a sufficient amount of it would no doubt produce the vaporization of the most refractory substances, yet a high degree suddenly applied to liquids vaporizes them more slowly than a lower degree. Water thrown on a plate of iron, or silver, heated to redness, instead of instantly flashing into steam, rolls upon its surface in globules, and is a long time in disappearing. This is occasioned by an atmosphere of vapor that is at once formed around the globules of water, which, being a poor conductor of heat, cuts it off from the action of the hot plate, and by its elasticity actually interposes a cushion between them and elevates the globule slightly above the plate. This elevation of the drop above the plate is perceptible by the eye. The apparatus for showing this is represented in *Fig.* 72.

---
191. Explain the spheroidal state.

THE SPHEROIDAL STATE EXPLAINS 161

A lamp, called an eolopile, is mounted upon a foot, provided with screws, so that it may be adjusted to an exact level. Immediately over it is placed a smooth plate of silver, which is heated red-hot by the inflammation of the alcohol in the eolopile. In the middle of this plate is placed a hollow cylinder, open at both ends, also of silver, and having a longitudinal slit on two opposite sides, at equal distances from each other. Three or four grains of water, blackened by lamp-black, are then poured into the cylinder, and its top is covered by a small disk of metal. The water is immediately thrown into the spheroidal state, and if a candle be placed directly opposite to the slit on one side, and the eye applied to the other, it will be seen that the water does not rest upon the hot plate, but is supported above it. The electric spark can also be seen through the same interval, between the plate and the drop. Thus situated, water is said to be in the spheroidal state, from the spheroidal form it assumes in rolling upon the red-hot plate. The apparatus for performing these experiments is represented in *Fig.* 73. The red-hot capsule of silver or copper may be filled nearly full of water without its boiling, and if a thermometer be dexterously introduced, the temperature will be found to be about 205°, instead of 212°. Under similar circumstances the temperature of alcohol is 168°, instead of 176°, its boiling point; ether 93°, instead of 96°; sulphurous acid only 13°, considerably below the freezing point of water. For water to pass into this state it is necessary that the plate or capsule have attained the temperature of at least 340°. If at this mo-

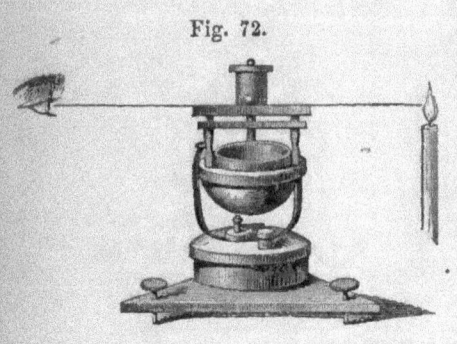

Fig. 72.
Space between the Hot Plate and the Drop.

Fig. 73.
205°
Temperature of Water in Spheroidal State.

Describe the experiments.

162   THE EXPLOSIONS OF BOILERS, ALSO

ment the red-hot capsule, nearly full of water, be quickly and carefully removed from the flame and placed upon a tripod stand, it gradually cools, and the water being less and less repelled, at length comes into direct contact with the metal, bursts into steam with explosive violence, and is projected in all directions, affording an excellent illustration of increased activity of ebullition produced by diminution of temperature, *Fig.* 74. Even if the water be boiling, its temperature sinks from 5° to 7° below the boiling point at the moment it falls on the heated surface, i. e., from 212° to 207°.

Fig. 74.

The Lamp Removed.

192. It explains the explosions of Steam Boilers. If a copper flask be heated red-hot by a powerful lamp, a large quantity of water may be introduced into it through a fine tube, without its boiling, and a cork securely fitted to its mouth. If now the lamp be extinguished, as the flask cools, the water at length comes into contact with the metal, flashes into steam, and the cork is driven out with great fury. This is thought by some to be the state of things in the interior of steam boilers when explosions are produced by diminishing the heat of the fire; *Fig.* 75.

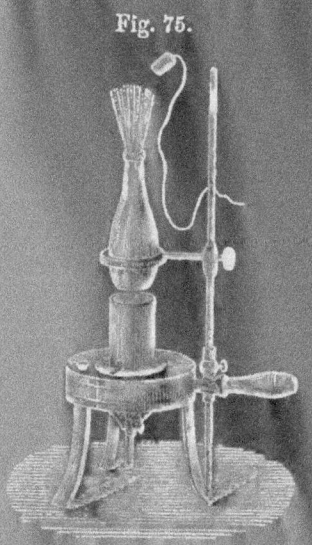

Fig. 75.

Explosion of Boiler. Lamp Extinguished.

On the same principle a red-hot copper ball may be introduced into water at the temperature of 75°, and remain visibly red-hot for a few seconds. The vapor of steam which surrounds the ball for a time prevents the contact of the fluid; *Fig.* 76. As soon as the ball has sufficiently cooled, the water ceases to be repelled by the envelope of steam, and coming into contact with the hot copper, is at once converted into steam, scattering the liquid in every direction; *Fig.* 77.

---

192. Show how it may explain the explosions of boilers. Explain the red heat of a copper ball under water. Show how water and mercury may be frozen in a red hot crucible.

THE RED HEAT OF METALS UNDER WATER. 163

Fig. 76.

Ball of Copper Red-hot under Water.

Fig. 77.

Red-hot Ball Cooled.

On the same principle the human hand, moistened with water, may be dipped with impunity into a vessel of melted lead, or iron, the vapor that is formed by the moisture, for a certain length of time, keeping off the melted metal. In pouring glass into wooden moulds it is usual to introduce first a small portion of water. By passing into the spheroidal state it is repelled from the glass, so that it does not injuriously cool it, and at the same time protects the wood. In performing these experiments, provided the hot surface be a sufficiently good conductor of heat, the nature of the material is unimportant. Silver, platinum, copper and iron, may all be used. One liquid may be thrown into the spheroidal state upon the surface of another, as water, alcohol, or ether, on the surface of hot oil. Solids can also be thrown into the spheroidal state by being placed on hot plates, as iodine on hot copper. The iodine is melted and thrown into the spheroidal state, emitting but little vapor; but if the lamp be removed so as to permit the capsule to cool, it suddenly bursts into a magnificent cloud of rich violet vapor. Liquefied sulphurous acid passes into the spheroidal state at 13°, notwithstanding it is in the interior of a red-hot crucible. If a drop of water be introduced into the acid, under these circumstances, it is instantly frozen. Solidified carbonic acid and ether pass into the spheroidal state at so low a temperature that, if a globule of mercury be introduced into the mixture, it is immediately solidified, and may be turned out solid upon the table.

193. Distillation. The difference between the boiling

Fig. 78

Distillation of Water.

LIEBIG'S CONDENSING TUBE. 165

points of liquids is sometimes made use of to separate them from each other, and to clear them of impurities. This process is called distillation. It consists in raising liquids into vapor by boiling, and then condensing the vapor by causing it to come into contact with some cold surface. This is usually accomplished by having a tube of considerable length leading from the top of a closed boiler and passing, in the form of a spiral, through a vessel which is kept filled with cold water, changed as fast as it becomes warm; *Fig.* 78. A is the boiler; C is the head of the still; D the pipe leading to the condenser; F the spiral tube in which the vapor is condensed; K the point where it is discharged into the bowl P; R is a discharge cock, by which water is constantly supplied to the vessel I J K L, so that a

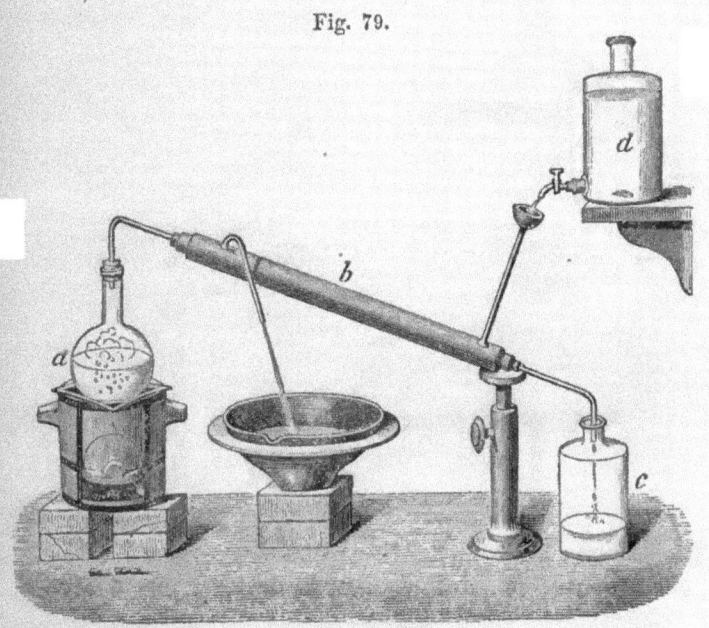

Fig. 79.

Liebig's Condensing Tube.

current of cold water is continually passing through it, entering at the bottom and issuing at the top. Sometimes, in place of the still, a condensing tube, *Fig.* 79, is employed. The principle is the same as in the still, but it is more convenient for use

---

193. Describe the process of distillation. The still. Liebig's condensing tube. The alembic.

in the laboratory when it is desired to distil small quantities of liquid, as it can readily be adapted to a flask of any size, as seen in the figure. It consists of a tube of copper, b, through which passes a large glass tube, closed at both ends by corks, by means of which connections may be formed at either end with smaller tubes. Through the copper tube cold water is continually circulating, entering by the funnel into the lower end, and flowing out above into the bowl. The vapor formed in the flask a, is condensed in b, and is collected, drop by drop, in the bottle, c. Again, the same process may be carried on in the Alembic, of which a representation is given in *Fig.* 80. It consists of a glass boiler, to which a head is adapted by grinding, in such a way that the vapor which is condensed upon its sides trickles into a gutter and issues, drop by drop, through the spout. This is a very convenient instrument for distillation on a small scale.

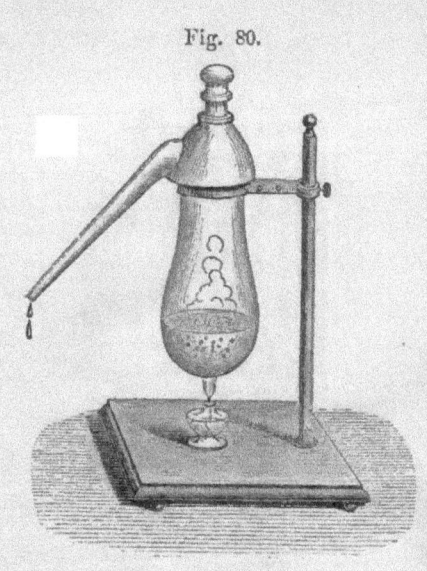

Fig. 80.

Alembic.

194. Uses of Distillation. One of the most important uses of distillation is the purification of liquids from the foreign substances with which they may be charged. Thus muddy water can be made clear by boiling it and condensing the vapor. The foreign particles are too heavy to rise with the vapor, and remain in the boiler. Sugar and salt dissolved in water can not rise in vapor; consequently they are left behind in the boiler, while the water is distilled off. In such cases the liquid left behind is concentrated, and this is sometimes one object of the process.

195. The separation of two Liquids by Distillation. Two liquids, thoroughly mixed, may be separated by this process, provided their boiling points are different. Thus, alcohol boil-

---

194. Explain the uses of distillation.—195. Show how two liquids may be separated by distillation.

THE USES OF DISTILLATION. 167

ing at 176°, while water boils at 212°, it is quite evident that the alcohol can be boiled and raised into vapor before the water is hot enough to do the same; and this being condensed, it will trickle down into the receiver, leaving the water behind it. To ensure the success of this process the temperature must be kept as near as possible to the boiling point of alcohol, and below that of water. On the same principle a volatile substance might be boiled off, and the liquid left behind made stronger and purer. This last process is sometimes called Condensation. The distillation of pure water from salt water, which is sometimes done on shipboard, is accomplished on the same principles. The salt and other impurities dissolved in the water can not rise with the vapor of water, on account of their greater specific gravity. The vapor, therefore, produced by the boiling of sea water, is comparatively pure, and when condensed in the worm of the still, proves a tolerably wholesome water. These processes, it can be readily seen are matters of great practical importance in the arts.

Experiments:—Effects of Heat: Vaporization.

1. **Vaporization.** Heat the cause; shown by heating water or alcohol.
2. Solids are sometimes vaporized without liquefying; shown by heating, in a Florence flask, camphor, sulphur, benzoic acid, sal ammoniac, arsenious acid. Let a second flask be inverted over the first, that the vapors which are formed may be collected and condensed. This is called sublimation.
3. **Ebullition.** Different liquids boil at different temperatures; this may be shown by placing a thermometer in boiling water, ether and alcohol. The last two should not be boiled over a lamp, but by immersion in boiling hot water, in test tubes.
4. Boil water in a metallic vessel and in a glass vessel, successively, using the same thermometer to show the effect of nature of the vessel upon the boiling point.
5. Call attention to the fact that in the boiling of water steam is formed at the bottom of the liquid, and not upon its surface.
6. The boiling point of liquids is elevated or depressed by the diminution or increase of the pressure of the atmosphere. Water, ether, alcohol, under the exhausted receiver of an air pump, boil respectively at 70°, −44°, and 36°.
7. The principal fact connected with vaporization, viz., the absorption and entire disappearance of a large amount of heat, is shown by placing a thermometer in a flask of water, and heating over a spirit lamp. The temperature of the water will rise until it reaches 212°. Above this point the mercury refuses to rise, though heat is continually entering the water at the same rate as before.
8. The same fact is shown by putting a thermometer into water at 90°, and placing the whole under the receiver of an air pump; exhaust, and as soon as the water begins to boil, the thermometer sinks, owing to the absorption of heat.
9. Again, if to a pound of water at 212°, 8 pounds of red-hot iron filings be added, the temperature of the water will be found, on trial, not to have been increased a degree. What has become of the heat of the red-hot iron?
10. If ether, at the ordinary atmospheric temperature, be subjected to diminished pressure by being placed under the exhausted receiver of an air pump, it will boil furiously, and the thermometer will immediately sink very rapidly, showing the absorption of a large amount of heat.
11. Place some pure water, at 62°, in a flask, over a good spirit lamp, and note the number of minutes it takes to rise to 212°, or to gain 150° of heat. Let it boil as many minutes more, and then note the temperature; it will be found to be still no higher than 212°; yet it has received actually 150° of additional heat. What has become of it?

12. Note the number of minutes that it takes the water in the last experiment to boil entirely away; multiply by the number of degrees of heat imparted per minute, and it will be found that 1000° of heat have been absorbed.

13. The heat thus absorbed is given out again when the vapor is condensed. Let a tall jar be filled with 11 cubic inches of water at 32°; condense steam at 212° into it until 2 cubic inches have been added to the 11, and it will be found that the temperature of the water has increased to 212°; i. e., the heat contained in steam at 212° is sufficient, when condensed, to heat $5\frac{1}{2}$ times as much water as that from which it was produced, from 32° to 212°; i. e., 180°. 180°$\times 5\frac{1}{2}$ = 990°. See *Fig.* 55.

14. The boiling point varies with variation in pressure; this may be shown by boiling water in a flask, tightly corked, having a thermometer in it. The steam being prevented escaping, reacts upon the water and soon exerts a powerful pressure, and the thermometer at once commences to rise. Remove the pressure, by allowing the steam to escape, and the temperature falls. This may be shown by Marcet's apparatus, or the steam flask. Shut the stop-cock of each, when the water commences boiling and the thermometer will rise above 212°; open it again, and it will immediately fall to 212°; exhaust the air from the steam flask, by the air pump, and it will boil at a temperature lower than 212°.

15. The Culinary Paradox. Boil water in a flask, close it quickly by a cork; remove it from the lamp, invert it, and apply cold water to the upper part; the boiling will recommence with violence; apply hot water and it will cease.

16. Wollaston's steam bulb and jar of cold water, shows the moving forces in the steam engine. Boil the water in steam bulb until the piston has reached the top of the cylinder; then dip in cold water, and the piston will descend.

17. That water expands 1700 times in vaporizing, may be shown by a cylinder in which there is a cubic inch of water, fitted with a piston. The water is boiled away and the piston is forced up until the capacity of the space below it amounts to 1700 cubic inches.

1. Spheroidal State. Heat a copper ball red-hot in a powerful lamp, and dip it quickly into water at temperature of 96°, in a glass jar. It will remain red-hot for a considerable length of time.

2. Drop water into a red-hot capsule of copper, until it is nearly full; then remove the lamp. The water will not boil until the lamp is taken away.

3. Drop water into a red-hot flask of copper and cork it tightly; remove the lamp; the cork, in a few moments, will be driven out with great violence.

4. Heat a copper dish, pierced with holes, red-hot, and drop a little water upon it gently from a glass dropping tube; the water will not run through; remove the lamp and the water will then readily flow.

5. Drop liquefied sulphurous acid into a red-hot capsule of platinum, and test the temperature with a thermometer.

6. Drop water into a red-hot platinum capsule until it is quite full, and then insert a delicate thermometer; the mercury will only rise to 205° F.

7. Throw a mixture of solidified carbonic acid and ether into a red-hot platinum capsule; the ether will almost immediately catch fire, producing a powerful blaze; introduce a thermometer into the mixture beneath the flame, and the mercury will be frozen. This is owing to the low temperature at which the carbonic acid is thrown into the spheroidal state.

8. Introduce into the same mixture a small platinum spoon filled with mercury; it will be frozen, and may be turned out upon the table in the solid state.

9. Introduce a little water in the same manner into the same mixture, and it also will be frozen, and may be turned out upon the table as ice.

10. Throw a few grains of iodine into a red-hot platinum crucible, over a lamp, and it will vaporize slowly in consequence of being thrown into the spheroidal state at a low temperature, and only a little heat reaching it; remove the lamp, and it will at once burst into a splendid violet cloud.

11. For these experiments there is needed a powerful alcohol vapor lamp, and thick capsules of copper, platinum, or silver, which retain heat for some time.

1. Distillation. Fill a common retort, half full of water, and boil it slowly over a spirit lamp; the vapor will condense in the neck of the retort and trickle drop by drop from its beak into a cup placed to receive it.

2. Take some well water and pour into it a few drops of sol. of oxalic acid; a white cloud will be produced, showing the presence of lime in the water. Pour the same water into a retort and distill as before; collect the distilled water and test for lime again; no lime will be found, showing that the water has been purified by distillation.

3. Dilute alcohol with water until it will no longer inflame when a taper is put into it; then pour the mixture into an alembic, having a thermometer in it; heat to 180°, not higher; vapor will rise and condense in the neck, and finally fall, drop by drop, into a wine glass placed to catch it; apply the taper and it will burn, showing that the alcohol

has been separated from the water. This will show how alcohol is separated from watery solutions.
4. Try the same experiment with wine.
5. Ditto with brandy diluted with water; with other liquors.
6. Boil muddy or turbid water in a retort, and observe the clearness of the residual water.

§ V. Effects of Heat:—Evaporation:

196. Evaporation. Evaporation has been described as the second mode of vaporization. It differs from ebullition, in taking place from the surface of liquids, while ebullition consists in the formation of vapor at the bottom of a liquid, immediately in contact with the surface of the boiling vessel, and accompanied by more or less commotion in the fluid as the vapor rises through it. Evaporation is a slow and quiet process, unattended by violent action; ebullition is rapid, and must be kept up by artificial means. Evaporation goes on at common temperatures, and may take place even at the lowest, and during the coldest seasons; while ebullition requires a high degree of heat, or at least the removal of atmospheric pressure.

197. Evaporation takes place at common temperatures; Heat its cause. To prove that evaporation takes place at natural temperatures, nothing more is necessary than to expose a quantity of water to the open air, in a shallow vessel; the liquid will be found gradually to diminish, and will finally disappear entirely. If a quantity of water, or ether, be carefully weighed, at the end of an hour it will be found to have lost weight very perceptibly. It was for a long time thought that the air was the cause of evaporation, and that, in consequence of its affinity for different liquids, it dissolved them with varying degrees of rapidity, as water dissolves the different salts; but it is impossible to attribute the effect to this cause, for it is an established fact that evaporation takes place *in vacuo*, that the air positively retards the process, and that one of the best means of accelerating it is to remove the air altogether. *The sole cause of evaporation is Heat.* We know that this is true in the case of ebullition, because we perceive the actual application of the heat; but in the case of evaporation it is not so apparent, be-

---

196. What is the second mode of vaporization? In what respects does evaporation differ from ebullition?—197. Prove that evaporation takes place at common temperatures. Show that it is produced by heat, and not by the action of the air.

cause there is no actual application of heat, and the amount required is gathered up silently and quietly on every hand. It would appear that in the liquid state the particles of matter having already begun to separate from each other and acquire facility of motion, are readily pushed still further apart by the heat which liquids, at ordinary temperatures, collect, that they at length cease to oppose any barrier to the passage of light, become invisible, and lighter than air, and finally rise and escape. The experiments of Dr. Dalton not only prove that heat is the true cause of the formation of vapor, but also that the actual quantity which can exist in any given space is dependent solely upon temperature. If a little water be placed in a dry glass flask, a quantity of vapor will be formed proportionate to the temperature; at 32° the flask will contain but a very small quantity of vapor; at 40° more vapor will exist in it; at 50° it will contain still more; and at 60° the quantity will be still further increased. If, then, under these circumstances, the temperature of the flask be again suddenly reduced to 40° a certain portion of the vapor will be reconverted into water; the quantity which retains the form of vapor remaining precisely the same as when the temperature was originally at 40°.

198. The amount of Vapor formed, and its elasticity, are proportionate to the temperature. Vapors, like gases, possess a certain elastic force; by this is meant that they possess a tendency to expand indefinitely, and are only prevented from doing so by the pressure of counteracting forces, of which the most important is the pressure of the atmosphere. If confined in a closed vessel a vapor exerts a certain pressure upon the sides of the vessel, in consequence of its elasticity or tendency to expand, and the degree of this pressure, and the amount of vapor formed, will depend upon the temperature to which the vessel is subjected. If the vessel be a bottle, tightly closed, and containing a small amount of water, while the remainder of the space is filled with air, the air within the bottle will not prevent the liquid from evaporating; a certain amount will pass into the state of vapor, depending upon the temperature; its elastic force will be added to the elastic force of the air confined in the bottle, and a pressure exerted upon the inside, tending to burst it. If, under these circumstances, the stopple of the bottle be removed, a portion of the mixed air and vapor will rush out: if

---

198. Prove that vapors, like gases, possess elasticity, and exert pressure upon the inside of a vessel containing them. What effect has increase of temperature upon the elastic force of vapors? What degree of force may be exerted by this means?

THE AMOUNT OF VAPOR AND ITS 171

the vessel employed be a bell glass, closed at the top, and open at the bottom, having a small quantity of water in it, and placed in a bath of mercury, the mercury will be depressed as the vapor is formed, showing that the elastic force of the gaseous contents of the bell glass has been increased. If the temperature be steadily raised the amount of vapor formed, and the elastic power of the mixed air and watery vapor, will increase at an equal rate, and the pressure upon the sides of the vessel will be correspondingly augmented. When 212° is reached the water will begin to boil, and the pressure be still further augmented; as the temperature rises beyond this point the pressure will go on, increasing in force, and eventually reach such a degree that no amount of external pressure can resist it, and the vessel will be rent in twain. The tendency, therefore, for a liquid to pass into vapor, is not only due to heat, but is heightened as the temperature increases, and when a certain degree has been attained, becomes irresistible.

Fig. 81.

199. These truths illustrated by experiment. Let D C A be a glass tube, curved into a siphon, the upper extremity open to the air, the other closed; let the tube be half filled with mercury, so that it will enclose about an inch of air in the short leg, and a drop of liquid ether be introduced in such a way as to rise through the mercury, and enter the space filled with air; this may be readily done by a skillful manipulation of the apparatus. As soon as the liquid reaches the confined air the mercury in the short leg will be depressed below its former level; this depression is due to the elastic force of the vapor of ether formed. If the tube be dipped into warm water, at temperature of 100° *Fig.* 81, the column of mercury will be still further depressed, and the more as the temperature rises; if, on the contrary, the temperature be diminished, the column of mercury in the short leg will rise, showing that the elastic force is diminished. From this experiment, it is clear

The amount and elasticity of Vapor proportioned to Temperature.

---

199. Prove this fact by experiment. Describe *Fig.* 81.

that the liquid ether introduced into confined air is not prevented from passing into vapor by the pressure of the confined air, nor by the pressure of the excess of the column of mercury in the long leg over that in the short leg, nor by the atmospheric pressure which is operating upon the mercury through the open end of the tube, but that it proceeds in spite of these opposing forces, and even acts against the whole pressure of the atmosphere at D. It further appears that this elastic force is increased by heat, and is diminished by cold. If, instead of leaving a space filled with air in the short leg of the tube, it be entirely filled with mercury, and a drop of liquid ether introduced, the same effect will result; the mercury will be immediately depressed in the short leg, and the more, the higher the temperature employed; it will also be seen that the vapor formed is an elastic, transparent, and invisible fluid, like the air.

200. The rapidity of evaporation varies with the pressure to be overcome; in a Vacuum, it is instantaneous. In the preceding experiment the evaporation of the liquid goes on very slowly and gradually, on account of the pressure of the mercury and of the atmosphere, which must first be overcome; if this pressure be diminished it will proceed more rapidly; if it be entirely removed, the evaporation will be instantaneous. In a vacuum, this counteracting pressure is entirely removed, and consequently, if a small portion of any vaporizable liquid be introduced, its vapor will immediately fill the whole of the vacant space. The quantity and elasticity of the vapor will depend upon the temperature, and they will both be precisely the same as though the evaporation had taken place in air at the same temperature, instead of a vacuum; the only difference in the two cases will be that, in a vacuum, the evaporation takes place instantaneously, while in the air, time is required for its diffusion, owing to the pressure which the air exerts; and in the vacuum, the elasticity of the vapor is the only force tending to depress the mercury, while in air, the elasticity of the vapor added to that of the air, is the depressing force, and consequently produces a greater effect. This may readily be proved by the following experiment. Let A, *Fig.* 82, be a glass tube, about 36 inches in length, open at the lower end, and let it be completely filled with mercury, closed with the finger, and inverted, in a vessel also of mercury. As soon as the finger is withdrawn, the mercury

---

200. What effect has pressure upon the rapidity of evaporation? How does evaporation proceed in a vacuum?

THE RAPIDITY OF EVAPORATION 173

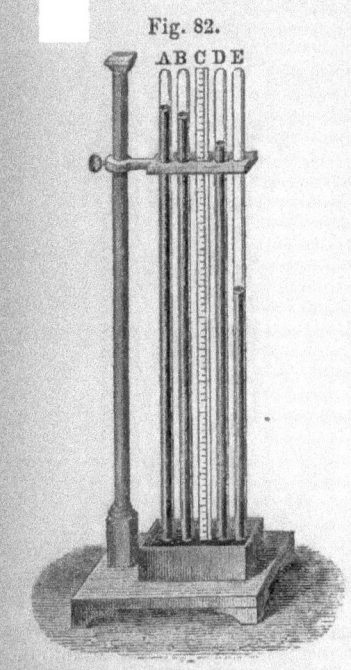

Fig. 82.
A B C D E

The rate of evaporation of different Liquids unequal.

will at once sink in the tube till the height of the top of the column above the level of the mercury in the lower vessel is about 30 inches. The reason of this is, that the weight of a column of mercury of this height is exactly equal to the weight of a column of air of an equal base, extending to the extreme limits of the atmosphere; and the column of mercury, and that of air, exactly balance each other. All the space in the interior of the tube, above 30 inches, is entirely free from air, and a perfect vacuum, sometimes called the torricellian vacuum, after Torricelli, a celebrated Italian philosopher. If now, a drop of ether be introduced into the open end of the tube, beneath the mercury, it will rapidly rise, in consequence of its superior lightness, until it reaches the vacant space; a portion of it will then immediately flash into vapor, and the elasticity of the vapor formed will at once depress the mercury considerably below the point at which it stood a moment before, as is seen in the tubes B, C, D, E. The quantity and elasticity of the vapor will in all cases be exactly proportional to the temperature, and the mercury will continue to sink until as much of the liquid ether has evaporated as the temperature is capable of sustaining in the vaporous state. The vacuum will then be saturated with vapor, i. e., it will hold as much vapor as is capable of existing in it at that particular temperature. If the temperature be elevated above this point, more ether will be evaporated, and the mercury still further depressed; if the temperature be lowered, some of the vapor will be condensed into the liquid state again, and the mercury will rise.

201. The amount of evaporation of different liquids in a vacuum, at the same temperature, is unequal. Let the four

Describe the experiment by which this is proved.—201. Show that the rapidity of evaporation of different liquids in a vacuum is unequal.

174   VARIES WITH PRESSURE.

Fig. 83.

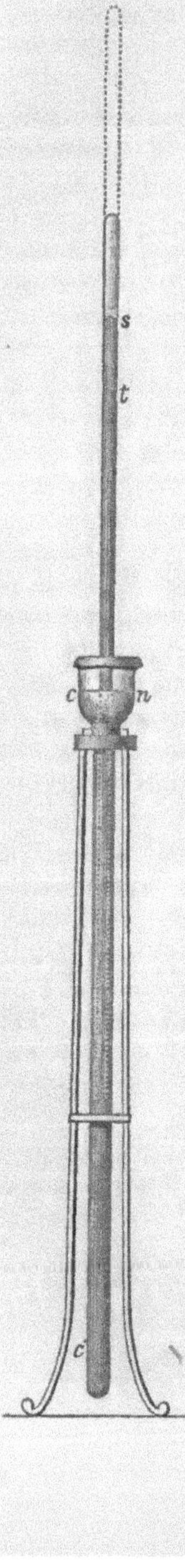

Variation in pressure makes no change in the elastic force of Vapor.

tubes, A, B, D, E, *Fig.* 82, be all filled with mercury, in the manner already described, and let the mercury in each have sunk to 30 inches, leaving a vacuum above it in each tube; let the tube A be preserved, unchanged, as a standard for the others, and into the tubes B, D, and E, let some drops of water, alcohol and ether, be respectively introduced. As soon as they reach the vacuum in the upper part of each tube, the mercurial column in each case will be depressed, but not to the same extent in all. In the tube D, containing the alcohol, it will be more depressed than in the tube B, and in the tube E, much more depressed than in either B, or D. This shows that, at the same temperature, the vapors of different liquids do not possess the same elastic force; at 68° the elastic force of the vapor of ether is nearly 25 times greater than that of the vapor of water.

202. **The elastic force of the vapor in a saturated space does not vary with the pressure to which it is subjected; but it does vary with the temperature.** Let *Fig.* 83 represent a barometer tube, completely filled with mercury, dipping into a deep cistern of iron, c' also filled with the same fluid. On introducing a few drops of ether beneath the lower edge of the tube, it will rise to the upper part, and will there evaporate. By this formation of vapor, the mercurial column will be depressed, and at the same time a small portion of liquid ether will float upon its upper surface, at *s*. The elastic force of this enclosed vapor is measured by the distance to which it depresses the mercurial column. If its elasticity be increased, the column of mercury is lowered; if it be diminished, the mercurial column rises; if it remains unchanged, the height of the mercurial column above the level of the mercury in the vessel below, remains unchanged. Now, if the barometer tube be depressed by the hand in the lower vessel, this will tend

to drive the mercury farther up the tube, and compress the vapor; if, on the contrary, the tube be raised out of the vessel, the mercury will tend to fall, and the pressure on the vapor will be diminished. In either case, no effect whatever is produced in the height, s, of the mercurial column, t, above the level, c, n, of the mercury in the vessel below. The elastic force of the vapor, therefore, whether it be compressed, or expanded, remains the same. When compression takes place, in consequence of driving the tube down, a portion of the vapor is condensed into the liquid state again, and the elastic force of the vapor which remains, continues the same as before. When the pressure is diminished by drawing the tube up, an additional amount of the ether evaporates, which, adding its elasticity to that of the original vapor, preserves its elastic force, unchanged. The height of the column of mercury remains, therefore, the same, whether the tube be elevated, or depressed; but the amount of liquid ether above the mercury varies considerably. As the tube is lowered, the mercury rises, and the space occupied by the vapor contracts at the same rate, while the amount of liquid ether increases; as the tube is elevated, the mercury sinks, and the space occupied by the vapor increases at the same rate, while the amount of liquid ether is diminished.

Fig. 84.

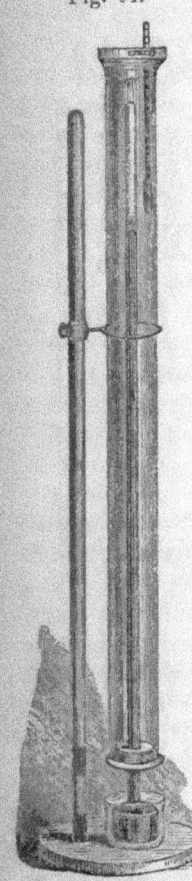

Elasticity varies with Temperature.

It is far otherwise when the *temperature* is made to vary. Let a similar barometer tube have placed over it another tube, considerably larger than itself, and closed at the bottom, *Fig.* 84, and let hot water be poured into this tube, the increased temperature causes an additional portion of ether to evaporate in the barometer tube, and a cor-

---

202. Does the elastic force of a vapor vary with the pressure to which it is subjected, or with its temperature? Prove this by experiment. Explain the increase in the volume of liquid ether by increasing the pressure. Explain the diminution in its volume by the removal of pressure. Why, in both cases, does the height of the column of mercury remain the same? What is the effect of applying hot water to a portion of the tube only? Why can not the elastic force of vapor rise above that due to the temperature of the coldest part of the vessel?

responding increase in the elasticity of the original vapor, by which the column of mercury is rapidly depressed. As water of higher temperature is employed, the effect is increased, and finally, when the boiling point of the ether is reached, the elasticity of the vapor is great enough to drive the mercury entirely out of the tube; or, in other words, its elastic force is exactly equal to that of the surrounding air; if a higher temperature than the boiling point be employed, its elasticity becomes greater than that of the surrounding air, and can be made to sustain a column of mercury varying in height with the temperature employed. On the contrary, if this process be reversed, and the temperature surrounding the barometer tube be diminished, the elastic force of the vapor will be diminished, and the mercurial column will rapidly rise until it has attained the height of 30 inches. The above statements, however, only hold good so long as the tube is heated uniformly through its *whole extent;* if only a portion of the tube be heated, a very different result takes place; the additional vapor formed in the hot portions of the tube is condensed again in those which are not thus heated, and consequently there is no steady and progressive increase of the elastic force; this force can never exceed that which the vapor formed in the coolest part naturally possesses, because the excess of vapor is at once condensed as soon as it reaches this colder space. In other words, its elastic force can never rise above that due to the lowest temperature which prevails anywhere within the tube; thus if, instead of applying hot water along the whole length of the tube, in the last experiment, the hand be simply applied at the upper part of the tube, the ether may be made to boil, but the height of the column of mercury is but little affected, for the additional ether vapor produced is at once condensed, and its elastic force destroyed in those parts of the tube which remain unheated. From what has been said it is evident that, in order to increase the elastic force of vapor, it is necessary to confine or compress it, and at the same time raise its temperature. If it be compressed only, the effect is merely to condense a portion of it into water, leaving its elastic force unchanged; if it be heated, simply, without being compressed or confined, it expands indefinitely, and its elastic force also remains unchanged. These facts are of fundamental importance in the steam engine. To obtain mechanical power from steam, it must be both compressed and heated, and this is the reason why a very strong boiler, and a very hot fire, are necessary to develop the mechanical

THE ELASTIC FORCE OF VAPOR IN TWO CONNECTING 177

power of steam from the inert state in which it exists at the time of its first formation.

Table of the elastic force of the vapor of Water at different temperatures:

Temperature.	Pressure.		Volume of Vapor compared with that of the Water producing it as 1.
	Inches of Mercury sustained.	Pounds per square inch.	
—4°	0.052	0.0255	650588
14°	0.104	0.05	342984
32°	0.199	0.10	182323
50°	0.373	0.18	102670
100.°4	1.873	0.92	22513
150.°8	7.530	3.69	6114
201.°2	24.062	11.80	2075
212.°	29.921	14.67 or 15	1696

The elastic force of all vapors, if compared at temperatures equally distant from their boiling points, whether above or below them, is very nearly equal. Thus water, at 242°, i. e., 30° above 212°, its boiling point, has an elastic force of 52.90 inches of mercury. Ether, at 134°, 30° above 104°, its boiling point, has an elastic force of 50.9 inches. Water, at 182°, 30° below 212°, has an elastic force of 16 inches. Ether, at 74°, 30° below its boiling point, 104°, has an elastic force of 16.10 inches, i. e., the elasticity of these two vapors, at the above temperatures, is very nearly equal.

203. The elastic force of vapor in two connecting vessels of different temperature can not rise above the elastic force of the colder vessel. When two vessels, containing the same liquid, at different temperatures are connected by a tube commanded by a stop-cock, so long as the stop-cock is closed, the elasticity of the vapor in the hotter vessel is proportionably greater than that of the vapor in the colder. If the stop-cock be opened, and a communication established between them, the elasticity of the whole apparatus will not be the mean of that which existed in the two vessels previously, but that which corresponds to the temperature of the colder. Let the vessel A, in *Fig.* 85, containing water at the temperature of 32°, be placed in a vessel of pounded ice, and let the vessel B, contain water at the temperature of 212°. As long as the vessels do not communicate, the pressure in the vessel A, will be measured

---

203. What is the elastic force of vapor contained in two connecting vessels which are unequally heated? Prove this fact by experiment.

Fig. 85.

The elastic force of vapor in two connecting vessels of different temperature can not rise above the elastic force of the colder vessel.

by a column of mercury 0.199 inches in height; in the vessel B, by a column 29.921, inches in height. But as soon as the communication is established, by opening the stop-cock c, the vapor in B, in consequence of its high pressure, rushes over into the vessel A, where it is immediately condensed, thereby diminishing the pressure in B, and continues to do so until the pressure in B is brought down to the same point as the pressure in A. In such cases the pressure becomes equal in the two vessels, and can not rise above that which is proper to the lowest of the two temperatures. This is a principle of the greatest importance in the operation of the steam engine, and shows how it is that when the communication is opened between the condenser and the end of the cylinder towards which the piston is moving, the pressure, or tension of the steam in that end of the cylinder is brought down at once to the degree corresponding to the temperature of the condenser, and this without at all diminishing the temperature of the cylinder. If the temperature of the condenser be kept at 32°, the steam from the cylinder is condensed into water as fast as it enters, and the elastic force of the vapor eventually left in the cylinder is reduced to the tension

---

What connection has this fact with the escape of steam from the cylinders of the steam engine into the condenser? In what did the improvement of Watt, in the steam engine, consist? Show how a vacuum may be produced in the cylinder. What suggested the idea to Mr. Watt?

due to the temperature of 32°, i. e., 0.199 in. This tension is so small that a nearly perfect vacuum is thus produced throughout both the cylinder and the condenser. This was the capital improvement made in the steam engine by Mr. Watt. Being asked, in 1817, whether he recollected how the first idea of his great discovery came into his mind, he replied. "Oh yes, perfectly; one Sunday afternoon I had gone to take a walk on the green of Glasgow, and when about half way between the Herd's house and Arn's well, my thoughts having been naturally turned to the experiments I had been engaged in for saving heat in the cylinder, at that part of the road the idea occurred to me that, as steam was an elastic vapor, it would expand and rush into a previously exhausted space; and that if I were to produce a vacuum in a separate vessel, and open a communication between the steam in the cylinder and the exhausted vessel, such would be the consequence."

204. The rate of the evaporation of different Liquids in the air is different. It has been shown that the rate of evaporation of different liquids in the torricellian vacuum is different. The same is also true of their evaporation in air. If the tubes in the apparatus before described, *Fig.* 82, be half filled with mercury, and then inverted in a vessel of the same liquid, the upper part of each tube will be filled with air; now let a few drops of water, alcohol and ether, be introduced into the three tubes respectively, and it will be found that almost immediately the mercury will be unequally depressed in each tube. The greatest depression will take place in the tube into which the ether has been introduced, and the least in the one into which the water, while the tube containing the (alcohol) will exhibit a depression intermediate between the two. This shows conclusively that different liquids evaporate in air with different degrees of rapidity. The same fact may be proved by exposing to the air equal quantities of the same liquids in vessels of equal size; the ether will disappear with the greatest rapidity, water with the least; and those liquids will be found to evaporate with the greatest rapidity whose boiling point is the lowest. Most liquids are susceptible of this gradual dissipation, and even some solids, such as camphor and ice, both of which waste away when exposed to the air without undergoing liquefaction. That mercury evaporates, may be shown by suspending a bit of gold leaf in a bottle partly filled with this liquid; in a few weeks the

---

204. Is the rate of evaporation of different liquids in the air, as well as in a vacuum, different? Prove this by experiment.

lower part of the gold leaf will become white from the condensation of the vapor of mercury upon it. In general, the process of evaporation, for every liquid, goes on precisely the same in air as in a vacuum, except in rapidity. In the case of a vacuum, the vessel acquires the full complement of vapor due to the temperature instantaneously; in the case of air, there is a mechanical impediment to the rise of vapor which retards the process, but eventually the vessel will contain the same quantity of vapor when the thermometer is at the same height, whether it be empty, or full of air.

205. The presence of Vapor in Air affects its bulk and density. When a liquid evaporates into the air contained in an open flask, a portion of the air is expelled, in consequence of the additional bulk imparted to it; and the gaseous contents of the flask will consist of a mixture of air and the vapor of the evaporating liquid. Whether these gaseous contents gain in weight, or not, will depend upon the density of the vapor in question; if it be lighter than air, the gaseous contents of the flask will weigh less than before; if heavier, they will weigh more. Watery vapor is considerably lighter than air, and consequently air, saturated with moisture, weighs considerably less than perfectly dry air; this may be one reason of the fall of the barometer just previous to a storm, viz., the gradually increasing quantity of watery vapor in the air. If, on the other hand, the vapor of the liquid be heavier than air, as in the case of the vapor of bromine, the weight of the gaseous contents of the flask will be increased, and it will support a higher mercurial column.

Table of density of Vapors at the boiling point of their liquids respectively compared with that of Air.

Air,	1.000	Bi-Sulphide Carbon,	2.6447
Steam,	0.6235	Spirit of Turpentine,	3.0130
Alcohol,	1.6138	Mercury,	6.976
Ether,	2.5860	Iodine,	8.716

From this table it is apparent that the density of steam, at 212°, and of watery vapor in general, is much less than that of air. This fact explains the rapid rise of steam in the air when discharged from the escape pipe of a steam engine.

---

205. What effect has the presence of watery vapor in the air upon its bulk and density? Why does moist air weigh less than an equal bulk of dry air? What effect has the moisture in the atmosphere upon the height of the mercury in the barometer?

206. Circumstances which influence evaporation. The same liquid evaporates with different degrees of rapidity at different times. The circumstances which chiefly influence evaporation are, extent of surface, and the state of the air, as to temperature, dryness, stillness, and density.—1st. *Extent of Surface.* As evaporation takes place only from the surface of liquids, it is obvious that its rapidity must depend upon the extent of surface exposed; a given quantity of water will evaporate four times as quickly from a vessel two feet square, as it will from a vessel one foot square.—2d. *Temperature.* The effect of heat in hastening evaporation may be shown by putting an equal quantity of water in two saucers, one of which is placed in a warm, the other in a cold situation; the former will be quite dry before the liquid in the other is perceptibly diminished. Elevation of temperature in the air, in the evaporating liquid, and in the vessel containing it, always quickens evaporation.—3d. *State of the air as to moisture and dryness.* As the amount of vapor which can exist in the air is limited, and depends upon its temperature, it is evident that if the air be saturated with moisture, no more can be evaporated, and that, in proportion as it approaches saturation, must the process of evaporation be retarded. Whereas, if the air contain but little vapor, it can readily take up a large additional amount, and the process of evaporation must be proportionably hastened. In dry, cold days, in winter, the evaporation is exceedingly rapid; whereas, if the air contain much moisture, it proceeds very slowly, even though the air be warm.—4th. *Stillness of the air.* Evaporation is much slower in still air than in a current. The air immediately in contact with the water becomes saturated with vapor, and a check is soon put to evaporation; if, however, the air be removed as fast as it has become charged with vapor, and its place supplied with fresh, dry air, the evaporation continues without interruption. This is the reason why evaporation proceeds with so much rapidity upon a windy day.—5th. *Pressure* has also a marked effect upon evaporation; if the atmospheric pressure be diminished, evaporation goes on more rapidly, because there is less resistance to be overcome; on the other hand, increase of pressure, by increasing the resistance to be overcome, tends to retard the process.

207. Absorption of Heat in Evaporation.—Diminution of Temperature. The most important fact connected with evapo-

---

206. State the circumstances which influence evaporation. What is the effect of extent of surface? Of temperature? Of moisture and dryness? Of stillness? Pressure?

ABSORPTION OF HEAT IN EVAPORATION.

ration, as with ebullition, is the absorption and disappearance of a large amount of heat; and what strikes one at first as very singular, more heat is absorbed in this process than when water boils at 212°. For it has been found that the lower the temperature at which a vapor is formed, the greater the amount of its latent heat; and that the sum of the insensible and sensible heat in vapor formed at all temperatures is very nearly a constant quantity; the higher the sensible heat of vapor, the smaller the amount of its insensible heat, and the lower the sensible heat, the larger the amount of its insensible heat. Thus, a certain weight of vapor at 100°, condensed in a receiver containing water at 32°, gives out according to clement §187, p. 157.

Sensible heat, ... 68°.
Latent heat, ... 1062°.   Total, . . 1130°.

The same weight of vapor at 212°, condensed at 32°, gives out

Sensible heat, ... 180°.
Latent heat, ... 950°.   Total, . . 1130°.

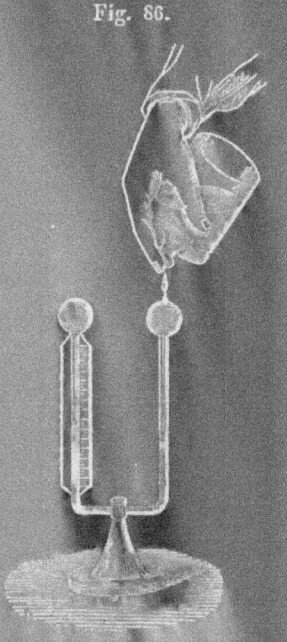

Fig. 86.

Cold produced by Evaporation.

It is quite evident, then, that the vapor formed at 100° contains more latent heat than the vapor at 212°, in the proportion of 1062° to 950°. In consequence of the large amount of heat absorbed in evaporation, the temperature of the evaporating liquid is much reduced, and great cold is the result. The fact of the absorption of heat, and of the production of cold by evaporation, can readily be proved by pouring a little ether on the hand, or on the bulb of a thermometer covered with linen, *Fig.* 86. The more volatile the liquid, and the more the process be hastened by artificial means, the greater the degree of cold. Consequently, ether produces a greater degree of cold than water or alcohol, and if a current of air be blown over it, the cold becomes sufficiently intense to freeze water without difficulty.

207. What is the most striking fact connected with evaporation? Is the absorption of heat more, or less, than in ebullition? What effect has evaporation upon temperature? How can this fact be proved?

THE CAUSE OF THE COLD   183

208. Removal of atmospheric pressure hastens Evaporation and increases the intensity of the Cold. It has been shown that water boils at a lower temperature, and with much greater rapidity, when the atmospheric pressure is diminished; and if the pressure of the atmosphere be entirely removed, water may even be made to boil at 70°, i. e., 142° below its ordinary point of ebullition; for the same reason the rapidity of evaporation is greatly increased by the diminution of the atmospheric pressure, and it becomes most rapid when this pressure is entirely removed by the use of the air pump. The more rapid the evaporation, the greater is the degree of cold produced. In the open air, the cooling effects produced by the evaporation of water are not strikingly apparent, because the process is comparatively slow, and therefore the quantity of heat abstracted from any substance by the vapor, in any given time, is but little more than it receives from surrounding objects; its temperature, therefore, is but slightly diminished. But when water is placed in a vacuum, its evaporation is very rapid, and did not the vapor speedily completely fill the vacuum, and thus prevent further evaporation, its temperature would soon sink low enough to freeze. If the vapor that rises from the water be removed as soon as it is formed, by some substance placed within the receiver which has a strong chemical affinity for water, like sulphuric acid, or chloride of calcium, so that the completeness of the vacuum is permanently maintained, water can readily be frozen by its own evaporation. In *Fig.* 87, the upper pan is filled with water, and the lower with sulphuric acid; the watery vapor is absorbed by the latter nearly as fast as it is formed, and a gentle working of the pump is generally sufficient to freeze the water in a few moments. Or, if water be placed in small quantity, as a drop, for instance, upon a piece of cork, or some other substance of poor conducting power for heat, so that it will not readily supply to it the heat which is carried off in evaporation, the drop of water may be readily frozen under the exhausted receiver of an air pump. In *Fig.* 87, if the up-

Fig. 87.

Water freezing in a Vacuum.

---

208. What effect has the removal of atmospheric pressure upon the degree of cold? Show how water may be frozen by the evaporation of ether under the receiver of an air pump. Show how water may be frozen by its own evaporation.

per vessel be removed, a thermometer be placed in the lower vessel, ether poured in, and a watch glass, containing a small quantity of water, be placed in the ether, as soon as the exhaustion of air commences, the ether will begin to boil at a temperature considerably below 32°, and the water will be speedily frozen. By the application of this principle water may be frozen in considerable quantities. By an exhaust pump, worked by a steam engine, the atmospheric pressure is removed from the surface of ether confined in a metal cylinder placed horizontally in a tank of salt water. The ether flashes into vapor, taking the heat necessary to its existence in this condition from the surrounding salt water, which is thus cooled down to 25°. Salt water is used because it does not congeal at this low point. The salt water thus cooled, is then made to circulate around copper vessels, tinned on the inside, and containing pure water, which, in a few moments, is frozen solid. The salt water, in performing this process, increases in temperature only 5° or 6°, and is returned by a pump to the original tank, where it is again reduced to 25° by the evaporation of the ether. Thus, by the continual working of the exhaust pump, evaporation is effected, heat absorbed, cold produced, and ice made to the amount of four tons daily. The vapor of ether removed by the pump, is conveyed through a spiral tube, surrounded by a large quantity of cold water, and condensed again into a liquid to be used a second time.

209. The cause of the cold produced by Evaporation. The cause of the reduction of temperature by evaporation is simply this:—In the change of any substance from the liquid to the gaseous state, a large quantity of heat is absorbed and rendered latent, and this heat must be supplied from the water which remains unevaporated. For every drop of water which is vaporized, the water which is left behind in the cup will be deprived of as much heat as would be sufficient to raise the temperature of a similar drop 1000° if it were to remain liquid. This immense loss of heat reduces the temperature of the water in the cup to the freezing point, and compels it to congeal. The cold produced is due, therefore, to the large amount of heat made latent in the passage of a substance from the liquid to the gaseous state.

210. The Cryophorus. This is a curious instrument, in-

Describe the process by which water may be frozen upon a large scale by the evaporation of ether.—209. State the cause of the cold produced by evaporation.—210. Describe the Cryophorus.

vented by Dr. Wollaston, and intended to illustrate the freezing of water by its own evaporation. It consists of two bulbs of glass joined by a tube. One bulb is half filled with water and boiled over a lamp. As soon as the steam has completely filled the whole apparatus, and entirely expelled the air, through an orifice left at the extreme end of the other bulb, this aperture is hermetically sealed by the blow-pipe. Nothing, therefore, is left within the apparatus but water and watery vapor; if this vapor be condensed, a vacuum is at once produced, which of course favors rapid evaporation. To use the apparatus, all the water is made to collect in one bulb, and the empty bulb is then immersed in a freezing mixture of ice and salt, as represented in *Fig.* 88; the effect is to condense the vapor into water,

Fig. 88.

The Cryophorus.

with the production of a vacuum, and such a rapid evaporation from the water in the other bulb, that it is soon frozen. The bulb containing the water is prevented from receiving heat from surrounding objects by a jar covered with a pasteboard lid, as represented in the figure. Instead of immersing the bulb in a freezing mixture, the instrument may be mounted vertically in the bell glass of an air pump, in such a way that its empty bulb may dip into a vessel filled with ether, placed on the plate of the air pump, while its tube passes through the top of the bell, and its bulb containing water is supported in the air above. On exhausting the air of the bell glass, the ether evaporates, cold is produced, the watery vapor in the bulb is condensed, and in a few moments the water in the upper bulb is frozen by its own evaporation; care should be taken to protect it from the heat of surrounding objects. The name *cryophorus* signifies frost-producer.

Show how it may be made to act by insertion in an exhausted receiver.

211. The Pulse Glass. This is an instrument similar to the cryophorus, except that it is partially filled with ether and its vapor, instead of water. On applying the hand to one bulb, the vapor expanding drives all the fluid into the other bulb, and at length produces the appearance of violent boiling. At this instant a sensation of cold is experienced in the hand; *Fig.* 89. The boiling is produced by the rapid vaporization, from the heat of the hand, of the film of liquid lining the inside of the empty bulb.

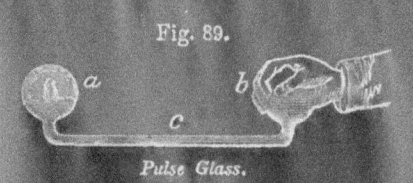

Fig. 89.

Pulse Glass.

212. The cold produced by Fountains and Earthen Water Jars. Evaporation is frequently employed to produce cold. Thus fountains, by throwing up a large quantity of water in the air, in fine spray and drops, expose a large surface of liquid, and the evaporation which this produces cools the air very perceptibly. On the same principle, a bottle of wine, surrounded by a piece of cotton or linen, wetted with water and suspended in a draught of air, will have its temperature reduced several degrees. The famous wine coolers used in Spain, called Alcazzarras, depend on the same principle. These are large earthen vessels, made of porous clay, and unglazed. The bottles of wine, or other substances, which it is desired to cool, are placed in the inside, and the remaining space filled with water; owing to the porosity of the clay the water oozes to the outside, and evaporating, soon reduces the temperature of the interior of the jar several degrees. The degree of cold produced is much increased by a current of air.

213. Effect of Evaporation upon Animal Life. Evaporation takes place constantly from the surface of our bodies, and thus it assists powerfully in maintaining the equable animal temperature essential to comfort and health. The natural temperature of the human body, in health, is about 98°, and it can not be raised much above this point without producing serious discomfort, and permanent injury. Violent exercise always tends to increase the animal heat, but the more violent it is the greater the quantity of perspiration which is poured forth upon the surface of the skin, and the more abundant the evaporation,

---

211. Describe the pulse glass.—212. Explain the coolness produced by fountains and water jars.—213. What is the effect of evaporation upon the animal economy?

and consequently, the greater the amount of heat absorbed and carried off. In this manner nature regulates the heat of the system, and during health, sustains the equilibrium of animal temperature. If this evaporation be checked, the temperature of the system rises, fever supervenes, and the most injurious consequences often result. In summer, when the temperature of the air is nearly as great as that of the human body, the least exertion is attended with a very great increase of the animal temperature, and is inconvenient and oppressive; but at the same time a copious perspiration is poured forth, the evaporation of which not only tends to carry off all the superfluous heat that would be injurious to the animal economy, but also enables man to perform much physical and mental labor, which otherwise would be impossible.

214. Effect of Evaporation on the temperature of the Earth and on Climate. The effect of the evaporation of the immense quantity of water, which is continually taking place, is to lower the temperature of the earth and the sea, and to prevent them from becoming excessively heated by the powerful influence of the sun's rays. Were it not for this, many portions even of the temperate regions of the earth would be absolutely uninhabitable in summer. The temperature of the atmosphere is also lowered by the same cause. A portion of the heat required by the vapor is drawn from the air, as well as from the earth and the sea, and thus it is rendered much less oppressive. The high temperature of summer is mitigated by the passage of water from the liquid to the vaporous state, in the same way as the excessive cold of winter is moderated by the passage of the water from the liquid to the solid state; in the former case, vast amounts of heat become latent; in the latter, vast amounts of heat previously latent, become sensible; it is strictly true that the evaporation of water greatly cools the atmosphere, while its congelation into ice and snow powerfully heats it.

215. The effect of the condensation of the watery vapor of the air. As the formation of watery vapor cools the air by the immense amount of heat which it renders latent, so the condensation of this watery vapor into the liquid state again, tends powerfully to heat the air, by the immense amount of heat previously latent, which it gives out. It is estimated that one lb. of steam at 212°, in undergoing condensation, would raise 3657 cubic feet of air 10°, and cause it to expand, in so doing,

---

214. On the temperature of the earth, and on climate?—215. What is the effect upon the air of the condensation of its watery vapor?

to 3733 cubic feet. Every pint of rain which falls indicates an equivalent expansion. This is also the reason why, in the very cold weather of winter, the temperature of the atmosphere rises the instant a violent snow or rain storm commences.

216. The amount of watery vapor contained in the air. The amount of watery vapor contained in the air is enormous. It is estimated to be at least 50,000,000,000,000 tons. The total annual fall of rain is estimated at 188,452,000,000,000 tons. The whole of this vast quantity is raised into the air from the waters of the ocean by the process of evaporation, and this shows that the process is carried on upon an immense scale. It has been estimated that in summer the number of pounds evaporated from the surface of water, under favorable circumstances, is $104\frac{1}{2}$ per minute to the acre, and the number of gallons per acre, in 24 hours, is 15,048. In consequence of this, the atmosphere is at all times charged with vapor, the amount of which is perpetually varying, but it is almost always below the proportion which the atmosphere might contain if it were loaded with as much moisture as it could possibly hold at its actual temperature. It is owing to the circumstance that the air is seldom thoroughly saturated with watery vapor, that wet bodies become dry, and that the surface of the soil, however moist it may be, in a very brief period becomes parched and dusty. By this process of evaporation a natural distillation is maintained, by which a perpetual circulation of water is kept up. The water is raised in a perfectly pure state into the atmosphere, is transported to distant regions, and being condensed in rain, not only falls upon the land in grateful showers, but also carries with it various gaseous products useful to vegetation, such as Ammonia and Nitric acid, which are diffused through it. The waters thus condensed, descend through the valleys into the rivers, whence they are returned to the ocean, or else sinking into the earth eventually reappear as springs. Were it not for this process the earth would be destitute of rain, and a desert, producing no vegetation, and incapable of supporting animal life. If evaporation were to cease, all living things would perish; there would be no rivers or brooks; no clouds or brilliant sunrises, or sunsets; the earth would be shorn of its beauty, as well as deprived of life.

217. Hygrometers. The quantity of watery vapor existing

---

216. State the amount of watery vapor contained in the air. What is the amount of evaporation from the surface of water per acre? What becomes of the water raised into the air by evaporation? State the advantages of this process of natural distillation.

in the air at any particular time, depends entirely upon the temperature, other things being equal, and the exact amount can be ascertained by an instrument called the hygrometer. These are constructed upon very different principles. One of the simplest is the hygrometer of Saussure, which depends upon the property possessed by hair, of lengthening in dry, and contracting in moist air. A single hair is fastened firmly by one end, and at the other is wound once or twice around an axle carrying an index. As it contracts or expands, it causes the index to traverse a graduated circle, a greater or less distance, and thus it furnishes an approximate indication of the amount of the moisture present in the atmosphere; *Fig.* 90. A thermometer is also attached to the instrument for the purpose of indicating the temperature of the atmosphere at the time when the observation is taken.

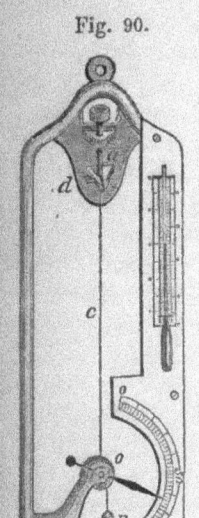

Fig. 90.

Hygrometer of Saussure.

218. Daniell's Hygrometer. This is a more accurate instrument than the last. It consists of two bulbs, one of which is half filled with liquid ether, while the other bulb and the tube connecting them contain nothing but the vapor of the same substance. The bulb A encloses a thermometer, for the purpose of indicating its temperature; the bulb B is enveloped with muslin. There is a second thermometer for the purpose of indicating the temperature of the atmosphere. The principle on which the instrument acts is, that when the atmosphere contains as much moisture as it can hold at the particular temperature which it possesses, a very slight reduction of temperature will cause a portion of this vapor to be deposited in the form of water. When the air does not contain as much vapor as it can hold at its actual temperature, it must be reduced to that at which the vapor contained in it will be sufficient to saturate it, before any will be deposited; and this reduction will be more or less, according to the degree of saturation of the air. The number of degrees, therefore, which the temperature of the atmosphere must be reduced before it will deposit its watery vapor, is then a meas-

---

217. How may the degree of moisture in the atmosphere be ascertained? What are Hygrometers?—218. Describe Daniell's Hygrometer.

Fig. 91.

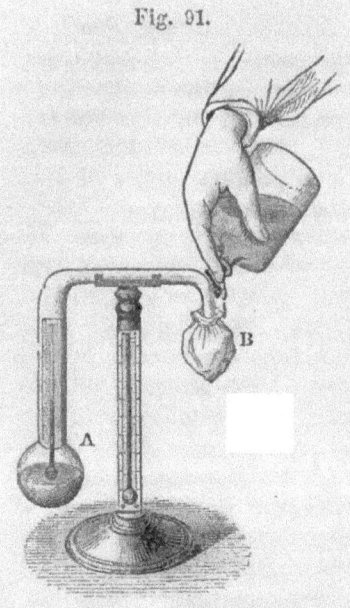

Hygrometer of Daniell.

ure of the amount of vapor in the air. To use this hygrometer, we first note the temperature of the air, by the thermometer on the stem of the instrument. We then pour sulphuric ether, drop by drop, on the muslin. By its evaporation it cools the bulb B, and condenses a portion of the vapor within it; a partial vacuum is formed in A, in consequence of which the ether in it begins to evaporate rapidly, and its temperature, and that of the whole bulb, to sink as indicated by its thermometer. Presently, a degree of cold is attained at which the outside of the bulb becomes suffused with a fine dew; at this instant we note the thermometer in the bulb and observe the difference between it and the thermometer on the stem. This gives us the number of degrees which it has been necessary to reduce the temperature of the air, in order to make it part with its moisture, and as a consequence the amount of vapor contained in the atmosphere. As it is possible, if the reduction of temperature has been rapid, that the loss of heat may not have been perfectly uniform throughout the interior of the bulb A, and the thermometer in it not have become cooled as soon as the outside surface of the bulb, it is well to observe the temperature of A a second time, at the moment when the ring of dew disappears, during the return of the instrument towards the temperature of the surrounding air. The temperature at which the dew is formed and disappears, is called the *dew point*, and the mean of these two observations will give it with perfect exactness. By means of a table constructed for the purpose, the degree of saturation of the air can be calculated, the dew point having once been ascertained. Let the temperature of the air be 60°, and the dew point 50°, calling 1000 the amount of watery vapor which the air can possibly hold at 60°, and observing from the table that the tension of watery vapor at 60° is 0.518, while at 50° it is 0.361, and knowing that the quantity of vapor is directly proportioned to its tension, we have this proportion: $0.518:0.361::1000:x. = 695$. The proportion of watery vapor actually contained in the air, to that which it might contain at the temperature in question, is as 695 to 1000. Tables have also been constructed for showing the actual rate of evaporation at any given time, or the number of grains of water which will evaporate from a given surface, such as a square foot, freely exposed to the air in a certain time, for it is this which determines the drying influence of the atmosphere upon substances exposed to its action.

219. The effect of reducing the temperature of the air, upon the amount of watery vapor contained in it. As the presence of aqueous vapor in the air is due to heat, it is evident that if the temperature of air, charged with moisture, be reduced below the dew point, this vapor will be compelled to resume the liquid state. This reduction of temperature is effected by a variety of natural causes, and results in the production of clouds, of rain, of snow, of dew, and of frost. When a stratum of warm air, charged with moisture, is suddenly mixed with a stratum of cold air, the amount of vapor being greater than the temperature produced by the mixture can sustain, a portion is condensed into rain, and if the temperature be low enough, into snow. Again, if a portion of air, charged with watery vapor, be carried from the lower part of the atmosphere to the higher, its volume will be rapidly increased by the diminution of the atmospheric pressure to which it is subjected, and its temperature will be proportionably lowered. The result will probably be the condensation of its watery vapor, and the production of clouds and rain. On the other hand, if air, containing clouds, be brought from the higher regions of the atmosphere to the lower, its temperature will be raised by the additional pressure to which it is subjected, it will be able to sustain a larger amount of water in the state of vapor, and the clouds will probably disappear. Again, if portions of air, charged with moisture, be swept from the sea against the cold sides of some lofty mountain, the moisture will be at once condensed, and descend in the form of showers of rain.

220. Dew is produced by the diminution of the temperature of the air. Dew is nothing but the watery vapor of the air condensed by diminished temperature. The cause of the dimi-

---

219. What is the effect upon the moisture of the air of reducing its temperature? What is the effect upon the watery vapor of the air of increasing or diminishing its volume? What is the effect of transporting air from a low to a high point upon its watery vapor?—220. What is dew?

nution of the temperature of the air is its contact with bodies that have been cooled by the radiation of the heat of the earth during the night, after the influence of the sun's rays has been withdrawn. During the day, the earth receives from the sun more heat than it radiates, and its temperature rises; but as soon as the sun begins to decline towards the horizon, this process is reversed; the earth then begins to radiate more heat than it receives, and its temperature rapidly sinks. The air in contact with the earth is also cooled, and when its temperature has sunk below the degree necessary to retain its aqueous vapor, this vapor is condensed into minute drops of water, and is deposited upon the cooled surface of the earth. That the cold results from radiation, and not from the general cooling of the atmosphere, is shown by the fact that the surface of the earth is often found to be very cold, and to be suffused with dew, when the air above is warm enough to retain all its vapor. The air a few feet above the earth is sometimes warmer than the surface of the ground by 20° or 30°. Should the radiation continue long enough, the dew is frozen as soon as formed, and becomes frost. In some countries ice is made in this way, and on this principle. Those substances which are the best radiators of heat, are always the most drenched with dew, because they part with the greatest amount of heat, and become the coldest at night, such as rough, dark and filamentous substances, while poor radiators have hardly any dew deposited upon them at all. Rough-leafed plants will be drenched with dew, while smooth and polished leaves remain quite dry. For the same reason, the former are the soonest frozen in the fall of the year. The greatest amount of dew is always deposited on clear and moonlight nights, because then there is nothing whatever to return to the earth any portion of the heat which it has radiated, while on cloudy nights the clouds themselves radiate back as much heat as the earth radiates to them, and consequently its temperature is not sufficiently reduced to admit of the formation of dew. For the same reason, there is no dew formed beneath the trees, or high awnings; and thus it is, that in the autumn a thin covering, by preventing radiation, protects plants from frost even on very severe nights. These facts are illustrated in *Fig.* 92, where the arrows represent the direction of the rays of heat. On the left is indicated the state of the temperature of the

---

How is it produced? Show that radiation is the cause of dew. Explain the effect of clouds on the formation of dew.

THE PHENOMENA OF DEW.

Fig. 92.

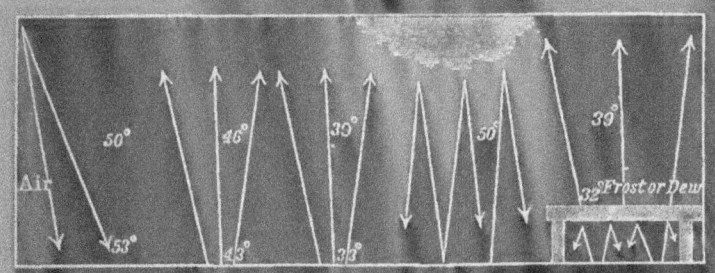

Phenomena of Dew.

earth in the fall of the year, produced by the sun's rays falling on it, viz., about 53°, the air above it being at 50°. A little farther to the right is represented the state of things immediately after sunset, the temperature of the earth having fallen to 43°, and the heat rapidly radiating from it. Still farther to the right is indicated the same process, a little farther advanced, the earth cooled by radiation to 33°, about the freezing point of water, and the atmosphere above at 39°. To the right of this we observe the effect of a cloud, in sending back the rays of heat which the earth had radiated, indicated by the reversion of the arrows. And finally, there is seen the effect of an awning or covering in returning to the earth the rays of heat which it had radiated, while the upper surface of the awning or screen itself is cooled down to the freezing point by the same process, and is found in the morning covered with frost. It is quite evident that the largest amount of dew and frost must be deposited upon bright and clear starlight and moonlight nights; and in those countries where the atmosphere is distinguished for its brightness and clearness, the reduction of temperature effected by radiation, is often sufficient to freeze considerable bodies of water. In India, near the town of Hoogly, about 40 miles from Calcutta, the principle of radiation is applied to the artificial production of ice. Flat, shallow excavations, from one to two feet deep, are loosely lined with rice straw, or some similar bad conductor, in order to cut off the conduction of heat from the ground, and upon the surface of this layer are placed shallow pans of porous earthenware, filled with water to the depth of one or two inches. Radiation, after the sun goes down, rapidly reduces the temperature below the freezing point, and thin crusts of ice form, which are removed as they are produced, and deposited in suitable ice houses until night, when

9

the ice is conveyed in boats to Calcutta. Winter is the ice making season, viz., from the end of November to the middle of February.

221. The constitution of Gases.—Difference between Vapors and Gases. From the above mentioned facts it is evident that diminution of temperature has the effect of condensing vapors into liquids. There are vapors not so easily condensed as the vapor of water, and which, at all ordinary temperatures, retain their aeriform condition. These are called gases. They may be regarded as the vapors of liquids, which vaporize at a degree lower than any of the natural or artificial temperatures which have been yet observed. In this view oxygen is the vapor of a liquid, which vaporizes at a temperature vastly lower than any yet discovered. This gas, consequently, has never been liquefied. The gases resemble vapors in being equally invisible and elastic aeriform fluids. They differ from vapors in this respect, that while the gases obey the law of Marriotte, (§ 9,) at all common temperatures, and diminish in volume, and increase in elastic force, as the pressure to which they are subjected is increased; vapors, on the other hand, at the point of maximum elasticity for their temperature, if their volume be diminished, are in part changed into liquids. By a sufficient increase of pressure, combined with diminution of temperature, many of the gases may, however, be reduced to the state of liquids, and then if these liquids be allowed to evaporate very suddenly, they absorb, in so doing, so much heat, that a portion of the liquid is often frozen. By this process some of the most permanent gases have been reduced, first to the state of liquids, and then to that of solids, a conclusive proof that the state of matter, as solid, liquid and gaseous, depends upon heat.

222. Pressure required for condensing the Gases.—The process. The method of condensing the gases consists in exposing them to the pressure of their own elasticity, continually increased by the production of fresh portions of gas. The process is exceeding simple, and may be performed by any one, though without care and experience, it may be attended with much danger to the experimenter. The materials to form the gas are put into a strong glass tube, closed at one end, and bent, as in *Fig.* 93; after which the orifice is hermetically sealed, or closed by means of a metallic cap, strongly cemented. In most instances, it is necessary that the materials should be kept apart

---

221. What are gases? State the difference between vapors and gases.—222. Show how gases may be condensed into liquids.

THE CONDENSATION OF GASES. 195

Fig. 93.

Condensation of Gases.

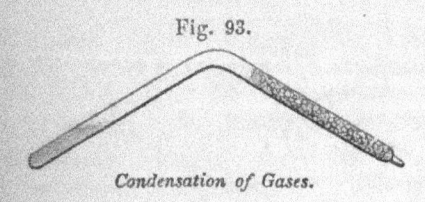

until the tube is closed, and afterwards, by a change of position, be brought to act upon each other. Thus, in order to produce carbonic acid gas, dilute sulphuric acid is poured into the tube, and then pieces of chalk or marble are introduced; after the end of the tube has been hermetically sealed by melting the glass with a blow-pipe, taking care to keep the tube in the position shown in the figure, the apparatus is inverted, the sulphuric acid immediately descends upon the marble, and the carbonic acid gas is instantly evolved. Marble is a compound of carbonic acid gas and lime; the sulphuric acid, however, having a stronger affinity for the lime, seizes upon it, and at the same moment drives the carbonic acid out. Every fresh portion of gas produced tends to compress that which existed in the tube before, and the gaseous particles finally become so closely forced together, and condensed, as to pass from the gaseous into the liquid state.

223. The amount of pressure required varies with the Gas. The amount of pressure required to liquefy the different gases is variable. Thus sulphurous acid gas requires only the pressure of two atmospheres, or 30 lbs. to the square inch, at the temperature of $45°$; carbonic acid gas requires thirty-six atmospheres, or 450 lbs. to the square inch, at a temperature of $32°$; while the gaseous protoxide of nitrogen requires no less than fifty atmospheres, or a pressure of 750 lbs. to the square inch. Suppose, then, that the area presented by the interior of the tube to be eight square inches, the total pressure upon the inside of the tube, in which the protoxide of nitrogen is condensed, is $750 \times 8 = 6000$ lbs. This is a force which few glass tubes are capable of resisting. The process is greatly expedited if the end of the tube containing the gas in question is immersed in a mixture of ice and salt; this maintains a steady temperature of $-4°$, and tends to bring the particles of gas still nearer together. Sometimes, two separate vessels, connected by a tube, are employed, one to hold the materials for producing the gas, the other to condense it. In this case, the former is called the generator, the latter the receiver.

---

223. Is the pressure required the same for all gases? What is the degree of pressure often required? How may the process be expedited?

196   THE SOLIDIFICATION

224. Thilorier's process for solidifying Carbonic Acid. By the application of these principles Thilorier, a French philosopher, was enabled not only to liquefy carbonic acid, but actually convert it into a solid. In this apparatus, both pressure and reduction of temperature are employed to liquefy the gas, and the solidification is accomplished by allowing a portion of the liquid acid to evaporate very suddenly; so much heat is absorbed that a portion of the liquid acid is frozen and condensed into white, flaky solid, resembling snow. The apparatus represented in *Fig.* 94, is the form in which it has been arranged by Deleuil & Son, of Paris. Two very strong vessels are provided, made of the best cast iron, enclosed in a wrought iron casing,

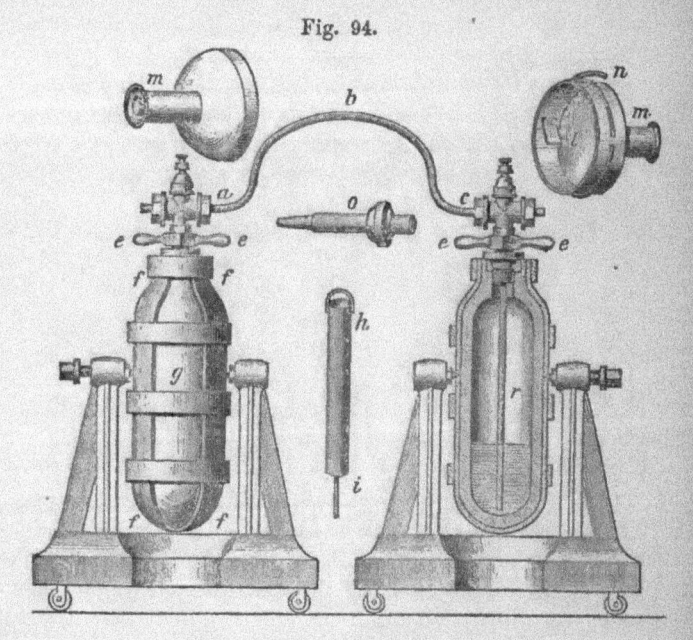

Fig. 94.

The Solidification of Carbonic Acid.

and strongly hooped. One is used as the generator of the gas, the other as the condenser; but as they are made of the same size, and exactly alike, each may be used equally well for either purpose. The tube *a b c*, can be removed at pleasure, and the iron stoppers screwed into the top of the cylinders can be unscrewed by the handles, *e, e*. In *g* there is placed 1800

---

224. Describe Thilorier's process for solidifying carbonic acid.

grammes, or about 4 lbs. of the best bicarbonate of soda, and upon this about 1½ gallons of water at temperature of 100° F. The vessel, h, is then filled with strong sulphuric acid, and carefully lowered into the generator, an entrance having previously been made for the rod, i, through the soda, by means of a long stick. The stopper, e, e, is then to be replaced and forcibly screwed down. On oscillating the generator, which can readily be done in consequence of its suspension upon pivots, the sulphuric acid is thrown from the brass vessel, h, upon the bicarbonate of soda, which is a compound of carbonic acid and soda, and having a superior affinity for the soda, it seizes upon it, dispossessing the carbonic acid, which escapes in the form of gas, and collects in the upper part of the vessel, where it soon commences to compress itself most powerfully. About 7 minutes is the estimated time for the completion of the chemical reaction. The carbonic acid is in part liquefied by the great pressure to which it is subjected, and mixed with the water, &c., used in its preparation. The tube, a, b, c, is now to be screwed into its place upon the top of the receiver, r, and then firmly attached in a similar manner to the generator, g. The receiver is shown in section, and it will be observed that the tube, r, leading from the generator, reaches to the lower part of it. Up to this time there is no connection between the two vessels. A stop-cock is now opened upon the summit of g, and a second upon r, by means of keys not shown in the figure, and a connection formed between the two vessels. The receiver being colder than the generator, the gas rushes into it with force, and is partially condensed into a liquid around the lower part of the tube, r. This condensation is produced, partly by the pressure of the gas, and partly by the difference between the temperatures of the generator and receiver. The temperature of the generator is from 90° to 100°, while that of the receiver is not greater than that of the surrounding air, or about 60°. The pressure of the carbonic acid corresponding to the former temperature is 75 atmospheres, while that corresponding to the latter is only 50. Consequently, according to the principle laid down in § 203, as soon as a connection is formed between the two vessels, the carbonic acid rushes over into the receiver, and continues to do so until the pressure in both vessels corresponds to that which is proper to the temperature of the receiver. The result is, that in the space of a minute, the greater part

---

Explain the intense cold produced by the evaporation of the liquid acid.

of the carbonic acid in the generator is transferred to the receiver. The quantity condensed may be greatly increased by placing the receiver in a cask, and surrounding it with ice and salt, having the temperature of —4°. The stop-cocks are then closed, the tube, a, b, c, removed, the stop-cock of the generator opened, and the gas remaining in it suffered to escape. The stopper is then to be unscrewed, and the interior of the generator cleansed. It is then to be charged anew, and the whole process is to be repeated seven times, when about half a gallon of liquid acid will be collected. With each repetition, more of the gas is liquefied in the receiver, where it at length creates prodigious pressure. The escape pipe, o, is then to be adjusted to the stopper of the receiver, and its end inserted into the circular brass box, l, through the tube, n; m, m, are the two opposite sides of the box, which can be firmly fastened together by a simple arrangement. The stop-cock of r is then to be opened, when the liquid acid, tending strongly to assume the gaseous state, will be driven forcibly through the tube into the brass box, and then, suddenly expanding, so much of its heat becomes latent that a portion of the still liquid acid is frozen, and the box becomes filled with a white snow-like substance. The temperature of the box will be reduced to —94° by this process, and its handles must be covered with leather, or other non-conducting substance, in order to protect the hands of the operator.

225. Solid Carbonic Acid. If exposed to the air, the solid acid slowly evaporates; but covered with cotton, it may be preserved for some hours. This is owing to the extremely poor conducting power of the solid. Its temperature is about —108° or 140° below the freezing point; yet, notwithstanding this low temperature, a mass of it may be held upon the hand without producing any special sensation of cold; nor does a mercurial thermometer, dipped loosely into it, exhibit the low temperature that might be expected. This is due, in part, to its poor conducting power, in virtue of which the external heat can not readily enter it, and in part to its being surrounded by a thin stratum of carbonic acid gas, of extremely poor conducting power. If pressed between the fingers, however, the skin will at once be blistered, as if scalded; and the same result will follow if it be mixed with some liquid which is not readily frozen,

---

225. What is the temperature of solid carbonic acid? Describe the experiments which may be performed with it.

like ether; this increases its conducting power by filling up the pores of the acid, and greatly accelerates the evaporation. A little of this mixture placed upon the hand will produce a deep and painful blister, and almost immediately solidify mercury, though this requires a temperature of —40°; if a glass tube, containing liquid carbonic acid, hermetically sealed, be introduced into such a mixture, the acid will be immediately congealed. If some of the frozen mercury be placed in water, the mercury will melt, but the water will be frozen, showing that the process of liquefaction, even in the case of frozen mercury, as in all other instances, is attended with the disappearance of heat. If the mixture of carbonic acid and ether be thrown into a red-hot platinum crucible, the whole mass will at once be thrown into the spheroidal state, and receive heat from the crucible so slowly that liquid mercury introduced into it in a spoon, will instantly be frozen, and may be turned out upon the table in a solid form. The ether may even take fire, and actually blaze with a powerful flame from the mouth of the crucible, and yet liquid mercury be frozen; this is one of the most extraordinary experiments in chemistry. By accelerating the evaporation of the bath of carbonic acid and ether in the vacuum of the air pump, it is said that a temperature as low as —166° F. has been attained. By immersion in such a bath many liquefied gases have been frozen, and obtained in the form of clear and transparent solids. Without the aid of pressure, many of the gases, including chlorine, ammonia, and carbonic acid, have been obtained in the liquid form by simple immersion in a bath of carbonic acid and ether in air. The tubes used were of green bottle glass, bent as represented in *Fig. 93*, and to these, brass caps and stop-cocks were securely attached, by means of a resinous cement. The cold bath was applied at the curvature. When pressure was required it was obtained by the employment of two condensing syringes. By condensing the gaseous protoxide of nitrogen into a liquid, mixing it with bi-sulphide of carbon, and placing the bath *in vacuo*, Natterer succeeded in producing a temperature of —220° F., which is much colder than that produced by carbonic acid and ether, and the lowest temperature ever observed.

226. The solidification of other Gases. The following table represents the point of congelation of several of the gases:

Explain the freezing of mercury in a red-hot crucible.—226. State the point of congelation of other gases.

Sulphurous Acid,	—105° F.
Cyanogen,	—30° "
Iohydric Acid,	—60° "
Ammonia,	—103° "
Sulphydric Acid,	—122° "
Protoxide of Nitrogen,	—150° "
Carbonic Acid,	—70° "
Bromohydric Acid,	—124° "
Fluoride of Silicon,	—220° "

Seven gases, viz., air, oxygen, hydrogen, nitrogen, carbonic oxide, bi-oxide of nitrogen and marsh-gas, have resisted all attempts to liquefy them; although air was reduced to $\frac{1}{615}$ of its bulk, oxygen to $\frac{1}{531}$, hydrogen to $\frac{1}{500}$, carbonic oxide to $\frac{1}{278}$, and bi-oxide of nitrogen to $\frac{1}{660}$ of its original volume.

227. Pressure exerted by condensed Gases. In order to estimate the pressure which the condensed gases exerted upon the interior of the tubes in which they were contained, and to determine the force requisite to overcome the repulsive energy of their own particles in the gaseous state, small air gauges were enclosed in the condensing tubes. The pressure was estimated by the degree to which the air in the gauges was compressed. Many of the liquefied gases expand upon the application of heat more rapidly than in the gaseous state. It has also been found that Marriotte's law, that the elasticity of a gas increases directly with the pressure, although correct for pressures at a considerable distance above the point of condensation, does not hold good as this point is approached; in this case the elasticity is not proportioned to the pressure, but is considerably less; probably because the distance to which the particles of the gas are separated is no longer able to overcome the attraction of cohesion, this attraction increasing in power the more nearly the point of condensation is approached. These experiments have been prosecuted with great success by Cagniard de la Tour. Various liquids, such as water, alcohol, and ether, were enclosed in strong glass tubes, hermetically sealed, so as to fill somewhat less than one-fourth their capacity. These were then cautiously heated; the liquids expanded until their bulk was nearly doubled; expansion then ceased, in consequence of the immense pressure to which they were subjected, and then as the heat was increased, they suddenly passed into the state of vapor and disappeared. Water was found to become gaseous in a space

---

Name the gases which have resisted all attempts at solidification.—227. How is the pressure in the interior of tubes in which gases are condensed estimated? At what rate do the liquefied gases expand? Describe the experiments of De la Tour.

equal to about four times its original bulk, at a temperature of about 773° F., that of melting zinc. As the vapors cooled, suddenly a sort of cloud filled the tube, and in a few moments after, the liquid reappeared. Space must be allowed for the full expansion of the liquid, otherwise the strongest vessels will give way. Thus it has been ascertained, from these and other experiments, that there exists for every liquid a temperature at which no amount of pressure will retain it in the liquid state, but it will inevitably assume the form of a gas. This being true, it is not strange that for some gases there is a temperature above which no amount of pressure is sufficient to reduce them to the liquid state. These are the gases which, like air and oxygen, have remained uncondensed, whatever the pressure to which they have been subject.

228. The present constitution of the Globe entirely dependent on its temperature. From these and other experiments, we justly conclude that the state of matter, as solid, liquid, or gaseous, depends chiefly on the temperature to which it is subjected. At a sufficiently high temperature, the most infusible forms of matter, such as refractory minerals, and the metal platinum, would naturally exist in a state of vapor, as aeriform fluids, perhaps, colorless, inodorous, and invisible. And at a former period in the history of our planet, it is, chemically speaking, a possible thing that all the matter of which the earth consists may have been in an invisible and aeriform state, or perhaps a nebulous mass. On the other hand, at a sufficiently low temperature, probably the most volatile of substances, like the atmosphere and oxygen and hydrogen gases, would eventually become as solid as the most solid rocks and metals, and all the aeriform fluids be condensed. In such a state of things there would be no atmosphere and no water, nor any other substance on the face of the whole earth, whose particles would possess any power of movement among themselves. Either of these extreme temperatures would be fatal to the existence of man and animals, as well as to that of plants, and strip the earth of everything pleasant to the eye, as well as of all articles good for food. That neither of these extremes exists, but exactly that happy mean in virtue of which all the three states of matter can exist and co-exist side by side, the solid rock, the liquid water, the gaseous atmosphere, is surely a conspicuous proof of most refined design in the arrangement of the realm

---

228. Show that the present constitution of the globe is entirely dependent upon its temperature.

of Nature, and a sure proof to us of the goodness and the beneficence, as well as of the wisdom and power of the Creator.

Experiments:—Effects of Heat: Evaporation.

1. Evaporation. Heat is absorbed in the process of evaporation, as well as that of ebullition. This may be shown by dropping ether upon the bulb of a thermometer: the mercury falls, because its heat is absorbed by the vaporization of the ether.

2. The rapidity of evaporation is greatly increased by the removal of the atmospheric pressure. Place ether under the receiver of the air pump, and exhaust the air: the ether begins to boil, and a thermometer introduced into it sinks below 32°.

3. Pour ether upon the surface of water in a watch glass, and evaporate rapidly by means of the air pump: the water will be frozen. The watch glass should be placed in the interior of a large vessel, also filled with ether. To make these experiments succeed with promptness the water, ether, and sulphuric acid, as well as the vessels employed, should be previously cooled by being placed on ice. The watch glass should be supported upon a ring of tin, wound with woolen cloth.

4. Place water in a watch glass, in strong sulphuric acid, and exhaust the air by an air pump. The water will be frozen by its own evaporation. The vapor, as fast as it rises, is condensed by the sulphuric acid. The air pump must be kept very steady.

5. A single drop of water placed on the plate of an air pump may be frozen simply by its own evaporation; also a single drop of water placed upon a piece of burnt cork, hollowed upon its upper surface.

6. Provide an unbaked clay cup,—one of the cups of Grove's battery will answer very well,—pour water into it, and introduce a thermometer As the water percolates through the cup and evaporates, the thermometer sinks. The effect is greater if ether or alcohol are used.

7. Drop ether or alcohol upon the bulb of the large air thermometer, previously described, *Fig* 45, and the sinking of the liquid in the stem will be very marked.

8. Place deep wine glasses of water, alcohol, and ether, under the same receiver of an air pump, with a thermometer in each, and note the difference in the cold produced when the air is withdrawn, owing to the difference in the rate of evaporation.

9. If ether be allowed to fall, drop by drop, upon a thin vial of water, covered with muslin, in a current of air like that produced by a bellows, the water will be frozen.

10. That heat is absorbed by evaporation, under all circumstances, is shown by the cryophorus of Dr. Wollaston. The empty bulb must be placed in a freezing mixture of equal parts of snow and salt; the vapor within it is condensed; rapid evaporation takes place from the liquid in the other bulb, and it soon freezes. Both bulbs should be protected from draughts of air, and previously somewhat cooled; the experiment should not be attempted in a warm room.

11. The pulse glass held in the hand, as soon as it boils, produces a sensation of cold, on the same principle.

12. The water hammer, made to boil in the same way, also illustrates the same truth.

13. That the amount of moisture existing invisibly in the air depends upon its temperature, may be shown by placing a bottle of moist air, tightly corked, upon ice and salt, in a bowl. As the air cools, a cloud appears within the bottle.

14. Ice and snow mixed, and placed in a jar, will soon induce a deposit of moisture on the outside, from the air, which is cooled by contact with it.

15. The Dutch weather house; the sponge balance hygrometer; the hygrometer of Saussure, may all be used to demonstrate the varying amount of moisture in the air, by removing them from a damp to a dry atmosphere, and the reverse.

16. Daniell's hygrometer will illustrate the same fact on a different principle.

17. Place a square piece of copper upon the surface of a mixture of ice and salt, and observe the minute drops of moisture formed. This illustrates the mode in which dew is formed upon the earth, the difference being that in one case the copper is cooled by the ice, in the other the earth is cooled by radiation.

18. Expose different plates of different substances, such as glass, wood, rough copper, polished copper, all of the same size, on a cool night in summer, and observe the different amounts of dew collected upon them.

19. Place a thermometer upon the ground on a clear night, suspend a second thermometer 10 or 12 feet above it, in the air, and note how much lower the first sinks than the second, showing that dew is caused by the radiation of the heat of the earth, and not by the general coolness of the atmosphere.

20. Solidified Carbonic Acid. The dry solid acid may be held in the hand with impunity; mixed with sulphuric ether, it is dangerous to handle.

21. Place a small quantity on stout plate glass, no effect takes place so long as it remains dry; pour ether on it and the glass is broken at once by the intense cold which is produced.
22. Mix the solid carbonic acid with sulphuric ether, upon the surface of mercury in a wooden bowl. The metal will almost immediately be frozen.
23. Place a medal at the bottom of the bowl, and an impression of the medal will be taken in the mercury.
24. Introduce a mercurial thermometer, and observe the rapid fall of the fluid into the bulb, and its subsequent congelation and great contraction.
25. Introduce a spirit thermometer, and note the difference of effect.
26. Throw some of the solid acid upon cold water.
27. Throw some of it upon hot water.
28. Place some of it at the bottom of a jar in which a candle is burning, and observe the going out of the flame.
29. Introduce a taper into such a jar.
30. Throw some of the solidified mercury into water: the mercury melts, but the water at the same time freezes. This is an excellent illustration of the absorption of heat always attendant upon liquefaction.
31. Place some of the solid carbonic acid and ether under the receiver of an air pump, with a spirits thermometer graduated very low, and exhaust; note the extremely low temperature produced; $=-166°$ F.
32. Heat a silver or platinum capsule to a full red heat, over a powerful spirit vapor or gas lamp; throw in a quantity of mixture of solid carbonic acid and ether; introduce quickly a little mercury in a platinum spoon; the ether will probably take fire and burn, but notwithstanding, the mercury will be frozen, and may be turned out a solid mass upon the table.
33. Treat water in the same manner; it will also be frozen.

§ VI.—Specific Heat:—Capacity for Heat.

229. The amount of Heat in different bodies of the same temperature unequal.—Specific Heat. It has been seen that, in the important processes of liquefaction and vaporization, a large amount of heat disappears and becomes latent, without producing the smallest effect upon the temperature of the solid and liquid in question. It is evident, therefore, that heat can exist in a body without being free or sensible. Heat, in this state, is called heat of *composition*, because it has, so to speak, combined with the body which it has entered, producing a compound substance which, in some respects, does not exhibit all the properties of its component parts; and as it is one of the characteristics of chemical combination that the properties of the elements are never displayed in the compound produced, it is supposed that some such union has taken place in this case between the heat absorbed, and the body in question. The heat thus absorbed is called Latent Heat. It has also been seen that equal weights of different bodies of the same temperature do not contain the same amount of heat. Thus a pound of ice at $32°$(§§

---

229. What is meant by heat of composition? By latent heat?

141 and 142) may have 140° of heat added to it, and be converted into a pound of water without having its temperature elevated 1°. It is evident, therefore, that the pound of water at 32° must contain at least 140° more heat than the pound of ice of the same temperature. The same is true of a pound of steam at 212°, and a pound of water at 212°; the former contains at least 1000° more heat than the latter, and yet they are both of the same temperature. It is, therefore, a general truth, that equal weights of the same substance contain equal quantities of heat, but equal weights of different bodies, at the same temperature, contain unequal quantities of heat. This difference in bodies, in regard to the amount of heat which they contain at the same temperature, was described by Dr. Black, who was the earliest experimenter upon this subject, by the term *capacity for heat*, "a word apparently suggested by the idea that the heat present in any substance is contained within its pores, or in the spaces left between its particles, and that the quantity of heat is regulated by the size of its pores." This term is now discarded, and in place of it that of *specific heat* has been generally substituted. Every substance is said to have a specific heat, peculiar to itself. By specific heat is meant, the quantity of heat required to raise the temperature of any given substance 1° F., compared with the quantity of heat required to raise the temperature of an equal weight of water 1°. The specific heat of water is taken as unity, and that of all other bodies is different from it, because an equal weight of each requires more or less heat than water to raise its temperature 1°. The specific heat of water being 1, that of mercury is .033, because it requires 33 times less heat to raise the temperature of mercury 1°, than it does to raise the temperature of an equal weight of water 1°. The specific heat of bodies is one of their most important properties, and a vast amount of labor and skill has been expended upon the different methods for ascertaining it. It is sometimes called *calorimetry*, and the instruments for determining it calorimeters.

230. Proof that equal weights of different substances contain unequal amounts of heat.—Specific heat determined by mixture. That equal weights of different bodies at the same temperature contain unequal quantities of heat, may readily be

---

How can it be proved that equal weights of different bodies, at the same temperature, contain unequal amounts of heat? What is meant by the term capacity for heat? What term is now substituted for it? What is meant by specific heat? Give the specific heat of water and mercury. State what is meant by this.—230. Prove that equal weights of different substances contain unequal amounts of heat by the process of mixture.

proved by observing that the same number of degrees of heat communicated to two different bodies, will raise their temperatures very unequally. Thus, if to a pound of water, and a pound of mercury, at the same temperature, equal amounts of heat be added, the temperature of the mercury will rise 33 times as much as that of the water. In other words, water requires 33 times more heat than an equal weight of mercury in order to be raised to the same temperature. The equal amounts of heat may be added to the different substances in several modes. Thus, if to 1 lb. of mercury at 40°, 1 lb. of water at 100° be added, the temperature of the mixture will stand at $98\frac{1}{4}°$, i. e., the $1\frac{3}{4}°$ lost by the water has heated the mercury $58\frac{1}{4}°$. While on the other hand, if to 1 lb. of water at 40°, 1 lb. of mercury at 100° be added, the temperature of the mixture will be only $41\frac{3}{4}°$, i. e., the $58\frac{1}{4}°$ lost by the mercury will have heated the water by $1\frac{3}{4}°$. The amount of heat added in both cases to the colder substance has been the same, but the effect has been to raise the temperature of the cold water only $1\frac{3}{4}°$, while the temperature of the mercury has actually been increased $58\frac{1}{4}°$. Water, therefore, has a greater power of holding heat, or, as it is called, a greater capacity for heat, compared with mercury, in the proportion of 33 to 1, nearly. In the same way, if to 1 lb. of water at 50°, 1 lb. of spermaceti oil at 100° be added, the temperature of the mixture will be $66\frac{2}{3}°$, i. e., the $33\frac{1}{3}°$ lost by the oil, has heated the water only $16\frac{2}{3}°$, while if the experiment were reversed, the water being at 100°, and the oil at 50°, it would be found that the oil had gained $33\frac{1}{3}°$, and the water lost $16\frac{2}{3}°$, whence it appears that the capacity of the water for heat is twice as great as that of spermaceti oil, and consequently, that in order to warm a certain weight of water to the same degree as an equal weight of oil and mercury, twice as much heat must be given to the water as to the oil, and 33 times as much as to the mercury.

231. Specific heat determined by the different times required to heat equal weights of different bodies an equal number of degrees. The same fact may also be proved by noting the time required for equal weights of different substances, to be heated by the same number of degrees. Let a pound of water, of oil, and of mercury, placed in three separate flasks, be brought severally to the temperature of 50°, and then placed in a bath of warm water at 100°. It will be found that when

---
231. Prove the same thing by the different times required to heat equal weights of different bodies by an equal number of degrees.

206   BY RATE OF COOLING,

the mercury has reached the temperature of 80°, the oil will stand at 52°, and the water at 51°, and that though eventually they all reach the same temperature, the water takes 33 times longer to acquire that heat than the mercury, and twice as long as the oil. They are all, however, receiving heat at the same rate; and the only explanation which can be given of the fact is, that the water has more capacity for receiving and containing heat in an insensible form than the other substances, or that its constitution is such that it requires more heat in order to have its external and sensible temperature raised to the same point.

232. Specific heat determined by the rate of cooling an equal number of degrees. Again, on heating a pound of water, oil and mercury, each to 212°, in separate flasks, and immersing them in melting ice, which always stands at the constant temperature of 32°, it will be found that the times required for each to cool through 50°, or any other equal number of degrees, will be in the proportion of 33 to 2 and 1. The water will be 33 times longer in cooling than the mercury, and twice as long as the oil.

Fig. 95.

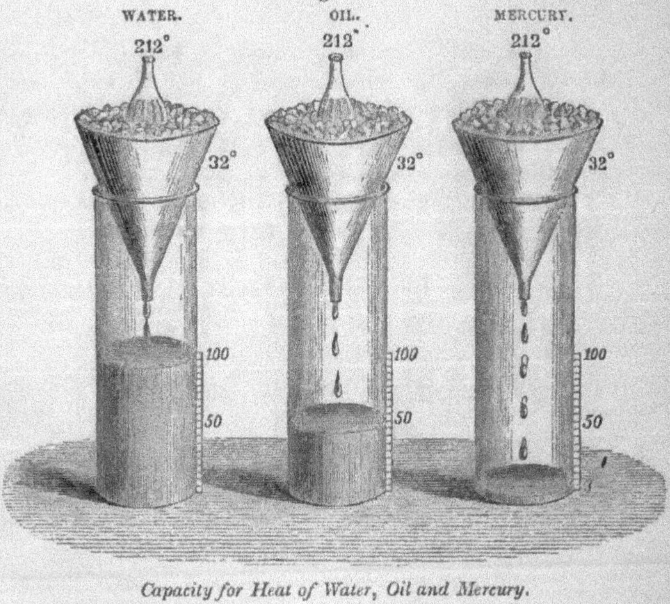

Capacity for Heat of Water, Oil and Mercury.

232. Show how specific heat can be determined by the rate of cooling.

233. Specific heat determined by the quantity of ice melted by equal weights of different substances in cooling from 212° to 32°. If this be true, it is quite evident that when water cools a certain number of degrees, it must give out 33 times as much heat as mercury in cooling an equal number of degrees, and twice as much as oil. The amount of heat given out can readily be estimated by measuring the amount of water produced by the melting of ice in each case. Thus, let a pound of water, a pound of oil, and a pound of mercury, contained in separate flasks, be brought to the temperature of 212°, by immersion in boiling water, and then be surrounded by ice in funnels, placed over graduated glass jars, as in *Fig.* 95, and the quantity of water produced in the cooling of the three flasks from 212° to 32°, be carefully measured; it will be found to be in the case of the vessel of water, 33 times as much as that produced by the cooling of mercury, and twice as much as in the case of oil.

234. The Calorimeter of Lavoisier and Laplace. The celebrated calorimeter of Lavoisier and Laplace, was constructed on this principle; *Fig.* 96. The apparatus consists of three

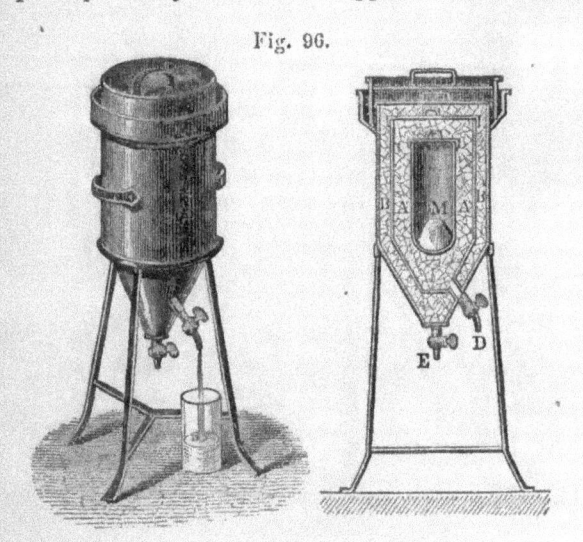

Fig. 96.

The Calorimeter of Lavoisier and Laplace.

concentric vessels of sheet brass, arranged one within the other.

233. Show how specific heat can be determined by the quantity of ice melted by bodies in cooling from 212° to 32°.—234. Describe the calorimeter of Lavoisier and Laplace. Describe a more simple mode of determining the same thing by a vessel of ice.

In the inner is placed the substance whose specific heat is to be determined, having been previously heated to 212° by immersion in boiling water. The two exterior compartments, A and B, are filled with pounded ice; the ice of the compartment A, is intended to be melted by the hot body, M; the ice in the compartment B, is intended to cut off the radiant heat of the external air, in order that the ice melted in A may be due solely to the heat proceeding from the body M. Two stop-cocks are provided, D and E, for the purpose of drawing off the water. The hot body is first introduced, and covered with a double lid; the stop-cock D is then opened, and the water formed allowed to trickle into a measuring glass. When the temperature of the hot body has fallen to 32°, the water will cease running, and the amount is then carefully measured and compared with that produced by the cooling of an equal weight of water from 212° to 32°. It has been objected to this instrument, that a portion of the water formed is detained by adhesion within the inner vessel, and that a portion may be frozen a second time, and thus the indications of the instrument may be vitiated. A more simple mode of determining specific heat is to place the body previously heated to 212°, in a piece of ice which has been scooped out to receive it *a Fig. 97*, and covered with a lid, *b*, of the same material. When the substance has cooled to 32°, the water should be poured out and measured; this amount compared with that produced by an equal weight of water in cooling from 212° to 32°, will give the specific heat required.

Fig. 97.

Specific Heat.

235. Specific heat determined by the rise of temperature produced by the immersion of equal weights of different bodies, for the same time in equal weights of water. In this process, equal weights of water, and the substances in question, are heated to 212°, and then immersed for the same length of time, in equal weights of water, of exactly the same temperature. The difference in the temperature of the water, tested by a delicate thermometer, will give the specific heat. The difference in the time required for heating the water in each vessel an equal number of degrees by the different substances, will give the same result.

---

235. Show how specific heat may be determined by the number of degrees of heat imparted to water in the same time.

236. The specific heat of Water. The specific heat of water, or the capacity of this substance for heat, is greater than that of any other liquid, and also of all solids, and consequently to change the temperature of large masses of water, is a work of time. Water may have a very large amount of heat poured into it without any perceptible effect upon its temperature. And on the other hand, a vast amount of heat may be abstracted from water without any sensible diminution of its temperature. This is due to its immense capacity for heat. Water, therefore, in consequence of the slight effect produced upon it by variations of atmospheric temperature, would make a very poor thermometric fluid. Mercury, on the contrary, whose specific heat, or capacity for heat, is 33 times less than water, readily yields to the slightest change of temperature, and is therefore admirably adapted to thermometric purposes. The susceptibility of bodies to changes of temperature is always in the inverse proportion to their specific heat.

237. Specific Heat of Solids. The determination of the specific heat of bodies is necessarily attended with great difficulty, owing to the variety of the sources of error, and the number of precautions required; and much careful consideration and experiment has been bestowed upon it. The following table gives some of the results of M. Regnault, one of the most successful of the later experimenters on this subject, obtained by the processes of immersion and mixture, and they bring to light some very curious facts:

Specific Heat of Solids of equal weight between 32° and 212°.

Water,	1.	Silver,	0.05701
Charcoal,	0.24150	Tin,	0.05623
Glass,	0.19768	Mercury,	0.03332
Iron,	0.11379	Platinum,	0.03243
Zinc,	0.09555	Gold,	0.03244
Copper,	0.09515	Lead,	0.03140
Brass,	0.09391		

238. Specific heat of Liquids. The specific heat of liquids is determined by the same methods as that of solids. Water is taken as the standard, and the specific heat of all other liquids is compared with it. The specific heat of water is greater than that of all other liquids, without exception. A body in the

---

236. How does the specific heat of water compare with that of other bodies? What are some of the results of this peculiarity?—237. Give some of the results of Regnault's table.—238. How is the specific heat of liquids determined? Give the table.

liquid state has a higher specific heat than the same substance when in the solid form. This is very marked in the case of water, in which the specific heat is double that of ice, water being 1.000, ice is 0.505.

Table of Specific Heat of Liquids.

Water,	1.00000		
Oil of Turpentine,	0.42593	Bi-Sulphide of Carbon,	0.2303
Alcohol,	0.615	Bromine,	0.1060
Ether,	0.5113	Chloroform,	0.2293

239. Specific heat of Gases. The determination of the specific heat of gases is attended with unusual difficulties, on account of the facility with which their bulk and weight are influenced by external circumstances, and though conducted by many philosophers of distinguished experimental skill, the best results can be viewed only as approximations, requiring to be corrected by future research. Dr. Crawford, the first careful experimenter on this subject, conducted his experiments in the following manner. He selected two copper vessels, made as light as possible, and exactly of the same form, size and weight, exhausted one of them, and filled the other with the gas, to be examined. They were heated to the same temperature by immersion in the same vessel of hot water, and then plunged into equal quantities of cold water, of the same temperature. Each flask heated the water; but while the exhausted flask communicated solely the heat of the copper, the other gave out the heat of the copper plus that of the gas which it contained. The number of degrees by which the cold water was heated by the former, deducted from the number of degrees by which it was heated by the latter, gave the heating power of the confined gas. By repeating the experiment, with air and different gases, their comparative heating powers, or specific heats, were ascertained. These experiments, though correct in principle, are not considered reliable, on account of the superior heating influence of the copper globes compared with the small amounts of gas that were employed. The same subject was next investigated by Lavoisier and Laplace, with the aid of their *calorimeter;* § 234. A current of gas was transmitted through a spiral tube placed in boiling water, in order to be heated to a fixed temperature, and was then made to circulate within the calorimeter, in a similar

---

239. How is the specific heat of gases determined? Describe Crawford's process. Describe Lavoisier's method.

tube, surrounded by ice. Its temperature, in entering and quitting the calorimeter, was noted by means of thermometers, and the number of degrees of heat lost in cooling from 212° to 32° was estimated by the quantity of ice liquefied. These experiments, though very ingenious, and conducted with great care, are thought to be inaccurate, for the reason previously given, that, in the use of ice, a portion of the water formed may be frozen a second time in consequence of the low temperature of the apparatus, and a portion also detained and prevented from escaping into the measuring glass, by the adhesive action of the ice. A similar set of experiments was afterwards undertaken by Delaroche and Berard. They transmitted known quantities of gas, heated to 212°. in a uniform current through the calorimeter, and instead of ice, surrounded the serpentine tube with water. The temperature of the gas, at the moment of its exit, was carefully noted, and the number of degrees of heat which it imparted to the water, in cooling from 212°, was also carefully ascertained by delicate thermometers. The results of their experiments are contained in the following table, which for a long time was thought to furnish the most accurate determination of the specific heat of gases. Equal weights of the gases were used in all cases. In the first column the specific heat of water is taken as the standard of comparison; in the second column the specific heat of air is taken for the standard:

Delaroche and Berard's Table of the Specific Heat of Gases.

Gases, equal weights.	Water the Standard.	Air the Standard.
Water,	1.0000	
Watery Vapor,	0.8470	
Air,	0.2669	1.0000
Oxygen,	0.2361	0.8848
Nitrogen,	0.2754	1.0318
Hydrogen,	3.2936	12.3400
Protoxide of Nitrogen,	0.2369	0.8878
Heavy Carb. Hydrogen,	0.4207	1.5763
Oxide of Carbon,	0.2884	1.0805
Carbonic Acid,	0.2210	0.8280

It is very evident, from this table, that equal weights of the different gases differ very much in the quantity of heat which they contain. The specific heat of hydrogen is twelve times

---

Describe that of Delaroche and Berard. Give some of the results of their table. How does the specific heat of hydrogen compare with that of other gases, and even with the metals.

greater than that of air; that of nitrogen and oxide of carbon about the same as air. Compared with water, the specific heat of hydrogen is more than three times greater, and larger than that of any other known substance. Out of nine gases, on which experiments were made, none, except hydrogen, has a specific heat equal to that of water; but they all have a specific heat much greater than that of any of the metals. Thus hydrogen, the lightest known substance, has the greatest specific heat, while the metals, the heaviest of all bodies, possess the least.

240. Regnault's determination of the specific heat of Gases. Within a few years the same subject has been investigated by Regnault. The method adopted was, in the first place, to condense the gas in a strong receiver; a known weight was then allowed to escape at a perfectly uniform rate through a spiral tube plunged into a vessel of hot oil, which was maintained at a fixed temperature; the gas was in this way, during its passage through the spiral, raised to a known temperature equal to that of the oil in the bath; it was then made to pass through a metallic vessel, surrounded by a known weight of water; and finally, was allowed to escape slowly into the air, ample time being given for its temperature to be reduced to that of the surrounding water. By this process the rise of temperature experienced by a known weight of water when a given weight of each gas, after it had been raised to a fixed standard temperature, was passed through it, was ascertained. The different gases treated in this way, were found to impart unequal quantities of heat to the water, and this became a measure of their specific heat. The results are given in the following table:

Regnault's Table of the Specific Heat of Gases.

Gases, equal weights.	Water the Standard.
Water,	1.0000
Watery Vapor,	0.4750
Air,	0.2377
Oxygen,	0.2182
Nitrogen,	0.2440
Hydrogen,	3.4046
Protoxide of Nitrogen,	0.2238
Heavy Carb. Hydrogen,	0.3694
Oxide of Carbon,	0.2479
Carbonic Acid,	0.3308

240. Describe Regnault's process. Give some of the results of his table.

On comparing this table with that of Delaroche and Berard, considerable diversity is found, but not more than might be expected from the improved methods of experimentation that have been introduced since their time. The important fact is proved by both tables, that equal weights of different gases of the same temperature, and the same density, contain very unequal amounts of heat, and that there is, therefore, no relation between the thermometric temperature of a body and the actual amount of heat which it contains; also that the specific heat of hydrogen, the lightest substance known, is not only greater than that of all the gases, but actually nearly $3\frac{1}{2}$ times greater than that of an equal weight of water of the same temperature; and as the specific heat of water is superior to that of every other liquid and solid, it follows that the specific heat of hydrogen is greater than that of any other known substance.

241. **The specific heat of a body may be changed by altering its density.** The specific heat of a body is not a permanent property, but may be altered by changing its density. Any influence which alters the distance between the particles of a body, affects its specific heat. If the particles be brought nearer to each other, specific heat is diminished; if the particles be separated and removed to a greater distance from each other, the specific heat of the body is increased. If, by mechanical compression, the particles of a piece of soft, well annealed copper, whose specific heat varied from 0.09501 to 0.09455, be brought nearer to each other, the specific heat will be found to be reduced to 0.0936 to 0.0933; on being again thoroughly annealed, so as to recover its former density, its specific heat will be nearly restored to what it was before,—0.09493 to 0.09479. When water, or any other liquid, is compressed, its specific heat is diminished; when it is allowed to expand to its former dimensions, its specific heat returns to the same amount as before. The same is true of gases; if they are compressed, their specific heat is diminished; but if allowed to expand, their specific heat is greatly increased. Regnault denies this in the case of the gases, but his conclusions are in direct opposition to those of Delaroche and Berard, and nearly all other experimenters, and they must, therefore, be received with some hesitation. As the distance between the particles of bodies is very much affected by change of temperature, a removal of the particles from each

---

241. What effect is produced upon the specific heat of bodies by altering their density? Give illustrations. What effect is produced upon specific heat by elevation of temperature? Give the table.

other, and expansion being produced by a rise, while contraction is the result of a diminution of temperature, it follows that the specific heat of a body is greater at a high temperature, than at a low one. This is true of solids, liquids, and gases. In the case of gases, it is denied by Regnault; but the correctness of his opinion may be doubted. That it is true of solids, may be plainly seen from the following table:

Rise of Specific Heat with rise of Temperature.

	Specific Heat from 32° to 212°.	Specific Heat from 32° to 572°.
Mercury,	0.0330	0.0350
Platinum,	0.0335	0.0355
Antimony,	0.0507	0.0549
Silver,	0.0557	0.0611
Zinc,	0.0927	0.1015
Copper,	0.0949	0.1013
Iron,	0.1098	0.1218
Glass,	0.1770	0.1900

242. **The specific heat of a body changed by altering its physical state.** A body in the liquid state has a higher specific heat than the same substance when in the state of a solid. On the other hand, a substance in the gaseous state has a lower specific heat than the same substance in the liquid state. When ice passes into the liquid state, its specific heat is doubled; but when water is converted into vapor, its specific heat is diminished one half. Different solids have the amount of their specific heat differently affected by a change of state, and they vary very much among themselves.

243. **A change in the specific heat of a body always changes its temperature; an increase of specific heat diminishes temperature, and a diminution of specific heat increases it. Change of Density, or of the State of bodies, always produces change of temperature.** It has been shown, in the case of soft copper, that a change in the specific heat of a body is always produced when a change is made in its density; if its density be increased, its specific heat is diminished; if its density be diminished, its specific heat is increased. Besides this effect, and as a consequence of it, a change in the *temperature* of the body whose density is altered, is always produced. In the case of soft copper, if density be increased, and specific heat diminished, temperature rises; if density be diminished, and specific heat be

---

242. What effect is produced upon specific heat by change of state?—243. What effect is produced upon temperature by change of specific heat?

increased, temperature sinks. So great is the effect upon temperature, in consequence of a change of specific heat, produced by a change in density, that if a piece of iron be rapidly hammered it immediately becomes hot, and by a skillful blacksmith, may even be made red-hot by this process. This rise in temperature may be thus explained. The distance of the particles of bodies from each other is in general determined by their specific heat. This specific heat spends its energy in keeping the particles apart, and in resisting the attraction of cohesion which is constantly tending to draw them together, and it no longer possesses the power of affecting temperature. Whenever heat is expended in producing any mechanical effect of this kind, it loses its power of affecting the thermometer and the senses, and passes from a sensible to an insensible state. Heat can not produce an effect upon temperature and a mechanical effect, at the same time. A definite amount of heat made to pass into a body may cause the temperature of the body to rise, or it may spend itself in increasing the distance between its particles, and expanding it, but it can not do both at the same moment. Heat which has caused a body to expand, can not at the same time raise its temperature. When a piece of iron is held near the fire, the first effect of the heat is to expand the iron, and this it does without raising its temperature; this heat becomes latent in the iron, and the temperature of the body does not rise unless it receives more heat from the fire than can be employed in effecting expansion. But the heat that has been expended in this manner, and become latent in any substance, is not lost; it will again become heat of temperature as soon as it is no longer needed for the purpose of keeping the particles of the body apart. If mechanical force should violently compress the body and bring the particles nearer together, the heat which had previously kept them apart being now no longer needed for this purpose, will make itself apparent as heat of temperature. This is what takes place when cold iron is hammered; the heat which had kept the particles asunder, and which had remained latent while thus expended, being now no longer able to exert this effect, is compelled to appear as heat of temperature, and the iron at once becomes very hot. If, on the other hand, the particles of iron had been separated from each other by mechanical violence, they could not have

---

What effect is produced upon temperature by the compression and expansion of bodies? Of passing from the solid to the liquid or gaseous state? Give illustrations. Explain the heating of iron red-hot by hammering. From what source is this heat derived?

remained permanently separated except by the agency of heat, for which there would be, therefore, an imperative demand. All the heat in the neighborhood would be drawn upon for the purpose of satisfying this demand, and the first source would be the free, sensible heat of the body itself. This would at once be transferred into the latent state, and be expended in maintaining the distance between the particles; it would cease, therefore, to appear as heat of temperature, and the iron would at once become cold. The quantity of heat latent in the metals, and which becomes apparent when they are compressed, is admirably illustrated by the faint flash of light which is emitted when a bullet from a steam gun strikes a wrought iron target. The bullets are completely flattened, and when directed against a plate of lead placed in front of the target, the two surfaces of lead become firmly united as if melted or soldered together. The flash of light is only visible in a darkened room. Another still more striking illustration is seen in the flash of light produced when the 80 lb. hexagonal bolts fired from the Whitworth gun strike the thick iron-plated sides of a floating battery, *Fig.* 98. "Notwithstanding the immense resisting power of the

Fig. 98.

The Latent Heat of Iron Shot and Plates rendered Sensible by Compression.

iron plates, the hexagonal bolt passed completely through them. *The shot when discovered was found to be so hot that no one*

Explain the heat and light, produced by the shot from the Whitworth guns. Give other illustrations.

could touch it, and was ascertained to have been compressed to the extent of an inch in length. It was noticed that at the instant of concussion between the shot and the vessel, a broad sheet of intensely bright flame was emitted, almost as if a gun had been fired from the vessel in reply." The same effect has been repeatedly noticed when the balls from the heavy Dahlgren guns of the Monitors struck the stone fortifications against which they were directed. The heat, in these cases, was that previously latent in the iron, made sensible by the compression of the metal and the diminution of its specific heat. In like manner, the intense heat which is evolved when iron bars are subjected to the process of rolling, and not unfrequently by the axles of cars and carriages when in rapid motion, and in the processes of boring and planing metals, is due to the same cause. It is the heat previously latent in the metals, evolved and converted into heat of temperature by the diminution of their specific heat in consequence of compression. The heat set free in the simple operation of boring a hole with a gimlet, is sufficient to inflame a friction match. The heat produced by the rapid drawing of a string tightly around the neck of a glass flask, is sufficient to crack it. And in the whale fishery, the heat evolved by the inconceivably rapid motion of the rope over the side of the boat, after the whale is struck, would be sufficient to set it on fire if it were not kept cool by the continual pouring of cold water. In the best constructed steam engines, the bearings of the shafts are made hollow, and a steady stream of cold water caused to circulate through them, in order to prevent them from becoming excessively heated, and the axles from expanding to such a degree as to be incapable of moving. These are illustrations of a general principle. *Whenever any body is expanded, heat is absorbed and temperature sinks. Whenever any body is compressed, latent heat is given out and temperature rises.* This is true of solids, liquids, and gases. Liquids, if compressed, grow warm; if relieved from compression, they grow cold again. Gases, if compressed, grow hot; if released from compression, temperature declines. So, in like manner, when bodies change from the solid to the liquid or gaseous state, there is an absorption of heat, because of the large amount which is expended in making the change. The difference between the

---

_{What effect is produced upon temperature of the passage of a solid into the liquid and gaseous state? Of the passage of gases and liquids into the solid state? When a liquid is vaporized, what effect is produced upon temperature? What when a vapor is condensed into a liquid?}

same substance as a solid and as a liquid is that in the latter case the particles are so far removed that they can slip readily upon each other. This separation can only be maintained by the addition of a large amount of heat. Consequently, whenever a solid is liquefied there is an immense absorption of heat, and temperature sinks; whenever a liquid is solidified, the reverse takes place and temperature rises. The latent heat no longer required, becomes sensible. When a liquid is vaporized, heat is absorbed and temperature sinks. When a vapor is condensed into a liquid, latent heat is given out and temperature rises.

244. The Fire Syringe. These principles are admirably illustrated by the fire syringe represented in *Fig.* 99. It consists in its most improved form of a hollow cylinder of glass, into which a piston fits air-tight. Upon the under side of the piston is a cavity to receive a bit of tinder or punk, or a tuft of cotton moistened with ether. On driving the piston forcibly down, the tinder will emit smoke, and finally ignite: a match may thus be lighted with ease. This large amount of heat has proceeded from the air contained in the cylinder. By sudden and forcible compression its density is increased, its particles are brought nearer together, the heat previously expended in keeping them asunder and latent in the air is made sensible, becomes heat of temperature, and is sufficient to inflame the tinder. It is an experiment strictly analogous to the heating iron red hot by hammering. On rarefying air the opposite effects are observed. The mist observed in the receiver of an air-pump while it is undergoing exhaustion, is a proof of the production of cold. As the air is withdrawn, that which remains undergoes a corresponding rarefaction. A demand for heat is created to sustain this rarefied state. A large amount of heat becomes latent, and temperature sinks so low that the moisture in the air can no longer remain in the state of vapour, but

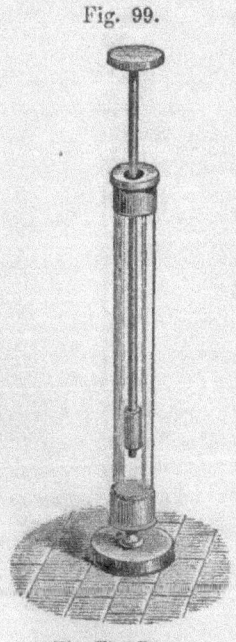

Fig. 99.

The Fire Pump.

---

244. Describe the fire syringe. Explain its principle.

is condensed in minute drops. A thermometer placed in such a receiver rapidly sinks as the air is exhausted, in consequence of the rarefaction, but when readmitted it rises again with equal rapidity, in consequence of the condensation. If the blast from an air gun be directed upon a delicate thermometer, the mercury will sink at the moment of discharge, owing to the enormous expansion of the air. And when steam from a boiler suddenly issues, under great pressure, from a small aperture into the atmosphere, its instantaneous expansion cools it to such a degree that instead of scalding the hand held in it, as is the case with ordinary steam, it scarcely feels warm.

245. The distribution of temperature in the Atmosphere, the formation and disappearance of clouds, the production of rain and snow explained by change of density in the air. These facts explain the great cold of the atmosphere of the earth at high elevations. In consequence of the diminution of pressure at high altitudes, the air is much more rare than it is at the surface of the earth. The sensible heat of temperature which it would possess if it were everywhere of the same density as it is at the surface of the earth, has been absorbed in consequence of its rarefaction, and is now latent. The higher we ascend, the greater the rarefaction, and consequently the greater the absorption of heat, and the lower the temperature. The average depression of temperature is about 1° F. for every 300 feet of ascent. If, therefore, a portion of air from the surface of the earth were suddenly carried to a great altitude, its temperature would fall, its watery vapor be condensed, and clouds be produced, § 202. If on the other hand, a portion of air, at a great elevation, were suddenly brought near the earth, its temperature would be greatly elevated in consequence of its condensation, and if it contained mists and clouds, these would disappear. Change of place among portions of the atmosphere is, of itself, able to produce great changes in its temperature, and in its clearness and cloudiness, and this, no doubt, has an important bearing upon many meteorological phenomena.

An excellent illustration of these principles is afforded by the fountain of Hiero, as it is called, at Schemnitz in Hungary. A part of the machinery for working the mines consists of a column of water 260 feet high, which presses upon a large volume of air, enclosed in a tight reservoir. The air is consequently enormously compressed by the immense weight of the water,

---

245. How do these principles explain the distribution of temperature in the atmosphere?

amounting to 8,089 atmospheres. When a pipe communicating with this reservoir of air is suddenly opened, it rushes out with extreme velocity, and instantly expanding, absorbs, in so doing, so much heat as to precipitate the moisture it contains in a shower of very white, compact snow, a hat held in the blast being immediately covered with it. So strong is the current of condensed air, that the workman who holds the hat is obliged to lean his back against the bank to retain it in its position. The snow in this case is due to the expansion of the air, and the conversion of its heat of temperature into latent heat.

246. The condensation of Vapors by pressure is explained on this principle. It is not the permanent gases alone, whose temperature is raised by compression and diminished by expansion. It is equally true of vapors. If vapor, after being separated from the liquid that forms it, be compressed into a diminished volume, or allowed to expand into an increased one, its temperature will be raised in the one case and lowered in the other, and at the same time its elasticity will be increased by the diminution of its volume, and diminished by the increase of it. It has been stated, § 202, that when vapor is subjected to mechanical compression, its elastic force remains unchanged, because a part of the vapor is condensed into a liquid. It is more correct to say, that the first effect of mechanical compression upon vapors is to increase their temperature, by converting their latent into sensible heat. Their elasticity is at the same time increased in proportion to the pressure, but as the elevation of their temperature above that of the surrounding medium, renders it very easy to abstract heat from them, and the instant any heat is abstracted, a portion of the vapor is reduced to the state of a liquid, this increased elasticity is almost immediately reduced to the point at which it was before the compression took place, and no perceptible depression is produced upon the height of the mercurial column. On the other hand, when the mechanical pressure upon the vapor is removed, it immediately expands, its temperature is proportionally lowered by the conversion of its sensible into latent heat, heat begins to enter it from the surrounding medium, a portion of the liquid begins to vaporize, and so the process goes on, until as much vapor has been formed as the temperature of the surrounding medium is able to sustain. Consequently, no perceptible elevation takes place in the height of the mercurial column, because the increase

---

246. State the eight principles that may be deduced from the above mentioned facts.

of elasticity produced by the influx of heat, keeps pace with the diminution produced by the removal of mechanical pressure. The condensation of vapor is then, in all cases, due to the abstraction of heat, and not to mechanical compression, just as truly as the formation of vapor is due to the addition of heat. In the liquefaction of gases, the process is accomplished by depriving them of heat as fast as their temperature is raised by compression. In this manner, so much heat is gradually abstracted as to compel them to assume the form of liquids. In all cases, vapor compressed, rises to the same temperature that would be necessary to produce it, under the same pressure, by the direct application of heat. Thus the vapor raised from water at the temperature of 68° has a volume 58,224 times greater than the water which produced it. Now let this vapor, having been separated from the water, be compressed until it be reduced to the volume which it would have had if it had been formed from boiling water, i. e., a volume only 1.696 times greater than that of the water which produced it, and its temperature will rise from 68° to 212° by the conversion of its latent into sensible heat, i. e., exactly the temperature it would have been necessary to give it, if it had been formed in the first place of this degree of pressure and elastic force. This is a conclusive proof, that the sum of the sensible and insensible heat in vapor is the same, whatever the temperature at which it may have been formed.

247. **Summary of Principles. Applications. Illustrations.** From the phenomena presented by liquefaction, vaporization, solidification, and the compression and expansion of solids, liquids and gases, we may deduce the following important principles:—

1. Change of density always produces change of temperature.

2. If a body pass from a denser to a rarer condition, or from the state of a solid to that of a liquid or a vapor, heat is absorbed, and the temperature of surrounding objects sinks.

3. If the reverse takes place, and a body becomes more dense than before, or passes from the state of a vapor to that of a liquid or solid, as when steam is condensed or water freezes, heat is given forth, and the temperature of surrounding objects rises.

4. Mechanical compression raises, and mechanical expansion diminishes the temperature of all bodies, solid, liquid and gaseous.

5. If the result of mixing two liquids be, that they occupy less space than before, heat is produced. Four parts, by weight, of sulphuric acid, and one part, by weight, of water, become condensed when mingled, and sufficient latent heat is set free to heat the mixture above the boiling point of water.

6. If the result of mixing two liquids be, the production of a solid, great heat is produced. One or two drops of sulphuric acid added to a solution of chloride of calcium, produces a solid, and gives forth a large amount of heat.

7. If a solid be dissolved in water, cold results. Nitrate of ammonia thrown into water will be at once dissolved, and great reduction of temperature will take place.

8. If a liquid be added to a solid, and be at once absorbed, heat results. If quicklime be thrown into water, the water disappears, and great heat is produced, sufficient to inflame matches, and set fire to buildings and vessels.

Many other phenomena of daily occurrence in nature and the arts may be explained on these principles.

Experiments: Specific Heat.

1. **Specific Heat.** To show that equal amounts of heat, added to different substances, increase their temperatures unequally, or that their capacities for heat are different, mix 1 lb. of water at 100°, with 1 lb. of mercury at 40°; the temperature of the mixture will be 98°. Then mix 1 lb. of mercury at 100°, with 1 lb. of water at 40°, and the temperature of the mixture will be 42° only. The same amount of heat has been added in both cases. Why this difference of result? Because the water has a greater capacity for heat than mercury.

2. Heat balls of zinc, copper, tin, iron, lead, of the same weight, to the same degree, by immersing them in boiling water, and then dip them all into different vessels, of the same size, all containing equal weights of water at 32°, each having a thermometer in it, and note the different heights at which the thermometers stand at the end of half an hour.

3. This experiment may be varied by observing the times occupied by the different metals in raising the temperature of the different vessels of water to the same degree.

4. Observe the amount of ice melted, and water formed, by the cooling of equal weights of different substances. This is the most satisfactory mode of ascertaining specific heat.

1. **Change of State produces change of Temperature.** Mix equal parts of snow and salt together; great cold results from their liquefaction.

2. Add a few drops of sulphuric acid to a strong solution of chlorohydrate of lime, (muriate of lime); a solid results, and great heat is produced.

3. Add water to quicklime; a solid results, and great heat is produced.

4. Potassium and sodium pressed together in a mortar, produce a liquid alloy; add mercury, and this liquid solidifies, and heat enough is produced to inflame the naphtha adhering to the potassium.

5. Hammer iron, and it becomes very hot.

6. Compress water by a powerful screw, and the thermometer rises; remove the pressure, and it sinks.

7. Compress air in the fire syringe, and a piece of well dried punk, or tinder, will be inflamed.

8. Exhaust the air from a bell glass, by the air pump, and the thermometer will sink; allow the air to enter again, which is the same thing as compressing it, and the thermometer will rise.

9. Mix equal volumes of sulphuric acid and water; an increase of density results, with great rise of temperature.

10. Mix equal volumes of alcohol and water; condensation results, and rise of temperature.

§ VII. The Sources of Heat.

247. The Sources of Heat. The sources of heat are numerous, but they may all be reduced to seven; viz: 1st, The Sun. 2d, The internal heat of the earth. 3d, Chemical action and combustion. 4th, Electricity. 5th, The absorption of moisture. 6th, Vital action. 7th, Mechanical action.

248. The Sun. Of all the sources of heat, the sun is the most intense. The cause of the sun's heat is unknown, but it is probably due to electrical or chemical action. The amount of heat which the earth receives from this source is enormous. Faraday has calculated that the average amount radiated by the sun upon an acre of land, on a summer's day, is equal to that which would be produced by the combustion of sixty sacks of coal. It has been estimated that the amount of solar heat entering the atmosphere of the earth in one year, is sufficient to melt a layer of ice completely enveloping it, from 90 to 100 feet in thickness; of this amount however, the earth only receives about two thirds, the rest being absorbed by the atmosphere. This vast amount is, however, but a small part of that radiated by the sun; calculating the area which the earth presents, and its mean distance from the sun, it has been found that the earth does not receive at any moment, more than $\frac{1}{2281000000}$ part of that which the sun emits. Indirectly by the various effects which solar heat and light produce when they reach the earth, the sun is really the cause of that which proceeds from some of the other sources of heat, and especially, that produced by the combustion of vegetable matter.

249. The Internal heat of the Earth. Besides the heat which it is receiving from the sun, the earth has also a nucleus of intensely heated matter within itself. This is proved by the steadily increasing heat of the earth at successive depths. At 30 or 40 feet beneath the surface, the thermometer is unaffected

---

247. How many sources of heat are there? State what they are.—248. Which is the most intense source of heat? What is the amount of heat received by the earth from the sun, per acre? What is the amount per annum, that enters the atmosphere? How much of this reaches the earth? How does the heat and light of the sun, indirectly produce the heat that seems to emanate from other sources?—249. What is the second source of heat? How may the nucleus of heated matter in the interior of the earth be proved to exist?

by the variations of the seasons. As we proceed below this point the thermometer is found to rise progressively, though not uniformly in all places, at the average rate of 1° F. for every 50 feet of descent. Some have estimated the rate at 1° for every 45 feet. In six of the deepest mines of the north of England the rate is 1° for every 44 feet. In the lead mines of Saxony it is 1° for every 60 feet, and the same rate was observed in boring the well of Grenelle at Paris. At this rate the temperature of the earth increases 100° for every mile; consequently at one mile and a half the temperature would be as high as that of boiling water, and at the depth of 40 miles a temperature of 4000° would be attained, which is considerably above the melting point of cast iron and even of platinum, and quite sufficient to completely fuse all known mineral substances. The central mass of the earth is probably now in a state of igneous fluidity, and the thickness of the external crust is not more than $\frac{1}{150}$ its radius, about the thickness of a sheet of paper upon a twelve inch globe. This thin crust is however so poor a conductor that the central heat is hardly felt on the surface, and it has been calculated that it does not elevate the mean temperature of the surface more than $\frac{1}{50}$ of a degree. It must however, exert a powerful effect in keeping up the general temperature of the globe.

250. Chemical action, Combustion. Chemical combination is generally accompanied with the evolution of heat, and this constitutes the chief source of artificial heat. When the combination takes place slowly, as when iron oxidises in the air, the heat disengaged is imperceptible, but when it proceeds rapidly the disengagement of heat is very intense, and combustion ensues. Every chemical combination which is attended with the disengagement of heat and light is called combustion. In the case of wood, coal, oil, gas, &c., it is the combination of carbon and hydrogen with the oxygen of the air which produces the heat and light. But there are numerous instances of combination in which oxygen plays no part, as when metallic antimony is dropped in powder into a jar of chlorine, or phosphorus is mixed with iodine. The quantity of heat produced by combustion varies greatly with the nature of the substances em-

---

What is the rate of increase? At this rate what is the temperature at the depth of 40 miles? How much of this heat reaches the surface of the earth? What effect has it upon the general temperature of the globe?—250. What is the third source of heat? What is combustion? In the case of the combustion of coal, oil, &c., what elements by their combination produce the heat? To what is the amount of heat produced in all cases of combustion proportioned?

ployed, but it is always constant for the same substances, and proportioned exactly to the weight of each which is consumed. The amount of heat produced is by no means proportional to the light. The flame of hydrogen is that which produces the most heat of any known combustible, but its light is so feeble that it can hardly be seen in the day time. The following table gives the amount of heat produced by various combustible substances when they burn in the air. The thermal unit is the heat necessary to raise a weight of water equal to that of the combustible, 1°.

Table of Heat produced by various Combustibles.

Hydrogen,	34.462 units of heat.
Light. Carb. Hydrogen,	13.063 " "
Illuminating Gas,	11.858 " "
Beeswax,	10.496 " "
Spermaceti,	10.342 " "
Turpentine,	10.662 " "
Alcohol,	7.184 " "
Wood Charcoal,	8.080 " "
Coke,	8.047 " "

251. Electricity. This is another source of intense heat, whether produced by the electrical machine or by the galvanic battery. Gunpowder may be inflamed and gases may be fired by a single spark, however small, from the electrical machine, and the heat produced by the galvanic battery is far greater than that proceeding from any other artificial source. If the wires from the poles of a powerful battery be tipped with well burned charcoal and brought near each other, a continuous current of electricity passes, producing intense light, and heat sufficient to fuse the precious stones, and dissipate the metals in vapour.

252. The Absorption of Liquids and Gases. The simple act of moistening any dry substance is attended with a slight disengagement of heat. With mineral substances reduced to fine powder and wetted, the rise of temperature does not exceed one or two degrees, but with vegetable and animal substances, such as cotton, hair, wool, ivory, dried paper, &c., the rise of temperature varies from 2° to 10° or 11° F. The absorption of gases by solid bodies gives rise to the same phe-

---

What substance produces the greatest amount of heat in burning? Give the table of the amount of heat produced by different combustibles. What is the thermal unit in the above table?—251. State the fourth source of heat. What heating effect can be produced by the electrical spark, by the galvanic battery?—252. What is the fifth source of heat? State the heating effect produced by the absorption of moisture by cotton, hair, wool, &c., by the absorption of gases?

nomena. If platinum, in the state of platinum black, be placed in oxygen gas the metal will absorb several hundred times its weight of the gas, and its temperature will rise high enough to produce intense combustion. In like manner, if a jet of hydrogen gas be directed upon a bit of spongy platinum suspended in the air, it will almost immediately take fire from the heat produced by the absorption of the gas.

253. Vital action. Both plants and animals produce a continued and definite amount of heat, by means of which their temperature is sustained considerably above that of the surrounding medium. This may be regarded as strictly due to the chemical action which at all times is going on within the vegetable and animal economy, regulated, however, by the vital power. There is, during life, a steadily continued combination going on between the carbon and hydrogen of the tissues, and the oxygen of the air. This is a case of combustion, and strictly analogous to the burning of coal and gas in the air, for the same amount of heat is produced by an equal weight of the elements employed in both cases, the only difference being, that in the one case the heat is produced rapidly, in the other, slowly.

254. Mechanical action.—Friction and Percussion.—The mechanical equivalent of Heat. The friction of two bodies against each other produces an amount of heat proportioned to the pressure employed and the rapidity of the movement. Among savage nations the friction of two pieces of wood is used as a means of lighting a fire, and the heating of machinery, and the axles of carriages and of locomotives, even to the point of igniting combustible substances placed near them, is a matter of daily occurrence. Sir H. Davy melted two blocks of ice by causing them to be rubbed violently against each other, in a vacuum, at a temperature below 32°. Count Rumford succeeded in boiling water by the friction from the boring of a cannon; a blunt steel borer was made to press against the end of the cannon, and surrounded by a box containing $18\frac{3}{4}$ lbs. of water, in which a thermometer was placed. The original temperature of the water was 60°; in an hour the temperature of the water had risen to 107°; in one hour and a half, to 142°; in two hours to 178°, and in two hours and a half from the commencement of the experiment, the water rose to 212°, and ac-

---

253. What is the sixth source of heat? To what is the heat produced by this source strictly due? What combustion is continually going on in the bodies of animals and plants?—254. What is the seventh source of heat? Explain the heat of friction. Describe Sir H. Davy's experiment. Count Rumford's.

tually began to boil. An apparatus has been invented in France, for generating steam by means of heat generated by friction. Mr. Tyndall succeeded in making water boil in two minutes and a half, in a brass tube which was made to revolve very rapidly between two pieces of oak, compressed tightly around it, and the cork with which the tube was stopped was projected twenty feet into the air by the pressure of the steam. Percussion is a combination of friction and compression, and often produces intense heat, as when the particles of steel detached by the flint, in the use of the ordinary tinder box, are ignited by the heat evolved by the sudden collision. Iron may be heated red hot by hammering, and bars of brass and copper which were quite cold when subjected to the pressure of the rolling mill, often issue in an extremely heated state. The heat derived from this source is, as has been previously stated, the heat previously latent in these substances converted into heat of temperature by the increase of density produced by compression. It is remarkable that the supply of heat from this source seems to be almost unlimited. The quantity of heat developed by friction is dependent solely upon the amount of force expended, and not upon the nature of the substances rubbed together. It was ascertained by Mr. Joule that when water was agitated by means of a brass paddle wheel, the expenditure of an amount of force sufficient to elevate 772 lbs. to the height of 1 foot, had the effect of raising the temperature of 1 lb. of water, 1°. When iron was rubbed against iron the expenditure of an amount of force sufficient to elevate 775 lbs. to the height of 1 foot, had the effect of raising the temperature of 1 lb. of water, 1°. When mercury was agitated by a cast iron paddle wheel, 1 lb. of water was raised in temperature 1° by the expenditure of an amount of force sufficient to elevate 774 lbs. to the height of 1 foot. The conclusion deduced was that the mechanical force adequate to raise 772 lbs. to the height of 1 foot, produced sufficient heat to elevate the temperature of 1 lb. of water from 55° to 56°, i. e., by 1°. There is good reason to believe that the reverse is also true. That the heat which will raise the temperature of 1 lb. of water 1°, will exert a mechanical force sufficient to raise 772 lbs. to the height of 1 foot, or is equivalent to this amount of

---

Mr. Tyndall's. Explain the striking of sparks by the flint and steel. Is there any limit to the amount of heat which can be produced by friction? Does the heat produced depend upon the nature of the substance employed, or upon the amount of force? How was this proved? How much heat is produced by a mechanical force sufficient to raise 772 lbs one foot high? How much mechanical force is produced by an amount of heat which will heat 1 lb of water, 1°. State the mechanical equivalent of heat.

mechanical force. This amount of force, viz: 772 lbs. elevated to the height of 1 foot, is consequently called, the *mechanical equivalent of heat*.

Experiments.

1. **Sources of Heat.** The heat of the sun may be shown by condensing its rays upon some inflammable material by an ordinary burning glass.
2. The heat of combustion may be shown by the inflammation of the ordinary illuminating gas of cities.
3. The heat of Electricity, by passing the charge of a Leyden jar through a jet of illuminating gas, as it issues into the air. For this purpose let a wire be attached to the stem of the burner, ascend by its side and rise two inches above it; then let it curve at right angles, and terminate in the center of the ascending column of gas; bring the knob of the Leyden jar near to the end of the wire, so that the charge will pass directly through the gas. It will be inflamed.
4. Chemical action produces heat, shown by pouring 1 ounce of Chlorohydric acid on 1 ounce of Ammonia; also by rubbing together Sulphur and Caustic Potash, equal parts, in a mortar. The Acid should be poured from a vessel tied to a stick several feet long.
5. Mechanical action produces heat, shown by boring a hole with a common gimlet, in wood, and then applying the iron to a piece of phosphorus. It will be inflamed.
6. The same may be shown by the compression of Air in the Fire Syringe.
7. Also by the admission of air into an exhausted Receiver, containing a Thermometer.

---

§ VIII. The nature of Heat.

255. The material theory of Heat. There are two theories in regard to the nature of heat. The first regards heat as an extremely subtile form of matter, and possessed of all its common properties except weight; able to enter into combination with bodies, and producing, when it does so, the phenomena of expansion, liquefaction and vaporization. It is supposed to be a fluid, and to pass, with great celerity, from one body to another, whenever they are brought into actual contact. When an appreciable interval separates two bodies, heat is thought to pass from one to the other with the velocity of light. Its particles are supposed to be very highly repulsive, and to have a strong tendency to fly apart, so that when it enters another substance it necessarily tends to separate the particles of which it is composed, and to expand the body. Being destitute of weight, heat is called an Imponderable. The theory of the material nature of heat is chiefly supported by the phenomena of liquefaction and vaporization, in which heat seems to en-

---

255. How many theories are there in regard to the nature of heat? Describe the material theory. On what is this theory chiefly supported?

ter, in certain regular proportions, into composition with other forms of matter, and to produce new substances differing from their component elements in most of their physical properties. In this respect there certainly is a close analogy between heat and other kinds of matter. The material theory of heat, is the one which has been generally received until within a short time.

256. The mechanical theory of Heat. The second theory is called the mechanical theory of Heat. It supposes that heat is altogether immaterial in its character, and simply a force produced by the vibrations of the molecules of bodies, or the infinitely small particles of which matter is believed to be made. The essence of heat is thought to consist in motion, so that it is always produced by motion, and also, itself always generates motion. The infinitely small particles of which bodies consist, are thought to be in a state of constant vibration, or to have a never ceasing oscillating motion. This motion is supposed to be the cause of heat, and when it exceeds a certain rate, to produce the sensation and all the other common effects of heat. According to this view, heat is a *mode of motion*. This is the theory which was suggested by Count Rumford, towards the latter part of the last century, supported by Sir H. Davy, and revived recently by Messrs. Grove, Joule, and especially by Mr. Tyndall.

257. Proof that heat is produced by motion. This is proved by the numerous instances in which heat results from the arrest of motion. If a lead ball be allowed to fall from a great height upon an iron plate, it is flattened by the fall, its motion completely checked, and its temperature will, at the same time, be found to be considerably elevated. The motion seems to have been transformed or converted into heat. In like manner, if a railway train under full headway, be stopped by the application of the brakes, as the motion is retarded, great heat is manifestly produced, and even the ignition of the wood and leather with which the wheels are pressed. When mercury is repeatedly poured from one vessel to another, its motion, in each case, being suddenly arrested by dashing against the sides of the vessel, its temperature is perceptibly elevated. In like manner, if air be blown violently against a fixed obstacle,

---

256. What is the second theory? Describe it. Who have been some of the principal supporters of this theory?—257. Give some of the proofs that heat is the result of motion. If a lead ball be allowed to fall from a great height, what effect is produced upon its temperature? If mercury be poured from one vessel to another? If a railway train, in rapid motion, be suddenly stopped? Give other instances.

the temperature of the latter, as well as of the air, if tested by a delicate thermo-multiplier, will be found to be considerably raised. The same fact is also conclusively shown by the experiment of Count Rumford, already described, upon the boiling of water in the boring of cannon. It is even asserted, with considerable confidence, that the water of the cataract is heated by its fall, and that of the ocean by the agitation of its waves.

258. Proof that motion is produced by heat. This is shown in the effect which is produced upon the dimensions of bodies whenever heat enters them. The particles are invariably moved farther apart, and the bodies expanded. If the heat, in the case of a solid, be pushed to the point of liquefaction, a further movement takes place, and the particles are removed so far from each other as to be susceptible of a ready interchange of place. Finally, if the heat be urged so far as to produce vaporization, a still further movement is produced in the particles, and they become actually self-repellent and elastic. The motion of the steam-engine is altogether the result of the heat derived from the fire of the furnaces. So is the motion of the caloric-engine of Ericsson. The heat of combustion is supposed to be produced by the violent clashing of the particles of carbon and hydrogen, of which common combustible matter is composed, and the oxygen of the air. The mechanical motion imparted to these particles by the force of chemical affinity tending to draw them together, is converted into the peculiar kind of motion producing the sensation and the effects which we call heat. In all cases therefore, the general effect of heat is the production of motion, and *vice versa*, heat is always produced by motion. They are therefore convertible one into the other.

259. Heat not the sole cause of motion, while motion is the sole cause of heat. Though motion is produced by heat, heat is not the sole cause of motion. There are many other sources of motion besides heat, such as gravity, electricity, and animal contractility; but heat is thought to be only produced by motion. Motion is regarded as the natural state of the molecules of matter. These are believed to be constantly in motion, even when the body of which they are a part, is at rest; and when this motion is, from any cause, quickened beyond a certain de-

---

258. Prove that motion is produced by heat. Show that this is the case in expansion, liquefaction and vaporization. The steam engine. The caloric engine. Are heat and mechanical force mutually convertible?—259. Is heat the sole cause of motion? On the other hand is motion the sole cause of heat, according to the mechanical theory? What proportion exists between the heat produced by a definite amount of mechanical motion and the motion produced by the same amount of heat?

gree, heat is the result. Consequently, mechanical motion is spoken of as the cause of heat, by which is meant, that it is the sole cause, while heat, on the hand, is never spoken of in this sense, as the sole cause of motion.

260. The amount of Heat produced by a definite amount of mechanical motion, and the Mechanical Motion produced by the same amount of heat, are precisely equal. It has been shown that the amount of force produced by the fall of 772 lbs. through 1 foot, is sufficient to raise the temperature of 1 lb. of water 1° F. i. e., this is the amount of heat which would be generated if a 772 lb. weight, after having fallen through 1 foot, had its moving force destroyed by collision with the earth. Conversely, it has been shown, that if the force produced by an amount of heat which would elevate the temperature of 1 lb. of water 1° were all concentrated, it would be sufficient to raise 772 lbs. 1 foot into the air. From these facts we draw the conclusion that the heat produced by motion, and the motion produced by heat, are not simply accidental circumstances, but, that there is, in these cases, a certain definite amount of mechanical motion converted into the motion which we call heat, which ceases to appear any more as mechanical motion; and on the other hand, a certain definite amount of heat motion converted into mechanical motion, and which ceases to appear any more as heat. These forces are not lost or destroyed, but merely converted from one kind of force into the other, and may be recovered again by the contrary conversion. It follows from this, that, in all cases where heat is used to produce motion, as in the case of the steam engine, an amount of heat disappears or is used up proportionate to the mechanical effect produced. It is believed that the heat possessed by the steam when it enters the cylinder of the high pressure steam engine, is not all found in the steam which issues from the same cylinder, after the piston has been moved, but that a portion of this heat has been consumed and converted into mechanical motion, and that this mechanical motion in spending itself, has produced again an equal amount of heat, by friction, in the various parts of the machine. According to the material theory of heat, none of the heat of the steam, which is used, is consumed,

---

260. What is the amount of mechanical motion produced by the heat necessary to raise 1 lb. of water 1°? Conversely, what is the heat produced by the mechanical force, necessary to raise 772 lbs. 1 foot? When heat is used to produce motion, does the whole of the heat appear at the conclusion of the process, or has a part been consumed in producing the motion? Illustrate this in the case of the steam engine. Is the heat which exists in the steam when it enters the cylinder of a high pressure engine all found in it when it leaves the cylinder? If not, what has become of it?

but the whole is found in the steam which issues from the cylinder, and may be collected in the condenser. The mechanical motion, according to this view, is not due to the conversion of heat into motion, but merely to its expansive effect in passing from the boiler to the condenser.

261. Some of the common phenomena of heat explained upon the mechanical Theory. According to this theory, the particles of bodies being in a state of incessant vibration, heat is supposed to be produced by increase in the intensity of the motion. When the atoms move beyond a certain determined velocity, and the vibrations become more extended, the heat evolved pushes the particles apart and separates them from each other, thus causing the body in question to increase in volume, and producing expansion. When the vibrations of the particles become sufficiently extensive, they are then loosened from each other to such a degree as to be able freely to interchange places, and liquefaction is the result. When the vibrations are pushed so far that the particles are separated too far from each other for cohesion to bind them together, they become self-repellent and elastic, and the vaporous state is produced. When a hot body, whose particles are in a state of vibration, is brought near to another, colder than itself, the vibration is communicated to the particles of the second body, which are thus, in their turn, set in motion, or conduction takes place. When heat is radiated it is supposed that the oscillating motion of the particles of the hot body is communicated to the particles of a very fine and delicate ether pervading all space, which, as soon as they begin to vibrate, produce a succession of undulations, that are propagated in right lines until they reach some material obstacle, to the particles of which their motion is then communicated. This is supposed to be the mode in which radiant heat is propagated through space and made to affect the temperature of bodies on which it falls. When a solid body is liquefied, it is well known that a large amount of heat becomes latent, which, it has been thought, combines with the solid, in order to form the liquid. According to the mechanical theory, this heat is not stored or combined, but has been simply consumed or used up in forcing the particles of the body apart, i. e., in the production of a certain amount of motion, and when these particles approach each other

---

261. Explain liquefaction according to the mechanical theory of heat. Vaporization. Conduction. Radiation. Explain the disappearance of heat, or heat made latent in liquefaction, according to the mechanical theory; also, the heat made latent in vaporization.

again, and the liquid returns to the solid state, the motion which then takes place reproduces exactly the amount of heat which had been consumed. The same thing takes place in the case of vaporization; there is no heat combined or made latent, but there is a larger amount consumed and used up than in the case of liquefaction, and this is again reproduced when the particles of the vapour move near to each other for the purpose of resuming the liquid or solid state. Thus all the common phenomena of heat are as well explained by the mechanical as by the material theory of heat.

262. The mechanical theory is confirmed by several simple facts. According to the material theory, the heat evolved by friction, as in the case of the celebrated experiment of Count Rumford, when water was boiled in the process of boring a cannon, is heat previously existing in the solid metal of the cannon and the borer, in a latent state, in other words, is a part of their specific heat which is forced to appear in consequence of the diminution of specific heat produced by compression. If this were the case it is evident that the specific heat of the chips and fragments of metal, produced by boring, should be less than before, to a degree sufficient to account for the increase in the temperature of the water. Count Rumford ascertained by experiment, that the capacity for heat, or the specific heat of the chips had not been reduced, but was precisely what it was before. The material theory fails, therefore, of explaining the heat produced in this case, and the only supposition that we can adopt is, that the effect has been caused by the motion of the particles produced by compression, and by the mechanical motion of the borer, converted, in part, into heat. Again, in Sir H. Davy's experiment, § 254, in which two blocks of ice were melted into water by the heat generated by rubbing them together in a vacuum, at a temperature below 32°, the explanation given by the material theory is the same as in the last case, that the melting is produced by the diminution of the specific heat of the ice. The specific heat of the water formed, ought therefore to be considerably less than that of the ice, but instead of that, its specific heat, or its capacity for heat is double; it is impossible, therefore, that the heat which melted the ice should be latent heat, become superfluous, and forced to appear, because the water

---

262 By what simple facts is the mechanical theory confirmed. State the experiment of Count Rumford of boiling water by means of friction; also, Sir H. Davy's experiment of melting ice by friction. Show how both are explicable upon the mechanical, but inexplicable on the material theory of heat.

could not retain it. It is certain, also, that in all cases when ice is melted, there is an enormous amount of heat absorbed, and none whatever given forth. The conclusion, therefore, is, that the melting of the ice is due to the conversion into heat of a part of the mechanical motion employed.

Lastly, it has been seen, that when gases are rarefied by a diminution of pressure, their temperature is greatly reduced, and this has been regarded as the cause of the low temperature which prevails in the higher regions of the atmosphere. The explanation given, has been that the specific heat of rarefied, is much greater than that of condensed air, and the demand for heat, caused by the expansion, is satisfied at the expense of the heat of temperature. It has been ascertained, however, from a calculation of the weight of the atmosphere, raised by the expansion of a heated body of air confined in a cylinder, under a piston moving freely, and open to the air above, that the amount of heat of temperature which disappears, is exactly proportioned to the weight raised, or the mechanical motion produced, and that these are in the precise proportion of 772 lbs. raised 1 foot for an amount of heat sufficient to heat 1 lb. of water by $1°$ F. It seems evident, therefore, that the diminution of temperature in the case of expanding air, is due to the consumption of heat, and its conversion into the mechanical motion of the molecules in the act of expansion; and the exact agreement of the proportion of heat to motion in this particular case, with the calculated proportion between heat and motion in the determination of the mechanical equivalent of heat, § 254, furnishes a very strong argument in favor of the mechanical theory of heat.

263. Heat may be converted into Light. If we intensify the vibrations of heat in any body, we convert it into Light, and cause the body to shine. This we can do by exposing a piece of platinum wire to heat of gradually increasing intensity. At first it emits only obscure rays of heat, then luminous rays of light of a very feeble red color, then those of a bright cherry red, then orange, yellow, white, and finally an intense blue. It has been calculated that all red light is produced by a temperature of $700°$, bright red $900°$, full red heat $1000°$, yellow $1100°$, white light $1400°$ to $3280°$. Even the dullest substances may thus be made to emit light of the greatest brilliancy and intensity. From this it would seem that Light is only the exceed-

---

Show how the diminution of temperature in the atmosphere, as we ascend, may be explained upon the mechanical theory.—263. Show how heat can be converted into light.

ingly rapid vibrations of the same ether, which when vibrating more slowly produces merely the effect and sensation of Heat. As these heat vibrations increase in rapidity they produce, first that kind of light which results from the slowest Light vibrations, then that color which is produced by vibrations of a more rapid character, and finally blue light, which has been found to be produced by the most rapid vibrations, and to be possessed of the greatest refrangibility. On the other hand, that Light may be converted into Heat, seems to be proved by the experiment of placing cloths of different colors upon the snow. The temperature of these cloths is shown by the depth to which the snow is melted beneath them; and this is found to be precisely the order in which they absorb the light: black destroys all light vibrations and it is found to be heated the most and sunk the most deeply in the snow; next comes blue, green, purple, red and yellow, white reflects all the light, and consequently is heated the least of all the colors. Light can also be resolved into heat through the medium of chemical action. Heat and Light are therefore produced by the same cause, acting with different degrees of intensity, and we naturally pass, therefore, from the study of radiant Heat to that of radiant Light.

264. The convertibility of the Forces, which act upon matter into each other and their indestructibility. The general conclusion at which modern science has arrived, is that the various forms of force which act upon matter are, many of them, if not all, capable of passing into each other, and that in all cases when a force seems to be destroyed, it is not really so, but simply converted into another variety of force of equal energy. Force is, then, believed to be as indestructible as matter. By this expression it is not meant that either force or matter are incapable of destruction, but simply, that in fact, as the material world is at present constituted, neither of them is destroyed in the various transmutations which they undergo, but are merely changed from one form to another. The primary form of force which is selected as the type of all the others is mechanical motion. Into this all the others are capable of being resolved, and out of it, most of them can be again elicited. From heat may be obtained light, electricity, chemical action and motion; from light may be obtained chemical

---

Show that light may be converted into heat.—264. What is the general conclusion of modern science in regard to the convertibility of the forces that act on matter, and their indestructibility.

236 WHICH ACT UPON MATTER.—NATURE OF LIGHT.

action and heat; from electricity, heat, light, chemical action and motion; from chemical action, heat, light, electricity and motion; from motion itself, heat, light, electricity and chemical action. The intimate connection of Heat and Light, and their mutual convertibility, will be seen more clearly from the following chapter.

CHAPTER III.

THE SECOND CHEMICAL AGENT:—LIGHT.

THE NATURE OF LIGHT; SOURCES; REFLECTION; REFRACTION; SOLAR SPECTRUM; SPECTRUM ANALYSIS; EFFECT OF LIGHT ON PLANTS; CHEMICAL EFFECTS OF LIGHT; PHOTOGRAPHY; RELATIONS OF LIGHT AND HEAT.

265. The nature of Light. The second of the great Imponderable Agents controlling the action of Affinity, and playing an important part in many chemical phenomena, is Light. There are two hypotheses in regard to the nature of light corresponding with those which have been explained in regard to the nature of heat. According to the first of these, light is a subtile material fluid, which is thrown off by all luminous bodies, composed of particles inconceivably minute, and moving with immense velocity. These particles falling on different substances are reflected, transmitted, or absorbed, and when they strike upon the optic nerve, produce the sensation of light. The second hypothesis supposes that light is the result of undulation, produced in an exceedingly rare and subtile medium, pervading all space, and filling the interstices of all forms of matter. This medium is not light itself, but it can be thrown into the vibrations which constitute light by impulses communicated to it by all luminous objects. The latter is the theory now generally received, as it affords the most complete explanation of all the phenomena of light. It is strongly supported by the analogy of sound, which, as is well known, is produced by the undulations of the air, and is in like manner susceptible of transmission, reflection, and absorption; it also corresponds with

---

265. What is the second imponderable? How many theories are there in regard to the nature of light? State the material theory. The undulatory theory.

the undulatory theory of heat already explained, and now beginning to be generally received.

265. The sources of Light.—Solar Light. The first and most important source of light, is the sun and the heavenly bodies. The origin of the light of the sun and the stars is unknown, but it is generally supposed that the inflammable matter which appears to surround the sun is gaseous in its character, because the light which it emits is the same as that which proceeds from gaseous, inflammable substances, and does not afford any trace of polarization by the instruments intended to detect it. Astronomical investigations have rendered it probable that the sun consists of two parts, a central mass, emitting light of great brilliancy, and an external luminous atmosphere, also emitting light, and called a photosphere. This view of the constitution of the sun is supported by the recent discoveries connected with spectrum analysis.

267. Ignition of Solids a source of Light. Whenever any solid body is raised to a temperature of 900°, or 1000°, it begins to emit light, and becomes luminous, or incandescent. Even gaseous matter, if heated to 2000°, becomes feebly luminous. If any solid matter be introduced into a current of gas at this high temperature, the brightness of the light is greatly increased, and it is upon the ignition of s lid matter in the interior of currents of intensely heated gas, that all processes of artificial illumination in common use, depend. In the case of illuminating gas, kerosene, candles, and oil, the solid substance emitting the light, is carbon in a state of intense ignition, precipitated from the gas in which it previously existed in combination with hydrogen. This very curious and beautiful process, on which so much of the comfort and enjoyment of man depends, will be more particularly described hereafter. One of the most remarkable instances of the production of light in this manner is seen in the case of the Drummond light, in which a jet of mixed oxygen and hydrogen is directed upon a piece of solid lime. The gases burning alone produce a flame which is hardly perceptible, but the moment the lime is introduced, the brilliancy of the light becomes at once too great for the eye to bear. Even a piece of platinum, or of china, introduced into

---

266. What is the first source of light? Why is the light of the sun and stars supposed to be of gaseous origin? What is supposed to be the constitution of the sun?—267. What is the second source of light? How can solid matter be made to emit light? On what do all processes of artificial light in common use depend? What is the ignited solid substance which emits light in the burning of illuminating gas and candles? Explain the Drummond light. Does the ignited solid in this case undergo any change?

this flame, or any other solid substance, will instantly begin to emit light. In all these cases the solid itself undergoes no change, and remains unconsumed. The color of the light varies with the intensity of the heat; when first perceptible, it is of a dull red, and gradually passes into orange, yellow, white, and violet. The temperature at which bodies begin to emit red light in the dark, is about 700°, but in broad daylight, solid matter does not become incandescent until heated to 1000°. Platinum begins to emit light in the dark, at 977°. If platinum, brass, antimony, gas-carbon, porcelain, black-lead, copper, and palladium, be introduced into a clean gun-barrel, which is then raised to a dull red heat, they are found, on looking into the barrel, to emit red light at the same moment, showing that they all require nearly the same temperature to make them incandescent. Chalk and marble, under the same circumstances, require a lower temperature, and begin to emit light before the gun-barrel is red-hot.

268. Electricity a source of Light. This is a powerful source of light, as may be seen in the case of the sparks produced by the ordinary electric machine, and also by the excessive brightness of a flash of lightning. The galvanic battery produces a steady and permanent light, too bright for the unprotected eye to bear, if the wires from the two poles are tipped with charcoal, and brought near enough to each other for the electric current to pass. Attempts have been made to employ this light in light-houses, but with indifferent success. In the galvanic battery, chemical action is the source of the electrical current; but this may also be produced by the revolution of wound armatures before the poles of powerful magnets, and if this current be allowed to pass through charcoal points, light of equal intensity to that of the galvanic battery may be obtained. The motion required may be generated by a small steam engine. This is the form in which electricity is now chiefly used for the production of artificial light. Here we have a striking instance of the conversion of forces; heat produces motion; motion is resolved into electricity, and this electricity into heat and light. The electric light from the battery is frequently substituted for the sun, in optical experiments, on account of its excessive brightness.

What is the temperature at which red light in the dark is emitted? In broad daylight? Do all bodies require nearly the same temperature to render them incandescent? —268. What is the third source of light? What is said of the light produced by the galvanic battery? To what purpose has it been applied? By what other means has light of equal intensity been produced? Can motion be converted into light? What illustration does this afford of the conversion of forces?

269. Exposure to the sun's rays, and to electricity, a source of Light. There are some substances, like the diamond, and other minerals, which, after being exposed to the sun's rays for some time, appear luminous when carried into a dark place. This property of emitting light without the application of an elevated artificial temperature, is called phosphorescence. Fluor spar, the diamond, and white marble, acquire phosphorescence, on the discharge through them of a succession of electric sparks. Again, if fluor spar be heated quite hot, it will become phosphorescent, and emit a beautiful blue light.

270. Decaying animal and vegetable matter a source of Light. Sea fish, and especially the herring and mackerel, become phosphorescent shortly after death. By placing such fish in weak saline solutions, such as sea salt; these solutions become luminous, and this appearance will continue for some time. In like manner, certain species of wood, in a state of decomposition, become phosphorescent, and shine with considerable brilliancy in the dark. In all these cases the light ceases to be given forth if the temperature be reduced below 32°. The light is probably due to a species of slow combustion, produced by the combination of the substance in question with the oxygen of the air. Phosphorus, a simple substance extracted from bones, also emits quite a brilliant light, when exposed to the air, on account of its rapid union with oxygen, and as this substance exists to a limited degree in all animal and vegetable matter, it is not unlikely that their phosphorescence may be due to this cause.

271. Luminous animals a source of Light. The glow-worm and the fire-fly have the power of giving out light, and in tropical climates there are numerous insects which, on being irritated, emit sufficient light to allow of reading. The waters of the ocean, in tropical latitudes, emit a beautiful phosphorescent light, on agitation, which is thought to be due to the presence of minute animalcules. Two of these animalcules placed in a bottle of water, have been known to diffuse a luminous influence through the whole mass.

272. Crystallization a source of Light. If sulphate of soda, and a few other salts that have been fused by the action of fire, be dissolved in water, and crystallized, the formation

---

269. What is the fourth source of light? What is phosphorescence? How do fluor spar, the diamond, and white marble, acquire phosphorescence?—270. What is the fifth source of light? To what is this light probably due? What is said of phosphorus as a source of light?—271. What is the sixth source of light? Give illustrations.—272. What is the seventh source of light? Give illustrations.

and separation of each crystal will be attended by a flash of light. The same result is produced if transparent arsenious acid is dissolved in hot chloro-hydric acid, and allowed to crystallize; if the process be watched in a darkened room, a faint flash of light will be seen to accompany the deposition of each crystal. The cause of this light is not known.

273. The reflection of Light. Light, whatever be the source from which it emanates, proceeds in straight lines, and these radiate from the luminous centre equally in all directions. These fine radiations are called rays, and a collected bundle of them is called a beam of light. The intensity of light diminishes according to the square of the distance from the luminous centre; so that a body receives one-quarter the light at a distance of two feet from the source of light, that it did at the distance of one foot. When these rays fall upon the surface of solid bodies they are reflected, absorbed, transmitted, and refracted, in the same manner as rays of heat under similar circumstances. The law of reflection is, that the angle which the incident ray makes with a perpendicular at the point of contact with the reflecting surface, is equal to the angle which the reflected ray makes with the same perpendicular. The phenomena of the reflection of light from mirrors, are the same as for the reflection of heat, § 73. There are different kinds of light, distinguished from each other by color, just as there are different kinds of heat, distinguished from each other by temperature; and when a beam of common light falls upon a solid body, some of the kinds of light of which it is composed may be absorbed, and some reflected. It is by this absorption of certain rays, and the reflection of others, that the colors of bodies are produced; the color of the body in question being that of the rays which are reflected. If all the rays are absorbed, except the red, the body will appear to be of a red color; if all are absorbed except the yellow and the blue, the body will seem to be of a green color, green being produced by a mixture of yellow and blue. There are certain bodies which transmit light freely, without absorption, and allow objects to be seen through them; these are called transparent: those which do not allow the light to pass through them are called opaque. There are no substances, however, which are perfectly transparent. The purest

---

273. In what direction do rays of light proceed? What becomes of these rays when they fall on other substances? What is the law of reflection? How does the reflection of light compare with that of heat? Explain the colors of bodies. What are transparent, and what opaque bodies? Are there any substances perfectly transparent or opaque?

atmosphere, and the clearest glass, arrest a portion of the light. It is estimated that not more than $\frac{1}{3000}$ part of the light of the sun's beams reach the earth, the remainder being absorbed. On the other hand, there are no bodies which are perfectly opaque; gold, one of the densest of the metals, may be hammered into very thin leaves, which transmit a green light, if the metal be pure gold, and purple, if alloyed with silver.

274. The refraction of Light. If a ray of light fall perpendicularly upon any transparent medium, it will continue on its course without any deviation; but if it fall obliquely, it will be bent more or less out of its original course. This sudden bending of a ray of light is called refraction. The refracted ray passes on in its new direction, through the refracting medium, in a straight line; but on issuing again upon the opposite side, it is refracted a second time in a contrary direction, and is restored to a course parallel to that which it had at first, provided the two refracting surfaces are exactly parallel. Refraction always takes place when rays of light pass from a rarer to a denser medium, or from a denser into a rarer medium, as from air into glass or water, and from glass or water into air. This is illustrated in *Fig.* 100, where s a represents the incident ray, and N M the refracting medium. As soon as the ray of light passes out of the air into the plate of glass at A, it is bent out of its course towards D; and again, when it passes from the denser medium of the glass, into the rarer medium of the air, it is refracted in the opposite direction, and takes the direction, D B, parallel to its original course. In general, the denser a substance is, the greater is the refraction which it produces in a ray of light. But this is far from being universally true, for ether, alcohol, and olive oil, which are lighter than water, have a higher refractive power. Observation has shown that *inflammable*, or *combustible* bodies, such as the diamond, phosphorus, sulphur, amber, camphor, olive and other oils, have a refractive power from two to seven times greater than that of incombustible sub-

Fig. 100.

Refraction of Light.

---

274. What is meant by the refraction of light? In what direction does the light pass through the refracting medium? Describe *Fig.* 100. What effect has density upon refractive power? What has been noticed in regard to combustible substances?

stances of equal density. The laws and phenomena of refraction are among the most interesting and important of all those connected with the subject of light, and upon them depends the operation of the microscope, telescope, and many other optical instruments. Their consideration, however, belongs more particularly to Natural Philosophy, and the student is referred, for their full explanation, to some extended treatise upon Optics.

275. Double refraction and polarization of Light. Light is not only susceptible of simple, but also of double refraction, as is the case with rays of heat. If a ray of light be allowed to fall at an oblique angle upon a rhombohedral crystal of Iceland spar, *Fig.* 101, it will be separated into two refracted rays, one of which, o, will follow the ordinary law of refraction; the other, E, pursues a totally different direction, and in a different plane. The former is called the ordinary, the latter the extraordinary, ray. Light that has been doubly refracted is found to have undergone a remarkable modification, and is no longer capable of reflection, refraction, or transmission in the same manner as before. Each ray on emerging, has acquired new properties. The rays, in fact, appear to have acquired sides, and to have new relations to certain planes within the crystal; such rays are said to be polarized. Light may be polarized by reflection, and also by transmission through bundles of plates, as well as by certain crystals. Polarized light is possessed of many peculiarities, which have been applied to some important practical purposes. A portion of all reflected light is polarized, and thus the astronomer can ascertain whether the light proceeding from a heavenly body had its origin in the body itself, or has been derived from some other source. Light proceeding from incandescent bodies, such as hot iron, glass, and various liquids under a certain angle, is polarized; and from a gaseous substance, such as illuminating gas, is in its unpolarized condition. On applying this principle

Fig. 101.

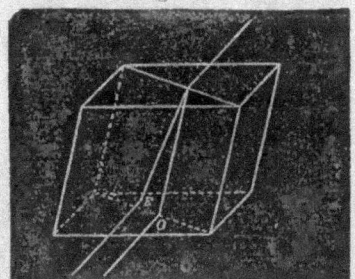

Double Refraction of Light.

---

275. What is meant by double refraction? By polarization? Are there any other means by which light can be polarized? What peculiarity is possessed by all reflected light? What is the difference between light proceeding from ignited solid bodies, and ignited gases? What application has Arago made of this principle to the light of the sun?

THE DECOMPOSITION OF LIGHT   243

to the sun, Arago is said to have discovered that the light which it emits is of gaseous origin. On transmitting polarized light through transparent media, whose structure is not perfectly homogeneous, and then allowing the light to be reflected to the eye of the observer, at an angle of 56°, the most brilliant colors will appear. From the production of these colors, we can infer the want of homogeneity in the transparent medium; and by an extension of observations of this kind, instruments have been constructed by which a quantity of crystallized matter existing in any solution may be ascertained, too minute for the power of ordinary chemical analysis to detect. This has been practically applied in the manufacture of sugar, and to the determination of the progress of diseases in the human body. For details, in reference to this interesting, but difficult subject, reference must be made to some treatise on Optics.

276. The compound nature of Solar Light.—The Illuminating Rays. A beam of solar light does not consist of one single kind of light, but of several, possessed of different colors when separated, but when united, producing upon the eye the impression of white light. These different kinds of light are possessed of different refrangibility, and consequently, when made to pass through the same refractive medium, they are not all bent to the same extent from their original course. By this unequal refraction, they are separated from each other, and each can be made to exhibit its own proper color. Sir Isaac Newton was the discoverer of the compound nature of white light, and he employed for this purpose a solid piece of glass, of triangular shape, known under the name of the *prism*, *Fig.* 102. Sometimes the prism is made hollow, and filled with water, or some other liquid. On placing the prism in such a position that one of its faces may be horizontal, as at A, *Fig.* 103, and allowing a beam of sunlight, admitted through a very small circular aperture, to fall at an oblique angle upon one of the other faces, the beam of sunlight, in passing through the prism, will be refracted twice, once at its entrance, and again at its emerg-

Fig. 102.

Prism.

What effect takes place when polarized light is transmitted through bodies whose structure is not perfectly homogeneous? What applications have been made of these principles?—276. How can the compound nature of solar light be shown? In what respects do the different kinds of light differ from each other? Who discovered the compound nature of light? What is a prism? How can it be used to decompose light?

Fig. 103.

The Decomposition of Light.

ence from the prism, and the rays of which it is composed being bent from their original course unequally, will be separated from each other, and caused to diverge. In consequence of this divergence, the differently colored rays will become distinct, and be beautifully displayed if a screen be placed to receive them. The colored rays are seven in number, and are always arranged in the same order. The oblong spot of colored light which they form is called the *solar spectrum*. At the upper end of the spectrum, where the most refracted rays fall, the color is violet; then comes the indigo ray, the blue, green, yellow, orange, and red, which is refracted the least. The shape of the spectrum depends upon the shape of the aperture; if this be circular, the spectrum will be bounded laterally by vertical straight lines, and at the ends by semicircles; its breadth is always equal to the diameter of the aperture; its length varies with the refracting angle of the prism, and the substance of which it is made. As in the original beam of white light, the various colored rays are all superimposed, it follows that if the spectrum formed be only slightly elongated, in consequence of the feeble refractive power of the prism, the different colors will overlap each other, be more or less blended, and none of them will present a clear and decided tint. In order to increase the brilliancy of the spectrum, it is necessary that the aperture through which the light is admitted should be very small, in order to obtain the finest possible beam of light, and then that the screen should be placed at a considerable distance from the prism, so that the rays may not strike it until they have widely diverged, and become completely separated from each other; in this manner a spectrum may be obtained in which the different rays will display clear and decided tints of great brilliancy and beauty. The most effective mode of producing this result is to form a

---

Describe the solar spectrum. What is its shape? How can it be displayed to the best advantage? How may the brilliant line of colored light produced by this means be widened?

minute image of the sun by means of a convex lens, and allow the light which proceeds from it to fall upon a screen, pierced with a very small aperture. The light which passes through this aperture may be considered as emanating nearly from a physical point, and the overlapping of the different colors is almost entirely prevented. Another cause of the imperfect separation of the different rays exists in the prism itself. Ordinary prisms are full of striæ, by which the light is irregularly refracted, and the different colors intermingled. This difficulty may be overcome to a certain extent by transmitting the rays as near the edge as possible. The effect of this reduction in the diameter of the aperture will be to diminish the width of the spectrum, and reduce it to the form of a mere line of light of the most brilliant colors. In order to give breadth to this line it is necessary to convert the circular aperture into an extremely narrow slit, formed by perfectly parallel knife edges, only a very small fraction of an inch apart; a spectrum will thus be formed, horizontal and rectangular, having its upper edges, as well as its sides, parallel. This arrangement is the one best adapted for making accurate observations upon the spectrum. The colored spaces do not occupy an equal extent in the spectrum; the violet is the most extended, and the orange the least; if the prism be of flint glass, and the spectrum be divided into three hundred and sixty equal parts, it is found that the red rays occupy forty-five of these parts, the orange twenty-seven, the yellow forty-eight, the green sixty, the indigo forty, and the violet eighty. If the screen on which the spectrum is formed be perforated opposite any of the colors, as the violet, for example, a small beam of pure violet light will pass through, which may be examined separate from the others. If this beam of violet light be allowed to fall on a second prism, and its image received on a second screen, it undergoes no decomposition into light of various colors, but simply produces a spot of violet light, of the same shape as the incident beam. This beam may be again and again refracted by prisms and lenses, but it will undergo no further change. The same is true of all the colors. Hence it appears that the different rays of the spectrum are incapable of further separation into rays of different colors, by subsequent refraction, and that

---

What will be the shape of the spectrum formed by knife edges? Do the different colors occupy the same space in the solar spectrum? What is the proportion? Show that the different colors are not susceptible of further decomposition. Are the colors confined to one part of the spectrum?

the solar spectrum gives us the ultimate analysis of white light. From these and other experiments, Sir Isaac Newton inferred that white light is composed of seven colorific rays; later experiments have led to the opinion that the seven colors of the spectrum are occasioned not by seven, but by three simple or primary rays, viz., blue, yellow and red. These rays are concentrated at those points in the spectrum where each of these colors appears the brightest, but each color is in reality spread over the whole spectrum, forming, with the others, a variety of mixtures,—red and yellow producing the orange; yellow and blue the green; red and blue, with a little yellow, the violet. The prismatic colors also differ in their illuminating power; the orange illuminates in a higher degree than the red, the yellow than the orange. The maximum of illumination lies in the brightest yellow, or the palest green; beyond the full deep green, the illuminating power sensibly diminishes; the blue is nearly equal to the red, the indigo is inferior to the blue, and the violet is the lowest on the scale. If the seven colors of the spectrum be received upon seven distinct mirrors, so arranged as to reflect them all to one point, the original white light of the solar beam will be reproduced.

277. The number of vibrations required to produce the different colors of the solar spectrum. According to the undulatory theory of light, the average length of a wave in white light is estimated at $\frac{1}{50000}$ of an inch; in red light, at $\frac{1}{34000}$ of an inch; in violet, at $\frac{1}{60000}$ of an inch. The number of vibrations in white light is estimated at 500,000,000,000,000 per second; in red light, at 482,000,000,000,000; and in violet light, at 707,000,000,000,000.

278. The heat rays of the solar beam. Besides the different kinds of light of which the sunbeam consists, it also contains rays of heat, and heat of different kinds. These rays of heat are distributed through the spectrum, and are not concentrated at one point; consequently, they possess different refrangibilities, and are distinguished from each other by this property. If these rays of heat were exactly similar, they would be equal in refrangibility, and be all collected at one point, after passing through the prism. They not only differ in refrangibility, but also in heating intensity, in the same manner as the rays of

---

According to later experiments, of how many colors is the solar spectrum thought to consist? Where is the point of maximum illumination situated?—277. What is the length of a wave in white light? In red? In violet? What are the number of vibrations in white light? In red? In violet?—278. Show that there are different kinds of rays of heat in the solar beam.

light differ in illuminating power. This fact was first observed by Sir W. Herschel, who observed that in viewing the sun with large telescopes, through differently colored glasses, he sometimes felt a strong sensation of heat, with little light; and at other times he had a strong light, with little heat. His experiments were made by transmitting a solar beam through a prism, receiving the spectrum on a table, and placing the bulb of a very delicate thermometer in different parts of it. The thermometer was found to stand at different points in the different rays; thus, if in the blue rays, it marked 56°; on moving it down to the yellow rays, the instrument indicated a temperature of 62°; while at the lower end of the spectrum, at the extremity of the red rays, the temperature was found to be as high as 79°, i. e., 23° higher than in the blue rays. It was also observed that not only the red was the hottest ray, but that there was a point a little beyond the red, altogether out of the spectrum, where the thermometer stood higher than in the red itself. The most intense heat was always beyond the red ray, where there was no light at all, and the heat, in all the experiments, was found to diminish progressively, from the red to the violet, where it was least. These invisible rays of heat were found to exert a very considerable effect at a point $1\frac{1}{2}$ inches below the extreme red ray, even though the thermometer was placed at a distance of 52 inches from the prism. Other experimenters have placed the point of maximum heat within the red rays; and the point is found to vary with the material of which the prism is made. With a prism of rock salt, Melloni succeeded in separating the point of maximum temperature to a much greater distance from the colored parts of the spectrum than had previously been done. On moving the thermometer below this point, it was found that the rays of heat extended a considerable distance below the colored parts of the spectrum. The conclusion, therefore, is irresistible, that there are in the solar beam invisible rays of heat, of different refrangibilities, and so much less refrangible than the light that the central ray fall considerably below the lower, or red end of the spectrum. The shape of the thermal spectrum does not coincide with that of light, but is curiously discontinuous, consisting of several distinct parts, and forming at the lower end three round spots, B, C and D; see spectrum of heat, *Fig.* 106.

Where is the point of maximum heat? How was this determined? What effect has the nature of the prism on the point of maximum heat? What is the shape of the thermal spectrum?

279. The chemical rays of the solar beam. It has long been known that the light of the sun possesses extraordinary chemical power; the di-chloride of mercury, or calomel, and the chloride of silver, commonly called lunar caustic, are blackened; transparent phosphorus becomes opaque; and the coloring principles of vegetable origin are destroyed, by its action. Solar light will also produce the instantaneous combination of the two gases, chlorine and hydrogen. On the other hand, it confers upon the green cells of the leaves of plants the power of decomposing carbonic acid; and it has also a wonderful influence in producing the green cells of plants. This chemical energy is not concentrated at any one point in the spectrum, but is extended through several of the colored rays, and outside of them above the violet; whence we conclude that there are different kinds of chemical rays in the solar beam, distinguished from each other by a difference in refrangibility, just as there are different kinds of heat, and different kinds of light. The point of maximum chemical effect does not correspond with the maximum point for light, nor with the maximum point for heat, but is found at the violet, or upper end of the spectrum, *Figs.* 103 and 104. Scheele noticed that the effect of the violet rays upon the chloride of silver is more perceptible than that of the other rays. Dr. Wollaston ascertained that the greatest effect is produced just outside of the violet rays. The spot next in energy is the violet itself, and the effect gradually diminishes in advancing to the green, beyond which it seems to be wholly wanting. Nitrate of silver placed in the red rays is not blackened at all. The chemical rays are, therefore, more refrangible than those of light, in consequence of which they are dispersed over the blue, indigo, and violet spaces, and even extend a considerable distance outside of, and above this end of the spectrum; they are often called *actinic* rays. It is also said that other rays have been discovered in the spectrum which do not exercise any chemical action of themselves, but have the property of continuing it when once commenced; they are thought to extend from the indigo beyond the violet, and are called phosphorogenic rays. They are so named because they are believed to be the rays which are absorbed by the substances called phosphorescent, already described, and being emitted again when

---

279. Give some illustrations of the chemical effect of the sun's rays. Is this chemical energy concentrated at one point in the spectrum? Are there different kinds of chemical rays? In what respect do they differ? Where is the point of maximum effect? What are phosphorogenic rays? What is the shape of the chemical spectrum?

these bodies are carried into the dark, constitute the phenomena of phosphorescence. Some experiments of Sir John Herschel seem to show that the shape of the chemical spectrum is not the same as that for light, and is also discontinuous, like that of heat, consisting of a broad band between the orange and the yellow, then omitting the yellow, commencing again at the green ray, and continuing far above the upper end of the violet, gradually tapering to a blunted point. See *Fig.* 106.

280. The range of the chemical rays in the solar spectrum. —Fluorescence. The invisible rays extend beyond the violet extremity of the spectrum for a distance nearly equal in length to twice that of the luminous portion; but in the electric light obtained by the ignition of charcoal points, the invisible spectrum can be traced nearly six times as far; *Figs.* 104 and 106. On transmitting, however, these invisible rays through certain substances, such as a solution of sulphate of quinine, the decoction of the bark of the horse chestnut, tincture of chlorophyll, &c., the rays become visible in consequence of a diminution of their refrangibility. Thus, if a tube, filled with a solution of sulphate of quinine, be placed in the invisible rays, entirely outside of the spectrum, and above the violet ray, a ghostlike gleam of blue light will shoot directly through the tube, and on examining the blue light thus obtained, it is found to contain rays of much less refrangibility than the violet, and not much exceeding those of the green ray. The explanation of this singular effect is, that the invisible rays have had their refrangibility reduced by passing through the quinine, and on emergence, possess the refrangibility, color, and other properties of the colored rays of the upper part of the spectrum; in other words, the invisible rays have been absorbed and re-radiated in a condition of lower refrangibility, such as ordinarily produces the impression of blue light. According to the undulatory theory of light, the rate of undulation, or the number of vibrations per second which produces the invisible rays, is reduced by transmission through the sulphate of quinine, and when they issue again, they possess only the number of vibrations which produces blue light. This change of refrangibility is not limited to the invisible rays outside the luminous spectrum, but can be accomplished also in the case of the visible and colored rays. In every case, the altered rays are

---

280. How far do the chemical rays extend above the violet? What is the effect of a solution of quinine on the invisible chemical rays? Explain fluorescence. State what is meant by the degradation of light?

changed into those which are less refrangible, and the change is never to rays of greater refrangibility. This singular change of refrangibility has received the name of the *degradation* of light, and is analogous to the change of refrangibility produced in rays of heat when they are absorbed by certain substances, constituting another point of resemblance between these two chemical agents. Bodies which have the power of effecting it are called *fluorescent*, from fluor spar.

281. The triple character of solar light. A beam of solar light is therefore composed of three distinct sorts of rays, viz., the heating, the illuminating, and the chemical, and hence is capable of producing three different kinds of effects: first, the effect of heat; second, that of light; third, that of chemical influence. In a beam of natural sunlight, the different rays are, as it were, intertwined, like the triple strands of a cord, and their influence is exerted at one and the same spot; but if transmitted through a prism, they are separated, in consequence of the difference in their refrangibility, and their maximum influence is manifested at three distinct points. This is clearly shown in *Fig.* 104, in which the ray of sunlight, *a*, by the refraction of the prism, is elongated so as to extend from *c* to *b*. The rays of heat being less refrangible than those of light, exhibit their maximum effect at H, below the red rays, while, however, their general influence extends from *b* to V, or to the upper end of the illuminating rays. The chemical rays, on the other hand, being more refrangible than those of light, exhibit their maximum effect at C, a point considerably above the most refrangible of the illuminating rays, while their general influence extends from *c* to R. The illuminating rays extend from V to R, and the maximum effect

Fig. 104.

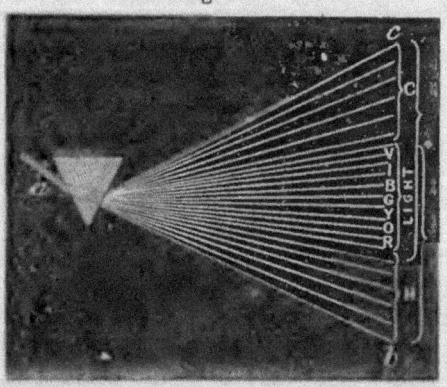

Unequal refrangibility of the Chemical, Illuminating and Heating Rays in the Solar Beam.

---

281. Prove the triple character of solar light. Why are the foci of a lens for light, heat, and chemical effect, not found at the same point?

DISSECTION OF 251

Fig. 105.

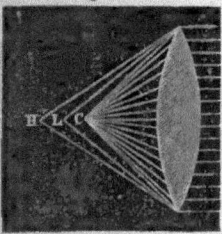

The different Foci for Heat, Light and Chemical Rays.

is exerted at Y, while, within the same limits, a certain amount of heating and chemical influence is also displayed. From this, it is evident, that the solar beam is possessed of a triple nature, and exerts, wherever it falls, three distinct sorts of influence. On account of the different refrangibility of these three sorts of rays, if a beam of solar light be transmitted through a lens, they will not all be concentrated at the same focus, the chemical rays being the most refrangible, will have their focus at a point C, nearer the lens than the focus for light, L, while the rays of heat will be collected at the point H, more remote from the lens than the focus for light; *Fig.* 105. It follows from this, that, if the greatest chemical effect of the sun's rays be desired, the object must be placed, not in the illuminating focus, but a little nearer to the lens; if the greatest heating effect of the sun's rays be sought, the object must be placed a little farther from the lens than the focus for light. In order to form a correct idea of the solar spectrum, it is necessary, also, to bear in mind that the different spectra are not all continuous, nor possessed of the same shape. In *Fig.* 106, this discontinuity, as well as the relative extent of the different spectra, and the points of maximum intensity, are well represented, together with the fixed dark lines crossing the spectrum at right angles, which are presently to be described. It will be observed that in the spectrum for light, the maximum point of illumination is in the yellow ray, and that the fluorescent rays extend a considerable distance above the upper end of the violet ray. In the spectrum for heat, the shape is peculiar, and the effect at the lower part limited to the four round spaces, A B C D while the point of maximum intensity is considerably below the yellow, at the extreme end of the red ray. In the spectrum of chemical rays, the point of maximum intensity is outside the violet ray, and the continuity of the spectrum is also broken. In the case of Fraunhofer's lines, it will be noticed that they have been traced a considerable distance outside of the illuminating rays of the spectrum, in both directions, above the violet, and below the red. In the spectrum formed by the solar beam, these spectra are not separated from each other, as in the

What is their position in reference to the lens? Describe *Fig.* 106.

Fig. 106.

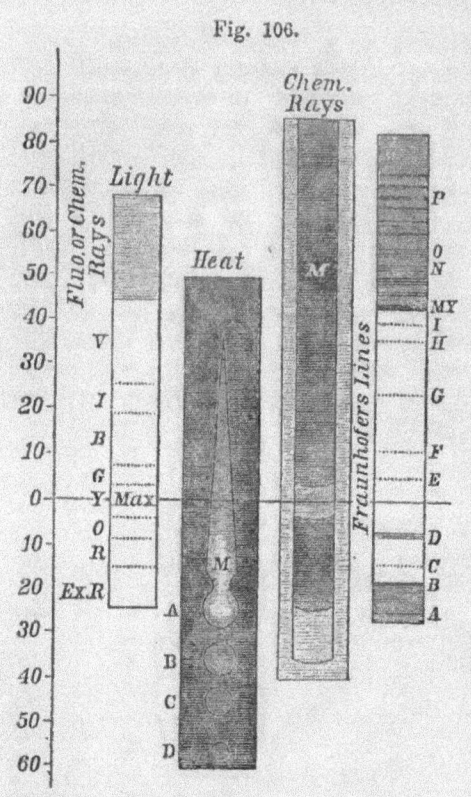

The Light, Heat, and Chemical Rays, and the Dark Lines of the Solar Beam.

figure, but are superimposed; and in the case of any unrefracted solar beam passing through a circular aperture, into a darkened room, are all intertwined, and concentrated in the small round spot of light produced.

282. The spectra produced by artificial light and colored flames. If artificial light, emanating from different luminous bodies, be transmitted through a prism, it is decomposed in the same manner as the solar beam, and a spectrum is formed, consisting of the various colors which produce white light, but never in the same relative intensity and proportions in which they appear in the solar spectrum. The color which predominates in the artificial light, predominates in its spectrum; a red flame produces a spectrum in which the prevailing hue is red; a blue flame a spectrum in which it is blue. If the flame be a pure red or blue, the spectrum will present a continuous band of a red or blue color. There is no artificial light which is not deficient in some of the elements of solar light. Colored artificial flames may be produced by placing the salts of different metals in the flame of an alcohol lamp, or gas burner, and the peculiar colors imparted have long been used by chemists as indications of the presence of these metals; thus a yellow flame is caused by the salts of sodium; a violet flame is produced by those of potassium; lithium and strontium salts give a red flame, and

---

282. Can artificial light be decomposed? Does the spectrum formed differ from that of the sun? Can metals be detected by the color they impart to flames?

the salts of barium tinge the flame green. The value of these colored flames, as a means of detecting the metals, is diminished when several of these metals are present at once, because the color produced by one metal obscures that produced by another, though this difficulty may be in part removed by the use of colored glasses, or liquids, through which the flame is observed. If, however, these colored flames be subjected to the action of a prism, and the spectrum formed be examined by a powerful telescope, certain characteristic peculiarities may be observed which make this the most delicate means of qualitative analysis yet discovered.

Fig. 107.

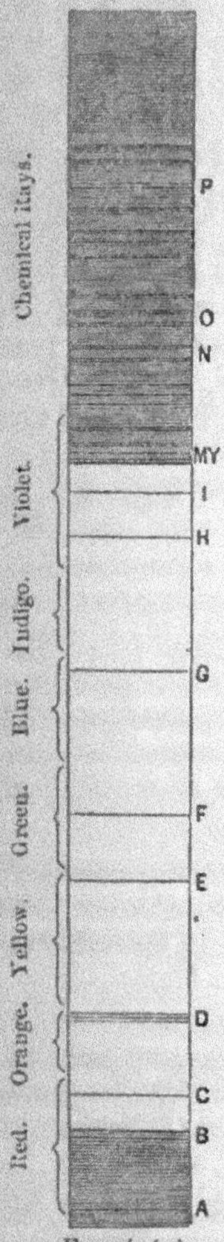

Fraunhofer's Lines.

283. The solar spectrum not continuous, but crossed by fixed dark lines.—Fraunhofer's lines. The solar spectrum not only contains heating and chemical, as well as illuminating rays, but also exhibits, when carefully examined, a great number of *dark lines*, crossing the spectrum at right angles to the order of the colors, and always occupying the same relative positions. In other words, the solar spectrum is not continuous, but is separated into a great number of portions, of unequal size, by dark lines of division, in which there is no light. That these dark lines indicate the absence of light, is shown by their want of blackening effect, and their correspondence with the inactive spaces which are observed when a photograph is taken of the solar spectrum. These lines were first noticed by Dr. Wollaston, in 1802, on transmitting solar light through a very narrow slit, and viewing it directly by the eye placed immediately behind the prism. In 1815, Fraunhofer, a distinguished optician, of Munich, examined the solar spectrum thus produced by a *lens*, and ascertained the existence of nearly 600 dark lines; of these he published an accurate map, selecting seven, on account of their distinctness, and the ease with which they may be recognized, and distinguishing

---

283. By what is the continuity of the solar spectrum broken? Describe Fraunhofer's lines. Do they extend beyond the limits of the visible spectrum?

them by the letters B, C, D, E, F, G and H. They have, since his time, been ascertained not to be confined to the colored parts of the spectrum, but to extend beyond the violet ray, and through the whole of the space occupied by the chemical rays. These lines are represented in *Fig.* 107, and are known by the name of Fraunhofer's lines. B is in the red space, near its outer end; C which is broad and black, is beyond the middle of the red; D is in the orange and is a strong double line, the two lines being nearly of the same size and separated by a bright one; E is in the green, and consists of several lines, the middle one being the strongest; F is in the blue, and is a very strong line; G is in the indigo, and H in the violet. Between B and C, there are 9 lines; between C and D, there are 30; between D and E, there are 84; between E and F, 56; between F and G, 185; and between G and H, 190. In order to observe them, the sun's light must be admitted through a narrow, vertical slit, *o*, into a darkened room, and allowed to fall upon a prism, *p*, placed with its axis parallel to the slit, *Fig.* 108, and at a distance of about 24 feet from it. The prism is fixed before the object-glass of a telescope, *l*, in such a position that the angle formed by the incident ray with the first face of the prism, is equal to that formed by the refracted ray with the second face; so that the position of the prism is that in which the light is subjected to the minimum amount of dispersion. These lines are always found, whatever be the solid or liquid medium used in the construction of the prism, and whether its refracting angle be great or small, and under all circumstances they always preserve exactly the same relative position in the respective colored spaces in which they occur. The line B, for instance, is always found at the same relative

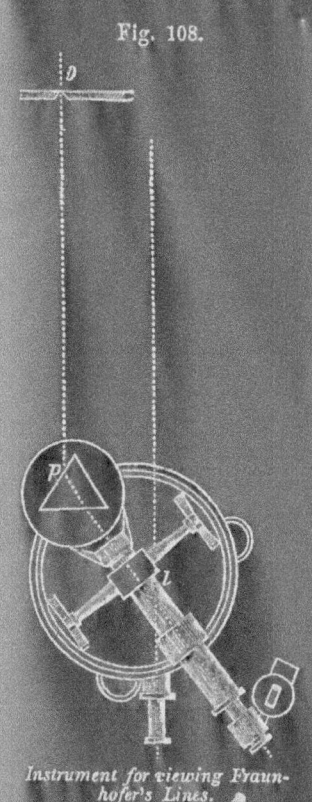

Fig. 108.

Instrument for viewing Fraunhofer's Lines.

How can these lines be best observed? What is their number? How can they be displayed upon a screen?

distance from the extremity of the red space in the spectrum, whatever the material of which the prism is made. These lines differ very much in appearance; some are extremely fine, and are hardly visible; others are very near each other, and resemble a cloud, rather than distinct lines; and there are some which seem to possess a perceptible breadth. Fraunhofer counted 590 lines; but Sir D. Brewster has since extended the number to 2000. These lines indicate the absence in the solar beam of rays of certain refrangibilities, and the reason that they do not appear in the spectrum as ordinarily formed, is the superposition of spectra, which, in the more perfect spectrum of Fraunhofer, does not exist. The greater the elongation of the spectrum, and the more widely the colored spaces are separated, the more distinct do these lines become. If it be desired to throw the spectrum upon a screen, it may be done by the arrangement shown in *Fig.* 109. It has been found that all light proceeding directly from the sun, or indirectly from it by reflection, such as the light of the moon and the planets, and the light reflected from the clouds and the rainbow, gives a spectrum crossed by lines exactly identical. It is a point of great interest to determine the cause of these dark breaks in the continuity of the solar spectrum. The spectra produced by the light of Sirius, Castor, and other fixed stars, are also all crossed by black lines, but different from each other, and from the sun, though in nearly all, some of the most important black lines found in the solar spectrum, are seen. Thus, in Procyon, the double line, D, is found; and in Capella and Beltegeux, the lines D and b. Arcturus, Aldebaran, β Pegasi, and δ Virginis are particularly remarkable for the strength and number of the lines by which their spectra are crossed.

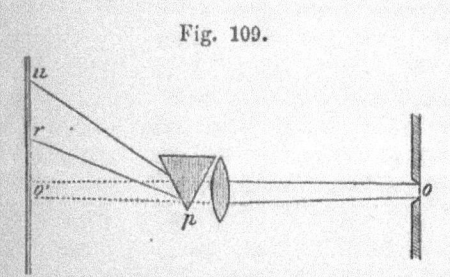

Fig. 109.

Fraunhofer's Lines displayed upon a Screen.

284. **Spectra produced by the light of the Nebulæ, and by artificial light, are crossed by bright, instead of dark, lines.** While, however, the spectra of the sun and the fixed stars are found to be crossed by black lines, it is a singular fact that the

---

What kind of lines are formed in the spectra of the moon, and the planets? Of the fixed stars?—284. What kind of lines in the spectra of the Nebulæ? Of artificial lights?

spectra of the Nebulæ, in the heavens, are crossed by *bright*, instead of dark lines; and this is also the case with the spectra produced by the various sources of artificial light, by the electric light, by gas, oil, alcohol, and hydrogen. The spectrum of the electric light gives a very bright line in the green ray; those of hydrogen, alcohol, and oil, give two extremely bright lines in the red and orange. The spectra furnished by colored flames, produced by the introduction of different substances into the flame of an alcohol lamp, give lines of various degrees of color and brightness scattered through the whole spectrum.

285. Spectrum Analysis. By observations upon the spectra of colored flames, it has been discovered that the bright lines formed are always the same whenever the same metallic salt is introduced into the flame, and that the appearance of these lines, in any spectrum, is a sure indication of the presence of the substances in question in the flame from which the spectrum has proceeded. The bright lines in the spectrum, produced by the introduction of a chemical substance into the flame of an alcohol lamp, or gas burner, constitute a new mode of qualitative analysis. It is not those bodies alone which have the power of imparting a color to flame that yield characteristic spectra, but this property belongs to every elementary substance, metallic, or non-metallic, solid, liquid, and gaseous. All that is necessary is, that the substance should be heated to the degree at which it is vaporized, and this vapor made luminous, for then each element gives forth the characteristic bright lines emitted by itself alone. Many of the metals can be made to give their characteristic lines, if heated in the flame of an ordinary chemical gas burner; but most of them require the intense heat of the electric spark, derived either from the galvanic battery, or from Ruhmkorff's coil, an instrument to be described hereafter. The spark, in passing between two points of the metal in question, volatilizes a small portion, and heats it so intensely as to enable it to give off its peculiar light. The permanent gases also yield characteristic spectra if a discharge from a powerful Ruhmkorff's coil be passed through them. Thus, if the spark be passed through an atmosphere of hydrogen, the light emitted is bright red, and its spectrum consists of one bright red, one green, and one blue line, while in nitrogen, the light is purple,

---

285. What effect is produced upon the lines in the spectra of artificial light by ignited metals? Is the power of producing characteristic lines in the spectrum confined to the metals? Can the gases be made to give characteristic lines? How can we trace the lines beyond the limits of the visible spectrum?

and the position of the lines entirely different. When a compound gas, or vapor, is ignited by the electric spark, the spectra produced are those of the elementary components of the gas. At these intense temperatures, chemical combination seems to be impossible, and the various elements are able to coexist in a separate form, mechanically intermingled. If photographs of these spectra be taken, the impression obtained contains all the lines characteristic of the elements in question. The photograph being produced by the chemical and extra violet rays, gives a spectrum which extends much beyond the limits of the violet ray, and contains lines not seen when the spectrum is viewed through the telescope; see *Fig.* 107. The minutest quantities of the different elements, if ignited, will give the characteristic lines with perfect distinctness, and if several elements happen to be contained in the same flame, the lines peculiar to each are as plainly seen as they would have been had no others been present. Sodium gives a single or double line of yellow light in a position corresponding to that of the orange rays in the solar spectrum. Potassium gives a red line in the red end of the spectrum, and a violet line at the violet end. Lithium gives a dark spectrum, with only two bright lines, one a pale yellow, corresponding to the yellow portion of the spectrum; the other a bright red, in the red end of the spectrum. Strontium presents eight characteristic bright lines. Calcium gives one broad green band, and one bright orange band, besides several smaller orange lines. Messrs. Kirchoff and Bunsen, to whom we are indebted for the first investigation of this subject, state that the amount of sodium which can be detected in this manner need not exceed the 190,000,000th part of a grain; of lithium, the 70,000,000th part; of potassium, the 60,000th part of a grain; bromine the same; strontium, the 1,000,000th; calcium, the 100,000,000th part of a grain. The yellow line of sodium, No. 3, *Fig.* 111, is always found, whatever be the kind of light employed. This is owing to the extensive diffusion of this element in the atmosphere, and its presence in every substance which has been exposed to the air for however short a time. Lithium, which was formerly supposed to be contained in only four minerals, by the aid of spectrum analysis, has been observed in almost all spring waters, in tea, tobacco, milk, and blood, but existing in such

---

State the characteristic lines of sodium. Potassium. Lithium. Strontium. Calcium. How minute a quantity of each can thus be detected?

minute quantities as to have eluded detection by the less delicate methods of analysis.

286. The Spectroscope. The instrument used in these researches is called the Spectroscope, *Fig.* 110. It consists of a

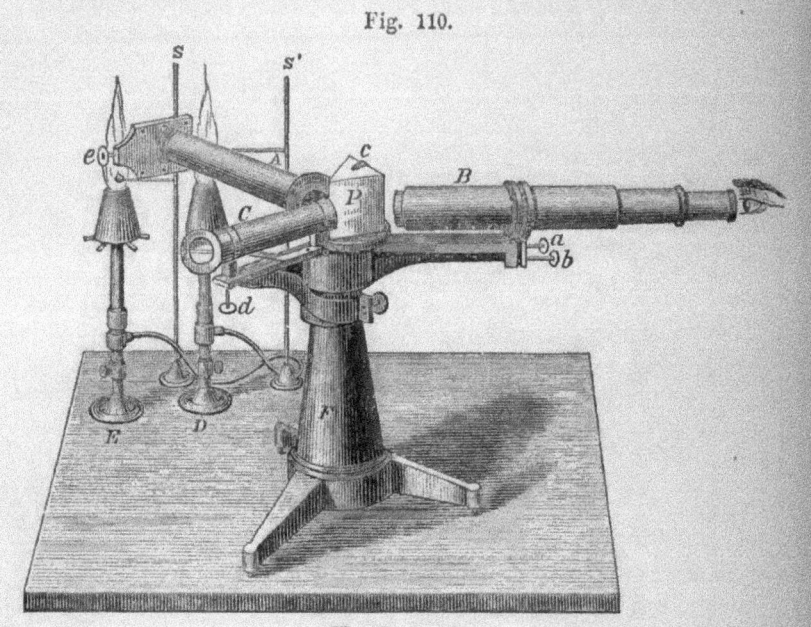

Fig. 110.

The Spectroscope.

prism, P, mounted vertically upon a firm iron stand, F, and a tube, A, carrying a lens at the end nearest the prism, and at the other extremity having a very fine vertical slit for the admission of the light. The width of this slit can be regulated by the small screw, e. The stand, s, carries a sliding rod, which supports the substance to be analyzed, in the flame of the gas burner, E. This burner is placed opposite one half of the slit, and its light passes directly down the tube to the prism; opposite the other half of the slit is placed a small rectangular prism, the object of which is to reflect the light proceeding from some other source, as the sun, or any artificial light, D, also down the axis of the tube. By this arrangement, spectra, proceeding from two different sources, are formed, one above the other, and can readily be compared, so as to decide whether

---

286. Describe the Spectroscope.

their lines coincide, or differ. The light having been refracted by the prism, is received by the telescope, B, and the image of the spectrum magnified before reaching the eye. The telescope is movable in a horizontal plane, upon the tripod, and can be adjusted so as to observe every part of the spectrum formed by the prism. The tube, C, contains a lens at the extremity nearest the prism, and at the other, a scale formed by transparent lines on an opaque ground; this tube is adjusted in such a way that a light being placed at the open extremity, the image of the scale is reflected by the prism into the telescope, B, for the purpose of reading off the position of the bright and dark lines of the spectrum, as both will appear simultaneously placed side by side in the field of the telescope. When the instrument is used, stray light is excluded by covering it with a loose black cloth. The dispersion of the spectrum may be much increased by using several prisms instead of one. The prism is sometimes made hollow, and filled with bi-sulphide of carbon.

287. The new metals discovered by spectrum analysis. In the course of his researches upon the bright lines in the spectra produced by the alkalies, the German chemist, Bunsen, observed several lines which could not have been produced by them, and which led him to suspect the existence of a new metal. On evaporating 40 tons of the mineral waters of Durckheim and Baden, he obtained 105 grains of the chloride of a new metal, which, on being introduced into the spectroscope, gave two splendid violet lines, and is called Cæsium, from *cæsius,—bluish gray*. In the waters of Hallein and Gastein, there was discovered another new metal, Rubidium, from *rubidus, dark red*, because it has two splendid red lines in its spectrum. A third metal, called Thallium, has since been discovered, so called from $\theta\alpha\lambda\lambda\dot{o}\varsigma$, a *budding twig*, in allusion to the brilliant green line presented by its spectrum. Indium was recognized by the presence of a hitherto unobserved fine dark blue line. The peculiar appearance of the spectra of several of the metals, as seen through the spectroscope, is represented in *Fig.* 111, the dark lines of the solar spectrum being represented in black, the differently colored lines of the other spectra in white. No. 1 represents the solar spectrum; No. 2, that of potassium; No. 3, that of sodium, its bright line being identical in position with the dark solar line, D; No. 4, that of the new metal, rubidium; No. 5, that of another new metal, cæsium.

---

287. What new metals have been discovered by spectrum analysis? Describe *Fig.* 111.

Fig. 111.

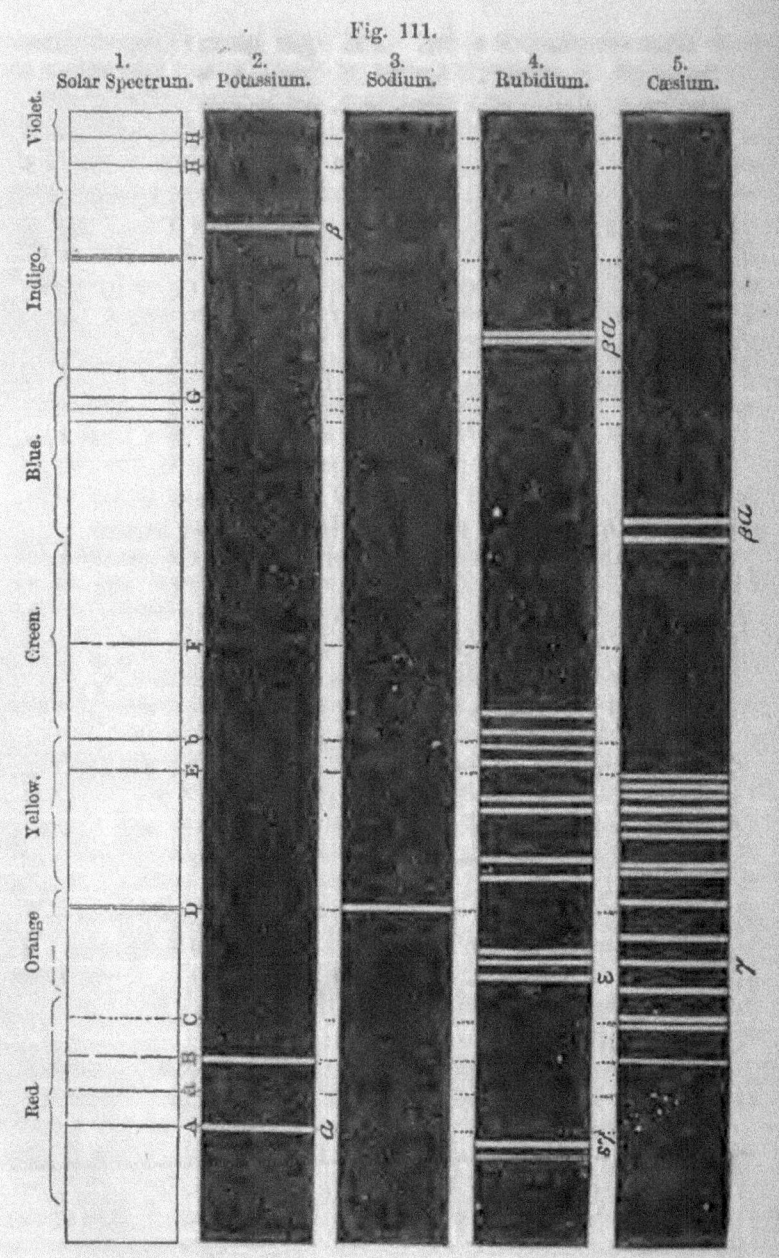

The dark lines in the Solar Spectrum, compared with the bright lines in the Spectra of Potassium, Sodium, Rubidium and Cæsium.

288. The dark lines of the solar spectrum exactly coincident with the bright lines of spectra produced by the metals. Kirchoff, in experimenting on the bright lines found in the spectra produced by the burning metals, discovered that these bright lines are in many cases exactly coincident with the dark lines mapped by Fraunhofer, in the solar spectrum, so that when the two lights are thrown into the tube through the same slit, and their spectra are seen through the same telescope, B, *Fig.* 110, arranged one above the other, the bright lines of the one are found to be continued, without the slightest interruption, into the dark lines of the other. Thus sodium, for example, when ignited, emits an intensely brilliant yellow light, which is concentrated into two closely contiguous bands, or bright lines, coincident in position with Fraunhofer's double black line, D, in the solar spectrum; it was also found that the bright lines characteristic of potassium, chromium, magnesium, iron, and nickel, exactly correspond with certain of the black solar spectra lines; vaporized iron gave about 60 bright lines, coinciding in position, and in breadth, with the same number of black lines produced by the sun. It seems impossible that this should be an accidental coincidence, and it at once suggested the idea that they are due to the same cause, and that the dark lines in the solar spectrum are produced by these metals, ignited in the atmosphere of the sun. The only difference is, that in the one case the lines are bright, in the other they are dark.

289. The bright lines afforded by metallic spectra converted into dark lines.—The dark lines of the solar spectrum explained. Now it has been found that the bright lines of the metallic spectra may be converted into black lines, by placing behind the flame in which the metal is ignited another flame, much more intense than the first, and containing the same metal in a state of more intense ignition. For instance, if through the flame of a common alcohol lamp, colored by sodium, the more powerful light of sodium, heated by hydrogen, or by the electric light, be transmitted, the bright lines found in the spectrum of the first sodium light, are instantly changed into black lines, occupying the same position; the bright lines in the spectra of potassium, lithium, barium, and strontium, may be converted into black lines, in a similar manner. In other words, if any element be ignited, it emits rays of light of a definite degree of refrangibility, and these rays have the power of absorbing

---

288. What connection has been discovered between the dark lines of the solar spectrum, and the bright lines of the spectra of the metals?—289. How may the bright lines of the metallic spectra be converted into dark lines?

all rays of this identical refrangibility which may fall upon them, emanating from another portion of the same element, in a state of more intense ignition, thus destroying the light of its bright lines, and turning them into dark lines, destitute of light. If now, in the atmosphere of the sun, the vapors of the various metals be present in a state of intense ignition, their light, passed through a prism, and decomposed, would produce a spectrum filled with *bright* lines; but if, behind this external luminous atmosphere of the sun, there be another source of heat still more intense, and containing these same metals in a state of ignition, the first bright lines will be converted into *dark* lines. Now, this is precisely the view which astronomers are disposed to give of the constitution of the sun. Within a luminous external photosphere there is supposed to be an internal nucleus, in a more intense state of ignition. It is therefore highly probable that the dark lines of the solar spectrum are produced by this cause, and that the vapors of the following metals, sodium, potassium, magnesium, calcium, iron, chromium, and nickel, and possibly zinc, cobalt, and manganese, are present in the sun's atmosphere; hydrogen, aluminum, barium, and strontium, are also probably present, but not lithium, copper, and silver. For the same reason, it is thought that many of the metals of the earth may be detected in the atmosphere of the different fixed stars. Aldebaran contains hydrogen, sodium, magnesium, calcium, iron, tellurium, antimony, bismuth, and mercury, while in Sirius, only sodium, magnesium, and hydrogen, have been detected. The spectra of the stars resemble that of the sun, inasmuch as each consists of colored rays, intersected by dark lines; the spectra of the Nebulæ, on the other hand, differ from those of the sun and stars, as they consist simply of bright lines, crossing the colored rays, like the spectra produced by the various kinds of artificial light, by the metals and other elements, like hydrogen and nitrogen. Hence we conclude that the Nebulæ are merely masses of glowing gas, and do not consist, like the sun, of an incandescent solid or liquid mass, surrounded by a gaseous atmosphere; and that the stars on the other hand possess a constitution identical with that of the sun. Spectra have even been taken from the showers of meteors, in which the sodium line has been clearly distinguished. This is the most brilliant generaliza-

How may the dark lines of the solar spectrum be explained? What substances have been discovered in the sun? In Aldebaran? What conclusions have been drawn in regard to the spectra of the Nebulæ, and of the fixed stars?

tion of modern chemistry, and in this way does the chemist possess the power of extending his researches beyond the earth, and determining the chemical constitution of the sun and stars, and that too with a degree of exactness far surpassing that of the ordinary means of analysis.

290. The effect of Solar Light on the Vegetable Kingdom. The combined influence of the three kinds of rays contained in the sunbeam upon all objects exposed to their influence, is undoubtedly very great. This is seen especially in the case of plants. Without the influence of the heating rays of the sunbeam, plants evince no signs of life, and in general, the higher the temperature, the more abundant and luxuriant the vegetation. The effect of the illuminating rays is equally marked. In the dark, it is well known that the growth of plants is checked, and that their tissues are soon almost entirely deprived of their green color, and turn white; their juices, also, lose their peculiar characteristic properties and become tasteless and watery. All plants tend to grow towards the light, and if placed in cellars, are soon bent in the direction of the windows. There is also a certain mechanical effect exerted by the solar beam; under its influence the stomata of the leaves are opened, and the amount of air and watery vapor exhaled and inhaled is greatly increased; if this influence be withdrawn, the stomata are at once closed, and the respiration of the plant is entirely suspended. Plants, therefore, placed in absolute darkness, speedily die. There is another effect, however, exerted by the chemical rays of the solar beam, of at least equal importance. The green parts of leaves and stems acquire the power, under the influence of sunlight, of decomposing carbonic acid, appropriating the carbon, and exhaling nearly pure oxygen. In the dark, this process is reversed, and carbonic acid is exhaled; but as the amount of oxygen produced is much larger than the amount of carbonic acid, the general effect of plants is to diminish the amount of carbonic acid in the atmosphere, and to increase the amount of oxygen. They tend, therefore, to fit the air for the support of animal life, and to neutralize the injurious influences exerted upon the atmosphere by the carbonic acid produced by the breathing of animals. There are two periods in the growth of plants when the amount of car-

---

290. What is the effect of the heat rays of the solar beam on plants? Of the illuminating rays? What is the effect of light on the stomata of leaves? What happens if plants be placed in complete darkness? What effect has light on the decomposition of carbonic acid by plants? Is this process ever reversed? At what two periods in the life of the plants is carbonic acid produced in excess? What effect has light on oxidation? On de-oxidation?

bonic acid evolved is greatly increased, viz., the germination of the seeds, and the bursting of the flower-buds; especially the former. This is owing to the fact, that in both these processes a large amount of carbon is removed from the starch contained in the seed and flower, in order that it may be converted into sugar. Oxygen is, therefore, absorbed from the atmosphere to unite with this carbon and convert it into carbonic acid, which is then exhaled. Both these processes are greatly assisted by the absence of light, and one of the indispensable conditions of vegetation is, that the seed be buried in the ground, and kept in the dark. The absence of light tends, therefore, to accelerate combination with oxygen, or to produce oxidation; the presence of light to set free oxygen from substances containing it, or to produce de-oxidation. It is by this latter process that all the carbon contained in plants has been abstracted from the atmosphere, by the agency of leaves, and also all the coal now found buried in the bowels of the earth. These influences are exerted chiefly by the chemical rays of the sunbeam, and they are greatly increased by covering plants with blue glass. This has the effect of absorbing the rays of heat and light, and leaving the plant to the exclusive influence of the chemical rays.

291. Summary of the effects of Light on Vegetation. The general effect of sunlight on plants may be thus summed up: 1st. The illuminating rays prevent the germination of seeds. 2d. The chemical rays, formed at the violet extremity of the spectrum, and extending a considerable distance beyond it, quicken germination. 3d. The luminous rays effect the decomposition of carbonic acid by the leaves. 4th. The chemical and luminous rays are both essential to the formation of the coloring matter of leaves. 5th. The chemical and illuminating rays, unassisted by the calorific rays, prevent the development of the reproductive organs of plants. 6th. The heat rays, corresponding with the extreme red rays, assist the development of the reproductive organs of plants. There seems to be a nice adaptation of sunlight to the varying condition of vegetation, at the different seasons. In the spring, when the process of germination is going on, there is a large excess of chemical rays, which, as we have seen, tend powerfully to hasten the process. The excess of the chemical rays, at this season of the

---

How has all the coal been abstracted from the atmosphere? By what rays of the solar beam has this been done? What effect has blue glass upon plants?—291. Give a summary of the effects of light on vegetation. How does sunlight seem to be adapted to the varying condition of vegetation?

year, is proved by the greater facility with which photographic operations may be carried on. As summer advances, and the influence of the illuminating rays is required to promote the decomposition of carbonic acid by the leaves and the consequent growth of vegetation, the quantity of the illuminating and heating rays both increase in a very great degree relatively to the chemical rays. In the autumn, as plants approach maturity, and seeds are to be formed, and fruit ripened, the illuminating and chemical rays both diminish, and the heating rays are increased. This furnishes a very extraordinary and curious instance of design in Nature. Advantage is often taken of these principles by the horticulturist, in the cultivation of plants. When the seeds are to be forced, they are covered with dark blue glass, because this absorbs all the illuminating and calorific rays, and allows only the chemical rays to reach the plant. As the plant advances towards maturity, light is needed, and yellow glass is substituted in place of blue. When the period of maturity arrives, heat has become more essential, and red glass is employed in place of the yellow. In this manner the gardener closely imitates the changes in the composition of sunlight which are made in Nature.

292. The effect of Solar Light on Chemical Compounds. Several instances have already been adverted to, of the chemical effect of the sun's rays; chlorine and hydrogen will unite with explosion, and the chloride of silver will be blackened if placed in the bright sunlight. In all these cases the effect is produced by the chemical rays of the sunbeam, and not by those of heat or light, for if the beam be decomposed by a prism, and the different rays separated from each other, those of heat and light may be entirely excluded, and yet the effect remain the same. An important application is made of this influence of the chemical rays in the art of Photography, or the formation of pictures by the agency of the sun. These pictures are generally produced by the action of the chemical rays of the sunbeam on some salt of silver. The explanation of the chemical part of the process must be deferred for the present, and the mechanical details only given here. The outline of any object can be taken by the following simple process. Let a piece of white paper be moistened with a diluted solution of common salt, and then washed over with a solution

---

How does the gardener imitate Nature in this respect?—292. What is the effect of sunlight on chemical combination? On chloride of silver? By what rays in the sunbeam is this effect produced? How is this proved? What art depends upon this effect of light?

of nitrate of silver. Common salt consists of chlorine and sodium, and by the action of the chlorine the nitrate of silver is converted into the chloride of silver, a substance which speedily turns black on exposure to the sunlight. This black color is due to a chemical change in the chloride, in virtue of which, either an oxide, or some peculiar form of chloride of silver, of a black color, is produced. If, on paper thus prepared, before it has been exposed to the light, any small object be placed, which is perfectly opaque, and then the whole exposed to the action of the sun, the paper will be blackened, except where it has been protected by the article in question; thus a white spot will be produced upon a dark ground, having the exact outline of the article employed, and this white spot may be prevented from turning black on exposure to the light, and preserved permanently white, by washing the paper immediately in a saturated solution of common salt, by which all the chloride of silver is dissolved out, and the paper left in its natural condition. If the article in question be not entirely opaque, but partially translucent, the paper under it will have been more or less blackened, corresponding with the amount of light transmitted, and in this way various degrees of shade produced which may be rendered permanent in the manner above described. It was on this principle that Wedgewood and Davy, about 1802, undertook to prepare photographic pictures, by projecting the shadow of the article intended to be copied, upon white paper and leather, saturated with a solution of nitrate of silver; but unfortunately their attempts failed in consequence of inability to fix the pictures, and render them indestructible by diffused light.

293. The Daguerreotype process. The next improvement in taking photographic pictures consisted in the use of the camera obscura. By this instrument a luminous image can be formed in the interior of a darkened box; and if this image be allowed to fall upon a polished silver plate, or upon properly prepared paper, a picture will be formed which only needs protection from the action of diffused light, after being taken from the camera, in order to be permanent. M. Daguerre, who was the inventor of the process which bears his name, made use of plates of silver coated with iodine, by exposure to the fumes which rise from this substance on the application of heat; in this way a thin film of iodide of silver is formed upon the

---

How may the outline of an object be taken? Who first undertook to prepare photographic outlines by this process?—293. Describe the Daguerreotype process.

surface. It is then exposed for a few moments to the action of light in the camera, the effect of which is to decompose the iodide of silver, and expose the pure metal to a greater or less degree, according to the light and shade of the image within the instrument. The plate is then removed from the camera, and as quickly as possible transferred to a darkened room, where it is held over the fumes of heated mercury; these mercurial fumes act upon the silver wherever it has been laid bare by the action of the light, and to a degree proportioned to this action, and thus a difference of surface and color are produced between the image and the other parts of the plate, and it now only remains to remove the undecomposed iodide of silver from the other portions of the plate, and render it incapable of being affected by the action of the diffused light of day, in order to make the picture complete. This is effected by washing the plate with a solution of the hypo-sulphite of soda, which dissolves off all the remaining sensitive coating. It is then covered with a very thin film of reduced gold, for the purpose of giving to the picture a richer and warmer tone. This is accomplished by pouring upon the plate a solution of chloride of gold, and heating it over the flame of a spirit lamp.

294. Photographs. About the same time that the process for taking pictures upon iodized silver plates was introduced by M. Daguerre, Mr. Talbot invented a similar process for taking pictures upon paper prepared with a solution of iodide of silver. The paper is placed in the camera in the manner just described, and the invisible picture which is formed is developed by washing it with a solution of gallic acid, the superfluous iodide of silver being quickly removed by washing with a solution of hyposulphite of soda. The picture thus formed is then placed upon a second sheet of iodized paper, and both are exposed to the direct rays of the sun. In consequence of the partial transparence of the paper, the rays of light are enabled to pass through the first sheet more or less, according to the degree of light and shade of the picture, and falling upon the lower sheet, speedily develop a second picture upon its sensitive surface. As the darkest portions of the first picture were produced by the most highly illuminated parts of the object, the picture of which was taken, it is quite evident that in the second, the lightest portions will be produced beneath the darkest portions of the first, in consequence of the obstruction which these offer to

---

294. Describe the simplest photographic process.

the passage of light, and that the darkest portions of the second picture will correspond with the lightest portions of the first, and consequently the lights and shades of the second picture will exactly correspond with the lights and shades of the original object. This process not only possesses the advantage of cheapness and portability, but also the additional one of allowing the multiplication of impressions indefinitely, without again having recourse to the camera, and of giving an exact reproduction of the original object; but it is defective in delicacy in consequence of the coarseness of the fibre of paper, even when manufactured with the greatest care and expressly for photographic purposes. The next improvement consisted in the substitution of glass plates, coated with iodide of silver through the instrumentality of a delicate and transparent paste, made of the whites of eggs. The transparent medium now most commonly employed, is collodion; this is a solution of gun cotton in ether. The plate of glass is first rubbed very dry and clean, with linen and leather; it is then placed in a horizontal position, and upon the middle portion a quantity of liquid collodion, having some iodide of potassium dissolved in it, is poured, and the superfluous liquid allowed to drain off. The collodion soon evaporates, and the plate acquires a cloudy appearance. It is then immediately plunged into a bath containing 4 grains of nitrate of silver, to every 10 grains of water; the iodine at once quits the potassium and unites with the silver, to form an iodide of silver, which is deposited in a thin film over the whole plate; the process is carried on in a dark room, in order that it may not be affected by the diffused light. After remaining about a minute in the bath, the plate is drained, dried, and placed in a closed frame, fitting tightly into the grooves of the camera. When it is adjusted in its proper place, the slide which protects it is removed, and the iodized plate of glass exposed to the action of the luminous image formed in the interior of the camera. The iodide of silver is everywhere decomposed to a degree proportioned to the light, the brightest parts of the image producing the deepest impression, but without exhibiting any apparent picture. It is then removed from the camera into a darkened room, and washed with a solution of pyro-gallic acid, containing a slight amount of crystallized acetic acid. Wherever the iodide of silver has experienced the beginning of decomposition, there is

---

Describe the collodion process. How is the superfluous iodide of silver removed? What is a negative? A positive? How are the lights and shades of the negative picture reversed in the positive?

formed the black gallate of silver, and the image immediately appears. The shaded parts of the object whose picture is made, having produced no effect upon the iodized glass plate within the camera, at these points no darkening effect is produced when it is dipped into the gallic acid, and the undecomposed iodide remains entirely unchanged. As this would speedily become blackened under the influence of diffused daylight, it is quickly washed off by a solution of hypo-sulphite of soda. Thus there is formed upon the glass plate a representation of the original object, in which the lights and shades are reversed, the bright parts being dark upon the plate, and the dark parts of the object being perfectly colorless and transparent; consequently, the picture thus obtained is called a *negative*. In order to produce a *positive* picture, or an exact reproduction of the original object, the negative plate is laid upon a piece of paper prepared with chloride of silver, and the two sheets being compressed between two plates of glass, the whole is exposed to the action of bright sunlight. The dark parts of the plate become the light parts of the new picture, and the light parts of the plate the dark parts, thus forming a perfect reproduction of the lights and shades of the original object. The paper is then washed in a solution of hypo-sulphite of soda, in order to remove the superfluous chloride of silver, and the picture is complete. It is evident that from a single negative on glass, of this description, an indefinite number of positive pictures may be obtained by a process which may be considered a kind of printing by the sun. This constitutes the art of photography, in its most perfect form.

295. The Photographic Camera. In *Fig.* 112 is represented the arrangement of the camera obscura, for the taking of daguerreotypes and

Fig. 112.

The Photographic Camera.

. 295. Describe the photographic camera.

photographs. The lens is placed at A, and turned towards the person or object the image of which is to be taken. Its focus can be altered by means of the screw D. The glass, or the silver plate, is fastened upon a frame, which is slid into a groove, E B, made capable of adjustment in reference to the lens by moving it in or out of the body of the instrument, C. It will be observed that the image of the object is inverted. The images produced by single lenses are always inverted, but this evidently presents no practical difficulty. In the actual use of the instrument, an additional slide is employed, not seen in the figure, by which the light of the room is entirely cut off from the plate, and the process carried on in total darkness. For full particulars in reference to this beautiful art, reference must be made to special treatises on Photography.

296. Photographs are produced solely by the chemical rays of the solar beam. The process of forming daguerreotype and photographic pictures depends solely upon the chemical rays of the solar beam, i. e., upon the rays that are found in the solar spectrum, above the violet, and entirely outside of the luminous limits of the spectrum, extending in *Fig.* 104, from V to c. The name photography, which means "Light drawing," is therefore misapplied to this art, because the light of the solar beam, instead of producing the pictures, actually tends to prevent their formation. That this is true, may be proved by taking a daguerreotype in the dark, by the use of the obscure, or chemical rays, alone. Let a large solar spectrum be thrown upon a screen, and at the point C, between V and c, *Fig.* 104, beyond the luminous rays, where the chemical rays are situated, let a lens be placed in such a way as to throw these rays into a darkened apartment, upon the object whose picture is to be produced; from the object they may be received upon sensitive photographic paper arranged in the camera and a picture taken in the ordinary manner. That it is the actinic, or chemical rays, which produce the picture, is also proved by the following experiments. Throw the prismatic spectrum upon a table, and place in it slips of photographic paper, prepared with chloride of silver; then bring out the effect by means of some developing agent. It will be found that the darkening is the deepest in the indigo and violet spaces, and that it extends upwards to a considerable distance beyond the visible spectrum. If traced in the opposite direction, it is found to diminish rapidly in intensity, until it

---

296. By what rays in the solar beam are photographs produced? How may this be proved by photographic paper? By flowers and pieces of glass of different colors?

ALL SURFACES ARE AFFECTED 271

reaches the green colored space, and then to cease entirely. *Fig.* 113 illustrates this, and shows very plainly that in the red, orange, yellow, and green, there is no darkening effect whatever produced. Again, take a vase of flowers, of different shades,—scarlet, blue, and yellow,—and make a photographic copy of them upon iodide of silver. The blue tints will be found to act most violently upon the sensitive paper, while the red and yellow are scarcely visible. Again, take a sheet of sensitive paper, prepared with chloride of silver, and place upon it strips of blue, yellow, and red glass. On exposure to the sun's rays for a few minutes, the part beneath the blue glass darkens rapidly, while those covered by the red and yellow glass, are perfectly protected. This is the more striking from the extreme transparency of the plate of yellow glass, and the ease with which the light strikes through it, and the nearly complete opacity of the plate of blue glass, hardly allowing of the passage of light at all.

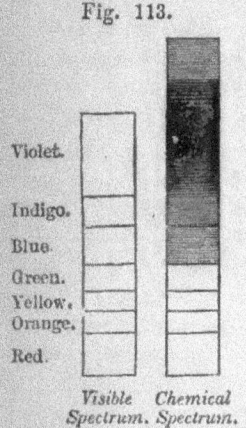

Fig. 113.

Violet.
Indigo.
Blue.
Green.
Yellow.
Orange.
Red.

Visible Chemical Spectrum. Spectrum.

297. Practical importance of distinguishing between the illuminating and chemical rays of Light. As the Photographist requires the use of the chemical rays of the solar beam, it is necessary for him to pay constant attention to the peculiar properties of these rays, and the various circumstances which affect them. As they are more refrangible than the illuminating rays, they are brought to a focus at a point somewhat nearer the lens than the rays of heat and light, *Fig.* 105, and in the arrangement of the camera, the plate must be adjusted accordingly. In the copying of natural objects, it will be found that the less refrangible colors, from green to red, inclusive, send forth no chemical rays, and therefore make no impression upon the sensitive surfaces which are employed, and produce no picture. Figures, therefore, of green, yellow, and red, have of late years been very generally introduced for the purpose of preventing the counterfeiting of government and other notes. In the taking of photographs, it is not always the brightest day that is

---

297. Why must attention be paid to the chemical rays of sunlight in adjusting the camera? What is the advantage of introducing colored figures into bank notes? Why is the brightest day not necessarily favorable to photography? Why are the windows of photographic artists glazed with blue glass?

the most favorable, on account of the predominance, on such days, of the yellow rays; and for the same reason, the autumn, —when such hues predominate in the landscape,—is not favorable for pictures of natural objects. The sensitive plates are a faithful index of the light of the atmosphere. The artist will frequently have occasion to notice, on prolonging his labors until the evening, that a sudden diminution of the sensibility of the plates begins to take place, at a time when, perhaps, but little difference can be detected in the brilliancy of the light; the setting sun has sunk behind a cloud, and all chemical action is soon at an end. If the light is at all of a yellow cast, however bright it may be, its chemical powers will be very small. For this reason, in order to cut off the yellow and red rays which may be reflected from common objects, upon those which are to be photographed, it is usual to glaze the windows of the apartment with blue, or violet colored glass. This imparts a blue tinge to all the objects in the room, and at the same time effectually absorbs the yellow and red rays that may exist in the atmosphere; thus the object to be photographed emits a larger proportion of chemical rays, and its outline becomes much more distinct.

298. All surfaces are affected by the sun's light. It has been seen that certain substances are peculiarly susceptible to impressions from the chemical rays of the solar beam; but it has been ascertained that the sun's rays can hardly fall upon a surface of any kind without producing a molecular change, and leaving a permanent impression. If an engraving, which has for some time been kept in the dark, be exposed to the sunlight upon one-half of its surface, while the other is covered, and then be removed to a dark room, and a piece of prepared photographic paper laid upon it, the part of the engraving which was exposed to the light is taken upon the sensitive paper, while the covered part produces no effect. An engraving which has been subjected to the action of the sun's rays, and then placed in the dark, will reproduce an image of itself upon photographic paper, at the distance of quarter of an inch, without contact. Indeed, one object can hardly touch, or approach another, without producing some impression upon its surface. The effects exerted upon bodies by the action of sunlight are

---

298. Do the chemical rays of the sunbeam produce an impression upon any except specially prepared surfaces? How is this illustrated in the case of an engraving exposed to the light and carried into a darkened room? What effect is produced upon these influences of light during the night? Is a period of darkness essential to the normal condition of matter?

obliterated during the night, and a period of darkness seems to be essential to restore the normal condition of all the various forms of matter.

299. The relations of the rays of Heat, Light, and chemical effect in the Solar Spectrum. It is thought that the undulations which give rise to the sensation of heat, are slower than those of light and chemical influence, but that all are produced by the exceedingly rapid vibrations of the molecules of bodies, communicated to the particles of an all-pervading ether, and carried along by it with wonderful celerity. The slowest and longest of these vibrations cause undulations of a low degree of refrangibility, which produce the sensation and other effects of heat; as they increase in speed, the degree of refrangibility is increased, and the intensity of the heat also augmented; as the vibrations become more frequent, the refrangibility is still further increased, and the effect of dull red light produced. By a still further increase in speed, the heating effect is diminished, refrangibility is still more increased, and the effect of bright red light produced. By a still further increase in speed, the effect of heat altogether ceases, the red brightens, and passes into the orange, and from orange to yellow, where the maximum effect of light is attained. The speed of the undulations rising still higher, the effect of light is diminished, the yellow passes into the green and blue, refrangibility is still further increased, and chemical effect first begins to show itself. This increases rapidly, as the blue passes into violet, and attains its maximum a little beyond that end of the spectrum; after which, this effect also diminishes, and the vibrations probably cease altogether. The conversion of heat, light, and chemical power, into each other, is thus seen to be simply a change in the rate of undulation. The conversion of these forces into ordinary motion, and their production from it, are also seen to be readily explicable as a mere change of the mode of motion, affording another illustration of the convertibility of Forces.

Experiments: Light.

1. The ignition of solids is a source of light; this may be shown by setting fire to a jet of hydrogen gas, and introducing into the flame, which is almost invisible, a piece of platinum wire; the light is at once greatly increased. Introduce fine iron, steel and copper wire; a piece of glass tube; the finely sharpened end of a piece of porcelain,

---

299. How do the ethereal vibrations which produce heat, compare in rapidity with those which produce light and chemical influence? Trace the gradual passage of the rays of heat into those of light and chemical effect. May these forces be regarded as only different rates in the motion of the molecules of matter?

chalk and marble; shake some calcined magnesia, and powdered charcoal, through the flame; in every case there is a great increase in the brilliancy of the light. The hydrogen may be prepared by pouring sulphuric acid, diluted with five times its volume of water, and allowed to cool, upon granulated zinc in a glass flask, fitted with a cork, through which passes a glass tube, drawn out to a fine nozzle. The gas must be allowed to escape from the nozzle for at least five minutes before lighting, in order to completely expel the atmospheric air, otherwise there will be an explosion.

2. Galvanic electricity is a source of light; this may be shown by binding a piece of well burned charcoal, or prepared carbon, to each of the wires attached to the poles of a battery of 12 Grove's cups, bringing the points near enough for the current to pass, and then drawing the charcoal points slowly apart to a short distance; the light is very vivid.

3. Crystallization is a source of light; this is best seen by dissolving *transparent* arsenious acid, or common arsenic, in boiling chlorohydric acid, until a saturated solution is made, and then allowing it to cool in a darkened room; a flash of light may be seen to accompany the deposition of each crystal

4. Chemical action is a source of light; this will become apparent from many of the experiments which are to follow, especially the burning of phosphorus in oxygen.

5. The law of the reflection of light may be shown in the same way as that of the reflection of heat. See experiment 30, page 78.

6. The reflection of light may also be shown by the large parabolic mirrors; see § 75, p. 51. If one of these mirrors be placed opposite to the sun, a spot of extremely intense light and heat will be formed in its focus; many of the metals will be made red-hot, and combustible substances inflamed.

7. The refraction of light; this may be shown by a large double convex lens; also by a solid prism of flint glass; or still more effectively by a hollow prism of glass filled with bi-sulphide of carbon.

8. The solar spectrum may be displayed to the best advantage by allowing a beam of sunlight to enter a darkened room through an exceedingly fine slit, in the manner described in § 276, and receiving the spectrum upon a screen of white cotton cloth, placed at a distance of 20 feet from the prism.

9. The different heating power of the rays may be shown by placing a very delicate thermometer successively in the colored spaces, from the violet to the red, and finally a little below, and outside of the red ray.

10. The different illuminating power of the rays may be shown by holding a printed page successively in the different colors.

11. The different chemical power of the rays may be shown by placing slips of unglazed white paper, that have been dipped in a colorless solution of nitrate of silver, and immediately afterwards in a solution of common salt, in the dark, successively, one slip in each color, from the red to the violet, and beyond the violet, for about one minute each; or by exposing a piece of prepared paper to the action of the whole spectrum. See §§ 278 and 279.

12. The power of sunlight to produce chemical combination, may be shown by mixing equal volumes of chlorine and hydrogen in a small glass tube, supported over mercury, in the dark, or diffuse daylight, and reflecting a beam of sunlight upon it by a mirror; only a small quantity of the gases should be employed. If a large quantity be used, the mixture should be placed in a bottle of white glass, in a wooden box, with a movable cover, which may be drawn off by a string from a convenient distance. The explosion is violent. The mode of preparing these gases may be seen by referring to the experiments under each.

13. The power of decomposing carbonic acid, imparted to green leaves by sunlight, may be shown by placing a thriving plant in a jar of carbonic acid gas, and exposing it to the sunlight for some days. Test the presence of the carbonic acid at the beginning of the experiment, by inserting a lighted taper; it will be extinguished. Prove the conversion of the carbonic acid into oxygen at the close of the experiment, by introducing the same taper, re-lighted; it will now burn with increased brilliancy.

14. That the leaves of plants emit oxygen in the sunlight, may be shown by placing a sprig of mint in a white glass globe, filled full of spring water, and then inverted in a tumbler of water, and placed in the sun; in a short time bubbles of gas will collect, which may be proved to be pure oxygen by their effect on a lighted taper.

15. The effect of sunlight on chemical compounds, may be shown by pouring a little solution of common salt into a wine glass containing a solution of nitrate of silver, and exposing the white precipitate to the action of the sun; it is almost immediately blackened.

16. The different chemical effect of light of different colors, may be shown by exposing slips of paper, prepared by dipping in a solution of nitrate of silver, and then in one of common salt, in the dark, under pieces of blue, yellow and red glass, to the action of sunlight. The effect will be decidedly the greatest under the blue, and least under the red glass.

ELECTRICITY. 275

17. Fraunhofer's lines may readily be seen by means of an instrument, arranged as in § 283, or by the Spectroscope, § 286, substituting sunlight, in place of artificial light.

18. The existence of chemical substances in flames, may be shown by employing the Spectroscope, as described in §§ 285 and 286, or by receiving the spectrum on a screen, as in § 284.

19. The conversion of the bright lines of the spectra of artificial light into dark lines, may be shown by forming a spectrum upon a screen, by means of the Spectroscope, and the light of a powerful lamp, and noting the bright double sodium line in the orange; this is due to the universal diffusion of sodium: then ignite a piece of sodium in a small platinum spoon, in a gas burner, placed so as to intercept the light of the original lamp in its passage into the Spectroscope, and the bright sodium lines of the spectrum will be at once converted into dark lines. The same experiment may be tried with equal effect with potassium and other metals.

20. The daguerreotype and photograph process may be illustrated by strictly following the directions contained in §§ 293 and 294, with the aid of a good camera obscura, taking care to protect the prepared plates carefully from the action of diffused light. The proportions of the solutions required are as follows:

1. Collodion,—5 or 6 grs. of gun cotton, to 1 oz. of mixture of 1 part of alcohol to 2 of ether, then add 2½ grs. each of iodide of potassium, and iodide of cadmium.
2. Nitrate of Silver Solution,—480 grs. of crystallized nitrate of silver, to 2 oz. of water, with addition of 4 grs. of iodide of potassium, or cadmium.
3. Pyro-Gallic Acid Solution,—1 gr. of pyro-gallic acid, 30 minims of alcohol, 30 minims of glacial acetic acid, 2 grs. of citric acid, dissolved in 1 oz. of water.
4. The Hypo-Sulphite of Soda Solution should be saturated. If any difficulty be encountered, further instruction should be sought from some experienced photographer.

CHAPTER IV.

THE THIRD CHEMICAL AGENT:—ELECTRICITY.

STATICAL ELECTRICITY; GALVANIC ELECTRICITY; ELECTRO-MAGNETISM; MAGNETO-ELECTRICITY; THERMO-ELECTRICITY; ANIMAL ELECTRICITY; THE RELATIONS OF THE CHEMICAL AGENTS.

§ I. Statical Electricity.

300. Electricity. The third of the three great imponderable agents by which the action of chemical affinity is controlled, and which is either produced in all cases of chemical action, or has a powerful effect in producing them, is Electricity. There are two different states in which electricity is manifested, statical and galvanic. The former is electricity in a state of repose; the latter is electricity in movement. Statical electricity is principally produced by friction; it accumulates upon the surfaces of bodies, and exists in a state of tension, which is manifested by sparks, and by the attraction which it exerts. Gal-

---

300. What is the third imponderable? In what two states does it exist? Describe them.

vanic electricity is principally produced by chemical action; it flows for hours in a steady and continuous current; and is particularly distinguished from statical electricity by its chemical effects, and its connection with magnetism.

301. The nature of Electricity. There are two hypotheses in regard to the nature of this powerful agent analogous to those which have been mentioned in regard to the nature of heat and light. The first regards it as an exceedingly subtile fluid, so light as not to affect the most delicate balances; moving with immense velocity, and pervading all substances. The second regards it as the result of a special modification made in the state of bodies, depending upon a peculiar vibration of the particles of matter communicated to the same ether, whose undulations produce heat and light. The latter theory is the one which is now generally received. The full discussion of all the phenomena of electricity would require a volume, and it properly forms a part of the sciences embraced in Natural Philosophy. We are concerned with it here only so far as it is connected with chemical phenomena, and as a knowledge of its fundamental facts is necessary to the full understanding of the various chemical processes which are soon to come under our notice. The subject of galvanic electricity is of more importance to the chemist than that of statical, and our attention will, therefore, be chiefly directed to it. The fundamental facts on which the whole science of statical electricity is founded may be stated in a few words.

302. The fundamental facts of Statical Electricity. If a piece of glass, amber, or sealing-wax, be rubbed with the dry hand, or with flannel, silk, or fur, and then held near small light bodies, such as straws, hairs, or threads, these bodies will fly toward the glass, amber, or wax, thus rubbed, and, for a moment, will adhere to them. The substances having this power of attraction are called *electrics*, and the agency by which this power is exerted is called *electricity*. Some bodies, such as certain crystals, exert the same power when heated, and others become electric by pressure. Although these are the simple facts on which the science is based, yet electricity exhibits a vast number of curious and interesting phenomena, depending on the variety and kind of machinery, and the quantity of the electri-

---

301. State the two theories in regard to the nature of electricity. Which is now generally received?—302. State the fundamental facts of electricity. What happens when glass, amber and sealing-wax are rubbed, and brought near small pieces of paper? When is a body said to be excited with electricity? What are the most common electrics?

cal influence employed. When a piece of glass, or other electric, has been rubbed, so as to attract other bodies, it is said to be *excited with electricity,* or *electrified,* and it is found that many substances are capable of this excitement, when managed in a peculiar manner. The most common are amber, glass, rosin, sulphur, wax, and the fur of animals.

303. The sources of Electricity. The principal source of electricity for experimental purposes, is friction. Whenever two surfaces of any kind are rubbed together, one becomes excited with negative, the other with positive, electricity. This, however, is only a special case of a much more general law, for it has been found that when the equilibrium of the *molecules* of any body is disturbed, a development of electricity takes place. The mere compression of many crystals is attended by electric action. A crystal of Iceland spar, if compressed, exhibits signs of electrical excitement, which it retains, sometimes, hours and days. The same is true of fluor spar, of mica, of arragonite, of quartz, and several other substances. Sometimes, elevation and depression of temperature are sufficient to develop electricity. This is especially true of the mineral, tourmaline. If a crystal of this substance be gently heated, it becomes powerfully electrified while the temperature is rising, one extremity being positively, and the other negatively excited. When the temperature becomes stationary, the excitement ceases; as the crystal cools, the electric excitement returns, but the polarity is reversed; the end of the crystal that was before positive, now becomes negative. The temperature should not rise above 300°. The electrical excitement of the crystal may be shown by its power of attracting and repelling light substances brought near it. Fracture also produces electricity; this may be shown by suddenly breaking a stick of roll sulphur. The rending of crystals along the line of cleavage, as when the laminæ of a sheet of mica, or talc, are quickly separated in a dark room, is attended with a feeble electrical light. A melted substance, in the act of solidifying, is often electric. Melted sulphur, solidifying in a glass vessel, is negatively excited, while the glass becomes positive. Ice is also often electric. This is probably due to molecular movements. Chemical action always produces electricity. Electricity is also developed in the process of combustion; carbon, or charcoal, when it burns, becomes

---

303. What is the principal source of electricity? To what is electrical excitement, in all cases, thought to be due? What is the effect of compressing crystals? Of heating and cooling tourmaline? Of fracture? Of solidification of sulphur? Of combustion?

negatively electric, while the carbonic acid which it forms, is positive. In like manner, hydrogen, when it burns, is negative, while the watery vapor produced by it is positive. It is said, also, that evaporation is a source of electricity, but this may be regarded as a case of chemical action. The evaporating surface is negative, while the vapor is positive. The atmosphere is also another source of electricity, not only during storms, but also in fine weather. Fogs, snow, and rain, are almost always charged with positive electricity. The clouds are also commonly highly positive. In general, all these sources of electricity may be resolved into the movement of the molecules of bodies, and their violent separation; all then become oppositely electrified. Thus electricity, like light and heat, may be considered as due to motion.

304. Electrical Attraction and Repulsion. When an excited electric, like a rod or tube of glass, which has been violently rubbed with a piece of flannel, is presented to a small ball made of pith, or cork, and suspended by a silk thread, the pith ball is attracted to the glass, and adheres to it for a moment, as in A, *Fig.* 114. Soon, however, it is repelled, and occupies the position indicated by B. If now, to this pith ball, thus repelled, another pith ball be presented, this is first in like manner attracted, and then repelled, and so on with a succession of similar balls, which are each in turn attracted, and repelled. From this experiment we draw the following conclusion, that if any electric be excited by friction, it will first attract, and then repel, a light substance placed near it, and that this light substance, when repelled, is itself in a state of elec-

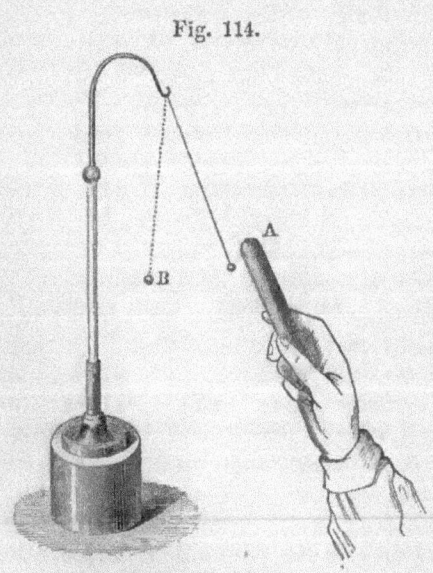

Fig. 114.

Electrical Attraction.

Of evaporation? What is the electrical state of the clouds? What is the relation of electricity to motion?—304. What happens when an excited glass rod is brought near a pith ball? When a second pith ball is presented to the first? What conclusion do we draw from this experiment?

TWO KINDS OF ELECTRICITY. 279

trical excitement, similar to the glass, proved by the fact that it first attracts, and then repels, another light body placed near it. A metallic rod being presented to the electrified pith ball, it will lose its excitement and return to its natural condition.

305. Two bodies similarly electrified repel each other. If to a pith ball, thus excited, another pith ball, excited from the same piece of rubbed glass, be presented, they will mutually repel each other. And, in like manner, if a rod of sealing-wax, or sulphur, be violently rubbed with a piece of flannel, and then brought near to a pith ball, suspended by a thread, the pith ball will at first be attracted by the sealing-wax, and then repelled, and will be found to have become excited with electricity, similar to that of the original sealing-wax: then, if to this pith ball thus excited, a second pith ball be presented, that has been excited by the same piece of rubbed sealing-wax, we shall find that these two pith balls, which have derived their electricity from the same source, will mutually repel each other.

306. Two bodies differently electrified attract each other. —Two kinds of electricity, Vitreous and Resinous. But if to a pith ball, excited by the rubbed *glass*, there be presented a pith ball that has been excited by a piece of rubbed *sealing-wax*, the two will mutually attract each other. Hence we conclude that while bodies *similarly* electrified repel, bodies *differently* electrified attract one another. We also conclude that there is an apparent difference between the electricity produced by glass when rubbed, and the electricity produced by sealing-wax, and it is usual to speak of two kinds of electricity, vitreous and resinous, or positive and negative, and they are often denoted by the algebraic signs $+$ and $-$.

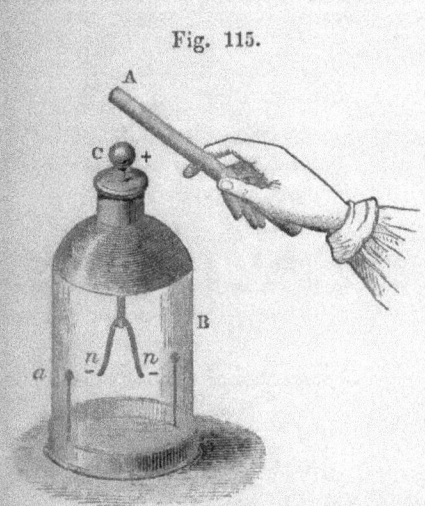

Fig. 115.

The Electroscope.

307. The Electroscope. On these properties is

---

305. What is the effect of two bodies similarly electrified upon each other?—306. What effect have two bodies, differently electrified, upon each other? What is meant by the signs $+$ and $-$?—307. Describe the electroscope.

founded the instrument called the Electroscope, intended to indicate the presence of electricity in any body, and the kind of it. The two bits of gold leaf, n, n, in the accompanying *Fig.* 115, which are both connected with the brass head of the instrument, are similarly electrified when any excited electric is brought near to them, and repel each other more or less, according to the degree of this excitement. Let A be a rod of electrified sealing-wax, brought near to the knob, c; the two bits of gold-leaf will be electrified, and will diverge from each other, indicating the existence of electrical excitement in A. The kind of electricity can be ascertained in the following manner. First, electrify the gold leaf with vitreous electricity, and then see, when the body whose electricity it is wished to determine, is brought near c, whether the slips continue to diverge, or come together; if the former, the electricity is vitreous; if the latter, it is resinous. The operation of this instrument will be more fully explained hereafter.

308. Conductors and Non-conductors.—Insulation. If, in the preceding experiments, the pith balls be suspended from metal chains, having a direct metallic communication with the earth, none of the above phenomena will be manifested, for the electricity will pass off into the earth as soon as it reaches the balls, while the electrical excitement invariably makes itself apparent if these be suspended from silk or glass. Hence we conclude that some substances conduct electricity very easily, and do not permit it to accumulate, while others deny it a passage. This is the foundation of the division of all bodies into conductors and non-conductors. A substance is said to be insulated when it is separated from all direct communication with good conductors of electricity by the intervention of a non-conductor, as when any body is placed upon a stool with glass legs, or a metallic rod is provided with a glass handle. No substance is capable of being permanently electrified which is not a non-conductor itself, or made so by insulation. Thus, in *Fig.* 116, we have a bit of brass rod with a glass handle, and notwithstanding the conducting power of the metal, in consequence of its having a glass handle, it will, when rubbed, exhibit all the ordinary marks of electrical excitement. All substances exhibit electricity when rubbed,

Fig. 116.

Metallic Rod with Glass Handle.

Show how the kind of electricity may be detected.—308. What is meant by conductors and non-conductors? By insulation?

THE INDUCTION 281

but those which are good conductors lose it immediately; consequently, there are no signs of electrical excitement, except the escape be prevented by insulation. The metals, charcoal, plumbago, water, and substances containing water in a liquid state, and therefore more or less damp, are conductors of electricity. Glass, resins, sulphur, diamond, dried wood, silk, hair, and wool, also the air and gases, are non-conductors; but these are often rendered conductors by the presence of water. For this reason, in damp weather, many electrical experiments can not be performed, because of the deposition of moisture upon the surface of insulators, and the good conducting power imparted to air by watery vapor.

309. Vitreous electricity can not be produced without a correspondent amount of resinous electricity, and vice versa. When two substances are rubbed together, both vitreous and resinous electricity are developed, the rubber being charged with one, and the substance rubbed, with the other; and the presence of both may be made manifest if the two substances in question are insulated. Thus, if a glass rod be rubbed with a piece of flannel, while the glass will be charged with vitreous electricity, the flannel itself will be charged to an equal degree with resinous electricity. And on the other hand, if a rod of sealing-wax be rubbed with a piece of dry flannel, while the wax will be excited with resinous electricity, the piece of flannel will be charged to an equal degree with vitreous electricity. It is impossible to produce one kind of electricity without at the same time producing an equal amount of the opposite kind. This is the most marked peculiarity possessed by electricity, and this is the reason why it is called a *polar force*. By the term polar force, is meant a force which, whenever it is produced, always develops an equal amount of force over against, or opposite to itself, just as the poles of the earth are opposite to each other. The peculiar nature of a polar force is well illustrated in the case of a straight bar magnet, or a common magnetic needle, while one end is excited by one kind of magnetism, and points to the north, the other end is excited with the opposite kind of magnetism, and points towards the south; and these two magnetic forces are mutually attractive of each other. In like manner, if one end of an insulated cylinder of brass be kept in a state of electrical excitement with one kind of electri-

---

Mention some of the best conductors. Some of the best non-conductors. What is the effect of damp weather on electrical experiments?—309. Can vitreous electricity be produced without the manifestation of an equal amount of negative? Why is electricity called a polar force? What is meant by the term polar? Give an illustration of this.

city, the other extremity will be excited with an equal amount of the opposite kind. This polar peculiarity of electricity will become more apparent as we proceed.

310. Induction of Electricity. One of the most curious facts connected with electricity is, the power that a highly electrified body has of throwing all other bodies near it into a state of electrical excitement. Thus, an electrified glass globe, or other body, placed in the centre of a room, will produce electrical excitement in all objects in the apartment, and if they be insulated, sparks may be drawn from them. This is called the induction of electricity. When careful experiments are performed, it is found that if the body in question be charged with vitreous electricity, it will induce resinous electricity in the extremities of those bodies which are nearest to it, while vitreous electricity will be manifested on those ends which are the most remote. This is illustrated by *Fig.* 117. Let A be a rod of glass, positively electrified, and let it be brought near the metallic cylinder, B, insulated upon a stand of glass. B will immediately begin to give signs of electrical excitement, and it will be found, on examination, that the end of B nearest A will be negatively, while the most remote end will be positively electrified. If A be withdrawn, the signs of electrical excitement in B will disappear. If it be again brought near, they will reappear. Should a connection be formed between the remote end of B and the earth, the positive electricity will escape, and B will then contain only negative electricity, which will remain after A is withdrawn. B is then left negatively electrified upon

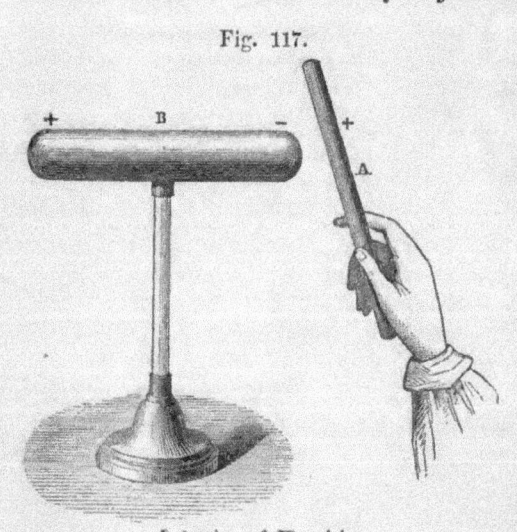

Fig. 117.

Induction of Electricity.

---

310. What is meant by the induction of electricity? Is the electricity induced of the same kind as that of the excited body? Explain *Fig.* 117. Is it possible to electrify a body without the actual contact of the excited substance?

its insulated stand, and if any body be now brought near to it, the negative electricity will escape with a spark. Thus an electrified body drives off electricity of the same kind, and puts bodies near it in an electrical condition opposite to itself. The polar relation of the positive or vitreous electricity, and the negative or resinous electricity, at the opposite extremities of the cylinder, B, is apparent; and also the fact that one kind of electricity can not be developed without a corresponding development of the other.

311. The intervention of solid matter no obstacle to Induction. This effect takes place even through glass and metallic obstacles placed in the way. Thus, in *Fig.* 117, if a plate of glass were held between the rod, A, and B, the effect would be the same. And so, in *Fig.* 118, if A be a metallic disk, insulated upon a glass stand, B be a plate of glass, and C be another metallic disk, and if A be electrified positively by an electrical machine, C will be immediately electrified also, through the glass, B, which will oppose no impediment to the process, and the right side will be charged with positive electricity, while the left side will be negative. If C be now touched on the right side with the finger, its positive electricity will escape, and it will remain negatively electrified, as represented in the figure. If, instead of using two disks, we paste a piece of tin foil on one side of a frame of glass, leaving a margin of an inch on every side, and on the other side a similar piece of tin foil, and electrify that on one side, the foil on the other side will be charged with the opposite electricity, if a connection be formed between it and the ground. Or, if a bottle be filled with cop-

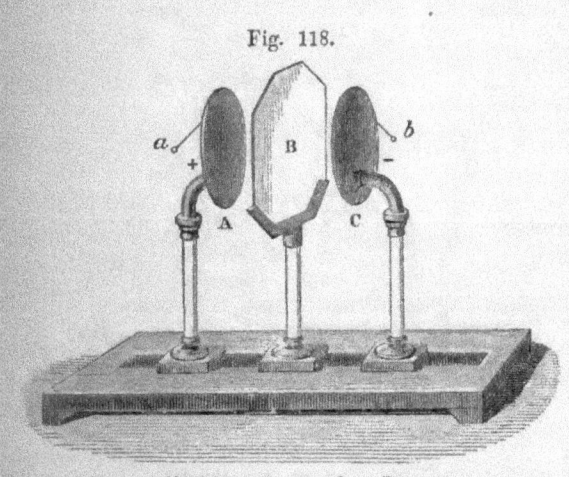

Fig. 118.

Solid Matter no obstacle to Induction.

---

311. Show that the intervention of a solid body is no obstacle to induction. Describe *Fig.* 118. Show how induction operates in the case of the electroscope.

per leaf, or have tin foil pasted on the inside, and the outside be covered with tin foil extending over the bottom, and three-fourths of the body of the bottle, and a connection be formed between the inside and an electrical machine, the outer side will also be electrified with the opposite electricity. This is the arrangement of the famous Leyden jar. In the case of the Electroscope, *Fig.* 115, the rod A, of sealing-wax being negatively electrified when brought near to c, induces in the knob positive electricity, as is seen in the figure, and negative electricity in the leaves of gold; but both being similarly electrified, they repel each other in proportion to the degree of electrical excitement in A, until they touch the metallic slips, *a, a*, on each side connected with the earth. At the moment of contact, the negative electricity escapes, and there is nothing but positive electricity left in the knob, c, and the leaves. At first, these fall together, but almost immediately begin to repel each other under the influence of the positive electricity with which they are now both affected.

312. The theory of Induction. The difference between the conduction and induction of electricity consists in the mode in which the electrical influence is propagated from atom to atom, through bodies, so as to exert an effect at a considerable distance. If, when an electrified body is brought near to a body which is in its natural state, there be an instantaneous passage of the electricity through the particles of the second body, the process is said to be *conduction*, and the body in question is called a good conductor. If, however, there is not an instantaneous transmission of the electrical influence through the particles of the second body, but a certain amount of resistance offered to the passage of the electricity, the particles become polarized by induction; and as each particle that is electrified induces electricity in those near it, and throws them into a polar state, the effect may be propagated to a great distance. This is well illustrated in *Fig.* 119. Let P represent any body charged with positive electricity, and *a b c d* rows of particles of air, intermediate between P and a second conductor, N. Air, as we know, is a poor conductor of electricity, and opposes some impediment to its passage; consequently, the particles of air between P and N, all become polarized; i. e., their electrical

Fig. 119.

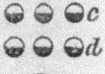

Theory of Induction.

---

312. State the theory of induction. Show that it is accomplished by a process of polarization. Describe *Fig.* 119.

state is disturbed, and the negative electricity in each is drawn towards the positively charged body, P, while the positive electricity in each particle is driven to the opposite pole and turned towards the conductor, N. The body, N, is also similarly affected, its negative electricity being strongly attracted towards the positive electricity of the particles in d, immediately contiguous to it, and its positive electricity being repelled to the greatest possible distance. This state of things will continue as long as P remains in its position; but if that body be removed, the state of polar tension will cease, and the electricity of N, and the particles of air will return to its natural state.

313. Electricity confined to the external surface of Bodies. This may be proved by the following experiment devised by Coulomb. A hollow sphere of brass, *Fig.* 120, is mounted upon a stand of glass, and pierced with a circular aperture. It is highly electrified by contact with an electrical machine, and its inner surface is touched by a stick of glass or gum lac, tipped with a small bit of brass, c. This piece of brass is then applied to the gold leaf electroscope, *Fig.* 115, and no divergence of the leaves can be observed. The bit of brass is next applied to the outside surface of the globe, and then to the same electroscope, when a manifest divergence of the leaves is seen. Hence we conclude that there was no accumulation of electricity except upon the outside surface. This fact may be proved by other experiments of a still more satisfactory character. It is found, also, that smoothness of the external surface has a great effect in retaining electricity and preventing it from escaping, while points and sharp edges greatly favor its escape. For this reason the prime conductors of electrical machines, and

Fig. 120.

Electricity confined to the Surface.

313. Show that electricity is confined to the external surface of bodies. What is the effect of the smoothness and roughness of surfaces on the escape of electricity?

all the parts of Leyden jars, should be made as smooth as possible. On the same principle, perfectly smooth surfaces, brought near to highly charged electrified bodies, receive electricity from them with great difficulty and always with a spark and shock, while edges and points will receive it from a distance, and silently, without either spark or noise. This is the principle on which lightning rods are constructed. They disarm the highly electrified clouds from a distance, noiselessly and quietly. These rods were first set up by Dr. Franklin, shortly after he made his great discovery of the identity of lightning and electricity, by means of a kite raised in a thunder storm, in the neighborhood of Philadelphia.

314. Theories of Electricity. Two different theories have been proposed to account for the phenomena of electricity, that of Dr. Franklin, and that of Dufay. To account for electrical phenomena, Dr. Franklin supposed, as above stated, that all terrestrial things had a natural quantity of that subtile fluid, but that its effects became apparent only when a substance contained more or less than the natural quantity, and that this state is produced by the friction of an electric. Thus, when a piece of glass is rubbed by the hand, the equilibrium is destroyed, in consequence of the electrical fluid passing from the hand to the glass, so that now the hand contains less, and the glass more, than their ordinary quantities. These two states he called *positive* and *negative*, implying the presence and absence of the electrical fluid. If now a conductor of electricity, such as a piece of metal, be made to touch a positive body, or brought near it, the accumulated fluid will leave this body and pass to the conductor, which will then contain more than its natural quantity of the fluid. But if the conductor be made to touch a negative body, then it will impart a share of its own natural quantity of the fluid to that body, and consequently will contain less than usual. Also, when one body, positively, and another negatively electrified, are connected by a conducting substance, the fluid rushes from the positive to the negative body, and the equilibrium is restored. This theory, originally invented by Dr. Franklin, will account satisfactorily for nearly every electrical phenomenon. There is, however, another theory, that of Dufay, which is also very generally received. This theory supposes that there are two kinds of electricity, which are termed the *vitreous* and *resinous*, corresponding with the positive and

---

Explain the principle of the lightning-rod.—314 What is the theory of Franklin? Of Dufay? Which is preferred?

negative of Franklin. This supposition is founded on the fact, that when two pith balls, or other light bodies, near together, are both touched by an excited piece of glass, or sealing-wax, they repel each other. But if one of the balls be touched by the glass, and the other by the wax, they will attract each other. Hence, Dufay concluded that electricity consists of two distinct fluids, which exist together in all bodies; that these two fluids attract each other, but that they are separated during the excitation of an electric, and that when thus separated, and transferred to non-electrics, as to the pith balls, the mutual attraction of the two electricities causes the balls to rush towards each other. The electricity corresponding with the positive of Franklin, is called vitreous, because it is obtained from glass, while the other is called resinous, because it is obtained from wax and resin. In respect to the merit of these two theories, we can only say here, that while Franklin's is the most simple and accounts equally well for nearly all electrical phenomena, the preponderance of opinion is at the present time in favor of the theory of the polar character of electricity. It is regarded not as a fluid, but as a force, which acts at the same moment in opposite directions.

315. Development of large quantities of Electricity.—The Electrical Machine. When large quantities of electricity are desired, it is obtained by means of the friction of a large surface of some non-conducting electric, such as glass; this is accomplished by means of what are called Electrical Machines. There are two kinds, called the *cylinder* and *plate* machines, depending on the form of the glass used to excite the electricity. The plate machine is considered much the best, since both sides are exposed to electrical friction, while in the cylinder machine only the outside can be excited. The plate machine is represented in *Fig.* 121. It consists of a plate of glass, F, F, turning on an axis of wood, by the handle, M, and supported by a frame fixed to a platform, also of wood. On opposite sides are two cushions of leather, made to press against the plate by springs. From D, or some other part connected with the rubbers, a rod descends to the ground as a conductor of electricity to the machine. The electrical fluid accumulates on the surface of the prime conductors, C, C, which are insulated by glass supports in order to prevent the escape of the fluid. By means of such a machine, especially if the cushions are covered by soft mercurial

---

315. Describe the electrical machine.

288   MACHINE.

Fig. 121.

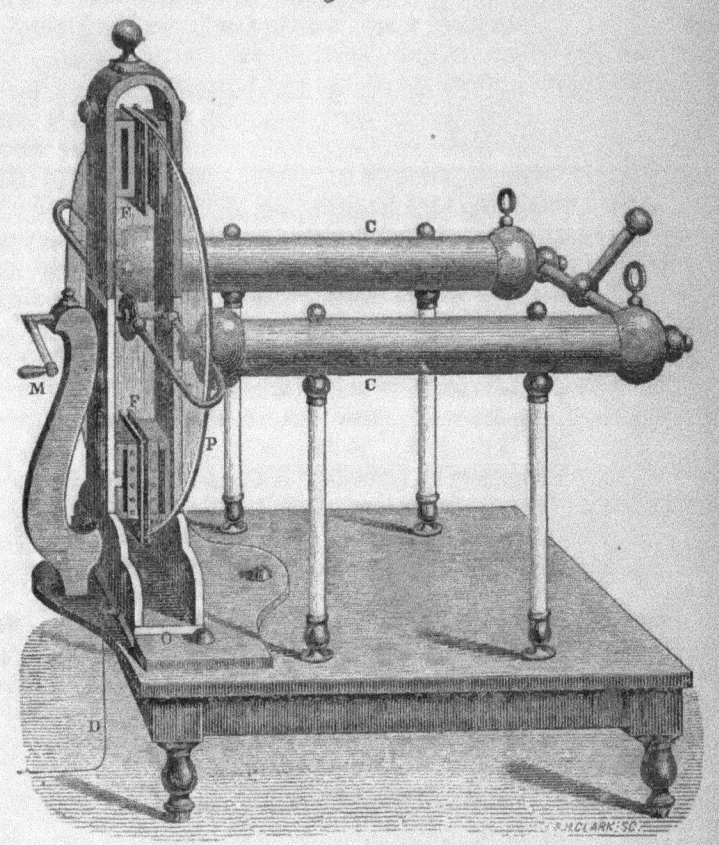

The Electrical Machine.

amalgam, large quantities of electricity may be collected. On turning the plate, sparks are seen to pass from its surface to the prime conductors, being attracted by sharp points of brass wire, which issue from their smooth and brightly polished surfaces. A plate of two feet in diameter is sufficient for all ordinary purposes, but they are often made much larger, requiring the strength of several men to turn them.

316. The Leyden Jar. An indispensable companion to the electrical machine is the Leyden Jar, so called from having been invented at Leyden, in Holland. It depends for its action

316. Describe the Leyden jar.

THE LEYDEN JAR.

upon the principle of the induction of electricity, above explained. It is necessary to bear in mind that glass is no impediment to the induction of electricity by a highly charged electric. The apparatus is delineated in the accompanying *Fig.* 122. It consists of a glass jar, coated both inside and outside with tin foil, except a part around the top, as shown in the figure. The inside is sometimes also filled with gold or copper leaf. Through a varnished wooden stopper, or through an ordinary cork, a wire having a knob at its top is passed, and extends to the inside coating. Now, if either positive or negative electricity be communicated to the knob, it is immediately diffused over the whole of the inside coating, and by its inductive influence the outside coating takes on the opposite kind. When in this state, the two coatings being oppositely electrified, the jar is said to be charged. The more the inside is charged, the more also, and to the same degree, is the outside also charged. In this state, as soon as a communication is established between the inside and the outside coatings, the two electricities being mutually attracted, rush together with a bright flash and loud report, and the equilibrium is at once restored. The discharge may be effected through a short metallic circuit, as in the accompanying *Fig.* 123, or through a long chain, or through the fingers, or through a larger part of the body, the outside of the jar being grasped in one hand, and the knob touched with the fingers of the other hand; or in fine, several persons may form a circuit, by taking hold of hands, and the one at one extreme touching the outside coating, while the one at the other touches the knob. All will feel the shock

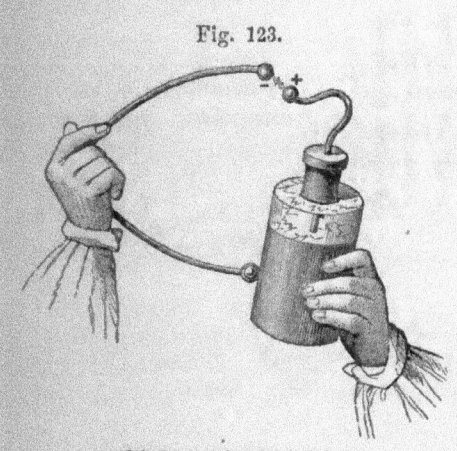

Fig. 122.
Leyden Jar.

Fig. 123.
Discharge of a Leyden Jar.

How may it be discharged?

at the same instant. It is usual to charge the jar from the electrical machine, but it may also be charged from the Electrophorus, an instrument to be presently described.

317. Mode of charging the Leyden Jar. While the jar is receiving the charge, it must not be insulated, i. e., the outside must communicate, through some good conductor, with the earth. As the positive fluid collects on the inside, the outside becomes negative, by the expulsion of the positive fluid natural to it, and the accumulation of the negative fluid in its stead, drawn from the earth. But if the outside is insulated, these transfers to and from it can not take place, and therefore the jar can not become charged.

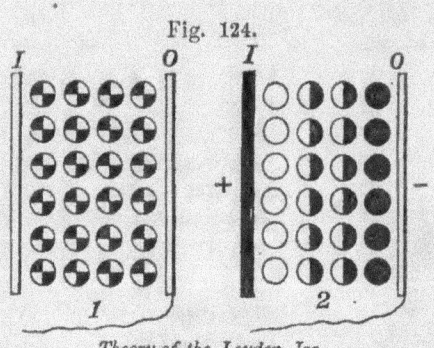

318. The theory of the Leyden Jar. As the Leyden jar is charged by induction, the theory of the process is the same as that given for every process of induction, viz., that it is accomplished by the polarization of the particles of an imperfect electrical conductor. Let No. 1, in *Fig.* 124, indicate a section of the glass side of a Leyden jar in its natural or uncharged state; all the particles composing it are represented as in an indifferent electrical condition. No. 2 represents a section of a similar jar in its charged condition. The inside surface, *I*, having been connected with the prime conductor of an electrical machine, is charged with positive electricity. The effect of this has been to expel all the positive electricity from the row of particles nearest the inside surface, and to force it into the next row; this has compelled the positive electricity of this row to take refuge in the third row, the positive electricity of which it has expelled and driven into the fourth row; and this in turn has been compelled to escape from the jar by the agency of the conductor connecting it with the ground, leaving the outside of the glass in a highly excited *negative* state, while the inside is maintained in a highly excited *positive* state by its

---

317. Why can the Leyden jar not be charged if it be insulated?—318. State the theory of the Leyden jar.

connection with the electrical machine. Let the jar be now disengaged from the electrical machine, and the two surfaces thus oppositely excited be connected through the agency of a metallic conductor, and the equilibrium will be restored by the sudden rush of the two charges towards each other, accompanied by a shock and a spark of unusual brilliancy.

319. The Electrophorus. This is an instrument for readily obtaining small quantities of electricity. It consists of a plate of resin from nine to twelve inches in diameter contained in a shallow dish of metal, and a metallic disk, A, a little smaller than the plate of resin, provided with a glass handle. See *Fig.* 125. To charge the Electrophorus, the plate of resin is briskly

Fig. 125.

The Electrophorus.

rubbed with a piece of warm dry flannel, or struck several times with a dry silk handkerchief, folded up for the purpose, or by the skin of a cat, by means of which negative electricity is excited. If now the plate of metal be brought down upon the resin, its lower surface, under the influence of induction, will become positive, while its upper surface will be negative. Let the upper surface be now touched with the finger, *Fig.* 125,

---

319. Describe the electrophorus.

292   THE HYDRO-ELECTRIC

the negative electricity will be withdrawn, and the plate will become wholly charged with positive electricity to such a degree that sparks can readily be obtained from it. This electricity being merely the result of induction, the resin has lost none of that produced by the original rubbing, and the process may be repeated many times without any additional friction. This instrument is of great use in the laboratory, for exploding gaseous mixtures.

320. The Hydro-Electric Machine. Electricity may also be generated by the friction of steam of very high pressure against the sides and edges of an aperture, through which it is violently rushing. The apparatus is called the Hydro-Electric machine; *Fig.* 126. A strong iron boiler and furnace, arranged

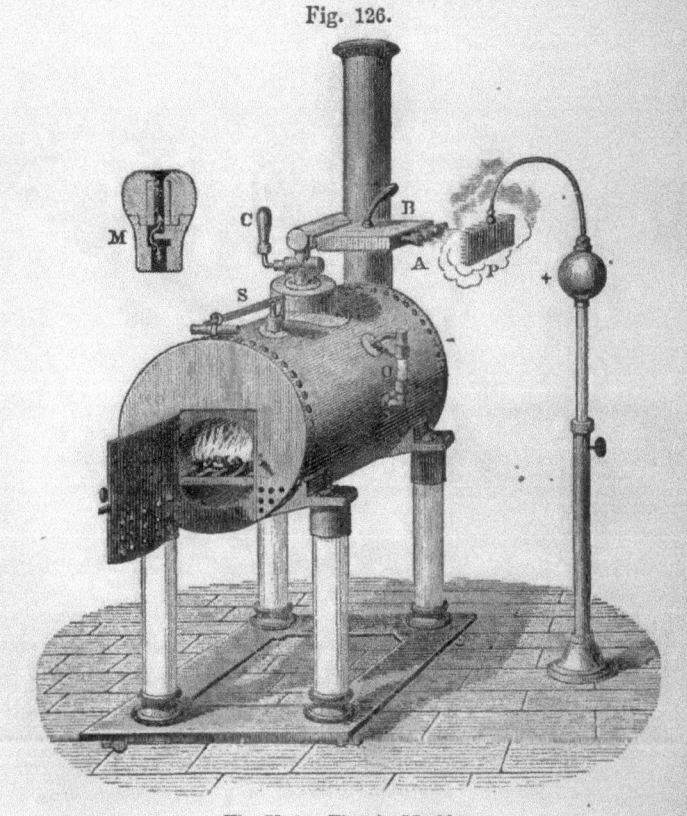

Fig. 126.

The Hydro-Electric Machine.

---

320 Describe the hydro-electric machine. To what is the electricity produced by this process really due?

MACHINE. 293

upon the plan of the boiler of a locomotive, is mounted upon four stout glass insulators, well varnished. The boiler is provided with a safety valve, s, and with a gauge for showing the water level, o ; b represents the smoke chimney; a, a row of apertures for the escape of steam; c, a stop-cock, commanding these apertures. The apertures are all lined with wood or ivory, and are each provided with a partition nearly closing the passage, for the purpose of increasing the friction of the steam as it escapes; one of them is shown in section at m. p is a collection of bright metallic points, for the purpose of collecting the electricity, and these are mounted upon a movable stand. The pressure of steam required is about 90 lbs. to the square inch. On opening the stop-cock, the steam rushes out with great fury, a portion is condensed into globules of water, and these, as they are carried forward, are pressed violently against the sides of the apertures. This friction decomposes their natural electricity, the negative remaining on the jets, while the positive is carried out by the steam and deposited upon the conductor, p. The interior of the tubes plays the part of the rubber of the ordinary machine, while the steam acts as the glass plate. Sparks have been obtained from this machine at the distance of 22 inches.

321. The effects of Electricity. These are marked and powerful, and may be classified as Physiological, Luminous, Calorific, Mechanical, Chemical, and Magnetic. The shock produced by the discharge of a Leyden jar is an instance of the physiological effects. The bright spark, and the flashes of light, that may be drawn from the electrical machine in the dark, show its luminous effects. Its calorific effects may be shown by the inflammation of gunpowder, and of alcohol, when a powerful discharge is passed through them from the Leyden jar, *Fig.* 127, and by the expansion of

Fig. 127.

Inflammation of Alcohol by Electricity.

---

321. State the effects of electricity.

294   THE EFFECTS OF

air in a confined vessel, *Fig.* 128. The expansion is indicated by the rising of the water in the glass tube, as soon as the discharge from the Leyden jar takes place. Its mechanical effects are exhibited by the splitting of plates of glass, through which a charge is transmitted, by the piercing of a card, *Fig.* 129, and by the generally destructive results of severe lightning. Its chemical effects are shown by the decomposition of many compound bodies, and its powerful influence in determining chemical combination. When a succession of electric discharges from a powerful electric machine is sent through pure water contained in a glass tube, by means of gold or platinum conductors, which nearly touch each other in the liquid, the water is decomposed, and resolved into its two elements, hydrogen and oxygen, which immediately assume the gaseous state, and form a collection of gas at the upper end of the tube. This experiment was performed in 1798, in Holland, and it conclusively shows the power of electricity in effecting chemical decomposition. It is equally efficacious in bringing about chemical combinations, for if this mixture of the two gases be introduced into a tube, closed at the upper end, *Fig.* 130, over water, so arranged that an electric charge can be passed through it by means of the wires *t* and *c*, and one single spark be transmitted, the oxygen and hydrogen will re-unite with a brilliant flash of light, great commotion result, and a minute portion of water will be formed. If the end of such a tube were to be corked, and then the tube removed from the water, on the

Fig. 128.

Expansion of Air from an Electric Discharge.

Give illustrations of these effects.

ELECTRICITY.

Fig. 129.

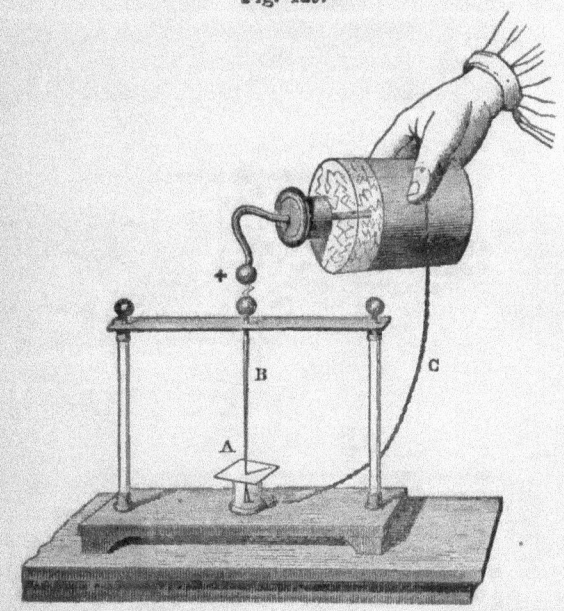

Card Split by an Electric Discharge.

Fig. 130.

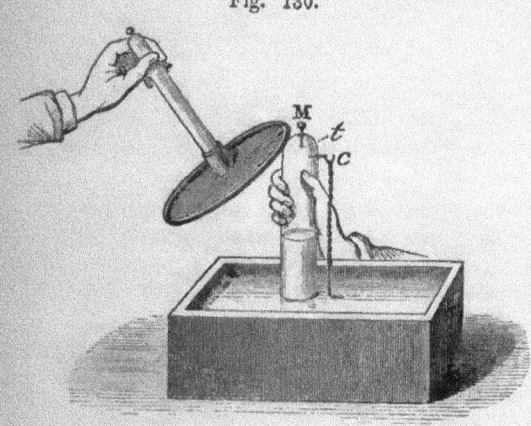

Chemical Effect of Electricity.

passage of the spark, a loud explosion would take place. This is by no means the only instance of the chemical power of this wonderful agent. Chlorine and hydrogen can be made to unite in the same manner, with an explosion forming chlorohydric acid: illuminating gas, and oxygen, forming water and carbonic acid: and the same with many other gases. Finally, electricity produces powerful magnetic effects. If a succession of strong electric shocks be transmitted through a steel needle, it becomes a permanent magnet.

The needle should be placed upon some non-conducting material, on a plate of copper, about two inches in length, and at right angles to the course of the current. Both chemical and magnetic effect is much more powerfully exerted by the galvanic current.

Experiments :—Electricity.

1. To show that electricity may be excited by friction, rub a bit of amber, a glass rod, a stick of sealing-wax, and rod of sulphur, with a piece of silk, and hold each in turn near a pith ball, suspended by a silk thread from an insulated hook, as in *Fig.* 114; the ball will, in every case, be first attracted, and then repelled.

2. To show that compression produces electricity, press in the hand a piece of Iceland spar, and then apply it to the electroscope, *Fig.* 115; the leaves will immediately diverge. Rub together two round uncut stones of quartz, chalcedony, and cornelian, and a strong phosphoric light and odor will be produced.

3. That elevation and diminution of temperature produce electricity, may be shown by dipping the mineral tourmaline into boiling water, and then applying it to the electroscope; as it cools, the leaves will diverge. This will continue during all the time of cooling, and one end of the crystal will exhibit positive, and the other negative electricity

4. That fracture produces electricity may be shown by suddenly breaking a stick of roll sulphur, and applying either piece to the knob of the electroscope, or holding it near a pith ball; also, by warming a piece of talc, splitting it rapidly, and holding one of the pieces near the electroscope; also, by splitting mica, and by doubling a large card, and tearing it across.

5. Melt sulphur, and pour it into a wine glass; both will become electrified,—the sulphur negatively, and the glass positively, and first attract, and then repel, a pith ball.

6. To show that electricity is developed in the process of combustion, support a piece of brass upon the top of a delicate gold leaf electroscope, in such a way that one end will project considerably over the side of the instrument; then take a cylindrical piece of charcoal, with flat ends, 2 inches high, and 1 inch in diameter. Place this piece of charcoal vertically about 3 inches below the projecting brass plate. The charcoal must communicate with the ground, and be lighted at the centre of the upper end, taking care that the fire does not reach the sides. A current of carbonic acid gas rises and strikes against the plate, and in a few minutes the electroscope will show signs of electric excitement. This is a delicate experiment.

7. That evaporation produces electricity, may be shown by placing a small tin dish upon the top of a gold leaf electroscope, having in it a red-hot coal, just taken from the fire Sprinkle a few drops of water upon the coal and the evaporation will at once cause the gold leaves to diverge. This will not succeed either with charcoal or coke. It does best with a hot iron put into the water.

8. To show that hydrogen, when it burns, produces electricity, set fire to a jet of hydrogen, so as to form a flame about 3 inches in length; then place a coil of platinum wire so as to be about 4 inches distant from the external surface of the flame, then let the upper extremity of the coil be bent so as to touch the plate of the electroscope, and signs of positive electricity will make their appearance.

9. To show electrical attraction and repulsion, perform the experiments described in § 304; also, rub a glass rod with a piece of silk, and hold it near small pieces of paper, these bits will be first attracted, and then repelled.

10. To show that bodies similarly electrified repel, and differently electrified attract each other, electrify two pith balls by a piece of excited glass, and on bringing them near each other, repulsion will take place; electrify one with a glass rod, and the other with a stick of sealing-wax, and bring them near each other, and attraction will ensue. These experiments may be multiplied indefinitely by means of the electrical machine.

11. To show the induction of electricity, insulate a metallic conductor upon a glass stand, and suspend from one extremity two pith balls by distinct threads; then bring near to the opposite extremity an excited glass rod, as in *Fig.* 117, and it will be found that the pith balls will become excited with positive electricity, and repel one another; remove the glass rod, and the pith balls will immediately return to their natural state; bring it back again, and the electrical excitement will be restored.

12. If the insulated conductor be touched by the finger when excited by induction, a spark will be drawn from it, and the pith balls will collapse. By this process the positive electricity will be withdrawn, and only negative electricity left upon the conductor, with which the pith balls will almost immediately become charged, and again repel each other.

13. Walk rapidly over a brussels carpet, on a cold day in winter; this will charge the carpet with electricity, and the effect will be to electrify, by induction, all the articles in the room; apply the hand to the gas fixtures, and a spark will be perceived; this spark, if made to pass through the current of gas issuing from the burner, will be sufficient to inflame it. All persons moving upon the carpet will become electrified, and communicate sparks to those who enter the room. These effects are not prevented by the intervention of glass screens between the excited electric and the conductor on which the electricity is induced. See *Fig.* 118.

14. An amalgam for the rubbers of the electrical machine may be made by melting ½ oz. of zinc in a ladle, and stirring into it 2 oz. of mercury; when cold, pound it with a little wax or grease, and then spread it smoothly upon the leather with a hot spatula.

15. The electrical machine, for successful action, must have the plate thoroughly cleaned, be well dried and warmed, the rubbers provided with fresh amalgam, and the prime conductor carefully cleaned from dust; a metallic conductor should also lead from the rubbers to the ground.

16. The principle of the Leyden jar may be shown by pasting a piece of tin foil upon each side of a pane of glass to within an inch or more of the edge; fasten a thread holding a pith ball to the tin foil on each side, with a piece of wax; connect one coating with the ground, and touch the prime conductor with the other; the plate of glass will become charged, and the pith balls fly out to some distance; then establish a connection between the two sides by a bent wire; a shock will immediately pass, and the two balls will fall.

17. To show the mechanical effects of electricity, repeat the experiment indicated in *Fig.* 129.

18. To show the heating effect, pass an electrical charge through two wires nearly touching each other, in the bulb of a large air thermometer, *Fig.* 45; the liquid will immediately rise in the tube.

19. To show the physiological effect, pass the shock from a Leyden jar through a circle formed by several persons joining hands; the person at one extremity should grasp the outside of the bottle with moistened hands, and the one at the other should touch the knob with his moistened finger. The jar, in order to avoid the danger of falling, should be placed firmly upon a table.

20. The chemical effects may be shown by the apparatus indicated in *Fig.* 130; also, by passing a spark through a jet of hydrogen issuing from a small tube; or, through a jet of common illuminating gas; also, by passing a succession of sparks over a piece of paper moistened by a mixture of a solution of iodide of potassium and common starch; the iodide is decomposed, iodine is set free, and a blue color struck by combination with the starch; also, by passing a succession of sparks through gold or platinum wires inserted in a tube filled with water; at each discharge bubbles of oxygen and hydrogen will rise from each wire; when the tube is filled with gas so as to expose the wires, the next shock will cause the recombination of the gases with the formation of a small amount of water.

21. The magnetic effects may be shown by twisting a fine platinum wire into a spiral, inserting a fine steel needle, wound with silk thread, in its axis, and passing a succession of electric shocks; the needle will speedily become magnetic.

For a more complete list of electrical experiments, the student is referred to a small work entitled "Electrical Experiments, by G. Francis."

---

§ II. Galvanic Electricity.

322. Galvanic Electricity. This is the name given to that peculiar form of electricity which is produced by chemical action. It is generally called after its discoverer, *Galvani*, Galvanic Electricity, or Galvanism. As distinguished from Statical Electricity, it is called Dynamical, because it is electricity

---

322. By whom was galvanic electricity discovered? Why called voltaic? What is the difference between galvanic and statical electricity?

in action, producing force, and flowing like a current. It is also sometimes called Voltaic Electricity, from Volta, one of its most successful investigators. Galvanic electricity differs from statical, in this respect, that the latter is more intense in its character and effects, producing more vivid sparks, and giving more violent shocks; while the latter is produced in a continuous and steady flow, and apparently in larger quantity. This difference will become more manifest as we proceed.

323. Discovery of Galvanism. The discovery of galvanic electricity was made by Galvani, the Professor of Anatomy in the University of Bologna, in the year 1790, and it was not known to exist until some time after the most important principles of statical electricity, or the electricity of the machine, had been well established. The discovery is said to have been made in the following manner. It happened that several frogs lay upon the table of the laboratory, near to which Galvani's assistant was engaged in experimenting with an electrical machine. While the machine was in action, the assistant accidentally touching one of the frogs with the knife which he held in his hand, the limbs of the frog became suddenly affected with convulsive movements. When the circumstance was reported to Galvani, he commenced a series of experiments for the purpose of discovering the cause of the strange phenomenon. With this view, he dissected several frogs, separating the legs, thighs, and lower part of the spinal column, from the remainder, so as to lay bare the lumbar nerves. He then passed copper hooks through the flesh above the legs, and suspended some of them by these hooks from the iron bar of the balcony of his window, in order to ascertain if they would be affected by the electricity of the atmosphere, and found that, whenever the wind, or any other accidental cause, brought the muscles of the leg into contact with the iron bar, the limbs were affected with convulsive movements, similar to those produced by the sparks taken from the prime conductor of the electrical machine.

324. Galvani's Theory. Galvani imagined that he had here discovered the cause of muscular contraction in living animals, and ascribed it to the influence of electricity. He supposed that this animal electricity originates in the brain, and is distributed by the nerves to every part of the system; the different parts of each muscular fibril, he believed, were in oppo-

---

323. In what manner did Galvani make the discovery?—324. State his theory.

VOLTA'S THEORY. 299

site states of electrical excitement, like the outer and inner surface of a charged Leyden jar, and that contractions of the muscle take place whenever the electricity is allowed to pass. This discharge, he supposed, was made during life, through the medium of the nerves, and in his experiments by means of the copper hooks and the iron. Thus, if, as represented in *Fig.* 131, the spinal cord of a frog were touched by a zinc rod, z, to the

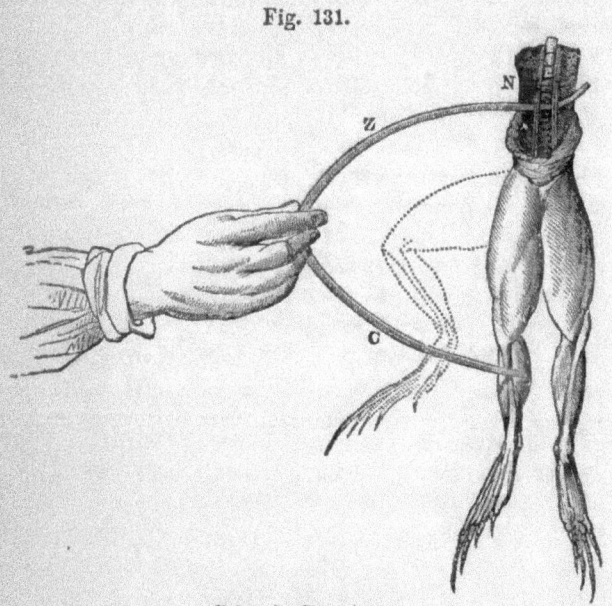

Fig. 131.

Galvani's Experiment.

opposite extremity of which is attached a piece of copper c, and the copper wire then brought into contact with the outside of the frog's leg, the convulsive movements which take place he supposed were owing to the passage of the electricity from the nerve to the muscle, through the metallic conductors, exactly as a Leyden jar is discharged by a curved discharging rod, as shown in *Fig.* 123. These views were very generally adopted, and the new agent passed under the name of the *galvanic fluid*, or animal electricity.

325. Correction of Galvani's theory by Volta. Volta, a celebrated Italian philosopher, and then professor at Como, afterwards at Pavia, already known by his invention of the

---

325. Give Volta's correction of Galvani's theory.

electrophorus, the condensing electrometer, and the eudiometer, repeated the experiments of Galvani, and came to a precisely opposite conclusion. He found that the convulsive movements of the frog never took place when the metallic connector was formed of one single metal, but only when a compound connector was employed, composed of two metals, such as zinc and copper, as represented in *Fig.* 131. Hence he concluded that the electricity was produced by the contact of these two dissimilar metals, and that it was the nerve and the leg which constituted the discharger; precisely the reverse of the opinion of Galvani. After a long contest, Volta finally established his position, and showed that when two metals are made to touch each other, they become excited, the one with positive, the other with negative electricity, in all cases. Thus, when a piece of silver is placed upon the tongue, and a piece of zinc under it, and then their two edges are made to touch each other, there will be a passage of electricity from one to the other, which will be made sensible, not only by a peculiar metallic taste, but also by a slight flash of light before the eyes, especially if these be closed. Again, on touching the knob of a delicate condensing electroscope, containing two slips of gold leaf, as in *Fig.* 115, with a piece of polished zinc, the leaves diverge, and it can be shown that they are electrified negatively. This leads to the conclusion that by its contact with the zinc, the copper knob of the instrument becomes charged with positive electricity, while the zinc is charged with negative. The quantity of electricity evolved by two pieces of metal being very small, Volta tried the experiment of uniting many pieces in one series, and arranging them in pairs, with a conductor between them, and found that the electrical influence was increased in proportion to the number of plates thus combined.

326. The Voltaic Pile. These experiments finally led to the construction of the Voltaic Pile, the wonderful apparatus which, under the name of the Galvanic Battery, has immortalized his name, and conferred lasting benefits upon man. The Voltaic Pile consists of several pairs of zinc and copper plates, placed one upon the other, with discs of thick fibrous paper, moistened with a solution of sulphate of soda, placed between each pair, and the pair immediately above it. Thus, first we have copper, then zinc, then paper; after that, copper, zinc, paper, again.

Give illustrations of the production of electricity by the contact of two metals.—326. Describe the voltaic pile. How may shocks be taken from this pile? How may several piles be connected?

Fig. 132.

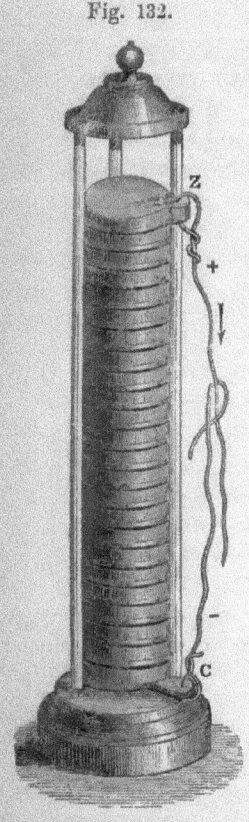

The Voltaic Pile.

It is quite evident that this order being strictly observed, while a zinc disc terminates the upper end of the pile, a copper disc will terminate the lower end. A wire being then attached to the extreme plate at each end, and the opposite extremities being brought together, a flow of electricity takes place, which makes itself manifest by a faint spark when the wires are separated, and also when they are again united. The power of this pile increases with the number of pairs of plates employed. A pile composed of two dozen plates of each metal will give a slight shock, which, when taken by the hands, may be felt up to the elbows. The mode of receiving the shock is to wet the hands, and then placing one of them in contact with the zinc plate which terminates one end of the pile, to touch with the other hand the copper plate which terminates the other end; or, these two plates may be touched with wires wound with wet rags, and held one in each hand. When the galvanic current is to be passed through any substance, this is done by connecting a wire with each terminating plate; the two wires are then brought near each other, and the substance being placed between them, the fluid passes from one wire to the other, and so through the substance in question. Any number of these piles may be connected together by making a metallic communication between the last plate of the one, and the first plate of the other, always taking care to connect the copper end of each pile with the zinc end of the preceding pile. In this manner, a galvanic battery may be constructed, the power of which will be proportionate to the number of plates employed.

327. True theory of the Pile. Volta was of the opinion that the mere contact of the two dissimilar metals, zinc and copper, generated the electricity, and that the moistened discs only served as conductors to convey the electricity generated by one

---

327. What is the true theory of the pile?

pair to the lower plate of the pair immediately next it; and so on through the whole apparatus. It has since, however, been conclusively shown that the sole cause of the electrical current is the chemical decomposition of the saline solution by the zinc plates employed. In all cases of galvanic action, there must be a liquid composed of at least two chemical elements, susceptible of decomposition by one of the metals, and not by the other; the latter metal acting only the part of an electrical conductor.

328. Chemical constitution of the substances used to produce Voltaic Electricity. Simple chemical action of one simple substance upon another, such as bromine upon iron, is not sufficient to excite galvanic electricity. It must be such chemical action as to produce the separation of the elements united in some compound substance. This separation can be effected by introducing some third simple substance, which has a stronger affinity for one of the elements in the compound than this has for the other. In all such cases the new element introduced goes to the formation of a new compound substance, by uniting with one of the original elements, and the other element, existing in the original compound, is set free. It is also essential that the compound to be decomposed should be in the liquid state, and the new element, introduced for the purpose of decomposing it, must be a solid. A second plate, consisting of a good conductor of electricity, must also be provided. The word, element, is here used in its strict chemical sense, as explained in § 30. It would appear that as the molecular disturbance created by friction is sufficient to produce the manifestation of statical electricity, so the molecular disturbance produced by violently rending one chemical element from another, by means of the chemical affinity exerted by a third element, is sufficient to produce the manifestation of galvanic electricity. The compound liquid which is generally used in practice, is common water, slightly acidulated with sulphuric acid, and the third element employed is metallic zinc; for the conductor, the metals copper and platinum are often employed, and sometimes common charcoal. Water is composed of the two elements, hydrogen and oxygen; the oxygen is violently separated from the hydrogen by the zinc under the influence of affinity; an oxide of zinc is formed on the one hand, and hydrogen is set free upon the other, and at the

---

328. Is the simple chemical action of one substance upon another sufficient to produce galvanic electricity? What sort of chemical action must it be? In what state must the compound substance to be decomposed be? Is molecular disturbance really the cause of galvanic electricity? What is the compound liquid generally used? What is the decomposing metal employed?

PROOF THAT CHEMICAL ACTION 303

same time a certain amount of electricity is evolved. In all those instances in which the simple contact only of different metals, without the employment of any liquid agent, has been found to produce electricity, it is always the case that the moisture of the air is really decomposed by the most oxidisable of the metals, while the electricity set free, is carried off by the other.

329. Proof that Chemical Decomposition is the source of Galvanic Electricity. That chemical decomposition is the source of the electricity of the voltaic pile is well shown by what is called a simple galvanic circle. Let a glass cup be provided, *Fig.* 133, fill it about two-thirds with a mixture of 8 parts by volume of water to 1 of sulphuric acid; then immerse in it a piece of brightly polished zinc, 6 inches in length, and as wide as the cup will admit. On immersing the zinc in the acidulated water, bubbles of hydrogen are at once abundantly discharged upon its surface, set free by the abstraction of oxygen from the water by the zinc, and these bubbles rising through the liquid, at length escape into the air. Now place in the same vessel a slip of polished copper, and so long as it does not touch the zinc, no change will be observed, and the bubbles of hydrogen will continue to escape as before, at the surface of the zinc plate. The instant, however, that any metallic communication is made between the two plates, as in *Fig.* 134, where the two plates have been inclined so that the upper edge of the copper plate has been brought into contact with the zinc, it will be observed that the bubbles of hydrogen are no longer discharged upon the zinc, but upon the *copper*. There is no visible transfer through the liquid, but the fact is certain, and it is quite evident that an influence of some sort has been set in motion, by which the point of discharge for the gas has been transferred to the copper, and a current produced, indicated in the

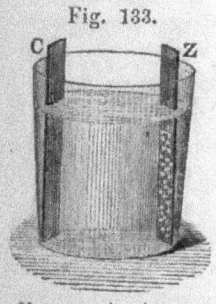

Fig. 133.
No connection between the Plates.

Fig. 134.
Connection formed between the Plates.

---

329. Prove that chemical decomposition is the source of galvanic electricity. Describe *Fig.* 133. *Fig.* 134. What is the effect of amalgamating the zinc plates? What other effects can be produced by the wires besides the evolution of gas?

figure by the direction of the arrow. Separate the two metals, and the gas ceases to be discharged upon the copper, and rises again from the zinc. If, instead of bringing the plates themselves into contact, the connection be made by wires, or any other good electrical conductor, the result will be the same; *Fig.* 135.

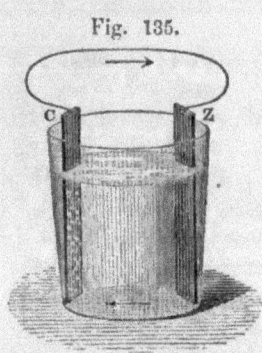

Fig. 135.

The Plates connected by a Wire.

If the zinc, after being thoroughly cleansed by immersion in the acidulated water, be rubbed with mercury, it immediately acquires a bright amalgamated surface, and when restored to the water, it no longer exerts any decomposing action, and particles of hydrogen are no longer seen to rise from it. The instant, however, that a connection is made by a wire, or otherwise, with the conducting plate, hydrogen bubbles at once begin to be discharged from it as before. The cause of this is not understood, but constant use is made of the fact to protect the zinc plates from corrosion, except during the period when the battery is actually in action. The evolution of gas is not the only effect observed; the wires, if separated, will emit a spark of electricity. If they are wound around the bulb of a delicate air thermometer, (*Fig.* 45,) the liquid will rise in the tube, indicating the production of heat; if they are wound about a piece of soft iron, the iron will become magnetic, and attract iron filings; if one wire be applied to the crural nerve of a frog, and the other to the outside of the muscle, the leg will be violently convulsed; if dipped into acidulated water, it will be decomposed, oxygen will appear at one pole, and hydrogen at the other. In short, the wires will emit sparks, produce heat and magnetism, give shocks, effect chemical decomposition, and indicate the passage of a continuous current of galvanic electricity.

330. The decomposing plate is the point of departure of the electrical current. At the same time that hydrogen is discharged upon the copper plate, a corresponding portion of oxide of zinc is formed on the zinc plate by the affinity of the zinc for the oxygen of the water, and this oxide is eventually united with the sulphuric acid, converted into sulphate of zinc, and finally dissolved in the remaining water. If it were not for the

---

330. What is the point of departure of the electrical current?

sulphuric acid, the oxide of zinc which is formed, being an insoluble substance, would speedily cover the zinc plate with a thick deposit, and put a stop to its decomposing action upon the water. By the introduction of the sulphuric acid, the oxide is removed as fast as formed, and converted into the soluble sulphate of zinc, which is at once dissolved in the water. Thus the zinc plate is kept bright, and its decomposing action is sustained until the water has dissolved all the sulphate of zinc of which it is capable. As soon as this point is reached, the oxide of zinc begins again to coat the zinc plate, and to diffuse itself in a cloudy precipitate through the water, thereby hindering the ready transference of the molecules of gas, and obstructing the passage of the electric current. By the combined operation of both these causes, the process is brought to a conclusion. If some other chemical compound be employed, instead of water, which is capable of decomposition by the copper, and not by the zinc, the electrical current will be reversed, and will set out from the copper towards the zinc. In all cases, it is the metal which exerts the decomposing action by which the current is set in motion, and from which it starts.

331. Mode of transfer of the Hydrogen. The mode in which the hydrogen is made to appear upon the copper plate is believed to be as follows. Oxygen is thought to be naturally charged with negative, and hydrogen with positive, electricity; consequently, as oppositely electrified bodies attract each other, when brought into close contact, these two substances unite under the influence of this electrical attraction, and form water. Every particle of water consists, then, of two elements, and a row of them extending from the zinc to the copper plate, may be represented, as in *Fig.* 136. If now we suppose the oxygen of the particle of water, next the zinc, to quit the hydrogen with which it is united, and to connect itself with the zinc, as represented in the figure, and that a certain amount of electricity

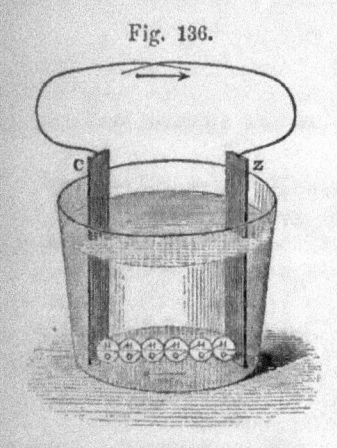

Fig. 136.

Mode of Transfer of Hydrogen.

What is the use of the sulphuric acid? How is the process brought to a conclusion?—331 How is the hydrogen made to appear upon the copper plate?

is excited by the transfer, which concentrates itself upon the deserted particle of hydrogen, then this particle of hydrogen, in consequence of the good conducting power of the copper, will be attracted towards it; but coming into contact with the particle of water next it, by its superior electrical excitement it appropriates its oxygen to itself, forming a new particle of water, and then communicates its electricity to the second particle of hydrogen thus set free. This second particle of hydrogen is in turn started towards the copper plate, but in its way meeting with the next particle of water, it seizes upon its oxygen in the manner represented in the figure; and so the process goes on, every particle of hydrogen set free, decomposing the particle of water next it in the shortest line of direction to the copper plate, until finally the last particle of water immediately touching the copper plate is decomposed, and its hydrogen having nothing to unite with, is discharged, together with the accumulated electricity, upon the copper plate, and escapes. The electricity thus produced finds its way back through the copper and the connecting wire, to the zinc, and thus returns to the point from which it set out. In this manner there is a continual precipitation of particles of hydrogen upon the copper, and a steady current of electricity kept in motion, until the effect of the zinc upon the liquid ceases, and no more water is decomposed. In all cases, it will be seen that the current is from the zinc to the copper. There is good reason for doubting whether the theory described above, of the opposite electrical state of the oxygen and hydrogen is strictly true; but there is no doubt of the transfer of the hydrogen, and that it is probably effected in the manner indicated.

332. The part played by the Copper. It is evident that it is the zinc which is the generating plate, and that the copper acts simply as an electrical conductor. Consequently, any good conductor of electricity will answer equally well, provided only, in all cases, it be not one which itself acts upon the acidulated water, because, in this case, an opposite current would be set in motion, which would neutralize the first. The conductor need not necessarily be metallic. Charcoal is employed in many of the best batteries, and in others, slips of platinum. In all cases, the conducting plate is charged with positive electricity, and the

---

Describe the process of circulation which takes place.—332. What is the part played by the copper? Must the conducting plate be made of metal? What is the electrical condition of the two plates? What is meant by a negative electric? By a positive electric?

THE POLARIZATION 307

Fig. 137.

Positive and Negative Plates.

generating plate with negative. In *Fig.* 137, the two plates are distinguished simply by the signs + and —. The ends of the two wires, connected respectively with the two plates, are called positive and negative poles, or sometimes positive and negative electrodes. Every chemical element which appears at the positive pole is called a *negative* electric, and every one appearing at the negative pole a *positive* electric. This is in accordance with the theory of electricity previously explained, that a body positively electrified will attract negative electrics, and a body negatively electrified positive electrics.

333. The polarization and transfer of the elements of the Liquid, and the polarization of the Solid particles of the circuit necessary for the electrical force to circulate. The transference of the particles of hydrogen, and the production of the electrical force, as just described, is supposed to be preceded by the polarization of the entire circuit, both solid and liquid. By polarization is meant,—as has been previously explained in describing the discharge of the Leyden jar, § 316,—the disturbance of the natural equilibrium of the electricity residing in the molecules of a substance, and its distribution at the opposite poles of each molecule. Thus in *Fig.* 138, the upper row represents a series of particles of water, each composed of oxygen and hydrogen, in an unpolarized state; the second row represents the same particles of water in a polarized state, in which the particles have been turned around, and the negative oxygen made to alternate with the positive hydrogen. This polar state is produced by bringing a highly charged positive electric into proximity with the negative oxygen, on the right of the figure. The oxygen is at once attracted, the hydrogen repelled and at the same time its positive electricity greatly intensified by in-

Fig. 138.
Unpolarized Particles of Water.

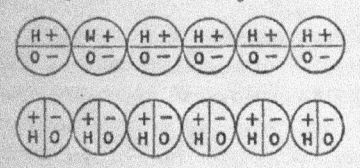

Polarized Particles of Water.

---

333. What is meant by the polarization of the liquid, as well as solid, part of the circuit? What is polarization? Describe *Fig.* 138.

308 OF THE ENTIRE CIRCUIT.

duction; a similar change takes place in all the molecules, and the polarization is propagated throughout the series. In the case of the simple galvanic circuit, the polarization is supposed to be produced in the following manner: when the plate of zinc is introduced into the acidulated water, the part which touches the liquid, in consequence of the chemical action which takes place between it and the oxygen of the water, immediately becomes highly charged with positive electricity, while the opposite extremity, which is outside the cup, becomes negative; this immediately polarizes the molecules of water, in the manner shown in *Fig.* 138. As soon as the copper plate is introduced, its molecules also become polarized, and the whole series extending to the extremity of the wire connected with that plate, is thrown into a similar state. The same process also takes place in the zinc plate, and is propagated to the extreme end of the wire connected with it, as shown in *Fig.* 139. As the ends of the wires, however, do not touch each other, there can be no discharge; there is a state of polar tension produced, extending through the circuit, but no discharge, and no current or manifestation of electricity. Every thing, however, is ready for the discharge, and the instant the metallic connection is completed, it takes place. The first movement occurs on the right, at the lower part of the zinc plate. The first particle of oxygen is drawn off by the zinc, and its negative electricity seizes hold of the positive electricity of the polarized particle of zinc next it, the positive electricity of this particle of zinc seizes upon the negative electricity of the polarized particle immediately adjoining, and thus the transfer of *negative* electricity proceeds from particle to particle up the whole length of the zinc plate, and through the wire connected with it. On the opposite side, at the foot of the copper plate, the reverse process is going on; the hydrogen of the last particle of water is released from its oxygen and escapes into the air; its positive

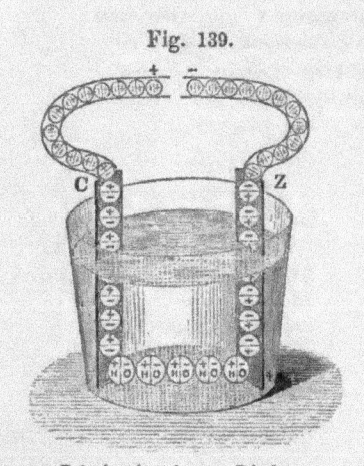

Fig. 139.

Polarization, but no Discharge.

State what takes place as soon as the zinc plate touches the acidulated water. Is there any discharge so long as the poles remain disconnected? Trace the process.

electricity seizes hold of the negative electricity of the polarized particle of copper nearest it, and sets free its positive electricity; this seizes upon the negative electricity of the next polarized particle; the positive electricity thus set free seizes hold of the negative electricity of the particle next adjoining, and thus the transfer of *positive* electricity proceeds from particle to particle up the entire length of the copper plate, and through the wire connected with it. Consequently, there is a steady discharge of positive electricity from the wire connected with the copper plate, and of negative electricity from the wire connected with the zinc plate, and when the two wires are connected, these mutually attract each other, remain united for a moment, and then separate, and pass on in opposite directions. Thus, as soon as the metallic connection is completed between the plates, the polar tension previously existing immediately springs into action, and a continued double circulation of electricity, in opposite directions, from molecule to molecule, is set up through the whole circuit, solid, as well as liquid; *Fig.* 140. In order to prevent confusion, however, whenever the direction of the electrical current is referred to, the direction of the positive current is alone mentioned.

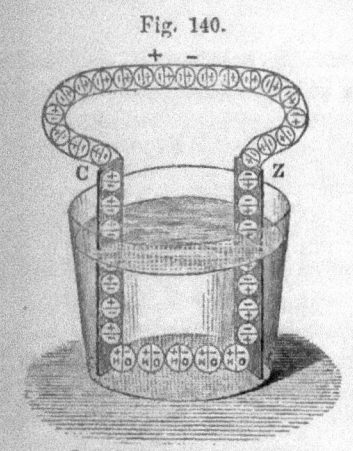

Fig. 140.

Polarization and Discharge.

334. Proof that a state of electrical tension exists in the plates before the actual passage of the current. That this state of polar tension actually is produced as soon as the zinc generating plate and the copper or platinum conducting plate are introduced into the acidulated water, may be shown by the following experiment. A plate of zinc, z, *Fig.* 141, and another of platinum, P, are immersed in acidulated water, and the wire proceeding from each is insulated and connected with the two gilt disks, a and b, of the electroscope, E; these disks are insulated by the glass of the apparatus; they slide easily to and fro in sockets, and can be brought within a quarter of an inch of each other; a single gold leaf connected with the

---

What takes place when the connection is made? Show that a double current circulates.—334. Prove that a state of electrical tension exists before the passage of the current.

310   BEFORE THE PASSAGE OF THE CURRENT.

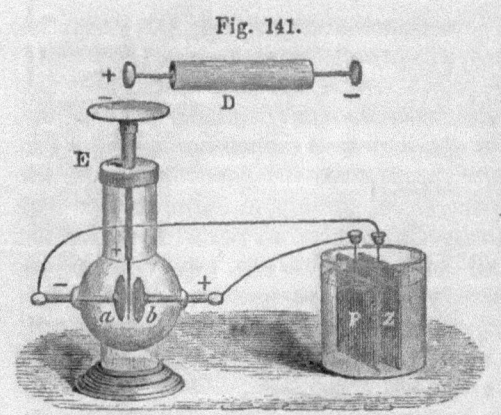

Fig. 141.

Electric Tension before the passage of the Current.

plate of the instrument is suspended between them. Now, if the positive end of a De Luc's dry pile, D,—an instrument to be presently described, § 349,—be brought near the plate, this will become negative by induction, and the gold leaf positive, as indicated in the figure. Under these circumstances, however, if there were no electrical tension existing in either a or b, there would be no attraction of the gold leaf toward either, and it would continue unmoved; but if there be an opposite state of electric tension in the two disks, it will be drawn towards that which is charged with negative, and repelled from that charged with positive electricity. On examination, it is found to be attracted towards the disk, A; and the conclusion, therefore, is irresistible, that the zinc plate is in a state of negative electric tension. If now, the negative end of the De Luc's pile be presented to the plate of the instrument, this will become charged with positive electricity by induction, and the slip of gold leaf with negative electricity. In this state of things the gold leaf is attracted towards the disk, b, a conclusive proof that the plate, P, is in a state of positive electric tension, and this at a time when there is no direct connection between it and the plate, z. It is evident, therefore, that a state of electric tension is produced the instant the plates are introduced into the acidulated water, before the metallic circuit is completed.

335. The energy of the current proportionate to the chemical activity. If a metal be employed, in place of the zinc, which has a more powerful affinity for oxygen, and which will decompose water with greater energy and promptness, the intensity of the electrical current will be greatly increased. And as potassium—the metallic basis of common potash,—has a stronger affinity for oxygen than any other metal, this would form theoretically, the best generating plate for a galvanic current; there

---

335. To what is the energy of the current proportioned? What metal is the best generator?

are, however, insuperable objections to its use, arising from the intensity of its action,—its softness and want of durability, and its high cost. The experiment, however, admits of trial, by forming an amalgam of potassium with mercury, for it has been ascertained that the galvanic relations of all amalgams are those of the most oxidizable metal which they contain. On the other hand, the conducting plate must be composed of some metal exerting as little chemical action upon the water, and having as little affinity for oxygen, as possible. On this account, copper, and still more, platinum, are admirably fitted for this purpose. The reason for this necessity is, that in proportion to the affinity of the second, or the conducting plate for oxygen, does it tend to produce a counter current of electricity which neutralizes the primary current proceeding from the zinc, and proportionably reduces the energy of the circuit. Thus, in *Fig.* 140, if the copper plate had an affinity for oxygen equal to that of the zinc, it would tend to decompose the water, and set in motion a succession of particles of hydrogen, charged with positive electricity, towards the zinc; the result would be, that two opposing states of polar tension would be produced, and at the point of meeting, a particle of hydrogen on the one side, would be found arranged opposite to a particle of hydrogen on the other, and positive electricity against positive electricity, repelling each other with equal strength, and entirely preventing the passage of any current. In proportion as the conducting plate possesses an affinity for oxygen, does it tend to produce this result, and to stop the flow of the current. For this reason, it is necessary that the conducting plate should have the least possible affinity for oxygen, and be made of platinum, copper, gold or silver, all of which have a feeble affinity for this substance; and that the generating plate, on the other hand, should possess the greatest possible affinity for the same element.

336. **The direction of the current is dependent upon the direction of the chemical action.** In all these cases the positive electricity sets out from the more oxidizable metal which constitutes the generating plate, and traverses the liquid towards the less oxidizable metal which forms the conducting plate. The negative current, on the other hand, starts from the generating plate, and turns its course in the opposite direction, i. e., passes up the plate, instead of through the liquid. Consequently,

---

What metal would, in theory, make the best generating plate? Why must the conducting plate be formed of some metal which exerts no decomposing action on water?—336. What is the direction of the current?

there is a current of positive electricity passing from the wire connected with the conducting, or copper plate, and of negative electricity passing from the generating, or zinc plate.

337. Direct metallic connection between the generating and conducting plate not necessary. That direct metallic contact between the two plates is not necessary for the production of the current, may be shown by the apparatus represented in *Fig.* 142. Let z be a zinc plate, and p a platinum plate, having a platinum wire attached to it, and bent so as to touch a piece of paper, *a*, moistened with a solution of starch and iodide of potassium, and immersed in water, strongly acidulated; in this case, it will be observed, there is no direct metallic connection between the two plates. Iodide of potassium is a substance composed of iodine and potassium; the starch is a test for iodine, and is turned blue the instant any of the iodine is detached from the potassium; and as the electric current has the power of detaching the iodine, if there be any electrical current transmitted from the platinum to the zinc plate, it will be at once manifested by the formation of a small blue spot at the point where the platinum wire touches the paper. Hence we conclude that the direct metallic connection of the two plates is not necessary for the passage of the current, but that any good non-metallic conductor of electricity will answer equally well. This experiment also shows very satisfactorily that the contact of two dissimilar metals is not the cause of the galvanic current, and that the hypothesis suggested by Volta, in regard to the theory of the Voltaic pile is not strictly correct.

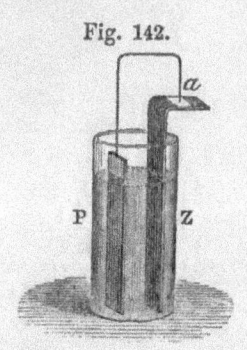

Fig. 142.

Contact not necessary.

338. Effect of the discharge of hydrogen on the conducting plate. It will be observed in all the cases heretofore described, that as long as the circulation of the electrical current continues, there is a constant discharge of particles of hydrogen gas upon the conducting plate, whether it be made of platinum, or copper. The bubbles of hydrogen are discharged upon the surface of the plate at every point beneath the level of the water, and gradually stream upwards towards the air. In this way most of them escape, but a portion are detained by the strong

---

337. Show that direct metallic connection between the plates is unnecessary.—338. What is the effect of the discharge of hydrogen on the conducting plate?

THE PLATINUM PLATE COATED WITH HYDROGEN. 313

attraction of adhesion which is exercised upon this gas by platinum, and to such a degree that the plate will really be covered with a thin film of gaseous particles, too small to be discovered by the eye, but capable of detection by other means, even after it has been removed from the liquid. In this manner platinum plates may be coated with hydrogen. Now hydrogen has a very strong affinity for oxygen, and tends, therefore, to exert a decomposing action upon water, in the same way that metallic zinc does. If, then, a platinum plate, coated with hydrogen in the way above described, be placed in acidulated water, and a perfectly clean platinum plate be placed opposite to it, and the two plates be connected by a wire, the hydrogen of the coated plate will tend to decompose the particle of water next it, and seize upon its oxygen, forming with it a new particle of water, and a state of polar tension will be at once produced through the whole circuit, precisely as there would be, if there were a zinc plate in the place of the one coated with hydrogen. Under these circumstances, an electrical current will circulate from the coated plate to the clean platinum through the liquid, and then back through the wire, and continue until all the hydrogen adhering to the coated plate has been exhausted by uniting with particles of oxygen, and been converted into water. From this experiment, it appears that any substance which has a strong affinity for oxygen, even though it be gaseous in its character, may be used in place of an oxidizable metal, as a generating plate.

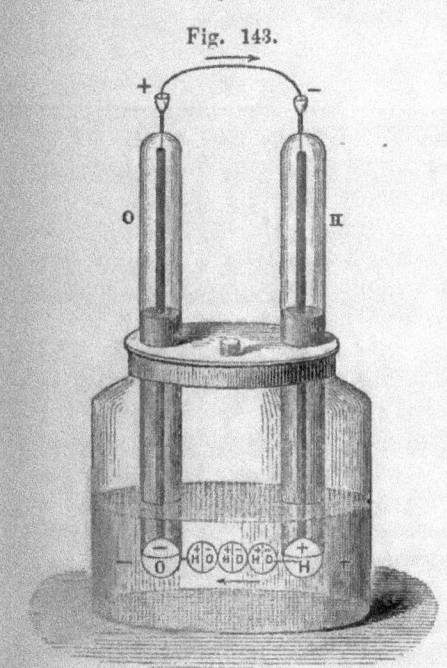

Fig. 143.

The Gas Battery, Simple Circuit.

339. The Gas Battery. Advantage has

How may platinum be coated with hydrogen? Can such a coated plate be used as the generating plate of a battery?—339. Describe the gas battery.

been taken of this property to form what is called a gas battery; *Fig.* 143. Two glass tubes, closed at one end, have suspended within them plates of platinum, each plate terminating in a cup filled with mercury, placed upon the summit of each tube. The tubes are then filled with acidulated water, and inverted into a glass vessel partially filled with the same mixture. The tube marked H, is then connected with the negative pole of a second galvanic battery, not shown in the figure, and the tube marked O, with the positive pole, by means of the cups filled with mercury, and the galvanic current passed through them, descending through O, and ascending through H; as the current passes, the water in these two tubes is decomposed, and the hydrogen collects in the tube H, and the oxygen in the tube O, gradually expelling the acidulated water with which they are filled, into the lower vessel. The tube H is made of twice the capacity of the tube O, and the process is continued until both tubes are completely filled, H with hydrogen, and O with oxygen. The second battery is then entirely removed, and the two mercury cups connected by a wire, as shown in the figure. We have then a platinum plate in the tube H, surrounded by hydrogen, and dipping down into the acidulated water of the lower vessel, and a second platinum plate in the tube O, surrounded with oxygen, and dipping down into the acidulated water, and the plate in O connected with the plate in H, by a wire above. Under these circumstances, the hydrogen gas in H will act like a zinc plate similarly situated; a state of polar tension is at once produced, running through the whole apparatus; the lower end of H becomes positively electrified, as shown in the figure; it seizes hold of the oxygen of the particle of water nearest it; its hydrogen appropriates the oxygen of the succeeding particle; and so on, until the last particle of water is reached. The hydrogen of this particle is discharged into the oxygen of the tube, O, and at once resolved into water. At the same time, a current of positive electricity is set in motion through the liquid, from H to O, then up the plate O to the wire, and finally is returned to the plate H, its course being indicated by the arrows. As particle after particle of hydrogen in the tube H, is united to the oxygen of successive particles of water, fresh portions of water are formed in the tube H, which gradually fill it. At the same time, an equal number of particles of water are formed in the tube O, by which it is also gradu-

---

Explain how both tubes become gradually filled with water.

BATTERY OF INTENSITY. 315

ally filled; and when this takes place the process is brought to a conclusion. This very curious instrument establishes the important fact that hydrogen gas is capable, by its action on acidulated water, of generating a current of positive electricity. By connecting 8 or 10 such cells in succession, *Fig.* 144, in

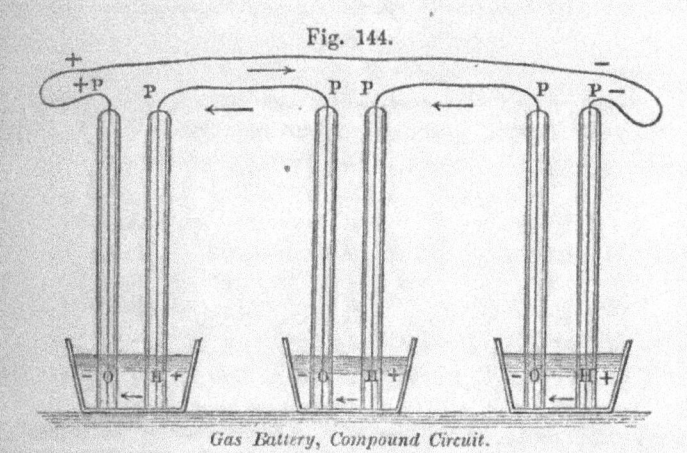

Fig. 144.

Gas Battery, Compound Circuit.

such a way that the oxygen tube of one cell shall be connected with the hydrogen tube of the adjoining cell, very decided manifestations of the electrical current may be obtained; bright sparks can be produced between charcoal points, and various chemical decompositions effected.

340. The Galvanic Battery. If the wire proceeding from the conducting plate, be it charcoal, or platinum, or copper, instead of being carried directly to the generating zinc plate, be attached to the zinc plate of a second pair, in a second vessel, as is represented in *Fig.* 145, the electricity generated

Fig. 145.

Crown of Cups, Battery of Intensity.

---

340. Describe the arrangement of the galvanic battery. By whom invented. By what name originally called.

316   BATTERY OF QUANTITY.

by the first zinc will be communicated to the second, and being united to the electricity generated by it, will be transmitted through the fluid in the second vessel to the second conducting plate. The electrical current of the second pair is increased by the addition of the electricity of the first; by the addition of a third pair, the power of the current is trebled; and so we may proceed indefinitely, increasing the intensity of the electrical current by every additional pair; but when we reach the end of the series, we must connect the conducting plate of the last cup with the zinc, or generating plate, of the first cup, in order to make the circuit complete, and restore the electrical equilibrium. Such an arrangement of connected cups and plates is called a Galvanic Battery, from the powerful effects which it is capable of producing. It was first devised by Volta, after his invention of the Pile, and called by him the "*couronne des tasses*," or, crown of cups. As the entire merit of this celebrated instrument belongs exclusively to Volta, and not at all to Galvani, it should be more properly called the Voltaic Battery.

341. Batteries of Intensity and Batteries of Quantity. It might be thought that an equal generating surface of zinc being employed in both cases, it would make no difference in the effect produced, whether we employed a great number of small plates, or a small number of large plates. It is found, however, in practice, that there is an important difference between the effects of the two arrangements. The former will yield electricity of great efficacy in effecting chemical decompositions, the latter, electricity of great heat-producing power and magnetic energy. A battery that is adapted for the former is called a Battery of Intensity, and one that is adapted for the latter is called a Battery of Quantity. A battery of intensity may be con-

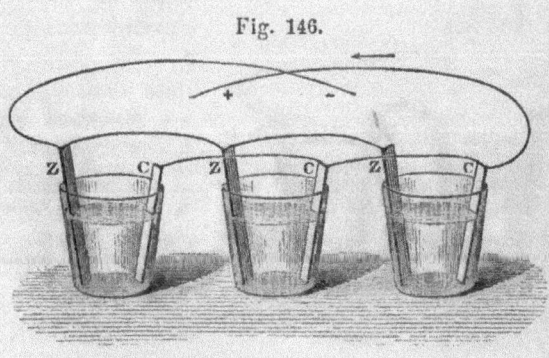

Fig. 146.

Battery of Quantity.

341. What is a battery of intensity? Of quantity? Describe the arrangement of each.

IMPROVED BATTERIES.   317

verted into a battery of quantity, by breaking all the connections between the coppers and zincs of different cups, and uniting all the zincs together, then all the coppers, and at last establishing a connection between all the coppers and all the zincs by one single wire. In this way we practically convert all the zincs into one large zinc, and all the coppers into one large copper plate; *Fig.* 146.

342. Improved Batteries. Instead of having the different pairs of plates in different cups, we may solder the zinc and copper plates together, and sink them into grooves in a trough, as in *Fig.* 147. In this case the plates themselves form the cups. The spaces between the plates are filled with the exciting liquid to the same height. The electricity generated by the first zinc on the left is conveyed through the liquid to the opposite copper, and by it transferred to its companion zinc; it is then transmitted through the next division of liquid to the succeeding copper, and so through the whole series, until it reaches the last cell at A. Into this, a conducting copper plate, a, is inserted and connected with the wire which carries back the electrical current to the beginning of the battery, where it is attached to another conducting plate, h, by which it is transferred to the first zinc plate. In *Fig.* 148, the same apparatus is seen in perspective. It is called

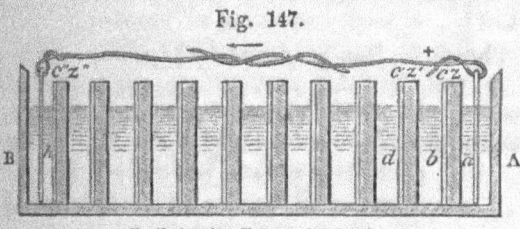

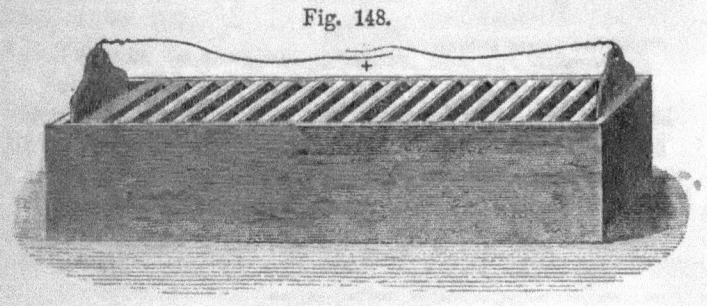

Fig. 147.

Cruikshank's Battery in Section

Fig. 148.

Cruikshank's Battery.

---

342 Describe the arrangement of Cruikshank's battery.

Cruikshank's Battery, and is a very convenient form of the apparatus.

343. The Sulphate of Copper Battery. There is a second form of the galvanic battery in which the liquid to be decomposed is not acidulated water, but water which holds in solution a quantity of sulphate of copper, sometimes called blue vitriol. Copper is employed for the conducting plate, and zinc for the generating plate. The sulphate of copper is composed of sulphuric acid and the oxide of copper. Sulphuric acid is composed of sulphur and oxygen, and its composition may be represented by SO^3, i. e., one proportion of sulphur, and three of oxygen. Oxide of copper is composed of copper and oxygen, and its symbol is CuO, i. e., one proportion of copper, and one of oxygen. The symbol of the whole is $CuO\ SO^3$. When the zinc plate is introduced into this solution it seems to produce a double decomposition, and at the same time set on foot two processes of polarization and circulation; *Fig* 149. In the first place, it produces a chain of polarized particles of water, and second, a chain of polarized particles of sulphate of oxide of copper, both extending to the conducting plate; then, the zinc draws off the oxygen from the water, and the hydrogen seizes upon the oxygen of the adjoining particle, as has been already described, until finally the last particle of hydrogen is projected upon the conducting plate. The oxide of zinc thus formed upon the zinc plate seizes upon the sulphuric acid of the sulphate of copper in contact with it, setting free the oxide of copper, and forming sulphate of zinc, which is at once dissolved in the liquid. The oxide of copper, thus set free, seizes upon the sulphuric acid of the next particle of sulphate of copper; and thus the process goes on, until finally a particle of the oxide of copper is projected upon the conducting plate, at the very moment when the particle of hydrogen just spoken of, reaches the same point. (See the figure.) This hydrogen at once seizes upon the oxygen

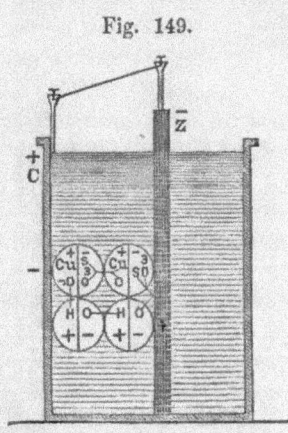

Fig. 149.

The Sulphate of Copper Battery dissected.

---

343 Describe the sulphate of copper battery. What is sulphate of copper? Give its symbol. What double decomposition takes place? What becomes of the hydrogen? Explain the deposition of the copper. What is the advantage of this battery.

Fig. 150.

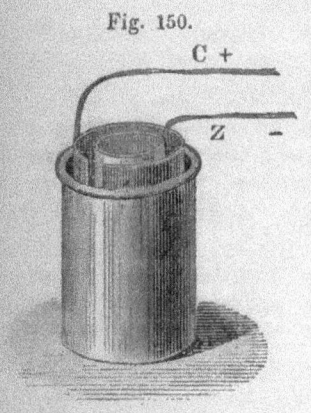

The Sulphate of Copper Battery.

of the oxide of copper, forming a particle of water, and setting free metallic copper, which is immediately discharged upon the copper conducting plate. From this, it appears, that in this form of the battery the copper plate does not receive a deposit of particles of hydrogen, but, in its place, a deposit of copper. Consequently, there is no counteracting current of electricity, produced by hydrogen, tending to neutralize that which is produced by the generating plate, as has been shown to be the case in the simple galvanic circuit, and thus a great addition is made to the power of the battery. This form of the galvanic battery is of special use for the production of electro-magnetism, as will be shown hereafter. It is represented in perspective in *Fig.* 150.

344. Daniell's Sulphate of Copper Battery. There is a practical difficulty in the operation of the sulphate of copper battery, that the zinc plate, is itself more or less covered by the particles of reduced copper, which act as so many secondary conducting plates, and tend to dissipate the force of the principal current, and divert it into smaller channels. Another difficulty consists in the decomposition of the sulphate of zinc by the operation of the current, and the deposition of metallic zinc upon the copper plate, thus converting it practically into a zinc plate, and causing it to set up a counter current. These difficulties are overcome by separating the zinc plate from the copper plate by the intervention of a porous cup, and thus preventing the sulphate of copper from coming into direct contact with the zinc, and the sulphate of zinc with the copper. This form of the instrument constitutes Daniell's battery, and the arrangement is as follows; *Fig.* 151. z represents a solid bar of zinc, placed in a cup of porous earthen ware, and filled with acidulated water; c represents the copper plate, made in the form of a cylindrical cup, open at the top, and closed at the bottom, and filled with a solution of sulphate of copper. On the inner side of the rim of this cup is supported a copper shelf, pierced with holes, for the purpose of containing some crystals

---

344. What are some of the difficulties connected with the operation of the common battery? Describe Daniell's battery.

320   DISSECTED.

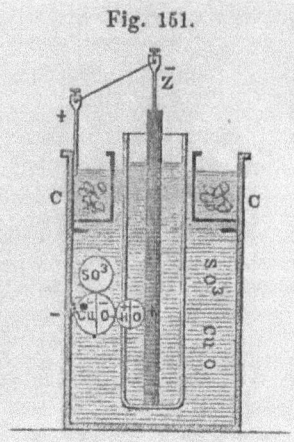

Fig. 151.

Daniell's Battery Dissected.

of sulphate of copper, which, by its gradual dissolving, may maintain the strength of the sulphate of copper solution placed below. As soon as the zinc and copper plates are connected by a wire, a steady current of electricity begins to circulate, which will continue to flow for many hours. The zinc, as soon as it is introduced into the acidulated water, decomposes it in the usual manner, and the liberated hydrogen is carried towards the conducting plate, directly through the porous cup. As soon as it enters the sulphate of the oxide of copper, it seizes upon the oxygen of the oxide, and is re-converted into water, giving up its electricity at the same moment to the copper of the oxide, which is at once deposited upon the surface of the copper cylinder. The sulphuric acid which is set free from the sulphate of copper, represented in the figure by SO^3, finds its way into the porous cup, where it assists in keeping up the strength of the acid solution, and is ultimately converted into sulphate of zinc by uniting with the oxide formed upon the surface of the zinc rod. The porous cup, though it is sufficiently firm to prevent the two liquids from mingling, opposes no impediment to the passage of the hydrogen through it in one direction, and of the sulphuric acid in the other, by the polarization of the chain of liquid particles which penetrates it. By this arrangement, the hydrogen is prevented from reaching the copper plate and setting up a counteracting current, and the copper set free from the oxide, cannot pass through the porous cup and attach itself to the zinc plate. At the same time, the sulphate of zinc is prevented from passing over to the copper, depositing metallic zinc, and converting it practically into a second zinc plate, directly opposed to the first. The result is, that such a battery will keep up a steady current of electricity for many hours, and hence is often called the constant battery. The actual form of this battery is shown in *Fig.* 152. v represents a glass, or earthenware jar; G, the copper cylinder, pierced with holes; c,

---

What becomes of the hydrogen? How is the copper plate prevented from being covered with zinc?

GROVE'S BATTERY.   321

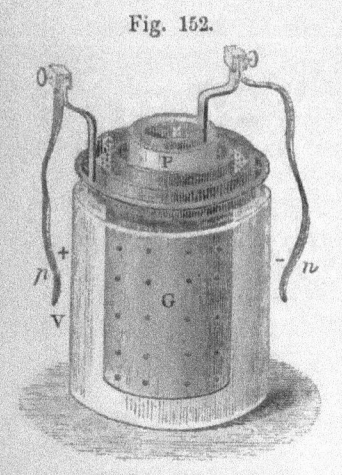

Fig. 152.

Daniell's Battery.

the colander, filled with crystals of sulphate of copper; P, the porous cup; z, the rod of zinc; p and n are thin strips of copper, for connecting with other cells. In this battery, the hydrogen is removed by chemical means.

345. Grove's Battery. In this battery, the hydrogen is also removed by chemical means, and it depends for its action upon the peculiar effect of this substance on nitric acid. This acid is a compound of nitrogen and oxygen, and may be represented by the symbol NO^5, i. e., five proportions of oxygen, to one of nitrogen. Hydrogen discharged into this substance, decomposes it by appropriating one proportion of oxygen, forming water, and converting NO^5 into NO^4, or, nitric into nitrous acid. The latter differs from the former, in possessing a deep red, or mahogany color, and emitting deep red acid fumes. By this action, the hydrogen is transferred from the gaseous into the liquid state. In Grove's battery, the conducting plate is made of platinum, and is immersed in a porous cup, of clay, filled with strong nitric acid, and placed in the centre of a zinc cylinder, surrounded by acidulated water. In *Fig.* 153, z represents the zinc cylinder, open at both ends, and placed in a jar of glass or earthen-ware, filled with acidulated water; P represents the platinum plate, placed in the interior of the porous cup, filled with strong nitric acid. The hydrogen, set free by the zinc, instead of being permitted to strike directly upon the platinum plate, passes through the porous cup into the nitric acid, where it is converted into water by uniting with one proportion of the oxygen contained in the acid, as represented in

Fig. 153.

Grove's Battery, Dissected.

345. Describe Grove's battery. With what liquid is the porous cup filled?

14*

the figure, and converting it into nitrous acid; at the same moment, it yields up its electricity to the nitrous acid, by which it is conveyed to the conducting platinum. By this process, the nitric is rapidly changed into nitrous acid, a substance emitting a large quantity of red and acid fumes, and is also rapidly diluted by the drops of water steadily added to it. The strength of the nitric acid is therefore continually diminishing, and the constant action of this battery is not so great as Daniell's. By the complete and energetic absorption of the hydrogen in this battery, power is amazingly increased, and it constitutes the best form of the instrument, being distinguished for the steadiness and intensity of its action; and 12 or 24 cups of it are quite sufficient for performing all the most brilliant galvanic experiments. In order to use several cups at once, the platinum plate of one pair must be connected with the zinc of the succeeding pair, and the terminating polar wires attached, one of them to the extreme platinum, and the other to the extreme zinc plate. The actual form of the instrument is seen in *Fig.* 154, where z represents the zinc cylinder, surrounded by acidulated water; v, the porous cup, filled with nitric acid, and containing the platinum plate, p; *b* and *a*, are screws, for the attachment of wires. This battery discharges a large amount of acid fumes, and it should always be placed in the open air, or in the strong draught of a chimney.

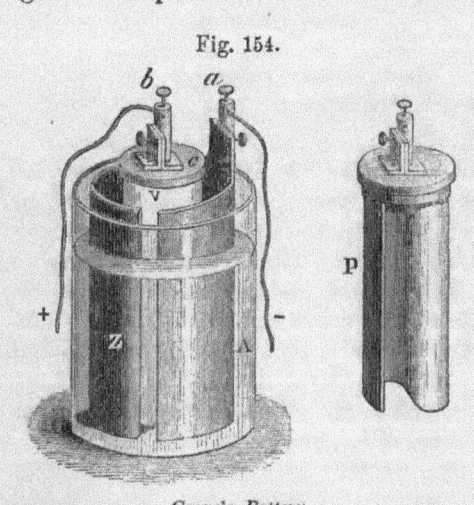

Fig. 154.

Grove's Battery.

346. Bunsen's Battery. It is not necessary that the conducting plate be made of metal; any good conductor of electricity will answer equally well. Advantage is taken of this in Bunsen's battery, which resembles Grove's, exactly, except in the substitution of carbon cylinders for the platinum plates.

What becomes of the hydrogen? What is said of the intensity and constancy of this battery?—346. Describe Bunsen's battery.

SMEE'S BATTERY.   323

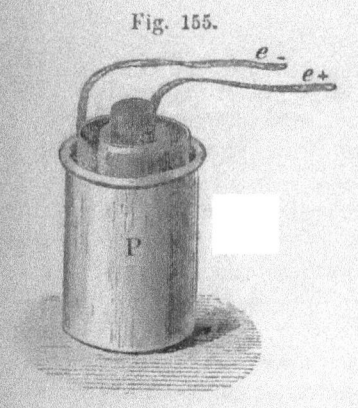

Fig. 155.

Bunsen's Battery.

Carbon is an excellent conductor of electricity, and on account of its great cheapness, compared with platinum, which is a very expensive metal, is much to be preferred. The form of the apparatus is much larger. The carbon cylinders are composed of solid gas coke, found in the interior of illuminating-gas retorts, or else of powdered coke, mixed with sugar, and baked. Porous cups, of corresponding size, filled with nitric acid, are used. These batteries are sold in Paris for about 5 Francs the cup. *Fig.* 155.

347. Smee's Battery. This form of the battery is also designed to increase power by favoring the escape of the hydrogen. It does so, however, by mechanical means, instead of chemical, and not so perfectly as in Grove's and Bunsen's batteries. It has been found that the bubbles of hydrogen adhere with considerable force to the smooth surfaces of conducting plates, but escape readily from the angles and edges. The conducting plate in Smee's battery is made of silver, roughened by the deposition upon it of spongy platinum from some solution in which it has been dissolved, and by this roughness of surface the discharge of the gas is much facilitated. *Fig.* 156.

Fig. 156.

Smee's Battery.

348. Management of Batteries. In all these batteries, it is to be noted that the real source of the electric current is the decomposition of water by zinc; but this water must be acidulated with sulphuric acid in the proportion of 1 part, by measure, of acid, to 8 parts of water. When very energetic action is required, the solution may be made stronger. As great heat is produced on mingling the acid

---

347. Describe Smee's battery.—348. What precautions must be adopted in the management of batteries?

and water, the mixture should be made some time before use, and allowed to cool. The nitric acid should be the strongest that can be procured, and never diluted. It is always decomposed by the action of the battery, producing a large quantity of corrosive fumes, and should not be employed, therefore, in a closed room, or in one in which there is any nice apparatus. It is essential that the zincs be well amalgamated by dipping them into mercury, upon the surface of which floats a quantity of diluted chlorohydric acid, (muriatic acid.) The zinc is cleaned as it passes through the dilute acid, and the mercury immediately amalgamates with it, giving it a bright and smooth surface. They should always be thoroughly washed in abundance of pure water, after use in the battery. The wires for connections should be of copper, well annealed, so as to be very flexible. The ends of these wires should be carefully brightened with a file, or by amalgamation with mercury before attachment to the binding cups; in all cases, the ends of the binding screws should be brightened by a file, or sand paper, before use, and all metallic connections carefully examined. Not unfrequently the action of a very powerful battery is greatly impeded, or entirely stopped, by a slight film which has formed on some connecting surface. Where the electrical charge is to be passed through water for the purpose of decomposing it, the water must be acidulated. It is advantageous to have the couplings of the cells of a battery arranged in such a way that it can be used either as a battery of intensity, or a battery of quantity. The effects of these arrangements are widely different, as will be seen hereafter. If it is desired to use a battery of intensity, the conducting plate of the first cell should be connected with the generating plate of the second cell, and so on, in a regular series, as represented in *Fig.* 157. On the

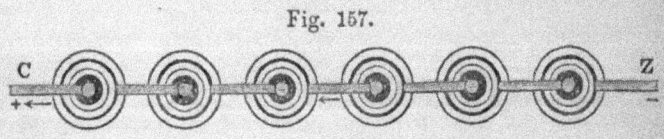

Fig. 157.

Arrangement of a Battery of Intensity.

other hand, if a battery of quantity be desired, the generating plates, i. e., the zincs, of all the cells, should be connected together, and the conducting plates in the same manner, as repre-

---

How may a battery of intensity be converted into one of quantity?

Fig. 158.

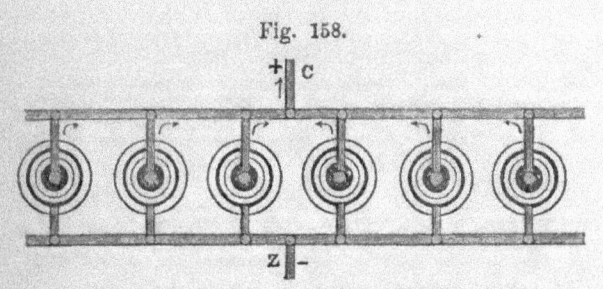

Arrangement of a Battery of Quantity.

sented in *Fig.* 158. By such an arrangement, the various zincs practically become one large zinc plate, and the various conducting plates one large conducting plate, and the quality of the electricity produced is materially changed.

349. De Luc's Pile.—Dry Pile. This is a galvanic arrangement, not requiring the use of any liquid, and named from its inventor. It was introduced shortly after the invention of the voltaic pile. It consists of a number of alternations, of very thin sheets of metal, with paper interposed between them. Thin paper, coated with gold or silver leaf on one side, should be covered on the uncoated side with thin zinc foil. This paper should then be punched out into circular discs of about an inch in diameter, and these arranged in such a way that the same order of succession, viz., zinc, paper, silver, zinc, paper, silver, should be preserved throughout, exactly as the discs are arranged in the voltaic pile. From 500 to 1000 such pairs are required to produce an active column, and they are most conveniently placed in a glass tube, perfectly clean and dry within, and surmounted at each end by a brass cap, perforated by a screw, which may serve to compress the discs, and also act as the poles of the pile, the screw at one end being in contact with the silvered side of the disc, and constituting the positive pole, and that at the other with the zinc discs, and forming the negative pole. The electrical current in this pile is due to the slight oxidation of the zinc discs by the moisture contained in the paper. If the paper be artificially dried, the pile loses its activity, but again recovers its energy as the paper re-absorbs moisture from the air. Provided the two extremities of this pile remain unconnected, it will retain its activity for years; but if the two poles are connected by a wire, the zinc discs become

---

349. Describe De Luc's dry pile. To what is the electrical current in De Luc's pile due? What is the effect of drying the paper artificially?

gradually oxidized, and the electrical power is destroyed. With a De Luc's pile containing 20,000 discs of zinc paper and silver, sparks have been obtained, and a Leyden battery charged sufficiently to produce shocks. A more effective instrument is prepared by using finely powdered peroxide of manganese, in place of the gold or silver leaf. One surface of the paper disc is coated with zinc, the other with the peroxide, either dry or attached by honey and water. A metallic plate is placed at each end for a conductor and the whole series is tied together by silk thread; the outside is then coated by dipping it in melted sulphur. The superior power of this instrument depends upon the affinity of the hydrogen, produced by the action of the zinc upon the moisture of the paper, for the oxygen of the peroxide, in virtue of which it is reconverted into water, and the paper kept continually moist.

350. Proof of the similarity of the electricity of the Battery and that of the Electrical Machine. The relation between the electricity of the voltaic battery and that of the electrical machine, may be readily ascertained by means of a De Luc's pile. On applying such a pile, containing 500 or 1000 discs, by that extremity which is in contact with the last silver disc, and which, consequently, represents the end of the conducting plate in the common voltaic battery, to the knob of the gold leaf electroscope, *Fig.* 115, whose leaves have been made to diverge with positive electricity, its leaves will still continue divergent. If the opposite, or zinc, end of the pile be then applied to the electroscope, its divergent leaves will first collapse, and then diverge again. Consequently, we infer, (see § 307, p. 280,) that the silver end of the pile, or the conducting end of the common battery, is excited with *positive*, and the zinc end with *negative* electricity. Thus a connection is established between the electricity of the conducting end of the battery, and that of the prime conductor of the electrical machine, and the electricity of the zinc end and that of the rubber of the same machine. If the wires attached to the two ends of a De Luc's pile be made to terminate in two small discs, which are brought within an inch and a half of each other, and carefully insulated, an insulated slip of gold leaf, suspended midway between the two discs, will first be attracted to the positive disc, then repelled and attracted towards the negative disc, and thus a state of per-

---

Explain the use of paper coated with the peroxide of manganese in place of the silver leaf?—350. How may the similarity of the electricity of the battery, and that of the electrical machine, be proved by De Luc's pile? How may it be proved by the ordinary battery?

pctual oscillation produced which will continue uninterruptedly for months or years. The oppositely electrified state of the two poles of the voltaic pile may also be shown with the ordinary battery, by attaching the wire connected with one pole of a powerful battery to the foot of the electroscope, and the wire connected with the other pole to the knob or plate of the instrument, the gold leaves will diverge powerfully, the platinum end furnishing positive, and the zinc end negative, electricity.

351. The difference between Galvanic and Statical Electricity. Galvanic electricity differs essentially from that of the electrical machine in possessing feeble intensity; and therefore but little power of overcoming obstacles placed in its path, giving shocks and the like. It is incapable of producing many of the effects of the electrical machine, and its influence upon electrometers and electroscopes is extremely slight. A Leyden jar can only be charged with great difficulty by making a communication between one of its surfaces and one pole of the battery, while the other surface is connected with the opposite pole. When the polar wires are brought near each other, only a feeble spark will pass, and on establishing the communication between them by means of the hands previously moistened, a shock is felt, but only for a moment. On the other hand, it is developed in much larger quantity than ordinary electricity, and in a steadily flowing current; it possesses, also, heating power of much greater intensity, extraordinary powers of chemical decomposition, and a wonderful influence in producing magnetism. Moreover, if the current from a powerful battery be passed through the great centres of the nervous system, the most astonishing muscular contractions are excited. It is capable of producing, therefore, remarkable heating, chemical, magnetic, and physiological effects.

352. Galvanic Batteries of Historic Note. Among memorable apparatus of this class which have obtained celebrity in the history of physical science, may be mentioned the pile of 2000 pairs of plates, each having a surface of 32 square inches, at the Royal Institution, London, with which Sir H. Davy made his great discovery of the decomposition of the alkalies, —potash and soda; also the great pile of the Royal Society, of nearly the same magnitude. In 1808, the Emperor Napoleon presented to the Polytechnic School, at Paris, a battery of

---

351. State the chief points of difference as to intensity, quantity, chemical decomposition, magnetic influence, &c., between the electricity of the machine, and that of the battery.—352. Mention some of the galvanic batteries of historic note.

600 pairs of plates, having each a square foot of surface. It was with this apparatus that several of the most important researches of Gay Lussac and Thenard, were conducted. Children's great battery, in London, consisted of 16 pairs of plates, each plate measuring 6 feet in length, and $2\frac{2}{3}$ feet in width, so that the copper surface of each amounted to 32 square feet; and when the whole was connected, there was an effective surface of 512 square feet. Dr. Hare's Deflagrator, in Philadelphia, consisted of 80 pairs of plates, each zinc surface measuring 54 square inches, and each copper 80 square inches. Pepy's battery, at the London Institution, consisted of pairs of enormous size, composed of a sheet of copper, and a sheet of zinc, measuring each 50 feet in length, and 2 feet in width. These were wound round a rod of wood with horse hair between them. Each bucket contained 55 gallons of the exciting liquid. With these batteries most extraordinary effects were produced. When the poles were dipped beneath the surface of water, a large quantity of oxygen and hydrogen was produced, and the water speedily grew very hot; iron wire melted and fell down in globules, and steel burned with brilliant scintillations. With Children's great battery many substances were fused which were exposed to the best wind furnaces without any effect. A piece of platinum wire, 1-30th of an inch in diameter, and 18 inches long, became instantly red, then white hot, with a brilliancy insupportable to the eye, and in a few seconds was fused into globules. When charcoal points were attached to the poles of the battery of the Royal Institution, a magnificent display of light was produced, the flame darting from one point to the other when they were four inches apart, and curving upwards in an arch. When any substance was held in this arch it became instantly ignited, platinum was melted in it, like wax in a candle, quartz, sapphire, magnesia, lime, all fused, and the diamond and plumbago entered into combustion and disappeared in the air. These batteries, however, and all similar apparatus, powerful as they were, and memorable as the discoveries in physics are to which they have been instrumental, have fallen into disuse since the invention of the batteries of Grove and Daniell, with two liquids. These, with a number of pairs of plates, not exceeding 40, and exposing a surface not exceeding 100 square inches each, produce a power equal to the largest of the batteries above described.

Describe the effects produced by Children's battery, and that of the Royal Institution. Why are these great batteries no longer used?

353. Heating effects of the Galvanic Current. In all cases where electricity is in motion, the force is conveyed by the entire thickness of the conductor, and not by the surface alone. If the wire connecting the poles of a small galvanic battery be made to pass through, or be carried around, the bulb of an air thermometer, as soon as the current circulates, a very perceptible effect will be produced upon the instrument. If the battery be large, and the wire small, the latter will become very hot, sometimes be made red-hot, and actually melted. This is owing to the smallness of the diameter of the conducting wire, by which a large quantity of the electrical current is compelled to traverse a limited number of conducting particles in a given time. The rise of temperature in the wire is inversely proportional to its conducting power, and therefore the poorer the conductor, the greater the heat produced. This may be shown by forming a chain of alternate links of silver and platinum, and transmitting through it a current from a powerful battery. The silver being a good conductor of electricity, and not obstructing the passage of the current, exhibits no intense heat, while the links of platinum, in consequence of the poor conducting power of that metal, almost immediately become red-hot. The conducting power of the metals for electricity varies nearly in the same order as their power of conducting heat. Charcoal, however, though a bad conductor of heat, is an exceedingly good conductor of electricity. Elevation of temperature diminishes the conducting power of the metals. This may be proved by transmitting through a platinum wire a galvanic current sufficient to make it red-hot; and while the current is still passing, igniting a small part of the wire by the flame of a spirit lamp; the rest of the wire immediately ceases to glow, in consequence of the obstruction at the point of ignition, and the consequent diminution in the flow of the current.

354. Ignition produced. The heat produced by the electrical current may rise so high as to produce ignition of the most refractory substances. Carbon is the only substance which can not be melted by the pile, though with six hundred Bunsen cells it has been softened to such a degree that adjoining pieces will adhere, which seems to indicate the commencement of fusion.

---

353. How may the heat of the connecting wire be shown by an air thermometer? What effect is produced upon the heat of the wire by reducing its size? To what is the rise of temperature in the wire inversely proportional? How may this be shown by a chain of alternate links of platinum and silver? What effect has elevation of temperature on the conducting power of the metals?—354. Describe cases of ignition produced by the current.

Platinum, which can not be melted by the most intense heat of a wind furnace, is immediately made white-hot, and fused by a powerful battery. It is said that if two platinum-pointed pencils, connected with the poles of the battery, be presented point to point, so that the current may pass between them, they will be fused and soldered together, and that this effect will be equally produced under water. The other metals are not only melted, but volatilized, and dissipated in vapor. Iron and platinum burn with a shining white light; lead, with purple; tin and gold, with bluish light; zinc, with white and red; copper and silver, with a greenish light. These effects are displayed with increased splendor if the metal to be burned be attached to a wire connected with the positive pole, and then applied to the surface of mercury connected with the negative pole. If a piece of steel watch spring, thus attached, be brought near the surface of a cup of mercury connected with the negative pole, the most beautiful scintillations will be produced; a steel file will answer nearly the same purpose. If two steel or iron wires, connected with the two poles, be brought near each other, vivid sparks will pass from one to the other, and if they both be coated with lamp-black, by holding them in the flame of an oil lamp, the sparks will be much brighter, especially if the two wires be held opposite each other, directly in the flame of the lamp.

355. Luminous effects. All combustible substances, whether solid or liquid, such as ether, alcohol, phosphorus, and gunpowder, may be inflamed by passing the galvanic current through them. A platinum wire, several yards in length, can be made to glow with intense brilliancy; and the effect is greatly increased if the wire be wound into the form of a spiral helix. Oxygen and hydrogen gases; also, hydrogen and chlorine, are combined by the spark, with a bright flash, and loud explosion. When pieces of well burned charcoal are attached to the wires, and become the poles of the battery, on bringing them near each other, a most brilliant arc of flame, emitting the brightest artificial light known, flashes between them. The compact coke of gas retorts is better adapted to this purpose than any other form of charcoal. The points must be brought near each other, and then gradually separated, *Fig.* 159; *a* is the positive pole, *b* the negative. As they are drawn apart by the rack and

---

How may the splendor of the light produced by the burning metals be increased?— 355. Describe the luminous effects produced by charcoal points. What arrangement of the points increases the luminous effect?

DUBOSCQ'S ELECTRIC LIGHT.   331

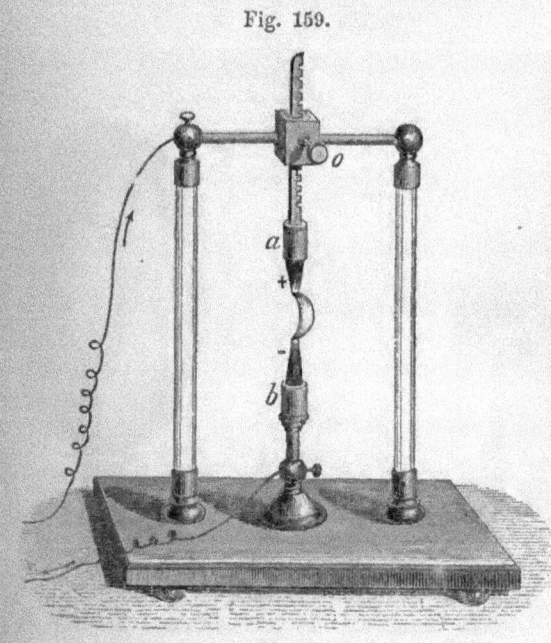

Fig. 159.

Luminous Effects of the Battery.—Charcoal Points.

pinion, the light and flame still continue, assuming the form of a curved arc. If the different metals are placed in this flame they are volatilized at once, and pass off in fumes. So intense is the light, that it may be used in optical experiments in place of the light of the sun. The luminous effect is found to be increased if the upper piece of carbon be made the positive, and the lower the negative pole. And if the two carbon points are arranged in a horizontal position, at right angles to the magnetic meridian, the length of the luminous arc is said to be greater in the proportion of 20.8 to 16.5, when the positive pole is to the east, than when it is to the west.

356. Duboscq's Electric Lamp. During the production of this dazzling light there is a considerable transport of the particles of carbon from the positive to the negative pole. A cavity is always produced in the carbon connected with the positive pole, and a deposit, continually increasing in length, is formed upon the negative pole. In *Fig.* 160 is represented an exceedingly ingenious apparatus for keeping this light at a fixed point in space so that it may be used in the solar microscope. Ordinarily the position of the light is continually changing as the negative pole is increasing at the expense of the positive; and this unfits it for use in connection with lenses; but in this apparatus this difficulty is overcome, and when placed in the

---

356. What change takes place in the length of the charcoal points during the passage of the current? If the position of the light be made fixed, for what purpose may it be used? Describe *Fig.* 160.

Fig. 160.

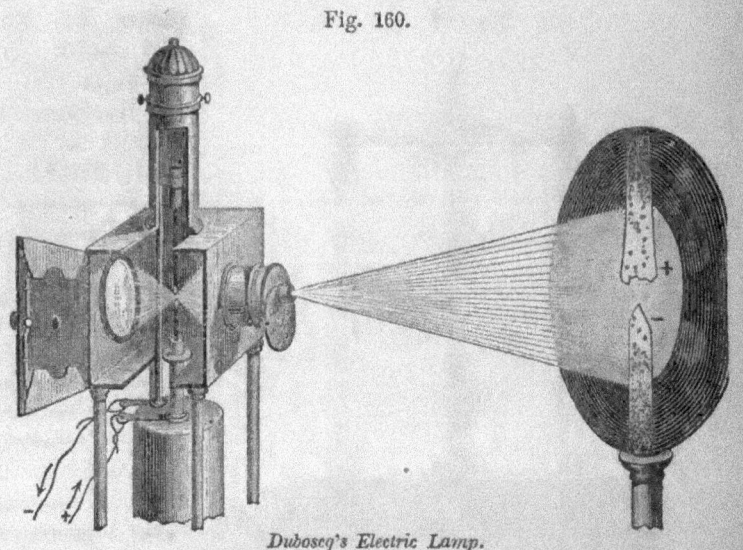

Duboscq's Electric Lamp.

microscope, the image of the two points is formed upon a screen at some distance, upon an enlarged scale. From this image, as shown in the figure, the peculiar shape assumed by the two poles can be plainly seen, and also the process of transport, by which one increases at the expense of the other. This exceedingly elegant instrument is the invention of M. Duboscq, of Paris, and is intended to be used in the performance of optical experiments, in place of solar light.

357. Discovery of the Electric Light. Sir H. Davy, in 1801, at London, was the first to perform the experiment of the electric light, and with the great battery of the Royal Institution, consisting of 2000 pairs of plates, obtained an arc of flame between two charcoal points, 4 inches in length. This charcoal had been prepared by heating it red-hot, and then quenching it beneath the surface of mercury. Despretz, however, with 600 cells of Bunsen, arranged consecutively, succeeded, when the points were placed vertically, the positive pole being above, in obtaining an arc 7.8 inches in length.

358. The Electric Light is not produced by Combustion. That this is not a case of ordinary combustion of charcoal in air, simply increased by the action of the galvanic current, may

---

357. Who was the discoverer of the electric light? What results did he attain? What length of arc was obtained by Despretz?—358. Show that the electric light is not produced by combustion

INTENSITY OF THE ELECTRIC LIGHT. 333

be shown by placing the charcoal points in the interior of a glass vessel, from which the air has been withdrawn by the air pump, *Fig.* 161. It will be found that the light is quite as great as before. It can even be produced beneath the surface of water, but is considerably diminished in splendor. The light is in great part due to the continued transport of minute particles of carbon in a state of intense incandescence.

Fig. 161.

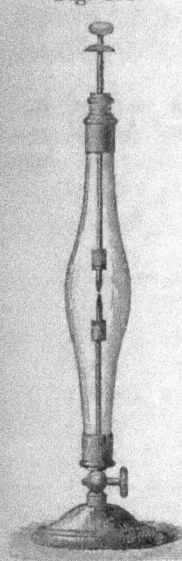

Charcoal Points in Vacuo.

359. The properties and intensity of the Electric Light. The heat produced in the voltaic arc is of the most intense kind. Platinum, iridium, and titanium, which resist the greatest heat of the most powerful wind furnace, readily melt, when placed in it. The light is powerful enough to produce the combination of chlorine and hydrogen at a considerable distance, and without any direct contact, and to act upon the chloride of silver, in the same way as the light of the sun. It also possesses the singular property of being attracted by the magnet. Transmitted through a prism, the electric light is decomposed, and produces a spectrum like that of the sun, with lines analogous to the lines of Fraunhofer, except that they are bright, instead of dark. The character of these lines depends upon the metal with which the poles are tipped. The light produced by 18 cells of Bunsen, has been estimated as more than that proceeding from 572 candles; under the most favorable circumstances, it has been estimated as equal to one-third of the intensity of solar light, and is so bright that it can not safely be regarded by the naked eye.

360. Connection between the heat of the Battery and the mechanical equivalent of Heat. The chemical action within the battery always produces heat, and a definite amount of chemical action a definite amount of heat; no more and no less. It has been ascertained, however, that if heat is developed at any point in the circuit outside the battery, the amount of heat produced within the battery is diminished in an equal ratio,

---

359. What degree of heat is produced by the voltaic arc? Of light? If the light be transmitted through a glass prism, what may be observed? How does it compare with the light of the sun?—360. If a portion of the power of the battery be used to produce motion, what effect is produced upon the heat of the battery?

334   THE CHEMICAL EFFECTS OF THE CURRENT.

and that if the electrical current be used to produce motion, as it may be, when employed to generate electro-magnetism, a portion of the heat of the entire circuit disappears, having been converted into mechanical effect or motion. The quantity of heat which disappears corresponds very nearly to that which Joule's law, (§ 254,) would require for the production of an equal mechanical effect. This serves to confirm, very strongly, the mechanical theory of heat.

361. Heating effects are best produced by batteries of quantity. In experiments on the heating effects of the galvanic current, the battery should be arranged so that the zinc plates may all be connected together, practically forming but one zinc plate, and the platinum plates, in the same manner, forming but one platinum plate, as shown in *Fig.* 158.

362. The chemical effects of the galvanic current.—Its decomposing power. The chemical effects of the voltaic current are even more remarkable and interesting than the heating. It had been noticed in Holland, in 1798, that a succession of charges of statical electricity transmitted for a long time through water, by means of platinum or gold conductors which nearly touched each other, effected the decomposition of water; and in 1800, shortly after the invention of the voltaic pile, it was discovered by Nicholson and Carlisle, two English chemists, that a current of galvanic electricity would not only decompose water, but that the oxygen would invariably be discharged at the positive pole, and the hydrogen at the negative. This experiment led to the application of the galvanic current to other chemical compounds, with a view to effect their decomposition, and enabled Sir H. Davy, a few years afterwards, to decompose the alkalies, potash and soda, which heretofore had been regarded as simple substances, and to prove that they were composed of oxygen, and two different metals, potassium and sodium. This great discovery was the prelude to others of a similar kind, and led to the establishment of an entirely new theory in regard to the constitution of the various rocks, minerals, earths, and salts, of which the earth is composed, viz., that they all possess a metallic basis, and have been produced by the combination of different metals with other simple substances, chiefly gaseous.

363. The constitution of Water. Pure water is a compound

Is there any correspondence between the amount of heat thus converted into motion, and that which is required by Joule's law?—361. Which kind of battery produces the greatest heating effect?—362. Who discovered the chemical effect of the current? What use did Sir H. Davy make of it?—363. Describe the composition of water by volume, and by weight, as shown by its decomposition

THE DECOMPOSITION OF WATER 335

of two gaseous chemical elements, oxygen and hydrogen, and hence is called a binary compound. It is also composed of these substances, united in certain definite proportions, both by weight and by volume. By weight, the proportion of oxygen to hydrogen is 8 to 1; by volume, it is as 1 to 2. Hence, if we wish to produce water by the combination of these two substances, we must use 8 parts by weight of oxygen, to 1 part by weight of hydrogen; but by volume, 1 measure of oxygen, to 2 measures of hydrogen; and these 8 parts by weight of oxygen, combined with 1 part by weight of hydrogen, make exactly 9 parts by weight of pure water. On the other hand, if we decompose pure water, we always obtain one volume of oxygen, to two volumes of hydrogen, and every 9 grains of water decomposed produce just 8 grains of oxygen, and 1 grain of hydrogen. From this, it appears that the proportions in which elements unite, *by weight*, to form compounds, are very different from the proportions in which they unite *by volume*. When one volume of oxygen, and two volumes of hydrogen, or which is the same thing, eight parts by weight of oxygen, and one part by weight of hydrogen, are introduced into a closed receiver, and a spark from the electrical machine is passed through them, an explosion results, the gases disappear, and watery vapor is formed, which, on the cooling of the vessel, condenses into little drops of water. The weight of the water formed is always precisely equal to the sum of the weights of the two gases employed.

364. The decomposition of Water by the Battery. If two platinum or gold wires be attached to the poles of the battery, and then be brought near each other beneath the surface of water slightly acidulated with sulphuric acid, bubbles of oxygen gas will appear at the positive, and of hydrogen at the negative pole. If a tube, closed at the upper end, and open at the lower, be completely filled with water, so as to retain no bubbles of air whatever, and then inverted over each pole, the bubbles of each gas, as they arise, will be collected separately in the two tubes, the oxygen in the tube over the positive pole, and the hydrogen in that over the negative pole, and twice as much of the latter as of the former; *Fig.* 162. As the hydrogen is collected in double the quantity of the oxygen, the tube containing it should be made twice as large as that for oxygen; the process may be continued till both are filled; and this will take place at the same instant.

Can water be reproduced by uniting these elements in the same proportions?—364. Describe the decomposition of water by the current.

Fig. 162.

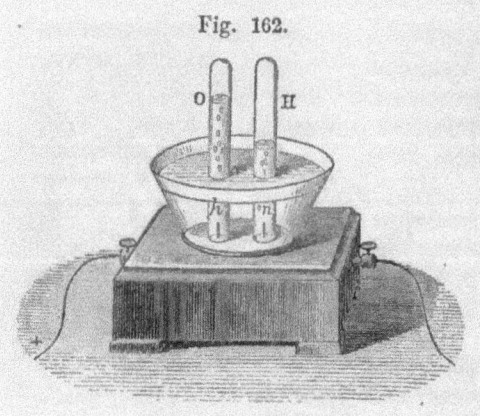

Decomposition of Water.

On carefully closing the oxygen tube beneath the water, and inverting it, so that a lighted taper can be introduced into it from above, the taper will be found to burn with extraordinary splendor, and if blown out in such a way as to leave a small smouldering spark upon the wick, it will be relighted when it is introduced again into the gas. On the other hand, if the hydrogen tube be removed with equal care, but not inverted, and a lighted taper introduced into it from below, the hydrogen will take fire, and burn with a lambent flame, but the taper will be extinguished. Thus, these two gases may be distinguished by their opposite effects upon a lighted taper. If, instead of using two tubes, one tube be filled with water, and inverted over both poles, the two gases will be collected together, and if a spark from the electrical machine be passed through the mixture, there will be a flash of light, and an explosion; the two gases will unite to form a very small portion of water, and will entirely disappear, and the water from the vessel will rush up so as to completely fill the whole of the tube. In performing this experiment, it is necessary to use a platinum wire for the positive pole at which the oxygen is discharged, for if a copper wire be employed, or any other metal which has a strong affinity for oxygen, the gas will unite with the metal to form a solid oxide, instead of escaping and rising through the liquid. Platinum and gold have only a very slight affinity for oxygen, and, therefore, when these are used, nearly the whole of the gas is collected. It is advantageous in all such experiments to have both wires made of platinum. From this experiment, it is evident that the galvanic current has the power of decomposing water, and separating it into its constituent elements.

365. The decomposition of Water is effected by the polarization and transfer of the component elements. It has been

---

Which gas collects in the larger quantity? How may they be tested, and proved to be different? Why must the decomposing wires be made of platinum?

AND TRANSFER OF THE ELEMENTS. 337

already stated that the galvanic influence is propagated by a polarization of the liquid, as well as the solid, part of the whole circuit. When the two platinum wires are dipped into the acidulated water, the liquid becomes a part of the circuit, and the particles between the poles become polarized; so that the atoms of oxygen are all turned towards the positive, and the atoms of hydrogen towards the negative pole, in the manner represented in *Fig.* 163. On the right, the polarized platinum wire, P, connected with the zinc end of the battery, z, enters a vessel of acidulated water, represented in section. On the left, a similar platinum wire, P, connected with the copper end of the battery, enters the same vessel of water. The polarized wire, P z, on the left, is then the negative pole of the battery, and the polarized wire, P c, is the positive pole. In consequence of the highly excited negative electricity accumulated in P z, all the atoms of hydrogen in the chain of particles of water being naturally charged with positive electricity, are drawn towards it; and all the atoms of negative oxygen are repelled from it, and at the same time attracted towards the positively excited platinum wire, P, c; on the principle that bodies electrified differently attract each other, while those electrified similarly repel one another. The next instant, the superior negative excitement of the wire completely separates the atom of hydrogen from the atom of oxygen, and as it can not unite with the platinum, it is discharged into the water, and escapes into the air. At the same moment, the negative oxygen at the opposite extremity of the chain is drawn powerfully towards the positive platinum wire, and as it can not unite with the platinum, it is also discharged, and escapes into the air. This necessitates a movement throughout the whole chain, and a flow, in opposite directions, of the two gases, and also of the negative and positive current. It is obvious, from the figure, why it is necessary that the positive pole should be made of some unoxidizable metal; if it were not, the oxygen discharged upon it would unite with it to form a solid oxide, and there would be no escape

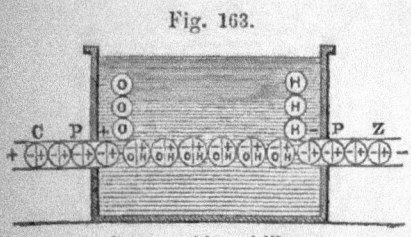

Fig. 163.

Decomposition of Water.

---

365. Describe *Fig.* 163. Show that the decomposition of the water depends upon the polarization of the circuit. Why is the water acidulated?

of gas. If the oxide be insoluble, it may adhere to the pole, forming a crust upon it; in this case, if the oxide be a conductor of electricity, it will itself become the pole; if it be not a conductor, it will interfere with, and finally arrest the course of the current, and put an end to the decomposition. If the oxide be soluble, it will be dissolved as fast as formed, and the water will become a solution of the oxide. If the water contain acid, the acid will unite with the oxide to form a new substance, and the liquid will become a solution of this substance. In the experiment just described, the sulphuric acid is not itself decomposed, but it tends to favor the passage of the current through the water. It is exceedingly difficult for the electrical current to pass at all through pure water, but on adding from one to fifteen per cent. of acid, its passage is greatly facilitated. Common salt, dissolved in water, produces the same effect. These substances all seem to act by lessening the affinity which binds the particles of oxygen and hydrogen to each other.

366. The decomposition of other compound Liquids. Water is not the only substance susceptible of electrical decomposition; a large number of compound liquids may be decomposed in a similar manner. It is always necessary that the substance should be a liquid, or soluble in a liquid, otherwise there can be no transfer of the elements which it contains on account of their immobility. If water be solidified, it immediately arrests the passage of the current. A solid substance can not be decomposed in this manner; but sometimes, merely moistening a solid, will be sufficient to allow the transfer of its elements. Binary compounds, or those which consist of one atom of each element, are those which are most readily decomposed, as is seen in the case of water. In like manner, chloro-hydric acid, a compound substance, composed of chlorine and hydrogen, and whose symbol is ClH, is readily polarized and decomposed by the electrical current; the chlorine being discharged at the positive pole, and the hydrogen at the negative. Ammonia, composed of nitrogen and hydrogen, and whose symbol is NH^3, is also easily decomposed, the nitrogen collecting at the positive pole, and the hydrogen at the negative.

367. The decomposition of Metallic Oxides in solution. Oxygen unites with most of the metals to form a new class of substances called oxides. Thus, common iron rust is a com-

---

366. Why must the compound substance to be decomposed be in the liquid state? Mention various compound liquids which may be decomposed by the current.—367. Describe the decomposition of the metallic oxides, potash and soda.

pound of iron and oxygen; soda is a compound of the metal sodium and oxygen; potash is a compound of the metal potassium and oxygen. Many of these oxides are soluble in water, and some of them can be decomposed by the galvanic current. In all these cases, the metal appears at the negative, and the oxygen at the positive pole. Thus, if perfectly pure potash, moistened, and placed upon a platinum plate, connected with the negative pole of the battery, be touched with a platinum wire connected with the positive pole, small metallic globules of pure potassium will be formed upon the platinum plate, and oxygen will be discharged upon the wire. The same is true of soda and sodium. If the platinum be formed into a cup, and filled with mercury, and the potash be placed upon it, the potassium amalgamates with the mercury as fast as formed, and may be obtained pure by distillation in an atmosphere of nitrogen.

368. The decomposition of Metallic Salts in Solution. The metallic oxides are capable of uniting with acids, to form a class of substances called salts. Thus potash, or the oxide of potassium, can unite with sulphuric acid, to form the sulphate of potash. In like manner, the oxide of copper can unite with sulphuric acid, to form the sulphate of copper; the oxide of lead can unite with acetic acid, to form the acetate of lead; the oxide of silver with nitric acid, to form the nitrate of silver. These salts, if dissolved in water, can often be decomposed by the galvanic current, and in all cases, the acid appears at the positive, the metallic oxide at the negative pole; sometimes, however, the oxide itself is also decomposed, and then its oxygen joins the acid, and appears at the positive pole, while the metal alone appears at the negative pole.

369. The Decomposing Tube. These decompositions can be very clearly shown by the apparatus represented in *Fig.* 164. It is a glass tube, curved twice at right angles. The liquid, or solution to be decomposed, is poured into it, and the poles inserted, one in each leg. They should be of platinum, and long enough to reach the curve, so as to come as near as possible without touching. On pouring into such a tube,—technically called a U tube,—a solution of sulphate of soda, mixed with a little tincture of blue violets, the salt will be decomposed. The sulphuric acid will be discharged at the positive pole, and will change the blue color of the solution to red; while the soda will

---

368 Describe the decomposition of metallic salts. At which pole does the acid appear? At which the oxide?—369 Describe the decomposing U tube, and the experiments that may be performed with it.

340 THE DECOMPOSING TUBE.

Fig. 164.

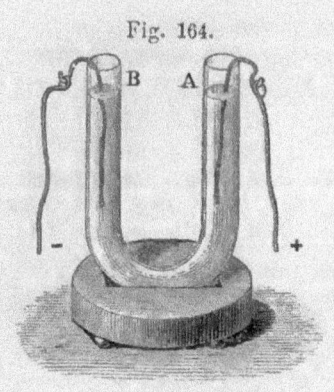

Decomposing U Tube.

be collected at the negative pole, and will change the blue color of that tube to green. On disconnecting the wires from the battery, and agitating the tube so as to mix the two colors, the original blue will be restored. If sulphate of copper be introduced, the sulphuric acid will be discharged in one leg and the oxide of copper in the other. If a solution of nitrate of silver be introduced, the nitric acid will be discharged at one pole, and the oxide of silver at the other; if acetate of lead be employed, the acetic acid, and oxygen from the oxide, will appear in one tube, and the pure lead in the other. · If a solution of iodide of potassium be used, the iodine will appear in the positive tube, and the potassium in the negative, and the presence of the iodine may be detected by pouring in a little solution of starch, which will at once be turned to a deep blue; the potassium will be immediately converted into potash by uniting with the oxygen of the water, and its presence may be shown by pouring in blue tincture of violets, which will at once be changed to a bright green. The same apparatus will answer equally well for the decomposition of chloro-hydric acid; the chlorine will appear in the positive tube, and may be detected by its odor and bleaching effect upon a few drops of solution of indigo, and the hydrogen will appear in the negative tube. In like manner, if acidulated water be introduced, the oxygen will be discharged in the positive tube, and the hydrogen in the negative; and if the end of the leg be stopped with a cork, through which passes a tube of glass, drawn to a fine aperture, the hydrogen, as it escapes, may be lighted, and will burn at the end of the tube with a small, but a steady flame.

370. Glass Cup with Porous Diaphragm. The same experiments may be well performed with the apparatus delineated in *Fig.* 165. It consists, simply, of a glass cup, divided in the middle by a porous diaphragm of plaster, confined in a frame, as represented in *a*. This porous diaphragm, inasmuch as it allows the penetration of liquids, and therefore of the establish-

---

What is the effect when sulphate of soda is decomposed? Iodide of potassium? Chloro-hydric acid? Water? How may the hydrogen be burned?—370. Describe the decomposing cell, and the experiments which may be performed with it.

SECONDARY 341

Fig. 165.

Decomposing Cell.

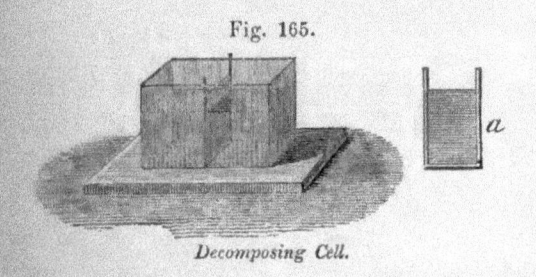

ment of a chain of liquid particles through it, offers no obstacle to the passage of the electric current, and the consequent transfer of elements in both directions through it.
In the decomposition of salts into acids and oxides, the acid will, in all cases, appear at the positive, and the oxide at the negative pole, and be manifested, one in each cell. The presence of the acid may be detected by pouring into the positive cell some tincture of a vegetable blue, like that of blue violets, when the blue color will immediately be turned to red. If the oxides formed belong to the peculiar class called alkalies, their presence will be indicated in the negative cup, by turning the same vegetable blue to green. Thus, if a solution of carbonate of potash, or sulphate of soda, or nitrate of lime be introduced into the glass cup, and colored blue by the vegetable tincture, it will be turned red in the cell into which the positive pole dips, and green in the cell containing the negative pole; because lime, soda, and potash, are alkaline oxides, and have the peculiar faculty of turning vegetable blues to green. But if a solution of the nitrate of silver, the sulphate of copper, and the sulphate of iron, be introduced into the glass cup, with the addition of the same vegetable solution, it will be turned red by the acids set free in the positive cell, but will remain unchanged in the negative cell, because the oxides of silver, copper, and iron are insoluble, and therefore manifest no alkaline properties.

371. Secondary Decomposition. When the poles of the battery are made of platinum, or some other equally unoxidizable metal, and the substance to be decomposed is a binary compound, composed of two elements only, and it is used in a pure state, there being no other compound, or elementary substance, of any kind, present, then the decomposing action of the current is of the simple character already described; but it is not often that the substances decomposed are thus situated. In the case of most of the solids which have been spoken of, they are used in the state of solution in water, and therefore, by the action of the galvanic current, the water may be decomposed as

---

371. What is meant by secondary decomposition?

well as the salt in question, and the oxygen thus set free at one pole, and the hydrogen at the other, may have a very important effect upon the other substances which appear at the same points. If, for instance, sulphate of copper, in solution in water, be the substance to be decomposed, as soon as it is subjected to the action of the electrical current, sulphuric acid will be set free at one pole, and oxide of copper at the other; but at the same time, a second current will be established, operating through the particles of water, and the result is, that hydrogen will be discharged at the same pole with the oxide of copper, and oxygen at the same pole with the sulphuric acid. The hydrogen will at once attack the oxide of copper, and uniting with its oxygen, will form water, and the copper will be deposited upon the platinum pole; at the other pole, the oxygen which is set free, having nothing with which it can unite, is discharged into the air. Consequently, in most cases of the decomposition of salts in solution, instead of the oxide of the metal being set free at the negative pole, the metal in a pure state is deposited in consequence of this secondary action of the hydrogen. This secondary action is indicated in *Fig.* 166, where the two platinum poles of a battery, P +, and P —, are inserted in a solution of sulphate of copper, represented by the upper circle, CuO SO^3; the whole of the liquid is supposed to be composed of similar globules, mixed with globules of water, HO. One row of these globules is represented as polarized, the positive oxide of copper, CuO, being turned towards the negative platinum pole, and the negative sulphuric acid, SO^3, turned towards the positive pole. Immediately beneath this row, is another, composed of particles of water, also polarized, the hydrogen being turned towards the negative, while the oxygen is turned towards the positive platinum pole. The instant the current begins to circulate, the oxide of copper is drawn to the negative pole, and at the same moment the globule of hydrogen is also attracted to the same point; the hydrogen immediately seizes upon the oxygen of the oxide, and

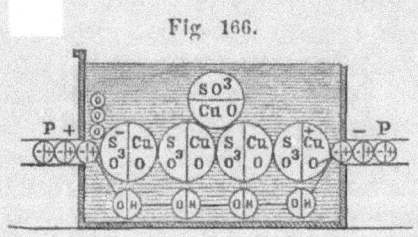

Fig. 166.

Secondary Decomposition.

What is the effect of the decomposition of the water at the same time with that of metallic salts? Illustrate this as shown by *Fig.* 166, in the case of sulphate of copper. What is the general effect of hydrogen on metallic oxides set free at the negative pole?

escapes into the liquid in the form of water, while the copper, being deserted by the oxygen, is deposited in the form of a film of metallic copper upon the platinum conductor. At the opposite pole, sulphuric acid is discharged, and at the same point oxygen gas; the former is at once taken up by the water, while the latter, being in the gaseous state, rises through the liquid, and passes off into the air. As water is present in almost all cases of the decomposition of chemical substances, it is evident that secondary action may be generally looked for, and there are few cases of decomposition in which it is not concerned. We shall presently see the importance of this action in all cases of electro-plating.

372. Experiment of three Cups connected by Syphons. These effects will also take place even if the solution is put in two distinct cups, placed side by side, provided only they be connected, by syphons of glass filled with the same liquid, and establishing a communication between the cups. The metal, in this case, will appear in one cup, and the acid in the other. Moreover, if three cups, as in *Fig.* 167, be used, and connected together by syphons, or by shreds of asbestos, moistened with the solution employed, and a solution of sulphate of soda be introduced into all the cups, colored by a vegetable blue, the acid will be found in the extreme right hand cup, C, with which the positive pole is connected, and will turn it red, while the soda will be found in the extreme left hand cup, A, and will turn it green, without the slightest change produced upon the blue color of the middle cup, B, notwithstanding the electric current must have passed through it. This very singular result is explained by the polarization of the entire circuit, in virtue of which, not a particle of acid or alkali is set absolutely free in their passage in opposite directions through the middle cup, until they reach the platinum poles; consequently, no effect is produced by either upon the color of the middle cup, though both pass through it. If the poles be reversed, i. e., if the right hand cup be connected with the nega-

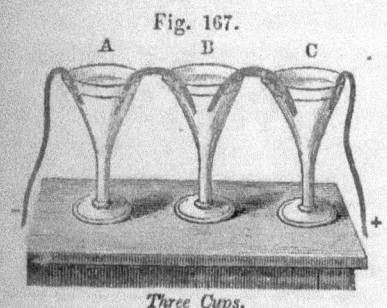

---

372. Describe the experiment of the three cups connected by syphons. How may this be explained by polarization?

tive end of the battery, instead of the positive, the acid will be collected in the left hand cup, and the alkali in the one on the right. This will be manifested by the changes in the color of the infusions. The liquid in C, which had been reddened by the acid, will first recover its original color in consequence of the neutralizing effect of the alkali, and will then become green as the alkali accumulates. In like manner, the liquid in A, which had been turned green, will gradually recover its original blue color, and then become reddened as the acid accumulates beyond the amount required to neutralize the alkali. During all these transfers, no change will be observed in the intermediate cup, B.

373. Sir H. Davy's extraordinary experiment, in which acids and alkalies, while under the influence of the current, seem to lose their ordinary affinity. Sir H. Davy ascertained that if the middle cup, B, be filled with a strong alkaline solution, for which the various acids have a powerful affinity, they may be transferred by the electrical current through this alkali, without any combination taking place between them. Thus, if sulphate of soda be placed in A, *Fig.* 167, and in B, a solution of potash, for which, ordinarily, sulphuric acid has a very powerful affinity, and pure water be placed in C, as soon as C is connected with the positive pole, and A with the negative, the sulphuric acid will be transported through the potash in B, without uniting with it, and make its appearance in C. The same acid may thus be transported through ammonia, and solutions of lime and soda, without affecting them, and so, in like manner, chlorohydric and nitric acids. This result is explained, as in the previous case, by the polarization of the entire circuit, in virtue of which, not a particle of acid is set free after it leaves the soda in the cup, A, until it reaches the positive platinum pole in the cup C, and consequently it passes through the potash without forming any permanent compound with it. This, however, supposes that the potassium of the potash also moves towards the cup A, and mingles with the soda, which is probably the case, and also that the composition of sulphuric acid is SO^4. The process of transfer is complicated, and will be more fully explained hereafter, when we come to treat of the binary theory of salts.

374. Exception in the case of the production of insoluble compounds. Chloro-hydric and nitric acids may be, in the same manner, transported through solutions of strontia and baryta,

---

373. Describe Sir H. Davy's experiment. How may this be explained?—374. State the exception in the case of insoluble products. How may this be explained?

and reciprocally, these substances passed through the acids without any combination, though they have a strong affinity for each other; but if it be attempted to pass sulphuric acid through strontia, or baryta, combination takes place, and the insoluble sulphates of strontia and baryta are precipitated to the bottom of the cup B. The same result followed when this acid was placed in the cup B, and it was attempted to transmit strontia and baryta through it; insoluble sulphates of these substances were always thrown down in B. The conclusion, therefore, seems to be that this transfer of acids and alkalies may take place when the resulting compound is soluble, but can not take place when the resulting compound is insoluble. This result is explained as in the two previous cases by polarization, the only difference being that the acid, when it strikes the baryta, in the cup B, forming an insoluble sulphate of baryta, can no longer transmit the current, no solid substance being able to do this, (see § 366,) and is immediately precipitated out of the line of voltaic influence to the bottom of the vessel.

375. The successive action of the same current on different vessels of water. In *Fig.* 168, if 1, 2, 3, 4, be a row of glass

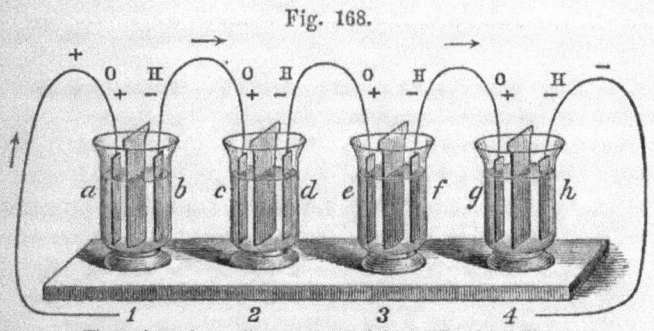

Fig. 168.

The action of one Current upon different Vessels of Water.

cups, containing acidulated water, and *g h*, *e f*, *c d*, *a b*, be slips of platinum, joined by wires, on forming the connection with the battery, oxygen will be discharged at the left hand slip, in each cup, and hydrogen at the right hand slip, and in all the cups at the same instant; and this will continue as long as the current passes. It is plain, from this, that there is a positive and negative pole formed in each cup, and not simply in

---

375. What is the successive action of the current on the four vessels of water shown in *Fig.* 168? How many poles are formed in each cup? How may this be explained by *Fig.* 169?

15*

the two extreme cups. This experiment shows, conclusively, that there is a state of polarization extending through the entire circuit. Thus, in *Fig.* 169, on the extreme right may be seen a wire of platinum, polarized by the action of the current; the connecting wires are also polarized, as well the wire connected with the positive pole. As soon as the current passes, the positive electricity moves towards the right, and the negative towards the left, and in doing so, the hydrogen particles are necessarily drawn in one direction, and the oxygen in the other, at teh points where the wires enter each cup. *In all cases where the metallic circuit is broken by the intervention of a liquid conductor, composed of two elements, two poles will be formed at each break, corresponding in position with the poles at the extremities of the series, and with the poles of the battery, and at each break decomposition take place.*

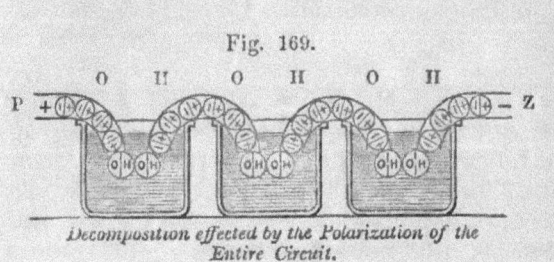

Fig. 169.

Decomposition effected by the Polarization of the Entire Circuit.

376. The successive action of the same current on vessels containing different compound liquids. If we take a series of four cups, arranged as before, *Fig.* 168, except that a piece of card, or three or four folds of blotting paper, are placed inside the cups, between the slips of platinum, and then introduce into 1, a solution of iodide of potassium, mixed with solution of starch, and into 2, a strong solution of chloride of sodium, colored blue by sulphate of indigo, and into 3, a solution of nitrate of ammonia, colored blue with tincture of purple cabbage, and into 4, a solution of sulphate of copper, and finally connect with the battery, we shall have iodine set free at the positive pole in 1, shown by changing the starch blue; chlorine set free at the same pole in 2, shown by its bleaching the vegetable blue; nitric acid set free in 3, shown by its reddening the vegetable blue; sulphuric acid in 4. On the other hand, at the negative pole in 1, we shall find potash; in 2, soda; in 3, ammonia; in 4, oxide of copper. These different substances are attracted towards their respective poles from the fact that they are themselves possessed, naturally, of the opposite kind of electricity. The iodine, chlo-

---

376. What is the successive action of the same current on various compound liquids?

rine, nitric acid, and sulphuric acid, are naturally charged with positive electricity, and the potash, soda, ammonia, and oxide of copper, with negative electricity. All the chemical elements seem to possess a definite electrical character, and this has led to their division into positive and negative electrics. Those are called positive electrics which appear at the negative pole in any decomposing cell, and those negative which appear at the positive pole, on the principle that oppositely electrified bodies attract each other.

377. Electro-Negative Bodies.

1. Oxygen.
2. Sulphur.
3. Nitrogen.
4. Chlorine.
5. Iodine.
6. Fluorine.
7. Phosphorus.
8. Selenium.
9. Arsenic.
10. Chromium.
11. Molydenum.
12. Tungsten.
13. Boron.
14. Carbon.
15. Antimony.
16. Tellurium.
17. Columbium.
18. Titanium.
19. Silicon.
20. Osmium.
21. Hydrogen.

378. Electro-Positive Bodies.

1. Potassium.
2. Sodium.
3. Lithium.
4. Barium.
5. Strontium.
6. Calcium.
7. Magnesium.
8. Glucinium.
9. Yttrium.
10. Aluminium.
11. Zirconium.
12. Manganese.
13. Zinc.
14. Cadmium.
15. Iron.
16. Nickel.
17. Cobalt.
18. Cerium.
19. Lead.
20. Tin.
21. Bismuth.
22. Uranium.
23. Copper.
24. Silver.
25. Mercury.
26. Palladium.
27. Platinum.
28. Rhodium.
29. Iridium.
30. Gold.

379. The law of chemical decomposition by the electrical current. Mr. Faraday has demonstrated the following law of chemical decomposition by the current. When the same current acts successively upon a series of solutions, as in *Fig.* 168, the weights of the elements which are set free at each pole are in the same proportion as their chemical equivalents. Thus, 1 being the chemical equivalent of hydrogen, and 8 the equivalent of oxygen, when water is decomposed, the proportion of hydrogen to oxygen produced, is always as 1 to 8. The chemical equivalent of potassium being 40, while that of oxygen is 8, in the decomposition of the oxide of potassium or potash, the proportion of potassium, by weight, to the oxygen, is always as 40 to 8. Consequently, when a current of electricity is passed through a series of cups, charged with different compound liquids, as in *Fig.* 168, the weight of the different elements set free at the poles in each cup, is not equal, as might be supposed from the equality of the force which acts upon them, but varies according to the chemical equivalent of the element. If cup 1

377. What is meant by electro-negative bodies? Which is the most highly electro-negative body?—378. What is an electro-positive body? Which is the most highly electro-positive body?—379. State Faraday's law of chemical decomposition. Explain this law by the atomic theory.

contain water, cup 2 chloride of sodium, cup 3 iodide of potassium, cup 4 chloro-hydric acid, while the weight of hydrogen set free in cup 1 compared to that of oxygen, is as 1 to 8, the weight of the elements set free in cup 2 is not the same, but as 35.5 of chlorine to 23 of sodium; in cup 3, it is 127 of iodine to 40 of potassium; in cup 4, it is 35.5 of chlorine to 1 of hydrogen. The reason of this is, because the atoms of the elements differ in weight according to these numbers, and when two substances unite, they do so atom to atom. It follows, as a consequence, that when these atoms are separated from each other, the weights of the elements produced are always those of their atoms; in other words, of their chemical equivalents. This will become clearer hereafter.

380. The amount of zinc dissolved from the generating plate is always proportioned to the amount of chemical decomposition produced, and vice versa. Not only is this true in respect to the decomposition effected by the current, after it leaves the battery, but also in reference to the chemical action within the battery itself. Thus, for every 9 grs. of water, consisting of 8 grs. of oxygen, and 1 gr. of hydrogen, that are decomposed by the electrical current, in cup 1, *Fig.* 168, exactly 32.7 grs. of zinc have united with 8 grs. of oxygen, and been dissolved in the acidulated water of each cup of the battery. And on the contrary, if 32.7 grs. of zinc have been dissolved in each cup of the battery, it will be found that the electrical current has decomposed exactly 9 grs. of water in cup 1, and set free 8 grs. of oxygen, and 1 gr. of hydrogen. If a smaller amount of zinc has been dissolved, a less amount of electricity has been produced, a less amount of acidulated water decomposed in the cells, and a less amount of the various solutions in the cups outside of the battery. The amount of decomposition effected becomes, consequently, a measure of the strength of the electrical current. Upon this principle depends the action of the voltameter.

381. The Voltameter. This is an instrument invented by Mr. Faraday, for the purpose of determining the voltaic power of any circuit. It consists of an upright glass cell, having a bent tube, *c*, fitted into its upper part by accurate grinding; *Fig.* 170. This tube is curved in such a way as to dip beneath the edge of the carefully graduated jar, *d*, which is entirely

---

380. Is there any proportion between the amount of zinc dissolved in the interior of the battery, and the amount of chemical decomposition effected outside of it? State the proportion of zinc dissolved, and of water decomposed.—381. Describe the voltameter. How may it be used to indicate the force of the current?

ELECTRO-PLATING. 349

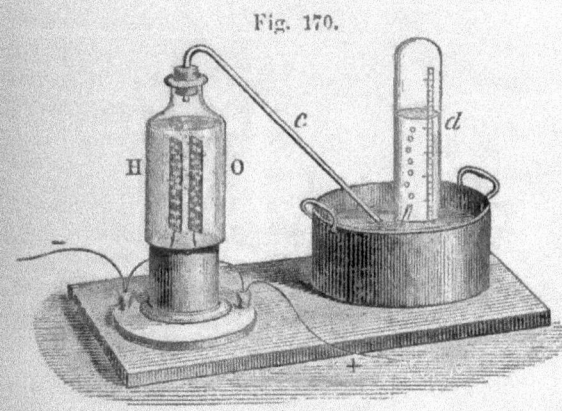

Fig. 170.

The Voltameter.

filled with water. Within the glass cell two platinum plates are arranged, H, connected with the negative pole of the battery, and o, with the positive. The cell is then entirely filled with acidulated water, and also the bent tube, *c*. The instrument is then connected with the battery by means of the wires, and made to form a part of the circuit; the acidulated water in the glass cell immediately begins to be decomposed, and the gases produced are conveyed by the bent tube to the graduated jar, *d*, by which their volume is measured. The volume produced is in proportion to the strength of the current, and the amount of zinc dissolved within the battery, and thus this instrument becomes a measure of voltaic intensity.

382. Electro-Plating and Gilding. A very important application is made of these facts in the arts. It will be recollected that in all the cases of decomposition of metallic solutions mentioned above, the oxide of the metal is deposited around the negative pole, the acid at the positive pole. If, then, any metallic article be attached to the negative wire of the battery, it becomes in effect the pole of the battery, and might be expected to become coated with the metallic oxide in question; and so it would be, if it were not, that at the same time, with the metallic salt, a small portion of the water is also decomposed, and its hydrogen appearing at the negative pole at the same moment with the metallic oxide, decomposes it, unites with the oxygen to form water, and sets the metal free, as in the case of the copper; see *Fig.* 166. The article attached to the negative pole consequently becomes coated with a covering of metal, instead of a metallic oxide. The nature of the metal deposited will depend upon the metallic solution employed. If it be a

---

382. State the principle of electro-plating and gilding.

solution of silver, the article attached to the negative pole will become coated with silver; if it be a solution of gold, with gold; if it be copper, with copper. It is evident, also, that while hydrogen is set free at the negative pole, a corresponding amount of oxygen must escape from the positive pole.

383. Electrotyping. In order, therefore, to coat or gild substances which are good conductors of electricity, with any metal, it is only necessary to attach them to the negative pole of a battery in full operation, and place them in a solution of the metal desired, the positive pole being introduced into the same solution, at a little distance from it. A small battery is quite sufficient, and in general one cup of Bunsen's arrangement will answer for all common purposes. The process is fully represented in *Fig.* 171, where o is the battery; c is the vessel con-

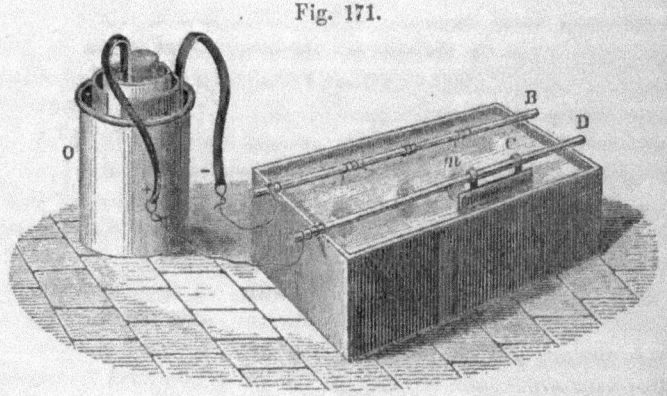

Fig. 171.

Electro-Plating.

taining the metallic solution, which in this case is the sulphate of copper; D is a metallic rod connected with the positive pole, and having a plate of copper suspended from it, and dipping into the liquid; B is another metallic rod, connected with the negative pole of the battery, from which the articles to be covered with copper are suspended. Thus, these articles are made the negative pole of the battery, and the copper plate suspended from D becomes the positive pole. The connections being formed, the sulphate of copper is decomposed into sulphuric acid and the oxide of copper; at the same time, a portion of the water of the solution is decomposed into oxygen and hydrogen. The sulphuric acid and the oxygen are drawn towards

---

383. Describe the electrotype process.

the positive pole, which is the copper plate suspended from D, and the oxygen immediately uniting with it to form the oxide of copper, this is immediately taken up by the sulphuric acid, converted into the sulphate of copper, and then dissolved in the solution, so that just as much copper is thus restored to the solution as is taken from it by the action of the current; and its strength sustained for an indefinite period. On the other hand, the oxide of copper, and hydrogen, are drawn towards the negative pole, which is the article, or articles, suspended from the rod B, and here the hydrogen uniting with the oxygen of the oxide to form water, the metallic copper is deposited. In this manner, exact copies may be made of all metallic articles. If the article be a copper medal, and it be desired to get an exact copy of it, every part, except the face, to be copied, is covered with wax, and it is then suspended from the rod B, in the sulphate of copper solution; it thus becomes completely covered with metallic copper upon the exposed surface; the thickness of the deposit will depend upon the duration of immersion. On removal from the solution, the deposited copper will tightly adhere to the original metal, but it may be separated from it by gently heating with a spirit lamp. The cast thus formed is the reverse of the medal, and if it be desired to obtain a copy in relief, it is only necessary to subject the cast to the same process, by attaching it to the negative pole of the battery, and immersing it in a solution of sulphate of copper. In this manner, faithful copies may be made of all metallic articles, by depositing metals upon them. The finest line engravings may be accurately reproduced. All the copper plates of the coast survey are formed by this process; the originals are never used, but only the copies, and any required number of these may be produced at a small expense. When the articles to be covered are not metallic, it is necessary to cover them with a fine powder which is a good conductor of electricity, and then treat them in the usual manner. The substance most commonly used for this purpose is plumbago, in very fine powder. The electrotype plates from which books are printed, are made by taking an impression in wax, of the original types; covering this plate of wax with a coating of plumbago, and immersing it in a solution of sulphate of copper, with an attachment to the negative pole of a battery. On the positive pole a large plate of copper is suspended, which is gradually dissolved at the same rate as the copper is deposited upon the wax, and the strength of the solution is thus maintained, until the whole plate has disappeared. The powdered wax receives a deposit of copper upon the whole of its surface, and in its finest lines, which gradually increases in thickness until it is strong enough to be separated from the wax, mounted upon wood or metal, and used for printing. The wax may be melted into a new sheet, and applied to another portion of types. This is by no means the only application in the arts. Gilding, silvering, bronzing, may all be accomplished by it, and it has grown to be a very important branch of industry.

384. The protection of the copper sheathing of Ships. By an ingenious application of the same principles the metals can be protected from the action of corrosive liquids in which they may be immersed. Thus, a zinc plate, placed in dilute sulphuric acid, will decompose the water with great rapidity, and itself be quickly oxidated, and finally dissolved. If, however, the plate of zinc be attached to the negative pole of a battery, and thus rendered negatively electric, at the same time that a slip of platinum, attached to the positive pole, is placed in the liquid immediately opposite, it will not decompose the water, will suffer no oxidation, and remain undissolved. The reason is, because the oxygen of the water is itself a negative electric, and therefore repelled from the negative zinc; for the same reason the acid is also repelled. In like manner, copper will rapidly decompose chloro-hydric acid, forming chloride of copper, and finally be itself wholly dissolved; but if the copper be rendered negatively electric, it will remain unaffected by the acid, because chlorine is also a negative electric, and is repelled from a body which is charged with electricity of the same kind. In this way it is possible to protect metals by means of galvanic arrangements from the influence of the most corrosive liquids. Sir H. Davy made an ingenious application of this principle to the protection of the copper sheathing of ships from the action of sea water. Sea water contains in solution a variety of metallic salts, the most important of which is chloride of sodium, or common salt. The chlorine contained in this substance has a very strong affinity for copper, and will attack it with great violence, forming a green chloride of copper, which is at once dissolved by the water, and thus the copper is rapidly wasted. Chlorine, however, is an electro-negative substance, and if the copper sheathing could be rendered also electro-negative, it

---

384. How may the metals be prevented from corrosion by the action of the electro-negative elements, such as oxygen and chlorine? On this principle, how may the copper sheathing of ships be protected? What disadvantages have arisen from this protection?

would be repelled, instead of attracted, and the metal would be perfectly protected from corrosion. This can be done by driving zinc nails into the copper, at proper intervals. The zinc at once becomes electro-positive, attracts the chlorine to itself, and sets on foot an electrical current, which is transferred to the copper; it thus becomes the generating plate of a battery, while the copper becomes the conducting plate. The copper is thus made electro-negative, and tends as strongly to repel the chlorine as the zinc does to attract it. By this arrangement, copper sheathing is completely protected, and kept entirely free from corrosion; but unfortunately, at the same time that the chlorine is repelled, other substances, such as lime and magnesia, being electro-positive in their character, are attracted to the copper. This earthy coating furnishes good points of attachment to sea weeds and shell fish, which soon make the bottom of ships very foul, and greatly impede their progress. It has become necessary, therefore, to discard the invention, and the same end is now partially attained by the use of a kind of brass sheathing, composed of zinc and copper, and called Muntz's yellow metal. On the same principle, metallic structures, such as iron pillars, fences, and the like, may be protected from atmospheric action by the insertion of small bits of zinc, at regular intervals. There are other applications of the same principles possessed of nearly equal interest.

§ III. Electro-Magnetism.

385. Magnetic effects of the Current. The power of lightning in destroying and reversing the poles of a magnet, and in imparting magnetic properties to pieces of iron which did not previously possess them, has been known for a long period, and led to the opinion that similar effects might be produced by the common electrical machine, and the galvanic battery. No results of importance were obtained, however, until the year 1819. In the winter of that year Professor Oersted, of Copenhagen, discovered that if a magnetic needle be brought near a copper wire, connecting the two poles of a battery, and through which the electrical current is passing, the needle is at once violently agitated, deflected from its position, and made to as-

---

385. What effect is produced upon the magnetic needle by a wire carrying the current, placed parallel to, and above, it?

354 THE MAGNETIC NEEDLE DEFLECTED.

sume a position at right angles to the wire. Thus, if the wire be placed upon the magnetic meridian, pointing north and south, the north end connected with the negative pole or zinc plate of the battery, and the south end connected with the positive pole, or the platinum plate of the battery, and the magnetic needle be placed below the wire, it will at once assume a position at right angles to the wire, the north pole moving to the west, and the south pole to the east, as represented in *Fig.* 172. If the needle be placed above the wire, the north pole will move to the east, and the south pole to the west. When the needle is placed in the same horizontal plane with the wire, it attempts to assume a vertical position, the north pole dipping when the wire is to the west of it, and rising when the wire is to the east of it. If the current be reversed, by changing the connections with the battery, and be made to pass from north to south, instead of from south to north, the movements of the needle are all reversed. The explanation given of these movements is, that two magnetic forces are generated by the passage of the current, circulating around the wire in opposite directions, along its whole extent, and at right angles to it; the tendency of one force is to cause the north pole of the needle to revolve around the wire in *one* direction; the tendency of the other is to cause the south pole to revolve in like manner in the *opposite* direction; the magnet, consequently, comes to rest in a position of equilibrium between these two forces, directly across the wire. Besides this *directive* action upon the magnet, the conducting wire also exerts an *attractive* action, as may be shown by suspending a magnetized sewing needle from a silk thread, and causing an electrical current to pass in an horizontal direction by the side of, and very near it. It also exerts an *inductive-magnetic* action, by which soft iron wires, or bars, placed across the conducting wire at right angles, are rendered magnetic as long as the cur-

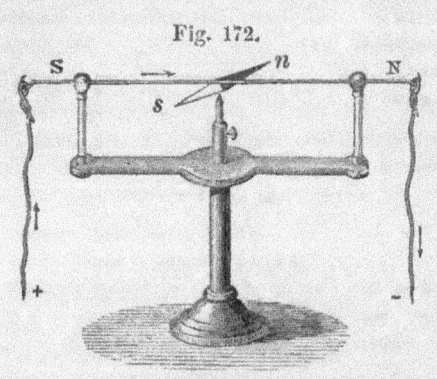

Fig. 172.

Effects of Galvanic Electricity on the Magnetic Needle.

By a wire placed below the needle? If the current be reversed, what is the effect upon the needle? What is the explanation given of these movements? What other magnetic effects are produced by the current?

rent circulates. The action of the conducting wire is, therefore, threefold.

386. What is a Magnet? A magnet is a body which possesses the power of attracting masses of iron, and a few other metallic substances, such as nickel, cobalt, and chromium. They are distinguished into natural and artificial. The natural magnet is an oxide of iron, first found in Magnesia, a district of Asia Minor, and from this has received its name. Artificial magnets are bars, or needles, of tempered steel, which do not naturally possess the properties of a magnet, but have acquired them by friction with another magnet, by the action of electricity, or by percussion in the magnetic meridian. They are more powerful than natural magnets, and possess identical properties. The attractive power of magnets is exercised at all distances, and through all bodies, but decreases with the distance, and varies with temperature; at a red heat, magnets lose their attractive power altogether.

387. The poles of the Magnet. The attractive force of the magnet does not reside equally at all points upon its surface; this may be clearly shown by holding a magnet immediately over iron filings placed upon a sheet of paper, when the filings will be seen to accumulate equally at the ends of the bar, while they will not be attracted at all at the middle; *Fig.* 173. These two ends, at which the force resides, are called the poles of the magnet. Every magnet possesses two poles, as one can not exist without the other. If a magnet be suspended upon a pivot, it will place itself very nearly upon a meridian line, and one pole will invariably point towards the north, and the other towards the south; if it be moved from this position, in a few moments it will resume it, the same pole pointing to the north as before; hence one pole of the magnet is called the north, and the other the south pole.

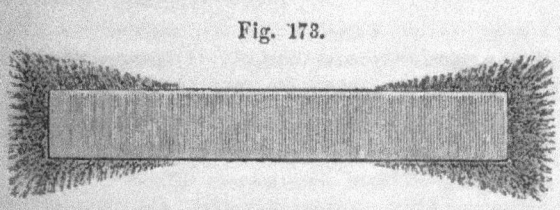

Fig. 173.

The Magnet.

388. The mutual action of the Poles. The two poles at-

---

386. What is a magnet? What is the origin of the name? What are artificial magnets? What is the effect of a red heat on a magnet?—387. Does the attractive force of the magnet reside equally at all points on its surface? What are the poles of the magnet?—388. State the difference between the polar forces of the magnet.

tract iron filings equally, and appear to be identical in their character; but in fact they possess different kinds of magnetism, endowed with properties opposite, but analogous to each other. Thus, if a small magnetic needle, *Fig.* 174, be suspended from a fine thread, and the north pole of a second needle be presented to the north pole of the first, a quick repulsion takes place; but if the same north pole be presented to the south pole of the suspended needle, attraction immediately takes place. The poles, *n* and *s*, are not then identical, since one is repelled, and the other attracted, by the same pole, N, of the magnet held in the hand. If the south pole of the second magnet be in turn presented to the north pole of the first, attraction will take place; and on the other hand, if presented to the south pole of the first, repulsion will ensue. Consequently, we deduce this principle, that magnetic forces of the same kind repel, and those of different kinds attract, each other. These two magnetic forces are always developed at the same time; one can not be produced without the other; they are equal in amount, are opposite in their tendencies, and are capable of exactly neutralizing each other. Forces which exhibit this combination of equal and opposite powers are called polar forces. Electricity is also a polar force, and the analogy between it and magnetism is so complete that it is obvious they must be closely connected.

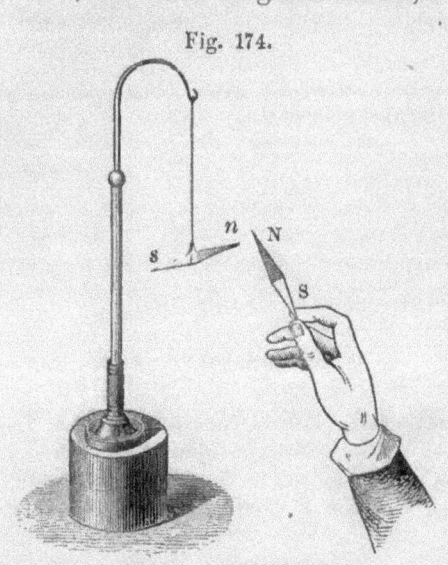

Fig. 174.

Mutual action of Magnetic Poles.

389. The directive action of the Earth upon Magnets. It has been stated that if a magnetic needle be suspended by a thread, or supported upon a pivot, on which it can readily turn, it will oscillate for a time, and finally take a position nearly north and south. If the needle be placed upon a cork, in a

---

What principle do we deduce from these facts? What are polar forces?—389. What is the effect of the earth upon a magnetic needle?

THE ASTATIC NEEDLE.   357

vessel of water, the same thing takes place; it assumes a position north and south, but does not advance either to the north or south. The action of the poles of the earth upon the magnet is not attractive, but *directive*, as though these poles were situated at an immense distance. The earth appears to be a vast magnet, whose poles are situated near the poles of the earth, the north magnetic pole being within the arctic, and the south magnetic pole within the antarctic circle. Consequently, as magnetic poles of the same kind repel, and of different kinds attract, each other, the pole of an artificial magnet which points towards the north pole of the earth must be its true south pole, and the pole which points towards the south pole of the earth its true north pole. *Fig.* 175.

Fig. 175.

The directive action of the Earth.

390. The Astatic Needle. The astatic needle is a magnetic needle, arranged in such a manner that it is no longer under the directive influence of the magnetic poles of the earth, and consequently, will remain fixed in any position in which it may be placed, without tending to point north and south. Two magnetic needles are placed, one beneath the other, and fastened firmly together by a pin, with their poles reversed, i. e., the north pole of the upper needle having the south pole of the lower needle directly beneath it, and the south pole of the upper needle having the north pole of the lower arranged likewise. Consequently, the attraction which the north pole of the earth exerts upon the upper needle is counteracted by the repulsion which it exerts upon the south pole of the needle fixed beneath it; the compound needle is therefore not drawn towards the north; for the same reason, it is not drawn towards the south, but remains indifferently in any position in which it is placed, without at

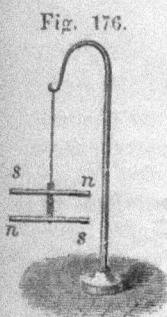

Fig. 176.

The Astatic Needle.

Is the action attractive, or directive? What is the true north pole of the needle? The true south pole?—390. Describe the astatic needle.

the same time losing any portion of its magnetic power; hence its name, derived from the Greek, which means *unsteady*, having no directive tendency.

391. Induction of Magnetism. A powerful magnet has the power of inducing magnetism in magnetizable substances placed near it, in the same way as a highly charged electrified body has the power of inducing electricity in all bodies in its vicinity. Thus, if a piece of iron be brought near the north pole of a powerful magnet, but not touching it, the end of the iron nearest the magnet will be affected with the opposite, and the remote end with the same, magnetism; consequently, the iron being thrown into the opposite magnetic state, will be attracted towards the magnet. This is the cause of all magnetic attraction, and is due to the magnetism induced in the body attracted; in the case of iron filings, each particle becomes magnetized. If, while the piece of iron is under the inductive influence of the magnet, another piece of iron be presented to it, and to this another, these pieces will all be magnetized by induction, with their poles reversed, and be attracted by the first piece; *Fig.* 177. If the magnet be removed, the induced magnetism of all

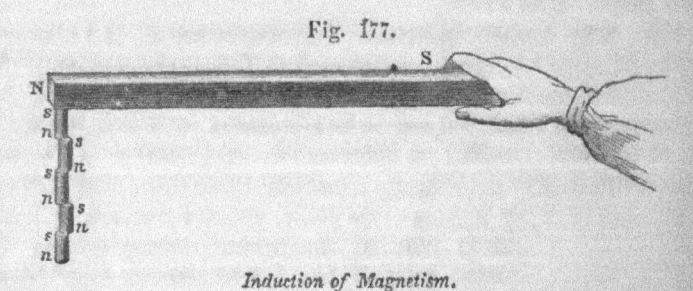

Fig. 177.

Induction of Magnetism.

the pieces of iron is destroyed, and they will fall to the ground; this induction is not prevented by the interposition of unmagnetizable substances between the magnet and the iron; a piece of glass inserted between them will not interfere with the effect.

392. All substances are either attracted or repelled by the Magnet.—Magnetic and Dia-magnetic Bodies. It was formerly supposed that iron was the only substance susceptible of attraction by the magnet; it was afterwards proved that the metals, nickel and cobalt, are also possessed of the same susceptibility, and more recently it has been discovered that all bodies are

---

391. What is meant by the induction of magnetism? How can it be proved?—392. What is the difference between magnetic and diamagnetic bodies? What other metals, besides iron, are susceptible of magnetization?

MAGNETIC AND DIA-MAGNETIC BODIES. 359

affected by the magnet, in some degree, and either attracted or repelled by it. Thus, if, in *Fig.* 178, N and S represent the poles of a powerful horse-shoe magnet, upon which the observer is looking down; the line A, X, connecting the two poles, may be called the axis of the magnetic field, and E, Q, which crosses it at right angles, its equator. If an iron needle be suspended by its centre, above such a magnet, it will take a horizontal direction, parallel to the axis A X, and is said to point axially. But if a stick of phosphorus be suspended between the two poles of the magnet, it will take the equatorial position. E Q, the phosphorus being repelled by each pole to the greatest possible distance; consequently, phosphorus is called a dia-magnetic body. Some of the metals, such as antimony and bismuth, exhibit this dia-magnetic property in a still higher degree. It is even possessed by many substances of an organic nature. In *Fig.* 179, is represented a bar of copper, occupying the equatorial position between the two poles of an electro-magnet, which project upwards through apertures made in the table. While iron is the most highly magnetic of all substances, there are many others not usually esteemed magnetic, which will take the axial position, if brought near the poles of a powerful magnet, such as the red oxide of iron, and even a sheet of writing paper, if rolled into the form of a short cylinder, will usually, owing to the iron or cobalt which it contains, assume a similar direction.

Fig. 178.

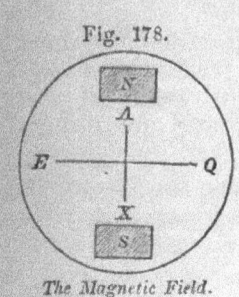

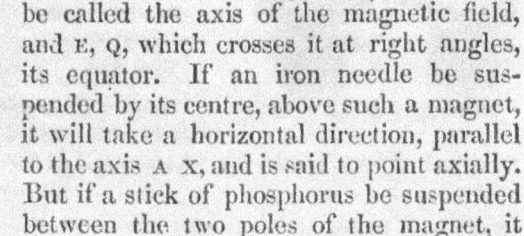

The Magnetic Field.

Fig. 179.

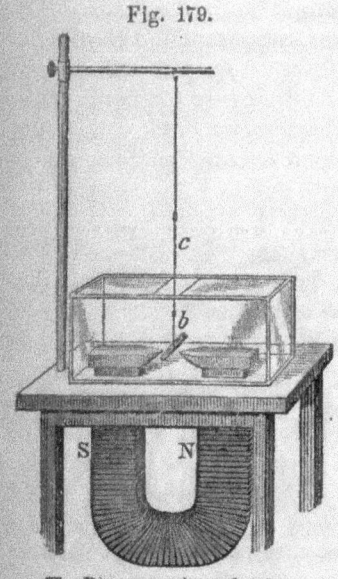

The Dia-magnetism of Solids.

393. The dia-magnetism of Gases. The property of dia-magnetism is not confined to solids and liquids; the gases also

---

What is the axis and the equator of the magnetic field? How can diamagnetism be illustrated by phosphorus and bismuth? By a sheet of writing paper?—393. How can the magnetism and diamagnetism of gases be shown?

Fig. 180.

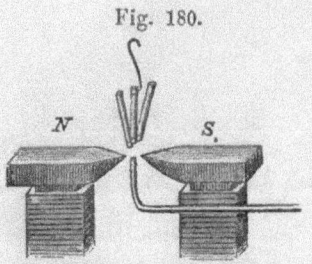

The Dia-magnetism of Gases.

possess it. Thus, if three tubes be arranged in the equator of the magnetic field, as shown in *Fig.* 180, and in each tube a piece of paper, moistened with chloro-hydric acid, be suspended, and another piece of paper, moistened with ammonia, be placed in a bent tube, conveying the gas in question, the gas will become charged with ammoniacal vapor, and as long as the electro-magnet is not brought into action, will pass directly up the centre tube; but as soon as the electro-magnet is in operation, those gases which are dia-magnetic will no longer pass up the centre tube alone, but will enter the side tubes, arranged in the equator of the instrument, and their presence will be made manifest in each tube by the white cloud which is always produced when the fumes of ammonia come into contact with those of chloro-hydric acid. The same fact can also be determined by blowing soap bubbles with the gas in question, and bringing them near the poles of the magnet; if attracted, the gas is magnetic; if repelled, it is dia-magnetic.

394. Oxygen a magnetic substance. By suspending a feebly magnetic glass tube between the magnetic poles, successively in oxygen and *in vacuo*, it has been found that it is less strongly attracted in oxygen than in the exhausted receiver, and on varying the experiment in different ways, it has been proved that oxygen is a decidedly magnetic body. A cubic French metre of oxygen, which is rather more than an English cubic yard, and which ordinarily weighs 22015 grs., if it were condensed until it had a specific gravity equal to that of iron, would act upon a magnetic needle with a force equal to that of a little cube of iron weighing $8\frac{1}{3}$ grs., and the magnetism of oxygen, is to that of iron, as 1 : 2647. The magnetic effect of the oxygen in the air is equal to that of a shell of metallic iron $\frac{1}{250}$ of an inch in thickness, surrounding the entire globe. Oxygen loses its magnetism when strongly heated, and recovers it again when the temperature falls. The diminution of its magnetic intensity as temperature rises, has been thought to explain the diurnal variations of the needle. It has also been ascertained that the

---

394. How can the magnetism of oxygen be proved? To what is this magnetic power equal when compared with that of iron? What is the effect of heat upon it? Is the flame of candles and the electric light magnetic, or dia-magnetic?

EFFECT OF CURRENT ON THE MAGNETIC NEEDLE. 361

flame of candles, and of the electric light, is dia-magnetic when placed between the poles of a powerful magnet.

395. Magnetic and Dia-magnetic Bodies. The following is a list of various substances, arranged in the order of their magnetic and dia-magnetic powers, as determined by Mr. Faraday.

Magnetic.	Dia-magnetic.	
Iron.	Bismuth.	Copper.
Nickel.	Phosphorus.	Water.
Cobalt.	Antimony.	Gold.
Manganese.	Zinc.	Alcohol.
Chromium.	Silico-borate of Lead.	Ether.
Cerium.	Tin.	Arsenic.
Titanium.	Cadmium.	Uranium.
Palladium.	Sodium.	Rhodium.
Crown Glass.	Flint Glass.	Iridium.
Platinum.	Mercury.	Tungsten.
Osmium.	Lead.	Nitrogen.
Oxygen.	Silver.	

396. Reason why a Magnetic Needle assumes a position at right angles to the Conducting Wire. From what has been said, it is evident that the magnetic needle assumes a position at right angles to the wire connecting the two poles of the battery, because of the creation of two magnetic forces circulating around the wire in opposite directions, and at right angles to its length; the north pole of the needle being controlled exclusively by the south magnetic force, and the south pole exclusively by the north magnetic force. A galvanic current can not traverse a wire without generating polar magnetic forces, circulating around it at right angles along its entire length. Thus, in *Fig.* 181, if A, B, represent a wire, through which an electrical current is passing, indicated by the dart, the small arrows indicate one of the magnetic forces, or magnetic currents, as they are sometimes called, which cross it at right angles, and the galvanic current can not be made to traverse such a wire without producing these magnetic forces. Not only does the electrical current generate these polar magnetic forces which cross it at right angles to its length, but it also becomes magnetic itself. This may be proved by the attraction which it exerts upon iron filings when they are brought near it; if the current be broken, the filings immediately fall. These filings are at-

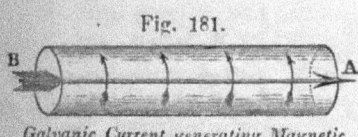

Fig. 181.

Galvanic Current generating Magnetic Force.

---

395. Mention some of the principal magnetic and diamagnetic bodies.—396. What is the reason that the conducting wire affects the magnetic needle? Does the wire itself become magnetic? How can this be proved? Is it possible for the current to traverse a wire without producing magnetism?

16

tracted to the wire by the magnetism which it induces, and as long as they are under its influence they are made temporary magnets, in the same way as they would be, if acted upon by a powerful permanent magnet. See § 391.

397. The galvanic current produces Magnetism.—Electro-magnets. Not only are iron filings thus inductively converted into temporary magnets by the wire, but larger pieces of iron, if brought near the wire, are similarly affected. If a small rod of iron be placed at right angles across the connecting wire, it will become strongly magnetic, and continue so, as long as the electrical current passes; if the connection of the wire with the battery be broken, the magnetism ceases. If the rod be placed in a small glass tube, and the conducting wire, instead of crossing once at right angles, be carried around it several times, forming a spiral coil, so that the electrical current is made to pass several times around the iron rod, its magnetic power will be greatly increased. The extremities of the rod will be the poles of the temporary magnet, and this will be the case even if the extremities of the iron rod project some distance beyond the coil. Such a spiral coil of wire is called a helix, and when wound to the right, constitutes a right-handed helix, *Fig.* 182; and when to the left, a left-handed helix; *Fig.* 183. In the right hand helix, the south pole is at the extremity of the coil, at which the positive electric current enters it; in the left hand helix, the south pole is always at the extremity, by which the current leaves the helix. If the direction of the current be reversed, the poles will also be reversed. It is not necessary to place the rod of iron in a glass tube; if the wire be wound with some good non-conductor of electricity, such as silk, or cotton, so as to compel the electrical current to circulate around the rod, without leaping transversely across the wires, or entering the rod itself, the same end will be attained. Such

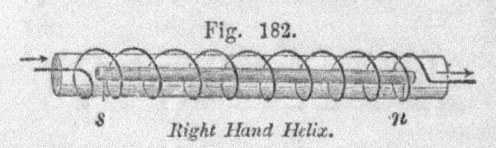

Fig. 182.

s   *Right Hand Helix.*   *n*

Fig. 183.

s   *Left Hand Helix.*   *n*

---

397. How can a rod of iron be made magnetic by the current? What is a right hand helix? A left hand? How are the poles of each arranged? What is the effect upon the poles of reversing the current?

MAGNETISM INDUCED BY THE CURRENT.

a bar of iron, converted into a temporary magnet, by the inductive influence of an electrical current, is called an electro-magnet. If a steel rod be substituted for the soft iron bar, it will become permanently magnetic. The same effect will be produced upon a steel needle placed in the centre of a spiral coil of wire, through which a powerful charge of frictional electricity from a Leyden jar is transmitted. If a wire, carefully wound with fine silk or cotton, and thoroughly coated with shellac dissolved in alcohol, in order to increase its non-conducting power, be wound several times around the iron rod, proceeding regularly from one end to the other and then returning, the magnetic power produced by the circulating current will be greatly increased, and the greater the number of coils, the more powerful is the effect. In *Fig.* 184, is represented a coil of this description, wound into the form of a hollow cylinder, so that the iron rod may be withdrawn at pleasure. If the rod be removed, and the connections established with the battery by means of the binding cups arranged below, it will be found that the ends of the coil have themselves become very strongly magnetic, as shown by their attraction of iron filings. If the rod be now inserted, this will become, by induction, very strongly magnetic, and support quite large pieces of iron brought near the poles; these pieces of iron become themselves possessed of magnetic power, and will support additional pieces, so that quite a long chain of magnets may thus be formed in the manner represented in the figure, in all cases the north pole of one being opposite the south pole of the next. If the connection with the battery be broken, so that the battery current ceases to flow through the coil, the magnetism of the rod, and of all the pieces of iron, is at once destroyed, and the keys fall; if the connection be reestablished, the magnetism is immediately restored, and the keys are again attracted. In this manner, by forming and breaking the connection with the battery, a piece of soft iron may be magnetized and de-magnetized at pleasure. If a magnetic needle be brought near the magnetized rod of a helix, it will be thrown into violent agitation for a few moments, and then have one of its poles strongly attracted towards one of the

Fig. 184.

Magnet, Made and Unmade.

What is the effect of carrying the wire several times around the iron bar? What is an electro-magnet? Describe *Fig.* 184. Is the coil itself made magnetic by the passage of the current? How can an electro-magnet be made and unmade?

poles of the rod. If it be the *north* pole of the needle which is thus attracted, we may know that it points to the *south* pole of the iron rod, and thus the character of its poles may be determined.

398. Molecular movements during the magnetization of Bars. The induction of magnetism, and the cessation of magnetism, are both attended with molecular motion throughout the rod of iron. The rod, on becoming magnetic, acquires a slight increase in length, and suddenly contracts to its former dimensions when the magnetism ceases. If the bar be supported at one end, so as to bend under its own weight, it becomes straightened to a greater or less extent when magnetized. Each time that the bar becomes magnetic, or loses its magnetism, a distinct sound is produced. Finally, the molecular movements, if repeated in quick succession by rapidly making and breaking contact between the helix and the battery, so as quickly to magnetize and de-magnetize the rod, produce an elevation of its temperature, which is entirely independent of the heat produced in the conducting wire by the flow of the electrical current. These facts are possessed of great interest, as connected with the theory of the convertibility of Forces. (See §§ 263 and 264.)

399. The Galvanometer. The degree of movement in a magnetic needle, produced by the passage of an electrical current, is proportioned to the strength of that current, and may be used, therefore, to measure its intensity. An instrument constructed for this purpose, is called a Galvanometer. Its use is restricted to the measurement of currents of feeble intensity, because, when the current reaches a certain degree of strength, the needle immediately assumes a position at right angles to the wire, and flies at once to the farthest point to which it can go, and it is evident that it can measure no degree of strength in the electrical current beyond that which will drive it into this position. For the measurement, however, of currents of electricity of low intensity, this instrument is invaluable. It is of two kinds, the common, and the astatic galvanometer; in the former, a common magnetic needle is employed; in the latter, an astatic needle. In the common galvanometer, instead of having the wire connecting the two poles of the battery pass once directly above or below the magnetic needle, it is bent, and carried first beneath the needle, and then brought back above

---

398. Describe the molecular movements which take place during the magnetization of bars? What effect is produced upon the temperature of the bar by rapid magnetization and demagnetization?—399. Describe the common galvanometer.

THE ASTATIC GALVANOMETER. 365

Fig. 185.

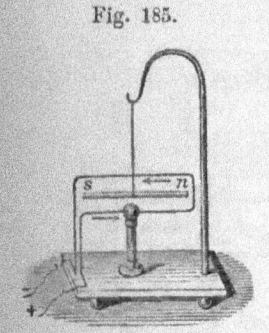

The Common Galvanometer.

it, as represented in *Fig.* 185; in this manner, the effect of the current upon the needle is doubled, and its sensitiveness to the passage of very feeble currents greatly increased. In the most perfect form of the instrument the wire is carried, not simply once around the magnetic needle, but several times, so as to constitute a longitudinal coil, within which the needle plays freely. When the instrument is to be used, it is placed, with the coil and the needle, in the magnetic meridian; the connection is then formed, and the electrical current transmitted; the needle is at once deflected to the east, or west, as the case may be, and more, or less, according to the strength of the current; when the current exceeds a certain strength, the needle assumes a position at right angles to the coil, and ceases to measure any additional degrees of intensity.

400. The Astatic Galvanometer. In the common galvanometer, the needle, when deflected by the electrical current, evidently moves in opposition to the magnetism of the earth, which tends to keep it in the magnetic meridian, and the distance to which it moves is not, therefore, a correct indication of the real strength of the current, but diminished by the amount of the magnetic attraction of the earth. If this attraction be neutralized, its sensitiveness to the influence of the electrical current is greatly increased. This is accomplished by the use of the astatic needle, which, as has been shown, (§ 390,) is constructed in such a way as to be free from this influence, in consequence of the counteracting influence of opposite poles. The conducting wire is carried, as in the last case, first under, and then above, the lower needle; *Fig.* 186. Such a needle is indifferent to the magnetism of the earth, and will remain without change in any position in which it may be placed; in practice, however, it is arranged so as to tend slightly to occupy a north and

Fig. 186.

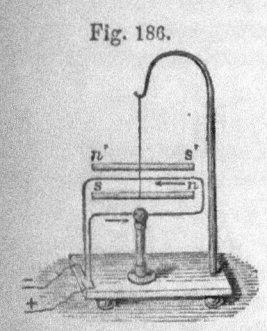

The Astatic Galvanometer.

---

400. Describe the astatic galvanometer.

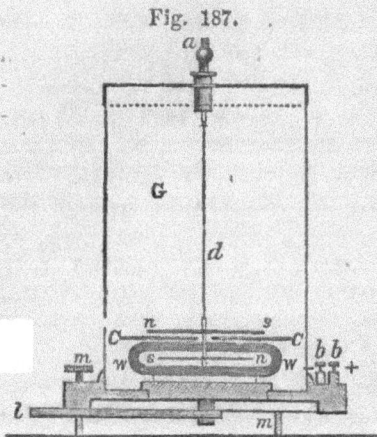

366 LIQUID PART OF CIRCUIT EXERTS MAGNETIC ACTION.

Fig. 187.

The Astatic Galvanometer, with Coil of Wire.

south direction, in order that it may possess a fixed point from which its motion may be measured. This galvanometer is represented in section, in *Fig.* 187; G is a glass case, protecting the instrument from dust, and currents of air; d is a fibre of silk, by which the needle is suspended; $n\ s,\ s\ n$, represent the compound needle with reversed poles; c, c, is a graduated copper plate, to mark the movement of the upper needle; w, w, is the coil of wire; b, b, are the binding cups, for making connections; m, m, are screws for leveling; and l, a small lever for adjusting the position of the needle upon the graduated copper plate. Such an instrument is sensitive to the feeblest currents of electricity, and will detect that which is produced by two bits of zinc and platinum wire, not half an inch in length, placed in acidulated water. This instrument is invaluable for the measurement of small degrees of heat, as well as of electricity, as we shall see hereafter.

401. The liquid part of the voltaic circuit acts upon the Magnetic Needle. That the electrical current, in every part of its course, acts upon the magnetic needle, i. e., in the liquid within the battery, as well as in the wire connecting the poles, may be beautifully seen in *Fig.* 188. A needle, n, s, is suspended over a dish of acidulated water; on one side of this dish a zinc plate, z, is placed, and on the other a platinum plate, P; the needle must be placed so that one of its poles point to one plate, and the other pole to the other. If the two plates be now connected by a wire, the needle will be deflected, and will place itself nearly parallel to the plates.

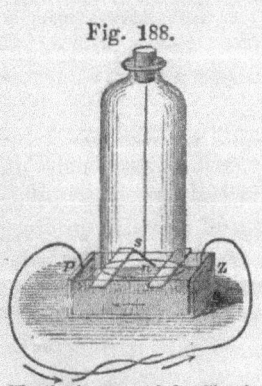

Fig. 188.

The liquid part of the Circuit magnetic.

---

401. Show that the liquid part of the circuit acts upon the magnetic needle.

THE LAWS OF ELECTRO-MAGNETISM. 367

402. The laws of Electro-magnetism. The following laws have been established in regard to the production of magnetism by the electrical current, so long as the battery current is maintained of uniform strength. 1st. The magnetism induced in any given rod of iron is proportioned to the number of coils of insulated wire which are wound upon the rod; and it makes no difference whether the coils are uniformly distributed over the whole length of the rod, or accumulated towards its two extremities. 2d. The diameter of the coils which surround the rod does not influence the result, provided the current be of uniform strength, the effect of increase of distance of the coil from the bar being compensated by the increase of effect produced by the additional length of the wire. 3d. The thickness of the wire has no effect upon the result. 4th. The energy of the magnetism is proportioned to the strength of the current. 5th. The retentive power of the magnet increases as the square of the intensity of the magnetism. 6th. The intensity of the magnetism is proportioned to the surface which the rod exposes; and in cylindrical rods is as the square of the weight; bundles of separate wires expose a larger surface than a solid rod, and hence are susceptible of a higher amount of magnetism than a solid bar of equal weight. 7th. The employment of long rods possesses this advantage over short rods, that the neutralizing influence of the two poles upon each other is lessened. 8th. The increase of magnetic energy by the increase in the strength of the electric current, proceeds up to a certain point, but there is a limit to the amount of magnetic force which can be developed in iron, although the amount of electric action may be indefinitely increased.

403. Ampère's theory of Magnetism. Ampère's theory of magnetism is, that in every magnet there are currents of electricity circulating around it at right angles to a line joining the two poles, *Fig.* 189, and that these currents are the source of the magnetic force. In the ordinary magnetic needle, which is pointing north and south, these electrical currents ascend on the western side, and descend on the eastern. This theory is founded upon the magnetic properties possessed by a helix, through which a current of electricity is circulating. If a

Fig. 189.

Ampere's Theory of Magnetism.

---

402. State the laws of electro-magnetism.—403. State Ampere's theory of magnetism.

AMPERE'S THEORY OF MAGNETISM.

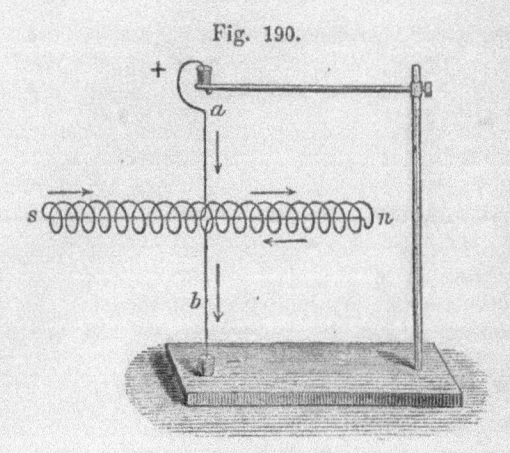

Fig. 190.

The Magnetism of a Wire Helix carrying the Current.

simple helix of thin wire be freely suspended in the manner represented in *Fig.* 190, by a hook dipping into a cup containing mercury, and supported at the lower end in a similar cup of mercury, as soon as the electrical current is made to circulate in a downward direction, the helix will acquire magnetic properties, as represented in the figure, and assume a north and south position; if suspended upon a point, it will assume a position parallel to the dipping needle. The helix will also be subject to attraction and repulsion by the poles of another helix, similarly mounted, and in short, exhibit all the properties of a common bar magnet; *Fig.* 191. Hence the supposition that the common magnet is nothing but an iron bar, around which a similar current of electricity is continually circulating. The cause of these currents is not known. The magnetism of the earth is supposed to be produced by currents of electricity circulating continually around it from east to west, perpendicular to the magnetic meridian; these are thought to be thermo-electric currents, due to the variations of temperature, resulting from the successive presence of the sun upon different parts of the surface of the globe from east to west, and by their circulation they produce the north and south

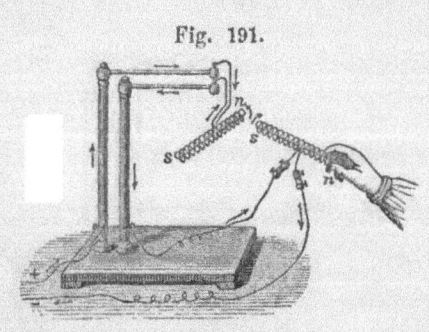

Fig. 191.

Two Magnetic Helices.

On what is this theory founded? Describe the movements of a helix carrying the current. Show how two mounted helices, carrying the current, affect each other. Explain the magnetism of the earth in Ampere's theory. Explain how the electrical currents of the earth circulate from east to west, while those of the magnet circulate from west to east.

magnetic poles of the earth, and give a fixed direction to the magnetic needle of the compass. That these currents circulate from east to west, while those of the ordinary magnet circulate from west to east, (see *Fig.* 189,) is explained by the fact, that the north magnetic pole of the earth really corresponds with the south pole of the ordinary magnet; and if the south pole of the ordinary magnet be turned towards the north, it will be seen that the currents, in this case, *Fig.* 189, really flow from east to west, just as in the case of the earth.

404. The magnetic effect of the wire carrying the galvanic current accounted for by Ampere's Theory. It has been found that when two wires are freely suspended near each other, and galvanic currents are transmitted through them, the wires will *repel* each other, if the currents pass in *opposite* directions, but they will *attract* each other if the currents be in the *same* direction. If the two wires, moreover, through which the current is passing in the same direction, be not exactly parallel, but cross each other at an angle, they will tend to place themselves in parallel lines. Now if it be granted that, in every straight magnet, electrical currents are continually circulating in a direction at right angles to a line joining the magnetic poles, we see plainly the reason why a magnet tends to place itself at right angles to a wire connecting the poles of the battery, and carrying the galvanic current, viz., that by such a movement the electrical currents in the wire, and in the magnet, assume a direction parallel to each other. Let P Q, in *Fig.* 192, represent a wire carrying the galvanic current in the direction of the arrow, and let N indicate the north pole of a bar magnet, around which electrical currents are supposed to be circulating in the same direction as in the wire; according to the above theory, these electric currents will necessarily tend to arrange themselves parallel to each other, and the magnet assume a position at right angles to the wire. On the other hand, if the magnet, N, be fixed in an upright position, so that it can not move, and the wire, P, Q, be suspended

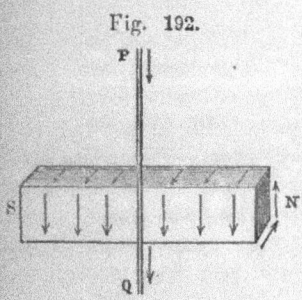

Fig. 192.

The magnetic influence of the Wire explained.

---

404. When the galvanic current is transmitted through the wires in opposite directions, what effect is produced? If in the same direction? If the two wires in the last case be not exactly parallel, what effect is produced? How does this explain, according to Ampere's theory, the effect of the wire on the magnetic needle?

16*

THE MAGNETIC EFFECT OF THE CURRENT.

freely parallel to it, as soon as the galvanic current begins to circulate from P to Q, the wire will tend to move, and assume a position at right angles to the magnet. Thus, the action of the magnet and the wire is reciprocal; they both tend equally to move into such a position, in reference to each other that the electric currents in both will be parallel, and that one, of the two, will actually move, which is the least permanently fixed. That the wire carrying the current does actually move, so as to adjust itself to the magnet, may be shown by the apparatus represented in *Fig.* 193. Let a plate of zinc, Z, be connected by a wire with the copper plate, C, and both be suspended in a little glass vessel containing acidulated water, which, by the aid of a piece of cork, D, is made to float in a vessel of water. In this case, the galvanic current is circulating, as indicated by the arrows, from west to east. If now the north pole of a permanent magnet be presented to the wire, as its electrical currents are also circulating from west to east, and are parallel to those of the loop, the little battery will maintain its position, the only effect being, that it will be attracted by the magnet, and finally place itself midway between its two poles; but if the south pole of the magnet be presented to it, the electrical currents of which are circulating from east to west, in the reverse direction from those of the wire, the floating battery will first be repelled from the magnet, then turned completely around, until the galvanic current circulates in the same direction as in the magnet, from east to west, and the two become parallel, and finally will be attracted as before, until it occupies a position midway between the two poles. If the magnetism of the earth be produced, as suggested in the last

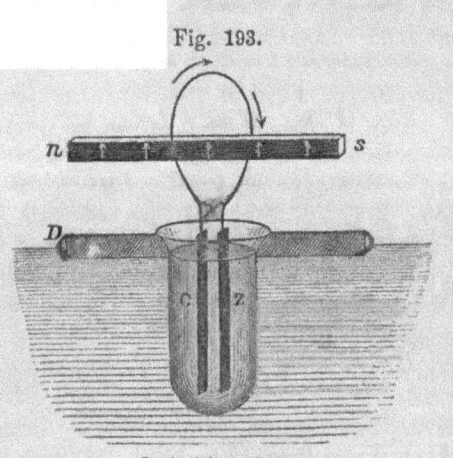

Fig. 193.

De la Rive's Ring.

What effect is produced upon a wire carrying the current, when freely suspended parallel to a powerful fixed magnet? What effect is produced upon the magnet if freely suspended parallel to a fixed wire carrying the current? Prove this by De la Rive's ring, *Fig.* 193.

article, by thermo-electric currents circulating around it from east to west, perpendicular to the magnetic meridian, it is evident that a wire, carrying the galvanic current, if freely suspended, ought to arrange itself, according to the above principles, parallel to these currents, and at right angles to the magnetic meridian. This is found to be the case, and it constitutes a remarkable confirmation of the truth of Ampère's theory. If the curved wire, *Fig.* 194, be suspended from mercury cups,

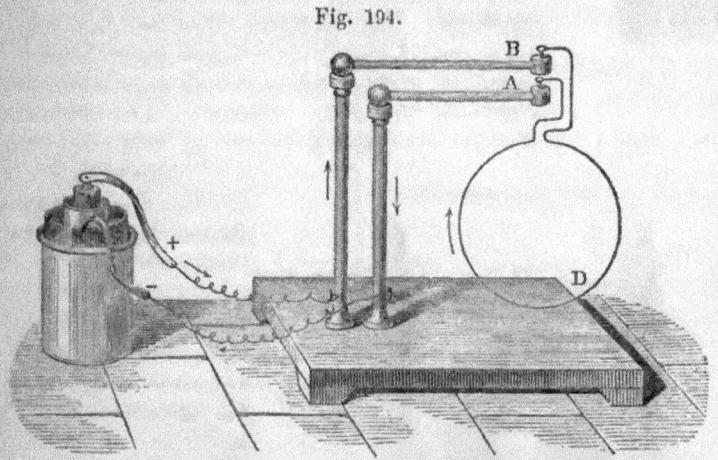

Fig. 194.

Effect of the magnetism of the Earth upon the wire carrying the Current.

so that it can move freely, and be turned so that its plane coincides with the magnetic meridian, it will remain in that position until a connection is formed with the battery, and a current passed through it. When this takes place, it will be seen to turn slowly around the pivots, so as to take a position at right angles to the magnetic meridian, and parallel to the thermo-electric currents supposed to be circulating from east to west. It will turn in such a direction that the current in the lower part of the hoop will also be from east to west. Other rotations, of a similar kind, may be explained upon the same theory, but it is not necessary to pursue the subject farther. The main fact is, that the galvanic current, traversing a wire, produces magnetic forces on lines at right angles to its length, and induces magnetism in a bar of soft iron placed across it perpendicularly.

Explain *Fig.* 194. What is the main fact?

372   AND THE MAGNET RECIPROCAL.

Fig. 195.

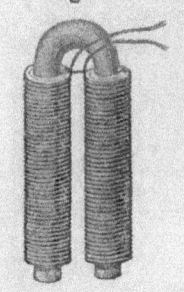

Horse Shoe Electro-Magnet.

405. The most powerful form of Electro-Magnets.—Horse-Shoe Magnets. By increasing the number of coils upon a straight rod of iron, its magnetic power may be indefinitely increased. But the best mode of arranging magnets of this kind is to bend the iron bar into the form of a horse-shoe, as shown in *Fig.* 195, and then to wind it with copper wire, well covered with cotton, or silk thread, and thoroughly insulated. The two poles can thus be brought very near to each other, and their combined magnetic power, concentrated upon the same object at the same moment. The two arms must both be wound in the same direction, in order that their effect may coincide and produce but two poles, one at each extremity of the curved bar. As soon as a connection is formed with the battery, the curved bar becomes a very powerful magnet, with its north pole at the end where the electrical current enters, and the south pole, at the end where it issues, as shown in *Fig.* 196, and will raise a very heavy weight; but as soon as the connection with the battery is broken, the magnetic power is destroyed, and the weight falls with a crash. Magnets have been constructed in this form which would suspend 2,000 or 3,000 lbs., and

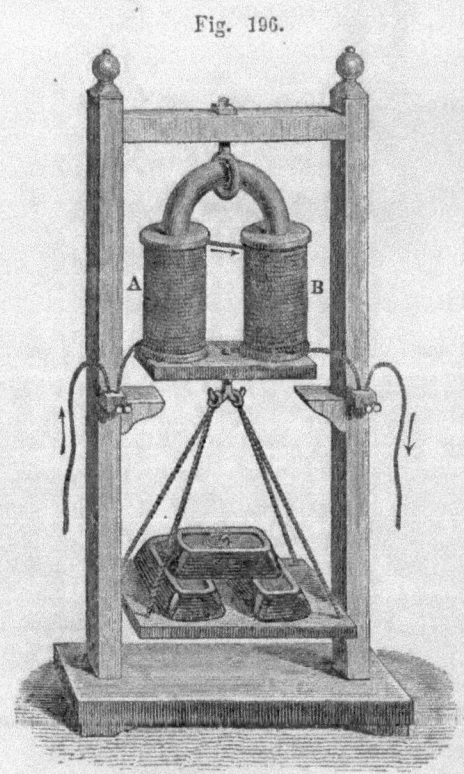

Fig. 196.

Large Electro-Magnet.

405. What is the most effective form of the electro-magnet? What effects have been produced by powerful magnets of this kind?

CURVED ELECTRO-MAGNETS. 373

in some cases 10,000 lbs. By making and then breaking the current circulating around such an electro-magnet, we can bring into play or annihilate at once this immense force. The iron bar below the poles is called the armature of the magnet, and the effect is very greatly increased if it also consists of an electro-magnet, inverted, with poles opposite to those in the upper magnet, and magnetized by the same current. As soon as the connection is formed with the battery, these two electro-magnets rush together with great power, and with a current of moderate intensity, are capable of supporting a weight of several tons. It has also been found that the power is greatly increased, if the helix, instead of being made of a continuous wire, be formed of several wires of limited length, each having its own connection with the battery. An electro-magnet, constructed on this principle, can be made to lift more than a ton with a single cylinder battery of small size. The same principle is well illustrated by what is called the magic circle, represented in *Fig.* 197. Two semi-circles are made of a stout bar of soft iron, and well fitted together so as to form a circle, and include a small helix of wound wire, II, the two ends of which are to be connected with the poles of a small battery. When the connection is made, it will be difficult to pull the semi-circles apart, and a very considerable weight may be raised; but the instant the connection is broken, the semi-circles fall apart of themselves.

Fig. 197.

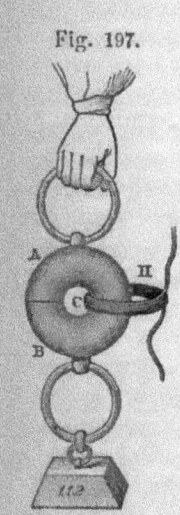

Magic Circle.

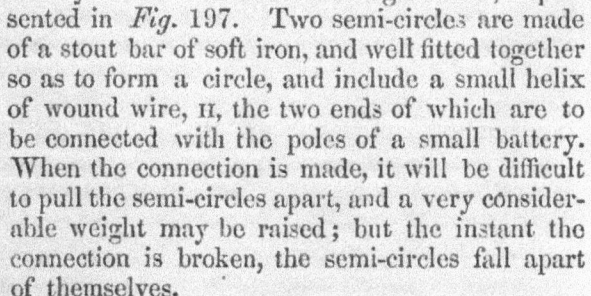

406. The Magnetic Telegraph. Advantage is taken of this power to make and to unmake a magnet, by means of transmitting and breaking a current of electricity, in the construction of the magnetic Telegraph. This is the most important of the uses which have been made of galvanic electricity, and it deserves a minute description. The electric telegraph consists of three parts, viz.: 1st, the battery, or source of electric power; 2d, the wire for the transmission of the current; and 3d, the electro-magnetic instrument for making the signals. 1st. The battery. Any form of the galvanic battery may be employed; but the most common form is Daniell's constant battery. Two batteries are required in order to establish telegraphic commu-

Describe the magic circle.—405. What is the magnetic telegraph?

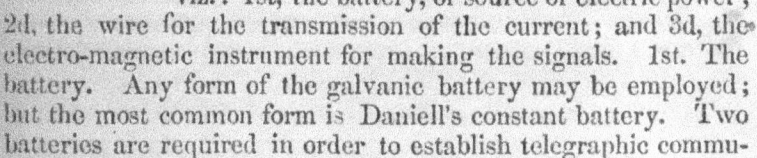

nication in both directions between two places, one at each end of the line. 2d. The wire. There must be a wire extending between the two places, in order to convey the current. This wire is connected with either pole of the battery, and is then carried upon posts, 15 or 20 feet in height, to the distant place. It is usually made of copper or iron, and is attached to the posts by some non-conducting substance. Sometimes it is insulated by a suitable covering and buried in the ground, but it is preferable to carry it through the air, on account of the facility with which breaks may be discovered and repaired. When it reaches the distant place, it is connected with an electro-magnet, which then becomes part of the line, and on leaving the electro-magnet, is conveyed to a large iron plate, buried in a moist spot in the ground, and there terminates. The electrical current, starting from the positive pole of the battery, traverses the wire to the distant place, circulates around the electro-magnet, then passes to the iron plate, and thence through the earth, back to the negative pole of the battery, and thus the circuit is made complete. It was at first supposed that a second wire was required to bring the current back from the distant point, after it had passed through the electro-magnet, in order that a connection might be formed with the opposite pole of the battery; but it was afterwards ascertained that the earth would answer as well as a second metallic wire, the great extent of conducting area which it exposes compensating for its feeble conducting power. In this manner a current is made to pass to any distant town, and to excite magnetism in an electro-magnet as soon as the wire is connected with either pole of the galvanic battery; and then when the connection with the battery is broken, this current can be made to cease, and the electro-magnet at the distant place de-magnetized. By this arrangement it is evident that a magnet can be made and unmade at any place, however distant, by simply making or breaking the connection between the wire and the battery. 3d. The instrument. Having now the means of creating a magnet at the point with which we wish to communicate, we have the means of producing motion, and giving signals. Two instruments are required, one at each end of the line, for the purpose of receiving messages from both directions, constructed on the following plan. Let an armature, consisting of a piece of soft iron, be suspended from one end of a

---

What are the three essential parts of the telegraph? How many batteries are required? How many wires? How does the electrical current return from the distant place? How many instruments are required?

THE LINE. 375

lever, about one-tenth of an inch above the poles of an electro-magnet, placed firmly upon a pedestal, and with its two arms projecting upwards, in the manner of the letter U. It is obvious that, when the current is circulating, this armature will be drawn to the magnet, and that the opposite end of the lever will be correspondingly elevated. If a steel point be attached to the upper side of the distant end of the lever, and a piece of paper be fastened firmly within one-tenth of an inch of it, a dot will be made upon the paper whenever the armature is drawn down, and the steel point flies up. When the connection with the battery is broken by the operator, at the place from which the message is transmitted, the armature is released, and the distant end of the lever falls. As soon as the connection is formed again, the steel point again flies up and strikes the paper a second time. If the paper, instead of being stationary, is in motion, and carried steadily along upon a roller, the second dot will not coincide with the first, and if the steel point be pressed for some minutes against it, a long mark will be formed. Thus the operator at the other end of the line has the means of impressing dots, and broken or continuous lines, upon paper, at the place to which the message is to be sent, each one of which may be made to represent a letter, and their combinations, words and sentences. The return message requires a similar arrangement; first, there must be a battery; for the wire, the original wire may be employed, disconnected from the electro-magnet just employed, and connected with the positive pole of the battery at that end of the line; then there must be an electro-magnet at the first place, which must be connected with the line on the one hand, and on the other, with an iron plate, buried in the ground. The operator to whom the original message was sent, must have the means of sending an electrical current back to the electro-magnet at the first place, and then establishing a connection between it and the ground, so that it may return to him through the earth, and he replies by making and breaking the connection between the wire and the battery under his control. Thus the electrical current is made to pass to the first place, there impress dots and lines on paper, in the manner already described, then descend to the iron plate, and so return through the earth to the opposite pole of the second battery. This is an outline of the system known as Morse's telegraph. A sketch of it is given in *Fig.* 198; c, z, represents the bat-

---

Explain the principle on which they are constructed.

THE INDICATOR.

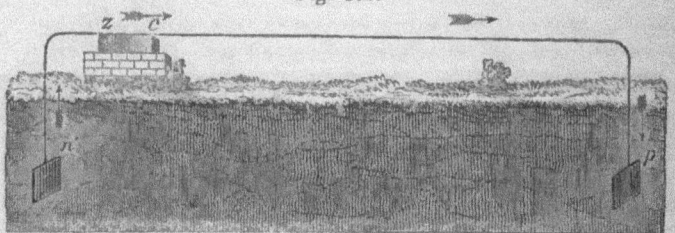

Fig. 198.

Current passing through the Earth.

tery; n and p, the iron plates; the arrows, the course of the current. There are other systems, but the principle is the same in all, the chief difference consisting in the arrangement of the electro-magnetic instrument.

407. Morse's Electro-Magnetic Indicator. In *Fig.* 199, is given an exact representation of the instrument used for mak-

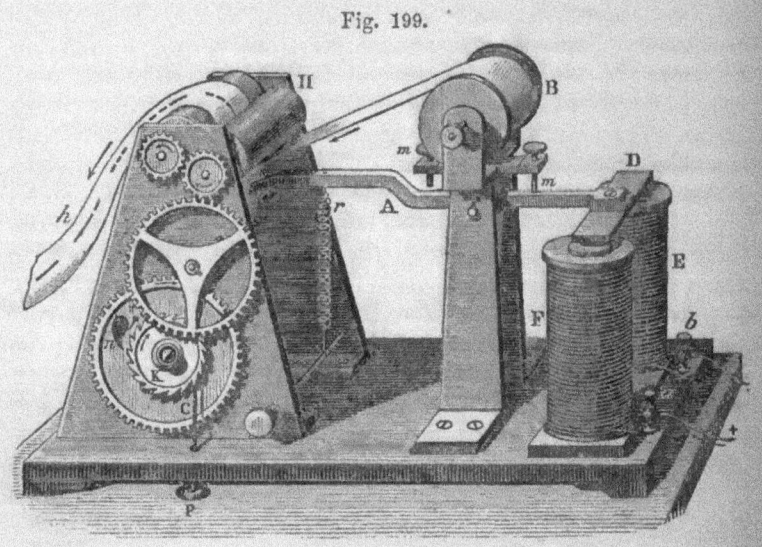

Fig. 199.

Morse's Telegraphic Indicator.

ing the signals. E represents the electro-magnet which is made and unmade by forming and breaking the electrical connection at the opposite end of the telegraphic line. The connection between the instrument and the main wire is formed at the points

---

Explain *Fig*. 198.—407. Describe Morse's indicator.

THE MANIPULATOR. 377

a and b; a is connected with the wire bringing the message, b with the iron plate buried in the ground. D is a piece of soft iron, which is drawn down upon the poles of the magnet whenever the circuit is completed, and is raised again, whenever the current is broken, by the spring r attached to the opposite end of the lever A; m, m, are two screws for regulating the play of this lever. At the extreme end of A, is a sharpened point which, when D is drawn down by the completion of the circuit, strikes against the band of paper upon the under side of the roller, H. This band of paper is continually moved forward by means of clock work carried by the weight, P. If the electrical circuit be formed, and then instantaneously broken by the operator at the station from which the message is sent, the sharp point merely strikes the paper, and is immediately withdrawn by the spring, r, leaving only a dot behind it; but if the circuit be maintained for an appreciable interval, the point, remaining longer in contact with the paper, leaves a line or mark behind it. Thus a long continuous, or broken line, may be produced, or a succession of dots; and a set of different signals constructed, corresponding with the letters of the alphabet. B is a roller, around which the band of paper is wound. With this instrument it is necessary to translate the signals that are formed into the letters which they represent; but instruments of a much more complicated character have been constructed, in which the message is recorded in printed letters. The instrument for accomplishing this, was invented by Mr. House, and is a wonderfully ingenious piece of mechanism. Mr. Bain has invented a telegraphic system, in which no electro-magnet is used, but only the chemical influence of the current operating upon paper prepared with cyanide of potassium.

408. The Telegraphic Manipulator and Morse's Alphabet. The instrument by which the message is transmitted to the distant place, is called the Manipulator. It consists of a wooden stand, *Fig.* 200, upon which is a metallic lever, a, b, turning upon a horizontal axis; L is a wire communicating with the line; B, a wire forming a connection with the local battery; and A, a wire connected with the iron plate in the ground. At x, there is a spring, by which the lever is raised and prevented from touching the metallic button under it; and so long as this is the case, there is no connection between the local battery and the line, and consequently no flow of the current to the distant place; but there is a connection with the local indicator, and,

---

408. Describe Morse's manipulator and alphabet.

Fig. 200.

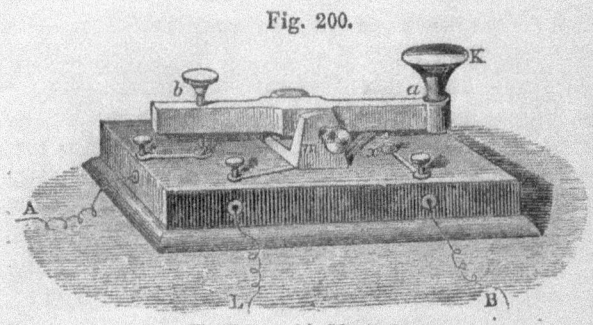

The Telegraphic Manipulator.

through it, with the line and the distant battery on the one hand, and with the iron plate, or the ground, on the other, so that the instrument, in this state, is always in a suitable condition for *receiving* a message. When it is desired to transmit a message, pressure is applied to the wooden knob, and the lever brought down upon the metallic button connected with the local battery, B, when a current immediately circulates through the point x, into the lever, then through m, into the line, and continues as long as pressure is applied upon the knob. Thus, by the depression and elevation of the knob, K, a succession of dots and broken lines may be impressed upon paper in the Indicator at the other end of the line, and it is only necessary to give these combinations a definite meaning. The alphabet adopted by Morse is represented in the following table.

A	·—	J	—·—·	S	···
B	—···	K	—·—	T	—
C	··—·	L	——	U	··—
D	—··	M	——	V	···—
E	·	N	—·	W	·——
F	·—··	O	· ·	X	·—··
G	——·	P	·····	Y	·· ··
H	····	Q	··—··	Z	··· ·
I	··	R	· ··	&	· ···

In this manner words and sentences can be arranged, care being taken to leave a space between each letter. During the process of transmission a continual clicking proceeds from the armature of the Indicator where the message is received, and so clear and definite are these sounds to the practised ear, that the message can be interpreted by these sounds alone, without having recourse to the paper, and in many telegraph offices no other Indicator is employed than an electro-magnet, and movable armature, the pen and paper being dispensed with. The same manipulator, when not used to transmit messages, is employed for their reception; the current from the distant place enters by

THE RELAY.   379

the wire, L, passes through m, to the metallic lever, thence through b, to the wire A, and by it is transmitted to the Indicator.

409. The Relay. In describing the Indicator, we have supposed that the current, after traversing the line, entered directly into the electro-magnet, and worked the armature; but when the current has proceeded a few miles, it can not act with sufficient force upon the electro-magnet to communicate the message. It can only be used to establish a communication between a fresh battery at the place where the message is sent, and the Indicator. The current then, instead of entering directly into the Indicator, is carried into another instrument, called the Relay, *Fig.* 201, enters the electro-magnet, E, through the

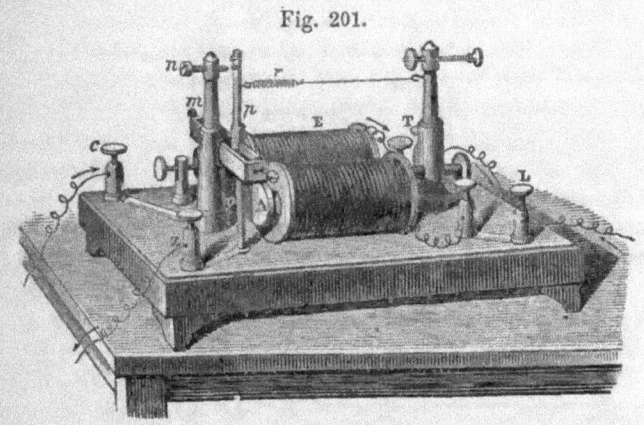

Fig. 201.

The Telegraphic Relay.

binding screw, L, and after traversing the coils, descends into the earth by the binding screw, T, and returns back to the battery from which it started. Each time that a current passes over the line, and traverses the electro-magnet, E, it attracts an armature, A, which is suspended from a horizontal axis, and is extended up into a vertical rod, p. Whenever the armature, A, is drawn towards the electro-magnet, it drives the lever, p, in the opposite direction, against a button, n; as soon as p touches n, a powerful current from the positive pole of a fresh battery placed beneath the table, and not seen in the figure, enters at c, passes up the pillar, m, to n, then down p, to o, and from that to the binding cup, z, whence it flows

---
409. Describe the arrangement and uses of the Relay.

to the electro-magnet of the Indicator, where it records the message in the usual manner, and thence returns to the negative pole of the supplemental battery. Thus, whenever the electro-magnet of the Relay is excited, however feebly, by the current of the line, the electro-magnet of the Indicator is also excited for the same length of time, by the current of the fresh battery, and all the feeble signals of the first electro-magnet are powerfully repeated by the second, and with sufficient force to transmit the message. As soon as the electro-magnet, E, ceases to act, the armature, A, is released, the spring, r, draws p away from n, and the current of the second battery ceases to circulate through the electro-magnet of the Indicator. With a battery of 25 of Grove's elements, the current is strong enough at 100 miles from its starting point to excite the electro-magnet of the Relay, and bring into operation the second battery, by which the Indicator is set in motion, and the message recorded. For a longer distance, a new current must be thrown into the line. This new current may be introduced at any station, from a battery of 20 or 30 elements, provided for the purpose, by connecting the wire from its positive pole with a metallic pillar placed immediately below the armature, D, *Fig.* 199, but not touching it, except when the armature is drawn down; when this takes place, the current enters the armature, and passes directly from it to the wire of the line, which carries it on to the following post. Thus, with every signal which is formed by the Indicator, a corresponding amount of electricity, of greater strength, from a fresh battery, is sent down the line, and so the despatch is transmitted from post to post. The battery used for this purpose is distinct from that used in connection with the Relay just described. The use of local batteries, and the restoration of the strength of the main current by supplemental batteries, seems to be due to Prof. Henry of the Smithsonian Institute. As messages are now generally interpreted by sound alone, the telegraphic Indicator, *Fig.* 199, is seldom employed except in small offices, and in place of it a simple electro-magnet with movable armature is substituted, arranged in such a manner as to intensify the sounds, and called the Sounder; this instrument is connected with the Relay in the same manner as the Indicator, by which its connection with the local battery is established, as already described.

Why is a supplemental battery required? What instrument is generally substituted in place of the Indicator? How does the operator send a message? State the rate of transmission by the Morse instrument. Why does the telegraph depend upon the use of constant batteries?

THE TRANSMISSION OF MESSAGES. 381

It will be noticed that the telegraphic wire and the earth, together form an immense electrical circuit, having a powerful galvanic battery included in it: one battery alone may be used to actuate the circuit, which may be placed at either end of the line or at any intermediate point, or several batteries, if one be found insufficient, care only being taken that their poles all point in the same direction. The telegraphic line, with its batteries and instruments, when in complete working order and prepared to transmit messages, constitutes a *closed circuit*, through the whole of which the electrical current is freely circulating, with the electro-magnets all actuated and their armatures drawn down tightly upon their poles. In order to send a message, the operator commences with breaking this circuit by applying pressure to his manipulator: this breaks the circuit in every instrument, and releases the armatures throughout the entire line: he then completes the circuit for a longer or shorter time, by removing the pressure from his manipulator, and thereby re-attracting the armature of his Indicator, an effect which is also repeated in every instrument upon the whole line: in this manner he produces a telegraphic letter, and by a succession of similar operations forms words and sentences, which are of necessity repeated in every instrument, unless the line is purposely broken and the current sent back through the earth at some nearer point. The Morse system is almost universally used in the United States, and more extensively in Europe than any other. In England, Cooke and Wheatstone's single or double-needle telegraph is commonly employed. The ordinary rate of transmission upon the Morse instrument is about 1,000 words an hour, although it can be worked as high as 1,500: upon the Needle instrument it is about 900. No electric telegraph could be put into actual operation without the use of constant batteries: these are of comparatively late invention, that of Daniell's not dating farther back than 1836, and Grove's about a year later. All previous batteries attained their maximum intensity in 5 or 10 minutes, and were altogether unable to maintain a steady current, continuing unchanged for hours and days. This affords an excellent illustration of the gradual steps by which great inventions attain perfection. In the thirty years that have elapsed since that period, the telegraph has been carried from the most eastern extremity of Asia, across Europe to the most western extremity of America, and at no distant day will completely encircle the globe.

410. The Transmission of Messages. If there are intermediate stations, the telegraphic current, in passing from one extremity of the line to the other, circulates through the instruments of all the stations, and every message is repeated simultaneously by every Sounder, even by those which are far in advance of the station to which the message is sent. When a message is to be transmitted from one end of the line to the other, or to an intermediate station, the operator first signals that station by sounding several times in rapid succession the first letter of its name, as s, for Springfield, B, for Boston, in order to call attention. This signal is repeated at every station down the whole line, to the most distant extremity, but it receives no notice except at the place to which it is sent. The operator at this point responds, to show that he is in readiness, and the message is then transmitted. No message is ever sent, until the operator at the proper station has been summoned. The reply is transmitted by means of a Manipulator, as already described, and this reply is also repeated by every Sounder on the line, both behind as well as in advance of the station from which it started, but receives no attention except from the operator who has been summoned. In consequence of this repetition of messages in every instrument, it is easy to transmit news to many points on the same line simultaneously. The news from New York City for the morning newspapers in New England, is transmitted simultaneously to all, by one operator at New York. The first thing done, is to call up the operators at the different points, by striking the signals appropriate to each place in succession, and when it has been ascertained by a reply that each is at his post, the news is transmitted. If it be desired, however, the operator who is summoned at any station can prevent messages from going further, by breaking connection with the line beyond him, and replying by his own battery and local ground connection. As only one message can be in process of transmission at one time, it is necessary to have more than one wire for the transaction of business between large cities.

411. Telegraphic Batteries. Several new batteries have been constructed within a few years, which are now generally employed for telegraphic purposes instead of the batteries already described. The most important are the sulphate of Mercury battery, Caillaud's battery, and the Sand battery.

The sulphate of Mercury battery, *Fig.* 202, No. 1, is generally arranged like Bunsen's battery, but the dimensions are less. In the outside cup, in place of water acidulated with

---

410. Explain the transmission of messages simultaneously to different stations.
411. Describe the new Telegraphic batteries: The Sulphate of Mercury battery.

CAILLAUD'S BATTERY. 383

Fig. 20

1.   2.

The Sulphate of Mercury Battery.   *Caillaud's Battery.*   *The Sand Battery.*

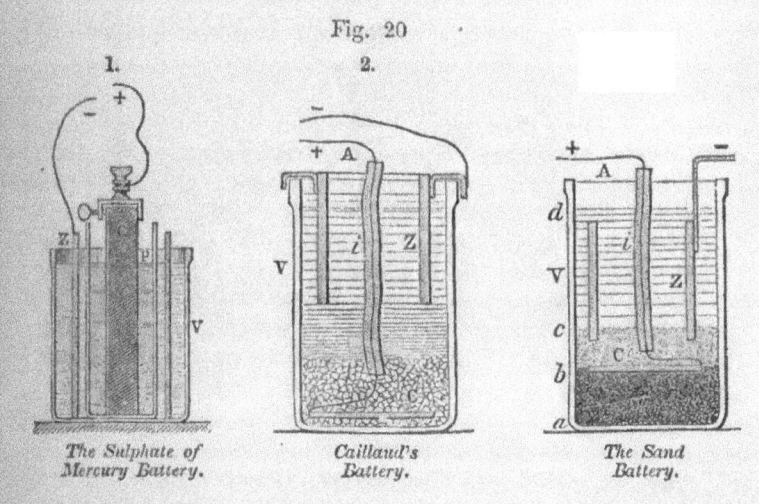

sulphuric acid, pure water is used or else water containing common salt—chloride of sodium—in solution; in the porous cup, in place of nitric acid, a solution of the sulphate of mercury is employed. This salt not being very soluble is mixed with three times its weight of water; the water is then decanted and a pasty residue left: the zinc plates, z, and the carbon cylinders, c, having been put into their places, the porous cups are then filled with this residuum, and afterwards the decanted liquid is poured in. The action of the battery is extremely simple: the water in the outer cell being decomposed, the oxygen unites with the zinc plate, the hydrogen penetrates into the porous cup, and de-oxidises the oxide of mercury, setting free metallic mercury and sulphuric acid; the former settles at the bottom of the porous cup, the latter passes through it, and unites with the oxide of zinc in the outer cup to form sulphate of zinc. The mercury may be collected and used to prepare a fresh quantity of sulphate, equal in amount to that which has been decomposed. This battery is soon exhausted when used continuously, but it can operate during three or four months so as to furnish interrupted currents like those which are used for telegraphic communication.

412. Caillaud's Battery This battery dispenses with porous cups and secures the separation of the two liquids which are required, by the difference in their density, assisted by the action of the current. At the bottom of the outside cup, v, *Fig. 202,*

---

412. Describe Caillaud's battery.

No. 2, a copper plate c, is deposited, to which is soldered a copper wire, insulated by means of a covering of gutta-percha, i. On the top of this plate is placed a layer of crystals of sulphate of copper. The remainder of the vessel is then filled with pure water; a cylinder of zinc, z, is then introduced, and so placed as not to touch the sulphate of copper. Thus the lower part of the liquid becomes saturated with sulphate of copper, while the upper part remains pure, the two liquids being prevented from mingling by a difference in density, and also by the passage of the current. The theory of this battery is the same as that of Daniell, §344: the water surrounding the zinc plate is decomposed, the oxygen unites with the zinc, the hydrogen passes into the sulphate of copper solution, and de-oxidises the oxide of copper which it contains, setting free metallic copper and sulphuric acid: the former attaches itself to the copper plate, the latter moves towards the zinc plate and unites with the oxide of zinc to form sulphate of zinc: the direction of the current is from z to c. This battery is extremely economical, and will furnish a steady current for several months: a little water must be added from time to time to replace that lost by evaporation.

413. The Sand Battery. In this battery, which is arranged upon the same plan as the last, Sand is employed in order to render the separation of the liquids more complete. The sulphate of copper broken into coarse powder, is introduced first, forming a layer from a to b, *Fig.* 202, No. 3: above it is placed the copper plate c, with its insulated wire i: on the top of this, a layer of sand, from b to c: then the zinc plate, z, and the remainder is filled with pure water. Sometimes, the sulphate of copper in crystals is placed on the top of the copper plate, and the sand immediately above it. The Sand battery is now very extensively employed in working telegraphic lines, on account of its economy and simplicity.

414. The Earth as a part of the Telegraphic circuit. One of the most remarkable facts connected with the working of the telegraph, is the extreme facility with which the Earth conducts the electrical current. It had been shown by Watson, in the last century, that a Leyden jar could be discharged through a circuit one-half of which consisted of moist earth, but Steinheil was the first to employ the earth to act the part of a conducting wire in a telegraphic circuit. While engaged

---

413. Describe the Sand battery.—414. What is said in regard to the earth as a part of the telegraphic circuit? Who discovered this fact?

in 1837, upon the railroad from Nuremburg to Furth, in experiments with a view to realize a hint thrown out by Gauss, that the two rails of a railway might be employed as conductors of the telegraphic current instead of wires, and finding it impossible to obtain an insulation sufficiently perfect for the current to reach from one station to another, he was led to notice the great conducting power of the earth, and to conjecture that it might be employed as a conductor in place of one of the telegraphic wires. His experiments were crowned with success, and he then introduced into telegraphy one of its greatest improvements, both in regard to economy from the suppression of one wire, and greatly increased facility in the construction of long lines. The two extremities of his telegraphic lines constructed at Munich in 1839, were attached to two copper plates, which were buried in the earth, and he attributed the transmission of the current to the direct conduction of the earth.

In 1841 it was proved, by Wheatstone and Cooke in England, that the earth may be employed to replace one-half the conducting wire, and be used for the return circuit; indeed they found that the same battery would work to a much greater distance, with a circuit half wire and half earth, than when altogether wire. It was noticed by Bain in 1841, that when a plate of copper was buried in moist earth, and connected by a wire passing through a galvanometer with a similar plate of zinc also buried in the earth at some distance from it, that a current of considerable intensity was generated by the action of the zinc on the moist earth; and on increasing the size of the plates, not only were powerful electro-magnetic effects obtained, but also electro-type deposits, even when the plates were more than a mile apart. The battery thus formed continued to work for a great length of time.

In 1844, Matteucci caused the current from a single Bunsen's element to circulate through a copper wire 9,281 feet in length, and through a portion of moist earth of the same extent, for the sake of comparison. It was found that the earth conducted so much better than the wire that its resistance must be regarded as nothing, and that the resistance of copper wire entering into the earth circuit, was less than that offered by the same wire when it entered alone into the circuit. It was ascertained by Bréguet, on the telegraph line between Paris

---
How was it discovered? What did Bain discover? Matteucci? Why is the conduction of the earth of great importance in telegraphy?

17

and Rouen, that when the current traversed a circuit half metal and half earth, the intensity was twice as great as when the circuit was metallic throughout—that is, a circuit 40 miles earth and 40 miles wire, presented no more resistance than a circuit of 40 miles wire, the earth in fact offering no resistance at all.

This is a fact of the greatest importance, as it not only permits the economy of a one line wire, but also renders the current twice as strong as it would be if returned by a second metallic wire. Two explanations have been given of this non-resistance of the earth; one, that as the conducting power increases in proportion to the area of a section of the conductor, the earth acting as a conductor with an infinite area, offers a smaller amount of resistance than the metallic part of the circuit; the other, that the earth acts as an immense reservoir which absorbs all the positive electricity poured into it on the one side, and the negative on the other. According to the first theory, between two stations very far apart, such as Washington and St. Louis, there must be a process of polarization like that described in §333, *Figs.* 139, 140, and a series of decompositions and recompositions of all the intervening molecules of water, with which the moist earth is charged, §365, *Fig.* 163: and the positive electricity, introduced into the ground at Washington, can only be neutralized by the negative electricity of the same battery, which has gone by wire to St. Louis, and thence back through the earth by a process of polarization and neutralization going on from molecule to molecule, of the intervening section of earth.

According to the second theory, the earth, on account of its immense size, has an unlimited capacity for electricity, and by absorbing all the positive and negative electricity which is generated by the battery, produces a flow of the electric current in the wire: or the earth may be regarded as an immense battery, producing electric currents that are passing in different directions, with some one of which the galvanic current forms a connection, making it part of the telegraphic circuit: thus the comparatively feeble current which traverses the line, runs into and is absorbed by the mighty current of the subterraneous battery below, and is hurried on with a greatly accelerated velocity. Objections may be raised in reference to both these theories, but the former is more in accordance with the principles pre-

---

State the two theories by which it is explained. Which is preferred?

viously laid down, in regard to the necessity for the polarization of the entire circuit before the current can be transmitted. The fact that the resistance of the earth to the passage of the telegraphic current is absolutely null, is certain, however difficult may be its explanation; and in reference to its influence upon the moral and social welfare of men by dispensing with the necessity of a second return wire of the same length with the first, and thus greatly facilitating the rapid extension of the telegraph over the whole earth, it is one of the most important discoveries of the age.

415. The velocity of the Telegraphic current. It has been ascertained by an ingenious apparatus devised by Wheatstone, that the velocity of statical electricity discharged through a copper wire half a mile in length, is 288,000 miles in a second, being greater than the velocity of light in the ratio of 286 to 192. In regard to the velocity of voltaic electricity traversing a wire, there is some discrepancy in the results of experiments, but they agree in showing it to be very great. Thus, according to

Prof. Walker of the U. S. Coast Survey, it is	18,780 miles per second.
Mitchell,	28,524 " " "
Fizeau and Gounelle, copper wire,	112,680 " " "
" " " iron wire,	62,600 " " "
Astronomers of Greenwich and Brussells, copper wire, of London and Brussells Telegraph,	2,700 " " "
Astronomers of Greenwich and Edinburgh, copper wire, of London and Edinburgh Telegraph,	7,600 " " "
Gould,	15,890 " " "

From the above table it would appear that the velocity of voltaic electricity is very much less than that of statical. It is probably not more than 20,000 or less than 12,000 miles per second. Taking Walker's estimate of 18,780 miles per second, it would require $1\frac{1}{3}$ seconds for the galvanic current to traverse a wire extending round the earth. The transmission of telegraphic signals must therefore be practically instantaneous.

416. The Sub-marine Telegraph. In the sub-marine telegraph, copper wires, coated with gutta-percha, are wound around a central rope of hemp, in such a manner as to form a compound rope, containing several strands of conducting wire; the whole

---

415. What is the velocity of statical electricity? Of galvanic electricity? Give the various results. What is the rate of transmission of the telegraphic current? How much time is required for its circulation around the globe?—416. Describe the submarine telegraph.

is protected by a flexible metallic covering of woven wire, and then this is covered with an exterior covering of gutta-percha, or tarred hemp. The metallic cable is coiled in the hold of a steamer, and one end having been made fast to the shore, and connected with a land telegraph, the rope is gradually paid out over the ship's stern, as she moves steadily forward, and from its weight sinks to the bottom of the sea. When the opposite shore is reached, the end of the cable is landed and connected with a land telegraph. In working a telegraphic line consisting of wires covered with gutta-percha, and sunk beneath a body of water, it has been observed that when the cable is connected with the battery, the signal is not instantaneously transmitted to the distant extremity; and on the other hand, if the connection with the battery be broken, there is not an instantaneous cessation of electrical action at the distant extremity. There is, in short, a retardation, and subsequent prolongation of the electrical current. This is owing to the action of the current upon the gutta-percha insulator. The insulated wire constitutes, in fact, a Leyden jar, of which the wire forms the inside surface, the gutta-percha constitutes the containing vessel; the external iron wire, or the water of the ocean, forms the outside metallic covering. The time lost at first, is that which is consumed in giving the gutta-percha its charge; being a non-conductor, its particles are all polarized in the manner represented in *Figs.* 119, 124, by the highly electrified wire. If the wire is carrying a current of *positive* electricity, the gutta-percha becomes highly charged with a proportionate amount of *negative* electricity, and as opposite electricities attract each other, this induced negative electricity reacts upon the positive electricity with which the wire is charged, exerts an attractive influence upon it, and tends to hold it fast, and to check the flow of the current in the wire. If the wire is carrying a current of *negative* electricity, the effect is reversed, the gutta-percha receives by induction a charge of *positive* electricity, and an equal retardation is produced in the flow of the current through the wire. On the other hand, when the connection with the battery is broken, and the current of electricity carried by the wire is stopped, there is a gradual cessation of the polarized state in the gutta-percha, and a steady decline in the tension of the induced charge which it had received, and this allows of the gradual escape of the electricity, which it had held back, during some seconds after the

---

Describe the retardation and prolongation of the electrical current. Show how the insulated wire constitutes a Leyden jar.

THE ATLANTIC TELEGRAPH CABLE. 389

connection with the battery has ceased. When wires, covered with gutta-percha, are suspended in the air, no such polarization takes place, on account of the non-conducting power of the air, which does not allow of the escape of the repelled electricity, and the wire is therefore like a Leyden jar, whose outside surface is not connected with the earth, §317.

417. The Atlantic Telegraph Cable. The Atlantic Telegraph Cable, which was successfully laid in 1866, is constructed of a core of 7 copper wires imbedded in gutta-percha, and protected by a twisted strand of ten steel wires covered with tarred hemp, *Fig.* 203. The total diameter of the cable does not exceed $1\frac{1}{10}$ inches. Three cups only of the weakest possible form of the galvanic battery are used, each consisting of a plate of copper, at the bottom of a glass jar about 8 inches in depth, filled in with saw dust dampened with pure water without the use of any acid, and a piece of zinc placed upon the top of it, *Fig.* 204. An insulated wire is attached to each copper plate leading to the zinc plate in the

Fig. 203.

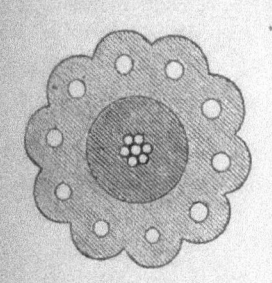

Section of the Atlantic Telegraph Cable.

Fig. 204.

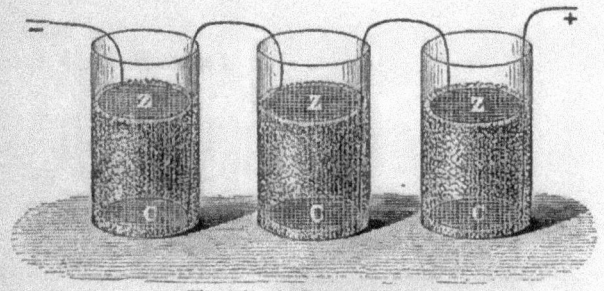

The Atlantic Telegraph Battery.

adjoining jar. A few pieces of sulphate of copper are dropped upon the copper plate previous to covering it with saw dust. No Indicator is employed like that described in §407, but instead of it an extremely simple instrument, called Thomson's Reflecting Galvanometer, *Fig.* 205.

---

417. Describe the Atlantic cable, and the battery used to work it.

390   THE SIGNAL INSTRUMENT.

Fig. 205.

Thomson's *Reflecting Galvanometer,*
in section.

It consists of a coil of wound wire, seen in section, at C, having a very small magnet, *m*, suspended within it by a single filament of silk; on the front of this magnet is fastened a small mirror, *n*, and the magnet and mirror are made to assume a fixed position, at right angles to the axis of the coil by the permanent horse-shoe magnet, S N.— A D, is a screen, at a distance of about 26 inches from the magnet, having a vertical slit, cut directly opposite to the mirror, *n*, and behind this slit is placed a lamp, B. The screen is graduated on each side of the slit, each division being about $\frac{1}{40}$th of an inch in length: L is a lens by which the light proceeding from the lamp is concentrated upon the mirror. The extremities of the coil, C, are connected with the telegraphic wire in such a manner that the current may at pleasure be made to circulate through it. An electrical current, passing through the coil, however slight, tends to counteract the attractive influence of the fixed magnet, S N, and to turn the magnet, *m*, into a position at right angles to its former position, and parallel to the axis of the coil. As long as no telegraphic current passes through the coil, the magnet, m, remains undisturbed in its fixed position, and the light proceeding from the lamp, B, passing through the vertical slit, and falling upon the mirror, n, is reflected back upon the same line and returns through the slit to the lamp, but the instant the current passes, the magnet is made to deviate from its fixed position either to the right or to the left, and a spot of light is reflected to the right or left of the slit, and made to fall upon the graduated scale, A D. If the positive current turn it to the right, and throw the reflected spot of light to the right of the vertical slit, a negative current will turn it to the left, and throw the reflected spot to the left of the same slit. The telegraphic operator has the power of transmitting a positive or negative current at pleasure, by means of the key, M, in *Fig.* 207: when it is moved so as to touch p, a positive current is transmitted; when it is moved so as to touch n, a negative current is transmitted. Thus the spot of reflected light is easily thrown either to the right or the left on the graduated scale, A D. When thrown to the right, a dot is indicated; when thrown to the left, a dash; and from these the characters of Morse's alphabet, §408 are readily produced. By this very simple apparatus, the longest messages can be sent from one side of the Atlantic to the other. The observer who receives the message sits upon the side of s N, opposite to B, and with the instrument, is placed in a dark room.

418. Thomson's Reflecting Galvanometer. The actual form of the Reflecting Galvanometer employed may be seen in *Fig.* 206: w represents a cylindrical box containing the coil of wire having the magnet and mirror suspended in it by a few fibres of unspun silk; in the front of the box at the opening of the coil, is placed a small lens, l: the coil with its connecting wires is mounted upon a stand, and provided with leveling screws. Upon a perpendicular rod mounted upon the top of this box, slides the horse-shoe magnet, m, by which, when brought down upon the sides of the box, the operator is enabled to give a fixed position to the internal magnet carrying the mirror. At R, is seen the screen, bearing the graduated scale; at L, the lamp, placed behind the screen, and at s, the vertical slit, through which the light passes to the lens, l, by which it is concentrated upon the mirror, and from this reflected upon the scale, R. As a very slight angular deviation of the magnet causes the spot of light to traverse the whole scale, this

---

Describe the Signal instrument, *Fig.* 205. How is the passage of the current manifested. How does the reflected spot of light communicate intelligence? Why does the observer sit in a dark room?—418. Describe the actual form of the Signal instrument.

instrument becomes an extremely delicate indicator of the passage of the current through the cable. The observer sits behind the box, w, in a darkened room. The coil, mirror and magnet, are seen in section, separately on the right of the engraving.

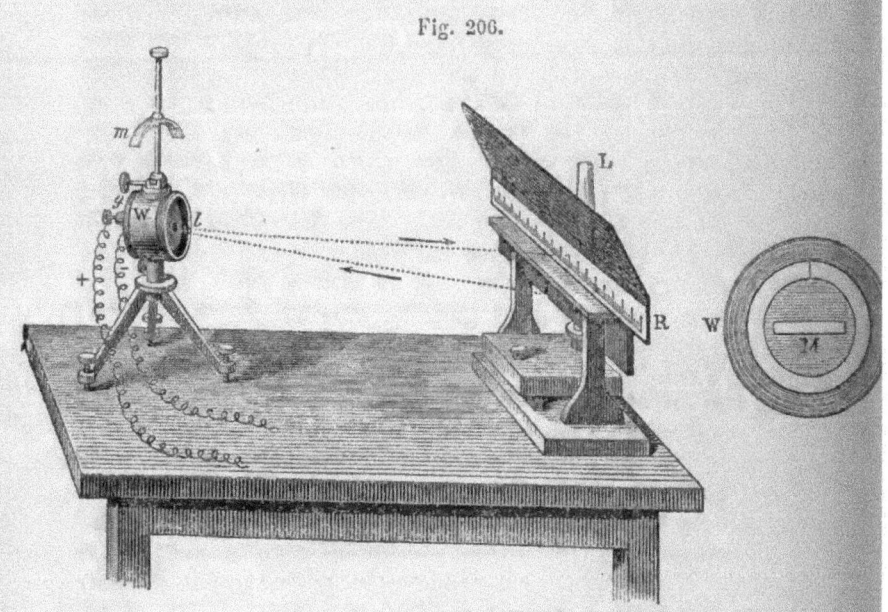

Fig. 206.

The Atlantic Telegraph Signal Instrument.

419. The actual arrangement of the Cable. The actual arrangement of the battery and cable is represented in *Fig.* 207: B and B', represent the two batteries, and E, the plate buried in the ground on one side of the ocean; M, is the key for sending at pleasure either a positive or negative current; A, the point at which the cable enters the sea; G, the signal galvanometer; F, the plate buried in the earth on the other side of the ocean. The current circulates from one pole of the battery through A to G, thence to the plate F, and from this returning through the ocean to the plate E, finally reaches the opposite pole of the battery to that from which it started. To use the cable advantageously, a uniform current of positive or negative electricity must not be employed, but the currrent should be often reversed; this is accomplished, in the instrument above described, by the constant alterations required to produce the dots and dashes, as already described.

---

419. Describe the actual arrangement of the Cable.

Fig. 207

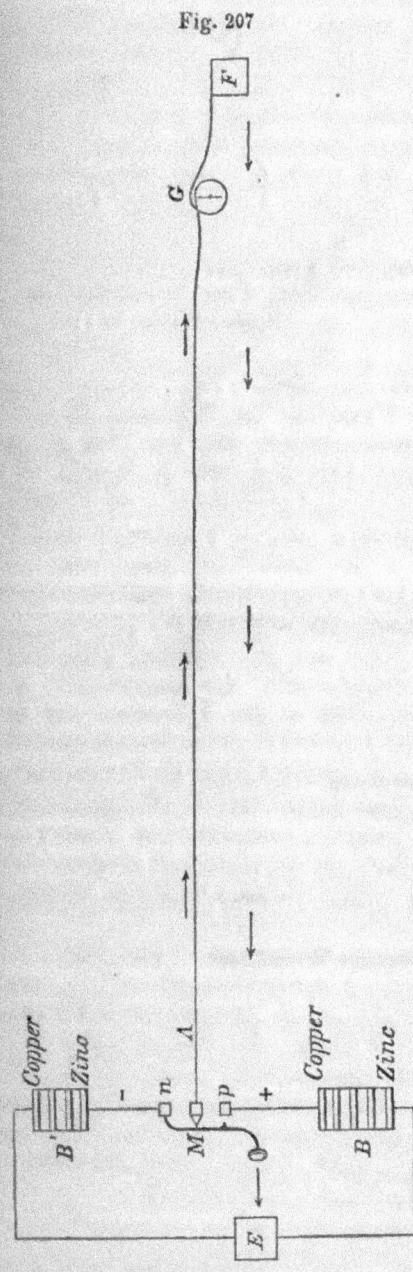

Transmission of the current across the Ocean.

420. The rate of transmission. The signal is transmitted instantly, but a slight delay of perhaps $\frac{3}{8}$ths of a second is experienced in freeing the cable. The rate of transmission is fifteen words or seventy-five letters per minute, but twenty words can be sent quite easily. There is no doubt that with the various land lines free from other duty, a despatch of twenty words could readily be transmitted from London to New York, or *vice versa,* in the time required to write it over four or five times; or in other words, it is possible to send it the entire distance in five minutes, every thing being in readiness for it. The difference of time being greatly in favor of New York, despatches often reach New York dated at a later hour than that at which they arrive. The news published in the New York afternoon newspapers, leaves London often at 3 P. M. of the same day. On one occasion a despatch was received at New York at about 11.30 P. M., dated London the *following* day. On another occasion a despatch from Rome reached New

York at 8 A. M. on the day of its date, was placed in a Western city at 8 A. M., and the reply which passed New York eastward about 11.30 A. M., doubtless reached Rome in the evening of the same day. On one occasion a despatch was sent from London to Washington in nine minutes and thirty seconds, and was received in Washington four hours fifty-eight minutes and thirty seconds in advance of the hour of its leaving London. On the morning of Feb. 1st, 1868, the wires of the Western Union Telegraph Company from San Francisco to Plaister Cove, Cape Breton, and the wires of the New York, Newfoundland, and London Telegraph Company from Plaister Cove to Heart's Content, were connected, and a brisk conversation commenced between these two continental extremes. Compliments were then exchanged betwen San Francisco and Valentia, Ireland, when the latter announced that a message was just then being received from London direct. This was said at 7.20 A. M., Valentia time, Feb. 1: at 7.31 A. M., Valentia time, the London message was started from Valentia for San Francisco; passed through New York at 2.35 A. M., New York time; was received in San Francisco at 11.21 P. M., *Jan.* 31, San Francisco time, and was at once acknowledged—the whole process occupying *two minutes actual time,* and the distance traversed about 14,000 miles! Immediately after the transmission of the message referred to, the operator at San Francisco sent an eighty-word message to Heart's Content in three minutes, which the operator at Heart's Content repeated back in two minutes and fifty seconds: distance about 5,000 miles! Notwithstanding the great length of the Cable no supplemental battery is required, because the whole force of the current is transmitted, none being lost as in the case of the Land Telegraph through imperfect insulation.

421. History of the Atlantic Telegraph. The construction of the Atlantic Telegraph is considered one of the most remarkable scientific achievements of the present Century. The first and second attempts at laying the cable in 1857 and 1858 were unsuccessful. The third attempt somewhat later in the year 1858 succeeded, and telegraphic communication across the Atlantic was maintained from Aug. 6th to Sept. 1st, two hundred and seventy-one messages having been transmitted from Newfoundland to Valentia, and one hundred and twenty-

---

420. State the rate of transmission. Mention instances of the rapid transmission of despatches. Explain how a message from London may be received at New York the day before it is sent.—421. Give the history of the Atlantic Cable.

nine from Valentia to Newfoundland. On August 31st two important messages were sent to the British government from Newfoundland, but the next day communication ceased, and no efforts to reestablish it proved of any avail. In 1865 the enterprise was renewed with an improved cable, which was successfully laid by the Great Eastern about half way across the Atlantic, when it parted, and all efforts at recovery failed. In 1866 the undertaking was renewed with a new cable, which was successfully landed in Newfoundland July 27th. The ships then returned to mid-ocean for the purpose of finding and raising the lost cable of the previous year. It was found without difficulty, and after many unsuccessful attempts, was finally raised, spliced to the remaining portion, and the whole landed at Newfoundland Sept. 7th. Both these cables are now in complete operation.

422. Application of Electro-Magnetism to the production of motion. Various applications have been made of the galvanic current to the production of motion. They all depend upon the instantaneous production and destruction of force by establishing and breaking the connection between the Battery and an Electro-magnet. One of the simplest instruments for this purpose is represented in *Fig.* 208. It represents an electro-magnet wound with covered wire, and supported vertically upon a stand: W is a brass wheel, carrying upon its circumference three armatures of soft iron, placed at right angles to the plane of the wheel. At B, on the shaft of the wheel, is a *break-piece*, consisting of a small metallic disc, from which project in a lateral direction three iron pins corresponding with the three iron armatures. The battery current entering at the binding cup, p, divides into two branches and ascends each of the legs of the electro-magnet, then descending, the two

Fig. 208.

Motion produced by Electro-magnetism.

422. On what does the production of motion by electro-magnetism depend? Describe *Fig.* 208.

branches unite and ascend by the single external wire, B, to the break-piece: thence it passes, whenever one of the three iron pins is in contact with the silver spring in which the wire terminates, into the shaft of the wheel, and so by the brass supports, S S, into the iron cores of the electro-magnet, finding its way, at M, into the binding cup, n, where it makes its final exit. The silver spring is arranged in such a way as to come into contact with each iron pin at the moment when the corresponding armature is within a quarter-revolution of the poles of the electro-magnet, and to cease its contact the instant each armature is brought directly over the two electro-magnetic poles. As soon as contact between the pin and spring takes place, the current passes, the electro-magnet is excited, and the armature is attracted forcibly towards the poles of the magnet: when it reaches them, contact is broken, the current ceases, and the electro-magnet loses its power: the wheel however, continues its revolution, in consequence of the momentum which it has acquired, until the pin of the second armature comes into contact with the break-piece, when the electro-magnet again becomes charged, the second armature is attracted, contact is again broken, and thus the process goes on. By these successive attractions a rapid rotary movement is imparted to the wheel, which continues as long as the current circulates. This is one of the most simple forms of an electro-magnetic rotary machine. There are others of a much more complicated construction, and possessed of sufficient power to be used in the movement of machinery.

423. Electro-Motor of M. Froment. *Fig.* 209 represents a machine constructed by M. Froment, at Paris, for the application of galvanic electricity as a motive force in place of steam. The principle is the same as in the preceding instrument, and its action depends upon the instantaneous generation and destruction of motive power by establishing and breaking the circulation of the current. It consists of four powerful electro-magnets, A, B, C, D, fastened upon an iron frame, X. Between these electro-magnets are two iron wheels, on the same horizontal axis, carrying eight soft iron armatures, M, M, mounted on their circumference parallel to the axis. The current from the battery enters at K, ascends the wire, E, and reaches the metallic arc, O, which transmits the current successively into each pair of electro-magnets. The current is broken in each pair, and their mag-

---

423. Describe the Electro-motor of M. Froment.

THE ELECTRO-MOTOR OF M. FROMENT. 397

Fig. 209.

Froment's Electro-Motor for driving machinery.

netism destroyed just as each armature comes opposite to their poles, and is made to circulate again and to re-establish their magnetism at the moment when each armature has passed one-half the distance which separates each pair from the pair immediately following. This adjustment is effected, and the proper connections established and broken at the required moment, by means of cogs arranged upon the arc, o. The current finally makes its exit, and returns to the battery by the wire, H. In this manner, the armatures, being attracted in succession by the four pairs of electro-magnets, the wheels to which they are attached acquire a rapid rotary motion, and this, by the wheel, P, and an endless band, is transmitted to any machine, a grinding mill for example, which it is desired to move. The machine employed in the workshop of M. Froment is of about one-horse power.

424. The Electro-Motor of M. Jacoby. Electro-magnetic engines of much greater power have been constructed. In 1838, M. Jacoby, at St. Petersburg, built an electro-magnetic engine of sufficient power to propel a boat containing twelve persons, upon the river Neva. The vessel was a ten-oared shallop, provided with paddle-wheels, to which motion was given by the electro-magnetic engine. The boat was 28 feet long, 7½ wide, and drew 2¾ feet of water. During a voyage which lasted several days the vessel went at the rate of four miles an hour. In 1839, a second experiment was tried in the same boat, the machine being worked by a Grove's battery of 64 platinum plates, each having 36 square inches of surface. The boat, with a party of fourteen persons on board, went against the stream at the rate of three miles an hour.

425. Electro-Magnetic Locomotives. About 1840, an electro-magnetic railroad engine was constructed by Mr. Davidson, in Scotland, and tried by the inventor on the Edinburgh and Glasgow railroad; it weighed, with its carriages, batteries, &c., five tons, but when put in motion it traveled only four miles an hour, exerting a power less than that of a single man. The arrangement of this engine was not unlike that exhibited in the machine, *Fig.* 208, the chief difference being that two electro-magnets were employed instead of one, and arranged in such a manner as to operate directly upon the shaft of the engine, the magnetism of the electro-magnets being perpetually induced and destroyed at the proper moment by making and breaking connection with the battery.

426. Page's Electro-Magnetic Locomotive. Some very efficient electro-motors have been constructed by our countryman, Dr. Page. With an electro-magnetic locomotive provided with two of these machines, rated at four-horse power each, actuated by a Grove's battery of one hundred pairs, a speed at the rate of nineteen miles an hour upon a level grade was attained: the car weighed eleven tons, and carried fourteen passengers. The engine employed was the *axial* engine. In all other engines the motion is produced by electro-magnets of soft iron, which are alternately magnetized and de-magnetized, as in *Fig.*

---

424. Describe the Electro-motor of M. Jacoby.—425. Describe Davidson's Electro-magnetic Locomotive.—426. Describe Page's Electro-magnetic Locomotive.

208, and in Froment's electro-motor, *Fig.* 209. In this machine the electro-magnets are dispensed with, and a long hollow helix is employed, consisting of several distinct helices, placed one above another, so as to make a hollow tube, each having independent connections with the battery, insulated from each other, and arranged in such a way that each helix can be magnetized and de-magnetized in succession.—It is well known that a helix of wound wire itself becomes magnetic, and possesses as much attractive power as the iron armature placed within it, *Fig.* 184, p. 363. If such a helix, mounted in a vertical position in such a way that an iron rod can be introduced into it from below, be connected with a battery, the iron rod will be at once drawn up into it and be sustained oscillating in its axis, even though it may weigh many pounds. On one occasion, by means of a huge helix, a weight of 2,000 lbs. was raised five inches from the floor, and caused to vibrate for an inch up and down by the pressure of the finger. The battery used was fifty pairs of Grove's, with platinum plates twelve inches square, ten inches immersed. This is called the *axial* force of magnetism. If the iron rod be suspended over the opening of such a helix, as *a b*, in *Fig.* 210, instead of under, it will be drawn down with equal force as soon as the wires, *p, n*, are connected with the battery.—In the interior of this compound helix a powerful steel magnet is suspended with its upper end upon a level with the top of the helix, and fastened to a connecting rod attached to a crank and axle. As soon as the helix opposite its lower end is magnetized, a powerful attraction is exerted upon the magnet, tending to draw it downwards: as it descends, it de-magnetizes, by means of a proper break-piece, every helix that it passes and leaves behind it, while it magnetizes in succession every helix in advance of it. When it reaches the bottom of the compound helix the process is reversed, every helix above it is successively magnetized, while every helix that it passes is immediately de-magnetized. Thus the magnet is made to rise again to the upper portion of the compound helix, and a reciprocating motion is produced which is imparted to the crank and axle. An axial engine of this description was exhibited at the Smith-

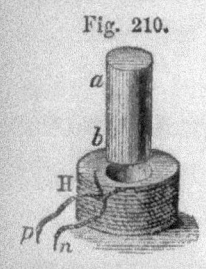

Fig. 210.

The axial electro-magnetic Force.

What is the *axial* force of magnetism? What extraordinary effects are produced by this force? Describe Page's axial engine.

sonian Institute of four or five horse-power, the battery of which was contained within the space of three cubic feet; it was a reciprocating engine of two feet stroke, and the whole, including the battery, weighed about one ton.

427. Stewart's Electro-Motor. Recently an electro-motor has been constructed by Mr. Stewart, in New York, in which a central axis about three feet in length, is surrounded by a series of electro-magnets so placed that magnetic action is maintained continually, and without intermission. The magnets are only magnetized twice in one revolution, instead of many times as in most other motors that have been constructed; it is claimed that much greater power is obtained, and at far less expense than any other machine that has been invented. The shaft makes five hundred revolutions per minute, with a battery of forty cells, producing one-tenth of one-horse power, and at an expense of about twenty-nine cents per cell for forty-eight hours.

428. The expense of Electro-magnetism compared with Steam. As yet electro-magnetic engines have not been introduced to any extent, because the expense of the zinc and acids which they consume is far greater than that of the coal required to produce an equal force by means of steam. Careful experiments have shown that the economic difference between a steam and an electro-magnetic engine, is as follows:

A grain of coal burned under the boiler of a Cornish
   engine, lifted . . . . 143 lbs. 1 foot high.
A grain of zinc consumed in a battery to move an
   electro-magnetic engine, lifted . . . . . . 80 lbs. 1 foot high.
The cost of coal is, per cwt., ... 9$d.$
The cost of zinc is, per cwt., ... 216$d.$

There is considerable diversity of opinion as to the amount of zinc consumed in the production of one-horse power. Page computes the consumption of zinc in his engine at 3 lbs. of zinc per day, for one-horse power. Joule calculates the consumption under the most favorable circumstances, at 45 lbs. per day, for one-horse power in Grove's battery, and in Daniell's battery at 75 lbs. There are also other disadvantages: the combustion of metals with a three or four-horse power engine, is very rapid at all the points where the current is broken in demagnetizing the electro-magnets. The power is also apppplied at a great mechanical disadvantage, and the conversion of elec-

---

427 Describe Stewart's electro-motor.—428. State the comparative expense of electro-magnetism and steam.

tro-magnetism into mechanical force is attended with much more loss than the conversion of heat into motion in the steam-engine. This is due in part to the very great reduction in the power of the magnet the instant the armature is separated from it; and the larger the magnets and engines, the greater the loss of power. These objections are less applicable to Page's engine, constructed on the axial principle, than any other. The cost per day, however, is not necessarily conclusive against these engines; notwithstanding the great expense they may, under certain circumstances, be usefully applied, especially in trades and occupations of small capital, where the absolute amount of mechanical power is a matter of less consequence than the facility of producing it instantaneously and at will: this would be the case even though the power should cost twenty times as much as the same amount furnished by a Cornish steam engine. To this must be added the important consideration of perfect safety and the entire freedom from the danger of explosion.

429. Electro-magnetic Clocks. Electro-magnets are often used as a motive power in clocks. The oscillation of the pendulum establishes and breaks the connection between an electro-magnet and a battery, in such a way as to give to the pendulum by the raising and dropping of an armature, sufficient impulse to maintain its motion. This interrupted connection may be communicated by a wire to all the clocks in a large city, and cause them to move at exactly the same rate, and thus one central clock may become the motor and regulator of an unlimited number of time-pieces. Such clocks, however, steadily deteriorate in consequence of the rapid combustion which takes place at the points where contact with the battery is made and broken; and for this reason a clock of ordinary construction moved by a weight and spring, is employed to furnish the standard time, and its pendulum as it oscillates is used to regulate the current which turns the hands upon an indefinite number of electrical dials. *Fig.* 211 represents a dial of this description, and *Fig.* 212, the mechanism by which its hands are turned. An electro-magnet, B, is used to attract an armature of soft iron, P, turning on a pivot, a. This armature transmits its motion to a lever, s, which by means of a ratchet turns the wheel A. This, by the pinion D, turns the wheel C, and

---

429. How may a pendulum be made to oscillate by electro-magnetism? How may one clock be made to indicate time on many dials in different places? Describe *Figs.* 211 and 212.

402 ELECTRO-MAGNETIC CLOCKS.

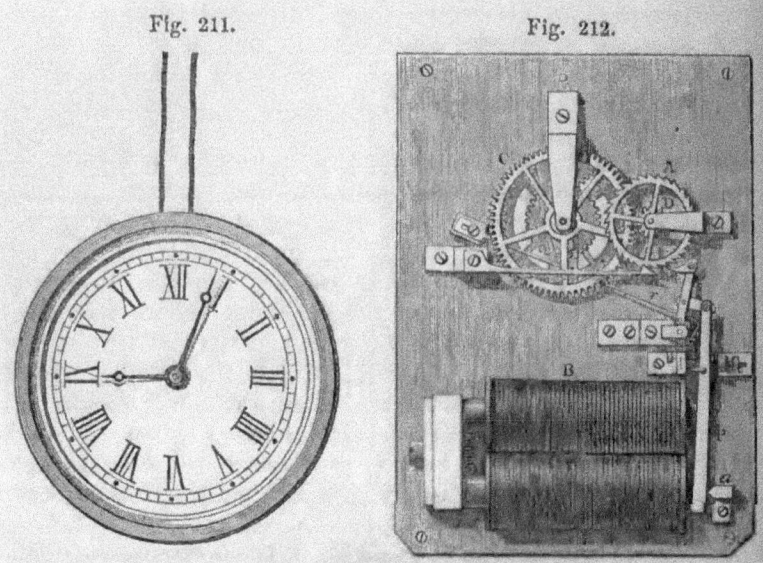

Fig. 211.   Fig. 212.

The Electro-magnetic Clock.

this, by a series of wheels and pinions, moves the hands. The regular motion of the hands depends upon the regularity of the oscillations of the armature P, and this regularity is maintained by making and breaking the connection between the electro-magnet B, and the battery, by the movement of the pendulum of the standard clock mentioned above. In this manner, all the clocks in a city, in a large hotel, or on the line of a railroad, may be made to indicate exactly the same time, for the electrical current, travelling at the rate of 18,780 miles in a second, takes but an inappreciable time to traverse the whole line. Mr. Bain has invented an electrical clock which is driven by the current derived from an earth-battery, consisting of one zinc and one carbon plate, imbedded in the ground, about four feet apart and three feet deep. §414, p. 385.

The exact time when the sun or a star crosses the meridian at one observatory, can be telegraphed instantaneously to others, and to distant places: and it is thus that the exact time of noon is flashed from a central observatory to many distant points. Time at Hartford is telegraphed from New York, and this from the Dudley Observatory at Albany. Other applications have been made of electro-magnetism to the bells of hotels and houses, and other minor conveniences of house-keeping.

How can time be transmitted from one place to another?

THE ELECTRIC 403

430. The Electric Fire-Alarm. One of the most interesting and useful applications of galvanic electricity is to the construction of the fire-alarm of cities. A central office is established, where a battery is placed which is always in action. From this a wire proceeds to every part of the town, and is carried at suitable points, into the interior of iron boxes fixed at the corners of the streets: after entering each box the wire again emerges, and is carried to the next box, and so on in succession through them all, and is finally returned to the opposite pole of the battery from which it started. Thus an electrical current is constantly kept in circulation through every part of the entire city circuit. The internal arrangement of the box is represented in *Fig.* 213. The current enters at o, by means of an

Fig. 213.

The Electric Fire-Alarm.

430. Describe the Electric Fire-Alarm. Describe the arrangement of the wire. How is the current broken?

insulated wire, taking the course indicated by the arrows, descending in the space between the outer and inner boxes, as far as R, and then ascending and passing into the interior circular box until it reaches B: B is a lever of wood, having its upper surface covered by a thin strip of metal, which by means of a spring is firmly pressed against the brass wheel w. By the side of the lever B, is a second lever which is concealed in the *Fig.*, constructed of wood, of the same dimensions, and having its upper surface covered also with a thin metallic strip, which is in like manner pressed firmly upon the wheel w, by means of a spring. Although these levers are placed side by side, there is no direct metallic communication between them, except by means of the wheel w. The current, when it reaches the first lever, B, descends upon the brass strip which covers its upper surface, to w, through which it passes to the second lever, behind B, and ascends by the brass strip which covers it, to the upper end, whence it passes by the wire as indicated by the arrow, to the electro-magnet E. After circulating through both arms of the electro-magnet, it emerges and passes by the wire in front of the bell G, to the lower part of the box, and thence by the wire P, ascends in the space between the outer and the inner box to the point O, where it again enters the iron tube through which it had descended, and passes on to the next adjoining box. It will be observed that so long as both levers, B, rest upon the wheel w, the electric current circulates uninterruptedly through the apparatus: and that when one or both the levers cease to press upon the wheel w, the current ceases to circulate. When a fire occurs, the box must be opened and the lever, L, pushed down as far it can be made to go. This movement winds up a spring and sets in motion a train of wheels by which motion is communicated to the wheel w. This wheel is not continuous, but is broken by notches in its circumference. As each notch comes successively beneath the levers B, their connection with the wheel w, is broken, and the current ceases to flow: this immediately de-magnetizes the electro-magnet E, and allows its armature A, to drop: at the same instant the current ceases to circulate through the entire city circuit, and by releasing an armature attached to an electro-magnet in a central tower, sets in motion a train of machinery by which a heavy blow is struck once by a powerful hammer upon the Fire Bell, and an alarm sounded. As the wheel w,

---

What must be done when an alarm is to be sounded?

revolves, and each notch passes on, the communication between the levers B, and the wheel W, is re-established, the entire city circuit is again rendered complete, the armature of the electro-magnet is again drawn up, and the machinery in the central tower is stopped, one blow only having been struck upon the bell. If, however, there be more than one notch in the wheel W, as it revolves the process is presently repeated, and a second blow is given upon the bell. These notches may be cut quite near each other, at regular intervals, or far apart and at unequal distances: thus many combinations may be effected, by which a variety of blows may be struck upon the bell, characteristic of each box, and determining the locality of the fire. Each box is distinguished by a number, and the notches are cut in such a manner as to strike this number upon the bell. Thus, if two notches be cut quite close together, and then, at some distance from them, four other notches at equal distances from each other, the effect will be to strike two strokes in rapid succession, and then, after a brief interval, four others, denoting the number 24, and indicating that box 24 is the one nearest the fire. By pulling the lever L, down once, the machinery is wound up just enough to make the wheel W, revolve five times, and thus the number 24, in the above case, will be repeated five times. With every completion of the circuit, the armature of the electro-magnet in each box is drawn violently back to the magnet, and a stroke given upon the bell G. The alarm is therefore repeated in every iron box in the city, and may be made to indicate the locality of the fire in every engine-house. The box is kept securely locked, and the lever L, is moved by means of a projecting pin, L, upon the inside of the open door, represented in the *Fig.* This pin extends through the door, and may be moved upon the opposite side while the door is closed: s s, are springs for the purpose of restoring the pin L, to its former position after being once thrust down. The whole box is closed by an external door not represented in the *Fig.*, the key of which is kept in some neighboring house. In some cases, the alarm is first telegraphed to a central office, and from that transmitted to a number of Fire-bells distributed over the city. The advantage of making use of a circuit which is constantly *closed*, instead of bringing the battery into use only at the moment when the alarm is to be sounded, is, that it furnishes evidence of being constantly in working order, and makes the

---

How is the number of the box struck upon the bell?

transmission of the alarm perfectly certain; for the instant any disarrangement takes place and the current ceases to circulate, the alarm-bell is sounded once. One stroke upon the central bell, not repeated, indicates that the circuit is broken and the line out of working order: for this reason there is no box in the system marked number 1. As one stroke indicates no alarm of fire, it may be employed to denote time and to signalize the exact hour of noon, by opening any one of the iron boxes in the system and breaking the circuit *once :* this gives one stroke upon the central bell, and also upon all the smaller bells distributed through the boxes. The battery required is about one hundred cells, of Daniell's. The iron tube which leads from each iron box to the ground has nothing to do with the regular working of the apparatus, but is intended to carry off lightning, and to furnish a connection with the ground whenever it becomes necessary to use the earth for a part of the circuit, as is done in the case of the ordinary Telegraph.—On the same principle, the burglar-alarms are constructed, which are frequently attached to windows and doors. The opening of the window, or door, breaks an electrical current circulating throughout the house from a central battery, and telegraphs the alarm and the particular door or window to some central apartment.

431. Electric Gas-lighting. An ingenious application of the above principles has been made by Mr. Farmer, of Boston, to lighting the street gas-lamps. A small iron box is placed directly beneath the jet, in which is placed a small electro-magnet, which is connected with a battery current circulating from lamp to lamp, throughout the town. As soon as this electro-magnet is actuated by the current, it attracts an armature, and opens a conical gas-stopper, thus allowing the gas to pass into the jet, where it is immediately lighted by an electric spark flashed from the battery, between two platinum points, which are placed directly over the aperture. On reversing the current, the conical stopper is pushed back into its place, and the gas-light is extinguished. The battery current in this apparatus is furnished by a thermo-electric pile, excited by a powerful gas-light. The dome of the capitol at Washington is illuminated by gas turned on and lighted by electricity. The battery consists of 200 jars, and consumes 600 lbs. of zinc, 80 lbs. of mercury, and 50 gallons of sulphuric acid, per annum.

How may the hour of noon be struck on the central bell? How large a battery is required?—431. What application has been made of these principles to the lighting of street lamps?

432. Progress of discovery in Electro-Magnetism. The successive discoveries which led to the construction of the powerful electro-magnets on which the Magnetic Telegraph and the various electro-motors above described depend, are as follows. The fundamental fact of the influence of a wire carrying the galvanic current upon the magnetic needle was discovered by Oersted, at Copenhagen, in the winter of 1819-20. The second fact, that the wire carrying the current is itself magnetic and will attract iron filings, was discovered by Arago and Davy, in 1820. The third fact, that two wires through which galvanic currents are passing in the same direction attract, and those in the opposite direction repel each other, was discovered by Ampère in 1820, and it was on this that he constructed his celebrated theory, §403, that magnetism is produced by currents of electricity circulating around the magnet at right angles to the line joining the two poles: it also led Arago in the same year to magnetize steel wire and sewing needles, by transmitting a current of electricity through a helix of wire surrounding a glass tube containing within it the needle or wire to be magnetized, *Figs*. 182, 183. The next important step was made by Mr. Sturgeon, at London, in 1825, by inventing the electro-magnet. He bent a piece of iron wire into the form of a horseshoe, covered it with varnish to insulate it, and surrounded it with a helix of soft copper wire, through which the battery current was transmitted, the spires of the helix being separated from each other to a considerable distance. When a galvanic current was passed through the helix from a small battery consisting of a single cell, the iron wire became magnetic and continued so during the passage of the current. When the current was interrupted the magnetism disappeared, and thus was produced the first temporary soft iron electro-magnet. This electro-magnet was very feeble in power, and could not be made to act by a current transmitted through a long wire. The next step in advance was made by our countryman, Prof. Henry, in 1828, by insulating the conducting wire itself with a well wound covering of cotton or silk, instead of the curved iron bar, and by winding the whole length of the horse-shoe with a series of coils in close contact, and then successive stratas of coils over the first, care being taken to secure insulation between each layer by a covering of silk ribbon. By this arrangement the power of the electro-magnet,

---

Describe the progress of discovery in electro-magnetism. Who constructed the first electro-magnet? Who constructed the first effective electro-magnet?

with the same amount of galvanic force, was increased several times, and it was found that a current transmitted through a long wire could be used to create a powerful electro-magnet at the distance of many miles, and make signals by striking a bell, especially if a battery of intensity, §341, consisting of many coils, was employed. This discovery made the construction of an electro-magnetic telegraph, which had been tried without success in England in 1825, a possibility, and served as the foundation for Morse's electro-magnetic instrument. Prof. Henry still further increased the power of the electro-magnet by using a number of separate coils, having independent connection with the battery, on the same horse-shoe, in place of one long single coil. In this manner the powerful electro-magnets capable of sustaining from three ten thousand pounds were made, which have since been used in the construction of electro-motors. He also exhibited the first mechanical motion ever produced by magnetic attraction and repulsion, by means of a vibrating beam placed horizontally over two upright magnets: a fly-wheel was subsequently attached to this, and afterwards a rotatory motion given. An account of this instrument is contained in Silliman's Journal for 1831.

Finally, the constant battery of Prof. Daniell was invented in 1836; the possibility of using the earth as a part of the telegraphic circuit, was discovered by Steinheil in 1837; and in the same year these principles were applied by our countryman, Prof. Morse, to the construction of the electro-magnetic telegraph. About the same time, Wheatstone and Cooke's needle telegraph was introduced in England; Daniell's and Grove's batteries were perfected in 1843; and the first telegraph line in the U. S. A. erected between Baltimore and Washington in 1844.

§ IV. Galvanic Induced Electricity.

433. Volta-Electric Induction. An induced secondary electrical current produced by establishing and breaking the primary current of a Galvanic Battery. We have seen that the frictional electricity of the machine induces electricity in all surrounding bodies, §310. The electricity of the battery acts in a similar manner, but only at the instant when the current begins, and at the instant when it ceases, to flow: during its continuous flow, no inductive influence whatever is exerted by it. This fact was discovered by Mr. Faraday, in 1831. He found that a wire transmitting a powerful current, induces a *momentary* current in a second wire parallel to the first, the two extremities of which are brought together, and united so as to form a *closed* circuit, whenever the connection of the original wire with the battery is *made*, or is *broken*. This he called *Volta-Electric Induction*. The effect is much increased, if instead of employing simple parallel wires, the wires of the two currents are coiled into two helices and arranged one within the other. The wire which conveys the primary current, or the primary coil, is placed in the axis of the coil for the secondary current, and the extremities of the secondary coil are joined together so as to form a closed or continuous circuit. A galvanometer is connected with the extremities of the secondary coil, in such a manner as to form a part of the closed circuit, for the purpose of demonstrating the actual passage of the current. The production of a secondary current under these circumstances, may be shown by the apparatus represented in *Fig.* 214. Let P

Fig. 214.

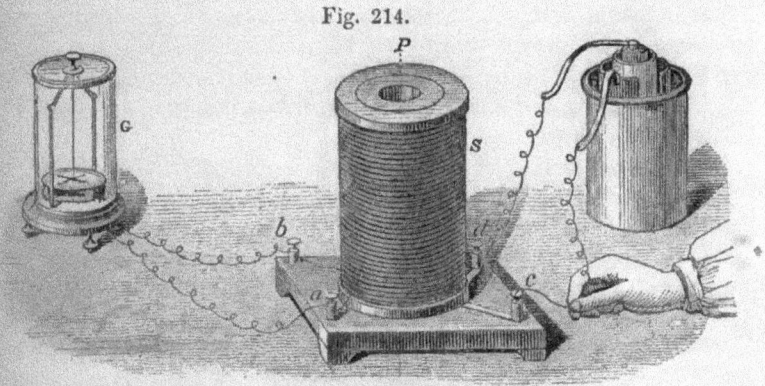

Volta-Electric Induction.

What is the effect of an electrified body on all others near it? What is the effect of a wire carrying a current upon a closed parallel wire? How can this effect be increased? Who discovered these facts? What name did he give to this inductive action?

represent the inner primary helix, composed of a short piece of stout wire carefully wound with silk or cotton and varnished with gum-lac, so as to be thoroughly insulated, and having its two extremities connected with the binding cups d and c, through which a connection is established with the battery. Let s, represent the outer secondary helix, composed of a great length of very fine copper wire, also carefully insulated, and entirely separated from the primary helix, and having its extremities connected with the binding cups a and b, through which a connection is established with the galvanometer G, thus forming a *closed* circuit, of which the galvanometer is a part. The connection of the primary helix with the battery is made or broken at pleasure by connecting or disconnecting the battery wire, by means of the hand, with the binding cup c. It is found that the moment the connection is completed with the battery, and the galvanic current begins to circulate through the inner primary coil P, a secondary current of positive electricity instantly circulates in an *opposite* direction through the outer coil, shown by the violent oscillations of the needle of the galvanometer. This secondary current continues only for a moment and almost immediately ceases. If the connection of the primary coil with the battery be kept up, the flow of the induced secondary current ceases, as is shown by the needle of the galvanometer returning to its position of rest. Again, the instant that the connection of the primary coil P, with the battery is broken by removing the battery wire from the binding cup c, and the primary current ceases to flow through P, a momentary secondary current of positive electricity, flowing in the *same* direction with the primary current, circulates throughout the entire coil, shown by the powerful impulse which it imparts to the needle of the galvanometer. These currents are only momentary, but are characterized by great power and intensity. *Though the current of positive electricity is only spoken of, according to the principle laid down, §333, p. 309, it must be understood, that a momentary current of secondary negative electricity is also produced at the same time, flowing in the opposite direction to that of the secondary positive:* when contact with the battery is completed, it circulates in the same direction with the primary current: when contact with the battery is broken, it circulates in the opposite direction. The secondary electric current thus induced is not derived from the battery, nor from

---

Describe the apparatus by which these effects may be demonstrated. Is a negative as well as a positive current induced?

the primary current; it is the electricity natural to the secondary wire, the equilibrium of which has been disturbed by the sudden production and cessation of the primary current in its vicinity: if the secondary wire be very short, the amount of induced electricity is very small, because the amount of matter exposed to the action of the primary current is very little, and the amount of electricity which it contains very trifling: if the wire be increased in length the induced electricity manifested is correspondingly increased, because of the larger amount of matter operated upon, and the larger amount of electricity whose equilibrium is disturbed by the operation of the primary current. It is essential to the complete success of these experiments, that the secondary wire should be much longer and finer than the primary.

434. Faraday's Experiments. In Mr. Faraday's original experiments the helices were arranged as follows: "About twenty-six feet of copper wire, one-twentieth of an inch in diameter, were wound round a cylinder of wood as a helix, the different spires of which were prevented from touching by a thin interposed twine: this helix was covered with calico, and then a second wire applied in the same manner. In this way twelve helices were super-imposed, each containing an average length of twenty-seven feet, and all in the same direction. The first, third, fifth, seventh, ninth, and eleventh, of these helices, were connected at their extremities, end to end, so as to form one helix: the others were connected in a similar manner; and thus two principal helices were produced closely interposed, having the same direction, not touching anywhere, and each containing one hundred and fifty-five feet in length of wire. One of these helices was connected with a galvanometer, the other with a voltaic-battery of ten pairs of plates four inches square, with double coppers, and well charged; yet not the slightest sensible deflection of the galvanometer needle could be observed. Then two hundred and three feet of copper wire in one length were coiled around a large block of wood: other two hundred and three feet of similar wire were interposed as a spiral between the turns of the first coil, and metallic contact everywhere prevented by twine. One of these helices was connected with a galvanometer, and the other with a battery of one hundred pairs of plates four inches square, with double

---

Is the secondary current derived from the battery or the primary current? What is its source? What is the effect of lengthening the secondary coil?—434. Give the history of Mr. Faraday's discovery.

coppers, and well charged. When the contact was *made*, there was a sudden and very slight effect at the galvanometer, and there was also a slight similar effect when the contact with the battery was *broken*. But whilst the voltaic current was continuing to pass through the one helix, no galvanometrical appearances nor any effect like induction upon the other helix could be perceived, although the active power of the battery was proved to be great by its heating its own helix, and by the brilliancy of the discharge when made through charcoal. Repetition of the experiments with a battery of one hundred and twenty pairs of plates, produced no other effects: but it was ascertained, both at this and the former time, that the slight deflection of the needle occurring at the moment of completing the connection, was always in one direction, and that the equally slight deflection produced when the contact was broken, was in the other direction; and also that these effects occurred when the first helices were used. The results which I had by this time obtained with magnets led me to believe that the battery current through one wire did in reality induce a similar current through the other wire, but that it continued for an instant only, and partook more of the nature of an electrical wave passed through from the shock of a common Leyden jar, than of the current from a voltaic battery, and therefore might magnetize a steel needle, though it scarcely affected the galvanometer. This expectation was confirmed; for on substituting a small hollow helix, formed round a glass tube, for the galvanometer, introducing a steel needle, making contact as before between the battery and the inducing wire, and then removing the needle before the battery contact was broken, it was found magnetized." In these experiments of Mr. Faraday, it will be observed that the secondary wire was actually shorter than the primary wire, and consequently the results obtained were extremely feeble; the current obtained from the secondary wire had in fact less intensity than that obtained from the primary: no effect was produced upon the tongue, no sparks, no heating of fine wire or charcoal, no chemical effects; the current was indicated only by the galvanometer and its magnetic effects; no additional effect was produced by increasing the size of the battery from 10 cells to 120. If the coil had been reversed, the shorter used for the primary and the longer for the secondary, very different results might have been obtained. This reversal

---

What effect would have been produced had Mr. Faraday used a longer secondary coil? Who first introduced the use of the long secondary coil?

of the relative length of the coils was first made by our countryman, Dr. Page: by making use of a short primary coil, and a secondary coil 320 feet in length he established the principle, that to obtain induced currents of high intensity from a battery of a single or only a few pairs of plates, the induced or secondary circuit must be much longer than the inducing or battery circuit. By employing a short primary coil, and a secondary coil of copper ribbon 220 feet in length and one inch wide, powerful shocks were obtained, a Leyden jar charged, and water decomposed, by the action of the secondary current: with a coil 320 feet in length, a secondary current was obtained of sufficient intensity to pass between charcoal points *before contact*. The establishment of this principle led to the construction of several important instruments for the development of secondary electricity, and eventually to that of Ruhmkorff's coil.

435. The inductive effect of the Primary current takes place through a considerable distance. The inductive influence of the primary current takes place even when the primary and secondary coils, are not placed one within the other, but are separated by a considerable distance. Thus in *Fig.* 215, let L,

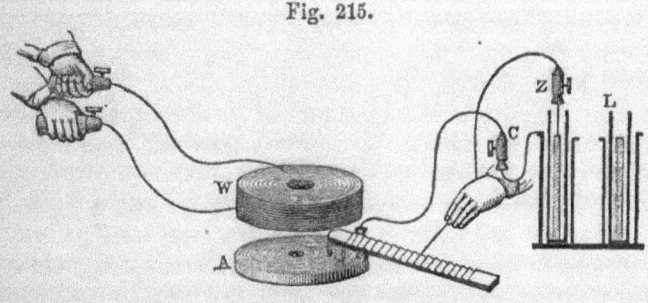

Fig. 215.

The Secondary Induced Current.

represent one cell of a Daniell's battery; A, the primary coil, composed of a short strip of copper ribbon, and having one of its extremities permanently connected with the positive pole of the battery, while the other is arranged in such a way that its connection with the negative pole may be made and broken at pleasure by drawing the negative wire over the ribbed piece of iron which terminates it: W, is the secondary coil, consisting of a great length of fine copper wire, separated

---

435. Will induction take place even if the coils are separated from each other? How can this be proved?

to a considerable distance from the primary coil A, and having its two extremities connected with the handles. As the wire, connecting the primary coil with Z, passes from one ridge of the piece of ribbed iron to another, the primary circuit is rapidly completed and broken, and a succession of powerful induced momentary currents alternately in opposite directions, circulates through the secondary coil W, by which a torrent of sharp shocks are given to the moistened hands. It will be observed that the extremities of the coil W, being connected with the handles, the body of the experimenter together with the secondary coil, constitutes a *closed* circuit. This inductive action is obtained even though a plate of glass be interposed between A and W, but if a plate of metal be interposed no inductive action takes place in the coil W, because it is transferred to the interposed conducting metallic plate. When the coil W, concontains several thousand feet of fine wire, the shocks are too intense to be endured. The intensity of the shocks, however, diminishes in a rapid ratio, as the distance between the coils is increased. With the arrangement represented in *Fig.* 215, shocks through the tongue are easily obtained when the wire coil is a foot or two above the ribbon coil, and the distance may be still further increased by using a larger ribbon coil or a more powerful battery. The shocks are made much more violent by wetting the hands with salt water. The intensity of the shock also diminishes rapidly as the secondary coil W, is raised from a horizontal position into an inclined one, and when it is elevated into a vertical position, its edge resting on the primary coil, they are no longer felt. These induced currents not only give powerful shocks, but also magnetize steel needles, and produce chemical decomposition: the former may be shown by placing a sewing-needle in the centre of the coil W, when it will instantly be made permanently magnetic; and the latter by disconnecting the extremities of the coil W, from the handles, and connecting them with platinum wires dipped into acidulated water, or into a solution of iodide of potassium. The character of the induced secondary current depends very much upon the arrangement of the secondary coil W: if it be composed of a long ribbon of copper, offering a large sectional area for the conduction of the current and diminishing resistance, at the same time that the different layers of the coil are approximated to each other with the smallest possible interval between them,

---

What is the effect of an interposed glass plate? What effect has increase of distance upon the intensity of the shocks? of placing the coils at right angles? What are the effects of the induced currents?

currents of large *quantity* are obtained like those required for magnetizing steel, or for igniting platinum wire, §341: but if it be composed of a very thin wire a secondary current is obtained of great *intensity*, producing powerful shocks, and intense chemical effects. During the uninterrupted circulation of the primary current no effect is perceived, but only at the moment of opening or closing the circuit. The secondary current which is obtained on closing the primary circuit, is called the *initial* secondary; and that which is obtained on breaking the primary circuit, is called the *terminal* secondary. When a battery of a single pair of plates is employed, the initial secondary is much inferior in intensity to the terminal, and gives a feebler shock: the intensity of the terminal secondary produced by breaking the circuit, is very little increased by adding to the number of the battery cells: with the initial secondary, on the contrary, every additional pair is found to increase its intensity, so that with ten cells it is found to equal the terminal, and with a larger number to exceed it: in quantity, however, the secondary currents both initial and terminal, are equal, those produced by a ribbon coil being much superior to those obtained from a wire coil.

436. Induction of a momentary Secondary current by the approach and removal of the Primary current. Similar effects may be produced by removing the primary helix P, in *Fig.* 214, from the secondary helix s, and causing the primary coil P, while it is still transmitting the battery current, suddenly to approach and recede from the secondary coil, as shown in *Fig.* 216. During the approach, a secondary current in an opposite direction is set on foot in the outer coil, as shown by the movement of the galvanometer: and again during the withdrawal a momentary secondary current, in the same direction with the primary current, is made to circulate. If the galvanometer be removed from the secondary circuit, and in its place a small wire helix substituted so as to make a continuous circuit, and a soft iron wire be introduced into the helix, it will be made temporarily magnetic: if a steel needle be introduced it will be permanently magnetized, and the intensity of the magnetism will be proportioned to the intensity of the current. These facts were also discovered by Mr. Faraday in 1831, at the same time with those described above, and his experiments were made in the following manner: " In the preceding experiments the wires were placed near to each other, and the contact

---

What is the effect of constructing the secondary coil of copper ribbon? of fine copper wire? What is the initial secondary current? the terminal secondary? How do they compare in intensity and quantity?—436. Show how induction may be produced by the approach and removal of the primary coil? Who discovered this fact?

416 APPROACH AND REMOVAL OF THE PRIMARY CURRENT.

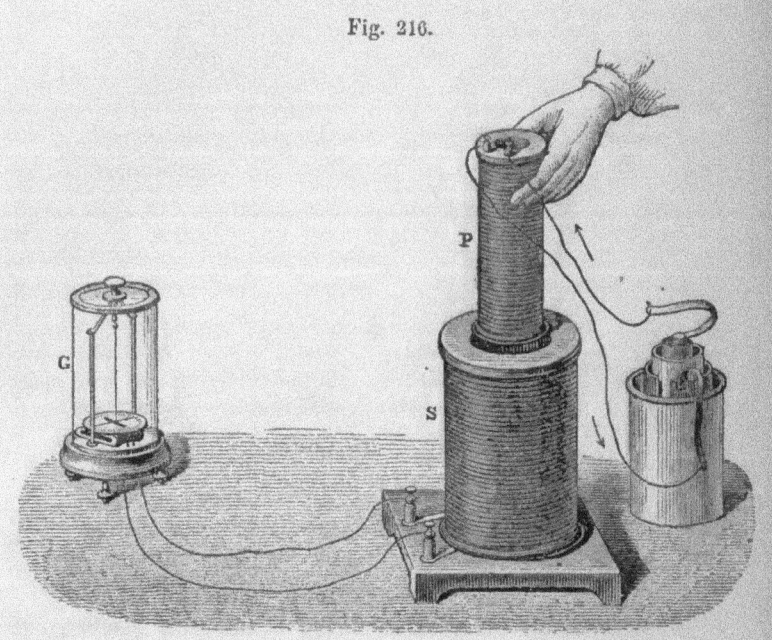

Fig. 216.

The Secondary current induced by the approach and removal of the Primary coil.

of the inducing one with the battery made when the inductive effect was required, but as the particular action might be supposed to be exerted only at the moments of making and breaking contact, the induction was produced in another way. Several feet of copper wire were stretched in wide zig-zag forms representing the letter w, on one surface of a broad board: a second wire was stretched in precisely similar forms on a second board so that when brought near the first, the wires should everywhere touch, except that a sheet of thick paper was interposed. One of these wires was connected with a galvanometer, and the other with a voltaic battery. The first wire was then moved towards the second, and as it approached, the needle was deflected. Being then removed, the needle was deflected in the opposite direction. By first making the wires approach and then recede simultaneously with the vibrations of the needle, the latter soon became very extensive; but when the wires ceased to move from or towards each other, the galvanometer needle soon came to its usual position. As the wires approximated, the induced current was in the *contrary*

How were his experiments conducted?

direction to the inducing current: as the wires receded, the induced current was in the *same* direction as the inducing current. When the wires remained stationary, there was no induced current. All these results have been obtained with a voltaic apparatus consisting of a single pair of plates."

437. The conditions of Induction, and properties of induced currents. From the experiments which have been described, the following principles may be deduced: 1st. The distance remaining the same, a continuous and constant current does not induce any current in an adjacent conductor. 2d. A current at the moment of circulation produces an *inverse* induced current in an adjacent conductor. 3d. A current the moment it ceases produces a *direct* induced current. 4th. A current which approaches a closed circuit, or whose intensity increases, gives rise to an *inverse* induced current. 5th. A current which is removed, or whose intensity diminishes, gives rise to a *direct* induced current.

The electricity of the induced current in the secondary coil is possessed of greater intensity, and will give more vivid and louder sparks and will produce more violent shocks than the primary current, especially at the moment when the connection of the primary coil with the battery is broken: it also decomposes water, metallic salts and the like, and acts upon the magnetic needle. Induced currents are more powerful, the longer the wires of the secondary coil. On the contrary, the primary coil should be made of large copper wire or ribbon, and of moderate length. The wires of both coils should be carefully wound with silk or cotton, and covered with a solution of shelllac, so as to secure perfect insulation. If the connection of the primary coil with the battery be completed or broken very rapidly, the effect of a *continuous* current of secondary electricity is secured. The direct secondary current produced by breaking connection with the battery and the primary coil, is ordinarily found to be much more powerful than the inverse secondary current produced by completing connection, §435.

438. Induction of a current on itself. The extra current on breaking and completing the primary circuit. If the wire connecting the two poles of a battery be short, and the circuit suddenly broken, only a scarcely perceptible spark is perceived. If the observer form part of the circuit by holding a pole of the battery in each hand, no spark is obtained unless the current

---

437. State the conditions of induction, and the properties of induced currents.—438. Does induction take place without the use of a secondary coil?

418 THE EXTRA CURRENT.

be very intense. If, however, the connecting wire be long and fine, and especially if it be made into a spiral with a great many turns so as to form a helix with very close folds, a very vivid spark is produced when the connection is broken, although only a feeble one passes when the connection is completed; and an observer in the circuit receives a shock, which is greater the more numerous the turns of the coil. This effect is explained by the inductive action which the current exerts upon the wire which it traverses, in virtue of which a *direct* induced current, or one in the same direction as the battery current, is induced in the wire connecting the poles of the battery, whenever the battery circuit is broken. To show the existence of this current at the moment of breaking contact, a battery may be arranged as in *Fig.* 217. Two wires form the poles of the battery, E and

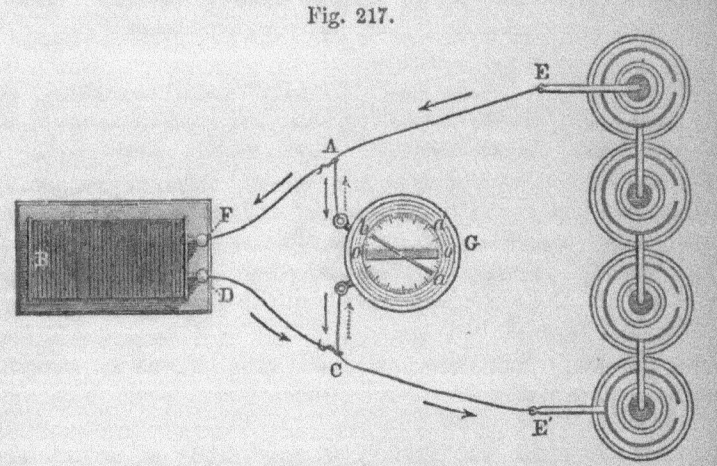

Fig. 217.

The Extra Current. The Induction of a current on itself.

E', and are connected with the two binding cups, F and D, at the extremities of a coil of long fine insulated copper wire. At the points A and C, on the wires, two other wires are connected with the galvanometer G, so that the current from the pole E, branches at A, into two currents, one circulating through the coil B, and the other through the galvanometer G, and both returning to the negative pole E'. As soon as the current circulates, the galvanometer needle is deflected from C to a, showing the tendency of the needle to move in that direction:

State the difference of effect in using a short and a long wire to connect the poles of a battery. Explain it. How can the existence of this induced current be proved? What is meant by the extra current? What effect has it upon the vividness of the spark on breaking the circuit? on completing it?

it is then brought back to zero, and kept there by the insertion of a pin which prevents it from turning in the direction G a, but leaves it free to turn in the opposite direction. Then on breaking contact at E, the needle is immediately deflected in the direction G a', showing the production of a current running contrary to that of the battery current; that is, from C to A. But the battery current having been cut off, this current C A, must traverse the closed circuit A, F, B, D, G ; that is, move in the same direction as the battery current. The current which thus appears when the battery circuit is broken, is called the *extra current*, or the *direct extra current*. This current moving in the same direction as the battery current, greatly heightens its intensity, and accounts for the vividness of the spark which is produced at the breaking of the battery circuit. A similar induced current is also produced on completing the battery circuit, but as this is an inverse current and moves in the contrary direction, it diminishes the intensity of the battery current, and therefore lessens the spark which appears on completing the circuit, and accounts for its feebleness.

439. Induction of a Secondary current in the Primary wire itself. From what has just been said, it appears that whenever the connection of the wires joining the poles of the battery is made or broken, a secondary current is induced in the primary wire itself. This induced electrical current is not derived from the battery current, but is simply a portion of the natural electricity of the wire, which has been disturbed, decomposed and thrown into an active state by the passage of the battery current: this inductive action is not confined simply to the wire which connects the poles, but also extends through the battery itself, because the natural electricity of the plates of which the battery consists has also been disturbed by the passage of the galvanic current through them, and the electrical current thus induced is added to that which has been excited in the wire joining the poles. This induced current being nothing but the disturbed natural electricity of the wire and battery, its strength and quantity must depend therefore upon the amount of matter which has been subjected to the influence of the battery current; i. e., upon the length of the wire and the number of plates in the battery : it is also affected by the manner in which the wire is arranged, whether wound into a coil or carried direct between the poles; also by the force of the primary current;

439. Is there a secondary current induced in the primary wire itself? What is the origin of this current? Is it confined to the primary wire? On what does its strength and quantity depend?

and by the suddenness with which it is broken. Thus, when the poles of a small galvanic battery consisting of a single pair of plates, are connected by a copper wire of a few inches in length, no spark is perceived when the connection is either formed or broken, or at the most only a very faint spark at the moment of breaking the circuit; but if the wire be thirty or forty feet in length, a bright spark appears at the moment when the connection is broken, though none is seen at the moment when the connection is made. By coiling the wire into a helix the vividness of the spark is increased; and a still greater effect is obtained if a piece of soft wire is introduced into the helix and converted into an electro-magnet. This increase of effect when a coil is used in place of a straight wire, seems to be due to the inductive action of the adjoining strands upon each other, as though they were so many independent wires; for it must be remembered that the secondary current is not a part of the battery current which is rushing through the wire as through a conductor, but is the natural electricity of the wire itself in a state of disturbance; and the greater the disturbance the greater the strength of the induced current: the breaking of the battery current produces a disturbance of the natural electricity of the wire, which is propagated through its whole extent; and then if this wire be coiled into a helix, the induced current in each strand is increased by the inductive influence of the strands on each side of it, in the same way as it would be if these strands were separate pieces of wire in a highly excited electrical state suddenly brought near it. The increased effect imparted to the current by the introduction of the soft iron, is due to the sudden disappearance of the magnetism of the iron as soon as the connection is broken, the sudden de-magnetization of an electro-magnet by interrupting the primary current which actuates it being always accompanied by the production of a secondary current in the same direction with the primary, as will be more fully explained presently, §443. So great is this increased effect, that though a battery may be so weak as to be altogether unable to produce any shock or emit the faintest spark when its extremities are connected by a short wire, the instant the conducting wire is lengthened and coiled into a helix, within which a rod of soft iron is placed, in consequence of the powerful induction which takes place, the

---

Give an illustration. Explain the increased effect produced by coiling the connecting wire into a helix. Explain the increased effect on inserting a rod of soft iron into the helix. Give experiments in illustration. Is there any difference in effect on making and breaking connection?

battery current on breaking contact acquires sufficient intensity to communicate powerful shocks and give vivid sparks. This is conclusively proved by the following experiments: a very small compound battery was formed of six pieces of copper bell-wire, each about 1½ inches long, and six pieces of zinc of the same size, a battery altogether too small to give the slightest shock or the faintest spark when the poles were connected: the connection between the poles was then made by means of a fine copper wire one-sixteenth of an inch in diameter, thoroughly insulated by a cotton covering, five miles in length, and wound upon a small core of soft iron: the shock on breaking connection between the poles, with this arrangement of the conducting wire, was distinctly felt at the same moment by twenty-six persons, who had formed a circle by joining hands and were placed in such a manner as to form a part of the galvanic circuit: the shock felt by the same persons on making contact with the battery, was hardly perceptible. A current is likewise produced when contact is made, but it is by no means as powerful, and is in a direction opposite to that of the battery. A thermo-electric battery which is ordinarily too weak to furnish sparks, can be made to do so on breaking contact, by means of a coil wound upon an iron axis. In the case of the large magnetic helix constructed by Dr. Page, described in §426, the length of the terminal secondary or separation spark, when the battery current was broken was immense: when the battery was allowed to attain its full power, the sudden separation of the wires produced sparks eight inches in length: when the separation was slow, the sparks were short and spread out more like flame. The effect is still further increased if the soft iron, instead of being solid, consists of a bundle of straight wires. To observe the effects of the induced extra current in the primary wire, suitable wires may be attached at A and C, *Fig.* 217, in place of the galvanometer: and thus it may be shown that this direct extra current gives violent shocks, bright sparks, decomposes water, melts platinum wire, and magnetizes steel needles. The brilliancy of the spark is much increased by employing a ribbon of sheet copper coiled into a spiral, instead of a helix of insulated wire. There is a difference in the character of the extra current when a coil of fine wire is employed, from that which is produced with a ribbon coil. In

---

What was the length of the spark produced by Dr. Page's large helix? What is the effect of substituting iron wires for the solid iron rod? How may the effects of the induced extra current in the primary wire be displayed? What are these effects? What is the effect of substituting a coil of fine wire for a ribbon coil?

the former case, it is more intense, gives more violent shocks, and effects chemical decomposition more rapidly: in the latter, it is of greater quantity, gives more vivid sparks, and exerts greater heating power. These direct and inverse extra currents, produced when the connection of the primary wire is broken or made, are not confined to the wire, but extend through the whole series of the battery, and increase in power with the extent of the series. They are probably due to the sudden polarization and discharge, §312, of all the molecules in the secondary circuit, on completing connection, and to the sudden de-polarization and discharge in the opposite direction, on breaking connection. It will be remembered that they do not exist, so long as the primary current circulates continuously through the battery. They spring into action momentarily only, the instant this continuity is interrupted.

440. Induced Tertiary currents. Induced currents of higher orders. Henry's Coils. The secondary current which is induced by the primary current of the battery, may be used to induce a tertiary current, and this tertiary a quaternary current, and so on. Thus, in *Fig.* 218, let L, represent one cell of Daniell's battery, and A, a primary coil of copper ribbon carrying the battery current: let the secondary coil be placed immediately over it, and its two extremities be extended so as to connect with the extremities of a third coil, D: these two coils will in effect form a closed circuit, and constitute but one secondary circuit: then immediately above B, let another ribbon coil be placed, whose extremities are extended so as to connect with the coil C: these two coils will in effect form but one closed circuit carrying the tertiary current: immediately above C, let another ribbon coil be placed whose extremities are extended so as to connect with those of the coil D: these two coils will in effect form but one closed circuit carrying the quaternary current: immediately above D, let another ribbon coil be placed the extremities of which are connected with the galvanometer G: these two coils will in effect form but one circuit carrying the quinquenary current. When the connection of the primary coil A, with the battery is formed or broken, a current will be induced simultaneously in all the coils, but inversely in each pair. Thus, if the connection of the coil A, with the battery be completed, a secondary current of negative electricity will be induced in the coil B; a tertiary current of pos-

---

440. Show how induced tertiary currents may be produced: currents of higher orders. State the relations of these currents when the connection with the battery is established:

HENRY'S COILS.

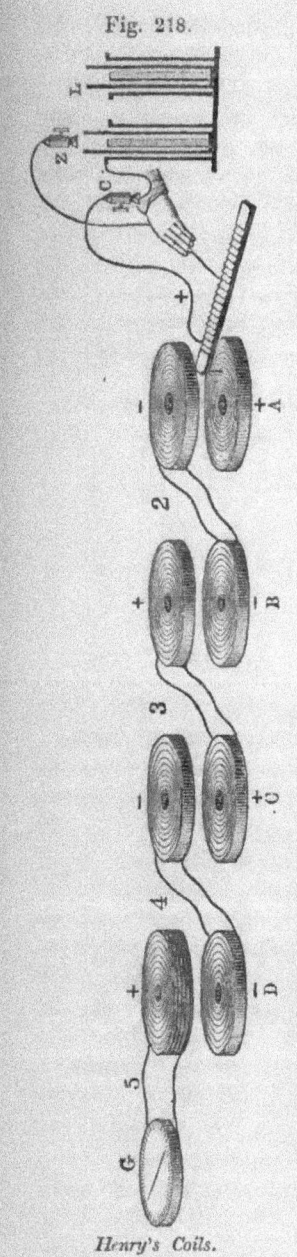

Fig. 218.

itive electricity, moving in the opposite direction, in C; a quaternary current of negative electricity, moving in the same direction, in D; and a quinquenary current of positive electricity, moving in the opposite direction, in the last coil, as shown by the galvanometer.—On breaking the connection of the primary coil with the battery, currents will be induced simultaneously in all the coils, but in the *inverse* direction; in the secondary coil they will be positive, in the tertiary negative, in the quaternary positive, in the quinquenary negative. By an extension of the series, currents even of the ninth order have been obtained, the successive currents being alternately positive and negative, direct and inverse. These coils are generally called Henry's coils, after Prof. Henry who first investigated this subject. They can be made to give currents of quantity or intensity, according as they are composed of copper ribbon or a great length of fine insulated wire. The two currents, direct and inverse, throughout the whole series, are exactly equal in quantity. They can be induced even if the coils are considerably separated from each other, though the effect is diminished by distance, and even when glass plates are interposed, but they are destroyed by the interposition of a plate of metal in any part of the series. They progressively diminish in energy from the beginning to the end of the series. The tertiary currents may be very satisfactorily exhibited by introducing a second double helix, in *Fig.* 214, between P, and the

Henry's Coils.

when it is broken. By whom was the discovery made? Give the history of the discovery.

battery, and connecting the outer helix of the second pair, with the inner helix, P, of the first; on every completion and break of the battery circuit, a secondary current will circulate in P, and a tertiary current in the opposite and in the same directions alternately, will be induced in the outer coil, S, as shown by the galvanometer. Shocks may also be obtained, which may be increased by placing a bundle of iron wires within the helix, as shown in *Fig.* 222. In the following table the direction of the successive induced currents, both at the establishment and break of the battery current are given: the sign $+$ indicating those which flow in the same direction as the battery current, and the sign $-$ those that flow in the opposite direction.

Table of the directions of the induced currents, up to the ninth order.

	At the beginning	At the ending
Primary current,	$+$	$+$
Secondary,	$-$	$+$
Tertiary,	$+$	$-$
Quaternary,	$-$	$+$
Quinquenary,	$+$	$-$
Sextenary,	$-$	$+$
Septenary,	$+$	$-$
Eighth order,	$-$	$+$
Ninth order,	$+$	$-$

441. History of the discovery. This induction of a secondary current in the primary wire itself, the peculiar action of a long conducting wire, either straight or coiled into a helix, and the increase of effect obtained by a ribbon of sheet copper, were discovered in 1831, by our countryman, Prof. Henry, now of the Smithsonian Institute, and published in the 22d volume of Silliman's Journal. The investigation was continued by him in 1834, and the results were communicated to the American Philosophical Society of Philadelphia, January 16th, 1835, and were published in a circular of that Society dated Feb. 1835, and reprinted in the Journal of the Franklin Institute, vol. XV. The same discovery was also made by Mr. Faraday, his attention having been called to the primary fact of the increase of effect produced by using a long wire, and especially one wound round an electro-magnet, to connect the poles of a battery, by a young man named William Jenkin, and was communicated by him to the Royal Society in a paper received Dec. 18th, 1834, and read January 29th, 1835, entitled "On the influence by induction of the electric current upon itself." In this paper many new facts were given, but the credit of the original discovery in 1831, clearly belongs to Prof. Henry.

§ V. Magneto-Electricity.

442. Magneto-electric Induction. The induction of a current of electricity is not limited to the primary current of the battery: a similar current is also induced by the action of a permanent magnet upon a closed wire, and also by the action of an electro-magnet actuated by a primary battery current. The former is called Magneto-electric induction; the latter, Volta-magneto-electric induction. In the case of magneto-electric induction, the conditions necessary to induce the secondary current, are as follows. There must be a closed circuit, with a galvanometer included for the purpose of indicating the existence of the current, as in the case of volta-electric induction, §433, and then a strong magnet must be rapidly brought near, and removed from the closed wire. Thus, in *Fig.* 219, a contin-

Fig. 219.

Magneto-Electric Induction.

uous wire, carefully insulated by silk, is wound into a helix, and its two ends are connected with a galvanometer in such a way as to form a *closed* circuit. On introducing a powerful magnet into the interior of the helix, which is made hollow for this purpose, the needle experiences a violent deflection, showing the

---

442. What is Electro-magnetic induction? What is Volta-electric induction? How can the induction of electricity by a magnet be proved? Describe the experiments. Why must the magnet not be introduced more than half way?

production of a current of electricity in the inverse direction from that which is circulating around the magnet, according to the theory of M. Ampère, §404. The magnet being allowed to remain motionless in the helix, in a few moments the needle resumes a stable position; but if the magnet be rapidly withdrawn from the helix, the needle is immediately deflected, and indicates an electrical current in the wire the reverse of the previous one, but in the same direction as that in the magnet. If the magnet, instead of being placed within the helix, be merely passed over it rapidly, the effect is the same. It is also found that in performing these experiments care must be taken not to introduce the magnet more than half way into the helix; for if passed wholly through at one motion, the galvanometer needle is deflected, is then suddenly stopped as by a blow, and finally is deflected in the opposite direction: the movement of the needle is reversed because as the magnet advances and appears at the opposite extremity of the coil, it comes at last to produce the same effect as withdrawing a magnet from a helix, when, as has been stated, a current the reverse of the first is produced. It is also found that the two poles of the magnet produce currents in opposite directions, i. e., if the north pole, on being introduced into the helix, produces a current from left to right as shown by the galvanometer, the south pole, on being introduced into the same helix, will induce a current in the opposite direction, or from right to left. It is also found, that, the pole of the magnet remaining the same, the winding of the coil to the right or the left, reverses the direction of the current: thus, when the north pole of a magnet is introduced into a right-hand helix, the induced current as shown by the galvanometer, will be in the inverse direction to that which is induced when the same pole is introduced into a left-hand helix.

443. Electricity also Induced by Induced Magnetism. The same effect may be produced by the rapid making and unmaking of a magnet by means of induction. If a piece of soft iron be introduced into the helix, *Fig.* 219, instead of a permanent magnet, and a powerful bar magnet be brought near the piece of soft iron, so as to induce magnetism in it, we find the same result produced as would be if a permanent magnet, having similar poles, were introduced into the helix. In *Fig.* 220, if N, s, be a powerful horse-shoe magnet, and *n, s,* be a piece of soft iron having a short piece of insulated

---

What is the inductive effect of the opposite poles? What is the effect of reversing the winding of the coil?—443. How may electricity be induced by induced magnetism? How can an electric spark be obtained from a magnet? Describe *Figs.* 220 and 221.

ELECTRICITY INDUCED 427

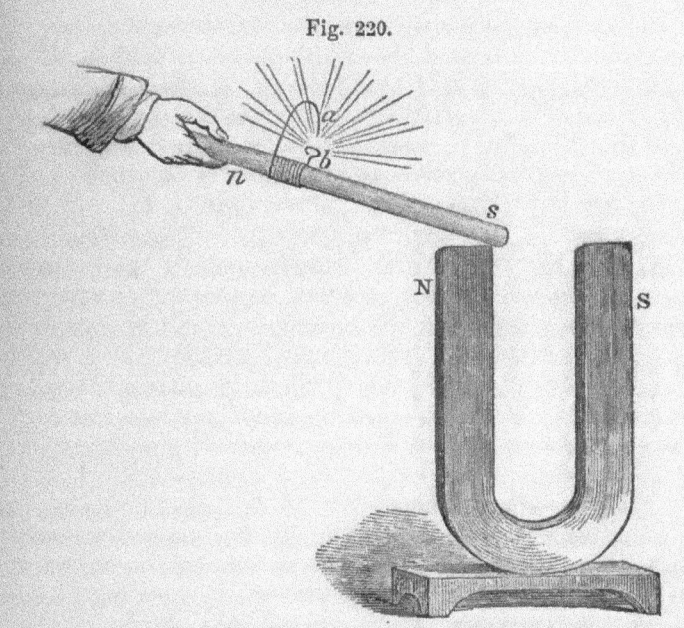

Fig. 220.

The Electric Spark obtained from a Magnet.

wire wound around it, the two ends of which, *a, b*, are brought together so as to nearly touch, then, whenever the piece of soft iron, *n, s*, is brought down on the magnet and becomes magnetized by induction, a current of electricity is generated in the coil, and a bright spark flashes between the extremities, *a, b*: a similar spark takes place whenever the soft iron bar is raised from the magnet and its induced magnetism disappears. Again, if *c*, in *Fig.* 221, be a bar of soft iron, curved and wound with wire, the two extremities of which are connected with a galvanometer, placed at some distance, and not seen in the figure, on bringing the powerful horse-shoe magnet, *a, b*, rapidly near the extremities, *m, n*, of the soft iron, the bar *c*, immediately becomes magnetized by induction, and at that instant a powerful deflection is made in the needle by the electrical current induced in the wire: the needle soon regains its equilibrium, but the instant that *a, b*, is removed, and *c*, ceases to be magnetized by induction,

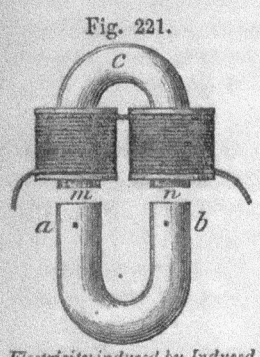

Fig. 221.

Electricity induced by Induced Magnetism.

there is a second violent deflection of the needle, showing the production of a current of electricity in the opposite direction.

444. History of the discovery of Magneto-electricity. The induction of electricity by magnetism was the discovery of Mr. Faraday, in 1831. His original experiment was arranged as follows.—" A combination of helices like that already described, §434, was constructed upon a hollow cylinder of paste-board; there were eight lengths of copper wire, containing altogether 220 feet: all the similar ends of the compound hollow helix were bound together by copper wire, forming two terminations, and these were connected with the galvanometer. One end of a cylindrical magnet, three-quarters of an inch in diameter and eight inches and a half in length, was introduced into the axis of the helix, and then, the galvanometer needle having become stationary, the remainder of the magnet was suddenly thrust in; the needle was immediately deflected in the manner in which it ought to be according to Ampère's theory: being left in, the needle resumed its former position, and then, the magnet being withdrawn, the needle was deflected in the opposite direction: these effects were not great, but by introducing and withdrawing the magnet so that the impulse each time should be added to those primarily communicated to the needle, the latter could be made to vibrate through an arc of 180° or more. In this experiment, the magnet must not be passed entirely through the helix, for then a second action occurs. When the magnet is introduced, the galvanometer needle is deflected in a certain direction; but being in, whether pushed quite through or withdrawn, the needle is deflected in a direction the reverse of that previously produced. When the magnet is passed in and through at one continuous motion, the needle moves one way, is then suddenly stopped, and finally moves the other way."—" Similar effects were then produced by the sudden induction of magnetism in soft iron. A soft iron cylinder was introduced into the axis of the hollow helix: a couple of bar magnets, each twenty-four inches long, were arranged with their opposite poles in contact at one end, and then spread out so that their other poles might be put in contact with the extremities of the soft iron cylinder, one pole being at one extremity of the helix, and the other at the other extremity, so as to embrace the iron core, and convert it into a magnet by induction: on breaking contact, or reversing the poles, the mag-

---

444. Who discovered the induction of electricity by magnetism? Describe his original experiment. How were the helices arranged?

netism was destroyed or reversed at pleasure. On making contact, the needle was deflected; continuing contact, the needle became indifferent, and resumed its first position: on breaking contact, it was again deflected, but in the opposite direction to the first effect, and then it became indifferent: when the magnetic contacts were reversed, the deflections were reversed."

445. An Electro-magnet magnetized and de-magnetized, will induce Electricity in a closed Wire.—Volta-magneto-electric Induction. In like manner, if, in *Fig.* 214, intended to illustrate Volta-electric-induction, a bar of soft iron be introduced into the centre of the primary coil, then, on establishing connection with the battery, not only is there a secondary current produced in the outer coil, on completing and breaking the circuit in the primary coil, but also an additional secondary current in the same direction as the first, by the magnetization and de-magnetization of the bar of soft iron, which takes place, whenever the connection of the inner coil with the battery is made and broken. The strength of this induced current will be proportioned to the power of the battery, to the length and fineness of the secondary wire, and also to the size of the soft iron rod employed, and the power of the electro-magnet produced. The power of an electro-magnet, other things being equal, depending upon the extent of surface which it presents, if the bar employed be very small, and introduced only a short distance, only a feeble electro-magnet will be produced, and a comparatively feeble secondary current generated. If the rod be large, and introduced to the extreme end of the coil, its electro-magnetic power will be proportionately increased, and also the strength of the secondary current. A bundle of wires is found to produce much greater effect than a solid iron rod, and this is proportioned to the number of the wires employed. This affords a very convenient mode of regulating the power of the secondary current; commencing with one wire, the strength of the induced current will be increased by every successive wire that is added. Thus, in *Fig.* 222, if P, represent the primary coil, s, the secondary coil, and G, the galvanometer, the strength of the secondary current induced by making and breaking contact with the battery, will be greatly increased with the addition of every wire that is introduced into P, indicated by the deflection of the needle and strength of the shocks.

---

445. What is the effect of making and unmaking an electro-magnet within a helix? What is the effect of increasing the size of the soft-iron core? of using wires instead of an iron rod? Describe *Fig.* 222. How can the strength of the shocks be regulated?

430   HISTORY

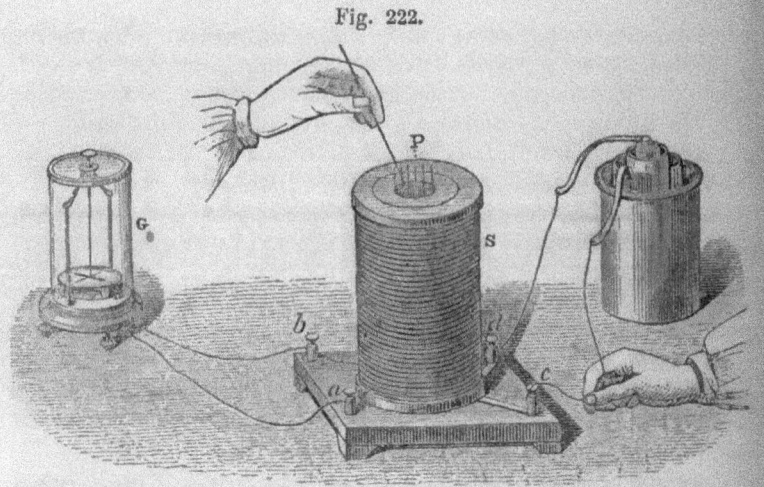

Fig. 222.

The strength of the Induced Current proportioned to the number of wires employed.

If a bar of copper were introduced into the coil, instead of an iron bar, or wires, the current would not be stronger than if the two coils alone were employed. Thus we may make use of the electricity of the primary coil to induce both electricity and magnetism, and then employ the magnetism so induced to add to the force of the induced secondary current of electricity.

446. History of the discovery of the Induction of electricity by Electro-magnetism. This was also the discovery of Mr. Faraday, in 1831. His original experiment was arranged as follows.—"A welded ring, *Fig. 223*, was made of soft round bar-iron, metal being seven-eighth's of an inch in thickness, and the ring six inches in external diameter. Three helices were put round one part of this ring, each containing about twenty-four feet of copper wire, 1-20th of an inch thick: they were insulated from the iron and from each other, and superimposed, occupying about nine inches in length upon the ring, or somewhat less than one-half of the circumference: they were arranged so as to be used separately or conjointly. On the other half of the ring about sixty

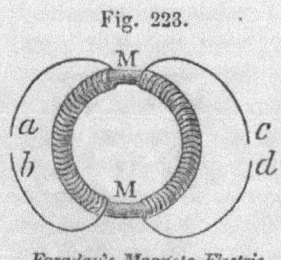

Fig. 223.

Faraday's Magneto-Electric Ring.

---

446. Who discovered the induction of electricity by electro-magnetism? Describe his original experiment. How were the helices wound upon the iron ring?

feet of similar copper wire, in two pieces, were applied in the same manner, also carefully insulated from the iron and from each other, and forming a helix which had the same common direction with the former helices, but separated from them by about half an inch of the uncovered iron at each extremity, M, M. This latter helix, a, b, was connected by copper wires with a galvanometer, three feet from the ring, so as to constitute a closed circuit. The first helices, c, d, were then united, end to end, so as to form one common helix, the extremities of which were connected with a battery of ten pairs of plates, four inches square. The galvanometer was immediately affected, and to a much greater degree than when a battery of helices of tenfold power, *not wound round soft wire*, were employed: but, although the connection with the battery was continued, the effect was not permanent, for the galvanometer needle soon came to rest in its natural position, as if quite indifferent to the attached electro-magnetic arrangement. Upon *breaking* connection with the battery, the needle was again powerfully deflected, but in the contrary direction to that induced in the first instance. Upon arranging the apparatus so that the last helix should be thrown out of action, and connecting the galvanometer with one of the three helices of the first series, the other two being separated from it and joined together, so as to form one helix, and connecting this with the battery, similar, but rather more powerful, effects, were produced upon the galvanometer needle. When the battery current was sent through the helix in one direction, the galvanometer needle was deflected on the one side; if sent through in the other direction, the deflection was on the other side. The deflection on breaking the connection with the battery, was always the reverse of that produced on completing it. On making contact, the deflection always indicated an induced current moving in the opposite direction to that of the battery, but on breaking contact, the deflection indicated an induced current moving in the same direction as that of the battery. No continuance of the battery current caused any deflection of the galvanometer needle. No making or breaking connection on the galvanometer side of the arrangement, produced any effect on the needle. Upon using the power of one hundred pairs of plates with this ring, the impulse when contact was completed or broken, was so great as to make the needle spin round rapidly four or five times, before

---

What was the effect on forming connection with the battery? on breaking connection? on reversing the current? What was the second arrangement? Which was found to be the most powerful?

its motion was reduced to mere oscillation, by the operation of the air and terrestrial magetism. Another arrangement was then employed, connecting our former experiments on Volta-electric induction with the present. A combination of helices like those already described, §434, was constructed upon a hollow cylinder of paste-board: there were eight lengths of copper wire, containing altogether about 220 feet; four of these helices were then connected end to end, and then with the galvanometer: the other intervening four were also connected end to end, and the battery of one hundred pairs discharged through them. In this form, the effect on the galvanometer was hardly sensible, although magnets could be made by the induced current. But when a soft iron cylinder, seven-eighths of an inch thick and twelve inches long, was introduced into the paste-board tube, surrounded by the helices, then the induced current affected the galvanometer powerfully, and with all the phenomena just described: it possessed also the power of making magnets apparently with more energy than when no iron cylinder was present. When the iron cylinder was replaced by an equal cylinder of copper, no effect beyond that of the helices alone was produced. The iron cylinder arrangement was not so powerful as the ring arrangement already described."

447. A Magnet will induce Electricity in a body in motion: and a Magnet in motion will induce Electricity in a body at rest.—Arago's Rotations. If a circular disc of copper, M, *Fig.* 224, be made to revolve with great rapidity beneath

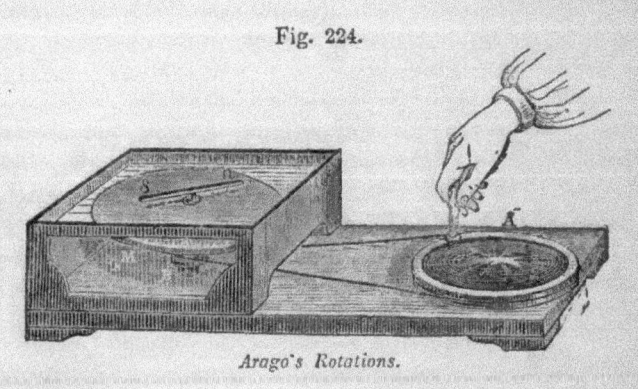

Fig. 224.

Arago's Rotations.

a magnetic needle, *n*, *s*, supported upon a flat piece of glass and in the same horizontal plane, the needle will be deflected in the

---

447. What is the effect of a magnet upon a body in motion? of a magnet in motion upon a body at rest?

direction of the motion, and stop from 20° to 30° out of the direction of the magnetic meridian, according to the velocity of the motion. If the velocity be increased, the needle is ultimately deflected more than 90°: it is then carried beyond this point, describes an entire revolution, and finally follows the motion of the disc until this ceases. Conversely, if a horse-shoe magnet placed vertically be made to rotate below a copper disc suspended on untwisted silk threads, the disc will rotate in the same direction as the magnet. The effect decreases with the distance of the disc, and varies with the material: the greatest effect is produced by the metals; with wood, glass and water, it disappears: if the action on copper be represented by 100, that on other metals is as follows: zinc 95, tin 46, lead 25, antimony 9, bismuth 2: if the disc be slit in the direction of the radius, the effect is much reduced, but is restored if a connection be completed again by soldering. These rotations were first observed by M. Arago, in 1825, after whom they have been named. He also noticed that the presence of a mass of unmagnetic metal, like copper at rest, diminishes the number of oscillations which a magnetic needle makes in a given time: in the case of copper, the number is reduced from 300 to 4. Mr. Faraday, in 1831, observed the converse of this, viz: that the presence of a magnet at rest diminishes the motion of a rotating mass of metal, and finally destroys it: if a cube of copper be suspended by a twisted thread, so as to rotate rapidly between the poles of an unactuated electro-magnet, it stops, the instant the electro-magnet is excited by the battery current. These facts were first explained by Mr. Faraday, in 1831. He showed that they are due to the secondary electrical currents which are induced in the discs of metal by the action of magnets, either the metal or the magnet being in motion. He found in all cases, that whenever a plate of conducting metal is made to pass either before a single pole, or the opposite poles, of a magnet, so as to cut the magnetic curves at right angles, electrical currents are produced in the metal at right angles to the direction of the motion: in the case of the revolving disc, the direction of these currents is from the centre to the circumference, following the direction of the radii: it is to the operation of these induced currents, that the effects in question are due. The magnetic curves here spoken of, are curved lines of magnetic force which pass through the axis of a magnet, or the line joining the poles,

---

Describe Arago's rotations. Give Mr. Faraday's explanation. What are the magnetic curves?

Fig. 225.

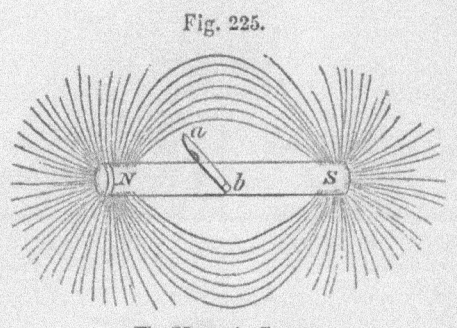

The Magnetic Curves.

and in the same plane with this line, *Fig.* 225. Whenever these curved lines of magnetic force are cut by the movement across them of any mass of matter which is an electrical conductor, as *a*, *b*, in the *Fig.*, whether it be a disc, a mass of metal, or a wire, induced secondary currents of electricity are produced.

448. The Magnetism of the Earth induces secondary currents of Electricity in metallic bodies in motion. Terrestrial magnetism, acting like an immense magnet placed in the earth, occupying the direction of the dipping needle, and according to Ampère's theory, §403, operating like a series of electrical currents, flowing from east to west parallel to the magnetic equator, will develop induced electrical currents in wires or metallic bodies that are moved across the magnetic axis of the earth parallel to the equator, and cutting the magnetic curves. This was proved in 1831, by Mr. Faraday, by placing a long helix of copper wire covered with silk, in the plane of the magnetic meridian, directed towards the magnetic pole of the earth, and parallel to the dipping needle: by turning this helix 180° degrees around its longitudinal axis, so as to revolve the strands of the helix across the magnetic meridian, he observed that at each turn, a galvanometer connected with the two ends of the helix, was deflected, showing the passage of an electric current. The same effect is always produced by moving a wire, whose ends are connected with a delicate galvanometer, at right angles across the magnetic meridian. This was beautifully demonstrated in laying the Atlantic cable at the bottom of the ocean, in a direction about due east and west: as the irregular motion of the steamship produced by the waves, drew the cable back and forth across the magnetic meridian, the secondary electrical current which it induced, inconceivably faint as it must have been, produced a perceptible deviation of the mirror and the spark of reflected light in the reflecting galvanometer, §418, at Valentia; so that it was literally true that

---

What effect has the magnetism of the earth upon metallic bodies in motion? How was this illustrated in laying the Atlantic cable?

they knew at Valentia every time the Great Eastern rolled. In this case, the ocean itself formed a part of the electrical circuit, together with the cable wire, and rendered it complete.

449. Magneto-electric Induction supports Ampere's theory. The induction of electricity by the magnet is exactly what might be expected if Ampère's theory be true, §403, 404, and confirms it. If, as is supposed by Ampère, magnetism is produced by a series of electric currents perpetually circulating around a magnet in a direction at right angles to its axis, the introduction of a magnet into the axis of a helix of insulated wire, must necessarily induce a secondary current of electricity, and its withdrawal another in the opposite direction, because the magnet corresponds to the internal helix of coarse wire carrying the primary current, *Figs*. 214, 216, in the case of Volta-electric induction, §433. The direction of the secondary current actually induced by the magnet, is also exactly what it should be if Ampère's theory be true. Magneto-electric induction is then, after all, only a case of Volta-electric induction.

It is obvious that the secondary electricity thus induced by the magnet, is not derived from the magnet, but is merely the natural electricity of the wire of the helix, which is momentarily disturbed by the approach and withdrawal of the magnet. The effect is greater the longer and finer the wire, and the more numerous the convolutions of the helix, on account of the larger amount of natural electricity which can be operated on by the magnet, and on account of the inductive action of the strands of the helix on each other, as already described in the case of Volta-electric induction, §439. The electricity thus produced is possessed of greater intensity than that which can be derived from any battery, however powerful, and very closely resembles the electricity of the machine in regard to giving shocks and producing light: if the circuit be broken at the moment when the magnetic induction takes place, sparks of extraordinary brilliancy will appear: it also possesses great power of effecting chemical decomposition, and may often be substituted with advantage, both for the common electrical machine and the galvanic battery.

450. Volta-magneto-electric Coils for inducing Secondary Electric Currents. Advantage is taken of these principles in the construction of apparatus for the production of steady and apparently continuous currents of induced electricity. Thus,

---

449. How does Magneto-electric induction support Ampere's theory? What is the source of the induced electricity? Why is the effect increased by lengthening the wire and multiplying the turns of the helix?

in *Fig.* 222, if the primary coil be arranged in such a way that its connection with the battery is rapidly completed and broken, by a mechanical contrivance adapted to the purpose, at *b*: then, so rapid a succession of secondary currents will be produced, as to have the effect of a continuous current, causing violent oscillations of the galvanometer needle, vivid sparks, and powerful shocks, the hands being previously moistened with salt water. The violence of these effects may be regulated by the number of wires introduced: with every successive wire, all the effects above described are proportionally increased, and when the coil is completely filled, the torrent of sparks becomes insupportable. Sometimes the regulation is accomplished by placing the coils in a horizontal position, and introducing a solid iron bar, or a bundle of wires, a shorter or longer distance. An instrument of this construction is often used by physicians for the administration of electricity to their patients.

451. Page's Separable Helices. One of the most perfect instruments for the exhibition and application of a secondary induced current, by the action of the primary current of the battery, combined with an electro-magnet, has been invented by our countryman, Dr. Page, and is represented in *Fig.* 226. It consists of an internal helix of coarse wire, P, of three strands, each about twenty-five feet long, and hollow in the axis, so as to admit of the introduction of a rod of soft iron, or of small iron wires. On the outside of the inner helix there is a second helix, s, consisting of from one to three thousand feet of fine wire. It is made entirely separate from the interior helix, and can be removed from it. The extremities of this helix terminate in two binding cups connected with the wires,

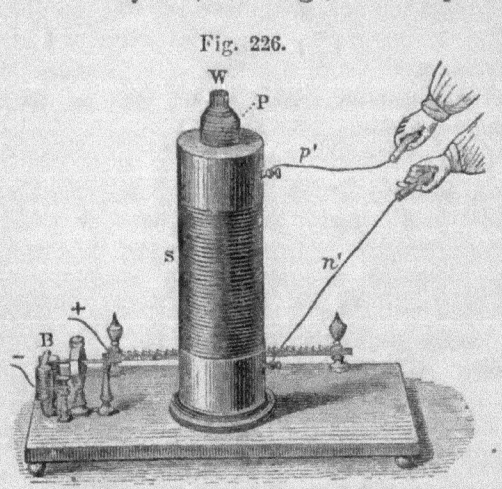

Fig. 226.

Page's Separable Helices, with Wires.

---

450. How can *Fig.* 222 be altered so as to produce a nearly continuous current of electricity? How can the violence of its action be regulated?

p', n'. The extremities of the inner helix are connected respectively with the binding cups, + and —, through the iron rasp, or else through a break-piece, B, attached to the instrument. One of the battery wires is connected with the binding cup, —, the other with the break-piece B, or applied to the iron rasp. The continual making and breaking the circuit in the inner coil, induces a momentary secondary current of electricity in the outer coil, alternately in opposite directions. If the two ends of the secondary coil, p' and n', are brought near each other, a bright spark flashes at every break in the primary current, even when no iron wires are employed. If a rod of soft iron, or a bundle of wires, w, is introduced into the centre of the helix, the spark is very much increased, brilliant scintillations are thrown off, and the shock becomes intolerable. The iron, in acquiring and losing magnetism whenever the connection with the battery is made and broken, induces a secondary current in *both* the coils, which is shown in the inner coil, in the increased scintillations which flash from the rasp; and in the outer coil, by the violent shocks which it imparts. Sometimes this instrument is provided with a mechanical contrivance moved by clockwork, for breaking the primary current, and in this case, none of the power being consumed in producing the mechanical motion which breaks the circuit, a very small battery will answer the purpose. If a silver dollar and a piece of zinc of equal size be used simply for the battery, and the inner helix be filled with soft iron wires, the shock is quite severe. If the extremities of the secondary coil are separated at the same instant that the battery current is broken, a spark will be seen, and a bright flash produced, provided these extremities are tipped with charcoal points, and held almost in contact. Water may be decomposed, if the wires are made of platinum, guarded by glass, and dipped into the liquid. The extremities of these wires shine in the dark, one constantly bright, the other intermittingly. Oxygen and hydrogen are given off in small quantities at each wire, and rapid discharges are heard in the water. A Leyden jar, the knob of which is connected with the inside coating by a *continuous* wire, may be feebly charged, and slight shocks rapidly received, by bringing the knob in contact with one of the cups of the outer helix, and grasping with the two hands respectively the outer coating of the jar, and a handle connected with the other cup. If a bundle of soft iron wires, w,

---

451. Describe Page's separable helices. How is the break-piece sometimes arranged? Describe the effects produced by this instrument. How may a Leyden jar be charged?

be introduced into the inner coil in place of the iron rod, the effects described above are much increased. The sparks and shocks may be varied at pleasure by increasing or diminishing the number of the iron wires, the addition of only one wire producing a decided effect. If a glass tube be introduced around the iron wires, between them and the inner coil, their inductive action on the secondary coil is not diminished, but if a brass tube be introduced instead of the glass, their inductive influence upon the secondary coil will be destroyed, so far as sparks and shocks are concerned: if the tube be only partially introduced, their inductive effect will be proportionably reduced, but not entirely destroyed: the distance to which the brass tube is introduced constitutes a second mode of regulating the intensity of the shocks. The brass tube neutralizes the inductive action of the wires by destroying the secondary induced current, and inducing a tertiary current in both the coils, flowing in an opposite direction, both when the battery current is established and is broken, and these tertiary currents have the effect of reducing, if not destroying, the secondary currents, which would otherwise be induced in the coils: this is always the effect of any closed wire circuit in the immediate neighborhood of a helix or coil carrying the secondary induced current.

As the two coils P and S, are separable, if the outer coil S be removed, and the inner coil be so arranged as to constitute a part of the battery circuit, which is broken at pleasure by the rasp or the revolving break-piece, the existence of the extra current, §438, shown by the increased vividness which it imparts to sparks and shocks when the battery current is broken, may be very satisfactorily exhibited; also the additional effects that are produced by inserting a soft iron rod into the interior of the helix. This instrument has been very extensively employed by physicians for the administration of electricity to their patients, on account of the facility with which the strength of the current can be regulated, by the number of iron wires introduced, by the distance to which a brass tube enclosing the wires is pushed in, or by the distance to which the iron wires or a solid rod is inserted: for greater convenience, it is usual in such experiments to mount the coils in a horizontal position.

452. The Circuit-Breaker. The effect of this instrument depends to a great degree upon the suddenness and complete-

---

What is the effect of using iron wires instead of an iron rod? of introducing a glass tube? a brass tube? Explain the latter effect. How may the existence of the extra current be displayed by this instrument? What is the arrangement of the coils when employed by physicians?

ness with which the primary current is broken. This is true in all cases of the induction of secondary currents by breaking the primary circuit. If the primary current be not broken suddenly, but gradually, there is a proportionate diminution in the power of the secondary current. In the ordinary modes of breaking the circuit, like the hammer break-piece of Ruhmkorff's coil, §453, the wires being slowly separated, there is an opportunity for the primary current to pass after the connection is actually sundered, by leaping across the small interval which separates them, in consequence of the conducting power of the air, and especially for the *extra secondary current* flowing in the primary wire to do so, on account of its extreme intensity, as is shown by the vivid spark which appears under these circumstances. The effect of this spark is to prolong the existence of the primary and extra currents in the inner coil, and consequently prolong the existence of the magnetism in the bundle of iron wires, and prevent them from being de-magnetized as quickly as they otherwise would be. This tends to prevent that suddenness in the break of the primary current, and de-magnetization of the iron on which the intensity of the induced current depends, and greatly reduces its power: the more sudden and complete the stoppage of the primary current and the annihilation of the magnetism of the iron wires, the more vivid and intense the secondary current in the outer coil, and the sparks and shocks which it produces. To obviate this difficulty, and to promote the suddenness and completeness of the break, the primary coil wire from one pole of the battery is made to terminate in a cup filled with mercury, whose surface is covered with a thin layer of spirits of turpentine: the wire from the other pole of the battery dips into the mercury, and is so arranged that when raised out of the mercury the current is broken, when depressed the current is established. The spirits of turpentine is an absolute non-conductor of electricity, and therefore the instant the wire leaves the surface of the mercury, its extremity being drawn up into a non-conducting medium instead of into the air, the flow of the current is instantaneously and completely arrested, no spark passes, the bundle of iron wires is instantly de-magnetized, and the power of the secondary current and the various effects which it produces, very greatly increased: water, alcohol and naptha are some-

---

452. On what does the effect of this instrument greatly depend? Why must the break be sudden and complete? Describe and explain the spark-arresting circuit-breaker. Explain the use of the spirits of turpentine.

times used instead of spirits of turpentine. This contrivance, which is called the spark-arresting circuit-breaker, was the invention of our countryman, Dr. Page, in 1838, and is one of the greatest improvements made in the construction of coils for the production of induced electricity by breaking the primary current: one of similar construction was introduced in France in 1856, by Foucault, and attached to Ruhmkorff's coil.

453. Ruhmkorff's Coil for inducing secondary electrical currents. One of the most interesting and extraordinary of the various machines for producing continuous secondary currents of electricity, is the coil of Ruhmkorff, a philosophical instrument maker at Paris, of which a section is given in *Fig.* 227. The principle of this instrument is precisely the

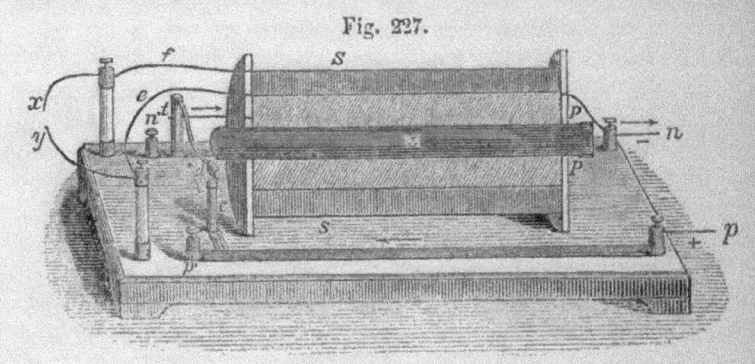

Fig. 227.

Ruhmkorff's Coil dissected.

same as the last. It consists of two concentric coils of copper wire: the primary or inner coil, P, P, consisting of five to twelve yards of copper wire, about 1-12th of an inch in diameter, coiled around two to three hundred times: and the outer or secondary coil, s, s, made of very long and thin wire, about 1-100th of an inch in diameter, and from three to five miles in length, the coil being formed by 20,000 to 25,000 turns of wire, and terminating in the wires f and e, which are directly connected with the points y and x. The inner helix is coiled directly on a cylinder of card-board, forming the nucleus of the apparatus, and inclosed in an insulating cylinder of glass or caoutchouc. Great attention is paid to the insulation: the wires are not merely insulated by being wound with silk, but each individual layer is insulated from the others by a coating of

---

453. Describe Ruhmkorff's Coil. How is the inner coil wound? the outer coil? How is insulation secured?

shell-lac. The length of the secondary coil varies greatly; in some of the larger sizes it is forty or fifty miles, and made of very thin wire: the thinner the wire the greater the tension of the secondary current: M, is a cylindrical bar composed of soft iron wires, firmly bound together, and is placed in the axis of the instrument. At p and n, are binding screws, for establishing a connection between the primary coil and a battery composed of three or four of Grove's cells. The battery current enters at p, passes on by the metallic band to the pillar c, thence to d; then through t, to the primary coil, P, P, and after traversing the whole length of that coil, finally rejoins the battery through n; its course through the instrument being indicated by the arrows. The circulation of the battery current through the primary coil admits of being broken at c and d. When d, which is a small hammer suspended from a pivot at t, is raised, the current is broken; when it is down, the current is continuous, passes on through the hammer, and after traversing the whole of the primary coil, eventually finds its way back to the battery, at n. As soon, however, as the current begins to circulate through P, P, the bundle of iron wires, M, becomes strongly magnetic, attracts d from the pillar c, and the *primary current is interrupted*; the instant this takes place, M loses its magnetism, and the hammer, d, falls; as soon as this occurs, the battery current immediately begins to circulate again, and M is again made magnetic, d is again attracted, the current is again broken, and is again renewed. The break in the current is made several times in a second, and by mechanical means may be made much more rapid. By each of these interruptions, a powerful secondary current is momentarily induced in the outer coil of fine wire, s, s, partly by the inductive influence of the primary current itself, and partly by the influence of the magnetism momentarily induced and destroyed in the bar M, according to the principles stated in the preceding sections: if there be a break in the secondary coil, as at y and x, Fig. 227, the electricity will leap across the interval with the production of vivid sparks. Every time the connection with the battery is broken, two direct secondary currents, one of positive and the other of negative electricity, are induced, moving in the same direction with the battery current. Two inverse secondary currents of positive and negative electricity, moving in the *opposite* direction from the battery current, are also induced at

---

Describe the arrangement of the coils. How is the current broken? How many currents are induced at every break and completion of the circuit?

every completion of the battery current: consequently each of the poles y and x, is alternately affected with positive and negative electricity, and if equal in quantity and tension, would exactly neutralize each other. But the currents induced when the current is completed, are not equal to those induced when the connection is broken: on breaking, the current is of shorter duration and more tension; on completion, of longer duration and less tension. When the two extremities of the outer coil, y and x, are connected by a continuous wire, the direct and inverse currents being nearly equal in aggregate power, the latter partially neutralize the former; but if the two extremities of the coil are separated at y and x, as in *Fig.* 227, the resistance of the air is then opposed to the passage of the currents, and only the current which has the superior tension, i. e., the direct current produced by breaking connection, and moving in the same direction with that of the battery, is able to leap over the interval and effect a passage: the separation of the two currents is more complete the greater the interval, up to a certain point, when neither pass, and there is then nothing induced at the poles y and x, but electrical tensions alternately in contrary directions. Consequently, in *Fig.* 227, as it is the direct current corresponding with the battery current only that passes between y and x, y must be taken as the positive pole, and x as the negative pole, because they discharge intermittent streams, the one of positive and the other of negative electricity exclusively. These currents are of extreme intensity, and produce vivid sparks which succeed each other in continuous succession. The intensity of these sparks may be greatly increased by increasing the suddenness with which the continuity of the primary current is broken. The power of the instrument may also be greatly increased by attaching to the primary coil a modification of the Leyden jar, called a Condenser. This consists of 150 sheets of tinfoil about 18 inches square, exposing a total surface of about 75 square yards. These sheets are pasted together so as to form two large sheets, and then attached to the two sides of a sheet of oiled silk, which completely insulates them, thus forming in effect a very large Leyden jar. They are then coiled several times around each other, so that the whole can be packed beneath the base of the instrument. One of these sheets, the positive, is connected with the binding cup n', *Fig.* 227, so as to communicate with

Explain why the direct currents alone can force a passage. How may the vividness of the sparks be increased? What is the arrangement of the condenser? What effect has it upon the extra-current spark? upon the spark of the secondary coil? Explain

the primary current when it emerges from the primary coil; the other, the negative, is connected with the binding screw p' which communicates directly with the battery current: these correspond with the binding screws G and H, in *Fig.* 228. The operation of this instrument seems to be as follows.—We have seen, §439, that, at each break of the battery current, an induced extra-current in the same direction is produced in the primary coil itself; and it is this which produces the spark that passes at each moment between the hammer and the anvil: being in the same direction, and prolonging the existence of the direct current in the primary coil, it tends to prolong also the magnetic effect, and to prevent the bundle of soft iron wires from being de-magnetized as quickly as it would be otherwise. By attaching the condenser to the primary current, the extra current, instead of producing a strong spark, darts into the condenser, the positive electricity into one sheet, and the negative into the other: they then combine quickly by the thick wire, by the battery, and the circuit, H, L, *Fig.* 228, and in so doing give rise to a current in a direction opposite to that of the primary current, which instantly de-magnetizes the bundle of soft iron wires, and renders the break of the primary current much more sudden and complete. The peculiar action of the condenser upon the coil by the absorption of the extra current, was discovered by Fizeau at Paris in 1853: by connecting the plates of the condenser with each side of the circuit-breaker, he found that the sparks discharged at the hammer by the extra-current were diminished, while those of the outer coil at y and x, were doubled in length. It was soon attached to the coil by Ruhmkorff, and the intensity of the secondary current so exalted as to lengthen its spark from one-eighth to a little more than half an inch. This was the first great improvement made upon the coil as constructed by Dr. Page. Other improvements were added in 1856 and 1857, by means of which the power of the instrument was gradually increased, until finally sparks of extreme intensity, from eighteen to twenty inches in length, were obtained from the secondary coil at y and x. The rapid de-magnetization is also greatly accelerated by making use of a bundle of iron wires instead of a solid bar of soft iron. This improvement was made by Dr. Page in 1838, in the construction of his separable helices, §451: this effect seems to be produced in great part by the neutralizing influence of the similar poles of the

---

its operation. Who discovered this fact? What effect is produced upon the suddenness of de-magnetization by the use of iron wires?

444 RUHMKORFF'S COIL COMPLETE.

wires on each other. Thus it appears that by the coils of Page and Ruhmkorff, galvanic electricity of low tension may be used to induce statical electricity as intense as that of the ordinary electrical machine, while its quantity is far greater; so that they may be substituted with great advantage for that machine in most cases, where a continuous discharge of sparks and shocks is required.

454. Ruhmkorff's Coil complete. The same instrument is represented in relief, in *Fig.* 228: K, represents a milled handle

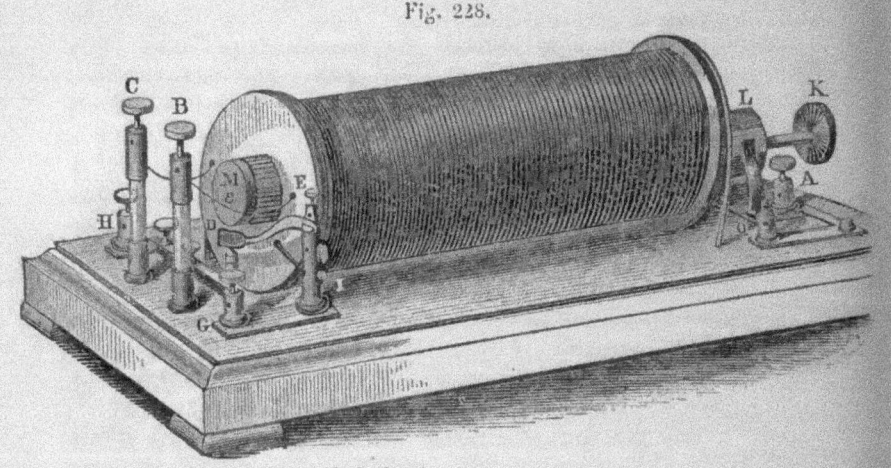

Fig. 228.

Ruhmkorff's Coil complete.

by which the cylinder L, called the Commutator, consisting of alternate pieces of copper and ivory, is turned so as to bring either piece into contact with the metallic spring O and reverse the direction of the primary current through the coil, by connecting at pleasure with the positive or negative pole of the battery: A, is the binding screw through which the positive current from the battery enters, and there is another on the opposite side of L, not seen in the *Fig.*, for the passage of the negative current: from A, the positive current passes up the spring O, into the commutator L, by which it is transmitted to the commencement of the primary coil, making its exit at I: it then proceeds to the hammer D, through G, to the binding cup H, whence it returns to the negative pole of the battery: M, is the bundle of soft iron wires, occupying the core of the instrument: C and B, are the binding screws connected with the extremities of the outer or secondary coil, and which may

Describe Ruhmkorff's Coil as represented in *Fig.* 228.

be brought into connection with each other by wires, as at *y* and *x*, in *Fig* 227: the condenser is attached at G and H. On turning the handle K, so as to bring the metallic piece L into contact with the spring O, the primary current immediately circulates through the inner coil, and a shower of vivid sparks flashes continually from B to C, when the proper connections are made by wires nearly touching each other. With large coils the hammer cannot be used, on account of the extreme violence of the spark produced by the extra-current; the surfaces become so much heated as to melt: to obviate this difficulty, and to promote the suddenness and completeness of the break in the circuit, a mercury circuit-breaker, §432, has been invented, by which the power of the instrument has been greatly increased and the use of the hammer discontinued: more recently, mechanical means have been employed for breaking the circuit slowly or rapidly, at the pleasure of the operator: by these and other improvements, this very interesting and remarkable instrument has been brought from a comparatively feeble state to a very high degree of efficiency, by our countryman, Mr. Ritchie, a philosophical instrument maker at Boston.

455. Ritchie's improved Ruhmkorff Coil. The length of the secondary spark which Ruhmkorff obtained in his original coil, did not equal one inch: in 1857, Hearder, in England, by more carefully insulating the coils, obtained sparks of three inches: it was found impossible to make larger and more powerful coils, in consequence of a discharge taking place within the coils, the current forcing a passage from strand to strand between the outer and inner portions and breaking down the insulation, the successive layers of wire being only separated by insulating media; and the longer and finer the outer coil, the stronger is the tendency for the secondary current to force a passage laterally through the adjoining layers in preference to passing through the immense length of the secondary wire, amounting in some cases to eighty miles. In 1857, Mr. Ritchie devised a mode of winding the wire of the outer helix in several different sections, carefully insulated from each other: the first section commences near the axis just upon the outside of the primary coil, and gradually extends to the outer circumference, in a plane perpendicular to the axis, (in the manner that sailors coil ropes on the deck); then continues to the next section, which is carefully insulated from the first, and wound from the outer circumference to the inner, and so on altern-

Describe Ritchie's Improved Ruhmkorff Coil.

446 IMPROVED

ately from section to section, until the coil is completed; in this manner, in consequence of the division of the outer coil into many sections, and their very perfect insulation, it becomes impossible for the secondary current to force a lateral passage and break through the coil. The result was, that in 1857, coils were made which gave sparks of twelve and eventually sixteen inches, in place of three. The instrument consists of a primary coil of copper wire about 1-6th of an inch in diameter and about 150 feet in length, wound in three courses, very carefully annealed, and mounted vertically, as in *Fig.* 229: this coil is completely covered externally with gutta-

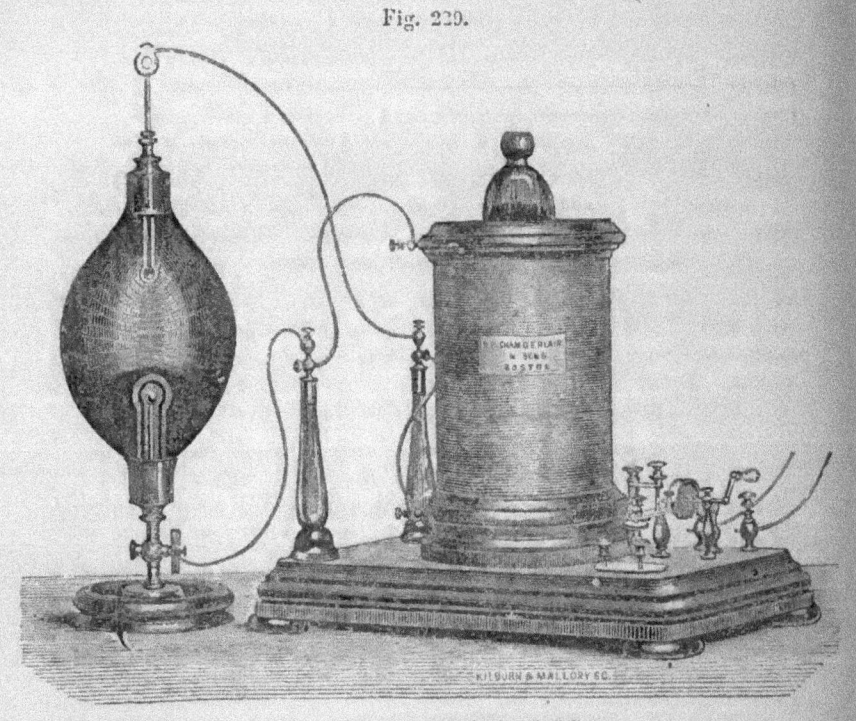

Fig. 229.

Ritchie's Improved Ruhmkorff Coil.

percha 4-10ths of an inch in thickness, and passing entirely through the basement to a plate of the same substance, to which it is united: within this coil is placed the bundle of soft iron wires: over the primary coil and magnet a thick glass cylinder or bell is placed, closed at the top, and provided with a knob by which it can be raised from its position. On the outside of this glass bell is placed the secondary coil, consisting of very fine copper wire, about 1-100th of an inch in diameter, very carefully insulated by silk winding, from three to thirty, and even eighty miles in length, wound in the manner above described, upon a cylinder of gutta-percha: the extremities of this coil are enclosed in rubber tubes and carried to insulated glass pillars, from which the induced current is taken by platinum wires in whatever direction it may be required: in *Fig.* 229, it is conveyed to the electric Egg, for the purpose of exhibiting its extraordinary illuminating power when discharged through a vacuum. The condenser is made of tin-foil pasted on tissue paper, of three thicknesses between each stratum: it is composed of three sections, of 50, 100, and 150 feet, which by means of screws can be used separately or in combination; this is packed beneath the basement and directly connected with the binding screws of the circuit-breaker. The interrupter, or circuit-breaker, is raised by means of a small crank worked by hand, operating upon a ratchet wheel, whose teeth strike the extremity of a delicately adjusted lever, from the other end of which the hammer is suspended: the rapidity of the break in the circuit may be varied at pleasure by turning the crank slowly or rapidly: the battery current is derived from two to four cells of Bunsen's carbon battery. When the crank is turned very slowly, the connection of the primary coil with the battery is prolonged, and the bundle of iron wires becomes very highly magnetized: the break then takes very suddenly, and instantaneously develops the entire force of the secondary current, producing sparks of great length and density, the discharge being surrounded by a kind of burr: if the velocity of the rotation be gradually increased, the spark assumes the luminous appearance of the sparks of the electrical machine: if the velocity be still further increased, the luminous discharge will disappear, for there will not then be sufficient time, between the establishment and break of the connection with the battery, to magnetize the iron core on which the intensity of the induced secondary current chiefly depends. The power of this instrument is vastly greater than that of any electrical machine; sparks of more than twelve inches in length can easily be obtained, discharges can be made so rapidly as to appear continuous, and a Leyden jar can be charged and discharged with so much rapidity as to exhibit hardly any perceptible interval, and with a noise almost stunning.

How is the circuit-breaker of Ritchie's machine arranged? What is the effect upon the power of the instrument?

This machine of Ritchie's excited much attention in Europe, in consequence of its immense superiority to all previous coils, and the obvious improvement in its mode of construction. Its mode of winding was almost immediately adopted by Ruhmkorff, and the secondary coil still further lengthened, amounting in some cases to 100,000 French metres, or even more,—from sixty to eighty miles,—and projecting sparks two feet in length: this took place in 1859; and in 1864, he received as a reward the prize of 50,000 francs offered by the French Emperor in 1852, for the most important discovery connected with the development of electricity.

456. The management of Ruhmkorff's Coil. The charging of a Leyden jar. The principal steps in the improvement of induction coils, as first constructed, are the increased length and fineness of the secondary coil, the employment of soft iron wires instead of the iron bar in the inner coil, and the spark-arresting circuit-breaker,—all inventions of Dr. Page: the discovery of the effect of the condenser by Fizeau, and its application by Ruhmkorff; and the peculiar mode of winding, combined with very perfect insulation, devised by Ritchie:—to the combined effect of these various improvements, made through a series of many years, the extraordinary power of Ruhmkorff's coil, in its most perfect form, is due. Several coils may be combined so as to increase the quantity of electricity which they will furnish, by placing them side by side and connecting them by wires in such a manner that the battery current will circulate through the primary helix of each coil in succession, thereby forming in effect one long primary coil: as only one hammer is required for the purpose of breaking the current, the remaining hammers should be removed: in like manner the secondary coils should all be connected by wires, so as to unite all the positive poles together into one pole, and all the negative poles into the other: the extreme positive and negative poles may then be brought together for the purpose of displaying the effects of the instrument in the usual manner: by this arrangement the quantity of electricity will be greatly increased, but no increase in the tension of the current will be obtained. If an increase of tension is required, each secondary circuit must be connected in a regular series, the positive pole of one to the negative pole of

---

What improvement was made by Ruhmkorff? with what result?—456. State the successive improvements. How may coils be combined so as to increase the quantity of the current? the tension?

A LEYDEN JAR. 449

the next, so as to form in effect but one secondary coil, each primary coil being excited by a separate battery. A Leyden jar may be charged by connecting the outer coating, *Fig.* 230, with

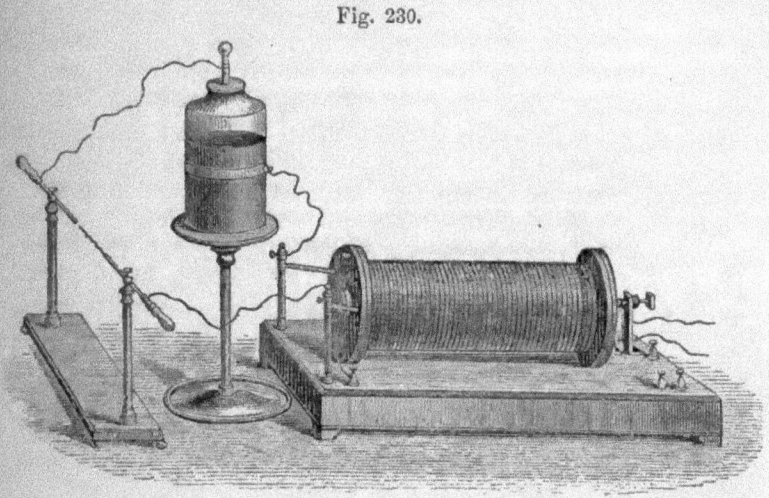

Fig. 230.

The charging of a Leyden jar by Ruhmkorff's Coil.

one of the poles of the coil, and the inner with one of the arms of a discharger, the other arm of which is in communication with the opposite pole of the coil: the extremities of the discharger should be placed two or three inches apart: after a few sparks have passed, the jar may be removed and discharged in the usual manner: with a large instrument an electrical battery containing several jars, and exposing ten square feet of surface, may be charged to saturation in a few seconds, and far more rapidly than by an ordinary electrical machine. If instead of the above arrangement, the outer coating of the jar be connected with one pole of the coil, and the inner with the other, the poles of the coil being at the same time connected by wires set about one inch apart, the Leyden jar will be constantly charged and discharged without cessation, the discharge taking place as a spark two or three inches in length, very bright, and producing an explosive sound, which seems to be continuous. If a platinum wire be twisted around the knob of a Leyden jar, and its ends be brought near enough to the poles of the secondary coil to almost touch them without quite doing so, a noise-

---

How can a Leyden jar be charged? What experiment may be tried with the coil and Leyden jar? What is the effect of charging large electrical batteries by cascade?

less spark of feeble light will pass from each pole to the end of the platinum wire nearest it, at both interruptions; if now the outer coating of the jar be connected with one of the secondary poles, the spark, at the interruption on that side, will suddenly become brilliant and noisy: the noiseless spark will kindle paper or other combustible objects, while the noisy flash from the Leyden jar will fail to kindle them. With Ruhmkorff's large coil, electrical batteries may be charged and discharged with a continuous and almost deafening noise. The most brilliant effects are produced by charging a series of jars by cascade. When six jars, each containing about two square feet of coated glass, are employed, a continuous stream of dazzling light six inches in length, is produced, accompanied by a noise that speedily becomes almost intolerable. With one jar, the discharge spark is two and one-half inches long; with two jars, three and a half inches; with three jars, four and one-quarter inches; with four jars, five inches; and with five jars, five and a half inches.

457. The Mechanical effects of Ruhmkorff's Coil. The effects of Ruhmkorff's coil are vastly more intense than those of the battery, and may be classed under the heads, Mechanical, Physiological, Heating, Luminous, and Chemical. The mechanical effects of the secondary current produced by this coil are disruptive in their character, and resemble those of a flash of lightning. For this reason it should be passed through glass vessels with the greatest caution. With the largest apparatus, glass plates two inches thick have been perforated. It should not be used for firing Endiometers, except with the greatest care and the employment of a very small battery.

458. The Physiological Effects. The physiological effects are extremely intense. The shocks are so powerful, that oftentimes careless experimenters have been prostrated by them. With two of Bunsen's cells attached to the primary coil, hares and rabbits have been killed, and a somewhat larger number would be sufficient to kill a man.

459. The Heating Effects. The heating effects are intense. If a thin iron wire be stretched between the two points y and x, it is immediately melted and burned with a vivid light: if each of the poles y and x, be terminated with a fine iron wire, whose extremities are brought near enough together almost to touch, *Fig.* 231, the wire connected with the negative pole will melt into a little globule of liquid iron, while the other will

---

457. What are the Mechanical effects of the coil?—458. What are the Physiological effects?—459. What are the Heating effects? Is there any difference in the temperature

THE HEATING EFFECTS. 451

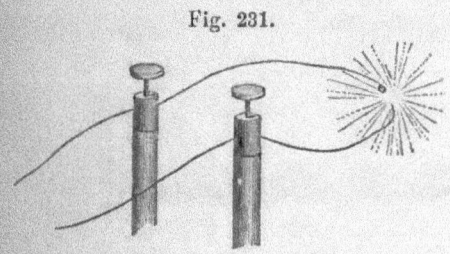

Fig. 231.

The heating effects of the poles of Ruhmkorff's Coil.

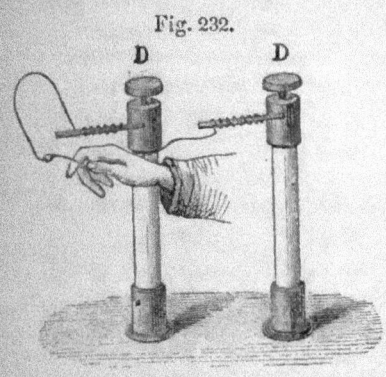

Fig. 232.

One pole cold.

remain cold enough to be held in the fingers, *Fig.* 232, and if a reflection of these points be thrown upon a screen by means of Duboscq's electric lamp, *Fig.* 160, a cone of vapor will appear to issue from the point of each wire, but that from the negative wire being the most powerful, apparently beats back the heated stream from the positive wire. These effects are the reverse of those produced in the voltaic arc of the galvanic battery, in which the greatest dispersion of matter and the highest temperature, are observed to occur at the positive pole. The heat is sufficiently intense to inflame all combustible substances, and to fuse and burn metals. Great use is made of this in Spectrum analysis, §285, 6, 7. Another very remarkable effect of Ruhmkorff's coil, first noticed by Dr. Page, is the ignition of disintegrated conductors: shreds of metal and other conducting substances in a pulverulent condition, are ignited and fused: a very small machine will ignite a pencil mark of plumbago, even through many miles of wire, and shreds of iron over an inch in length. Advantage has been taken of this in the construction of fuses for firing gunpowder in blasting, and in the discharge of fire-arms. A fuse has been invented called from its inventor, Statham's fuse, which depends upon the igniting action of the current upon the sulphide of copper. It has been found that in a copper wire covered with vulcanized gutta-percha or india-rubber, a layer of sulphide of copper forms, after some months, at the point of contact of the metal and its coating, which is sufficient to conduct the current. If a por-

---

of the poles? Which is the hotter? How do the poles appear, when seen by Duboscq's lamp? How do these effects compare with those of the battery? What is the degree of the heat? What effect is produced upon shreds of metal?

tion of the coating be removed from a wire loop, *Fig.* 233, and

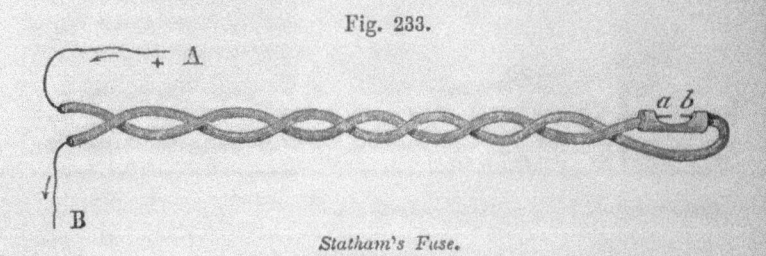

Fig. 233.

Statham's Fuse.

a quarter of an inch of the wire cut away, the current, interrupted at *a* and *b*, finds a passage by means of the sulphide of copper, which it ignites, and any inflammable substance like gunpowder or gun-cotton, placed in this cavity, takes fire. A very powerful battery would be required to ignite such a fuse, but with Ruhmkorff's coil, only one or two of Bunsen's elements are required, the ends of the secondary helix being connected with A and B. This fuse has been very successfully employed in exploding mines in the works at Cherbourg, in France: six mines were simultaneously fired at a distance of 1,500 feet from the apparatus. Recently a more sensitive priming material has been introduced, consisting of ten parts of sub-phosphide and forty-five of sub-sulphide of copper, and fifteen of chlorate of potash, finely powdered in a mortar, with the addition of sufficient alcohol to moisten it throughout: the mixture is dried and preserved until required, in close vessels. The magneto-electric machine to be presently described, §467, is now generally employed for firing such fuses, and it is stated that one such machine contained in a box of a cubic foot in size, worked by hand, in a telegraph office in Washington, has exploded a cartridge of powder in an office in New York, over 200 miles distant. Another very common application of Ruhmkorff's coil, is to the simultaneous lighting of theatres and large halls, by the discharge of the current through platinum points placed in the gas-jets.

460. The Luminous Effects. The Luminous effects of Ruhmkorff's coil are also very extraordinary, and vary as they take place in air, *in vacuo,* or in very rarefied vapors. In the air, a very bright and loud spark is produced, which, with the coils of the largest size, has a length of eighteen or twenty

---

Describe Statham's fuse. What applications are made of these fuses?—460. Describe the Luminous effects of Ruhmkorff's coil in air: *in vacuo.*

THE LUMINOUS   453

inches. If the discharge be made to take place *in vacuo*, in an exhausted receiver, an extremely beautiful auroral light is produced, extending through an interval of one or two yards. The experiment is made by connecting the two wires of the secondary coil with the extremities of the electrical egg, *Fig.* 229. This is screwed upon the plate of an air pump, and a vacuum, as complete as possible, produced. As soon as the sparks are allowed to pass, a beautiful luminous trail is observed to flow from one knob to the other, *Fig.* 234, No. 1, the negative ball

Fig. 234.

The Luminous effects of Ruhmkorff's Coil.

is surrounded by a quiet glow of light, whilst a pear-shaped luminous discharge takes place from the positive ball; between the two is a small interval, nearer to the negative than the pos-

How is the experiment performed? Describe No 1, in *Fig.* 234.

itive ball which is not luminous. The discharge is constant, and as bright as that obtained from a powerful electrical machine. When the exhaustion of the receiver is very perfect, the luminous portion is traversed by a series of dark bands or arches concentric with the positive ball, *Fig.* 234, No. 2: the presence of a little vapor of phosphorus renders these dark bands much more distinct. If the finger be applied at the side of the egg, the connection of the lower knob with the negative pole of the coil being broken, the trail suffers a curious deviation, and is drawn towards the finger, *Fig.* 234, No. 3. The positive pole possesses the most brilliancy, and its light is red, like fire, while that of the negative pole is feeble, and of a violet color. If, instead of using an electric egg, the receiver of an air pump be employed, containing a tumbler made of Uranium glass, lined with tin-foil about half-way up the inside, and a metallic rod be passed, air-tight, through the top of the jar, until it touches the metallic lining on the inside of the tumbler; then, on connecting one pole of the coil with the plate of the air-pump, *Fig.* 235, and the other with the sliding rod, a beautiful and continuous cascade of electric light will pour over the edge of the tumbler upon the metallic plate of the pump. The effect is heightened if the tumbler be placed upon a glass dish washed over with sulphate of quinine: a blue fluorescence will be produced which will contrast well with the yellow glass.— By introducing the vapors of different substances and different gases, the light of the electric egg is entirely changed, and a very curious stratified light produced, varying with the substance employed. The best method of procedure, is to seal wires of platinum into the extremities of a glass tube, introduce the gases, and then exhaust the tube more or less completely. Thus, if a long wide glass tube, *Fig.* 236, containing sticks of caustic potash, at P, be filled with carbonic acid gas, and exhausted by the air-pump, the residual carbonic acid will then be absorbed by the potash, and the vacuum thus made very nearly perfect. The effects observed on connecting the wires + and —, with

Fig. 235.

The Uranium Glass.

Describe No. 2: No. 3. What is the effect of using an Uranium glass? What is the effect of employing the vacua of different gases?

OF DIFFERENT GASES. 455

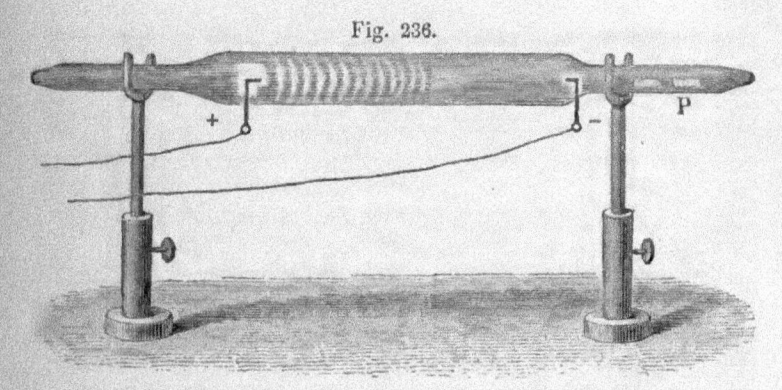

Fig. 236.

Luminous effects of Ruhmkorff's Coil in a vacuum of Carbonic Acid.

the poles of the secondary coil of Ruhmkorff, vary with the perfection of the vacuum. If it be merely that which can be produced by an ordinary air-pump, no stratification is obtained, and only a diffuse lambent light fills the tube; if the rarefaction be carried a step further, narrow striæ, like ruled lines, traverse the tube, *Fig.* 237, No. 1: a further rarefaction increases the

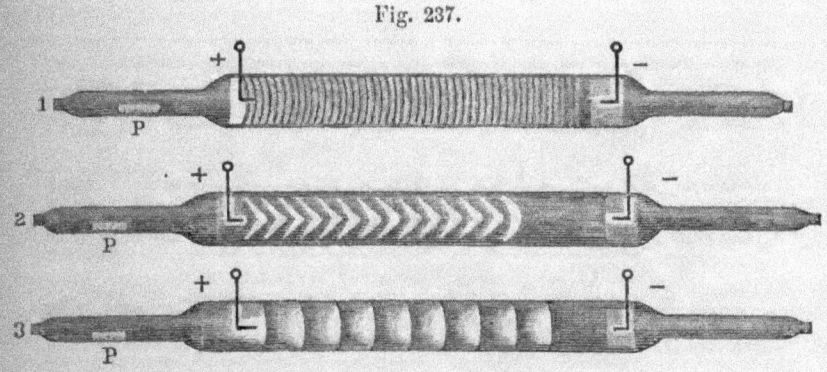

Fig. 237.

Luminous effects varying with the completeness of the vacuum.

breadth of the bands: if pushed still further, the bands assume a cup-shaped or conical form, *Fig.* 237, No. 2; and finally, a series of luminous cylinders, with narrow dark lines between them, *Fig.* 237, No. 3; lastly, when the vacuum approaches perfection, all the discharge and light absolutely cease. When

Describe the effect of a Carbonic acid vacuum made more and more complete? What is the effect when the vacuum is perfect?

the stratification is most distinct, a dark space appears at the negative pole, and the platinum wire is seen to be covered with a bluish glow of light, within which the metal glows as if red hot: as the experiment is continued and the wire rises considerably in temperature, portions of the negative wire are gradually thrown off in the form of fine metallic particles. The shape and color of the striæ vary with the gases employed. In hydrogen the light is white and red; in carbonic acid, greenish; in nitrogen, orange yellow. The light furnished by hydrogen, nitrogen, carbonic acid, and other gases, give different *spectra* when decomposed by the prism and viewed through a telescope. With oxygen, a good characteristic spectrum is not obtained, on account of its gradual disappearance and combination with the platinum of the pole; the bi-oxide of nitrogen is decomposed, giving, after a brief interval, the spectrum of pure nitrogen in great splendor; aqueous vapor is decomposed, and the spectrum of hydrogen produced: with ammonia, the spectra of hydrogen and nitrogen super-imposed, are obtained. If the vapor of spirits of turpentine, pyroligneous acid, alcohol, or bisulphide of carbon, are introduced into such tubes before the exhaustion, the aspect of the light is still further modified, and some very magnificent effects obtained. In an absolute vacuum, the current does not pass at all, the transport of some material particles being always necessary for its passage. Glass tubes containing highly rarefied gases and vapors, and of various forms and sizes, are constructed with great ingenuity by M. Geissler, of Bonn, and may be procured in this country of the principal philosophical instrument dealers. The light produced is oftentimes of the most beautiful and varied character, and the phenomena are sometimes made still more brilliant from the fluorescence which the discharge excites in the glass.

461. The Light intermittent, and affected by the Magnet. The stratified light of Ruhmkorff's coil is intermittent in its character, on account of the nature of the apparatus. This can be shown very beautifully by causing one of the vacuum tubes to revolve very rapidly upon an axle, the two arms projecting at right angles to the axis, like the spokes of a wheel, one extremity of the tube being in constant contact with one end of the coil, and the other with the other end. As the rotation goes on, the tube will be visible momentarily, the experiment being made in the dark, several times during each revolution, and

---

What is the effect upon the platinum wire? What is the color in Hydrogen? in Carbonic acid? in Nitrogen? Do the different gases give different spectra when their light is decomposed by the Prism?

will produce the appearance of a star of light, each arm of the star possessing distinct stratified bands, and appearing to be stationary on account of the briefness of the time for which it is visible. The phenomena of stratification are not owing to the undulations produced by the rapid succession of the secondary currents, for the same effects have been produced from a water-battery of 3,500 cells, also from 400 small Grove's cells; the quantity transmitted was so small, that the amount of water decomposed by the current, as estimated by a voltameter, §381, was almost inappreciable, but a beautifully distinct stratification was observed: this, however, was not the true voltaic arc; on bringing the two polar wires of the battery very near each other, the true voltaic arc was suddenly established, a great rise of temperature took place, and the arc seen to be also distinctly stratified. These stratified discharges are powerfully affected by the magnet, in accordance with the same laws with which it acts on all movable conductors: if one of the exhausted tubes be suspended vertically, with the negative pole undermost, it will be found on bringing one end of a powerful magnet near the extremity of one of the bands, in the direction of the axis of the tube, that the stratification will be changed and made to assume the appearance of a luminous spiral spring stretched out. The negative pole seems to be specially affected by the magnetic force, the lines of light assuming a position parallel to that of the magnetic curves, §447. It has also been ascertained by Mr. Gassiot, that by arranging a vacuum tube so as to cross the lines of magnetic force of a powerful electro-magnet, the discharge can be instantly arrested by magnetizing the electro-magnet; and by de-magnetizing the magnet the discharge is immediately renewed. De la Rive has shown that if one pole of a powerful bar electro-magnet be introduced into the axis of an electric egg, into which a little spirits of turpentine has been introduced, and then exhausted, the electro-magnetic bar extending up to the centre of the egg, and being covered with glass in such a way that the electric discharge from Ruhmkorff's coil is compelled to pass from its upper extremity, over the glass, to a copper ring at the bottom of the egg, producing a more or less irregular flow of light over the electro-magnet,—the instant the electro-magnet becomes magnetized by the passage of the battery current, the light ceases to stream from every point of the upper end of the magnet, and is con-

Describe the spectra of different gases.—461. How can the light be proved to be intermittent? What effect is produced by the magnet? Describe Gassiot's experiments: De la Rive's.

densed into a single luminous arc extending vertically from the top of the magnet to the bottom of the egg, and then, which is the most remarkable part of the experiment, it begins to revolve slowly around the axis of the magnet, turning in one direction or the other, according to the direction of the current in the electro-magnet, and the direction of the current from the coil. As soon as the magnet is de-magnetized, the vertical spark disappears and resumes its even flow. This is thought to prove that the rotary motion from east to west, observed in the Aurora Borealis, may be referred to the influence of terrestrial magnetism.

462. The Application of Geissler's Tubes to medical purposes and the illumination of Mines. The light of Geissler's tubes has been recently applied to medical purposes. A long capillary tube, *a*, *Fig.* 238, is attached to two bulbs, provided with platinum wires: this tube is bent in the middle, so that the two branches touch, and their extremities are twisted at *a*; the whole is filled with a highly rarefied gas. On the passage of the current, a sufficiently bright light is produced at *a*, to illuminate the nostrils, the throat, or any other cavity of the body into which the tube may be introduced, and allow of its thorough examination.

Fig. 238.

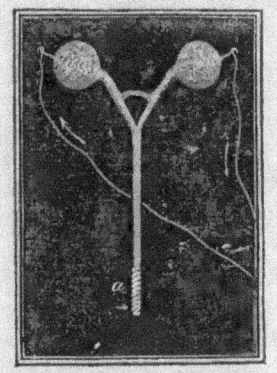

Ruhmkorff's Coil applied to Medicine.

M. Gassiot has devised a simple modification of Geissler's tubes for the purpose of illumination, *Fig.* 239. It consists of a carbonic acid vacuum tube, of about one-sixteenth of an inch internal diameter, wound in the form of a flattened spiral. The wider ends of the tubes, in which the platinum wires are sealed, are almost two inches in length, and half an inch in diameter, and are shown by the dotted lines. They are enclosed in a case of wood, indicated by the outside line, leaving the spiral only exposed. When the discharge from Ruhmkorff's coil is transmitted through the platinum wires, the spiral becomes intensely luminous, exhibiting a brilliant white light. The discharge may be transmitted through fourteen miles of copper wire, from a coil giving

What is this thought to prove in regard to the Aurora Borealis?—462. What application has been made of Geissler's tubes to Medicine? to illumination?

GEISSLER'S TUBES. 459

a spark one inch in length, without diminishing the luminosity of the spiral. The application of this light to mining purposes has been suggested by Dumas and Benoit. They have succeeded in constructing a battery in a convenient and portable form, of sufficient power to keep up a regular light for twelve hours. The advantage of this mode of illumination, is, that no heat is emitted by the light, and the tube remains cold: the gas of the mine has no access to it, so that there is no danger of explosion: there is no evolution of noxious gases and it can be lighted and extinguished at will.

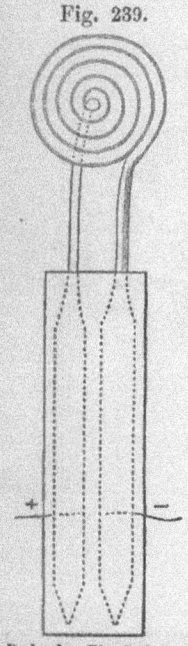

Fig. 239.

Ruhmkorff's Coil applied to Illumination.

463. Application of Ruhmkorff's Coil to spectrum analysis. One of the most interesting applications of Ruhmkorff's coil, is to the determination of the characteristic lines exhibited by the spectra of the various chemical elements, §285. Most of the metals require a higher temperature than that of common flame, in order that their vapors may become luminous, but they may be heated up to the requisite degree by means of the electric spark, which in passing between two pieces of the metal in question, attached to the poles of the coil, volatilizes a small portion, and heats it so intensely as to enable it to give off its peculiar light. The permanent gases also give characteristic spectra, as above described, if strongly heated by the passage of the electric spark. The arrangement of Ruhmkorff's coil for exhibiting the spectra of the metals, is shown in *Fig.* 240: + and —, represent the positive and negative wires connected with the two poles of the secondary coil: c, is a condenser, consisting of two sheets of tin-foil separated by a glass plate; between these plates and each polar wire a metallic communication is formed, as shown in the *Fig.*: t, is a support, the shaft of which consists of a glass rod: o, o, are balls made of the metal in question, and constitute the true poles of the secondary coil, between which the spark passes: s, is the spectroscope, constructed upon the same plan as the one previously described, *Figs.* 108, 110: s, is a screen for the protection of the eye of the observer. At each passage of the

463. How is Ruhmkorff's Coil employed for spectrum analysis? Describe *Fig.* 240.

Fig. 240.

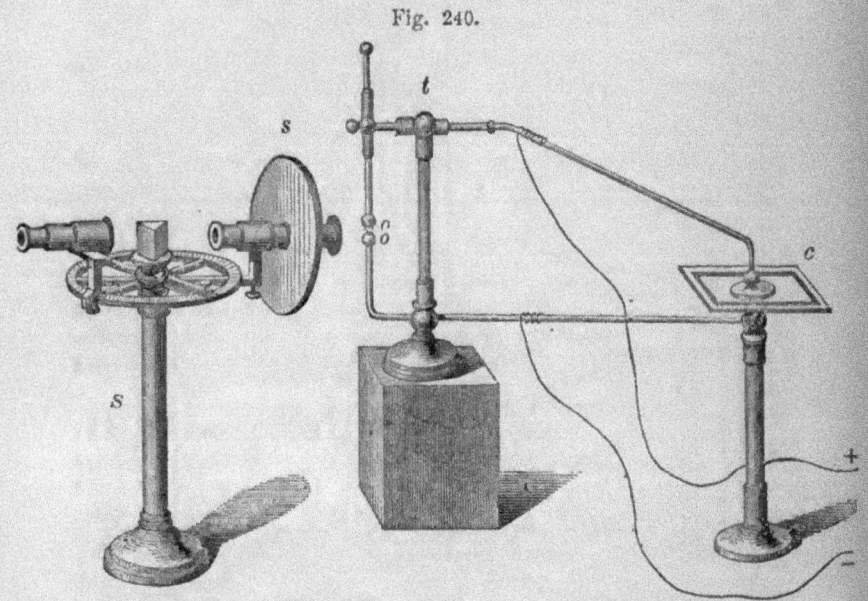

The Spectrum Examination of the Metals by Ruhmkorff's Coil.

spark, portions of the metal of the balls are torn off, and at the same moment intensely heated, and made to emit its peculiar light, which is then viewed by the telescope through the prism. For the determination of the spectra of the gases, it is only necessary to direct the spectroscope to the light emitted when the electric current of the coil is transmitted through the exhausted tubes already described. For a full description of the spectra of the metals, see §285, 286, 287.

464. Chemical Effects. The chemical effects of Ruhmkorff's coil are quite singular and very different from those of the battery. This is owing to the fact, that the secondary current possesses the double qualities of electricity of quantity, like that of the battery, and electricity of intensity, like that of the machine. Now it is well known that the chemical action of electricity is very different when it is electricity of intensity, and acts interruptedly by means of sparks, or electricity of quantity acting in a continuous current. In the first case, the decomposing action of electricity of intensity, like that furnished by the electrical machine, is to discharge a mixture of both

---

How are the spectra of the Gases determined?—464. State the chemical effects of Ruhmkorff's coil.

oxygen and hydrogen at *both poles*, while in the last case, the decomposing action of electricity of quantity, is to completely separate the two gases and set free *one at each pole:* consequently, as the secondary current produced by Ruhmkorff's coil, partakes of the qualities of electricity both of quantity and intensity, it might be expected that its chemical effects would be very various. Thus, according to the form of the platinum poles introduced into acidulated water, their distance from each other, and the degree of acidulation in the water, luminous discharges may be obtained between the poles, without decomposition of the water, or decomposition of the water with the separation of the gases from each other, and their discharge, one at each pole, similar to the decomposing effects of the galvanic current, or decomposition of water with the gases mixed and discharged at the same pole, there being no action at the other; or, finally, decomposition of the water and the gases set free mixed at both poles.

Gases may also be combined, and the compound gases and vapors decomposed by the action of the spark of the secondary current. Thus, if a tube filled with air be hermetically sealed, as in *Fig.* 241, the oxygen and nitrogen of the air combine under the influence of the current, and at the end of ten minutes to an hour it is filled with orange colored vapors of nitrous acid. This experiment illustrates the formation of nitrous acid in the atmosphere under the influence of electricity. If oxygen be enclosed in a tube with a solution of starch and iodide of potassium, as in *Fig.* 242, and a succession of sparks be passed through it, one by one, the mixture will soon exhibit the characteristic blue color of that peculiar modification of oxygen called ozone: the sparks must succeed each other slowly and gently. This experiment is also interesting as showing that the ozone which is

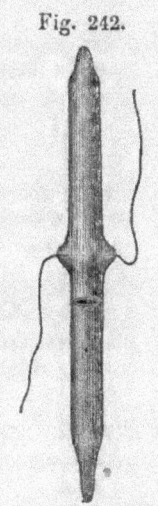

Fig. 241.

Conversion of Air into Nitrous Acid, by Ruhmkorff's Coil.

Fig. 242.

Oxygen converted into Ozone, by Ruhmkorff's Coil.

How do electricity of intensity and quantity differ in decomposing power? What is the effect of the coil on Air? on Oxygen?

462   EFFECTS OF

found to exist in the air, may also be due to the action of electricity on the atmosphere. The passage of the spark through compound gases and vapors, is attended by a partial separation of their component elements: in the case of steam, oxygen appears at the positive pole, and hydrogen at the negative; and long sparks are found to be more effectual in producing decomposition, than short ones. Thus, in *Fig.* 243.

Fig. 243.

Decomposition of Steam by Ruhmkorff's Coil.

A, is a half-pint flask, with a cork in which three holes are bored; in one of these is inserted the glass tube B, which dips beneath the lower end of H, in the trough of water C; in the others, the glass tubes D and E, are inserted, enclosing platinum wires projecting about one inch into the flask, and approaching within 1-16th of an inch of each other, so that the spark may readily pass between them: D and E, are connected by wires with the poles of Ruhmkorff's coil R. The water in the flask is boiled about fifteen minutes, until all the air which it contains has been displaced by steam; when this is the case, the bubbles of steam will condense in C, and no bubbles of air rise into the inverted tube H, filled with water: if at this moment, the water still boiling, the commutator of the coil be turned so as to establish a connection with the battery, sparks will flash through the steam in A, decomposing it, and filling the tube H with a mixture of oxygen and hydrogen, which may be tested by closing the tube with the thumb and applying a lighted match; a sharp detonation will take place. The power of the secondary induced current in effecting the combination or decomposition of gases and vapors, is much greater than that

What is the effect on the vapor of Water? Describe *Fig.* 243.

of the ordinary cylinder or plate electrical machine. As the condenser simply increases the intensity of the electricity of the secondary wire, and not its quantity, no gain in the amount of the substance decomposed is effected by its use.

465. The conversion of Carbon into the Diamond by the long-continued action of the Coil. M. Despretz, who for a long time has been engaged in experiments upon the effect of heat on carbon, is said to have succeeded in converting carbon into diamonds by the action of the induced current of Ruhmkorff's coil. He fastened a small piece of sugar, which, as is well known, contains a large amount of carbon in a state of absolute purity, to the lower positive ball in the electric egg, and to the upper ball a tuft of very fine platinum wire for the purpose of catching the sublimed carbon. A vacuum was then produced and the electric current allowed to traverse the apparatus for several months. At the end of this time the platinum wires were found to be covered with fine black powder, in which were discovered traces of crystallization. Among these crystals, some were found of a black color, others were perfectly translucid, and were found to be regular octoedra of a pyramidal form. When examined by a lapidary, they were found to be possessed of all the properties of the diamond. Rubies were very quickly polished with their powder, and the crystals burned in air without leaving any residue.

---

466. Magneto-Electric Machines.—The principles on which they depend. These are machines for generating currents of electricity by the revolution of coils, in front of the poles of powerful permanent or electro-magnets. In Page's and Ruhmkorff's coils, the secondary current is produced partly by the inductive influence of the primary current, and partly by that of the electro-magnet. In the magneto-electric machine, the electric current is produced by the inductive influence of powerful permanent magnets. By bringing a magnet near a coil composed of fine covered wire and forming a closed circuit, it has been shown, §442, *Fig.* 217, that a momentary current of electricity is induced; and again, that when such a magnet is removed from the coil, another momentary current, in the opposite direction, is induced. It has also been stated, that the two poles of the magnet induce currents in opposite di-

465. What is the effect of the coil on Carbon? Describe Despretz' experiments.—466. What are Magneto-Electric Machines? How is the Electric current produced?

rections, i. e., if the north pole of the magnet be introduced into the coil, *Fig.* 219, and a current observed to flow from left to right, as shown by the galvanometer, and then the north pole be withdrawn and the south pole be introduced, a current of electricity will be induced in the opposite direction, or from right to left:—moreover, that these effects are reversed if the direction of the winding is changed; i. e., if the north pole of the magnet be introduced into a right hand coil, the current will be in the inverse direction to that which is induced when the same pole is introduced into a left hand coil: if the south pole of the magnet be employed instead of the north pole, the same results follow; so that if two coils are wound in the *same direction*, and placed side by side, and a north pole of a magnet be introduced into one coil, and a south pole into the other simultaneously, a current will be induced in each coil, in *opposite* directions: but if the coils are wound in *opposite* directions, and a north pole be introduced into one, and a south pole into the other at the same moment, a current will be induced in each in the *same direction*. This is equally true, if instead of introducing permanent magnets into the coils, these are wound upon soft iron cores, and then the cores are magnetized and de-magnetized by the inductive action of powerful permanent magnets suddenly brought near and removed from their extremities. Consequently, if a coil of fine insulated wire be wound upon a core of soft iron, and a powerful permanent magnet be presented to one extremity of the iron core, first by one pole, and then by the other, the soft iron will become magnetized and de-magnetized, upon every approach and removal of the magnet; and a current of electricity made to circulate through the coil, first in one direction and then in the other. If there are two such pieces of soft iron, with coils wound in *opposite* directions, and having the ends of the wires soldered together so as to form, in effect, but one closed circuit, and the north and south pole of a horse-shoe magnet be presented at the same moment to both, they will become oppositely magnetized, and a momentary current of electricity *in the same direction* be induced in each coil at every ap-

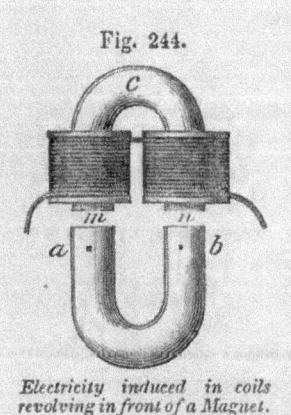

Fig. 244.

Electricity induced in coils revolving in front of a Magnet.

Why must the coils be wound in opposite directions? Describe the successive effects which take place when the wound armature, *c*, *Fig.* 244, is made to revolve.

proach and removal of the magnet. If, then, in *Fig.* 244, *a* and *b* be the poles of a powerful magnet firmly fixed, and *c*, a horseshoe armature, wound with two coils of fine wire in opposite directions, having their ends connected so as to form a closed circuit, and arranged to revolve about a vertical axis, so that *m*, after half a revolution, will be above *b*, and *n* above *a*, it is evident that so long as the armature is at rest, it is magnetized by the inductive influence of the permanent magnet, the poles being reversed; but the instant the armature begins to revolve, it is de-magnetized, and a momentary current of electricity is induced in the coils, which entirely ceases by the time it has made a quarter-revolution. Were the coils wound in the same direction, the momentary currents circulating in each, would move in *opposite* directions; but as they are wound in opposite directions, momentary currents in the *same* direction are induced in both. As the armature moves beyond the quarter-revolution, and its extremities approach the poles of the permanent magnet, they again become magnetized by induction, and it might be supposed that an electrical current would be induced in each coil, in a contrary direction to what it was in the first quarter-revolution, because, as we have seen, the currents induced by removing the magnet from a coil and restoring it, are always in the *opposite* direction; but as the extremities of the armature are now approaching *reverse* poles, this effect is neutralized, and the new currents of electricity induced in the coils in the second quarter-revolution, are in the *same direction* with those in the first quarter, so that in making half a revolution each coil experiences the induction of two currents of electricity in the *same direction*, in consequence of receding from and approaching opposite poles, alternately in the two quarter-revolutions, at the same moment. In the *second half-revolution*, two currents of electricity are induced in the same direction in each coil, but directly opposite to those induced in the same coils in the first half, because the coils are now receding from and approaching the reverse poles, *a* and *b* having interchanged places in reference to *m* and *n*. Consequently, if *c*, were made to revolve continuously around *m* and *n*, a succession of currents, *in opposite directions, in each half-revolution alternately*, would be made to circulate through both coils. In order that this effect may be produced, it is necessary, as has been stated, that the ends of the coils should be connected at

---

How many currents are induced in every half-revolution? Why may these be regarded as only one current? What is the final result?

both their extremities, so as to form a *closed* circuit; and on introducing a galvanometer into this circuit, these effects may be traced by the oscillations which are imparted to the needle. The currents thus induced are primary currents, and are not sufficiently intense to produce powerful shocks. For this purpose it is necessary that the circuit be broken at the exact moment, in each half-revolution when the induction of the primary current takes place. This break in the primary current produces in the coils a direct extra-current, § 438, of extreme intensity, moving in the same direction as the primary, and greatly increasing its power. When this extra current thus induced, is transmitted through the body, the shocks become almost insupportable, and if directed through carbon points, the sparks acquire great brilliancy. For the production of chemical decomposition, however, the primary current is sufficiently powerful, and no break in the circuit is required. These effects are manifested both at the removal and approach of the coils, but more vividly at the removal than at the approach, and their vividness is proportioned to the suddenness of the break in the circuit, and the rapidity of the revolution of the coils.

467. Saxton's Magneto-Electric Machine. The first magneto-electric machine for the production of continuous currents of electricity, was made by M. Pixii at Paris, in 1832: it consisted of two coils of insulated wire wound upon iron cores, in front of which, the poles of a powerful magnet were made to revolve with great rapidity. In 1833, Mr. Saxton, of Philadelphia, invented a machine of much greater power than that of Pixii, in which a curved armature with its coils, like that represented in *Fig.* 244, was rapidly revolved before the poles of very powerful permanent magnets. It is represented in *Fig.* 245, and a section of the armature and its coils in *Fig.* 246. It consists of a powerful horse-shoe magnet, M, placed horizontally upon one of its sides: in front of its poles, and as close to them as possible, without actual contact, an armature of soft iron is made to revolve upon a horizontal axis, which admits of being turned with great rapidity by means of a cord passing over a multiplying wheel, w. This armature consists of a curved piece of iron of such a shape that its two extremities, a and b, are at the same distance apart, as the two poles of the magnet, and each carries a coil of very fine wire, c and d, carefully insulated. The two extremities of the wires which form the

---

Why must the continuity of the circuit be interrupted in order to display the currents? Is the effect more powerful on the approach or removal of the coils?

MAGNETO-ELECTRIC

Fig. 245.

Saxton's Magneto-Electric Machine.

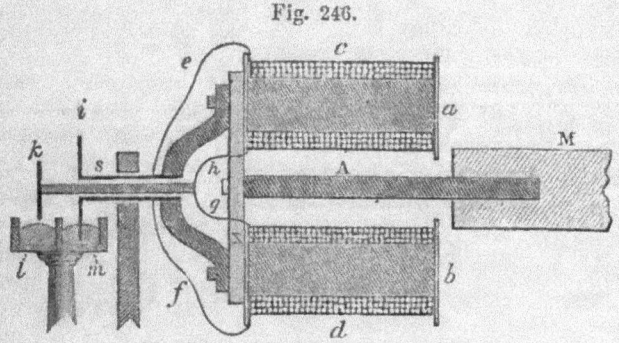

Fig. 246.

Armature and Coils of Saxton's Machine.

terminations of the coils, h and g, are united and soldered to a piece of copper passing through the axis of the spindle on which the armature rests, but *insulated* from it, and terminating in the copper cross-piece, k, which, at every half-revolution dips into the mercury cup, l, and immediately emerges from it again, thus breaking and completing the circuit once in every half-revolution; the other ends of the wire, e and f, are soldered to the spindle itself, and terminate in the circular disc of copper, i, which revolves in the mercury cup, m, thus maintaining a

---

467. Describe Saxton's Machine. How many currents are produced at every revolution of the coils?

constant connection between it and the extremities of the wires which form the commencement of the coils. The two mercury cups, l and m, are insulated from each other, but may be connected by a curved wire. This curved wire being inserted, it is evident that when either of the ends of k are immersed in the mercury cup, l, *a closed circuit is formed,* of which the coils and the two mercury cups form parts, and that whenever the cross-piece emerges from the mercury the continuity of the circuit is broken, and the extra-electric current has an opportunity to manifest itself. The cross-piece, k, is so arranged that its ends shall emerge from the mercury and break the circuit at the moment when the coils have just left the poles of the permanent magnet to which they have been opposed. Under these circumstances, if the wheel, w, in *Fig.* 245, be rapidly turned, four momentary currents of induced electricity, two negative and two positive, which may be regarded as, in effect, but *two*, one negative and the other positive, will flash through the wires in *opposite* directions, at every revolution; and these will be made manifest by bright sparks of light whenever either arm of k emerges from the mercury cup, l. If the wire connecting the insulated mercury cups be removed, and wires inserted into them, connected with the two metallic handles, H, H, which may be grasped by the hands, then these handles and the bystander become a part of the closed circuit, and at every revolution of the coils, four currents of electricity, in opposite directions, the first two in one direction, and the second two in the opposite, will flash through his body, producing an insupportable torrent of shocks. If the wires leading from the two mercury cups be attached to a galvanometer, the needle will be violently deflected, twice in each revolution, first in one direction, and then in the other, by the two opposite currents. If they be tipped with platinum, and dipped into a solution of acidulated water, this will be decomposed, oxygen set free at the positive wire, and hydrogen at the negative, in each half-revolution; but as the positive and negative currents in each half-revolution are in opposite directions, each polar wire becomes alternately positive and negative, and the oxygen in the second half-revolution appears at the same wire as the hydrogen in the first, and the hydrogen in the second at the same wire with the oxygen in the first; these immediately re-combine, and thus the chemical effect of the first half-

---

Why may these be regarded as in effect but two? Explain why the poles are alternately affected with opposite kinds of electricity. What are the physiological effects? the effects upon the magnet? the chemical effects?

revolution is neutralized by that of the second. In order to obviate this difficulty, it is necessary to turn up one of the arms of *k*, so that it will not touch the mercury, and thus suppress the current in every alternate half revolution. By this arrangement, only two momentary electrical currents are produced in every revolution; but as they are both in the same direction, and of the same kind, the poles are not alternately reversed. The power of the machine is thus reduced one-half; but thus arranged, this current of induced electricity may be used to produce chemical decomposition, in the same manner as the current from an ordinary galvanic battery.

468. **Page's Magneto-Electric Machine.** The mercurial cups in the instrument just described alternately receive a current of positive and negative electricity, but by the use of a pole-changer, their connection with the wires which terminate the coils may be changed twice in every revolution, and thus the electricity of each cup be made constantly the same, and a continuous flow of electricity of the same kind maintained from each cup, that may be used for any of the purposes for which the electrical current of the battery is generally employed. This object is best accomplished in Page's magneto-electric ma-

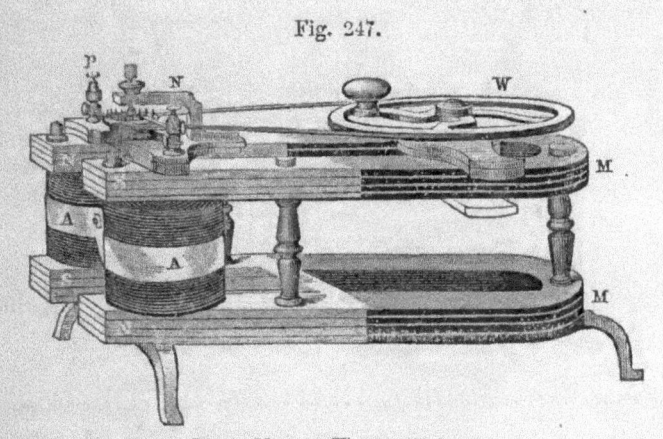

Fig. 247.

Page's Magneto-Electric Machine.

chine, *Fig.* 247: M, M, are two powerful permanent magnets, arranged one above the other in such a manner that the north pole of the upper magnet is above the south pole of the lower,

---

Why must the current in every alternate half-revolution be suppressed? What effect has this upon the power of the machine?—468. Describe Page's machine. How are the coils mounted?

and the south pole of the upper above the north pole of the lower: A, A, are two armatures, each wound with a coil of fine wire in opposite directions, and mounted vertically between the magnets, so that their iron cores are exposed at both extremities simultaneously to the inductive influence of the opposite poles of both magnets, instead of one extremity only, as in Saxton's machine, and become much more powerfully magnetized: these coils have their extremities connected with opposite sides of the pole-changer attached to the vertical shaft, on which the coils are made to revolve by the wheel W; P, N, are binding cups, filled with mercury, insulated from the magnets and each other, and connected with the pole-changer by wires which press tightly upon its surface. At every half-revolution the direction of the electrical current flowing through the coils is changed, and those extremities of the coils which, at the preceding half-revolution, discharged a positive current, now discharge a negative one; at the instant that this change takes place, their connection with the cups is changed, and the ends which formerly gave off positive electricity, but now negative, become connected with the cup which then received the negative current, and the ends which formerly gave off negative electricity, but now positive, become connected with the cup which then received the positive current; consequently, each cup receives, and gives off, the same kind of electricity in the second half-revolution, as in the first. This change of the ends of the coils is effected by the pole changer, represented in *Fig.* 248: S, represents a cross section of the vertical shaft on which the armatures revolve; A and B, are two pieces of brass, which encircle the shaft, but are separated from it by some non-conducting material; they are also insulated from each other by the bits of ivory, i, i; the wires which begin the coils are firmly fastened to A, and those which terminate them, to B: P and N represent wires connected

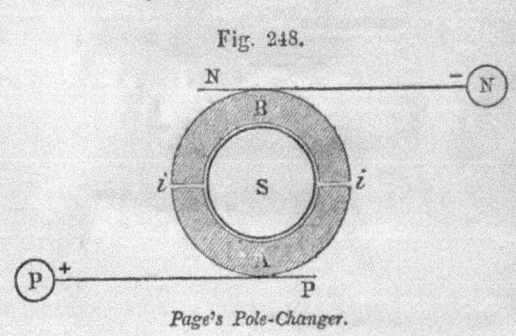

Fig. 248.

Page's Pole-Changer.

How is the electricity of each cup kept constantly the same? Describe the Pole-changer.

with the corresponding mercury cups, pressed tightly against the brass pieces, A and B. As the shaft revolves, A and B revolve with it and the coils; the instant that the half-revolution is terminated, the direction of the current reversed, and A begins to discharge negative electricity, instead of positive, the connection of A, with the positive wire and cup P, ceases, in consequence of the revolution, and is established with the negative wire and cup N; at the same instant, B is ceasing to discharge negative electricity, and beginning to discharge positive, and its connection with the negative wire N is broken, and established with the positive wire P. By this simple arrangement, the two cups, P and N, are made to discharge intermittent momentary currents of the same kind of electricity, which approach more nearly a continuous flow, as the revolution of the coils becomes more rapid, and by combining several of these machines whose armatures are so arranged that each shall in turn become magnetized just before the preceding one has entirely lost its magnetism, magneto-electric machines have been constructed by which a continuous current in a uniform direction can be steadily maintained. The break required, p. 466, for giving severe shocks is made by a wire pressing upon a toothed wheel, *Fig.* 247. This is removed when the instrument is used for chemical decomposition. See Expts., 160, 170, p. 524.

469. Magneto-Electricity used in the Arts, in place of Voltaic Electricity, especially for the illumination of Lighthouses. As the electrical current induced by magnetism possesses all the decomposing, heating and physiological powers of the electricity of the battery, and is much more manageable, because produced by a definite amount of motion, it is often substituted for the electricity of the battery, in electroplating. A single Saxton's machine, if kept in continuous revolution, will precipitate from 90 to 120 ounces of silver per week, from its solutions, and machines have been constructed by which $2\frac{1}{2}$ ounces of silver per hour, have been deposited upon articles properly prepared. They are employed with great advantage by physicians, for the administration of electricity to their patients, on account of the facility with which the rapidity of the shocks may be regulated by the motion of the wheel. They are also sometimes made use of for telegraphic purposes, where an occasional message only is to be sent, as in the case of the fire-alarm of cities for transmitting the alarm from the central office to every district of the city.

---

469. What applications have been made of Magneto-Electric machines? What results have been attained in electro-plating? in Light-house illumination?

These machines have also been employed for the production of a permanent electric light between two pieces of gas-coke, for Light-house illumination; the light can be maintained without interruption, so long as the magnetic armatures are kept in rotation, and the charcoal remains unconsumed. Many attempts have been made to use the intense light produced by the carbon poles of a powerful Galvanic battery for the same purpose. When these poles, as has been shown, §354, after having been brought into contact, are slightly separated, even in a vacuum, a light of extraordinary brilliancy is produced: Despretz has calculated that the light emitted by ninety-two of Bunsen's elements, arranged in two series of forty-six each, is equal to that of 1,144 candles, and is to the light of the sun as 1 to $2\frac{1}{2}$; and the light emitted by two hundred and fifty elements, in a grand experiment made by Profs. Cooke and Rogers, in the cupola of the State House, Boston, was calculated to be equal to that of ten thousand candles. Notwithstanding the intensity of this light, from the difficulty of maintaining a perfectly constant action in the battery, it is too irregular to admit of successful use for the illumination of Light-houses, and although tried under every conceivable circumstance, it has thus far proved, for these purposes, a complete failure. In the magneto-electric machine, in which the current is produced by a perfectly regular mechanical motion, much greater success has been attained. A machine for this purpose was first constructed by Nollet, at Brussels, in 1850, and was afterwards improved by Van Malderen. This machine is represented in *Fig.* 249. It consists of a cast iron frame, $5\frac{1}{2}$ feet high, on the outside of which eight series of five powerful horse-shoe magnets, A, A, A, are arranged on wooden cross-pieces. Upon a horizontal iron axis extending from one end to the other of the frame four bronze wheels are fastened, carrying 16 coils each, wound with 138 yards of insulated copper wire. These coils are made to revolve in front of the poles of the permanent magnets by an endless band, which receives its motion from a steam engine not seen in the *Fig.* To obtain the greatest degree of light, the most suitable velocity is 235 revolutions per minute. By this rapid revolution, magneto-electric currents of high intensity are induced, which, by the two binding screws a and b, are conducted by means of long copper wires, to two carbon points attached to the sockets of one of Duboscq's elec-

---

What advantage has this mode of illumination over the Galvanic Battery?

THE ILLUMINATION OF LIGHT-HOUSES. 473

Fig. 249.

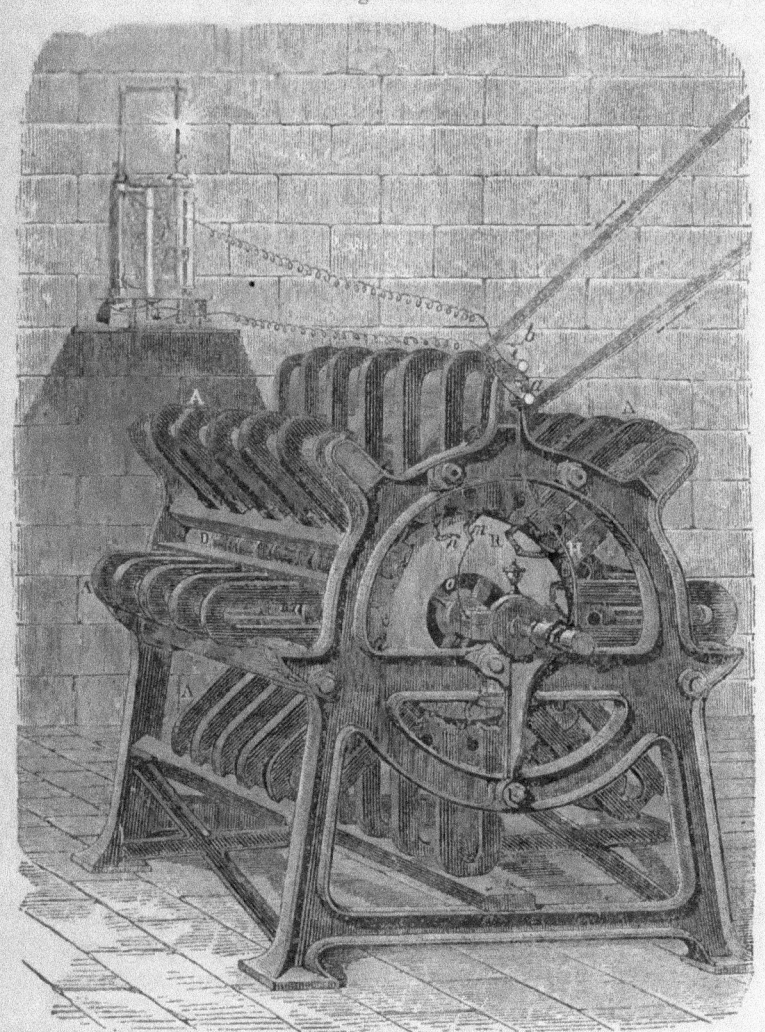

The Illumination of Light-houses.

tric lamps, §356, as shown in the *Fig.*, mounted upon the top of the Light-house Tower. In this machine, the current in each wire is not always in the same direction; each carbon is alternately positive and negative, and they are consumed with

---

Describe the machine of Nollet and Van Malderen.

nearly equal rapidity: for the production of the electric light, it is not necessary that the current should be uniformly in the same direction; when used for electro-metallurgy, however, this is absolutely requisite. A machine of four wheels gives a light equal to 150 Carcel lamps; a machine of six wheels, a light equal to 200 Carcel lamps.

470. Holmes' Magneto-Electric Machine for use in Light-houses. Mr. Holmes has succeeded, by the use of a powerful magneto-electric machine, in producing a light of great power and intensity, for use in Light-houses. The general arrangement of the machine is the same as in that which has just been described. It consists of 48 pairs of permanent compound bar-magnets, arranged in six parallel planes, so as to form a large compound wheel, between which the armatures, 160 in number, are arranged in five sets, the total amount of wire with which they are wound being about half a mile in length. The wires are insulated by cotton, and are so arranged as to maintain a continuous current in the same direction, varying from a maximum to exactly one-half the amount of the maximum, in rapid succession. To facilitate the change in the poles, the soft iron cores of the coils are not solid pieces of iron, but are tubes, single, double or treble, as it is found by experiment that the same weight of iron, when divided in this manner, loses or takes magnetism in much less time than when in a solid form. The steel bars weigh about one ton, and the wheel is made to revolve by a steam engine of one or two horse-power, at the rate of 150 to 250 times per minute. There is a limit to the velocity to be employed when the maximum of electricity is required. This light was for several months in successful operation at the South Foreland Light-house, on the English Channel, and afterwards at Dungeness, the actual expense of fuel in working the steam engine, being about the same as that of the oil formerly employed, and the light equal, photometrically, to 14 of Fresnel's first-class Light-house lamps. The same light is also used in the noble Light-houses of La Hève, near Havre. This light is nothing but the sparks first obtained from the magnet by Mr. Faraday, *Fig.* 220, made continuous by suitable machinery. It is said to possess extraordinary penetrative power for fogs, and that it shines so far at times, that even before it has arisen above the horizon, twenty-five miles off, it can be seen. This is justly regarded as one of the most

---

Describe Holmes' machine. What is the velocity of revolution? In what Light-houses has it been employed? How far can it be seen?

interesting scientific applications of modern times, and with the additional improvements which are steadily making, will no doubt in time be adopted in all the most important Lighthouses throughout the world. On the whole, however, up to this time, the preponderance of opinion is against the general introduction of magneto-electric machines into Light-houses, on account of their liability to get out of order, and the difficulty of securing the skilled labor required for their efficient management, there being, in the opinion of the Brethren of the Trinity House,—the English Light-house Board,—no advantages which can compensate for the want of certainty in Light-house illumination. In spite of all the care which the importance of the subject has rendered necessary, the Dungeness electric Light entirely failed, or was inefficient, for upwards of 119½ hours, between Aug. 1863, and Oct. 1864; and referring to this, the Brethren of the Trinity House say that it appears to them to be impossible to obtain entire immunity from such accidents, so long as human nature is subject to infirmity. These fallings off and cessations have frequently rendered it necessary that the ordinary oil Lamp should be re-lighted; and notwithstanding the power of the magneto-electric light, instances have occurred of vessels being stranded near Dungeness. The expense of maintaining an equal light from Colza oil, under the old oil-system, from wax-candles, Bunsen's battery, and the magneto-electric machine, being about the same, the question must be decided upon grounds of convenience and efficiency alone. The expenditure of a Light-house of the first-class, is about £400 per annum, the light burning four thousand hours, at an expense of about two shillings per hour.

471. Wilde's Magneto-Electric Machine. A great improvement has recently been made upon Holmes' machine by the substitution of powerful *electro-magnets*, in place of *permanent steel magnets*. It consists in the application of the current from a common magneto-electric machine, produced by the revolution of coils before the poles of a series of small permanent magnets, to the formation of a powerful *electro-magnet*. This is done by causing the current generated by the revolution of the coils to circulate through wires wound in the ordinary manner around a piece of soft iron, so as to convert it into a powerful horse-shoe electro-magnet. This electro-magnet possesses much more power than the original permanent magnets, on account

---

What are the objections to their use? What is the comparative expense of the different modes of Light-house illumination?—471. State the principle of Wilde's machine.

of the intensity of the induced current, produced by the revolution of the first pair of coils. In front of the poles of the electro-magnet thus formed, a second pair of coils is made to revolve with great rapidity, and a second induced current of still greater intensity than the first is obtained. This second induced current is then carried around a second horse-shoe of soft iron and a second electro-magnet formed, of still greater power than the first. In front of the poles of this second electro-magnet, a third pair of coils is made to revolve, and a third induced electrical currrent of still greater power than the preceding is obtained. Each electro-magnet and each induced current being more powerful than those which precede them, there is, theoretically, no limit to the power which may be thus induced. A small and weak permanent magnet may thus be made to actuate a series of electro-magnets of continually increasing power. Wilde's machine is constructed on this principle, *Fig.* 250. An armature S A, wound with insulated wire, is made to revolve with great rapidity by means of a band from a steam-engine B, in front of the poles of six permanent magnets, M M, each weighing one pound: from this armature the current is transmitted by the wires *p n*, through the cups *c c*, to an inverted electro-magnet E M, in front of whose poles a second armature, carrying coils, is made to revolve by means of a band B P, from the same steam engine: from this second armature the current which is produced by its revolution is carried by the wires *p' n'*, to a second electro-magnet, not seen in the *Fig.*, in front of whose poles a third armature, carrying coils, is made to revolve by means of the same steam-engine, and from these coils the induced current is carried by wires to the carbon points of a Duboscq's electric lamp, as in *Fig.* 249. The armatures employed in this machine are not wound or mounted in the ordinary manner, but according to the method of Siemen. A cylindrical piece of iron whose opposite sides are cut away, represented in a side view at G, No. 1, *Fig.* 251, and in an end view at E, is wound from end to end, lengthwise, with covered wire, until the grooves on both sides of the cylinder are completely filled: these longitudinal coils are then firmly bound with bands of brass H H, No. 2, *Fig.* 251, that they may not be displaced by the centrifugal force of the revolving cylinder: K is the wheel for the application of the band from the steam-engine: I I are axles; L L' is the pole-changer. The

---

How is the current induced by the permanent magnet made to create an electro-magnet of much greater power, and this, one of still greater power, and this a third? Is there any limit to this process theoretically?

MAGNETO-ELECTRIC 477

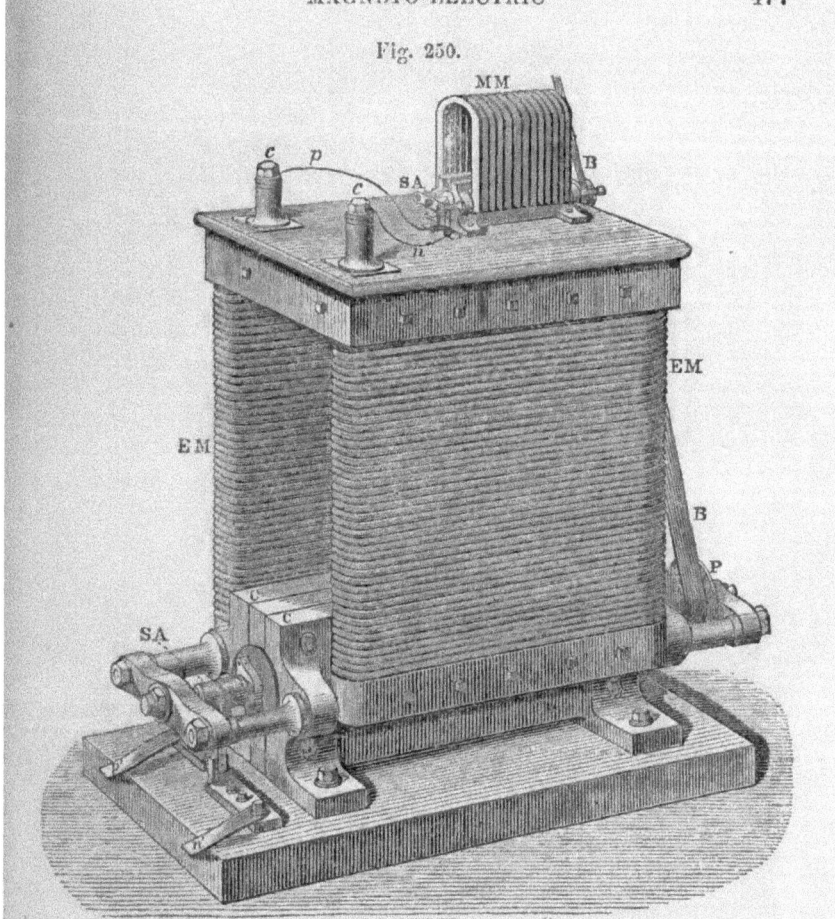

Fig. 250.

Wilde's Magneto-Electric Machine.

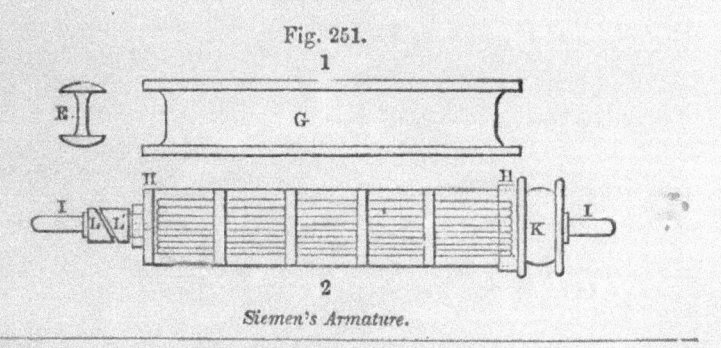

Fig. 251.

Siemen's Armature.

Describe the construction of Wilde's machine. Whose armature is employed? How is it wound?

armature thus arranged is then inserted into a cylindrical hole cut to receive it lengthwise through the pieces of iron c, c, which are firmly bolted to the lower ends of the inverted magnet E M, E M. These pieces of iron constitute, therefore, the true poles of the electro-magnet, and are separated from each other by pieces of brass. The cylindrical aperture is about 1-20th of an inch larger than the wound armature, so that it may revolve in very close proximity to the interior of the hollow cylinder without touching it. The armature is supported at each end by appropriate brass supports, and revolves with great accuracy. It is represented in place at S A, *Fig.* 250, and its opposite extremity, to which the band from the steam-engine is attached, at P. It is shown in transverse section, with the extremities of the covered wires, in *Fig.* 252, where *b b*, are the pieces of iron bolted to the lower extremities of the electro-magnet, and *c c*, the brass pieces by which they are separated. It is evident that by the rapid revolution of this cylinder the longitudinal coils, are continually brought near and removed from the poles of the electro-magnet E M, E M. The opposite electric currents thus induced are carried by the wires to the pole-changer arranged upon the axis at L L', *Fig.* 251, and at S A, *Fig.* 250, and there converted in the ordinary manner into permanent currents in one direction, whence they are transmitted to a second electro-magnet, or directly to the electric lamp. The upper armature S A, revolving between the poles of the permanent magnets M M, is arranged upon the same plan. In Wilde's largest instrument there is one set of permanent magnets, and *two* electro-magnets: its primary magneto-electric machine has a cylindrical armature of $1\frac{5}{8}$ inches diameter, actuated by six small permanent magnets weighing one pound each: the induced current from this armature is transmitted through the coils of an electro-magnet having a cylindrical armature of 5 inches diameter; and the induced current from this is finally carried to the coils of an electro-magnet having an armature of 10 inches in diameter: the

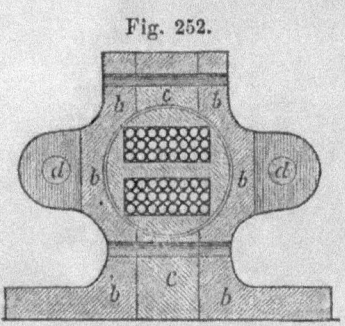

Fig. 252.

The Armature in its Socket.

How is the armature mounted? Describe the arrangement of Wilde's instrument of the largest size. How is the intensity armature wound? The quantity armature?

weight of the last ten-inch electro-magnet is nearly three tons, and the total weight of the instrument about four and half tons. The machine is provided with two armatures, one for intensity, the other for quantity, either of which may be used at pleasure by taking out one and introducing the other. The intensity armature is wound with a comparatively long and fine covered wire, 376 feet in length, and weighing 232 lbs. The quantity armature is wound with covered copper ribbon 67 feet in length, the weight of which is 344 lbs. With these three armatures driven at a uniform velocity of 1,500 revolutions per minute by a steam engine of about seven horse-power, an amount of magnetic force is developed in the large electro-magnet far exceeding any thing which has hitherto been produced, and an amount of induced electricity, when the ten-inch *quantity* armature is employed, so enormous as to melt pieces of cylindrical iron rod fifteen inches in length and fully one-quarter of an inch in diameter, and pieces of copper wire of the same length and one-eighth of an inch in diameter. With this armature in place, notwithstanding its tremendous heating power, the physiological effects of the current can be borne without inconvenience: immediately after fifteen inches of iron rod have been melted the terminals may be grasped, one in each hand, and the full force of the currrent sustained; the shocks are severe, but yet not inconveniently so. When an *intensity* armature seven inches in diameter was employed in another machine, consisting of one permanent and one electro-magnet, and driven at a speed of 1,800 revolutions a minute, the current melted seven feet of No. 16 iron wire, and heated a length of twenty-one feet of the same wire red-hot. The illuminating power of such a current is of the most splendid description. When an electric lamp, furnished with rods of gas-carbon half an inch square, was placed at the top of a lofty building, an arc of flame several inches in length was projected, and the light evolved from it was sufficient to cast the shadows of the street lamps a quarter of a mile distant upon the neighboring walls. When viewed from that distance, the rays proceeding from the reflector have all the rich effulgence of sunshine. With the reflector removed from the lamp, the bare light is estimated to have an intensity equal to 4,000 wax candles. A piece of ordinary sensitive paper, like that used for photographic printing, exposed to the action of the light for 20 seconds, at the distance of two feet

---

Describe the heating effects of this machine. When the quantity armature is employed ; when the intensity armature. Its physiological effects. Its illuminating effects.

from the reflector, was darkened to the same degree as a piece of the same sheet of paper when exposed for the period of one minute to the direct rays of the sun, at noon, on a clear day in the month of March. In the month of June, from a comparison of sunlight with the electric light armed with the reflector, by means of the shadows thrown by both from the same object, the electric light seemed to possess three or four times the power of sunlight. That the relative intensity was somewhat in this proportion, was evident from the powerful scorching action of the electric light upon the face, and the ease with which paper could be set on fire with a burning glass when introduced into its rays. The extraordinary calorific and illuminating powers of the ten-inch machine are the more remarkable, when we consider that they have their origin in six small permanent magnets, weighing only one pound each, and only capable of sustaining collectively a weight of sixty pounds. It has been calculated that with a 100-ton magnet, having an armature of 32 inches in diameter, and driven by a 1,000 horsepower steam-engine, light enough would be produced, if the lamp were placed upon the top of a high tower, to illuminate London by night, more brightly than the sunlight does by day. Twelve machines of the ordinary size would illuminate Broadway, from the Battery to Fourteenth St., at much less expense than gas.

One great advantage of this machine is its capability of enlargement to any required power. If, instead of using the current from the ten-inch armature of the second electro-magnet for the production of light, it were to be used in producing a still larger electro-magnet, a vastly greater development of power would be the result. The only apparent limit to this multiplication of power is the excessive heat which would be developed in the rotating armatures: this might, perhaps, be pushed so far as to burn up all the working parts, dissipate the electric lamp and conducting wires, destroy the attendants, and become in fact perfectly unmanageable.

A practical application of this Light has been made to Photography: an establishment has been fitted up at Manchester, in England, with one of these machines, by which more than two hundred negatives can be taken in one day. Its constancy renders it more reliable than an uncertain sunlight. The ordinary consumption of coal required to work a 7 horse-power steam-

---

How does the light compare with sunlight? What is its effect on photographic paper? What effect would probably be produced by an armature of 32 inches? Is there any limit to this multiplication of power? What practical application has been made

engine, midway between waste on the one hand and rigid economy on the other, is about 11¼ lbs. per hour, worth about one half-penny. To this expense must be added that of the carbon rods for the lamp, about ten inches per hour, worth perhaps an English penny, then interest on the cost of the machine, expense of maintenance and repairs, which will bring up the total expense per hour, of this enormous quantity of Light, not less than 4,000 wax candles, to six-pence or eight-pence. The British Commissioners of Northern Light-houses have ordered one of Wilde's machines, at a cost of £500.

472. Improvements upon Wilde's Machine.—Ladd's improvement. Wilde's machine has been greatly simplified and improved by throwing aside the permanent magnets M M, *Fig.* 250, and making use of the electro-magnet, alone E M, E M. This improvement is founded upon the fact, that a current can be obtained from the coil of an electro-magnet which has been powerfully excited, for some time, (in one case more than 25 seconds,) after the exciting battery current has been thrown off. An electro-magnet possesses the power of retaining a charge of electricity in its coil in a manner analogous to that in which it is retained in insulated sub-marine cables, §416, and in the Leyden jar, but not identical with it. This is evident from the appearance of a spark, at the point of disjunction of the insulated wires with which it is wound, a considerable time after all connection with the original exciting cause of the current has been cut off. The production of this spark arises from the comparatively slow manner in which large masses of iron return to their normal condition after having attained an exalted degree of magnetism. It is this important retentive property of the electro-magnet E M, which, in the case of Wilde's machine, maintains its magnetic power, notwithstanding the intermittent character of the electrical current generated in the armature of the permanent magnets M M, for, as is well known, no current whatever is produced from the armature of the magneto-electric machine when in certain positions during its revolution. The electro-magnet E M, in Wilde's machine, retaining its magnetic power for some time after its connection with a battery or magneto-electric machine has been suspended, is capable of exciting a current in its revolving armature without any further connection with the permanent magnets M M. On this principle, a modification in Wilde's machine was made soon after its invention, by Siemen, in Germany, and by Wheatstone independently in England. The steel magnets M M, were replaced by an electro-magnet, which was excited by a galvanic battery, the armature caused to rotate, and then the battery removed: or, instead of employing a battery, the soft iron of the electro-magnet was slightly magnetized by touching it with a permanent magnet. The residual magnetism left in the soft iron of the electro-magnet, after being under the influence of the battery or touched by the permanent magnet, is abundantly sufficient to induce a current of electricity in the coils of the rapidly revolving armature. In Wheatstone's apparatus, the extremities of the armature coil divide into two branches, one branch leading to the insulated wire which is wound round the actuating electro-magnet, and the other leading to the electric lamp. In this manner, a portion of the electric current induced in the coil is diverted to the primary electro-magnet, thereby increasing its magnetic power, and proportionally augmenting the secondary electric current which it induces in the armature coil; while the remaining portion is drawn off and used in the ordinary manner for the production of light, effecting decomposition, and the like. The residual magnetism of the electro-magnet is the original cause of the electric current, but this magnetism is immediately increased the instant the armature begins to revolve, by the flow of a portion of the induced current through the wire with which it is wound. This not only increases the intensity of the induced current, but also requires the application of a much more powerful force to produce the revolution of the armature, owing to the retardation exerted by the magnet; and the armature at the same time becomes very hot.

Mr. Ladd, a philosophical instrument maker in London, has greatly increased this effect by winding the Siemen armature of Wilde's machine with *two* distinct coils, insulated from each other, one coil being connected with the electro magnet E M, the other with the terminal wires $p'\ n'$, through the pole-changer, as in *Fig.* 250. These two coils operate entirely independent of each other. The instant the armature begins to revolve, a feeble current of electricity is generated in the coils by the slight amount of magnetism retained by the electro-magnet since its previous excitation; or if it should have entirely lost

---

Describe the improvement of Siemen and Wheatstone? What is the original cause of the electric current in these machines? Describe Ladd's improvement. How is the armature wound? With what are these coils connected?

its magnetism, this may be temporarily restored for the occasion by applying a powerful steel magnet to the poles of the electro-magnet; to this, the current from that one of the coils which is directly connected with the electro-magnet, immediately adds its magnetic power, and at the next revolution of the armature the current of electricity in both coils is greatly increased: this in turn adds to the magnetic force of the electro-magnet, which at once reacts again upon the coils, and so the process goes on as the rapidity of revolution increases. There is no limit to the power of the machine but the rapidity with which the armature is made to rotate, and this is entirely dependent upon the amount of mechanical force derived from the steam-engine. The great improvement in this machine is the introduction of the second coil upon the Siemen armature, which, although it gives off currents induced by the electro-magnet, does not at all detract from the intensity of the original coil; and when the former is attached to a Duboscq's lamp, it is found to give a light equal to 40 elements of Grove and Bunsen, from the expenditure of an amount of steam-engine force equivalent to one horse-power. One of these machines, at the Paris Exhibition of 1867, 24 inches in length, 12 in width, and 7 inches high, kept 50 inches of platinum wire 1-10th of an inch in diameter, incandescent, and when a small voltameter was placed in the circuit of the second armature, gave off about 16 cubic inches of gas per minute, and in connection with an electric lamp, emitted a light equal to that of about thirty-five Grove's elements, the driving force being less than one horse-power.

These electro-magnetic machines are all extremely interesting as illustrations of the conversion of Motion into Electricity, Heat, Light, and Chemical effect, and as connected with the theory of the Convertibility of Forces.

473. Points of difference between the electricity of the Electrical Machine and that of the Galvanic Battery. We have already noticed, §351, some of the points of difference between the electricity of the machine and that of the battery, viz: that the electricity of the machine possesses great intensity, but limited quantity; that of the battery, feeble intensity, but large quantity, that its influence upon electrometers and electroscopes, is extremely slight, that a Leyden jar can only be charged with difficulty, that when the polar wires are brought

---

What takes place as soon as the armature begins to revolve? What effects are produced by it?—473. State the points of difference between the electricity of the Electrical Machine and that of the Battery, in regard to quantity.

near each other only a feeble spark will pass, and on establishing a communication between them by means of the hands, previously moistened, a shock is felt, but only for a moment: we have also seen, §415, that its velocity is very much less, probably not exceeding 18,000 miles per second, while the velocity of statical electricity is 288,000 miles per second. On the other hand, galvanic electricity is developed in much larger quantity than statical, and in a steadily flowing current; it possesses also much greater heating, chemical and magnetic power, and exerts a peculiar effect upon the nervous system of animals. Notwithstanding these points of difference, it was believed from the earliest period in the history of galvanism, that it could be identified with statical electricity, and many attempts were made to establish the most conclusive test of identity, viz: the projection of the electric spark between the poles *before actual contact*, corresponding with the escape of vivid sparks from the highly excited prime conductor of an electrical machine. The electricity which is excited by rubbing a glass tube with a silk handkerchief, will pass without difficulty across half an inch of space, and give a bright and noisy spark, while the electrical current of a battery of several hundred pairs, will hardly force a passage through a stratum of air too thin to be appreciated, or produce a spark bright enough to be perceptible. Sir H. Davy asserted that 2,000 pairs of Wollaston plates, the most perfect form of the battery in his day, gave a spark 1-20th to 1-40th of an inch in air, and $\frac{1}{2}$ an inch *in vacuo*. Mr. Children stated that 1,250 pairs gave sparks through 1-50th of an inch. Daniell asserted that he had often seen sparks playing between the cells of his battery when they were approximated too much. Faraday stated that a spark would pass before contact even with a single pair. On the the other hand, many experimenters were inclined to deny the passage of any electrical spark at all before contact, even with the most powerful batteries. Jacoby found that the current from 12 pairs of plates in the most active operation, would not pass through 1-20,000th of an inch. Gassiot asserted that a battery of 150 pairs would not project a spark through 1-5,000th of an inch before contact, though it would give a minute but not brilliant spark on separating the poles, if tipped with charcoal: also, that a water-battery of 1,024 pairs, would not project a spark through 1-5,000th

---

What is the influence of galvanic electricity upon electrometers and the Leyden jar? What is the power of giving shocks and sparks? What is its velocity? How was the identity of the two attempted to be proved? Give the statements of Davy, Children, Daniell, Faraday, Jacoby and Gassiot, in regard to the projection of sparks by the battery.

of an inch, although a Leyden battery could be charged by it, so as to project a spark through 6-5,000ths of an inch. Walker proved that a constant battery of 99 cells would not project the spark through the thinnest measurable stratum of air. But it was finally determined by Crosse, in 1840, that a water-battery of 1,200 pairs, would give a constant small stream of sparks between the polar wires 1-100th of an inch apart, *before contact;* and Gassiot, suspecting that his previous battery series had not been sufficiently extended or insulated, constructed a water-battery of 3,000 pairs, and obtained sparks freely from its poles. By these experiments it came to be definitely settled that the galvanic battery would *project* a spark like a common electrical machine, and an actual identity was established between galvanic and statical electricity.

474. Points of resemblance between the Electricity of the Electrical machine and the secondary currents of Electricity induced by the primary current of the Battery and by Magnets. On the other hand, the secondary current of electricity induced by the primary current of the battery, on making and breaking connection, not being derived from the battery or from the primary current, but being simply the natural electricity of the secondary wire, disturbed and brought into activity by inductive influence, might be expected to exhibit a very close resemblance to that of the electrical machine, which is also nothing but the natural electricity of the glass plate of the machine thrown into a state of disturbance by means of friction. Thus, by the magneto-electric machine, the gold leaves of the electroscope may be made to diverge directly without the aid of a condenser, and a Leyden jar may be charged at every touch, provided one terminal wire of the coil is in connection with the outer coating of the jar, and the other carried to the knob by an insulated handle, the knob being connected with the inner coating by a wire instead of a chain: the sparks which are emitted are of the most vivid character, of great power, and violence, and often times extend through a space of several inches, surpassing all electrical machines except those of the largest size; the shocks are also extremely violent, and frequently dangerous, and the noise almost deafening.

475. The quantity of Electricity produced by the Battery immense, and its magnetic effect far superior to that of the Machine. Notwithstanding the extremely feeble intensity of

---

Give the experiment of Crosse, and the second experiment of Gassiot. What is the present opinion in regard to their identity?—474. State the points of resemblance between the electricity of the machine and that of the secondary current induced by the primary current and by magnets.

the electricity of the battery, its quantity is enormous. Mr. Faraday estimated the quantity of electricity furnished by the decomposition of a single grain of water, as equal to eight hundred thousand discharges of a battery of Leyden jars exposing thirty-five hundred square inches of surface, and charged by thirty turns of a powerful electrical machine. The experiment was performed in the following manner.—Two wires, one of zinc and one of platinum, each 1-18th of an inch in diameter, were immersed during 4-30ths of a second, to the depth of 5-8ths of an inch, and 5-16ths of an inch apart, in acidulated water prepared by adding a single drop of sulphuric acid to four ounces of water. The current produced by this exceedingly small battery, effected as great a deviation of the galvanometer needle, and decomposed the same amount of iodide of potassium, as thirty turns of a powerful plate electrical-machine: twenty-eight turns of the machine produced an effect perceptibly less than that produced by the two wires. The quantity of acidulated water decomposed within the battery in order to furnish this vast amount of electricity, was so small as to be incapable of measurement, and entirely inappreciable; but the electricity produced by it, if concentrated so as to be discharged in a single flash during a minute fraction of a second, from a Leyden battery having 3,500 square inches of surface, would kill a cat or a rat, and be intolerable to a man. From this experiment Mr. Faraday made the calculation that the electricity produced by the decomposition of a single grain of water in the battery by the action of the zinc plate, is equal to that furnished by eight hundred thousand discharges of an electrical machine, each equal to the one just described: or that the decomposition of one grain of water evolves a quantity of electricity sufficient to charge a surface of 400 acres, an amount hardly exceeded in the most violent storms. It has been calculated, that if this amount of electricity, furnished by one grain of water, were spread upon a cloud two-thirds of a mile distant from the earth, it would exert an attractive force upon the earth beneath it, of 1,664 tons! and that if the atoms of oxygen in this grain of water were attached to one thread 1-25th of an inch long, and those of hydrogen to another, the force required to separate the threads in one second, would be 7,250 tons! yet this amount of electricity is evolved, without

---

475. Describe Mr. Faraday's experiments upon the quantity of electricity produced by the battery. Give his conclusion in regard to the amount set free in the decomposition of a single grain of water. Describe the difference between the electricity of the machine and that of the battery in regard to magnetic effect.

noise, shock, or visible appearance of flame, in every case when rather less than six cubic inches of hydrogen and three cubic inches of oxygen, are set free by the action of four grains of zinc upon one grain of water. This, if concentrated into a single discharge, would be equal to a very vivid flash of lightning, whence it follows that the electricity set free in the decomposition of one grain of water by the four grains of zinc which are required, yields an amount of electricity equal to that of a powerful thunder-storm. Such is the difference between the electricity of the battery and the electricity of the machine, in regard to quantity. Their difference in regard to magnetic effect is equally remarkable. A piece of copper and a piece of zinc, the size of a cent, will produce a magnetic effect far superior to that exerted by the most powerful discharge of the electricity of the machine ever obtained. In experiments made upon the Atlantic cable, an electric current was sent through one thousand miles of it submerged in the water and a sufficient magnetic effect exerted upon the reflecting galvanometer, §418, to communicate a message, by a battery consisting of a silver wire and a zinc wire of the size of a pin, excited by a drop of acid supported between them by capillary action.

476. The action of Electricity and Magnetism on Light. Electricity, whether produced by the machine, by the battery, or by magnetism, has not only the power of producing light, but also a very singular effect on light after it is produced. Sir H. Davy ascertained, §359, that the light produced by the approach of two poles of a powerful battery, is influenced by the magnet, and is acted upon in the same way as any moveable metallic conductor traversed by the galvanic current: it is attracted and repelled by the magnet, and a rotary motion imparted manifesting itself by a change in the form of the arc. By holding the magnet in a certain position, the flame may be made to revolve, accompanied by a loud sound; and the form of the arc may even become broken by too great an attraction or repulsion. Fig. 253 represents the ordinary

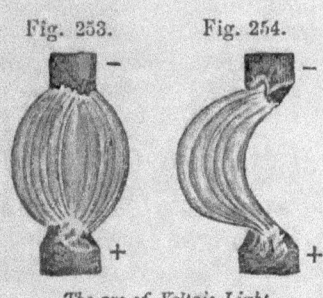

Fig. 253. Fig. 254.

The arc of Voltaic Light.

---

476 State the effect of the magnet on the electric light. How has it been shown that light is strongly diamagnetic?

488   THE EFFECT OF MAGNETISM

form of the voltaic arc between two cylinders of plumbago, and *Fig.* 254 the curved form which it exhibits under the influence of a magnetic pole. It has also been ascertained that light is strongly dia-magnetic, and assumes an equatorial position in the magnetic field. Bancalari observed that the flame of a candle placed between the poles of an electro-magnet, was repelled into a position at right angles to a line joining the poles, *Fig.* 255, as if blown by a current of air. M. Quet obtained a similar result by submitting the voltaic arc to the influence of powerful electro-magnetic poles, *Fig.* 256. It has been shown that the auroral light produced by Ruhmkorff's coil in the electric egg, *Fig.* 234, is made to revolve around an electro-magnet as soon as the connection is formed with the battery, that the stratified bands and luminous discharges of Geissler's tubes, §461, are powerfully affected by the magnet, and that the light from the negative pole is specially affected by the magnetic force. Finally Mr. Faraday has ascertained that a ray of light may be electrified and the electric forces illuminated. He observed that if a ray of polarized light were transmitted through a piece of glass placed between the poles of a powerful electro-magnet, on the line joining the two poles, on actuating the electro-magnet by connection with the battery, the ray of polarized light experienced a rotation, to the right or the left, according to the direction of the current. A polarized ray of light is one which by reflection, or by refraction through certain substances, has acquired certain peculiar properties different from those of ordinary light, which are summed up in the term polarization. Thus, when a ray of light falls upon a glass mirror at an angle

Fig. 255.

The effect of a powerful Electro-Magnet on the flame of a Candle.

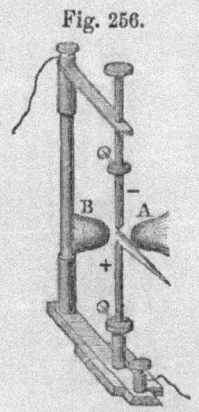

Fig. 256.

The effect of Magnetism on the Voltaic Light.

What is the effect of the magnet on the voltaic arc? on the auroral light of Ruhmkorff's coil and Geissler's tubes? What is the effect of Magnetism on polarized Light? What is polarized Light?

of 35° 25', it acquires the singular property of incapability of reflection from a second mirror of glass at the same angle, if the plane of incidence of the second mirror be perpendicular to the plane of incidence of the first: in other words, the ray becomes extinguished; it is partially reflected and re-appears, for every other inclination of the two planes, and the intensity of the ray reflected from the second mirror increases as the angle of the two planes of reflection diminishes. If, at the moment of extinction, a thin plate of quartz crystal, whose faces are perpendicular to its axis, be interposed between the two mirrors, the extinguished ray re-appears upon the second mirror, and in order to re-extinguish it the quartz must be turned by a certain angle to the right or the left. The quartz is said to exercise thus a rotary power, and to deviate the plane of polarization to the right or to the left, according to the direction in which it must be turned in order to re-extinguish the reflected ray. Several other substances besides quartz, such as oil of turpentine, solution of sugar, &c., possess the power of rotating the plane of polarization. The apparatus for showing that a similar rotating power is possessed by magnetism, is represented in *Fig.* 257. It consists of two very

Fig. 257.

The effect of Magnetism on Polarized Light.

What is the effect of quartz and some other substances upon the extinguished ray? Describe the apparatus, *Fig.* 257, by which it is shown that magnetism possesses a similar power of deviating a polarized ray of light.

powerful electro-magnets, M and N, mounted horizontally on two iron supports, o, o', which can be moved on a support K. The current from 10 or 11 Bunsen's cells, is transmitted by the wire A, to the commutator H, by which it may be sent in either direction through the coil M, thence by the wire g to the coil N, and then back again by the wire i, to the commutator H, finally emerging at B. The two cylinders of soft iron on which the coils M and N are wound, are perforated through their entire length by a cylindrical hole so as to allow a ray of light to pass completely through them both. At b and a, there are two of Nicol's prisms, each consisting of sections of rhombohedral crystals of Iceland spar, which have been cut diagonally, and then re-united by Canada balsam. These prisms serve instead of the two mirrors spoken of above, and exert a similar polarizing effect upon a ray of light. When the lamp is placed opposite b, and the eye at a, the ray of light is completely extinguished. If at this moment there be placed at c, a plate of ordinary or flint glass with parallel faces, the ray of light is still extinguished to the eye at a, so long as the electro-magnets remain unexcited, but the instant the current begins to flow and the electro-magnets become excited, the ray of light will reappear and cease to be extinguished by the prism a, and to extinguish it again it will be necessary to turn the index attached to a, to the right or left through a certain angle. If the current be broken the light reappears; if the current be reversed, and the poles of the electro-magnets changed, the direction in which the index must be turned in order to extinguish the ray, must also be reversed. Hence it appears that the electric current, or the magnetic power which it generates, possesses the power of rotating the ray of polarized light which passes through the core of the magnets, or else imparts this power to the piece of glass placed at c, and that this rotating power is to the right or to the left, according to the direction of the electric current, and is acquired and lost instantaneously, following the connection with the battery. "In this experiment," says Mr. Faraday, "we may justly say, that a ray of light is electrified and the electric forces illuminated." The general conclusion is, that the connection between Electricity, Magnetism, and Light, whether the light emanates from an electrical source, or from ordinary sources, is extremely intimate, and closely connected with the doctrine of the convertibility of Forces.

What is the general conclusion in regard to the connection between Electricity, Magnetism and Light?

477. Progress of discovery in the induction of Electricity by the Galvanic current, and the construction of Induction Coils and Magneto-Electric Machines. The successive discoveries which led to the construction of the powerful Induction Coils and Magneto-Electric machines now in use, are as follows.—The primary fact of induction, viz: the induction of a secondary current in the primary wire connecting the poles of a battery, and the increased effect obtained by using a long wire, and especially one coiled into a helix, was discovered by Prof. Henry in 1831. In the same year Mr. Faraday made the discovery of the induction of electricity by the battery current in a neighboring wire, distinct from it, and forming a closed circuit, whenever the battery circuit is completed or broken; also, whenever the battery circuit is brought near or removed from the closed secondary current. He also discovered at the same time, the induction of electricity by a magnet, whenever brought near or removed from a closed circuit consisting of a great length of wire coiled into a helix; also, the induction of electricity in a similar coil by the magnetization and de-magnetization of an electro-magnet by a battery current, and by the magnetization and de-magnetization of a piece of soft iron by the inductive influence of a permanent magnet brought near and removed from it. In 1833, Dal Negro, an Italian philosopher, discovered that the inductive influence of the current of the primary wire connecting the poles of a battery, was more intense if the wire were wound into a coil surrounding a piece of soft iron. In 1834, Mr. Faraday made the announcement of the same fact, communicated to him by a young man named William Jenkin, of London, viz: " that if an ordinary wire of short length be used as a medium of communication between the poles of a battery of a single pair of metals, no management will enable the experimenter to obtain an electric shock from this wire; but if the wire which surrounds an electro-magnet be used, a shock is felt each time the contact with the electromotor is broken, provided the ends of the wire be grasped, one in each hand." This fact Faraday confirmed by his own experiments. In 1836, Dr. Page discovered the principle that the intensity of the induced current in the secondary wire might be greatly increased by lengthening the secondary coil and making it many times longer than the pri-

---

477. Who discovered the fact of induction in the primary wire coiled into a helix? Who discovered the inductive action of the primary wire upon a neighboring wire? Who discovered the increase of effect produced by winding the primary coil around a piece of soft iron? What was the discovery made by Jenkin?

mary coil; constructed his compound-coil and spark-arresting circuit-breaker, and, in 1838, discovered the advantage of making use of a number of soft iron wires in place of a bar of solid iron in the axis of the inner coil. In 1853, Fizeau discovered the peculiar effect of the condenser, or Leyden jar, in absorbing the extra-current and increasing the intensity of the induced current in the secondary coil. In 1857, Ritchie invented his improved mode of winding and insulating the secondary coil and breaking the circuit, by which the length of the spark was increased to fifteen inches. And finally, in 1860, by adopting this improved mode of winding, and by greatly lengthening the secondary coil, Ruhmkorff succeeded in bringing his induction coil to its present state of perfection.

In the development of Magneto-Electric machines, the original discovery of the induction of electricity by the magnet, and the production of a current in a wire wound upon soft iron, by the approach and removal of a strong permanent magnet, was made by Mr. Faraday in 1831. In 1832, Pixii constructed his machine, in which a magnet was made to revolve in front of fixed coils. In 1833, Saxton constructed his improved machine, in which the magnets were fixed, and the coils made to revolve; and in 1833, Page made still further improvements by increasing the number of the magnets and inducing magnetism at both extremities of the iron cores within the coils, and invented his pole-changer, by which each pole always received the same kind of electricity, and one-half the electric current previously lost, was saved. In 1861, Holmes invented the combination of magneto-electric machines, which resulted in the production of the permanent magneto-electric light, and its introduction for Light-house illumination. This was followed by Wilde's machine in 1866, and by Ladd's in 1867, by which the Magneto-Electric machine has been advanced to its most perfect state, and brought to supersede the light of the sun for photographic pictures. All these wonderful inventions and their applications, directly connected with some of the greatest improvements in modern civilization, derive their origin from the discovery by Mr. Faraday, in 1831, of the induction of electricity by magnetism, and the production of the electric spark by a fixed magnet; and therefore, with justice might he say, in the latter part of his life, in speaking of the attempts by Mr.

Who discovered the advantage of lengthening the secondary coil? Who first made use of the Condenser? What was Ritchie's improvement? Ruhmkorff's? Trace the order of progression in the construction of Magneto-Electric Machines. To whose discovery is the Magneto-electric light of Light-houses strictly due?

THERMO-ELECTRICITY.   493

Holmes at introducing the magneto-electric light into the Light-house at the South Foreland, a subject in which he was much interested,—" I will not tell you that the problem of employing the magneto-electric spark for Light-house illumination, is quite solved yet, although I desire it should be established most earnestly, for I regard this magnetic spark as one of my own offspring."

§ VI. Thermo-Electricity.

478. Heat produces Electricity. We have seen that Electricity produces Heat: it is found that the reverse is also true, and that Heat under certain circumstances produces Electricity. If metallic bars of *unequal conducting power for heat* be soldered together at one extremity, and heat applied at the *point of junction*, the other extremity of the bars being connected with the galvanometer, an electric current will be at once produced, flowing from the hotter to the colder metal. Thus, in *Fig.* 258, let *m n*, be a bar of copper, whose ends are bent down and soldered to a plate of bismuth, *p o*, and let a magnetic needle be mounted upon a pivot in the space between the plates, and the apparatus be placed in the magnetic meridian; on applying the

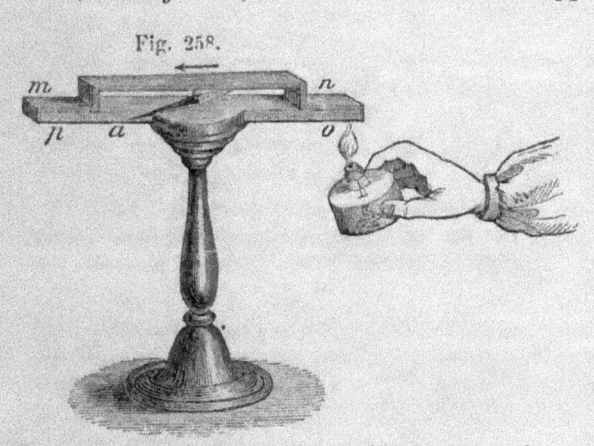

Fig. 258.

Electricity produced by Heat.

heat of a lamp at *o*, the needle will be at once deflected in such a manner as to show the passage of a current of electricity from *n* to *m*, in the direction indicated by the arrow. If instead of applying heat at *o*, a piece of ice be placed at that point, or cotton-wool moistened with ether, while the junc-

---

478 Prove that Heat produces Electricity. Describe *Fig.* 258.

tion at *m* retains its natural temperature, there will be a current in the opposite direction, from *m* towards *n*, and the energy of the current will be proportioned to the difference of temperature between the two junctions. The current is always from the hotter to the colder metal: it has been found that the currents are produced equally well *in vacuo* and in hydrogen, and therefore are not due to chemical action. The true cause is the unequal propagation of heat from the heated junction. Any obstruction to the equal distribution of heat in a metallic conductor, generates a current of electricity, in the same way that any obstruction to the flow of the electric current in a metallic wire produces a rise of temperature. Two metals are not necessary to the evolution of the current: any disturbance of the molecular arrangement so as to interfere with the equal propagation of the heat from the hot to the cold portions of a bar composed of a single metal, is sufficient to produce an electrical current. Thus a straight platinum wire stretched between the binding screws of a galvanometer, may be heated at any point without developing the slightest current in the instrument: but if the platinum wire be twisted into a loop so that its molecular arrangement is slightly altered at this point, and heat be applied close to the loop and to the right of it, a current will circulate through the galvanometer from right to left, owing to the unequal conduction of the heat. These facts were ascertained by Seebeck at Berlin, in 1821, and are of great interest as showing the intimate connection between Heat and Electricity. It may be stated in general that when two metals, of unequal conducting power for heat, are connected in any way so as to form a closed circuit, an electrical current is established flowing from the hotter to the colder, whenever a different temperature is produced between them, and the current is maintained as long as any difference of temperature continues. The metal from which the current proceeds is exactly analogous in situation to the zinc plate in the battery; the metal to which the current proceeds is analogous to the platinum plate. The different metals do not all possess this power when associated; and the direction of the current depends upon the metals which compose the circuit. When bars of antimony and bismuth are soldered together and heated at the junction, the current flows from the

---

Does the current flow from the hot to the cold metal or the reverse? What is the effect if there be any obstruction to the equal propagation of heat in a metallic conductor? What always takes place when two metals of unequal conducting power are connected so as to form a closed circuit and heated?

BATTERY. 495

cold end of the bismuth to the cold end of the antimony, as represented in *Fig.* 258. The following series represents the thermo-electric order of the metals, each metal being positive in reference to the metals which come after it,—Bismuth, Mercury, Lead, Tin, Platinum, Copper, Silver, Zinc, Iron, Antimony.

When heated together, the current proceeds from the cold extremities of those which are first on the list to the cold extremities of those which are last. The thermo-electric order is very different from the voltaic order. Other substances besides the metals will also produce electrical currents when soldered together and heated. Gas-carbon may be used in connection with German-silver, with silver, and with iron, and it has even been found that the point of a heated cone of porcelain, if brought into contact with a cold cylinder of the same material, will generate a thermo-electric current passing from the hot cone to the cold cylinder, each being connected with the galvanometer by cotton soaked in some conducting liquid.

When the process is reversed, and a weak galvanic current is transmitted through a thermo-electric series, heat is produced if the current be sent in the same direction as the thermo-electric current, and cold if in the reverse direction.

479. The Thermo-electric Battery. By connecting the cold bismuth end of a thermo-electric pair composed of antimony and bismuth, with the cold antimony end of a second pair, as shown in *Fig.* 259, the bismuth being represented by the white bar, and the antimony by the black, and so through a long series, a battery may be constructed, the power of which increases with every additional pair. While the ends of the pairs on one side must be heated, those on the other side must be kept cool, in order to obtain the most powerful effects. When arranged as in *Fig.* 260, the extremities of the series being connected with a galvanometer by means of wires, upon the application of heat at the upper ends, the needle is powerfully deflected, and iodide of potassium and acidulated water may be decomposed. The legs of a frog may even be thrown into convulsions by the current proceed-

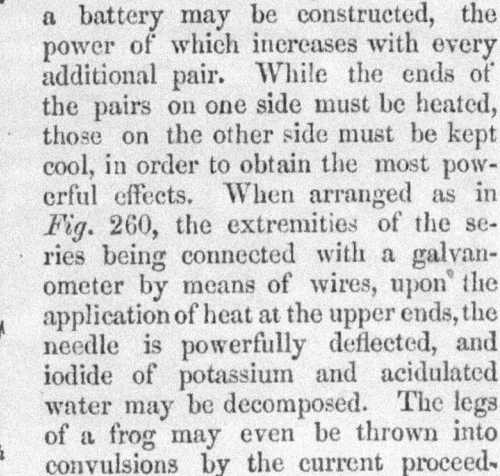

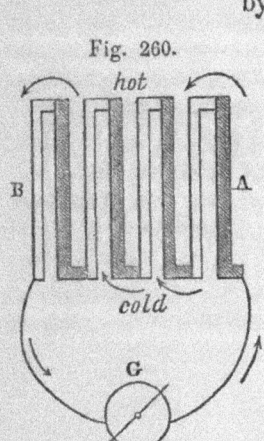

Fig. 259.

The Thermo-electric Pile.

Fig. 260.

Thermo-electric Battery, with Galvanometer.

ing from a single pair. If the lower ends of the pairs be heated while the upper are kept cool, the direction of the current will be reversed. The intensity of the current is feeble, but in quantity it closely resembles a weak galvanic circuit: its chief effect is therefore magnetic, and a battery composed of sixty pairs of bismuth and antimony bars, three inches long, three-fourths of an inch wide, and one-fourth of an inch thick, whose extremities on one side are heated by a hot plate of iron, and on the other cooled by immersion in snow mixed with half its weight of salt, will produce an electro-magnetic current sufficient to raise a weight of fifty pounds.

480. The Thermo-electric Battery of Nobili. The first thermo-electric battery was constructed by Oersted and Fourier, but Nobili was the inventor of the arrangement now generally used; he united bars of bismuth and antimony in such a way as to form a series of five pairs, the bar of bismuth *b*, being connected with the lower antimony bar of a second similar series placed vertically by the side of the first, *Fig.* 261, then the last bismuth of this series with the first antimony of a third, and so on for four vertical series containing 20 couples, the whole series commencing with a bar of bismuth and ending with one of antimony.

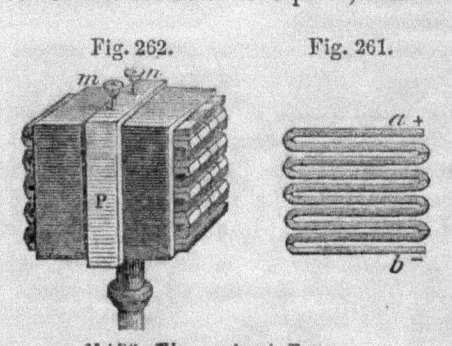

Fig. 262.   Fig. 261.

Nobili's Thermo-electric Battery.

The pairs were insulated by means of bands of paper covered with varnish, and then enclosed in a brass case, in such a manner that the junctions of the bars appeared at the opposite ends of the case, *Fig.* 262. Two binding screws, *x* and *y*, insulated by ivory and communicating, the one with the first antimony, and the other with the last bismuth bar, constitute the poles of the battery, and admit of the attachment of wires connecting with a galvanometer, as represented in *Fig.* 263. When thus connected, the slightest difference of temperature between the two ends of the battery is sufficient to excite a

---

What is the thermo-electric order of the metals? Will any but metallic substances answer? What is the effect of transmitting an electric current through a thermo-electric series?—479. Describe the thermo-electric battery. What are its effects? What is its magnetic power?—480. Describe the thermo-electric battery of Nobili.

MELLONI'S THERMO-MULTIPLIER. 497

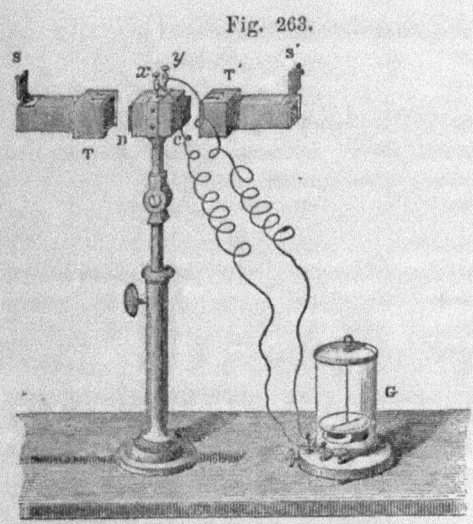

Fig. 263.

The Thermo-electric Multiplier for measuring heat.

current of electricity, and produce a very sensible deflection of the needle of the galvanometer.

481. The Thermo-Multiplier of Melloni. Nobili's battery thus arranged and connected with a galvanometer, is the instrument with which Melloni made his celebrated researches in regard to the transmission of heat through screens, § 88, and proved the existence of a *calorific* tint for heat in thin plates similar to the *colorific* tint for light. It was named by him the Thermo-Multiplier, *Fig.* 263. The

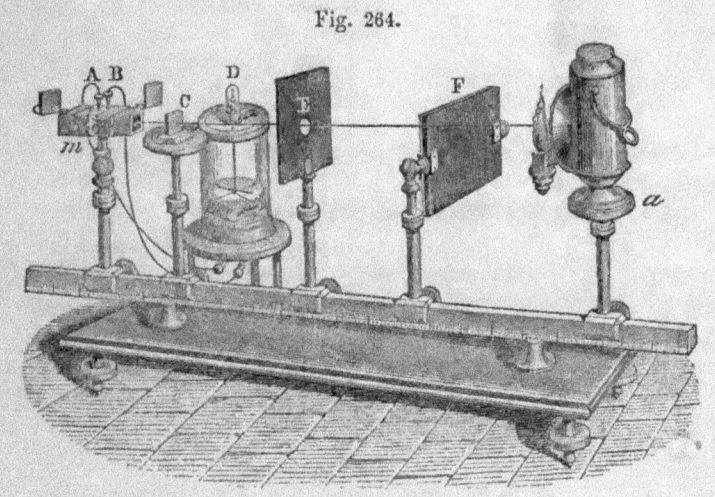

Fig. 264.

Melloni's apparatus for measuring the transmission of radiant heat by the Thermo-Multiplier.

arrangement of his apparatus was as follows, *Fig.* 264. Upon a tablet of wood, a brass rule was mounted, about a yard in length, and carefully graduated. This rule supported at varying distances the different pieces of which the apparatus was composed; on a stand a, was mounted the locatelli lamp, or other source of heat; then the screens F and E; then a second support C, on which were placed the substances whose diathermic power was to be determined; and finally the thermo-electric pile m, whose poles A and B, were connected with the galvanometer D, by short and thick wires. The diathermic power of the substances in question was determined by the degree of deflection in the galvanometer. A thermo-electric pile, with galvanometer attached, was also the instrument used by Tyndall in his experiments upon the absorption and transmission of radiant heat by gases, described in his work entitled, "*Heat a Mode of Motion*," and it constitutes the most delicate known instrument for measuring slight degrees of heat. The heat of the hand at the distance of several feet, warm air breathed from the mouth, or even the heat produced by the impinging of compressed air upon one end of the battery, the temperature of insects, *Fig.* 265, and, on the other hand, equally slight depressions of temperature at the opposite end of the battery, all produce a remarkable deflection of the needle, and are capable of being measured by it.

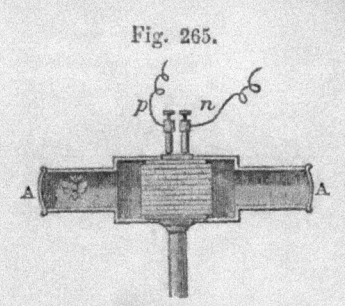

Fig. 265.

The temperature of Insects measured by the Thermo-Multiplier.

482. Farmer's Thermo-Electric Battery. A thermo-electric battery has recently been constructed by Mr. Farmer, the inventor of the Electric fire-alarm, § 430, which may be substituted with great advantage for the galvanic batteries and magneto-electric machines in common use. A series of pairs of German-silver and bismuth, are arranged with their soldered extremities pointing towards a common centre, in such a manner as to make a perfect circle, 1, *Fig.* 266; the electric current circulates from pair to pair, and finally appears at the polar binding screws; by means of these screws the current may be transmitted to the binding screws of a second series, 2, entirely

---

481. Describe Melloni's Thermo-multiplier. Describe the arrangement of Melloni's apparatus for measuring the transmission of radiant heat. What slight degrees of temperature can be measured by this instrument?

BATTERY. 499

Fig. 266.

Farmer's Thermo-Electric Battery.

insulated from the first, and producing a similar current, and thence to a third, finally emerging at the poles, p and n. In order to actuate this battery, it is only necessary to apply heat within the internal cylinder to which the pairs point. This may be done by means of charcoal, gas, or an alcohol lamp. In *Fig.* 266, G is a tube connecting with a gas-burner, B is the gas-burner of the battery, C is a deflector to keep the heat down in the centre. All that is required to put the battery in operation, is to turn on the gas and light the burner B; it acquires its maximum of activity in a few moments, and works continuously and constantly as long as it receives heat, producing a steady and perfectly uniform current of electricity for an indefinite period, without any perceptible variation in strength. It may be employed for any of the purposes for which a common galvanic battery is used,—for working the telegraph, precipitating metals from their solutions, exciting electro-magnets, operating fire-alarms, producing the electric light, or actuating Page's or Ruhmkorff's coils for medical use, and is particularly adapted to electrotyping, plating and gilding, because no acids, mercury, or liquids of any kind are required. There is no waste of the metallic pairs, as they remain as good at the end of the year as when first used. It requires no attention after being first lighted, and will run day and night without any change, as long as heat is applied. It is also very economical, as five or six pounds of coal will evolve as much electricity as one and a half pounds of zinc, five or six pounds of sulphuric acid, and one ounce of mercury. Ten pairs are estimated to be equal to one Smee's cell; twenty-four pairs to one Daniell's cell, and forty-four to

---

482. Describe Farmer's Thermo-electric battery. What is required to put this battery into operation? For what purposes may it be employed? What are its advantages?

one Grove's cell. The cost of working such a battery possessing half the power of a Grove cell, and five times that of a Daniell, is one-third of a cent per hour with gas, and two cents per hour with an alcohol lamp.

It has been estimated that a light equal to that of 5,000 candles, can be produced,

By a Grove's battery, at a cost of, per candle, per hour, of 5½ mills.
By Illuminating Gas, ... 1 "
By Smee's battery, ... 1 "
By the Magneto-electric machine, . . . 0.10 "

Also, that from one pound of coal used in the steam-engine to drive the magneto-electric machine, or in the thermo-electric battery, a light equal to that of about 144 candles can be obtained: also that the total electrical energy contained in one pound of pure carbon, completely burned into carbonic acid, and its heat used to produce electricity, and through electricity converted into Light, will furnish an amount equal to that of a candle burning 1 year and 5 months; and that if all the energy in a pound of carbon could be converted into Light by means of the electricity which it is capable of generating, it would be equivalent to the burning of a candle for 12,410 hours.

This will give some idea of the tremendous amount of energy capable of being furnished by the electricity derived from Heat.

§ VII. Animal Electricity.

483. Animal Life produces Electricity. The vital principle of the Animal economy in all animals produces Electricity, and in some animals is capable of generating very powerful electrical currents. The torpedo, a flat fish, found in the Mediterranean, is provided with two electrical organs, situated one on each side of the spine, near the head, and a powerful shock is received on simultaneously touching the back or belly of the fish at any part; but the strongest shock is obtained immediately over the two organs. The gymnotus, a fresh water fish, abundant in the waters of the Orinoco, has four electrical organs, running from the head to the tail of the animal. So great is the electrical energy

---

State the comparative expense of producing a light equal to that of 5000 candles from Grove's battery, Smee's, Illuminating Gas, and the Magneto-electric machine. State the total electrical energy contained in one pound of coal. State the illuminating power of one pound of Carbon if converted into light.

of the animal that a fish 40 inches in length, has given a shock which, it has been calculated, is equal to that emitted from a Leyden battery of 15 jars, exposing 3500 square inches of coated surface. The shocks from the gymnotus are sufficient to stun, and even kill, large fish; and give rise to electric currents of enough power to deflect the galvanometer, magnetize a needle, decompose iodide of potassium, and even produce sparks. It has been shown, also, that in all living animals an electrical current is perpetually circulating between the interior of the muscles and their external surface, probably due to the vital changes which are continually going on in the organic tissue. In warm-blooded animals, this current ceases in a very few minutes after death; but in cold-blooded animals, it continues for a much longer period. If five or six frogs be killed by dividing the spinal column just below the head, the lower limbs removed, and the skin stripped from them, the thighs separated from the lower legs at the knee joint, and then cut across transversely, a battery can be constructed from the pieces. Thus, let the lower half of the thighs be placed upon a varnished board, and arranged so that the knee joint of one limb shall be in contact with the transverse section of the next, and a muscular pile can be formed, consisting of ten or twelve pairs; the terminal pieces should be made to dip into small cavities, in which distilled water is placed. If the wires of a galvanometer be introduced into these cavities, by means of two thin platinum plates, a deviation in the needle will be observed in such a direction as to show the existence of a current passing from the centre, or cut transverse end of the muscle, towards its exterior. This muscular pile acts equally well in highly rarefied air, in carbonic acid gas, and in hydrogen; in the last gas the needle of the galvanometer, after being moved, remains stationary for several hours. This nullity of the action of the several gases is thought to prove that the oxygen of the air is not necessary, and that the origin of the current is in the muscle itself, and depends rather on the organization of the muscular fibre and the chemical actions going on within its structure. If a prepared frog be placed with its lumbar nerves plunged into one capsule filled with water, and its legs placed in another, the circuit being completed through the galvanometer, the instrument gives indications of an electrical current passing from the feet towards the head of the animal. The effect is very much

---

483. Can the vital principle of animals produce electricity? Describe the torpedo. What effects are produced by it? Is there an electrical current circulating in all animals? Describe the frog battery. How is it shown that the current is not produced by the action of the air?

502   THE PHYSIOLOGICAL

increased when several frogs are arranged on an insulated surface in the manner shown in *Fig.* 252, the spinal cord of each frog touching the legs of the following; every time the circuit is completed, the needle of the galvanometer moves, and the limbs of the frogs contract. It is probable that further investigation will develop a still closer relation between electricity and the vital force of the Animal economy.

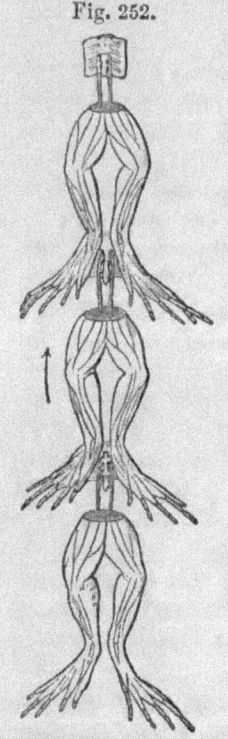

Fig. 252.

Battery constructed of the legs of Frogs.

484. The Physiological effects of the Galvanic Current. On the other hand the physiological effects of the galvanic current upon the animal economy are equally remarkable. The convulsive movements in the leg of the frog, noticed by Galvani, led to the invention of the voltaic pile, and the formation of a new science. When the wire from one pole of the battery is put in communication with the nerve of any limb of an animal recently killed, *Fig.* 253, and the wire from the other pole with the outside of the muscles, the limb will be contracted with great violence, the muscles of the face will be made to display the various emotions and passions of the mind, and many of the vital processes of secretion and digestion will be recommenced, so that there is good reason for supposing a close connection between the galvanic current and the nervous energy by which all the vital functions are maintained.

By means of a powerful galvanic current, small animals, such as rabbits and hares, which have been suffocated half an hour, have been brought to life. The face of a prisoner, who had been executed by hanging, exhibited such dreadful muscular contortions when excited by the galvanic current, as to horrify the spectators: the trunk partially raised itself, the hands were agitated and the arms swung wildly, the chest rose and fell as though respiration had recommenced, and nearly all the vital processes were set in motion; but the whole effect ceased as soon as the current

_{Describe the arrangement of the frog battery.—484. State the physiological effects of the current. What is the effect upon small animals that have been suffocated? Describe the effect upon an executed prisoner.}

was withdrawn. If the fingers be moistened and applied to the poles of the battery, a smart shock will be obtained, the strength of which will depend upon the number of plates or cells employed; if two metallic handles be connected with the two poles, and grasped by the moistened hands, the strength of the continued succession of shocks will be greatly increased. The

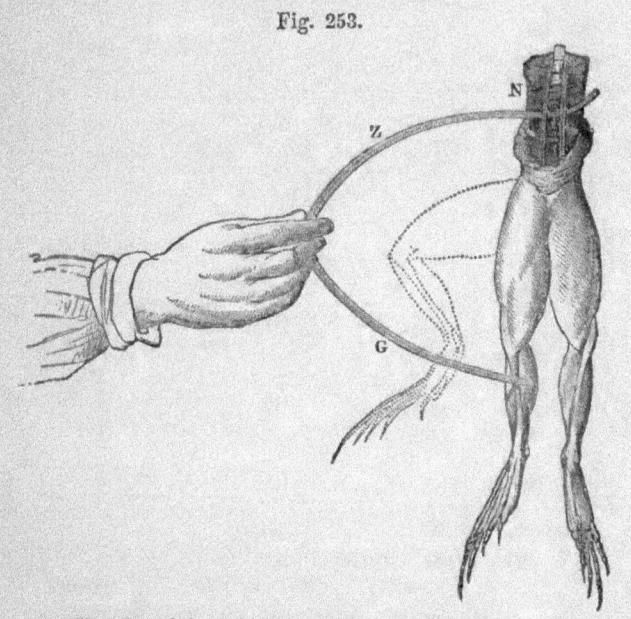

Fig. 253.

The effect of the Galvanic current on the Animal economy.

most severe shocks are given, however, not by the direct current of the battery, but by the induced currents of Page's and Ruhmkorff's coils, and the various Magneto-electric machines. Shocks of great violence can thus be given, and so firm a muscular contraction of the hands produced, that it will be impossible to relax the grasp. It has also been found that these induced currents exert a different effect upon the system, from the direct current of the battery, and do not produce the same chemical disturbance of the functions of the body. Various instruments have been invented for the application of these currents to medical purposes. Of these the most efficient is Page's sep-

How can shocks be taken from the battery? What is the effect of using metallic handles? By what instruments can the most severe shocks be obtained?

arable helices § 451, with the coils arranged horizontally, on account of the facility with which the shocks may be regulated. With this apparatus, there are some peculiarities in the shock depending upon the motion of the battery wire over the rasp: if it is moved slowly, distinct and powerful shocks are experienced; if the motion be more rapid, the arms are much convulsed: and if it be drawn very rapidly, the succession of shocks becomes intensely painful. The violence of the shocks can be easily regulated by the number of iron wires employed, and by varying the distance to which they are inserted. The power of the shock depends very much upon the extent of the contact surface between the hands and the metallic conductors; if two wires only are used, and held lightly in the fingers, the effect is much less than when metallic handles are employed especially if the hands are moistened with salt water. Shocks of a peculiar character may be given by placing the polar wires in two basins of water, and then dipping a hand into each basin; in this case the strongest sensation is experienced when the ends of the fingers only are immersed; if a large surface be exposed the shock will be felt strongly through the arms. These shocks will pass without much diminution of intensity through a circle formed of several persons, although different individuals are very differently affected, the shock which is felt by some only in the fingers or hands, in the case of others extending to the arms and breast. There is a difference in the strength of the shocks in the two arms; if the positive handle be held in the right hand and the negative in the left, the left hand and arm will experience the strongest sensations, and be the most convulsed. This remarkable difference of intensity is believed to be a purely physiological peculiarity, a greater effect being produced by the current, in the arm in which it flows in the same direction as the ramification of the nerves, than in the one in which it flows in an opposite direction. If both wires are put into the same trough at some distance apart, and a finger of each hand be placed in the water in a line between the two wires, a shock will be felt, because the current finds a passage through the body more readily than through the water, which intervenes between the fingers; but if the fingers be put in at right angles to the line between the wires no shock will be felt: if the conducting power of the water be made better than that

---

How can the violence of the shocks be regulated? What is the effect of taking the shocks through water? Is there any difference in the effect upon the two arms? How may the effect of the shock from water be increased?

of the body, by dissolving in it a little common salt, little or no shock can be perceived. It has also been ascertained that induced currents of different orders produce different effects upon the body. An induced current of the first order, produces strong muscular contractions, but has little effect upon the sensibility of the skin, while an induced current of the second order increases the cutaneous sensibility to such a degree, that it often cannot be applied to persons of great nervous susceptibility.

485. The various sources of Electricity, and its Relations to the other two Chemical Agents, Heat and Light. The study of Static and Galvanic Electricity has shown, that this wonderful agent can be produced by a great variety of sources:—by Friction; by Chemical action; by Magnetism; by Heat; and by Vital action. It has also shown that it is capable of producing, or of being converted into, all the Forces, which act on matter, except Gravity, viz,—Motion; Heat; Light; Chemical action; and Magnetism; and that it can imitate the effects, if not actually produce several of the properties of the Vital Force.

It is distinguished from the other Forces by producing more intense and powerful effects. The heat which it generates is the most intense heat known; the light, which it evolves is superior to the light of the Sun; the motion which it causes is infinitely more rapid and prompt than any which can be brought about by the more tardy operation of either Heat or Light: the physiological sensations which it exerts are more decided, and evident than those of the other forces. It is especially remarkable for the extraordinary influence which it exerts over chemical affinity. It is able to break up and destroy some of the most powerful combinations existing in Nature, and has disclosed the existence of a very large number of the chemical elements known to the chemist. It stands out, therefore, as in some respects superior to the forces of Heat and Light. Consequently it is a more prominent and valuable agent for the modification and control of Chemical affinity than either Heat or Light, and is emphatically the chief instrument which the chemist has at command in his investigations into the constitution of matter for the purpose of determining its composition and the nature of the elements which enter into it.

What different effects do induced currents of different orders produce?—485. What are the various sources of electricity? How is it distinguished from other Forces? Why more valuable to the Chemist?

§ VIII. Conclusion of the Chemical Forces.

486. The Relations subsisting among the three Chemical Forces, Heat, Light and Electricity. They are convertible, and probably due to the motion of the molecules of bodies. It is evident from what has been already said, that the three Chemical forces, Heat, Light and Electricity, are not independent of each other, but very closely related, and mutually convertible. Thus Heat, when accumulated to a sufficient degree in bodies, is capable of producing both Light and Electricity without the intervention of any other force. Light is capable of producing both Heat and Electricity not directly, but by the intervention of the force of Chemical affinity. Electricity is capable of producing Heat and Light directly, and by the rapid magnetization and de-magnetization of an iron bar, § 398, can also produce both Molecular motion and Heat. These Forces are all capable of being produced by the force of Mechanical motion; and it is thought by some can always be traced back to their origin, in Motion. If this be so, they are all due to one cause, viz—Motion of the molecules of bodies. Thus Heat, it is well known, can be produced by Motion, and every kind of Heat, as we have seen, § 258, p. 230, even the Heat of combustion, is susceptible of explanation on this principle. Light can also be produced directly by Motion, as is proved by the flash which accompanies the collision between projectiles and the target, § 243, p. 216. Electricity can also be produced directly by Motion, as is proved by the operation of the ordinary electrical machine and the revolution of coils in front of the poles of a magnet. The derivation of the three Chemical Forces from Motion, and their mutual convertibility are elegantly shown by the magneto-electric machines of Saxton and Page, *Figs.* 245, 247. In these machines coils of wound wire are made to revolve by means of mechanical motion in front of the poles of powerful magnets; by this revolution, the magnets are made to generate momentary currents of Electricity; by this electricity, when transmitted through carbon points, intense Heat and Light are produced, and chemical decomposition effected, as is shown by the use of the light for the illumination of Light-houses, and by the precipitation of the metals from their solutions in the various processes of electrotyping and plating. Thus Mo-

---

486. How can it be shown that the chemical Forces are convertible? How can they be traced back to Mechanical Motion? By what machines can the derivation of the chemical forces and their convertibility be shown?

tion may be converted successively into all the Forces and be made to appear as Heat, Light, or Electricity. The closeness of this relation is conclusively shown by the following elegant experiment of Mr. Grove. A prepared daguerreotype plate of silver coated with Iodine is enclosed in a box filled with water, having a glass front with a shutter over it. Between this glass and the plate is a gridiron of silver wire. The silver plate is connected with one extremity of the coil of a delicate galvanometer. The gridiron of silver wire is connected with one end of the helix of Breguèt's metallic thermometer, *Fig.* 50. The other extremities of the galvanometer and the thermometer, are connected by a wire, and the galvanometer needles are brought to zero. Thus a complete galvanic circuit is constructed: the prepared daguerreotype plate is the battery generating plate; the silver gridiron, the conducting plate; the water in the box, the exciting liquid, and the wire which runs to the galvanometer, thence to the thermometer, and then back to the silver gridiron, is the conducting wire. As soon as the shutter which covers the glass front of the box is raised, and a beam of day-light, or of the electric light or of the oxy-hydrogen blowpipe, is permitted to fall upon the silver plate, the needle of the galvanometer begins to move, and the index of the metallic thermometer to turn, showing the circulation of electricity, with the production of magnetism, and the evolution of heat. Thus Light being the initiating force, we get chemical action on the plate, electricity circulating through the wires, magnetism in the galvanometer, heat in the thermometer, and motion in the needles.

This process sometimes goes on upon a great scale in the operations of nature. Thus by the action of the Light of the Sun upon the leaves of plants, the carbonic acid which they inspire from the air is decomposed, and the Carbon, which constitutes a large part of the substance of plants, set free. It is by this process that the Carbon which now constitutes the vast depots of coal buried beneath the soil has been withdrawn from the ancient atmosphere of the earth. By this action of Light, in virtue of which this Carbon is withdrawn from chemical combination, an equivalent amount of chemical force is created, and the liberated carbon, recombining with the oxygen of the air, will produce an equivalent amount of Heat. The Heat thus set free produces by its effect on water, an equivalent amount of

Describe Mr. Grove's experiment. What is the initiating Force in this experiment? In what operation of nature is this process carried on upon a large scale? Describe this process.

molecular motion resulting in the formation of steam, and this in turn produces a definite amount of mechanical motion in the Steam-Engine, which if applied to the revolution of the coils of a Magneto-electric machine, would evolve a sufficient amount of electricity to set free, by means of carbon points, an amount of Heat and Light, provided nothing were lost in these repeated transfers, exactly equivalent to the Heat and Light of the original sunbeams whose active agency enabled the leaves to decompose the carbonic acid of the atmosphere. It was, therefore, not without reason that Mr. Geo. Stephenson, the inventor of the Locomotive, ascribed the power that drove it to the light of the sun. "Can you tell me," he said to Dr. Buckland, "what is the power that is driving that train?" "I suppose it is one of your big engines." "What do you say to the light of the sun?" "How can that be?" "It is nothing else; it is light bottled up in the earth for tens of thousands of years,—light absorbed by plants and vegetables being necessary for the condensation of carbon during the process of their growth—and now after being buried in the earth for long ages in fields of coal, that latent light is again brought forth and liberated, made to work as in that locomotive for great human purposes."

From the mutual convertibility of these three Forces, it is evident that, when any one of them disappears, and seems to be destroyed, it may in fact only be undergoing a process of conversion into one of the other two, and presently re-appear in another form. The motion of a rapidly moving ball seems to be annihilated by striking against the target, but in reality it is only converted into another force, viz., that of heat, as is proved by the rise of temperature both in the ball and target. Force, therefore, disappears in one form to re-appear in another. And not only is this true, but, the new Force thus produced by de-volution out of another, is exactly equivalent in amount to that of the Force which has disappeared.

487. In every case of the convertibility of the Chemical Forces, there is an expenditure of the original Force, and a reduction of its strength exactly equivalent to that of the new Force produced, into which it has been changed. In all cases where a given amount of force is in action, if the result be the production of a second force, the original force is reduced in

---

State Mr. Stephenson's opinion of the origin of the power driving the Locomotive. What becomes of the original Force in all cases of apparent disappearance?—487. Is there any proportion between the original Force and the new one into which it is converted?

strength to a degree exactly proportioned to that of the new force called into being. Thus when the movement of a definite amount of galvanic electricity produces a development of heat in a conducting wire, the amount of electricity in circulation is diminished to a degree exactly equal to the amount of heat brought into action. When the rapid motion of a wheel results in producing great heat in the axle, there is a retardation in the motion of the wheel, exactly equivalent to the degree of heat excited in the axle.

This is very beautifully and conclusively proved by the experiment of M. Favre, referred to in § 360. A voltaic battery, and an electro-magnet, which actuated it, were placed in two adjacent calorimeters somewhat similar to that of Lavoisier and Laplace, § 232, and the heat produced in a given time within the battery, when the connection with the electro-magnet was established, ascertained: the electro-magnet was then made to raise a weight, or in other words a portion of the power of the battery was converted into motion, and the amount of heat in circulation during a space of time exactly equal to the former again noted. It was found that the heat within the battery was diminished in exact proportion to the amount of mechanical effect exerted, and the amount of heat which disappeared was found by calculation to be exactly equal to the amount of heat which this mechanical power thus produced, was capable of evolving, according to Joule's Law, § 254, i. e, a definite amount of Heat had been resolved into a definite amount of mechanical motion, exactly equal to the mechanical motion required for the production of an equal amount of heat, the process being reversed.

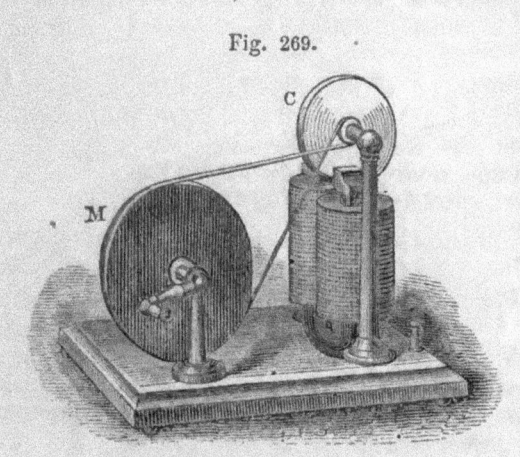

Fig. 269.

Motion Converted into Heat.

Describe M. Favre's experiment by which the equivalence of the new Force to the original Force is proved. What was the result?

510   FORCES.

The same fact is shown with equal conclusiveness by an experiment of M. Foucault; if a thin circular disc of copper c, *Fig.* 269, be mounted on a shaft between the poles of a powerful electro-magnet in the equatorial axis, it can be made to revolve with great rapidity by means of the multiplying wheel M, so long as there is no connection between the electro-magnet and the battery, and this movement will continue for some time after the propelling force is withdrawn, from the momentum it has acquired. If, at this moment, the connection with the battery be established so that the electro-magnet becomes powerfully magnetized, the motion of the disc is checked by the dia-magnetic action, § 392, exerted upon it, and by the secondary electrical currents, § 447, induced within it by the action of the electro-magnet, and it becomes exceedingly difficult to turn it; at the same time the temperature of the disc instantly rises; in other words, the force applied to the wheel remaining the same as before, and not being able to expend itself in the production of motion, is converted in part into heat, and the disc at once becomes very hot; in one experiment the temperature rose from almost 55° F. to 165°. It has been stated, § 472, p. 482, that when an armature carrying a coil is made to revolve between the poles of an electro-magnet it becomes much more difficult to turn it, and its speed is greatly reduced the instant the battery current is made to circulate through the electro-magnet: by enclosing such an armature in a glass tube filled with water, and causing the whole to revolve between the poles of the electro-magnet, Mr. Joule has endeavored to estimate the amount of heat into which a portion of the mechanical force has been converted, by the rise of a thermometer placed in the water.

In like manner, if the poles of a galvanic battery be joined by a thin platinum wire, the wire will be ignited and a certain amount of chemical action will take place in the battery, a definite quantity of zinc being dissolved, and of Hydrogen set free in a given time, resulting in the production of a definite amount of electricity circulating through the wire, of which a portion is converted into heat. If now, the platinum wire be placed in water, its conducting power will be increased in consequence of the diminution of resistance by the reduction of temperature, a larger amount of the electrical force will be converted into heat than before, and the chemical action on the generating plates within the battery will be found, on examination, to have been correspondingly augmented. If the experiment be re-

---

Describe M. Foucault's experiment. If a portion of the power of the battery be expended in the production of Heat, what effect is produced upon its chemical power?

versed and the wire be placed in the flame of a spirit lamp, by which its conducting power for heat is diminished, § 333, the chemical action is correspondingly reduced.

These instances might be multiplied indefinitely, and it is now a generally received truth that when one Force is converted into another, the strength of the original Force is proportionably reduced, and that the strength of the new Force is exactly equivalent to the diminution in the strength of the Force from which it has been derived.

488. The Convertibility and Equivalency of Force, true of all the Forces which act on Matter. Not only is the convertibility and equivalency of Force true of the Forces, Heat, Light and Electricity, but also, it is thought, of the other Forces which act on Matter, viz: the attraction of Gravitation and the attraction of Chemical Affinity. This seems to be pretty conclusively proved in the case of Chemical Affinity from the instances cited above, in which the amount of Chemical Force in action in the battery is increased or diminished in proportion to the increase and diminution of the strength of the Forces to which it gives rise. But the convertibility of Gravity into new Forces, and of other Forces into Gravity, has not as yet been so conclusively shown. This is a step which yet remains to be taken. At present we may be justified, perhaps, in regarding Gravity and Chemical attraction, i. e.,the Force of attraction which masses of inert matter exert reciprocally upon each other, by which they are drawn together; and the Force of attraction which the atoms of different elements and the more simple chemical compounds exert upon each other, by which they are bound together, and united into the various compound substances which we see around us,—as *Primary Forces* impressed upon all kinds of matter, no portion being exempt, and the latter made capable of modification and control, from the action of the *Secondary Forces*,—Heat, Light and Electricity, which have just been described.

489. The Indestructibility and Conservation of Force; the Correlation of the Forces. It results as a consequence, from this principle, that, when a new force seems to be developed by the action of one formerly existing, there is no creation of Force on the one hand, and no destruction of Force on the other, but merely a conversion of one Force into another.

---

488. Is the convertibility and equivalency of Force true of all the Forces? What is said in regard to the attraction of gravitation, and of chemical affinity?—489. What consequence results from this principle?

Force is therefore believed to be as indestructible as Matter. By this expression it is not meant that either Force or Matter are absolutely incapable of destruction, but simply that in fact, neither of them are destroyed in the various transmutations which they undergo, but are merely changed from one form to another. The sum total of Force in the Universe, as well as the sum total of Matter always remains the same, but both may be transmuted from one form into many others. There is never any fresh creation of either.

This is what is signified by the Term, now very generally introduced into Science, *the Conservation of Force*, i. e., no Force is ever destroyed; and the convertibility of the various kinds of Force into each other, in virtue of which this Conservation of Force is maintained, is often designated by the term, *Co-relation*, or *Correlation of the Forces*. These terms were first introduced, and the truths which they were designed to express, were first advocated in England by Mr. Grove, the distinguished inventor of the Nitric acid Battery, in 1842. The same general doctrine of the mutual relations of the Forces, was put forth about the same time by Mr. Joule, in England, noted for his determination of the mechanical equivalent of Heat; by Mayer, in Germany, and Colding, in Denmark. The idea that Heat and Motion are two different forms of the same Force, and mutually convertible, was first advanced by the celebrated Montgolfier about 1800. The same idea was set forth independently by M. Carnot, in 1824, and worked out more elaborately in his book upon "*The Motive Power of Heat*." Mr. Grove conceived the same idea at a somewhat later period, independent of both the former, and was the first to treat the subject in a systematic manner, and give it a scientific form. It is one of the most important advances made in Physical Philosophy in the present century, and is the line upon which research is now rapidly progressing. The most important works upon the subject are, Grove, on the "*Correlation of the Physical Forces*," and Tyndall, on "*Heat Considered as a Mode of Motion*."

490. Heat and Electricity the chief Agents used by the Chemist, in his investigations. The Lamp and the Galvanic Battery his chief Instruments. Of the three Chemical Forces, Heat and Electricity, are the most important to the chemist in carrying on his researches into the composition of

---

What is meant by the terms Indestructibility and Conservation of Force? How is this Conservation maintained? What is meant by the term Correlation of the Forces? Who introduced these terms? Give the history of the progress of these ideas.

CONCLUSION. 513

Matter, and in making the modifications which he desires, in the attraction of Chemical Affinity. While Light is extensively employed by Nature in carrying on some of her most remarkable chemical transmutations especially in the de-oxidation of Carbonic acid by the leaves of Plants, and generally in the chemistry of the vegetable kingdom, by the Chemist Light is hardly used in any process except that of taking Photographic pictures, and occasionally for effecting a few remarkable combinations, such as that of Chlorine and Hydrogen for the production of Chloro-Hydric acid.

The chief instruments which the chemist employs for the development and application of his two Principal Forces, are, for Heat, the Lamp, the Wind Furnace, the Gas-jet, the Oxy-Hydrogen Blow-pipe, the common Blow pipe,—all depending upon the process of Combustion,—and the carbon points of the Battery:—for Electricity, the Galvanic Battery, the Magneto-electric machine, the Thermo-electric Battery, and Ruhmkorff's coil. He also employs the carbon points of the battery, and the terminals of Ruhmkorff's coil, for the production of the most intense heat known to man, in his researches into the composition of matter by Spectrum analysis. The Lamp and the Furnace were known to the Alchemists; all the others, from the Galvanic battery down, have been the fruit of the scientific and inventive genius of the present century.

491. The Conclusion of the Chemical Forces. Thus we have briefly considered the nature and principal properties of the three active Agents or Forces, by which the attraction of Chemical Affinity is controlled and modified, and described the most important instruments employed in their application. We are now prepared to make this application and to enter upon the examination of the chemical character of the elements of which the various kinds of matter are composed, and the nature and laws of the Force of Affinity by which they are bound together. This constitutes the subject matter of Chemistry proper, and will be reserved for a subsequent volume devoted to the consideration of the chemical properties and relations of the various kinds of Matter, Inorganic and Organic, of which the Universe consists.

---

490. What are the chief Agents used by the Chemist? What use does he make of Light? What use is made of Light in Nature? What are the chief instruments employed by the Chemist for heat? for electricity? Which of them were known to the Alchemists?—491. When were the others introduced? State the conclusion of the subject.

Experiments: Galvanic Electricity, Electro-Magnetism, and Magneto-Electricity.

1. The Battery. A battery of 12 elements of Grove or 6 of Bunsen, will be large enough to exhibit nearly all the effects of Galvanic Electricity. The zinc plates should be well amalgamated by dipping them first in dilute chloro-hydric acid, until they are thoroughly cleansed, and then into a cup of mercury.

2. The charge for this battery is 1 measure of sulphuric acid to 6 or 8 of water, mixed, and allowed to cool. In case any of the zincs effervesce in the acid, they must be taken out and dipped anew in the mercury. The porous clay cups should be filled with the strongest Nitric acid which can be procured.

3. Bi-Chromate of Potash in solution, is often used in place of Nitric acid in Grove's and Bunsen's batteries, for the purpose of escaping the nitrous acid fumes, which are evolved in large quantity when Nitric acid is decomposed. Four parts of Bi-Chromate of Potash are dissolved in eighteen parts of water, and mixed with four parts of Sulphuric acid. The Hydrogen which penetrates into the porous cup, unites with a part of the Oxygen of the Chromic acid, and reduces it to the state of Oxide of Chromium, which remains dissolved in the Nitric acid; the strength of the battery however is much less than when Nitric acid is employed, owing to the increased resistance.

4. The Connections. The poles may be connected by means of copper wires, well annealed, so as to be readily twisted and bent. The ends of these wires should be brightened with a file, or amalgamated by acid and mercury. The tips of the screws connecting them with the battery, should also be brightened with a file. This is a precaution of great importance, as the full power of a battery can not be brought out if the connections be oxidated. The battery should, if possible, be so constructed as to admit of the zinc plates being all connected together by binding cups, so as to form one zinc plate, and the platinum plates so as to form one platinum plate, as in *Fig.* 158; or, of being arranged alternately, as in *Fig.* 157. The former arrangement should be adopted for experiments upon the heating and magnetic effects of the battery, and the latter for experiments upon its chemical effect.

5. Position. The battery must be placed in a draught of air, so that the noxious nitrous acid fumes may not be permitted to escape into the room.

6. The Sulphate of Copper Battery. The charge for this battery is a solution of the Sulphate of Copper in water; a saturated solution of this salt must first be made, and to this added an equal quantity of water. A pint of water at the ordinary temperature is capable of dissolving one-fourth of a pound of the salt, so that the half-saturated solution will contain about two ounces of the salt to the pint. The coating of oxide of copper which is formed upon the zinc plate, should always be removed immediately after using, by means of the card brush and plenty of water; if this is neglected the zinc becomes covered with a hard coating which can only be removed by scraping or filing. The deposit of copper must also be removed from time to time. The zinc plate must always be taken out of the solution when the battery is not in action, but the solution itself may remain in the copper cylinder. as it has no chemical action upon it, but tends to keep its surface in good condition. When the solution is exhausted, it is best not to attempt to renew its power by adding a fresh quantity of the salt; it should be thrown away, and a new solution prepared.

7. Daniell's Battery. The charge for this battery is a saturated solution of Sulphate of Copper acidulated with an eighth of its bulk of Sulphuric Acid, and placed in the outer cup: the solution is kept saturated by crystals of the same salt placed in the colander c, *Fig.* 151. The inner porous cup is charged with a mixture of one measure of Sulphuric Acid, and seven measures of water.

8. Smee's Battery. The charge for this battery is one measure of Sulphuric Acid to six measures of water: the strength of the charge may be increased by the addition of Sulphuric Acid, until the proportion is reached of one of Acid to four of Water.

9. The Gas Battery. The usual charge for Grove's gas battery, *Fig.* 144, is Oxygen and Hydrogen in the two tubes, dipping into a vessel of water acidulated with Sulphuric acid. Other gases however may be employed. Chlorine may be placed in one tube, and Hydrogen in the other, and connected by acidulated water: the Chlorine attracts the Hydrogen of the water, forming Chloro-hydric acid in the Chlorine tube, and the Oxygen which is set free unites with the Hydrogen to form water in the Hydrogen tube. Oxygen may be placed in one tube, and Nitrogen containing a piece of Phosphorus in the other: the Phosphorus attracts the Oxygen of the water and forms Phosphoric acid in one tube, while the Hydrogen which is set free unites with the Oxygen of the other tube to form water. With 50 pairs a decidedly painful shock can be given to a single person: the needle of a galvanometer will be powerfully affected; a brilliant

HEATING AND ILLUMINATING EFFECTS. 515

spark projected between carbon points: Iodide of Potassium and acidulated water may be decomposed, and gas enough set free in the last case to be collected and detonated. Twenty-six pairs were found to be the smallest number that would decompose water, but four pairs will decompose Iodide of Potassium. A gold leaf electroscope will be sensibly affected.

10. That chemical action is the source of the electrical current, may be shown by dipping an unamalgamated zinc plate into a mixture of sulphuric acid and water; bubbles of hydrogen will be formed on its surface, and rise through the water; the zinc will at the same time be oxidated. Introduce a copper plate, and establish a metallic connection between it and the zinc; the bubbles will then cease to be discharged upon the zinc, and will form upon the copper. If the plates be large, the wires connected with them will, when brought near each other, emit a spark, grow perceptibly warm to the touch, and deflect the magnetic needle. The source of the electrical current is evidently the decomposition of the water by the zinc. If several pairs of such plates be united, the copper of one being attached to the zinc of the next, a powerful battery may easily be constructed.

11. If the zinc be well amalgamated no effect will be produced when it is dipped into the acidulated water, and no bubbles of hydrogen will be formed upon its surface; but the instant a connection with the conducting plate is formed, by means of a wire, bubbles of hydrogen will be abundantly discharged upon the copper, as before.

12. **Heating Effects.** Wind a fine copper connecting wire several times around the bulb of an air thermometer, *Fig.* 45, and the liquid will rise rapidly in the stem. Touch the wire, and it will be found to be very hot.

13. Dip the two poles into water, or cause the current to circulate through a coil of fine copper wire, placed in a vessel of water or mercury, and the temperature of the liquid will be found to rise rapidly.

14. Stretch a fine platinum wire, three or four yards in length, between two fixed points, and transmit the voltaic current, it will become first red, and then white hot; if the wire be shortened, the effect will increase, until finally it will melt and drop in globules.

15. Try the same experiment with fine steel, iron and copper wire.

16. Construct a chain of alternate links of silver and platinum wire, and transmit the current; the platinum links will glow brightly, while the silver will remain entirely obscure.

17. Ignite a portion of a platinum wire, which has been made red hot by the passage of the current, in the flame of a spirit lamp, and the brightness of the wire will sensibly decline, showing the diminution of the current produced by the ignition of the metal at one point, and the consequent increased resistance.

18. If a loop of the same wire be cooled by immersion in water, the opposite effect is produced, in consequence of the diminution of resistance by the reduction of temperature, thus enabling a larger quantity of electricity to traverse the wire, and the metal will thus be raised to a white heat, almost approaching the point of fusion.

19. The burning of the different metallic foils may be effected by attaching a polished metallic plate, about 3½ inches broad, by 12 inches long, to the positive wire, and inclining the plate upon any convenient support, at an angle of 45°; then attach the metallic foil to be burned to the negative wire, and bring it into contact with the plate, taking care to change its position continually, so as to make it touch fresh surfaces; deflagration will immediately take place; gold leaf will burn with a bluish white light, crumbling into a dark brown oxide; silver, with greenish light; copper, a bluish white; lead, purple; zinc, a brilliant white, inclining to blue, and fringed with red.

20. Pour mercury into a small glass or iron cup, and connect with the negative pole of the battery, then fill the cup with copper, silver, or gold leaf, and touch the foil with a platinum wire attached to the positive pole; the foil will burn rapidly.

21. Attach a steel watch spring to the positive wire, and apply it to the surface of mercury connected with the negative pole, as in the last case; the watch spring will give forth a shower of sparks: try the point of a file, an iron nail, fine iron wire, zinc, tin, lead, copper, in like manner.

22. Attach a broad piece of charcoal to the negative wire, and bring down upon it wires of different metals, attached to the positive pole; they will all burn in like manner.

23. Attach silver leaf to the negative pole under alcohol, and apply the positive pole; inflammation of the silver will take place.

24. Try the effect of the two poles upon ether, alcohol, spirits of turpentine, naptha, &c.

25. **Illuminating Effects.** Attach a piece of gas-carbon, filed down carefully to a fine point, to each wire of the battery, by means of fine copper wire tightly bound. If the gas-carbon can not be procured, take pieces of box-wood, or lignum-vitae, cover them with sand, in a crucible, and expose them to an intense furnace heat for an hour, then cool suddenly by turning out upon an iron plate, or by plunging them, while red-

hot, into mercury, or into water; bring the points near each other, and an intensely brilliant flash will be produced; draw them slowly 1-10th of an inch apart, and a splendid arc of flame will be formed. The effect will be increased if the positive pole be uppermost, as in *Fig*. 159.

26. Perform the same experiment under water; the light will still be produced, but with diminished splendor, and at the same time the water will be rapidly decomposed.

27. Perform the same experiment in an exhausted receiver, *Fig.* 161: an equally brilliant effect will follow, and the points may be separated to a greater distance.

28. Apply a powerful magnet to the flame, and it will be repelled, assuming an equatorial position: by holding the magnet in a certain position the flame may be made to revolve accompanied at the same time by a loud sound, *Figs.* 253, 254, 255, 256.

29. Observe that the positive pole wears away, while the negative increases in length.

30. With Duboseq's electric lamp, *Fig.* 160, the image of the points may be thrown upon a screen, and the process of transport very plainly seen.

31. If the carbon poles be arranged vertically, as in *Fig.* 159, and the negative point be replaced by a carbon cup, on which small bits of the different metals are placed, they will burn with great brilliancy, and the emission of their characteristic colors.

32. If the negative carbon cup be filled with mercury, and a piece of moistened potash be placed upon it, the potash will be decomposed, and the metal potassium set free, forming an amalgam with the mercury, from which it may be obtained by distillation.

33. If mercury be placed in a small iron cup connected with the positive pole of the battery, and be allowed to trickle in a very fine stream, through a minute aperture into a lower iron vessel connected with the negative pole, at the moment of contact between the globules of mercury falling from the upper cistern and the lower cup, the mercury is heated to a white heat, and produces a dazzling white light. This is a splendid experiment.

34. Chemical Effects. Decomposition of Water. The poles, in this case, should be made of platinum, and inserted from below into inverted glass tubes, closed at the upper end *Fig.* 162. The water should be acidulated with sulphuric acid,—1 part of acid to 15 parts of water,—in order to increase its conducting power. The hydrogen will collect in the negative tube, the oxygen in the positive tube; the former in double the quantity of the latter. This experiment may be performed with the U tube, *Fig.* 164, which must be filled with acidulated water; the poles must be thrust far down into the tubes, so as nearly to touch, passing through corks at their mouths: a bent glass tube may be used to convey the gas from the oxygen end; and the hydrogen may be burned, as it is formed, from the extremity of another glass tube, drawn down to a very fine bore. This makes a very beautiful experiment.

35. Pass the galvanic current, in an apparatus similar to the last, through chloro-hydric acid. Hydrogen will be discharged in the negative tube, and may be burned from a fine orifice; chlorine will be discharged in the positive tube, and may be recognized by its odor, and its bleaching effect upon solution of sulphate of indigo, when poured into the tube; also, by its green color.

36. Repeat the same experiment, substituting tincture of litmus, of violets, or purple cabbage, for the indigo; they will at first be turned red by the acid, and then will be quickly bleached as the chlorine is disengaged. For the preparation of tincture of purple cabbage, see Expt. 16, p. 77.

37. Pass the current through a strong solution of common salt—chloride of sodium, colored blue in both tubes by tincture of cabbage; chlorine will be discharged in the positive tube, and almost immediately destroy the blue color, and sodium will be set free in the negative tube; this will be at once converted into soda by decomposing the water, and change the blue color to a bright green.

38. Pass the current through aqua ammonia, in a similar apparatus. Hydrogen will be discharged in the negative tube, and may be set on fire, as in Expt. 34, and nitrogen will be set free in the positive tube, as may be shown by its extinguishing a lighted taper.

39. Pass the current through nitric acid, in a similar tube. Oxygen will be discharged in the positive tube, as may be shown by its effect on a lighted taper, and red nitrous acid fumes in the negative tube. If a candle, having its wick glowing red-hot, but not lighted, be introduced into the oxygen tube, it will be re-lighted; also paper.

40. Pass the current through a strong solution of iodide of potassium; into the positive tube introduce a few drops of solution of starch, and into the negative some tincture of cabbage; iodine will be set free at the positive pole, and its presence shown by tinging the starch a deep blue, and potassium set free at the negative pole, which will at once be converted into potash by abstracting oxygen from the water, and its presence indicated by turning the vegetable blue to green.

41. Pass the current through a solution of sulphate of soda, in the U tube, tinged by tincture of cabbage: the salt will be decomposed into sulphuric acid and soda; the acid appearing at the positive pole, and turning the blue to red, and the soda at the negative pole, changing the blue to green; if the platinum wires be removed, and the contents of the two branches of the tube shaken together, the acid and the soda will again unite, the red will neutralize the green, and the blue color will be restored.

CHEMICAL EFFECTS. 517

42. Pass the current through a solution of nitrate of potash, colored blue by the tincture of cabbage; nitric acid will be set free at the positive pole, shown by the red color, and potash at the negative pole, shown by the change of blue to green.

43. Pass the current through a solution of chloro-hydrate of ammonia (sal ammoniac) in the U tube, colored blue by tincture of cabbage; chlorine will be set free at the positive pole, discharging the blue color altogether, and ammonia at the negative pole, changing the blue to green.

44. Pass the current through a solution of carbonate of potash, colored blue by tincture of cabbage; carbonic acid will be discharged at the positive pole, with effervescence, slightly reddening the blue tincture, and potash at the negative pole, turning the blue to a deep green.

45. Try the same experiment with a solution of carbonate of soda: carbonic acid will be set free at the positive pole, and soda at the negative.

46. Try the same experiment with solution of nitrate of lime; nitric acid will appear at the positive pole, and lime at the negative.

47. Repeat the same experiment with the solution of acetate of lead; acetic acid will be set free at the positive pole, reddening a vegetable blue, and pure lead at the negative pole.

48. Repeat the same experiment with the solution of nitrate of silver; nitric acid will be set free at the positive pole, and metallic silver at the negative.

49. Repeat the same experiment with the solution of chloro-hydrate of tin; the acid will be set free at the positive pole, and tin deposited at the negative pole.

50. Repeat the same experiment with the solution of nitrate of mercury; the acid will be set free at the positive pole, and the mercury at the negative.

51. Pass the current through a solution of chloride of calcium, colored blue by tincture of cabbage; chlorine will be set free at the positive pole, and discharge the blue color, while calcium will be set free at the negative, which will be at once converted into oxide of calcium or lime, and change the vegetable blue to green.

52. Repeat the same experiment with chloride of calcium, colored by the blue solution of litmus; the color will be removed in the positive tube, but no change produced upon it in the negative.

53. Repeat the same experiment with chloride of calcium, colored blue by sulphate of indigo; the color will be discharged in the positive tube, but remain unchanged in the negative.

54. Repeat the same experiment with chloride of calcium, colored by black ink; the black will be discharged in the positive tube, but remain unchanged in the negative.

55. Pass the current through a strong solution of corrosive sublimate (chloride of mercury) having a little blue tincture of cabbage in the positive tube; chlorine will be set free at the positive pole, discharging the blue color, and mercury at the negative pole, which should be made of gold foil; this will be at once whitened by the deposit of the mercury; a small gold coin will answer very well for the negative pole.

56. Pass the current through a solution of sulphate of copper; sulphuric acid will be set free at the positive pole, and copper deposited at the negative pole; sometimes the oxide of copper is deposited instead of the pure metal; but if the solution be of moderate strength, the hydrogen which is set free at the same pole will decompose the oxide, and set free metallic copper. This is a case of secondary decomposition (see § 371) and illustrates the art of electrotyping.

57. To decompose potash, pour a strong solution of caustic potash, which has been carefully protected from the air, upon the surface of mercury in a small iron cup; connect this cup with the negative pole of the battery, then apply to the surface of the solution a platinum wire connected with the positive pole; oxygen gas will be set free at the positive pole, and metallic potassium at the negative pole, which will immediately form an amalgam with the mercury, giving it a puffy appearance. The potassium may be extracted from the mercury, and obtained in a pure state, by distillation in an atmosphere of nitrogen.

58. Place a piece of solid caustic potash, slightly moistened, upon a flat piece of gas-carbon, hollowed into a cup, and attached to the negative pole of the battery in the instrument represented in *Fig.* 159, or in Duboscq's electric lamp, *Fig* 160, and then bring down upon it a piece of platinum wire, or gas carbon, attached to the positive pole; oxygen will be set free upon the wire, and the metal potassium in the carbon cup, burning, as it forms, with a beautiful red flame.

59. Another mode of performing the same experiment, is to excavate a small cavity in a piece of caustic potash, introduce into it a globule of mercury, and place the potash upon a plate of platinum; the positive pole is then to be connected with the platinum plate, and the negative with the mercury; the potash is slowly decomposed, oxygen set free at the positive pole, and potassium at the negative, which, as fast as formed amalgamates with the mercury; it may be obtained in a pure state by distillation in nitrogen, as described in experiment 57.

60. The decomposition of soda, and the formation of metallic sodium, may be accomplished by subjecting a piece of caustic soda, slightly moistened, to the same treatment; oxygen will be set free at the positive pole, and metallic sodium at the negative pole, which may be obtained, by distillation, from the mercury. If the experiment be performed with charcoal poles, the sodium, as it burns, will emit a yellowish light, and may thus be distinguished from potassium.

61. If some of the potassium or sodium amalgam, obtained in these experiments, be thrown into water, the potassium and sodium will quit the mercury, and decompose the water, on account of their strong affinity for oxygen, uniting with it to form potash and soda, and setting free the hydrogen, which will at once take fire and burn, with red flame for the potassium, and yellow for the sodium.

62. Repeat experiment 57, substituting for the solution of potash, a strong solution of chloro-hydrate of ammonia (sal ammoniac); the mercury will greatly increase in bulk, and an amalgam be formed with the so-called metal ammonium at the negative pole, while oxygen will be set free at the positive pole. This metal ammonium is supposed to be a compound of hydrogen and ammonia, and to have for its symbol, $N H^4$. This experiment may be varied by placing a piece of solid sal-ammoniac upon a platinum plate, and a globule of mercury in a small excavation made in its upper surface, with which the negative pole should be connected; the positive pole should be connected with the platinum plate; the ammonium amalgam will be formed as before.

63. Pass the current through 4 cups of acidulated water, connected by platinum wires, and arranged as in *Fig.* 168, and observe that two poles are formed in each cup, one of which discharges oxygen, and the other hydrogen, and always in the same order; on inverting a tube, closed at one end, and filled with water, over each pole, an equal quantity of hydrogen will be collected in all the hydrogen tubes, and an equal quantity of oxygen in all the oxygen tubes.

64. Arrange the apparatus as in the preceding experiment; at the same time introduce a voltameter into the circuit, (see *Fig.* 170,) having two tubes, closed at the top, inverted in it, and filled with water; the same amount of hydrogen and oxygen will be collected in these tubes as in those placed in any of the 4 cups. This shows the equality of the circulating force in every part of the circuit.

65. Arrange the 4 cups as before, except that instead of water, in the 1st cup let a solution of iodide of potassium be placed, mixed with starch; in the 2d, a strong solution of chloride of sodium—common salt, colored blue by sulphate of indigo; in the 3d, a solution of nitrate of ammonia, colored blue by purple cabbage; in the 4th, a solution of sulphate of copper; let the poles in each cup be separated by pieces of thick paper; connect with the battery, and observe the formation of two poles in each cup, as before, and that the iodine, chlorine, nitric acid, and sulphuric acid, on the one hand, and on the other, the potassium, sodium, ammonia, and copper, are set free at corresponding poles.

66. This experiment may be better performed with U tubes. Take 5 U tubes, fix them in supports, so that they may be placed in a line, and connect them by slips of platinum. Into the 1st, pour a solution of iodide of potassium, having starch mixed with it in the left hand leg, and purple cabbage in the right; in the 2d, a solution of chloride of sodium, colored blue in both legs by purple cabbage; in the 3d, a solution of nitrate of ammonia, also colored blue in both legs, by purple cabbage; in the 4th, a solution of sulphate of copper, colored blue in the left hand leg only, with purple cabbage; and in the 5th, acidulated water. Then connect the starch end of U tube 1 with the positive pole of the battery, and U tube 5 with the negative; observe that the iodine, chlorine, nitric acid, sulphuric acid, and oxygen, on the one hand, and the potassium, sodium, ammonia, copper, and hydrogen, on the other, are discharged at corresponding poles, showing the similarity of their electrical relations; the iodine may be known by the blue it imparts to starch; the chlorine by its bleaching; nitric acid, and sulphuric acid, by reddening purple cabbage; the oxygen by its effect on a taper; the potassium, sodium, and ammonia, by turning the purple cabbage green; the copper by its metallic lustre; the hydrogen by its quantity and inflammability.

67. Arrange three cups in the manner described in § 372, filling the three cups with solution of sulphate of soda, tinged blue by tincture of cabbage, and connecting them by shreds of asbestus, or syphons of glass tube filled with the same solution; on passing the current, the soda will collect in the negative cup, turning it green, and the acid in the positive cup turning it red, without producing the slightest change in the color of the intermediate cup, though both have passed through it.

68. Repeat this experiment, filling the cup A, on the left, with sulphate of soda, tinged blue; the cup C, on the right, with pure water, also tinged blue; and the middle cup B, with strong potash; on passing the current, the acid will collect in the right hand cup, turning the blue to red, and in so doing, pass directly through the potash in the cup, B, without any hindrance, though the affinity between them is intense; the soda will collect in the cup A, and turn it green, as before. If the sulphate of soda be placed in the right hand cup, the middle cup be filled with strong sulphuric acid, and the left hand cup with pure water, tinged blue, the soda will pass straight through the acid without affect-

ing it, notwithstanding the strong affinity between them, into the cup A, and its presence there may be detected by its turning the vegetable blue to green.

69. Arrange the three cups as before, and into the middle cup introduce a strong solution of caustic baryta, or strontia; in the left hand cup, sulphate of soda tinged blue; in the right hand cup, pure water colored blue; on passing the current, the sulphate of soda will be decomposed, the soda will collect in the left hand cup, turning it green, but the acid, in passing through the middle cup, will be caught by the baryta, and precipitated to the bottom, in the form of sulphate of baryta, while no effect at all will be produced upon the right hand cup. In like manner, if a solution of nitrate of baryta be placed in the right hand cup, strong sulphuric acid in the middle, and pure water colored blue, in the left hand cup, the nitrate of baryta will be decomposed, the nitric acid will remain in the right hand cup, but the baryta, on its way to the left hand cup, will be caught by the sulphuric acid, and precipitated to the bottom, in the form of sulphate of baryta; the left hand cup will remain unchanged. For an explanation of this, see § 374.

70. **Electrotyping, Plating, and Gilding.** Place a small silver coin, having a platinum wire attached to it, in a solution of sulphate of copper, and into the same solution introduce a small piece of zinc; no change will be produced in either metal so long as both are kept apart, but as soon as a connection is formed between them by means of the wire, copper will be deposited upon the silver; this shows the tendency of the metals to be deposited upon the conducting plate of the battery, which is always negative within the liquid, and positive without, *Fig.* 139, 140, 166.

71. Let two slips of platinum be connected with the poles of the battery, and introduced into a solution of sulphate of copper, the negative pole will at once be coated with copper, while oxygen will be discharged upon the positive. Repeat the same experiment with nitrate of silver; metallic silver will be deposited upon the negative pole. If acetate of lead be employed, a deposit of metallic lead will be obtained; and so with other metallic solutions.

72. To copy a coin, take an impression from it in beeswax; then blow over its surface some fine plumbago, in order to give it a conducting surface; then attach it by a wire to the negative pole of the battery, taking care that the wire actually touches the plumbago, and introduce it into a sulphate of copper solution; then bring the positive pole of the battery, which may be a slip of clean copper, into the same solution, and the wax mould will at once receive a deposit of copper, which will steadily increase in thickness; it may easily be separated from the wax and an exact reproduction of the coin obtained. The solution for depositing copper is best prepared by making a saturated solution of sulphate of copper, and then diluting it to one-half, or one-third, of its bulk, with a mixture of one measure of sulphuric acid with eight of water.

73. If the article to be copied be made of plaster, it should be dipped in melted stearine, and then coated with plumbago, as above described, before being placed in the bath; or, if it be a medallion, it may be wetted by holding it in water, with the face upward, until the liquid has thoroughly penetrated it; then tie a slip of paper around the rim, and pour melted white wax into the cup thus formed; the wax impression is then to be coated with plumbago, as above described; gutta-percha may also be used to take impressions.

74. In order to plate with silver, the articles must be well cleaned, and attached to the negative pole, in a solution consisting of two parts of cyanide of potassium, dissolved in 250 parts of water; to the positive pole, a silver plate must be attached, in order to keep up the strength of the solution.

75. For gilding, articles must be very carefully cleansed and attached to the negative pole, in a bath consisting of one grain of chloride of gold, and ten grains of cyanide of potassium, dissolved in 200 grains of water; a piece of gold must be suspended from the positive pole, in order to keep up the strength of the solution. In performing these experiments upon the deposition of metals, many points of detail connected with the strength of the solution, the power of the battery, and the degree of temperature can only be learned by practice. See Davis' Manual of Magnetism.

76. **Magnetism, and Electro-Magnetism.** The attractive power of the magnet may be shown by applying either extremity of a magnet to a mass of iron filings, or to any collection of small bits of iron; the filings and iron pieces will attach themselves strongly to each end of the bar.

77. That a magnet possesses two poles of opposite properties, may be shown by suspending a delicate magnetic needle by a thread, as in *Fig.* 174, and observing that its north pole is repelled and its south pole attracted by the north pole of a second magnetic needle held near each pole successively.

78. The repulsive power of the same poles, and the attractive power of the opposite poles of two different magnetic needles may be shown, by trying the effect of each magnetic pole of a bar magnet successively upon the poles of a delicate magnetic needle, suspended by a fine thread, *Fig.* 174.

79. The directive action of the earth upon a magnet may be shown by mounting a

magnetic needle upon a pivot, as in *Fig.* 175, and observing that it immediately takes a north and south position, and that the magnetic poles very nearly coincide with the extremities of its axis.

80. The effect of neutralizing the directive action of the earth upon a magnetic needle may be shown by fastening a second needle, with poles reversed, directly beneath the first, as in the astatic needle, *Fig.* 176, and observing that the earth no longer compels the needle to assume a north and south position.

81. The non-directive tendency of the astatic needle may be shown by observing that, when moved from the magnetic meridian, it does not tend to return to it again. That it has not lost its magnetic power, may be proved by the action of a bar magnet, when brought near it.

82. The induction of magnetism in a piece of soft iron may be shown by taking up a common nail by the end of a bar magnet, and observing that the extremity of the nail is itself possessed of attractive power, has become magnetic, and will attract a second small piece of iron, when applied to it, and this another, and so on in succession so long as the connection with the original magnet is maintained, *Fig.* 177.

83. To show the dia-magnetic effect of the magnet upon certain substances, suspend a delicate needle of bismuth or antimony by a thread between the poles of a powerful horse-shoe magnet, and it will at once assume an equatorial position, *Fig.* 179. Try the same experiment with a stick of Phosphorus.

84. The same dia-magnetic power may also be shown by suspending a small cube of copper between the poles of a powerful electro-magnet by a thread of twisted silk, which causes it to turn round with great rapidity; the instant, however, that the electrical current circulates, and the electro-magnet becomes excited, the motion of the cube is completely arrested; this is not owing to any attractive action exerted by the poles, for it is well known that no such attraction is exerted upon copper, but to a powerful dia-magnetic action, which acts at right angles to the magnetic axis.

85. The dia-magnetism of liquids may be shown by enclosing different solutions in small tubes of very thin glass; if the liquids are magnetic, like the solutions of iron, nickel, and cobalt, the tubes take up their position in the magnetic axis; if dia-magnetic, like water, alcohol, ether, spirits of turpentine, &c., they occupy the equatorial axis.

86. The dia-magnetism of gases may be shown by the apparatus indicated in *Fig.* 180; also, by placing a lighted candle between the poles of the electro-magnet, *Fig.* 255, the pillar of gas rising from the wick will cease to ascend, and be turned off at right angles upon a line corresponding with the magnetic equator.

87. To show that the wire carrying the battery current itself becomes magnetic, connect the poles of a series of several pairs of Grove's battery, by means of a short copper wire, and apply iron filings; they will adhere equally all around the circumference of the wire, forming circular bands; when the circuit is broken the iron filings will fall off; but if steel filings be employed, a part of them will remain attached.

88. To show the effect of the galvanic current upon the magnet, arrange the wire connecting the poles of a battery, and carrying the current, on a line running north and south, the direction of the current being from the south to north, and place a delicate magnetic needle, supported upon a fine point, directly beneath it, as in *Fig.* 172; the north pole will move to the west, and the south to the east; place the needle above the wire, and on either side, and observe the effect; finally, reverse the current, and observe the reversion of all the movements.

89. The effect of the wire carrying the current, upon the magnetic needle, may be best seen by making use of a magnetic needle half brass. In this instrument, the steel needle is wholly upon one side of the point of support, and is counterpoised by a brass weight on the other side. By this arrangement, the action of the electrical current upon the pole which points to the pivot (let it be the south pole,) can have no influence in turning the magnet, and its motion will be determined solely by the action of the current upon the north pole. The effect of this arrangement will be, to make the tendency of the magnet to rotate around the pole more apparent, but no actual rotation can be obtained.

90. That the galvanic current induces magnetism, may be shown by winding a piece of soft copper wire spirally around a glass tube, in a right hand direction, and connecting the two extremities of the coil with the poles of the battery; then introduce into the tube a rod of soft iron, and bring a magnetic needle near either end; it will be found that the iron rod has become strongly magnetic, the north pole being at the extremity at which the current leaves the coil; apply iron filings, or any small pieces of iron, to the rod, and they will be found to be strongly attracted; break the connection, and the magnetism will be destroyed, and the articles will fall; re-establish the connection, and the magnetism will be restored; *Fig.* 182.

91. Reverse the current, and the position of the poles will be reversed.

92. Wind a wire around a second similar tube, in the left hand direction, and the position of the poles will be reversed, the north pole being at the extremity at which the current enters the wire; *Fig.* 183.

VOLTA—ELECTRIC INDUCTION. 521

93. Connect a mounted helix, *Fig.* 184, with the battery: the helix itself becomes magnetic, before the introduction of the iron rod, as shown by its effect on the magnetic needle, and upon iron filings; then introduce the iron rod, and observe that the poles of the rod are the reverse of those of the helix, the rod being magnetized by induction.

94. To show the delicacy of the current, measured by the common galvanometer, *Fig.* 185, provide a piece of zinc, and another of copper, one inch square, and immerse them in a small quantity of acidulated water, taking care that they do not touch each other, then transmit the current through the galvanometer.

95. To show the extreme delicacy of the astatic galvanometer, immerse a piece of zinc, and another of copper, about ⅛th of an inch square, in acidulated water, and connect with the astatic galvanometer; *Figs.* 186 and 187.

96. To show the magnetic influence of the liquid part of the circuit, suspend a magnetic needle, as in *Fig.* 188.

97. To show the truth of Ampere's theory, mount a helix of wire, as in *Fig.* 190, and observe that one extremity is affected with north polarity, and the other with south, as shown by the magnetic needle, when brought near it.

98. Arrange two helices, as in *Fig.* 191, and observe that they act exactly as two magnets would, under similar circumstances.

99. To show that the wire carrying the current, and the magnetic needle, tend to revolve around each other, and that their action is mutual, try the experiment with De la Rive's ring, *Fig.* 192, first with one pole of the magnet, then with the other.

100. To show the confirmation of Ampere's theory, provide a ring, mounted as in *Fig.* 193, through which the current is passing, and observe that it arranges itself at right angles to the magnetic meridian.

101. Transmit the current through the magic circle, *Fig.* 197, and observe the heavy weights which it will support.

102. Suspend a heavy weight from a powerful electro-magnet, and observe the effect of breaking and forming the battery connection; *Fig.* 196.

103. To illustrate the principle of the telegraph, send the galvanic current through a wire, around a room, by connecting one extremity with the positive, and the other with the negative pole of a battery, and cause it to circulate through an electro-magnet, having a movable armature suspended over it, at the other end of the apartment, and observe the effect upon this electro-magnet of breaking and establishing the battery connection; or use Morse's indicator, *Fig.* 199.

104. To show the application of electro-magnetism to the production of motion, make use of the instrument represented in *Fig.* 208: also any of the electro-magnetic engines sold by the philosophical instrument-makers.

105. **Volta-Electric Induction.** The induction of a secondary current of electricity, by a primary current, may be shown by the apparatus represented in *Fig.* 214. A delicate galvanometer must be attached by wires to the extremities of the outer, or the secondary coil; then, on forming the connection between the primary coil and the battery, the needle of the galvanometer will be deflected in such a way as to indicate the passage of a secondary current in a reverse direction to that of the primary current; the instant the connection with the battery is broken, the needle will be deflected in the opposite direction, indicating the induction of a current in the same direction as the primary current.

106. That this effect takes place through a considerable distance may be shown by the apparatus represented in *Fig.* 215.

107. That a secondary current is induced by the approach and removal of the primary current may be shown by the apparatus represented in *Fig.* 216.

108. The induction of a secondary current, in the primary wire itself, or the extra-current, may be shown by the apparatus represented in *Fig.* 217.

109. The character of the induced extra-current may be shown by the apparatus indicated in *Figs.* 215, 226; vivid sparks are produced by drawing the wire of the battery over the piece of ribbed iron, and violent shocks are given.

110. The tertiary and quaternary currents may be shown by Henry's coils, *Fig.* 218.

111. **Magneto-Electricity.** That a secondary electrical current is induced by magnetism, may be shown by the apparatus represented in *Fig.* 219. On introducing the permanent magnet into the interior of the coil, the needle of the galvanometer is deflected powerfully, showing the induction of an electrical current in the inverse direction from the currents flowing around the magnet, according to the theory of M. Ampere. On reversing the magnet, the needle is deflected in the opposite direction.

112. Remove the magnet altogether, and introduce in its place a bar of soft iron: this will become magnetized by induction as soon as a magnet is brought near its free extremity: at the instant this takes place, the needle of the galvanometer will be deflected as before; when the magnet is removed, the iron bar will lose its magnetism and be deflected in the opposite direction.

113. The same effects may also be shown by the apparatus represented in *Fig.* 184.

114. The production of sparks by the current thus induced, may be shown by the ap-

paratus represented in *Fig.* 220. On touching the mounted permanent magnet A B, with the rod of soft iron, N S, wound with a coil of copper wire, the two ends of which nearly meet, the iron rod will be magnetized by induction, and at the same instant a bright spark flash between the wires.

115. If an electro-magnet, while actuated by the battery current, be brought near a coil of wire connected with a delicate galvanometer, a secondary current of electricity will be induced.

116. That an electro-magnet, magnetized and de-magnetized, will induce an electrical current in a closed wire may be conclusively shown by attaching a battery to one pair of the wires of Faraday's ring; *Fig.* 223.

117. The same fact may also be shown by introducing a bar of soft iron into the centre of the primary coil represented in *Fig.* 214, on completing and breaking connection with the battery the iron bar is magnetized, and de-magnetized, and a much more decided effect exerted upon the galvanometer than when the coils are used alone. This is a case of Volta-Magneto-electric Induction.

118. The same fact may be shown by the apparatus represented in *Fig.* 222, and also that the strength of the induced current of electricity as shown by the galvanometer is proportioned to the number of soft iron wires introduced, or in other words to the size and power of the electro-magnet.

119. Arago's rotations may be shown by the apparatus represented in *Fig.* 224.

120. Page's Separable Helices. The properties of the induced secondary currents may be exhibited by Page's separable helices, *Fig.* 226. If the handles connected with the extremities of the secondary coil be tightly grasped, shocks will be experienced, when the connection with the battery is rapidly completed and broken, either by drawing one polar wire over the rasp, or by the break-piece, even when there are no wires in the interior of the inner coil; introduce the wires one by one, and the shocks will gradually increase in intensity till they become intolerable, and the hands become so tightly fastened to the handles that it will be impossible to open them, and the scintillations upon the rasp and break-piece will become very brilliant.

121. Instead of the bundle of wires substitute a rod of soft iron, the shocks and sparks will be considerably diminished.

122. If the bundle of wires or the iron rod be introduced gradually, the spark and shock increase as it enters; in this manner the intensity of the shock may be regulated.

123. Pass a glass tube over the iron wires in the helix, and the effect will remain undiminished, but if a brass tube be employed, the shocks and sparks will cease altogether.

124. If the battery wire be moved slowly over the rasp, distinct, powerful single shocks are obtained; if moved more rapidly, the arms are convulsed violently.

125. The strength of the shock depends much upon the extent of contact surface between the hands and the metallic conductors; the shocks will be much lessened if two wires be used instead of handles, and still more if the wires are held lightly in the fingers. The shocks are greatly increased if the hands are moistened with salt water.

126. If the handle connected with the positive cup of the secondary helix be held in the right hand, and the one connected with the negative cup in the left hand, the left hand and arm will experience the most powerful shocks, and be the most violently convulsed. In determining the positive cup, the terminal secondary produced by breaking contact, should be alone taken into account; the initial secondary may be disregarded.

127. If the ends of the secondary wire be put into water, a peculiar shock may be taken by putting the fingers or hands into the water, so as to make the current pass through them. The current prefers a passage through the body to that through the water, between the fingers; if the conducting power of the water be made superior to that of the human body by the addition of a small quantity of common salt, little or no shock will be perceived.

128. If a delicate galvanometer be connected with the extremities of the secondary coil, the needle will be deflected in opposite directions, and equally far, whenever the battery circuit is completed or broken.

129. When the circuit is broken, over the surface of mercury by Page's circuit breaker, § 452, an intensely brilliant spark is seen in both cups, if the quantity of mercury is properly regulated, and the mercury is deflagrated in white vapor.

130. If water or oil be poured upon the surface of the mercury the sparks will become less intense, but the shocks more severe.

131. If prepared charcoal points (Expt. 25,) are attached to the ends of the secondary wires, and held almost in contact, a beautiful light will be produced.

132. If the ends of the secondary coil be connected with two fine platinum wires which have been inserted into glass tubes, that have been melted on the wires so as to cover the ends completely, and then filed away so as to expose the tips of the wires and then these are immersed in acidulated water, (Expt. 34,) not very far apart, the water will be decomposed, and Oxygen and Hydrogen set free, both on completing and breaking the circuit. As the platinum wires are alternately positive and negative, each gas will be given off alternately by both wires. The platinum wires may be coated with sealing wax instead of glass. The purpose of covering them is to confine the passage of the electrical current to one small and direct path from tip to tip, instead of allowing it to pass between the wires along the whole length of the portions immersed in the water.

133. In performing the above experiment, rapid discharges are heard in the water, with sharp ticking sounds audible at the distance of one hundred feet, and the extremities of the wires appear in the dark, one constantly, and the other intermittingly, luminous: this ticking noise and the sparks are produced only by the terminal current, on breaking connection with the battery.

134. A Leyden jar whose inside coating is connected with the knob by a continuous wire may be slightly charged, and feeble sparks be obtained from it, by grasping the jar with one hand, and bringing its knob into contact with one of the cups of the secondary helix, and then establishing a connection between the other cup of the helix and the outside coating of the jar, by means of a wire well insulated from the hand.

135. A gold-leaf electroscope, *Fig.* 115, will exhibit a considerable divergence of its leaves, if its cap be touched by a wire connected with either cup of the helix, provided the contact be made at the moment of breaking the battery circuit.

136. If the instrument be arranged horizontally, and a bar of soft iron enclosed in a brass tube be introduced into the helix, and a small key be applied to one end of the bar, although the magnetism of the bar is intermitted with every break in the battery circuit, yet being almost immediately renewed, the key will not fall. This experiment conclusively proves that a sensible time is required for a bar to lose its magnetic power.

137. Ruhmkorff's Coil. To display the action of this instrument advantageously, from four to eight cells of Grove's battery are generally quite sufficient. The wires leading from the battery are to be attached to the binding screws connected with the primary coil, and great care must be taken to avoid accidental shocks, by breaking connection with the battery, by means of the commutator, until the adjustment of the arrangements for the proposed experiment is complete. For the successful exhibition of the capabilities of the coil, the experiments must be performed in a darkened room. Care must be taken that the condenser is attached underneath the instrument, as described in § 453, pp. 442, 443.

138. The great power of the secondary current induced, can be shown by connecting two delicate steel needles with the binding screws of the secondary coil, and bringing them within a few inches of each other; on establishing the connection with the battery, a secondary current of great intensity will flash through the wires with vivid sparks; the distance may be increased, under favorable circumstances, to twenty inches, or even more.

139. The wire from which the current passes remains cold enough to be held in the fingers, *Fig.* 232; the other, the negative wire, becomes so hot that it melts into a globule of liquid iron, and if paper is held between the wires, it rapidly takes fire.

140. If a reflection of these points be thrown upon a screen by means of Duboscq's electric lamp, *Fig.* 160, a cone of vapor will appear to issue from the point of each wire, but that from the negative wire being the most powerful, seems to beat back the stream from the positive wire.

141. In place of the steel wires, substitute wires of copper, of zinc, of soft iron, of brass, &c.; in all cases combustion will take place with the production of the characteristic light of the metal.

142. On directing the discharge through balls of the different metals, *Fig.* 240, the spectrum lines peculiar to each metal may be seen to great advantage by means of the spectroscope.

143. On passing the discharge through an exhausted Electric Egg, *Fig.* 234, a beautiful luminous trail will flash from one ball to the other. Exhaust the receiver more perfectly and the luminous portion will be traversed by a series of dark bands concentric with the positive ball, *Fig.* 234, No. 2; the presence of a little vapor of phosphorus renders these bands much more distinct. Apply the finger at the side of the Egg, at the same time cutting off the connection of the lower knob with the negative pole of the coil, and the trail will suffer a curious deviation towards the finger, *Fig.* 234, No. 3.

144. Instead of the Electric Egg, place a tumbler of Uranium glass, *Fig.* 235, lined with tin-foil, upon the plate of an air pump beneath a receiver, and bring down a sliding rod until it touches the metallic lining, then, on establishing a connection with the coil, a beautiful cascade of light will pour over the edge of the tumbler.

145. Pass the discharge from the coil through Geissler's tubes, filled with different gases, which have been more or less exhausted, *Figs.* 236, 237, and observe the curious stratification which ensues.

146. Submit the light of Geissler's tubes to observation by the spectroscope, *Fig.* 240, and observe the beautiful spectra of the gases which are thus brought out.

147. A Leyden jar may be charged by connecting the outer coating, *Fig.* 230, with one of the poles of the coil, and the inner with one of the arms of a discharger, the other arm of which is in communication with the opposite pole of the coil, the extremities being two or three inches apart; allow a few sparks from the coil to pass, and then remove and discharge the jar in the usual manner.

148. Attach one of the secondary wires to the ball, or rod, of a self-discharging Leyden jar, and the other to the outside surface, so arranged that the discharger may be brought within half an inch of the ball; then, on turning on the battery current, the jar will be charged and discharged with great rapidity, and the snapping noise become continuous; if a piece of paper be held between the knob of the jar and the wire, it is instantly perforated, but not set on fire.

149. Twist a platinum wire around the knob of a Leyden jar, and bring its end near enough to the poles of the coil to almost touch them without quite doing so, and a noiseless spark of feeble light will pass from each pole to the extremities of the platinum wire; if at this moment the outer coating of the jar be connected with one of the poles of the secondary coil, the spark, at the interruption on that side will suddenly become noisy and brilliant; what is very singular, the noiseless spark will kindle paper and other combustibles, while the noisy flash will fail to kindle them.

150. Charge a large electrical battery by cascade, the jars being arranged horizontally and in succession, the knob of the first nearly touching the outside coating of the second, and so in regular series.

151. If the Leyden jar be coated with spangles, a spark will appear at each break, and the whole jar be lit up with hundreds of brilliant sparks each time it is charged and discharged.

152. When the continuous discharges from the Leyden jar are made to pass through the centre of a large lump of crystals of alum, sulphate of copper, or ferro-cyanate of potash, the whole of the crystal is beautifully lighted up during the passage of the electricity from one wire of the discharger to the other.

153. The chemical effects of the coil may be shown by causing the secondary current to pass through a tube of air hermetically sealed, *Fig*. 241: the Oxygen and Nitrogen combine to form Nitrous acid, with the production of red fumes.

154. Enclose Oxygen in a tube with solution of starch and Iodide of Potassium, *Fig*. 242, and pass a succession of sparks from the coil, one by one; the Iodide of Potassium will soon be decomposed, and the characteristic blue color resulting from the action of starch on free Iodine be produced, showing the conversion of Oxygen into Ozone.

155. Water may be decomposed by connecting the poles of the coil with two of Wollaston's dischargers, consisting of platinum wires covered with glass, the tubes being filled with mercury: Oxygen and Hydrogen will be set free at each pole alternately, and a mixture of the two gases may be collected in an inverted glass test tube filled with water.

156. The vapor of water may be decomposed by passing a continuous charge from the coil through steam in a glass flask, and a mixture of the two gases collected in an inverted tube, *Fig*. 243.

157. If the steel wires from the poles be applied to any small animal, such as a rat, or a rabbit, life will instantly be destroyed; two of Bunsen's cells are quite sufficient. With twelve of Bunsen's cells a man could probably be struck dead. A very feeble spark from one small Grove or Bunsen cell may be transmitted through a large circle of persons joining hands. These experiments, however, should be performed with the greatest caution.

158. Magneto-Electric Machines. The best machine for exhibiting the effects of Magneto-electricity is Page's, *Fig*. 247. On turning the wheel w, by means of the ivory handle attached to it, the coils A A, are made to revolve with great rapidity, and continuous currents of positive and negative electricity are discharged from the cups P and N, which, by means of wires, may be used for experiments in electromagnetism, decomposition of chemical compounds, the production of light, and the giving of shocks, in the same manner as the wires proceeding from the poles of a galvanic battery.

159. This instrument may be made to produce an electrical current of high or feeble intensity, by making use of coils, consisting of very long and fine wire, for the former, and of coils composed of short and coarse wire for the latter; the former is more useful for shocks and chemical decomposition, the latter for heating and magnetic effects.

160. By suddenly breaking the magnetic current, a secondary current in the same direction of much greater intensity can be induced; the breaking of the circuit is accomplished by means of a steel wire, thrust through the cup N, and bearing upon the toothed wheel mounted above the pole-changer. For giving shocks, this steel wire should be inserted and firmly fastened in its place; but for all other experiments it should be removed, and the primary current used alone.

161. Connect the wires proceeding from the poles P and N, with the extremities of a galvanometer, *Fig*. 185, and the needle will at once be violently oscillated.

162. Connect the polar wires with the extremities of an electro-magnet, *Figs*. 195, 196, 208, and a very considerable degree of magnetic power will be produced, quite

sufficient to raise weights, and produce motion in some of the most simple electro-magnetic machines.

163. Connect the polar wires with a telegraphic line, and it will be found that messages may be communicated by Morse's Indicator, *Fig.* 199.

164. By connecting the polar wires with the apparatus represented in *Fig.* 162, water may easily be decomposed, and the Oxygen and Hydrogen collected in separate tubes or in one ; in the latter case one cubic inch of the mixed gases will be liberated in five to ten minutes ; it is found that platinum terminal wires answer better with the magneto-electric current than strips of platinum foil for this experiment.

165. By placing a piece of unsized paper in the curved part of the U tube, *Fig.* 164, so as to separate the substances that are set free at the two poles, most of the experiments upon the decomposition of saline solutions described under Expt. 34, of the chemical effects of the Battery, may be performed. Sulphate of Soda, Nitrate of Potash, Iodide of Potassium, Sulphate of Copper, Acetate of Lead, Nitrate of Silver, Chloride of Gold, may be decomposed, and these metals, or their oxides, be obtained at the negative pole. The etherial solution of Gold prepared by dissolving a strong solution of the Chloride of Gold in Ether, may be substituted for the Chloride of Gold pure.

166. If the polar wires be connected with fine carbon points, *Figs.* 159, 249, a continuous light of great brilliancy will be evolved.

167. If the polar wires of the magneto-electric machine be attached to the primary coil of Page's separable helices, or Ruhmkorff's coil, all the effects of these instruments may be obtained in the same way as when a galvanic battery is employed.

168. The primary magneto-electric current has too low an intensity to afford strong shocks, but these may be increased by making use of armatures wound with a great length of very fine wire. Secondary currents, however, may be obtained by interrupting the primary circuit, as in the case of Page's separable helices : these have a much higher intensity, and give powerful shocks. The primary current is broken by means of a wire running from N, and pressing upon the pins rising from the circumference of a wheel mounted on the axle of the coils, *Fig.* 247. See Expt. 160.

169. To show that shocks may be obtained from the primary current, the wire that plays upon the pins must be removed, so that the circuit may not be broken ; the springs pressing on the pole-changer must neither of them leave the segment which it touches before it comes in contact with the opposite segment ; otherwise the circuit will be broken at the pole-changer, and strong secondary shocks obtained. Metallic handles are then to be connected by means of wires with the cups P and N, and the coils set in motion : slight shocks will immediately be experienced. These may be partially regulated by varying the speed.

170. To exhibit the shocks produced by the secondary current, the wire leading from N, and pressing upon the pins of the horizontal wheel must be inserted, and the coils set in motion. Whenever the wire is in contact with the pins, the primary current passes from P, through the magnets and axis of the instrument, by the pins and connecting wire to the cup N, in preference to passing through the body of the subject. But as soon as the wire ceases to press upon the pins, the primary current is broken, and the same instant a secondary current of great intensity is induced, which is in the same direction with the primary current, and not being able to traverse the instrument, is compelled to pass through the body of the operator, giving a shock of extreme intensity, increasing with the velocity of revolution ; the hands cannot be unclosed, and with a powerful machine, the person through whom it is discharged is prostrated, rolls on the ground, and is at the mercy of the operator. At the same time bright sparks of light sometimes an inch in length, will flash between the pins and the wires.

171. The shocks may be regulated by varying the speed of revolution ; also by placing an iron armature across the steel magnets, neutralizing their power ; also by passing the primary current through a piece of wet cotton wicking, one end of which is connected with one of the poles, P or N, and the other attached by a wire to one of the metallic handles. The handles are sometimes one-half of wood ; no shock is felt when either one handle or both is held by the wooden portion. Sometimes the handle is made of glass or porcelain, tipped with moistened sponge ; in this case no shock is felt when the handle is held by the glass. The arm connected with the negative cup will be most affected by the shocks.

172. Thermo-Electricity. Place a bar of copper upon a bar of bismuth, in the manner represented, *Fig.* 258, and apply a lamp at the point of junction ; a current of electricity will be produced circulating as represented in the figure.

173. Instead of heat apply cold at the point, O, and an electric current in the opposite direction will be induced as indicated by the motion of the needle.

174. Construct a battery of several pairs of plates of Antimony and Bismuth, as represented in *Fig.* 260, and observe the great increase of effect.

175. With a Thermo-electric multiplier, which may now be procured of any Philosophical instrument maker, observe the extreme delicacy with which slight changes of temperature are indicated.

176. With Farmer's Thermo-electric battery, repeat the various experiments described above, in connection with the galvanic battery; for the purpose of illustrating its decomposing, magnetic, illuminating, and physiological power: also use it instead of the battery to actuate Page's and Ruhmkorff's Coils.

177. Instead of applying heat transmit a current of electricity through a thermo-electric series, consisting of antimony and bismuth. Cold will be produced at the first junction, and heat at the second. If the electric current be transmitted in the same direction with the thermo-electric current, heat is the result; if in the contrary direction cold will be produced.

178. Animal Electricity. The electric current existing in the animal economy and circulating from the interior to the exterior of a muscle, may be shown by arranging a series of limbs of frogs in such a manner that the interior of one will come into contact with the exterior of the next, so that one of the extremities of the series is formed of the interior of the muscle, while the other is formed of the exterior; the terminal pieces should dip into cavities, in which a little distilled water is placed. On introducing the wires of a galvanometer into these cavities, and completing the circuit, a current is produced by which the galvanometer needle is deflected, iodide of potassium is decomposed, and the leaves of an electroscope, with the aid of a condenser, made to diverge.

179. The same current may also be shown, by stripping the flesh from the upper end of a frog's leg, so as to display the nerve, and then dipping the extremity of the nerve into one vessel of acidulated water, and the foot of the frog into another, and then connecting the two vessels of water by means of a curved wire; as soon as the circuit is completed, the leg of the frog is perceptibly convulsed.

180. A frog's leg may be used as a galvanometer, by stripping down the flesh so as to expose the nerve, and then inserting the rest of the limb in a small glass tube, the nerve hanging out: whenever an electric current, however slight, is made to pass through the nerve, the leg is immediately convulsed: it is said that such an arrangement is 50,000 times more delicate than the most delicate gold leaf electroscope.

181. Physiological Effects of the Current. Expose the nerve of the leg of a frog, and twist a bit of copper wire around a piece of zinc; then touch the nerve with the zinc, and the outside of the leg with the copper: at the moment of contact the leg is convulsed; disconnect the two metals, and the convulsions cease, though they may still be in contact with the animal. Each time the zinc and copper are made to touch, the convulsions are renewed.

182. Place a live flounder on a plate of zinc or pewter; and bring a silver spoon in contact with its back; there will be no convulsion, but if the spoon be made to touch the plate while it rests on the fish, the animal becomes strongly convulsed.

183. If a piece of silver be placed above the tongue, and a piece of zinc beneath it, no sensation is perceived so long as the metals are separated, but if they touch each other, a peculiar tingling sensation or taste is experienced. If the silver be placed between the upper lip and the teeth, instead of under the tongue, a flash of light will appear before the eyes.

184. Apparatus. The apparatus for the performance of the experiments described in this work, may be obtained of the following Philosophical instrument makers: E. S. Ritchie, N. B. Chamberlain, Boston; B. Pike & Sons, New York; W. Y. McAllister, Philadelphia.

VIRG. GEOR. II., 490.—"*Felix, qui potuit rerum cognoscere causas.*"

FINIS.

INDEX.

N. B.—The Numbers refer to the Pages.

A.

ABSORPTION of heat, 56.
" " in ebullition, 128.
Action of the same current on successive chemical solutions, 345.
Air, compression of, evolves heat, 218.
" specific heat of, 212.
" expansion of, by heat, 93.
" weight of, 6.
" thermometer, 101.
Aldebaran, spectrum of, 255.
Amalgam for electrical machine, 297.
Amount of vapor formed proportionate to temperature, 170.
Ampere's theory of magnetism, 367.
" " supported by magneto-electric induction, 435.
Animal electricity, 500.
Anomalous effect of heat on water, 95.
Apparatus, 526.
Applications of electro-magnetism to motion, 395.
Applications of expansion by heat, 85.
Arago's rotations, 432.
Arc, voltaic, 331.
" influence of magnetism on, 488.
Arcturus, spectrum of, 255.
Ascension of heated liquids and gases, 42.
Astatic needle, 357.
" galvanometer, 365.
Atlantic telegraph cable, 389.
" " battery, 389.
" " history of, 394.
" " signal instrument, 392.
Atlantic telegraph, rate of transmission by, 393.
Atmosphere, peculiar properties of, 5.

B.

BATTERIES, Cruikshanks,—Bunsen's, —Grove's, —Daniell's,— Smee's, — 317–323.
Batteries, management of, 323.
Battery of quantity and intensity, 316.
Betelgeux, spectrum of, 255.
Bismuth an eminently dia-magnetic substance, 359.
Black, Dr. Joseph, the discoverer of the Laws of Latent Heat, 124.
" discoverer of absorption of heat in vaporization. and evolution in condensation, 130.
" account of the successive steps in the improvement of the Steam Engine, 141.
Boiler of the steam engine, 146.
Boiler of locomotive, 152.
Boiling point influenced by atmospheric pressure, 131.
" measurement of heights by, 132.
" influence of adhesion on, 133.
" influence of air in water on, 134.
" influence of solids in solution on, 134.
" raised by increase of pressure, and lowered by diminution, 134.
Breguet's metallic thermometer, 110.
Bunsen's Battery, 322.

C.

CAESIUM, 259.
Caillaud's Battery, 383.
Calorescence of rays of heat, 74.
Calorimeter of Lavoisier and La Place, 207.
Capella, spectrum of, 255.
Camera, photographic, 269.
Carbonic acid, solidification of, 196.
Change of density produces change of temperature, 214.
Charges for batteries, 514.
Chemical constitution of water, 335.
" effects of the battery, 334.
" rays, range of, in solar spectrum, Fluorescence, 249.
" rays of the solar beam, 248.
Chemistry, origin of name, 1.

Chemistry, nature of, 1.
" a science of experiment, 9.
" differs from Natural Philosophy, 8.
" connected with the Arts, 10.
" medicine and agriculture, 11.
" depends upon the balance, 14.
" fundamental principle of, 15.
" active agents of, 19.
Circuit-breaker, 438.
Circumstances influencing evaporation, 181.
Cold produced by evaporation, 181.
Compensation pendulums, 88.
Compound nature of light, 243.
Condensation of steam, 139.
Condensing steam engine, 143.
Condenser, attached to Ruhmkorff's coil, 442.
Convection of heat in liquids, 37.
" in gases, 38.
Convertibility of Forces, and indestructibility, 236.
Copper plate of the battery, part played by, 306.
Copper sheathing, protection of, 352.
Crown of cups, Volta's, 316.
Cruikshank's battery, 317.
Cryophorus, 184.
Culinary paradox, 137.

D.

DAGUERREOTYPE process, 266.
Dalton's law of the tension of vapors, 174.
Daniell's battery, 319.
" hygrometer, 189.
" pyrometer, 190.
Davy, Sir H., extraordinary galvanic experiment, 344.
the discoverer of the electric light, 332.
Decomposition of water by the battery, 336.
Decomposing tube, 340.
Decomposition of metallic salts, 339.
" of metallic oxides by the battery, 338
" of water, 336.
De la Rive's ring, 370.
De Luc's pile, 325.
Despretz' experiments upon the conversion of Carbon into diamond, 463.

Dew, how produced, 191.
Dia-magnetism of gases, 359.
Dia-thermancy of solids, 61.
" liquids, 64.
" gases, 65.
Difference between galvanic and statical electricity, 327.
Different kinds of heat, 66.
Directive action of the earth, 356.
Disappearance of heat in liquefaction, 113.
Distillation, 164.
Double refraction and polarization of heat, 75.
of light, 242.
Draught of chimneys, 93.
Duboscq's electric lamp, 331.

E.

EARTH a part of the telegraphic circuit, 384.
Ebullition, 127.
Elastic force of vapor, varies with temperature, 174.
Elastic force of vapor in two connected vessels, that of the colder, 177.
Element, definition of, 16.
Electricity, nature of, 276.
" two theories of, 286.
" two kinds, Vitreous and Resinous, 279.
" statical, 275.
" galvanic, 297.
" sources of, 277.
" effects of, 293.
" induction of, 282.
" of the machine distinguished from that of the battery, 483.
" and magnetism, effect of on light, 487.
" induced by induced magnetism, 426.
" induced by the magnetism of the earth, 434.
Electric gas-lighting, 406.
" fire-alarm, 403.
" light, not produced by combustion, 332.
" lamp, 332.
" telegraph, 373.
Electrical insulation, 280.
" machine, 287.
" tension exists before the passage of the current, 309.
Electrified bodies repel each other, 279.

Electro-magnetism, 353,
" " laws of, 367.
" " experiments on, 515.
" magnets, 362.
" magnetic clocks, 401.
" " locomotives, 398.
" motor of Froment, 396.
" positive and negative bodies, 347.
Electrophorus, 291.
Electro-plating, 349.
Electroscope, 279.
Electrotyping, 350.
Electro-chemical order of the elements, 347.
Equatorial magnetic position, 359.
Evaporation, 169.
" of different liquids, different, 179.
" in a vacuum is instantaneous, 172.
Expansion produced by heat, 79.
" of liquids, 91.
" of gases, 92.
" of water in vaporization, 138.
Expansive power of steam increases with temperature, 155.
Expense of electro-magnetism compared with steam, 400.
Experiments on conduction, convection, radiation and transmission of heat, 76.
on effects of heat, — expansion of solids, liquids and gases, 110.
on liquefaction, 125.
on vaporization and steam, 167.
on evaporation, 202.
on specific heat, 222.
on sources of heat, 228.
on light, 273.
on electricity, 296.
on galvanism, electro magnetism, magneto-electricity, thermo-electricity, animal electricity, 515.
Experiment of the three cups, 343.
Explosions of steam boilers, 150.
" " " explained by the spheroidal state, 162.
Extra-current, 419.

F.

FAHRENHEIT's scale, 105.
" " reduced to Centigrade and Reaumur, 107.
Faraday's discovery of Volta-electric induction, 411.

Faraday's discovery of induction of electricity by electro-magnetism, 430.
discovery of the effect of magnetism on polarized light, 489.
Farmer's thermo-electric battery, 499.
Fire-syringe, 218.
Fizeau's discovery of the effect of the condenser upon Ruhmkorff's coil, 442.
Flame, dia-magnetism of, 488.
Fluidity, heat of, 115
Fluorescence, 249.
Fluxes, 121.
Foci for heat, light and chemical rays different, 251.
Force of expansion by heat, 82.
Forces, indestructibility and convertibility of, 235, 511.
Fraunhofer's lines in solar spectrum, 253.
explained by Kirchoff, 261.
displayed upon a screen, 255.
instrument for observing, 254.
Freezing mixtures, 119.
" of water in vacuo, 183.
" of water, anomaly in, 98.
" point of water lowered by salts and acids, 120.
" of water, heat evolved by, 117.
" of mercury in red-hot crucible, 199.
Friction a source of heat, 226.
Frog battery, 502.
" Galvani's experiment on, 299.
Froment's electro-motor, 396.
Fuel not economized in using other liquids than water, 158.
not economized in boiling water at a low temperature, 156.
Fusing point, why fixed, 116.
" " of different substances 113.

G.

GALVANI's theory, 298.
Galvani the discoverer of galvanism, 298.
Galvanism, discovery of, 298.
Galvanic electricity, 297.
Galvanic electricity produced by chemical action, 303.
Galvanic battery, 315.
Galvanic batteries of historic note, 327.
Galvanometer, 364.

23

Gases, dia-magnetism of, 359.
" dia-thermancy of, 65.
" expansion of, by heat, 92.
" nature of, 194.
" liquefaction of, 194.
" peculiar properties of, 5.
" constitution of, 194.
" poor conductors of heat, 34.
" condensation of, 194.
" solidified, 199.
Gas battery, 313.
Geissler's tubes, 455.
" " applications of, 458.
Globe, constitution of, dependent upon temperature, 201.
Graduation of thermometers, 105.
Grove's Nitric acid battery, 321.
" gas battery, 313.
Grove on the correlation of Forces, 512.
Gymnotus, 500.

H.

HARRISON's compensation pendulum, 88.
Heat, nature of, 22, 222.
" seeks an equilibrium, 25.
" conduction of, in solids, 26
" the cause of evaporation, 169.
" explained on the mechanical theory, 232.
" light and chemical effect, relations of, in the solar spectrum, 273.
" of the battery and mechanical equivalent of heat, 333.
" produced by motion, 229.
" converted into light, 234.
" rays of solar beam, 246.
" sources of, 223.
" evolved in solidification, 117.
" latent, 112, 115.
" specific, 203.
" produces expansion, 79.
" radiation of, effect of surface on, 43.
" reflection of, 48.
" refraction of, 67.
" double refraction of, 75.
" in voltaic circuit Favre's experiment, 360, 509.
" evolved in condensation of steam, 129.
" latent in steam, 128, 145.
" specific of solids, 209.
" " liquids, 209.
" " gases, 210, 211.
" " Regnault's table of, 212.

Heat, specific, altered by change of density, 213; diminished by compression; iincreased by expansion, 214.
" conduction of, in liquids, 33.
" " of, in gases, 34.
" convection of, in liquids, 37.
" " " gases, 38.
" propagation of, through liquids, 40.
" reflection of, by fire-places, 55.
" absorption of, affected by color, 57.
" Melloni's apparatus for measuring small degrees of, 63, 497.
" rays of solar beam, unequal refrangibility of, Sir H. Englefield's experiments, 68.
" Sir W. Herschel's experiments 69.
" experiments on conduction, radiation, reflection, transmission, effects of, 110.
Heated particles of liquids, their ascension how explained, 41.
Heating effects of galvanic battery, 329.
Henry's coils, 422.
" discoveries in electro-magnetism, 407.
" in telegraphy, 408.
" of the extra-current, 424.
High pressure steam-engine, 142.
History of Atlantic telegraph, 394.
" of discovery of induction of electricity by electro-magnetism, 430.
" of discovery of magneto-electric induction, 428.
" of discovery of extra-current, 424.
" of discovery of electro-magnetism, 407.
" of discovery of Volta-electric induction, 411.
" of discovery in the construction of induction coils, and magneto-electric machines, 491.
" of the theory of the correlation of the Physical Forces, 512.
Holmes' magneto-electric machine, 474.
Horse-shoe electro-magnets, 372.
Hydro-electric machine, 292.
Hydrogen, how transferred within the battery, 305.
cooling effect of, on red-hot wire, 36

Hygrometer, Daniell's, — Saussure's, 189.

I.

Ice, specific heat of, 210.
Indium, 259.
Induction, theory of, 284.
" on the approach and removal of the primary current, 415.
" conditions of, 417.
" takes place through a considerable distance, 413.
" coils, Page's, Ruhmkorff's, Ritchie's, 435.
" of magnetism, 358.
Insects, temperature of, measured, 498.

J.

Jacoby's electro-motor, 398.
Joule's Law, 227.
Joule, experiments of, on mechanical equivalent of heat, 227.

K.

Kirchoff's discovery of the coincidence between the dark lines of the solar spectrum and the bright lines of metallic spectra, 261.

L.

Ladd's magneto electric machine, 481.
Land and sea breezes, 39.
Latent heat, 203.
" " of condensing engine, 145.
Law of chemical decomposition by the battery, 347.
Leyden jar, 288.
" " charged by Ruhmkorff's coil, 449.
" " by Page's separable helices, 437.
Light, nature of, 236.
" sources of, 237.
" reflection of, 240.
" refraction of, 241.
" double refraction of, 242.
" solar, compound nature of, 243.
" " number of vibrations required to produce the different colors, 246.
" " heat rays of, 246.
" " chemical rays of, 248.
" " decomposition of, 244.
" " triple character of, 250.

Light, solar, spectrum of, crossed by dark lines, 253.
" " effect of, on plants, 263.
" " effect of, on chemical compounds, 265.
" " on daguerreotype plates, 266.
" " on photographic paper, 270.
" " relations of the rays of heat to those of light and chemical effect, 273.
" experiments on, 273.
" artificial, spectra of, 252.
" of magneto-electric machine applied to illumination, 473.
" brilliancy of that produced by Wilde's magneto-electric machine, 480.
" of the voltaic arc, 331.
" effect of electricity and magnetism on, 487.
" of Ruhmkorff's coil affected by the magnet, 457.
" comparative cost of producing by Smee's battery, Grove's, by illuminating gas, the magneto-electric machine, 500.
Liquefaction produced by heat, 113.
" always attended by reduction of temperature, 118.
Liquids poor conductors of heat, 33.
" peculiar properties of, 4.
Luminous effects of galvanic battery, 380.

M.

Magic circle, 373.
Magnet described, 355.
Magnetic and dia-magnetic bodies, 358.
  needle, influence of the battery current on, 354.
  needle acted upon by the liquid part of the circuit, 366.
  poles, mutual action of, 356.
  effects of the battery, 353.
Magnet, influence of, on the voltaic arc, 487.
Magnetism of a helix carrying a current, 368.
  of the earth affects the wire carrying the current, 371.
Magnetic curves, 434.
" field, 359.
" polarization of light, 489.
" telegraph, 373.
Magneto-electric induction, 425.

Magneto-electricity used in the arts, 471.
    electric machines, 463.
    electricity applied to the illumination of light-houses, 473.
Management of batteries, 323.
Map of solar spectrum, 253, 260.
Marcet's apparatus, 136.
Material theory of heat, 228.
Matter indestructible, 15.
    " three principal states of, 3.
Measurement of heights by boiling point, 133.
Mechanical theory of heat, 230.
    " equivalent of heat, 226.
Melloni's researches on heat, 62, 63, 64, 497.
    thermo-multiplier, 497.
Mercury, specific heat of, 205.
    " frozen in red-hot capsule, 164.
Metals, relative conductivity of, for heat, 27.
    conductivity of, for electricity, 28.
    thermo-electric order of, 495.
    deposited from their solutions, 339.
    discovered by spectrum analysis, 259.
Metallic connection between the plates not necessary for galvanic action, 312.
Mirrors parabolic, effect of, on rays of light, 50.
Molecular movements in magnetization, 364.
Morse's telegraphic indicator, 376.
    "   " alphabet, 376.
Motion produced by heat, 230.
Muscular electric current, 501.

N.

NEBULÆ, spectra of, 262.
Nicholson and Carlisle, their discovery of the decomposition of water by the battery, 334.
Nitrogen, spectrum of, 456.
Nobili's Thermo-electric battery, 496.

O.

OXYGEN, a magnetic substance, 360.

P.

PAGE's electro-magnetic locomotive, 398.
Page's pole-changer, 470.
    " magneto-electric machine, 469.

Page's separable helices, 436.
Papin's digester, 159.
Phosphorus a dia-magnetic body, 359.
Photography, 267.
Photographs produced by the chemical rays of the solar beam, 270.
Physiological effects of the battery, 503.
Plate electrical machine, 288.
Points of resemblance between static and galvanic electricity, 326, 485.
    of difference, 327, 483.
Polarization of heat, 75.
    " of light, 242.
    " and transfer of the elements necessary for galvanic action, 307.
Poles of voltaic battery, 307.
Positive and negative poles of the battery, how determined, 326.
Potassium, spectrum of, 260.
Pressure, how transmitted from boiler to cylinder, 150.
Prism, its effect on the solar beam, 243.
Procyon, spectrum of, 255.
Progress of discovery in galvanic induced electricity, and induction coils, 491.
    of discovery in electro-magnetism, 407.
Propagation of pressure through fluids, 149.
Pulse-glass, 186.
Pyrometer, Daniell's 110.

R.

RADIATION of heat, 42.
Rain and snow, production of, explained, 219.
Reaumur's thermometer, 106.
Reflection of light, 240.
    " of heat, 48.
Reflecting galvanometer, Thomson's, 390, 392.
Register thermometers, 108.
Removal of atmospheric pressure hastens evaporation, 183.
Refraction of light, 241.
Refractory substances, 121.
Refrangibility of heat, alteration in, 74.
    of light, alteration in, 249.
Retardation of telegraphic signals, 388.
Ritchie's improved Ruhmkorff's coil, 445.

Ruhmkorff's coil, induction coil, 440.
  mechanical effects of, 450.
  physiological effects, 450.
  heating effects, 450.
  luminous effects, 453.
  chemical effects of, 461.
  dissected, 440.
  decomposition of steam by, 462.
  conversion of carbon into diamond, 463.
Rumford's experiments on heat of friction, 233.
  experiments on conducting power of materials used for clothing, 29.
Rubidium, 259.

S.

SALTS, effect of, in lowering freezing point, 120.
  effect of, in raising boiling point, 134.
Sand battery, 384.
Saussure's hygrometer, 189.
Saxton's magneto-electric machine, 466.
Secondary induced currents of electricity, 409.
  " decomposition by the battery, 341.
Sheathing of ships, how protected, 352.
Sirius, spectrum of, 262.
Smee's battery, 323.
Sodium, spectrum of, 260.
Solar light, effect of, on plants, 264.
  " " " on chemical compounds, 265.
Solids, peculiar properties of, 4.
Solidification evolves heat, 117.
  " of carbonic acid, 196.
Sources of heat, 223.
Spark obtained from magnet, 427.
Specific heat, 203.
  " " determined by mixture, 204.
  " " determined by rate of cooling, 206.
  " " determined by time, 205.
  " " of gases, determined by Regnault, 212.
  " " determined by ice melted, 207.
  " " altered by alteration of physical state, 214.
  " " altered by alteration of density, 213.
  " " of solids, 209.

Specific heat of liquids, 209.
  " " of water, 209.
  " " of gases, 210.
Spectra of the Nebulæ and artificial lights, 255.
  of Potassium, Sodium, Caesium, and Rubidium, compared with Fraunhofer's lines, 260.
  of artificial light and colored flames, 252.
  projection of, on screen, 255.
Spectroscope, 257.
Spectrum-analysis, 256.
  " " made by Ruhmkorff's coil, 460.
Spheroidal state, 160.
Statham's fuse, 452.
Steam, latent heat of, 130.
  " elastic force of, 138.
  " used expansively, 155.
  " temperature of, at different pressures, 156.
  " electricity of, 292.
  " engine, the invention of, by Watt, 141.
  " condensation of, in condenser, its invention described by Watt, 179.
  " engine, condensing and non-condensing, how distinguished, 142.
  " super-heated, 158.
Still, for distillation, 164.
Submarine telegraphic cables, 389.
Sulphate of copper battery, 318.

T.

TABLE of conducting power for heat, 27.
  conducting power for heat compared with conducting power for electricity, 28.
  of Melloni, showing the amount of heat from different sources, transmitted by different substances, 60.
  of Melloni, showing the amount of heat from the same source that is transmitted by different substances, 63.
  showing the different temperature of the rays of heat of different refrangibility contained in the solar spectrum, 69.
  of relative expansion of different solids, 82.
  of Regnault, showing the pressure of steam at different temperatures, 156.

Table of Regnault, showing the sum of sensible and latent heat in steam at different temperatures, 157.
 of Regnault, showing the elastic force of watery vapor at different temperatures, 177.
 of density of vapors at the boiling points of their liquids, compared with that of air, 180.
 of temperatures at which different gases solidify, 200.
 of specific heat of solids of equal weight between 32° and 212°, 209.
 of specific heat of liquids, 210.
 of Delaroche and Berard, of specific heat of gases, 211.
 of Regnault, of specific heat of gases, 212.
 of rise of specific heat with rise of temperature, 214.
 of heat produced by various combustibles, 225.
 of electro-negative and electro-positive bodies, 347.
 of magnetic and dia-magnetic bodies, 361.
 of Morse's telegraphic alphabet, 378.
 of velocity of telegraphic current, 387.
 of direction of induced currents up to the ninth order, 424.
 comparative cost of light, 500.
Transfer of solids in voltaic arc, 331.
Tangent galvanometer, 365.
Telegraph, electric, 373.
Telegraphic batteries, 382.
 " manipulator, 378.
 " relay; 379.
Temperature, increase of with increase of depth beneath the surface, 224.
Thallium, 259.
Thomson's reflecting galvanometer, 390.
Thermo-chrosis, or calorific tint, 72.
 " electric battery, 495.
 " electricity, 493.
 " multiplier of Melloni, 497.
Thermometers, 100.
 " Breguet's metallic, 110.
 " Fahrenheit, 105.
 " Centigrade, 106.
 " Reaumur, 106.
 " maximum and minimum, 109.

Thermometers, Rutherford's self-registering, 109.
 " comparison of various scales of, 107.
 graduation of, 105.
 " tests of accuracy of, 105.
Torpedo, 501.
Transmission of heat, 57.
 " of telegraphic messages, 381.
Triple character of solar light, 250.

U.

URANIUM glass, 454.

V.

VALVES of steam-engine, 153
Vaporization, 126.
Vapor, amount of, in the air, 188.
 " in the atmosphere, affects its bulk and density, 180.
Vapors differ in latent heat, 130.
Velocity of telegraphic current, 387.
Vibrations, number of, required for different colors, 246.
Volta, the inventor of the voltaic pile, 300.
Volta's theory, 299.
Voltaic pile, 300.
 " " theory of, 301.
Volta-electric induction, 409.
 " magneto-electric induction, 429.
Voltameter, 348.

W.

WATER decomposed by a process of polarization and transfer, 337
 expansion of, in cooling, 97.
 freezing of, in red-hot capsule, 164.
 frozen by its own evaporation, 183.
 latent heat of, 210.
 evolution of heat of, in freezing, 117.
 maximum density of, 96.
 expansion of, in freezing, 98.
Weight of great importance in chemistry, 14.
Wilde's magneto-electric machine, 475.
Wollaston's Cryophorus, 185.
 " Hypsometer, 133.
 " Steam bulb, 140.

THE END.